Praise for Jennifer Fallon's Work

"Fallon merges epic fantasy with political intrigue and delivers a thrilling, page-turning saga. The complex characters and plot twists are perfect for those who like their sword-and-sorcery on a higher level. This is an ambitious, detailed epic whose end rips readers from a world they won't want to leave."
—*Romantic Times BOOKreviews* on *Warrior*

"Readers with a taste for detail and complicated plots will enjoy this story." —*VOYA* on *Wolfblade*

"Fallon sets the stage for another lively fantasy saga full of intriguing characters, smart dialogue, and twisty plotting." —*Publishers Weekly* on *Wolfblade*

"The battles are fierce, the losses heartrending in Fallon's beautifully created world, whose disparate inhabitants are once again completely convincing, making *Harshini* a chilling, thrilling conclusion to the trilogy."
—*Booklist* on *Harshini*

"A well-executed fantasy with complex characters and entertaining style."
—*Kirkus Reviews* on *Treason Keep*

Tor Books by Jennifer Fallon

THE HYTHRUN CHRONICLES

THE DEMON CHILD TRILOGY
Medalon (Book One)
Treason Keep (Book Two)
Harshini (Book Three)

THE WOLFBLADE TRILOGY
Wolfblade (Book One)
Warrior (Book Two)
Warlord (Book Three)

THE TIDE LORDS
The Immortal Prince (Book One)
The Gods of Amyrantha (Book Two)
The Palace of Impossible Dreams (Book Three)*

*Forthcoming

WARLORD

BOOK THREE OF THE WOLFBLADE TRILOGY

JENNIFER FALLON

TOR® fantasy

A TOM DOHERTY ASSOCIATES BOOK
NEW YORK

WARLORD

Copyright © 2005 by Jennifer Fallon

Originally published in 2005 by Voyager, an imprint of HarperCollins*Publishers*, (Australia) Pty Limited Group

Map by Ellisa Mitchell

A Tor Book
Published by Tom Doherty Associates, LLC
175 Fifth Avenue
New York, NY 10010

www.tor-forge.com

Tor® is a registered trademark of Tom Doherty Associates, LLC.

ISBN 978-0-7653-3475-6

First Tor Edition: August 2007
First Tor Mass Market Edition: May 2008

P1

For the adopted ones

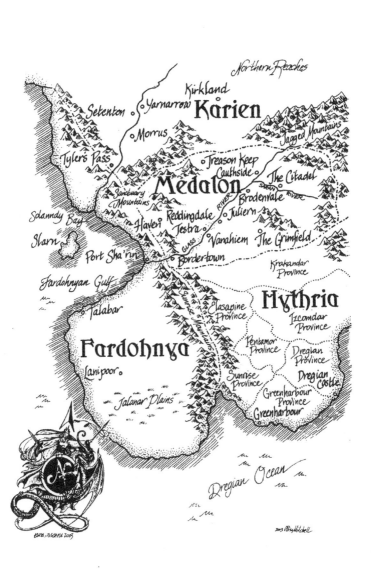

WARLORD

PART ONE

DUTY, DESTINY AND JUST DESSERTS

PROLOGUE

Damin Wolfblade had no need to stand sentry duty. With an army of more than two thousand men at his command, and while still in his own province, there wasn't even a need to post sentries at all. But Damin had been taught well. Just because an attack was improbable didn't mean it was impossible. So despite the fact they were still two days from the Elasapine-Krakandar border, and hundreds of miles from their nearest enemy, Damin had set sentries around the camp for the night and made a point of checking on their disposition personally.

The night was clear and crisp, the stars providing more than enough light to see by. He made his way forward accompanied by the busy sounds of night creatures and insects, without any attempt at stealth, his progress leaving a cautious silence in his wake. Damin's purpose for checking the sentries wasn't to catch them out. He wanted to alert them to the possibility that, at any time, their prince might happen by and they'd better be ready for it. It was a trick Geri Almodavar had taught him, one he claimed Laran Krakenshield was fond of. Damin didn't know if the old captain was just saying that to validate his suggestion, or if it really was a tactic favoured by Damin's late father, and in the end, it didn't really matter. It was a good thing to do, whoever thought of it.

Without warning, a silhouette detached itself from the

thin line of trees ahead, resolving into a man shape, a sword raised threateningly in Damin's direction.

"Halt! Who goes there?"

"Your prince."

The silhouette advanced, showing no sign of friendliness. "Show yourself!"

Damin did as the sentry ordered and stepped out of the shadow of the trees. The sentry studied him closely in the starlight and then sheathed his sword.

"Your highness," he said with an apologetic bow. "I didn't realise it was you."

"Don't apologise for doing your job, soldier."

"No, sire."

Damin stepped closer, surprised at how young the sentry seemed. He couldn't have been more than sixteen.

"Been with the Krakandar Raiders long?"

The lad shook his head. "Joined up so I could get out of the city." And then as he remembered who he was addressing, he added hastily, "Your highness."

Damin smiled wryly. "So did I."

"Sire?" the lad asked, looking confused.

"Nothing," he sighed. "Stay alert, eh?"

"Yes, your highness."

Damin patted the lad on the shoulder and continued along his way, thinking he should have thought to ask the boy his name. Almodavar would have done that. Then again, he probably didn't need to ask. Damin suspected Almodavar could address every Raider in Krakandar by name, and there were thousands of them. He probably knew the names of all their wives and children, too.

There's more to being a good general than knowing how to win a battle, Almodavar had often told him when he was a lad. *It's about knowing your men. Knowing what drives them. And sometimes it's knowing how to avoid a fight.*

Strange advice, really, he mused, *coming from a man so devoted to the God of War.*

Damin's thoughts were distracted by a faint light ahead of him through the trees. He stopped, wondering if the next sentry had been thoughtless enough to light a fire. He doubted it. Any man willing to do something so foolish wouldn't last long in any army over which Almodavar held sway.

Then again, the last sentry looked barely old enough to dress himself without his mother. Perhaps, with the Raiders' numbers so drastically reduced by the plague, there were raw recruits out here without the sense to realise how stupid such an action was. Drawing his sword, and fully intending to give the young man the fright of his life, Damin started forward, this time making as little noise as possible.

As he neared the light, he discovered it wasn't where the next sentry should be standing guard but some way off to the left, in a small clearing set back from the open grassland that marked the edge of the camp.

Curiosity replaced annoyance as Damin neared the clearing. A harsh white radiance beckoned ahead, not the warm yellow glow of a wood fire. Raising his sword a little higher, he felt himself drawn toward the light, the compulsion to discover the source of this strange illumination driving all thoughts of stealth or caution from his mind.

When he stepped into the clearing, Damin stared at the figure waiting for him and automatically fell to one knee, laying his sword on the ground in front of him.

"Divine One!"

"Scion of Wolfblade."

The voice was rich, the timbre so deep it resonated along his spine, prickling his skin with goosebumps. Even if he hadn't grown up surrounded by statues and paintings of his family's favourite god, Damin could feel the awesome presence of the gilded figure before him. Tall and proud, his shoulders broad, his long cloak billowing in the still air as if it was accompanied by its own breeze, and wearing armour Damin had only seen depicted in ancient Harshini murals, this was—he knew with a certainty—Zegarnald, the God of War.

It bordered on intoxicating to be in his presence, but for some reason, Damin found himself unsurprised. Maybe because he knew Wrayan Lightfinger spoke to the gods, he wasn't as shocked to meet one as he might have been. Whatever the reason for his calm acceptance of the miraculous, it made no difference now. He shielded his eyes against the light as he stared at Zegarnald in wonder and then bowed his head. "You honour me beyond words, Divine One."

"Yes," the god agreed. "I do."

As awestruck as he was, a small part of Damin wanted to smile at the god's solemn reply, but he thought better of it. Zegarnald was credited with many qualities, but a sense of humour wasn't among them.

"How can I serve you, Divine One?"

"You are riding to war."

Damin risked a glance upward, still squinting at the god's bright countenance, not sure if that was a question or an observation.

"We fear a Fardohnyan invasion, Divine One."

"Fear it?" Zegarnald asked. "Or welcome it?"

"I welcome it!" Damin assured him. Admitting he feared war wasn't what the God of War wanted to hear, he guessed.

Zegarnald appeared pleased with his answer. The god's light faded a little and he became easier to look upon. "You will honour me well, I think, young Wolfblade."

"It won't be for lack of trying, Divine One," Damin assured him, cringing a little at how trite he sounded. *Where was Wrayan when you needed him?* He was the expert when it came to talking with the gods.

Fortunately, Zegarnald took Damin at his word, seemingly unaware of any nuance of tone or meaning. "And I expect you to succeed. I expended much effort to ensure you were provided with the right guidance as a child."

Damin stared at the god in surprise. "You did?"

"I am well within my rights to do this, Scion of Hythria. Your father offered me your soul the night you were born."

"Every warrior in the country offers his firstborn son to you the night he's born, Divine One," Damin reminded him respectfully. "It's a tradition older than time. I claim no special privilege from it."

Zegarnald studied him with a frown. "Do you question

my right to arrange circumstances favourably for my disciples?"

"Of course not, Divine One," Damin hurried to reply. "It's just . . . well, you've got millions of disciples in Hythria and Fardohnya. Do you take a personal interest in the education of every boy offered to you?"

"The Hythrun heir is not *every* boy."

"But . . . I'm not the first Hythrun heir to be offered to the God of War, either," he pointed out, wondering as he said it why he was arguing with his god. If he had any sense he'd simply take this honour for what it was. But this wasn't about sense, Damin knew. Wrayan had taught him enough to make him a little suspicious, along with honoured, by the appearance of any god. There had to be a reason for this. The heirs of the last fifty-odd generations of Wolfblades had been sworn to Zegarnald the night they were born. To Damin's knowledge, the God of War had displayed a singular lack of interest in any of them until now.

"Your soul was offered to me by a true warrior, a man who genuinely and devoutly honoured his god," Zegarnald replied. Then he added in a somewhat more wistful voice, "It has been a long time since any Wolfblade prince truly honoured the God of War."

Damin fell silent as he realised Zegarnald meant Laran Krakenshield, suddenly humbled by his father's legacy. Laran had been a devout follower of the War God—Damin knew that much, even though he was barely two years old when his father was killed—and he could well imagine how Zegarnald would have reacted to a soul so earnestly proffered, no matter how trite the custom seemed to those who didn't believe.

"I hope I can prove worthy of your patronage, Divine One," Damin said, lowering his head. "To honour both you and my father's memory."

Zegarnald seemed pleased with his answer. "You will not disappoint me."

Damin couldn't tell if that was an order or a prediction, and wasn't brave enough to ask. He bowed his head again. "What must I do to serve you, Divine One?"

"Give me a decent war," the god replied.

Damin glanced up. "*Pardon?*"

"I have set the scene, Scion of Hythria. The game is now in your hands."

"I'm not worthy, Divine One," Damin declared with genuine despair at the thought that the entire weight of the coming conflict might rest on his shoulders.

"I ask nothing of you that you are not capable of," the god assured him. "And I will see you have what assistance you need."

"Assistance?" Damin asked, unable to keep the hope from his voice. "You mean more men?"

"I mean you will have *assistance*," the god repeated. "More than that, you do not need to know. Do not fear your ability to honour me, young Wolfblade. War and death suit me just as well as victory."

Damin hesitated, thinking that sounded a little ominous. "I will seek victory in your name, Divine One."

The god looked as if he expected nothing less. "You face a numerically superior enemy led by an experienced and intelligent general," the god warned. "You will have much opportunity to honour my name, Wolfblade. Do not disappoint me."

He knows where the Fardohnyans are, Damin realised. *How many they are. Who is leading them . . .* He desperately wanted to question Zegarnald further about the enemy, but the god either knew his thoughts or guessed his intentions and held up his hand to forestall him.

"Do not ask anything more of me," he warned. "It is enough to know I favour your endeavours. Any more than this would cheapen your victory."

Which is just fine by me, Damin thought irreverently. *If it means we're going to win.*

But he didn't say it aloud. He lowered his head again and, taking his dagger from his belt, pricked the tip of the fourth finger on his left hand. Some warriors—those who considered themselves particularly devout—sliced their forearm or their palm, even their thigh, when offering a blood sacrifice, but Damin had been raised by more pragmatic men. *The God of War wants the taste of your blood so he can know you in the heat of battle,* Almodavar used to say when he was a child, *not his disciples incapacitated and unable to fight.*

As the blood beaded around the small incision, Damin held his hand out to Zegarnald. "I live to serve and honour you, Divine One."

The god's countenance flared momentarily, perhaps because of the fresh blood so close by, and then he looked down at Damin with a grimace the young man thought might have been intended as a smile. "I accept your sacrifice, Scion of Hythria. Do not give me reason to regret it."

Damin bowed his head, closing his eyes to receive his god's blessing, but when he opened them again the clearing was dark. The night was unchanged—clear and crisp, the air still, the darkness filled with the sounds of nocturnal creatures going about their business.

Still on one knee, his sword on the ground in front of him, Damin wondered if he'd imagined Zegarnald had been here. And then he looked down at the bead of fresh blood dripping from the end of his finger, proof that he had been visited by his god.

Nobody's going to believe this, he thought. *If I go around telling people I've met Zegarnald, they'll think I'm as crazy as my uncle.*

Studying his cut finger for a moment longer, he cursed softly and wiped the blood away on his trousers. He wouldn't tell anyone, he decided. Not until he was certain himself that the pressure of command wasn't making him hallucinate.

Damin smiled grimly, thinking they hadn't even left Krakandar yet. If the pressure was getting to him already, there wasn't much hope for winning this war, no matter how much the God of War expected of him.

Feeling more than a little perplexed, Damin leaned forward and picked up his sword, sheathing it as he rose to his feet. What had Zegarnald said?

It is enough to know I favour your endeavours.

That's something, Damin decided as he turned from the small clearing. *The God of War favours our endeavours.*

Which would have been a lot more comforting, Damin thought as he resumed his patrol of the sentry positions, *if he hadn't added that bit about war and death suiting him just as well as victory.*

Chapter 1

Kalan Hawksword had discovered a great deal about herself in the past few days. And a great deal about her friends and family, people she thought she knew almost as well as herself. She'd learned her uncle Mahkas had a capacity for cruelty that defied reason and that her brother, Damin, wasn't nearly as asinine as she'd feared. She had learned her cousin Leila was capable of taking her own life out of despair, and that the coolest head in a crisis that she had ever encountered was Tejay Lionsclaw. She had learned Rorin Mariner's healing power had severe limits and that if you asked the gods for help, you'd better be prepared for the consequences if they said yes.

But mostly, she'd learned nothing was ever as simple or straightforward as it seemed.

Kalan glanced furtively along the narrow, crooked street before knocking on the door of the safe house. She wore a plain cloak over her silken gown to hide its obvious quality, but she suspected it meant little down here where the very air smelled of watchful suspicion. Although she'd left her horse with its silver-trimmed tack and imported Medalonian saddle back at the stables of the Pickpocket's Retreat and walked the few streets to the safe house, strangers were noticed down here in the back streets of the Beggar's Quarter. The locals might not know who she was, but they were certain she didn't belong here.

Fyora opened the door for her. Wiping her muddy feet on the coir mat, Kalan slipped into the small, unremarkable house as Fee closed and locked the door behind her. The *court'esa*'s face was grim as she pushed past Kalan and the narrow staircase into the dim main room with its barely adequate fire. Two narrow benches were lined up at right angles to the hearth and a rough wooden table with three stools was shoved against the wall on her right, but there was no sign of Starros. For a moment Kalan feared the worst. Before she could say anything, however, she heard something breaking in the other room and raised voices. Turning to Fyora, she raised her brow with a questioning look.

"He's not happy," Fee remarked unnecessarily.

"Would you be happy waking up to find the woman you love is dead and your friends have sold your soul to the God of Thieves?"

Fee shrugged. "In Starros's place, I'm not sure what I'd be feeling right now."

Fyora didn't seem all that interested in discussing it further. She left Kalan standing in the small front room, disappearing through another door near the staircase. The smell of something delicious cooking wafted in from the kitchen when she pushed open the door, and then faded again as it swung shut behind her. A few seconds later the door to the other room flew open and slammed against the wall, making the whole house shake. Starros stalked toward the front door, clearly planning to leave the house, but he stopped when he saw Kalan.

"Come to check on your handiwork, I suppose?" he asked, his voice heavy with scorn. "Take a good look, Kalan. You must be feeling very proud of yourself. See! Not a mark! Of course, I don't seem to own a soul any longer, but what the hell? Who needs a soul, anyway?"

He was right about his remarkable recovery. Three days ago they'd brought him here on a stretcher on the very brink of death—broken, bloodied and barely recognisable. The young man standing before her now was whole and unmarked, showing no sign of Mahkas's days of torture and beatings. But the cost had been prohibitive. It was obvious Starros was just beginning to understand that.

Wrayan emerged from the other room behind him and stopped in the doorway, leaning against the frame, his arms crossed. He looked weary. "There's no point getting angry at Kalan," he said. "It's not her fault."

"You told Leila I was dead!" Starros accused. "She was your friend. How could you do that to her? To *us*?"

"I'm so sorry, Starros," Kalan replied, tears welling in her eyes. She didn't need Starros to remind her how much of the blame she carried for Leila's suicide. "Mahkas made me . . ."

"You should have let me die, too!" he declared.

"We couldn't!"

"Why not? Because I'm so damned important to the royal house of Wolfblade? Or because none of you wanted the guilt of *two* innocent deaths on your hands?"

"If I'd realised bringing you back from the brink of death was going to turn you into an ungrateful halfwit," Wrayan remarked, still leaning against the door, "I *would've* left well enough alone."

"Nobody asked you to bring me back, Wrayan!" Starros pointed out furiously, turning on the thief.

"Actually, Damin Wolfblade asked me to bring you back," Wrayan corrected. "You remember him, don't you? Big blond chap with the power of life and death over you, me and everyone else in the province? Oh, that's right . . . he's your best friend, too, as I recall."

"A friend would never have sold my soul to a god!"

"Maybe that's something you should take up with Damin," Wrayan suggested. "In the meantime, lay off Kalan. She's on your side, in case you've forgotten."

"Where is my *friend*, then?" Starros demanded. "Where is Damin?"

"He left the city yesterday," Kalan explained. "Heading for Elasapine."

"Running away?"

Kalan shook her head, wondering how long Starros could sustain his rage. She'd never seen him like this before. "Hablet of Fardohnya is reportedly massing his troops behind the Sunrise Mountains for an invasion. Damin left with Adham and Rorin and Almodavar and two and a half thousand Raiders. They're heading to Byamor first, to collect Narvell and all the Elasapine troops Grandpa Charel will let him have, so they can hold Hablet off until Wrayan and I can get to Greenharbour to warn my mother."

Starros took a deep breath, as if his rage needed fuel to sustain it and it was being starved because nobody would fight with him. "So I was *what*? Just a passing aside? A footnote?" He turned to Wrayan again. "Did he ask you to put me back together again because he didn't have time to deal with me?"

"That's surprisingly close to how it happened," Wrayan agreed.

Starros's shoulders sagged suddenly. He sat down on the bench near the fire, putting his head in his hands for a time, and then looked up at them, his eyes filled with despair. "Does he know what he's done to me?"

Wrayan shrugged. "Probably not."

"Does he care?"

"Probably not."

"Why did you do it?" Starros asked Wrayan. He sounded more curious than angry now. "And don't give me any of that *he is my prince* nonsense. You're a Harshini sorcerer and the head of your own guild. You don't have to take orders from anybody."

"Two reasons," Wrayan replied, pushing off the doorframe. He crossed the room and took a seat opposite Starros on the other wooden bench. "The first was simple patriotism."

"What?"

"Damin might be arrogant at times and rather arbitrary when he decides to throw his weight around, but that doesn't mean he isn't right, occasionally. He has a war to fight and it needs his undivided attention. His best friend on the brink of death is a distraction he didn't need. Now you're all better and Damin doesn't have to worry about you."

"I never picked you for a raving patriot, Wrayan."

"Which just shows how little you know me."

"What was the other reason?"

"Selfishness."

"*Selfishness*?"

Wrayan smiled. "I've been offering you a job in the Thieves' Guild since you were fifteen, Starros. You're bright, well-educated and have a good head for politics and organisation. You kept knocking me back. Now you don't have a choice."

Starros looked at him, shaking his head in bewilderment. "You sold my soul to Dacendaran so you could recruit me into the Thieves' Guild?"

"Not the most orthodox way of going about it, I'll admit. But it is effective."

"What if I don't want to be a thief?"

Wrayan shrugged. "Doesn't matter. You're a thief now, whether you want to be or not."

"And what of my former life? You know . . . the one I had a few days ago?"

"Your former life ceased the minute Mahkas found you and Leila together," Kalan reminded him gently. She sat beside him and put her hand on his shoulder, hoping to convey her sympathy. "Even if she wasn't dead, there'd be no going back. Not now."

"What happened to Mahkas?"

She hesitated for a moment, and then decided the only thing to do was tell him the truth. "Damin tried to ventilate his windpipe with a battle gauntlet. Did a rather impressive job of it, too. Rorin healed what he could, but Mahkas is still bedridden and likely to be for a while yet. He can't speak in much more than a hoarse whisper. Xanda's taken over running the province while he's ill, but I'm not sure what will happen when he recovers."

"Why didn't Damin kill him?"

"Because he's not that stupid," Wrayan replied heartlessly.

Starros glared at him. "You think taking vengeance for Leila's death is stupid?"

"Taking vengeance for anything is stupid, Starros, when that vengeance is liable to do you as much harm as your enemy."

"So Mahkas is going to be allowed to get away with everything he's done?" Starros asked bitterly. "Is that what you're saying? And that I should just accept it?"

"I'm suggesting nothing of the kind."

"Then what *are* you suggesting?"

"I'm suggesting, Starros, that you are now a thief. Your soul belongs to Dacendaran. If you're planning to get even with Mahkas Damaran, do it in such a way that you hurt Mahkas and honour your god."

"You think I should *steal* something from him?"

"No, Starros, I think you should steal *every*thing from him."

Starros looked at Wrayan, a little baffled by what the thief was telling him, but before he had a chance to question him further, Fee came in from the kitchen carrying a large pot. She dumped it on the small table and, after eyeing the three of them curiously, announced that lunch was ready.

Kalan took Starros's hand and squeezed it, smiling at her foster-brother, hoping to let him know how much she empathised with his pain, but at that moment Starros wasn't thinking about pain, she suspected. The pain was too raw, his grief too overwhelming, for Starros to be thinking of anything other than revenge.

chapter 2

rakandaran the Halfbreed looked down over the plains around the Winter Palace at Qorinipor, shielding his eyes with his forearm against the bright sun resting on the horizon. It was chilly at this altitude, but he was dressed for it in a long, dark, fur-lined coat that reached almost to his ankles. It was a souvenir from a raid on a caravan belonging to a rather pretentious Hythrun merchant about six years ago. The man had cursed loudly as Brak relieved him of his precious coat, seemingly more upset about losing the garment than any other goods the bandits had taken from him in the raid. Brak pulled the coat closed against the bitter wind and scanned the plains below from his vantage point high in the foothills of the Sunrise Mountains on the Fardohnyan side of the border.

"It's depressing, isn't it?"

The Halfbreed turned to find Dacendaran, the God of Thieves, perched on a tree stump behind him, dressed in his motley array, seemingly unaffected by the cold wind, but looking just as displeased by the spectacle laid out before them as Brak.

"Hello Dace. What are you doing here?"

"Same as you." The boy-god shrugged miserably. "Looking at that army down there and cursing Zegarnald in every language I know."

Brak smiled at his forlorn expression. Jealousy among the gods was always entertaining. "He's really gone all out for this one, hasn't he?"

"How many of them do you think there are?"

Brak shrugged and buried his hands in the deep pockets of his coat for warmth. "Multiply the number of camp fires by six," he instructed the god. "That should give you a rough estimate."

"I'm the God of Thieves, Brak. I only count stolen property. What do I know about counting fires?"

"The mathematical principle is the same, Divine One. For fires *and* contraband."

"Easy for you to say," Dace grumbled. "Anyway, it's only late afternoon. Isn't counting camp fires something you can only do at night?"

Brak feigned a look of astonishment. "You mean there're some things beyond even a *god*?"

"Just answer the question, Brak. There's no need to be sarcastic."

The Halfbreed shrugged and turned back to stare down over the camp. "About thirty, maybe forty thousand men, I guess. He's probably got this many troops again down on the coast at Tambay's Seat, waiting for a chance at Highcastle, too."

The God of Thieves sighed. "Do you know what I'd give to be able to gather forty thousand thieves together all in the same place at the same time?"

"You can add that many again for the camp followers." He turned to the god and smiled. "Kalianah and Jelanna will be having a field day down there. Jondalup's probably doing a roaring trade, too. Soldiers love to gamble. Even Cheltaran will be licking his lips, given the likelihood of disease and injury that comes with war. Let's not even begin to talk about what Death is up to . . ."

"There's no need to rub it in, Brak."

He smiled, fairly certain he understood what had prompted this unexpected divine visitation. "Feeling a bit left out are we, Divine One, with the world about to be plunged into war?"

Dacendaran shrugged uncomfortably. "I was doing all right there, for a while. Things were moving along very nicely, even with a war on the way. All those soldiers . . . all those lovely fat purses . . . Hablet never forgets to pay his troops, I'll grant him that. And then the sacrilegious bastards chopped the hands off some poor *court'esa* who stole her customer's pay in my honour and now there's barely a larcenous thought in the whole damn war camp."

"That must have hurt."

"It *does*," the god agreed. "You have no idea how much it wounds me to see my followers abandon—"

"I was referring to the poor girl who got her hands chopped off, Divine One," the Halfbreed cut in. "I really don't give a fig about your followers."

Far from being offended, the god smiled knowingly. "You can pretend all you want, Brak, but I know you're mine."

"Is that right?"

"You're a *bandit*, Brakandaran," the god pointed out with a smug grin. "You have been for years, now. That puts you right up there with the burglars and the pickpockets."

"I am at the moment," Brak admitted, rubbing his chin thoughtfully, as if he was torn with indecision. "But there's a war about to start soon, you know. I can already feel myself being tempted to abandon my life of larceny for the noble pursuit of war."

"What do you mean?" Dace demanded.

Brak forced himself not to smile. "I'm just saying, Dace . . . It's going to be hard to resist swapping the joys of robbing fat merchants in the Widowmaker Pass when the higher calling of dealing out death to the poor, unsuspecting Hythrun beckons. All for the greater glory of Zegarnald, the God of War, of course."

"I hope you're joking."

Brak spun around to find Dace had vanished as Chyler Kantel approached from the trees behind him.

In her own way, Chyler Kantel was a queen and her kingdom was the Sunrise Mountains around the Widowmaker Pass. Admittedly, the bulk of her subjects made their living from robbing caravans in the pass, but there was far more to Chyler's Children than simple banditry. Every village in the mountains paid homage to her and in return, Chyler and her ragtag band supplied them with the protection Hablet's army wasn't interested in providing, along with selling them goods relieved from the caravans raided in the pass.

It was the reason, Brak knew, he'd stayed in the mountains with the bandits for so long. Here, among Chyler's Children, he could fight regularly and maybe if he was lucky, some young, hot-blooded caravan guard would get the better of him someday, and he might die. In the meantime, along with honouring Dacendaran, he occasionally got a chance to help the villagers in the region. It went some way to making up for what he'd done.

Chyler was bundled up against the cold in a fur-lined coat similar to Brak's (also stolen from a passing caravan), two layers of wool under her leather trousers and high, sheepskin-lined boots. There were silver streaks in her thick red hair these days, and laughter lines around her eyes that remained even when she wasn't laughing. Chyler was still as handsome and as lithe as a woman half her age. She was tough, too, in a way Brak found quite beguiling. He had seen her kill as coldly as an assassin and an hour later found her crying like a child when she was forced to put down a sickly dog.

Chyler stopped behind him on the ledge, looked around curiously and then fixed her gaze on Brak. "Who were you talking to?"

"The God of Thieves."

Chyler smiled. "If anybody else told me that, I'd swear they were crazy. But with you . . . Did he have anything interesting to say?"

"The gods rarely do," he said. "Mostly he was just whining about how Zegarnald and the other gods are getting stronger because there's a war on the way, which means he's getting weaker."

"He's got a point," Chyler agreed, stepping up next to Brak as she studied the vast war camp below. "We won't be robbing fat merchants—or any other kind—for quite some time, once that lot starts moving through the pass. I actually feel sorry for the Hythrun."

"*You*? Pitying the Hythrun? There's something I never thought I'd live to see."

She shrugged. "Well, first they get slaughtered by the plague and now, when they're at their weakest, Hablet's going to overrun them, and with the borders closed, they don't know anything about it. Doesn't seem fair, really."

"Not a lot about war is fair, Chyler."

"Do you think someone should warn them?"

"Who? The Hythrun?"

"No," Chyler replied, rolling her eyes. "The bloody Medalonians! Of course, the Hythrun!"

Brak shook his head emphatically. "Oh, no! Zegarnald would just *love* that."

Chyler looked at him in confusion. "What do you mean?"

"Tip off the Hythrun about the invasion and they'll be waiting for Hablet the moment he breaks through the pass."

She raised a brow questioningly. "And this is bad *because* . . . ?"

"Because it'll give Zegarnald a real war," he explained. "Right now, the chances are good Hablet will move through the pass as soon as spring arrives and be in Greenharbour before the Hythrun can say 'Oh my god! We're being invaded!' As you say, they've been decimated by plague and Lernen Wolfblade couldn't win a battle if it was between two toy ships in his own bathtub. With luck, this war might be over by the end of summer."

"But if the Hythrun get enough warning and find themselves someone capable of actually mounting a defence," Chyler concluded, "it might drag on for years."

"And the God of War would like nothing better."

"I thought you liked the Hythrun, Brak."

"I do. But I don't like pandering to Zegarnald's ego."

"But the Hythrun are bound to put up some kind of fight. How do you think the Fardohnyans will get past Winternest?"

"Don't know. Don't really care, either."

The bandit leader looked at him curiously. "Are you really going to stand by and do nothing about this war?"

"There's nothing I *can* do, Chyler."

"But you're Brakandaran the Halfbreed."

"I'm Brak the Bandit," he corrected. "I wish you'd give up this notion I'm anything more than that. It's not my responsibility to put the world to rights."

Chyler sighed. "You're rather disappointing for a legendary hero; you know that, don't you?"

"Then stop thinking of me as one. I'm really nothing of the sort."

Chyler slipped her arm through his and smiled. "I'm happy to keep your little secret, Brak, but no matter how much you try to forget it, you're still the Halfbreed. You're a legend, whether you want to be or not."

"Look, I've been here for the better part of twelve years, Chyler . . ." he began. It sounded a long time but to Brak it meant very little. Twelve years for a man who had lived for more than seven hundred was barely any time at all.

"Ever since I hauled you out of that pile of corpses they tossed over the wall at Westbrook the night we first met," she reminded him.

"Exactly. And in all that time, have you ever seen me do *anything* that might lead you to believe I have any sort of magical powers?"

"No," she conceded. "I believe it was releasing all the prisoners in Westbrook while looking for a child rumoured to be a sorcerer that convinced me. Or it might have been you making a hidden gate appear in a solid stone wall that you knew about because apparently you were at Westbrook when they built the place six hundred years ago. Or maybe it was the fact you survived being run through and tossed over the walls of Westbrook? Or the fact you seem to be able to speak to the gods at will. Should I go on?"

"That doesn't prove anything," he insisted. "Other people speak to the gods."

"But you're the only person I've ever met who gets a response."

"Maybe I don't," he suggested with a thin smile. "Maybe

I'm just some lunatic who hears voices in his head and *thinks* the gods are talking to him."

"Maybe. But that wouldn't account for Wrayan Lightfinger *telling* me you were the Halfbreed."

"You shouldn't believe anything a thief tells you, Chyler."

She laughed. "That's a bit rich, coming from the man who claims he was just talking to the God of Thieves."

Brak smiled. "Exactly my point. Never believe *anything* a thief tells you."

She looked at him curiously. "Does that mean I shouldn't believe you, when I ask if you'll keep an eye on things here for a while?"

"You're going somewhere?"

"I've been summoned."

"By whom?"

"The Plenipotentiary of Westbrook."

"What does he want with you?"

"He didn't say."

Brak was quite alarmed at the prospect. "You're not seriously thinking of going, are you?"

"Is there some reason you think I shouldn't?"

"Hmmm . . ." Brak said, feigning deep thought. "Can I think of a reason why you shouldn't meet with the Plenipotentiary of Westbrook? It couldn't possibly be because the last time you visited Westbrook you got arrested, I suppose? Or the fact there's a price on your head for killing the head of the Qorinipor Thieves' Guild? Maybe I just don't like the idea—"

"All right!" she cut in impatiently. "I get your point! And it's a crazy one. The last Plenipotentiary was killed eight years ago. And on the subject of being wanted for Danyon Caron's murder . . . well, that's all your fault, anyway."

"*My* fault?"

"It was *your* friend, remember, who set the guild straight on who exactly plunged a knife into the back of that perverted little cretin. Up until Wrayan Lightfinger opened up his big trap, nobody knew I had anything to do with it."

"I believe Wrayan *opened his big trap,* as you so eloquently put it, to set the record straight because the Qorinipor Thieves' Guild was threatening to have an assassin sent after him."

"He has no honour," Chyler declared with a wounded look. "He ratted on a fellow thief."

"You were going to let him die for a murder you committed, Chyler. Where's the honour in that?"

"He could have blamed someone else," she said, a little uncomfortably. "He didn't have to tell them the truth."

"So it would have been better to blame an innocent person?"

"That's not what I mean."

"No, what you mean is, you think Danyon Caron deserved to die and it seems patently unfair anybody should be called to atone for it, least of all you."

She glared at him. "If you know what I mean, Brak, why do you argue with me about it?"

"Because I can." He recognised the determined expression on her face. "You're still going to go to Westbrook, though, aren't you?"

"There might be a profit in it for us."

"There might be a gallows waiting for you, too," he countered.

She paused, appreciating his concern, although it was clear she had no intention of letting it get in her way. "Just promise me you'll look after things here while I'm gone, Brak. I can take care of myself."

"No."

"No, *what*?" She looked quite puzzled by his refusal. "Are you saying you don't think I can look after myself?"

"No, I'm saying I won't look after things while you're gone."

"Why not?"

"Because I'm coming to Westbrook with you."

"Why?"

Brak shrugged. "I'm supposed to be a legendary hero, remember? Maybe, if I go along to watch your back, I'll get to do something heroic."

Chyler looked at him for a long moment and then, instead of smiling at his joke, she nodded slowly in understanding. "You're leaving us, aren't you?"

Brak hesitated before answering, and then finally he shrugged. "I don't know," he replied honestly. "I've certainly contemplated the idea." He didn't add the reason he'd been thinking about it so much. *A man had a much better chance of dying in battle than while robbing trading caravans in the Widowmaker Pass.*

"I'll miss you. We all will."

"I actually haven't said I was leaving, yet."

"You don't have to," Chyler told him. "I can see it in your eyes."

"Chyler . . ."

She held up her hand to stop him saying anything more. "Look, you don't have to explain. Not to me. I don't know what you've been hiding from these past twelve years, Brak, and I don't really care. But it's eating you alive. I've always known that. And I've always known whatever you're trying to run from would eventually chew through that rock-hard shell you've so carefully built around yourself and finally hit a nerve. And when it did, you'd have to go."

"It's not you, Chyler, or anyone here."

"I know."

"You don't mind?"

"Of course I *mind*," she said. "You're the best sword I've got. But I'll cope. Chyler's Children drove fear into the hearts of caravan traders the length and breadth of the Widowmaker long before you came along, my friend, and we'll keep doing it long after you're gone. Nobody is indispensable, Brak. Not even the Halfbreed."

"I'll stay until after you've spoken to the Plenipotentiary," he offered. "Just in case he's planning anything nasty."

"I'd appreciate that."

"I won't forget you, Chyler."

"Ten years from now you won't even remember my name," she predicted.

"Ten years from now, Chyler," Brak replied seriously, with as much hope as conviction, "I'll be dead."

ChAPTER 3

Wrayan's suggestion that Starros should honour Dacendaran whilst seeking revenge against the man responsible for his lover's death struck a chord in the young man's heart. Over the next few days he found himself thinking of little else. The need to do something—anything—to make Mahkas pay for his crimes consumed every waking moment and more than a few of his dreams, too. Secretly, he welcomed the distraction. Plotting all manner of dreadful ends for Mahkas Damaran kept his mind off other things. It kept him from having to face his loss. It kept him from having to deal with his new status as a disciple of the God of Thieves.

But mostly, it kept him from having to feel anything, because that was the most terrifying thing of all.

Starros was coping with the discovery that Damin had ordered his soul traded for a quick recovery better than anybody—Wrayan and Kalan included—suspected. What he couldn't face was the emptiness, the certain knowledge that Leila was gone and it was his fault. If he'd only turned her away, the first time she came to his room. If he'd only faced the truth about their relationship and made Leila face it sooner. Perhaps then, it might have been over before it started. Over before they could fall in love. Over before Mahkas could find them in each other's arms. Over before Leila could be made to believe he was dead and she could take her own life to join him in the afterlife.

Despite what he'd said to her, Starros didn't really blame Kalan. His outburst a few days ago had been prompted by frustration as much as anger. He was helpless, hiding down here in the Beggars' Quarter. Helpless and hopeless, not sure where he belonged, just certain he no longer had a place in the life he'd once known as the Chief Assistant Steward of Krakandar Palace.

He was angry at Damin, too, for ordering this drastic change in his circumstances and then leaving him to cope with it alone. It might have been easier to deal with, had Damin been here. At least then, Starros would have something to rail at, a focus for his torment. But Damin had left Krakandar to attend to more important issues. He was Hythria's heir and the fate of a friend came a distant second to the security of the nation.

The thought both cheered and chilled Starros. Someday, Starros knew, when Damin ascended to the throne, Hythria would finally have a prince prepared to put his nation ahead of his personal concerns, something of which no High Prince had been capable for generations. At the same time, it meant Damin was far more ruthless than any of his recent predecessors. If that thought had occurred to Starros then, eventually, it would occur to the other Warlords, and it might begin to worry them. Worried Warlords, Starros knew, had a bad habit of sharpening their knives. Or hiring the Assassins' Guild.

"Why the long face?"

Starros, tucked away out of sight in a booth at the back of the Pickpocket's Retreat, looked up at the man who spoke. He was a tall, balding man in his late forties, his forger's fingers stained with ink.

Starros frowned, not appreciating the interruption. He'd sought refuge here in the hope of remaining anonymous. The heavy beams holding up the low ceiling, the dim lighting and the low hum of conversation gave the taproom a cosy, dark feel that suited Starros's mood well. "Was I looking miserable, Luc? How surprising, seeing as how I've got so much to sing and dance about, too."

Luc North, Wrayan's second-in-command, smiled grimly, taking the padded bench opposite Starros uninvited. "Wrayan said you might need cheering up."

"Can you raise the dead?"

"No."

"Then there's nothing you can do for me, Luc."

"How 'bout a little distraction then?"

"Like what?"

"We'll go honour Dacendaran," Luc suggested. "I know a house over on Weller Street where there's a jewellery box just begging to be lifted. And a very obliging lady of the house, too. She could teach you the finer points of 'taking more than the silverware.'"

"Isn't that what you thieves call rape?"

Luc was obviously offended by the question. "Let's get something cleared up right now, my friend. No thief rapes anyone while honouring Dacendaran and lives to tell about it."

"I never realized your people aspired to such a high moral standard."

"Hang around a bit longer," Luc advised. "You'd be surprised what us *people* believe."

"I'm sorry, Luc. I wasn't trying to be offensive. I'm just not in the mood for honouring anybody at the moment, least of all the god to whom I now apparently belong."

"It could be worse," the forger said philosophically.

"How?" Starros asked.

He smiled crookedly. "They might have sold your soul to Kalianah. You're a good-looking lad. I reckon you'd have been worn out in a month if you were stuck honouring the Goddess of Love seven or eight times a day."

Despite himself, Starros smiled, too. "There is that to be thankful for, I suppose."

"It's not such a bad life, you know," Luc told him. "And

considering what's happened to you lately, old son, it's a bloody miracle you're here to enjoy it."

"I suppose," Starros agreed, wondering what part of Leila killing herself constituted a miracle.

"So, you interested in a little excursion, or not?"

Starros shook his head. "Thanks, but I'm not sure I'm ready for any . . . excursions . . . just yet."

"Well, just let me know when you are. I'll see what I can arrange."

Starros looked at him curiously. "Wrayan's placed you in charge of my conversion to the God of Thieves, has he?"

"Only because he's going away."

That was something Starros hadn't known. "Where's he going?"

"Greenharbour," Luc replied. "He and Lady Kalan are leaving tomorrow. Didn't he tell you?"

"I heard Kalan talking about it, but I didn't realise they were planning to depart so soon."

"I gather if Lady Kalan had her way, they'd have ridden out of Krakandar on Damin Wolfblade's heels."

The feeling that his own woes were a secondary concern in the rapidly escalating threat facing Hythria left Starros feeling quite irrelevant. "Well, I suppose now I'm all better, they don't need to worry about me."

"It's not like you to be so petulant, lad." Luc was obviously trying to be sympathetic, but Starros wasn't in the mood for pity.

"Nothing's the same as it used to be, Luc," he replied, swallowing the last of his ale and climbing to his feet. "Me, most of all."

He turned for the door at the back of the taproom, thinking the solitude of the safe house he'd been so desperate to escape an hour ago was suddenly the most attractive thing on offer. Luc caught his wrist as Starros walked past him.

"Just remember, lad, 'taking more than the silverware' is a game two people have to play willingly. The last thief in

Krakandar who thought he could get away with rape died the very next day."

"Who killed him?" Starros asked, curious, in spite of himself.

"The man who takes care of all the guild's difficult problems," Luc replied. "The head of the guild. Wrayan Lightfinger."

CHAPTER 4

News that the plague was on the wane sent waves of relief through the citizens of Greenharbour. The discovery of an ancient Harshini text in the Sorcerers' Collective Library detailing the management of the disease had been a great boon. Marla had seen to it the news got about that old Bruno Sanval, the Lower Arrion of the Sorcerers' Collective, was responsible for this remarkable discovery and their subsequent triumph over the spread of the disease. Originally, Marla had helped fan the rumour to prevent Alija from taking the credit, but now the tale served an even better purpose. It gave the elusive Bruno Sanval standing with the people of Greenharbour, and with the other members of the Sorcerers' Collective. When Alija fell, there would be no power vacuum into which another despot could step. The transition of power in the Sorcerers' Collective once Alija was dead, she had decided, would be smooth and barely noticeable.

All the best transitions of power were.

There had been no new cases for days now and Marla was seriously considering opening the city gates for the first time in almost three months. Of course, as the problem of the plague began to wane, it merely highlighted all the other problems piling up around her. She sighed wearily. *It's going to take months to sort out the mess.*

"There's only one solution," Marla remarked aloud, without looking up from the report she was reading. This one detailed the woes of that popular disaster area known as the Greenharbour docks and was even more depressing than the report on the dire state of the felting business she'd just put aside because she was in no mood to deal with it. "The Retreat Season has to go."

When Marla received no answer, she looked up and realised she was alone in her brother's study with nothing more than his repulsive murals for company. The candles flickered faintly in the breeze coming from the open windows on her right. Once again, she realized with a start, she'd forgotten Elezaar was dead. Even though it was more than two weeks since they'd buried his child-sized body in the garden of her townhouse next to her late husband, Ruxton Tirstone, the habits of a lifetime were hard to break.

Marla's eyes misted at the pain of the dwarf's betrayal. It was not, however, the fact that he had told her worst enemy, Alija Eaglespike, her innermost secrets before taking his own life that both pained and infuriated the princess, it was his temerity in taking his own life afterwards to escape her wrath. Elezaar was a slave. By rights, he had no will of his own.

How dare you fear me? How dare you leave me to carry this burden alone?

"Did you call, your highness?"

Her brother's seneschal, Corian Burl, stood in the doorway, his hand on the latch, his features shadowed by the candelabra he held. He must have been waiting outside the door, in case the princess needed him.

Marla shook her head. "I was just thinking out loud. Do you think there'd be much of an outcry if my brother abolished the Retreat Season, Corian?" Although everything Marla did, she did in her brother's name, they both knew the High Prince barely even glanced at anything Marla put in front of him for his signature. If anybody was planning to abolish the custom of ordering the Warlords and their retinues out of the capital over the sweltering

Greenharbour summer, it certainly wasn't Lernen Wolf-blade.

The old slave shrugged. "I suspect opinion would be fairly evenly split, your highness. There are just as many highborn who look forward to the Retreat Season as there are those who curse it. Were you . . . or rather, the High Prince, thinking of abolishing the custom?"

"I'm not sure we're going to be able to afford the luxury of a three-month-long vacation this year, Corian."

The slave stepped into the room and closed the door behind him before answering. "If the High Prince abolishes this custom, even temporarily, it will be impossible to reinstate it, your highness. I'd be very sure I can live with the consequences before making such a decision if I were . . . the High Prince."

"Don't worry," she assured him with a faint smile. "I'll see to it the High Prince gives the matter his full consideration."

"I'm sure you will, your highness," the seneschal agreed with a courtly bow.

He'd been a *court'esa* once. And a very good one, if Elezaar's opinion was anything to go on. Even now, although he was well past sixty, Marla thought she could detect some hint of that smug self-confidence the very best *court'esa* somehow managed to convey.

"Will you be much longer this evening?"

Marla glanced toward the windows, a little surprised to find it was completely dark outside. When Corian had lit the candles earlier, it was barely dusk. "I hadn't meant to stay this late, to be honest."

"Can I have a tray brought for you?" the slave offered, walking toward her and stopping in front of the long gilded table that filled the centre of the room. "You've been here since dawn and barely had a bite to eat all day."

"Are you keeping tabs on me, Corian?"

"Always, your highness," the seneschal replied without embarrassment. "It is my job to ensure the ruler of Hythria maintains good health."

"My brother rules Hythria, Corian Burl," she reminded him. "Don't ever forget that."

"Of course, your highness."

Marla leaned back in her chair to ease the stiffness in her shoulders. "Where is the High Prince, anyway?"

"He's retired for the evening, your highness. He wearies easily, these days, and is having some . . . issues, with who his friends and foes might be."

Marla frowned. Her brother's tiredness and his paranoia were simply more symptoms of his failing health. This crisis with the plague had been more fraught for Marla than anybody knew. Hythria certainly couldn't afford the death of her High Prince now. Not with six long years until Lernen's heir came of age at thirty. For months now, she'd lived in fear for her brother and it only got worse after her husband died. If the disease could take down someone as hale and hearty as Ruxton Tirstone, Lernen had no chance. That he had survived the disaster unscathed was something of a miracle in Marla's opinion. Or perhaps a sign the gods were watching over her.

Muttering a silent prayer to Cheltaran, the God of Healing, to watch over her brother for another few years at least, she returned her attention to the seneschal. There was no point fretting about her brother anyway. She knew what was wrong with Lernen and it was likely to drive him mad, long before it killed him. One didn't lead the life he led and not be asked to pay the price eventually. Syphilis had no respect for rank or privilege.

"I should think about getting home too, I suppose." *Not that there's much point*, she added silently to herself. With both Ruxton and Elezaar gone there was nobody waiting for her at home these days. Nobody who cared how her day had been.

Sentimental fool.

"Shall I order your litter brought round, your highness?"

Marla put aside the report on the Greenharbour docks and the need to rebuild the ruined wharf district that had been decimated by fire several years ago. There was always something in the city that needed fixing. It would keep.

"Thank you, Corian," she agreed.

The seneschal bowed and withdrew, leaving Marla alone in the candlelit study with its gaudy, erotic murals, wondering if this was what life would always be like from now on . . .

And then she cursed her own weakness for wallowing in self-pity and rose to her feet. Alone she might be, but Hythria needed her and she'd been carrying that burden without help for more than two decades.

Marla Wolfblade was made of sterner stuff than this.

The house didn't look deserted when she got home. She had an efficient staff. The main rooms were lit brightly and the moment her litter pulled up in the small courtyard at the front of the house with its tinkling fountain dedicated to Patanan, the God of Good Fortune, they swung into action to ensure her slightest whim was catered to. Marla gave their actions little thought. She was too accustomed to their ministrations to even notice them.

"You have a visitor, your highness," one of the slaves—her housekeeper, Cadella—advised, as Marla stepped into the marbled entrance hall.

Marla frowned, wondering who would be so crass as to breach protocol by visiting a widow while she was still in mourning. Then she realised it was more than a month since Ruxton had passed away. *Closer to two months, actually,* she remembered with a start. It was probably the plague that had kept visitors from her door, not protocol. But now, with the plague waning, things were obviously returning to normal.

"I'm in no mood for visitors," she replied. "Tell whoever it is I'm indisposed. Have them make an appointment to see me at the palace tomorrow."

"He was very insistent, your highness," Cadella told her, as she took Marla's shawl and folded it over her arm. "He's been waiting nearly two hours."

"Who is he?"

"He wouldn't give his name, your highness."

She looked at the slave curiously. Cadella was a large middle-aged woman who ruled Marla's household with such military precision that at times she reminded Marla of Geri Almodavar. She'd inherited the slave from Ruxton, whom the woman had served faithfully for close to thirty years. "Are you telling me you allowed a man to wait in my house for two hours without bothering to establish if he was friend or foe, Cadella?"

"He wears the ring of the Assassins' Guild, your highness," the housekeeper explained. "I didn't think it would be polite to ask."

"Very well," she said, a little impatiently. "Have some refreshments sent in to him and tell our guest that I'll be with him shortly."

"As you wish, your highness."

Cadella curtseyed and hurried off to carry out her orders, leaving Marla to wearily climb the stairs to the first floor wondering why the Assassins' Guild was waiting for her in the parlour.

The first thing that surprised Marla about her visitor was h' appearance. She'd been expecting some seedy, furtive l' man, but the man who rose to greet her was well over si tall, his sleeveless, expensively embroidered shirt ra a physique any man half his age would be proi' looked to be in his late thirties or early forties id she himself with the unconscious sureness of a nob manner.

"Your highness," he said with a bow, takir offered and kissing her palm in the tra "Thank you for seeing me." .nis man made

"Who are you?" she asked coolly, th rhaps he'd been a living from being attractive to wom urt'esa, promoted court'esa trained. Perhaps he wa ld following his out-through the ranks of the Assassin iller. No doubt his spe-standing success as a professio n slitting their throats. Or cialty was seducing women an is a little too refined for any-maybe not, she mused. He se *thing so . . . messy. Maybe he smothers his undoubtedly grateful and gloriously sated victims with a pillow once he's had his way with them.*

"I am Galon Miar," the man informed her, still holding her hand.

Marla withdrew her hand, making no effort to hide her disdain. "Alija's latest plaything?"

Galon's perfectly groomed demeanour faltered for an instant. "If you know who I am, your highness, then you must also be aware of the rank I hold in the Assassins' Guild."

"I'm aware of a great deal about you, Master Miar."

He smiled languidly. "*Really*? Do I interest you?"

"Only in so far as I make a habit of knowing intimate details about those who try to ingratiate themselves into the lives of my friends."

"*Alija*?"

"You have *another* mistress?" Marla shrugged, moving around the table to take a seat on the low cushions opposite her visitor. "I take it your business here tonight is for your guild? I doubt Alija trusts you with anything other than her physical needs, so I think I can safely assume you're not here delivering a message from her."

Galon Miar hesitated, which gave Marla a great deal of satisfaction. She hadn't lost her edge.

"That's correct," Galon replied. He remained standing, ʰtely conscious of the fact that Marla had not given him ˙ssion to sit in her presence. "The Raven asked me to ⁄ou."

with ꞯnsiderate of him."

"My ꞎs to remind your highness of her agreement grape from ⁀t?" she asked, leaning forward to select a particularly hⁿtter on the low table. She wasn't feeling gesture made Gaⁿ but she needed the distraction. The "You promised uꞵk at her hand, rather than her face. Marla leaned back aⁿ, your highness."

ʸt the cushions. "Certainly, Master Miar. Did he say which one he wanted? My eldest son, Damin Wolfblade? The High Prince's heir? Or my younger son, Narvell Hawksword? The heir to Elasapine? My stepson, Rodja Tirstone, perhaps, who's now responsible for one of the largest commercial empires in Hythria? Or would you prefer his younger brother, Adham? He's off in Medalon somewhere, I believe. When you find him and inform him of his new career, you will give Adham my regards, won't you?"

Galon seemed amused by her deliberate misunderstanding. "You're a widow once more, your highness. And you're a very beautiful woman. The Raven has no doubt you'll marry again, and when you do it will be another fortuitous arrangement for you and the High Prince, both politically and financially. From the next union, you *will* provide us with the apprentice you promised when you entered into this agreement with the Raven two decades ago, even if you have to give birth to the child yourself."

"And if I don't?" she asked, privately gloating. *Alija's lover thinks I'm very beautiful. He'll want to hope his mistress doesn't find that out any time soon.*

"If you renege on your agreement with the guild, the first thing that will happen is the assassination you arranged all those years ago will become public knowledge. I'm sure that's an embarrassment both you and the High Prince would rather avoid."

Marla studied the man for a moment, and then came to a conclusion that left her almost faint with relief. "But you don't know who it was that I had assassinated, do you?"

"The Raven promised that information would remain secret, your highness. *He* hasn't broken his trust."

She popped another grape in her mouth, hoping she looked unconcerned. "So if the Raven died tomorrow, the secret would die with him and it wouldn't matter what you threatened me with, would it?"

That seemed to amuse Galon, too. "You'd try to have the Raven assassinated, your highness?"

Marla smiled. "Why do you ask? Looking for a bit of extra cash?"

The silence between them was laden with unspoken treachery.

"Thank you," the assassin said eventually, "but I rather like the idea of being the next Raven. Killing the present one would be a very bad career move. My guild takes a dim view of people who assassinate their superiors to expedite their own promotion."

"Not an unwise precaution in light of your profession."

"May I give the Raven your answer?"

"My answer, Master Miar, is what it has always been. I will give your guild an apprentice. As soon as I'm in a position to do so."

Galon bowed to her. "I shall convey your assurances to the Raven. He'll be most relieved."

"Do you have children, Master Miar?"

"If you know as much about me as you claim, your highness, you shouldn't need to ask."

He's quick, this lover of Alija's, which made Marla wonder what someone as obviously intelligent and astute as Galon Miar saw in that aging old whore.

"You have two daughters and a son, if my informants are correct."

"You're remarkably well informed."

"Remarkably," she agreed coolly. "Tell me, would you apprentice *your* son to the Assassins' Guild?"

"I already have."

She raised an eyebrow curiously. "Like father, like son?"

"Only if he grows up to be a legendary lover, a sparkling conversationalist and a brilliant assassin," Galon replied with a grin.

Marla found herself intrigued, despite herself. "You're pretty damn sure of yourself, aren't you, Galon Miar?"

"Comes with the job, your highness." He shrugged. "A lack of confidence in one's own abilities is fatal in my profession."

"I imagine it would be," she agreed, wondering what it would take to rattle that supreme self-confidence. "Is that what Alija sees in you, Master Miar? Or is it just your well-toned body she lusts after?"

He smiled. "Why don't you ask her?"

"Maybe I will," she replied. "Of course, I'm actually more interested in what you see in her. Is it the power a High Arrion of the Sorcerers' Collective represents that has you so enchanted with her?"

"Don't *you* find power arousing?" he challenged, shifting slightly from one foot to the other, the only sign Marla had that he might not be as at ease as he seemed.

"Not when it's Alija Eaglespike wielding it."

"You should try it sometime, your highness," Galon suggested persuasively. "You might find it even more stimulating than money, which—according to popular belief—is what *you* find attractive."

Marla's expression darkened. "Don't even presume to think you know anything about me, Galon Miar. Go back to your guild. Give your superior my answer. This audience is over."

Unapologetically, Galon bowed low, with all the courtly elegance of a nobleman. "As you wish, your highness."

Marla didn't answer. Instead, she ignored him, leaning forward to pick up a plum from the tray, examining it closely as if it was the most important thing in the room before biting into it, giving the blood-red fruit her undivided attention.

Taking the hint, the assassin turned and walked from the room, leaving Marla alone with the platter full of fruit and her racing pulse. She couldn't say for certain, however, if it was the looming threat of exposure by the Assassins' Guild that left her so unsettled or the unexpectedly disturbing presence of Galon Miar.

chapter 5

Damin Wolfblade reined in his horse and turned off the road, allowing the column of Raiders to ride by, the dust of their passage whipped away by the crisp breeze. It was a beautiful day. Too beautiful to be marching to war, even with the knowledge the God of War favoured his endeavour.

As he watched his Raiders riding along the road, their pennons snapping in the breeze, and tried not to dwell on the meaning of being visited by a god, Tejay Lionsclaw spied him and pulled away from the column, trotting over to where Damin was waiting. Dressed like a man in a tooled red leather breastplate bearing the rampant lion escutcheon of Sunrise Province, she didn't look like the mother of four small children. She looked more like the girl Damin had known when he was fostered at her father's stronghold as a child—fierce, determined and as tough as any Raider in her father's army.

Tejay circled her skittish mare and came to a halt beside him. "Something wrong?"

Damin debated telling her about Zegarnald's visit, but decided against it, for no reason he could readily identify. Instead, he shook his head. "I was just wondering what Charel Hawksword is going to make of me riding into Elasapine with my army."

"I'm sure, once you've had a chance to explain . . ."

He frowned. "I wrote him before we left, but if you were the Warlord of Sunrise Province and I was riding across your border with a couple of thousand troops, would you believe my explanation, or would you ride out to meet me with every sword you could muster at your back?"

"The latter, probably," she conceded. "Still, Narvell's effectively commanding Elasapine's troops these days, even if he isn't old enough to have the job officially. One assumes your half-brother will give you the benefit of the doubt."

"I hope so."

She looked at him askance. "You're kidding, aren't you?"

Damin grinned. "Yes."

"Well, it's good to see you joking around again. That's the first genuine smile I've seen since you got back to Krakandar from that cattle raid."

Damin's smile faded. "There hasn't been a lot to smile or joke about lately, Tejay."

"That never actually stopped you in the past."

He stared at her with a hurt look. "Are you accusing me of being shallow?"

"Wasn't that what you were trying so hard to make everyone believe?" she asked.

"I know, but . . . well, I thought my *real* friends would see the truth."

Tejay leaned across and patted his arm comfortingly. "Your real friends do see the truth about you, Damin. And we love you anyway. In spite of that."

"Tell me again why I let you come along?"

"You want to stop an invasion," she reminded him. "Which is going to come through my province."

"And is your husband likely to be waiting on *your* border with his army when we try to cross into Sunrise Province?"

"I doubt it."

He glanced at her, puzzled by her tone. "I gather that won't be because he welcomes our presence."

"More likely he won't be aware of it. Terin can be . . ." she hesitated as she searched for the right word.

"What?"

"Easily distracted," she finished eventually.

"What the hell does that mean?"

"He has other things on his mind." She shrugged.

Damin was getting a little tired of Tejay and her cryptic comments about her husband. "You promised me you'd tell me what's going on," he reminded her.

"And I will, Damin, it's just—"

"It's just *nothing*," he cut in. "Time's up, Tejay. Tell me now, or I'll have Adham escort you back to Krakandar and you can wait out this war doing needlework with my Aunt Bylinda and Luciena, and the rest of the women and children."

She glared at him. "You wouldn't dare!"

"Try me."

Tejay fumed silently beside him for a long time before she spoke again. The column continued to move past them. Adham waved as he rode by, sitting beside Rorin in the centre of the column. The dozen or more supply wagons were almost on them before Tejay deigned to answer his challenge.

"Terin is very conscious of the fact that his father was a bastard son promoted to Warlord," she said finally. "He believes I consider him beneath me. That I think I'm somehow better than he is because I come from a long line of Warlords and he's the son of a bastard soldier."

"Do you?"

She glared at him. "If I think myself a better person than Terin Lionsclaw, Damin, it's only because his actions lack nobility, not because of his birth."

"So he thinks you're a snob," Damin concluded.

"It's more than that," she replied heavily. She hesitated, and then the words began to tumble out of her as if they'd been pent up against a wall and Damin had finally forced her to breach it. "You can't conceive of what it's been like, Damin. His every waking moment is devoted to proving he's better than me. Better than my father, better than my brother, even better than his own father. It governs his every action. You can't draw breath without him reading something into it, some implied criticism or insult. To start with, it was just when we were alone, but the longer we're married the worse it gets. Even Chaine took him to task about it, on more than one occasion. He ridicules me in public every chance he gets because he thinks it proves he's better than me."

She hesitated, brushing away an annoying insect, but steadfastly refusing to look at him. "I stopped inviting my family to visit Cabradell years ago. I have no friends be-

cause he doesn't allow them in the palace. I can't go anywhere without having to explain where I am every moment
of the day and who I'm with. He doesn't love me, but he's
insanely jealous. I'm allowed no *court'esa* and when I once
made the mistake of getting a little too relaxed in the company of one of my bodyguards, he had the man falsely accused of adultery and put to death."

"Then how did you ever convince him to let you take the
children . . ." Damin's words trailed off and he stared at her.
"He didn't let you go, did he? You were leaving him."

"But then the plague got in the way," she said. "Which is
why I turned north to Krakandar when I realised I couldn't
get to Natalandar. There was no way I could face going
home. After Chaine died, I knew it was only going to get
worse. My father-in-law at least made it tolerable because he
had the power to curb the worst of Terin's excesses. I
couldn't turn back, Damin. Even if the thought of going
back to my husband hadn't been so unendurable, the
chances are good Terin would have had me killed the moment I stepped foot back in Cabradell Palace for taking the
children away."

"He knew you were leaving him?"

"Oh, yes. In my righteous indignation, I made the mistake
of leaving a letter, spelling out—in no uncertain terms—
what I thought about him."

"Then he's not likely to take your return to Sunrise
Province at the head of the armies of Krakandar and Elasapine in a very good light, is he?"

She shook her head. "I'm sorry, Damin."

He shrugged philosophically. "It's not your fault, Tejay.
It's just another problem we have to deal with."

"You say that because you've never been through the torment of living with someone like Terin Lionsclaw," she sighed.

Damin's frown deepened. "Did he hurt you, Tejay?"

She looked away, still refusing to meet his eye. "That's
not the issue, Damin."

"If he laid a hand on you in anger, my lady, I'll *make* it an
issue."

"You need to worry about Hablet and his invasion, Damin. Terin may be a cowardly little prick, but he's a loyal Hythrun. You need him *and* his army if you're going to defend Hythria."

"You said he was easily distracted," Damin reminded her. "The man you describe sounds quite the opposite. Almost obsessive, even."

"Terin's feelings of inferiority aren't confined to me, Damin. He thinks every vassal in Sunrise Province is looking down on him, criticising him, judging him. And that damned Karien just makes it worse."

"What damned Karien?"

"Renulus is his name," Tejay explained. "Chaine hired him to do a census of Cabradell City about two years ago. He moved into the palace and never left. Nor, incidentally, has he ever produced a count of Cabradell's population. But that doesn't seem to bother my husband. The two of them became great friends within days of meeting. Now he's all but running the province and Terin just lets the sly little maggot do whatever he wants."

"And he's a *Karien*, you say?" Damin asked curiously.

"Strange, isn't it? I always thought the Kariens couldn't bear to be parted from their precious god long enough to travel into the evil heathen south, but this chap seems to manage. And what's worse is Renulus has Terin believing the whole world is against him, including me. My husband spends most of his time trying to foil the plots Renulus has convinced him are going on all around him. Today it will be poor old Murvyn Rahan in Warrinhaven, tomorrow it'll be Lord Branador up at Highcastle . . ." She sighed, shaking her head. "You'll probably be halfway to Cabradell before either one of them notices your army, Damin, and when they do, it'll all be part of yet another dire conspiracy, as far as my husband is concerned."

"If he's behaving so erratically, they won't be imaginary plots for long, my lady," Damin warned. "Particularly not if people come to believe a Karien has his ear."

"I know that," Tejay agreed helplessly. "And *you* know it. But there's nothing I can do to convince Terin he's being a fool. It broke my heart, living in Cabradell, Damin. Sunrise should be the richest province in Hythria. We control the only trade routes into Fardohnya. We have fertile soil, rivers teeming with life, enough lumber in the mountains to see us through to the end of time. And Terin just lets it all go while he tries to consolidate his position in a world where a good half of his enemies are in his own mind."

"You know, Elezaar has a saying," Damin told her. "By the time you've killed your last enemy, burned his last village and slaughtered his last chicken, it's too late to discover you can't enjoy being a conqueror if all you have left to rule over is a field of smoking ashes."

"Elezaar seems to have a saying for every occasion."

"It's probably the most annoying thing about him," Damin agreed, "besides his nasty tendency to report every little thing I do to my mother."

"But at least you took some notice of what you were being taught," Tejay sighed. "It's a pity Elezaar, or someone like him, wasn't responsible for teaching Terin."

Damin leaned over and patted her arm encouragingly. "Then we'll have to re-educate Lord Lionsclaw ourselves. And maybe do something about his little Karien friend, while we're at it."

"Good luck," she replied sceptically.

The column had almost completely passed them by. As the last of the supply wagons trundled past, Damin gathered up his reins. "Race you to the head of the column?"

Tejay rolled her eyes. "You really are such a child sometimes, Damin Wolfblade."

He laughed. "You're just afraid you can't beat me."

"You think?" she challenged. Urging her mount into a gallop, Tejay charged forward leaving Damin staring after her in surprise.

"That's cheating!" he yelled after her.

Without looking back, Tejay indicated exactly what she thought of his opinion with a rather crude hand gesture more common to a Raider than the highborn wife of a Warlord. Damin laughed at her as he took off in pursuit.

Accompanied by the cheers of the watching troops, he overtook Tejay a few paces from the head of the column.

Panting from the effort of the short, sharp ride, Tejay caught up with him a moment later, her fair hair whipped back by the cool breeze. The sun was shining brightly, but there wasn't much warmth in it. Her cheeks and the tip of her nose were rosy from the brisk wind. "You just can't bear to lose, can you?" she accused as she reined in beside him.

"My mother says that's an admirable quality in a prince."

"Your mother is hardly objective, Damin."

"That doesn't mean she's wrong."

Tejay wasn't amused. "Well, I just hope Hablet appreciates your intolerably competitive spirit. I'm not sure Starros will."

Damin looked at her, puzzled by her abrupt change of subject. And her reproachful tone. He'd thought they were just fooling around. "What's that supposed to mean?"

"I mean, Damin Wolfblade," she scolded like a disapproving big sister as they rode at the head of the column, "that in your endless desire to win at all costs, you made a decision about your friend that really wasn't yours to make."

"How does that make me intolerably competitive?"

She rolled her eyes. "You won't even let death beat you, Damin. I think that qualifies as intolerably competitive."

He was wounded by her accusation. "You say that like it's a bad thing."

"Maybe it is."

Damin still wasn't sure why she was rebuking him. He certainly didn't feel like he'd done the wrong thing for Starros. "Would you rather I did nothing and left Starros to die?"

"What if he was *meant* to die?"

"You don't know that."

"Neither do you."

"I won't regret it," Damin told her. "No matter what you say."

"*Won't?*" she asked.

"I can't afford to regret anything, Tejay. Not if I want to rule Hythria someday and still maintain my sanity."

Tejay studied him curiously. "Is that another one of Elezaar's infamous Rules of Gaining and Wielding Power?" she asked. "Or one of your mother's pearls of wisdom?"

"Hard as it may be for you to believe, my lady," he informed her, "I actually came to that conclusion all on my own."

Before Tejay could answer, one of the scouts galloped toward them, his horse rearing as he hauled the beast to a halt in front of the column.

"We've got trouble," the man announced, turning his horse sharply to bring the excited beast under control. "On the border."

"What sort of trouble?" Damin asked.

"Your brother's waiting for us, your highness," the scout informed him. "And Lord Hawksword said to tell you that you're out of your mind if you think he's going to let anybody cross into Elasapine uninvited—even you—with an army at their heels."

Damin reined in his horse and brought the column to a halt. Almodavar, followed by Rorin and Adham, cantered forward to find out why Damin had stopped their progress.

When he explained what was going on, Almodavar nodded in understanding, apparently unsurprised. "Charel Hawksword is a wise man."

"Charel?" Adham asked. "I thought it was Narvell waiting for us at the border."

"On Charel's orders," Almodavar replied. "You can bet your life on it."

"But why?" Rorin asked. "Have you done something to upset the old man, Damin?"

"Not that I know of."

"It's because Charel's heir is the younger brother of Hythria's future High Prince," Tejay concluded, beginning to understand what Almodavar was getting at. "And he's trying to establish Narvell's independence."

"That's what this will be all about," the old captain agreed. "Just a show of force for the sake of appearances."

"Great!" Damin sighed impatiently. "We're facing a Fardohnyan invasion and Narvell decides to make a point with Elasapine's army. We really don't have time for this."

"Maybe, if you explained what is going on to Narvell?" Rorin suggested.

Damin thought about it for a moment, certain his younger brother wouldn't be trying to impede their progress if he knew the real reason for it. He turned to the scout who had delivered the news. "Did you actually speak to Lord Hawksword?"

The scout shook his head. "No, your highness. It was one of his officers who passed on the message. I don't think Lord Hawksword was even on the border at the time."

"How can you be sure?" Adham asked.

"When I arrived they were debating among themselves whether to send for him—to the manor house, they called it—but in the end, they decided not to disturb him. I'd gotten the gist of their intentions by then, anyway."

"The *manor* house?" Damin repeated, a little confused.

"They'll mean Zadenka Manor," Rorin suggested. "Lord Warhaft's estate. It's right on the border. He's probably staying there."

"Do you know where to find it?"

The young sorcerer nodded. "Sure. Keep going along the highway until you reach the village of Zadenka and follow the sign pointing left to Zadenka Manor. It's not really a great feat of navigation, Damin."

"Good," Damin said. "Then it shouldn't take you long to get there, should it?"

Rorin looked at him in confusion. "What?"

"I want you to ride for Zadenka Manor, Rorin, take that brother of mine aside and explain to him what's going on. Give him a chance to withdraw gracefully before we get to the border."

"Why me?"

"Because he ordered you to," Adham said. "He's the prince. They're allowed to give orders like that. Do it all the time, I've noticed."

Rorin seemed unimpressed by Adham's attempt at being witty. He turned his attention to the prince, ignoring Damin's stepbrother completely. "Anything else you want me to tell him while I'm there?"

"Just make him see how important this is, Rorin," Tejay said, before Damin could offer his suggestion. "Tell him Charel can prove he's not his big brother's lackey some other time. We don't have time for a border skirmish. Even a small one."

Damin indicated his agreement with a nod and turned his gaze on the sorcerer. "You heard the lady." To the scout he added, "Stay with Master Mariner. Don't let any harm come to him."

The scout saluted in acknowledgment of the order and gathered up his reins. Rorin did the same, smiling at the rest of them. "On the bright side, I guess this means I'll get to sleep in a real bed tonight."

"We'll see you at the border tomorrow," Damin promised.

"Count on it," the young man replied, turning his mount in the direction of the scout.

Annoyed more than concerned, Damin watched them cantering down the road until they disappeared behind the crest of the next rise and then gave the order to move out. As the column moved ahead he was left wondering why Charel Hawksword, a man he looked on as a beloved surrogate grandfather, would choose now, when they could least afford it, to start playing politics.

chapter 6

*S*tarros had just finished wearily pulling off his boots when he heard the sound of a door closing in the small room adjacent to his bedroom. The door inside the tiny dressing room clicked shut and a moment later Leila emerged from the slaveways, dressed in a nightgown, her long fair hair hanging loose around her face, rippled from being braided so tightly all day.

Even though Starros knew he was dreaming, in his mind's eye she crossed the small bedroom in three steps and wordlessly stepped into his arms. *He held her close, the feeling so real, so intense, that he felt almost overwhelmed by it; a moment of sheer bliss for both of them when neither had said a word, so neither of them was able to shatter their fragile happiness by speaking of reality.*

After a time she lifted her head from his shoulder and he kissed her, and then let her go and wiped a stray tear from her cheek. She smiled wanly, and sniffed back the rest of her tears.

"*I'm sorry,*" he remembered telling her, not sure why he was apologising.

"*It's not your fault, my love,*" Leila sighed.

"*You know, I don't think I ever really lamented the fact that I was common-born until tonight, when I realised how far out of my reach you really are.*"

"*I'm here in your arms, aren't I?*" she whispered, kissing him again.

"*Yes,*" he agreed. "*In secret. In the dark . . .*"

With a jerk, Starros sat bolt upright, splashing his ale on the stained wooden table of the booth, as he suddenly realised where he was. Despite both Wrayan and Luc warning Starros to stay out of sight, for fear news of his miraculous recovery might make its way to the palace, he found himself drawn back to the Pickpocket's Retreat. He sat alone in a corner booth and spoke to nobody, but he wasn't there for the conversation. It was the sound of other voices that he craved; the nearness of other living souls. Alone, Starros had only his memories of Leila, his guilt and her ghost for company, but even the close proximity of other people wasn't enough sometimes to fend off his despair.

And the uncomfortable urge to steal something.

"Another ale, lad? You've spilt more of that than you've swallowed."

Starros looked up, pulling his dripping sleeve out of the puddle of ale. Hary Fingle, the proprietor of the Pickpocket's Retreat, was looking down at him with concern. He glanced at the mess he'd made and looked up at the white-haired tavern owner. "Thanks, Hary, but I think I'll just sit on this one for a while longer."

"Well, just call Fee if you want another. Wrayan's picking up the tab. I daresay he'd prefer you drank it, though, rather than swim in it."

"That's nice of him."

"The Wraith looks after his friends."

"Wrayan the Wraith, eh? Odd to hear him called that."

"There's more people in Krakandar who know him by that name than any other," Hary said. "It's only you folks from the palace who think he's some sort of gentleman rogue who never actually gets his hands dirty."

"I'm not one of the 'folks from the palace' any longer, Hary."

"You'd be paying a damn sight more for that ale if you were, lad," Hary chuckled. "Keep your head down, eh?"

The tavern owner moved off to greet another customer in the noisy, crowded taproom, leaving Starros alone. He wasn't given long to enjoy his solitude, however. A moment later, Luc North slipped into the seat opposite with a fresh tankard of his own.

"You're going to be here a long while drowning your

sorrows at the rate you're drinking, Starros," the forger remarked. "You've been nursing that damn tankard half the morning."

"Are you watching me now?"

"Funny, but that's what I thought Wrayan meant when he asked me to keep an eye on you."

"I've been thinking about what Wrayan said, Luc."

"What did he say?"

"About stealing from Mahkas."

"Well, that's a step in the right direction. Dacendaran will be pleased."

"He said I should steal *everything* from him. He didn't mean that literally, did he?"

The forger shrugged. "Not unless you think you can organise the removal of the entire contents of Krakandar Palace without anybody noticing."

"Then what *did* he mean?"

"Take something that *means* everything to him, I suppose."

Starros frowned. "I would have thought that was Leila."

"Well, that's not really an option any longer," Luc remarked carelessly. "What else does he hold dear?"

"Krakandar," Starros replied without hesitation.

The forger pursed his lips thoughtfully. "Then if you really want to avenge your lover and honour your god, Starros, that's what you need to steal from Mahkas Damaran. Krakandar Province."

"And how do you propose I do that?"

Luc smiled. "I believe that's where the whole 'criminal mastermind' talent comes in."

"I'm not a criminal mastermind," Starros pointed out.

"You're going to have to be to pull this off, old son," the forger warned with a grin. He rose to his feet and tossed a few copper rivets on the table for his ale. "I imagine it'll keep you off the streets for a while, trying to figure it out, at any rate. Have you said goodbye to Wrayan?"

"He's going today?"

"Any minute," the forger said. "He's out in the stables with Lady Kalan getting ready to leave."

At that news, Starros abandoned his ale and hurried out the back of the tavern through the kitchens. It was raining outside, a gentle soaking rain so fine it was almost a mist. He found Wrayan and Kalan leading their mounts and a pack-horse out of the stables into the yard. Kalan was dressed in a dark green riding habit and a long matching cloak, her long blonde hair braided tightly against her head. Wrayan wore a long, dark leather coat that reached almost to his ankles, split at the rear to allow him to ride.

"You weren't going to leave without saying goodbye, were you?" Starros asked as Kalan grabbed a handful of mane and placed her foot in the stirrup.

"Of course not," she said, swinging up into the saddle. "I knew you'd come to see us off."

"That's why I sent Luc in to find you," Wrayan added. "Will you be all right once we're gone?"

Starros shrugged. "I'll survive."

"If you need anything, just ask Luc," the thief told him. "Or Hary. And stay out of sight. You're safe enough here in the Beggars' Quarter while Xanda's minding the shop, but you don't know what Mahkas will do when he's back on his feet."

"I'll be all right, Wrayan."

"Are you sure, Starros?" Kalan asked, looking down at him with concern.

"Yes, Kalan, I'm sure. Now go save Hythria and stop worrying about me."

"It's not too late to change your mind and come with us," Wrayan offered.

Starros shook his head. "I'd rather stay here. It's kind of hard to explain."

"I think I understand. Take care, my friend." The two men shook hands. "And I mean it about keeping your head down. Mahkas won't have forgotten you."

"I'm not likely to forget about him, either."

"Painful though it might be, you do know Leila's death isn't likely to have changed anything with Mahkas, don't you? I've known men like him before. You've as much chance of a change in him as you have trying to change the past."

"So don't do anything foolish," Kalan warned, as Wrayan climbed into the saddle.

"I'll be careful," Starros assured them both. "I promise."

"Really careful?" Kalan asked.

"Yes. And you be careful, too," he replied, stepping back to allow them to pass. "It's a long way to Greenharbour and there's more than just plague and the odd bandit out there to worry about."

Kalan looked across at her travelling companion. "I have Wrayan to protect me."

"But who's going to protect Wrayan from you?"

"I've been wondering the same thing," Wrayan agreed. "Now get out of this rain, Starros. We'll be fine. Just take care and don't let Luc depose me while I'm gone."

Starros figured Wrayan was joking. Luc North was probably the most loyal deputy any head of the Thieves' Guild had ever been blessed with. "I'll watch him. Just like he's watching me. On your orders, I believe."

"A man in my position can never be too careful," Wrayan replied. He tugged on the packhorse's lead rope to get him moving. "Be careful, Starros."

"You too, Wrayan," he replied. "Bye, Kalan."

Kalan looked down at him for a moment and then clucked at her horse to get her moving. Starros waited in the gentle rain until they'd turned down the lane behind the tavern and were out of sight, before heading back inside to the warmth of the Pickpocket's Retreat, his ale and the problem of how he was going to steal Krakandar Province from under the nose of Mahkas Damaran.

chapter 7

The Plenipotentiary of Westbrook was a fat, jolly little man who'd bought his position from Lecter Turon, King Hablet's eminently corruptible seneschal. He'd moved to the border fortress with his four wives and seventeen children and set about making the place his own personal kingdom some three years ago. After a series of commanders interested only in making a quick profit and returning to Talabar to enjoy the fruits of their labours as soon as they could possibly manage it, Blaire Baraban was actually a pleasant change. Interested in securing not just the fortress, but much of the surrounding countryside, he extended his benevolent corruption to the entire region and looked like he was settling in for a nice long stay.

Chyler had dealt with him before, usually when he tried to extend his influence into those lawless areas of the mountains that were traditionally Chyler's realm. The Plenipotentiary of Westbrook was a wily adversary, however, and after testing his limits in the early days of his reign, figured out just how far he could push Chyler before she reacted. Consequently, the mountains had been remarkably peaceful for the last three years and Baraban made a point of consulting Chyler before he did anything that might set her off, in the territory she considered her domain.

The man was, Chyler explained to Brak as they waited in his anteroom, as corrupt and self-serving as any previous incumbent in Westbrook, but at least he was honest about it. He didn't pretend to have any honour and didn't expect others to have it either. That made him much easier to deal with because you always knew exactly where you stood with him.

He greeted Chyler expansively as she and Brak were shown into his office, as if he was genuinely pleased to see her. After offering her a seat and gushing several insincere compliments about her health, beauty and good taste in fashion (she was dressed in men's clothes under a bulky, shapeless sheepskin-lined coat) he turned his attention to Brak.

"And who is this, Madam Kantel? Your bodyguard?"

"Something like that," Brak replied.

The Plenipotentiary of Westbrook smiled nervously and took a step back. Brak was a good foot taller than the tubby little man. He liked intimidating him.

"Well, then . . . that's as it should be, I suppose." He laughed warily, walking backwards until he had the bulk of his desk between himself and his visitors. "You know how dangerous the roads are . . . what with bandits, and all . . ."

"Why did you ask for this meeting, my lord?" Chyler asked impatiently, no more inclined to laugh at Baraban's jokes than Brak was.

Fixing his attention on the bandit leader, the Plenipotentiary of Westbrook assumed a businesslike air. "I have a proposition for you, Madam Kantel. One that should go some way to compensating your . . . *associates* . . . for their loss of income since the border was closed."

Chyler frowned. What Baraban euphemistically referred to as a *loss of income* meant near starvation for the families of her people, who relied on robbing merchants in the pass for their livelihood. "What sort of compensation?"

"I am talking gainful employment, madam. A chance for your people to earn an honest living for a change."

"We're quite happy with a dishonest living, Lord Baraban."

"And who am I to deny any man . . . or woman . . . the chance to honour the God of Thieves, Madam Kantel, but given the lack of traffic in the pass at present, perhaps a temporary shift of allegiance to the God of War might be prudent?"

"The God of *War*?" Brak asked, instantly suspicious.

"There is someone I'd like you to meet," Baraban said, picking up a small mallet resting in the cradle of a decorative brass gong. He tapped the gong twice. Before the metallic notes had faded, the office door opened and an aide stepped into the room.

"Ask General Regis to join us, would you?"

The aide saluted and closed the door again.

"Who is General Regis?" Chyler asked warily. Any high-ranking official made her wary, particularly military ones. Almost as wary as anybody from the Qorinipor Thieves' Guild, who still hadn't forgotten it was Chyler who had killed Danyon Caron some twelve years ago, right here in the great hall of Westbrook. Fortunately, the guild's objection to Caron's murder was more philosophical than actual. Once the identity of the thief's real murderer had come to light (thanks to Wrayan Lightfinger's perfectly understandable desire to save his own neck) and the reasons behind Chyler's actions became widely known, the guild seemed to lose its enthusiasm for seeing their poor dead leader's killer brought to justice. Danyon's successor had done very nicely out of his promotion and there wasn't a thief in the Qorinipor guild who didn't know about their late leader's predilection for youngsters. When all was said and done, the whole world was better off with him dead, so the guild, while officially denouncing Chyler Kantel as Danyon's killer, had made no further attempt to seek vengeance for his murder. But that didn't mean they couldn't change their mind about it and Chyler lived with the worry that they might.

"Axelle Regis," the Plenipotentiary of Westbrook explained. "He's the man King Hablet has placed in charge of the Hythrun invasion."

As Baraban was speaking, the door opened and a much younger man than Brak was expecting stepped into the office. He wasn't that tall, with a slender build, dark hair and an aristocratic bearing. He wore the pretentious silver and white dress uniform of Hablet's own Guard and appeared to be in his early thirties, which meant he was either exceptionally good or exceptionally well connected at court.

He eyed Brak and Chyler disdainfully. "These are the criminals you propose to employ?" he asked Baraban, without even acknowledging the presence of the Plenipotentiary's guests.

"Ah, yes, my lord, this is Chyler Kantel and her associate, Master . . ." He looked at Brak blankly as it dawned on him he didn't know his name.

"You can call me Brak."

"This is Master Brak."

"Lord Baraban has explained what I expect of you?" Regis asked the visitors.

"Lord Baraban has explained nothing," Chyler replied. "And you can expect all you want, my *lord*, but you won't be getting anything out of me or my people until I get some idea of what's going on here."

"I need more intelligence," Lord Regis announced.

Brak couldn't help himself. "Perhaps you'd be happier just learning to live with what you were born with, my lord."

Regis may have had a lot of friends at court, but apparently he didn't have much of a sense of humour. He glared at Brak. "If you're not going to take this seriously . . ."

"You'll do *what*, my lord?" Chyler asked, grinning broadly. She obviously thought Brak's joke was funny. "Find another band of border bandits to do your dirty work for you?" She rose to her feet, unconcerned. "Fine by me. Come on, Brak, if we leave now we can be back at—"

"Now, now, Chyler, there's no need to be hasty . . ." Baraban hurried to assure her. "Sit down, please, so we can talk about this, eh?"

With some reluctance, Chyler did as Baraban asked and resumed her seat. "What exactly are you offering?"

"Your people are familiar with the mountains," Regis replied, clasping his hands behind his back, standing unconsciously "at ease." Whoever this man was, Brak decided, he had a military background. "I'm led to believe you move quite freely across the border and have ways of doing so which don't involve using the Widowmaker Pass."

"You can forget it, my lord, if you want us to lead your army over the border without going past Winternest," Chyler warned, crossing her legs as she leaned back in her seat. "One man can make it if he knows the terrain, two or three at the most. There's a *reason* they built the road through here, you know."

"But your people *can* move in and out of Hythria without being detected, yes?" Regis was quite adamant about that.

"Yes," Chyler conceded.

"Then that is all I ask of you, Mistress Kantel," he said. "I just want to use your people to find out what's happening in Hythria."

"They're being wiped out by the plague," Brak reminded the general. "That's what's happening in Hythria."

"I'm more interested in their troop movements."

"Assuming they have any troops left to move."

Axelle Regis stared at Brak suspiciously. "You seem singularly unenthusiastic about this operation, Master Brak." His eyes narrowed as he studied Brak more closely. "You're not Fardohnyan, are you?"

"I was born in Medalon, actually, but that's not really the point, is it? What you're asking is no small favour. These people follow Dacendaran. You're asking them to change their allegiance to Zegarnald and risk being hanged as spies if they're caught in Hythria."

"No victory worth having comes without cost," Regis said.

"Which is all well and good when you're paying with *other* people's lives."

"Enough, Brak," Chyler warned, glancing up at him. "I think you've made your point." She turned back to Axelle Regis. "What are you offering?"

"Your people will be paid the same as troops in the regular army and given the honorary rank of non-commissioned officers."

Chyler shook her head emphatically. "Unacceptable! They'll be given the honorary rank of captain and paid accordingly, or we're not interested."

"That's preposterous!" Regis exclaimed. "You want me to accord your rabble the same rank as noblemen?"

"They're going to be taking the greatest risks," Brak pointed out. "Why shouldn't they be paid accordingly?"

"But as *officers*?" The general was appalled. "That's highway robbery!"

Brak smiled. "Did you miss the bit about us being thieves?"

Axelle Regis shook his head. "Absolutely not!"

"Then find your own intelligence." Chyler shrugged, rising to her feet again. She turned and headed to the door with Brak close behind her.

"What if we *paid* them as officers?" Baraban suggested hurriedly. "But they retain the rank of say . . . sergeants?"

Chyler stopped and looked up at Brak, before shaking her head and declaring, "They have to be captains."

"Why?" Regis asked impatiently.

"Because," Brak explained, with a faintly patronising air, "if one of our people is coming across the border with urgent intelligence, he needs to be able to get through your lines and back to the command post to deliver it, or he might as well find himself a nice little tavern behind enemy lines in Hythria somewhere, settle down and stay put for the duration of the war. An officer can commandeer a horse. An officer can make things happen. A non-commissioned officer is just as likely to be left languishing on the front lines, his intelligence rapidly becoming useless, while some jumped-up nobleman's son with more money than military training decides to take it upon himself to judge whether or not the information this *rabble* of ours is carrying is worth passing up the line."

Regis glared at Brak and then, with a great deal of reluctance, he gave in. "I see you have some experience in this area, Master Brak."

"I'm older than I look."

"Can I assume, given the appropriate rank and remuneration, you'll be volunteering your services?"

Brak glanced at Chyler before he agreed. She shrugged, apparently resigned to the inevitable. She knew the last thing he wanted was a war fought every inch of the way to Greenharbour. It would empower Zegarnald to an insufferable degree. If he spied for the Fardohnyans, maybe their victory would be a little swifter, a little cleaner. The fewer men who died fighting, the less the God of War could benefit from their deaths. "You can count me in, I suppose."

"Madam Kantel?"

Chyler sighed. "I'll speak to my men. How many do you want?"

"A dozen to start with. Maybe more if the Hythrun prove to be more organised than we anticipate."

An organised opposition, Brak thought. *That's all we need.*

Brak had no real interest in securing a victory for Hablet of Fardohnya, any more than he particularly cared if Lernen Wolfblade of Hythria was overthrown. He'd lived through dozens of monarchs in both countries. They had come in all varieties, good, bad, evil and benign. For a man who counted his age in centuries rather than years, this pending war was no better or worse than scores of others he'd seen fought.

The only thing about war that never changed, Brak knew, was that Zegarnald grew stronger with every innocent human death, and for no other reason than it irked Brak to see Zegarnald win at anything, he was prepared to do whatever it took to see this war was over and done with in the shortest time possible.

If that meant becoming a Fardohnyan spy, so be it.

Chapter 8

The Walsark Crossroads was the main junction of the roads that led from Krakandar City in the east of the province to Walsark in the north, Byamor, the capital of Elasapine Province in the west (the road Damin and his army had taken a few days ago) and the road south through Izcomdar and Pentamor Provinces to Greenharbour, some eight hundred miles away on Hythria's southern coast. There was a large inn located at the cross-roads and after a brief stop for lunch and some mulled wine to warm their chilled bones, Wrayan and Kalan pushed on, taking the south road, hoping to get as far as Kelvington before dark.

Even under ideal conditions, the journey to Greenharbour would take the better part of three weeks. With plague on the loose, refugees running from it, and the Warlords struggling to maintain control over the major cities with reduced numbers of Raiders, the highways of Hythria were in a state of anarchy. Even Wrayan's status as the head of Krakandar's Thieves' Guild was unlikely to impress a band of hungry refugees looking for food.

For that reason, they opted to stick to the major highways while they were still in Krakandar Province, riding past winter-brown fields, divided by tall green hedgerows and populated with countless woolly sheep waiting patiently for the spring shearing. Once they reached Izcomdar, they would turn off, taking the lesser-used roads in the hope of missing the worst of the marauders, which was the reason they had brought the packhorse along. Wrayan was quite certain he could live off the land if required, but he doubted it was a skill Kalan owned. They were travelling with many more supplies than he normally would have bothered with, had he been travelling alone.

Wrayan rode in silence for much of the way, worried less about Kalan's ability to travel in less than princely comfort than the wisdom of leaving Starros in Krakandar. He'd wanted to bring him along, certain the young man would be much safer under the protection of Princess Marla in Greenharbour than alone in Krakandar if Mahkas Damaran discovered The Bastard Fosterling was still alive. It was not meant to be, though. Starros wasn't going anywhere. He wanted to be near Leila and his grief would not allow him to turn his back on the place where she had been so recently laid to rest.

"What are you thinking about?" Kalan asked curiously.

Wrayan looked at her blankly. "What?"

"I was just wondering what you're thinking about, Wrayan. By the expression on your face, anyone would think you're riding to your own mother's funeral."

"I was just thinking about Starros." He straightened a little in the saddle and glanced at the rolling barley fields on either side of the road, relieved to discover the rain had stopped. The air was cold and although still overcast, a rainbow shimmered faintly on the horizon as the afternoon sun fought its way through the dark grey clouds.

"He'll be fine, Wrayan."

"I suppose."

"Starros was always the brightest of us and he's not impulsive. He won't go looking for trouble."

"I'm more worried about trouble finding him. Did you want to stop at Kelvington tonight or push on?"

"I'd rather push on," Kalan replied, leaning forward to pat her mare's neck encouragingly. "We need to get to Greenharbour as quickly as possible and we've a much better chance of avoiding the plague if we stick to ourselves."

"Are you sure?" he asked doubtfully. "It's going to be cold tonight."

"Don't you think I can handle roughing it a bit?"

"You rode into Krakandar with a baggage train, an honour guard and half a dozen slaves, Kalan."

She tossed her head, offended by what he was implying. "I'll have you know I can be every bit as rustic as you when the occasion calls for it, Wrayan Lightfinger."

"This isn't about being rustic. This is about sleeping on the wet ground on a cold night, probably without a fire because every twig and log in a thirty-mile radius is soaked through. There's nothing wrong with taking shelter in a comfortable inn when it's on offer, you know."

"Is it my comfort you're concerned about? Or your own?"

"Mostly my own," he admitted. "I'm not as young as I used to be. The romance of roughing it in the wilderness has long since lost its allure for me, I'm afraid."

"You're not old," she laughed. "Don't be ridiculous!"

"I'm a lot older than you, Kalan."

"But you're part Harshini," she reminded him. "So your chronological age doesn't really matter. Didn't you say Brakandaran was over seven hundred years old, and didn't look a day over thirty-five?"

"I'm not the Halfbreed, either," he pointed out, wishing she wasn't quite so enchanted by his ancestry.

But Kalan was totally dismissive of any concern he might have that he was getting too old for this sort of adventure. "I've known you since I was two years old, Wrayan. You haven't aged a day in all that time. You still look like a man in his late twenties."

"I may look it," he countered, "but that doesn't mean I feel it."

"Then we'll stop in Kelvington," she conceded. "So you can rest your weary, aching bones, you poor, decrepit, old thing."

"Thank you, my lady, I'd appreciate that."

She studied him, her face creased with concern. "You don't really think of yourself as old, do you, Wrayan?"

"I try not to think of it at all, actually."

"I never think of you that way."

"That's because you're a nice girl who's too polite to offend one of her mother's oldest friends."

"I think of you as *my* friend," she corrected, a little miffed. "Not my mother's friend. And I'll have you know, I'm not a 'nice girl' either. I'm a woman."

"I did notice that."

She looked at him sideways with a very suggestive leer. "Did you, now?"

Wrayan shook his head, recalling what Rorin Mariner had said about Kalan and the trail of cast-off lovers she left in her wake. For a brief moment, he was afraid she had plans to add him to her list. "Don't waste your *court'esa*-trained wiles on me, Kalan Hawksword. I've fought off far more irresistible creatures than you, in my time, and still emerged with my honour—and my sanity—intact."

"Who?" she demanded.

"A Harshini princess, for one," he admitted, thinking the truth of how different they were might be the easiest way of convincing Kalan her childhood crush was just that, and never likely to blossom into anything more. They would be on the road a long time together in the days to come and much of it alone. Better to get this cleared up at the outset.

"You turned down a Harshini princess?" she asked in surprise, although whether it was because he had met the Harshini or she was impressed by his strong moral fibre, Wrayan wasn't sure. "Weren't you even a little bit curious?"

"Don't worry, Kal, I had my curiosity sated plenty," he assured her, immediately wishing he'd never brought up the subject. He'd expected Kalan to shy away from the topic, not interrogate him about it.

Her eyes lit up at the news. "So you *did* sleep with your Harshini princess?"

"Actually, we didn't sleep much at all."

Kalan laughed delightedly. "You really are quite the lad, aren't you, Master Lightfinger? I always wondered what you really got up to with the Harshini. All those tales of wise kings, indescribably beautiful music, playful demons and learning how to use your magic properly, when in fact, you were just bed-hopping your way through Sanctuary. No wonder poor old Fee could never pin you down."

"I wasn't bed-hopping."

"Of course not," she laughed.

Her laughter was starting to irritate him. She simply didn't understand. "Well, before you get too envious of my conquests, Kalan, spare a thought for what it's been like for me since then. There's a reason the Sisters of the Blade set out to destroy the Harshini, you know. It was fear as much as vindictiveness."

"You mean the legend that once you've had a Harshini lover, nothing else can ever make you happy, is really true?"

"Painfully so," he admitted.

Kalan studied him curiously. "I gather that hasn't stopped you trying, though?"

Despite himself, Wrayan smiled. "I'm a thief, Kalan, not a Karien priest."

"Well, there's still hope, then," she said, and pulling the

lead rein of the packhorse, kicked her horse into a trot. Kalan rode ahead, towing the hapless beast behind her, leaving Wrayan staring after her, more than a little concerned by what she meant.

chapter 9

The need to prove to herself that she was unafraid of Marla Wolfblade prompted Alija's decision to hold the first social gathering Greenharbour had seen in months. A cautious optimism was infecting the city as the plague faltered, losing its grip with the same inexplicable speed with which it had spread. The Lower Arrion, Bruno Sanval, was being hailed as the author of Greenharbour's redemption, and while it annoyed Alija no end to have the gratitude of the city's citizens directed at her underling, rather than her, at least it was directed at the Sorcerers' Collective, and not Marla. Or the High Prince, Alija corrected. That was much more Marla's style.

And the reason she'd been so successful.

Marla had a remarkable lack of ego that for years had allowed her to stay in the background and let others take the credit for her work. It explained how Lernen Wolfblade had kept the throne for the better part of thirty years. When he'd first ascended to the throne, most of Hythria were predicting the length of his reign in months, not decades. To realise he'd lasted as long as this was quite a shock. To·take a step back and contemplate that not only had his reign been one of remarkable length, it was also one of the most prosperous in recent history and the most stable, was quite astonishing—until it became clear who was the true power behind the throne. When one realised that, Alija mused, it all began to make sense.

"My lady?"

Alija turned from the window. She had been staring sight-lessly out into the humid darkness as she pondered the dilemma that was Marla Wolfblade.

"Yes, Tressa?"

"The first of the guests have arrived, my lady."

"So early?" she sighed, already regretting her decision to host this evening's gathering, and it hadn't even begun yet. But she had to maintain the illusion that everything was as it had always been. She couldn't afford to tip her hand yet. Not until she was ready to implement her plan to destroy Marla, which she intended to do as soon as she actually *had* a plan.

"It's Master Miar," Tressa explained.

Alija smiled with relief. "Then show him in, Tressa. Don't leave him standing in the hall."

Tressa curtseyed and hurried away to admit Alija's guest. A few moments later, Galon Miar strode into the room. As usual, he acted as if he owned it, but this was her palace, and he was here at her invitation. Galon had an irritating habit of forgetting that.

The assassin stopped before her and raised her hand to his lips. "You're looking lovely as always, Alija."

"You're early."

"I thought it upset you when I . . . what did you call it? Oh, I remember . . . when I tried to make an *entrance*."

She eyed him sceptically. "And you think that arriving early so you can greet my guests as if you live here will annoy me less?"

He kissed her palm. "If I displease you, Alija, you only have to say so and I'll leave."

He would too, Alija knew. That was the problem with a man like Galon Miar. He knew his value to her. The support of the Assassins' Guild was something even Marla Wolf-blade's money couldn't buy and no matter how much he claimed he had no need to openly trade on his relationship with the High Arrion, she couldn't afford to offend him—a minor but important detail she hadn't taken into consideration before allowing herself to become entangled with such a dangerous man.

But she wasn't entirely without resources of her own. Her hand still resting in his, she briefly scanned his mind . . . and then broke the mental contact, snatching her hand away as if she'd been burned.

"You've been to visit Marla Wolfblade!" she accused.

Galon studied her curiously. "Yes."

"Why?"

"Don't you know," he teased, "oh, great and omnipotent sorceress?"

Alija scowled at him. "The only thing in your mind that I can clearly sense about your visit to Princess Marla, Galon, is that you're lusting after her."

Galon made no attempt to deny the accusation. "She is one of the great beauties of our time, my lady."

"I suppose," Alija conceded with ill grace. "If you go in for that pale, blond, washed-out sort of look."

Galon laughed. Now she'd let go of his arm, Alija was robbed of the opportunity to investigate his thoughts further. She would have to invite him to stay the night, she realised, although she hadn't been planning to. She needed to know the real reason behind his visit to Marla and didn't trust him to tell her the truth.

"You're jealous," Galon noted, highly amused by the idea.

"Not jealous," Alija corrected. "Just curious about what business the second most important man in the Assassins' Guild could possibly have with the only sister of Hythria's High Prince."

"Perhaps she wants me to kill someone for her."

"Anybody I know?" Alija asked, with a raised brow. *Is that sly little bitch thinking of hiring the guild to get rid of me?*

"You know I can't tell you that."

"Nor would I ask you to betray her confidence," Alija assured him, afraid that if she pushed the matter, Galon might realise how much his visit to Marla disturbed her. "Did you know she's coming this evening?"

"Actually, I didn't know."

"Will she be surprised to see you?"

"To be honest, Alija, I don't think she'll care one way or the other. Despite my famously irresistible personality, your cousin remained quite immune to my charms."

She probably knows who you're sleeping with, Alija answered silently, *and is too smart to let you rattle her.* Still, it was something of a relief to realise that even though Galon obviously found Marla attractive, she had not returned the sentiment.

"Marla may be a great beauty, Galon, but she's as cold as a blue-finned arlen. I wouldn't let the fact that she didn't melt in a puddle at your feet, as most women seem to, upset you too much."

"Ah, but how I do enjoy the challenge," Galon chuckled.

Before Alija could reply, Tressa entered the hall again and announced that Lord Marsh and his new wife, Lady Acora, had arrived, effectively ending any chance for private conversation for the rest of the evening. Galon turned to greet the new arrivals, leaving Alija with the uneasy feeling she was going to be sorry she ever mentioned the subject of Marla Wolfblade to her lover.

Marla arrived—fashionably late—several hours later, dressed in a dark red gown that clung to her well-formed body like a second skin from shoulder to hip, and then flared out in a wide skirt that swept the floor in her wake. It was the sort of outfit Alija would have worn ten years ago, before her waist had thickened just enough with the onset of middle age to make such a style look embarrassing, rather than alluring.

"Please forgive my late arrival," Marla begged, when she greeted her hostess, kissing the air beside Alija's cheeks. "I'm down so many slaves with this damned plague, I had to fix my own hair."

"How awful for you, my dear."

"You seem to be managing, though," Marla remarked, looking around the room at the several healthy-looking slaves offering platters of food and drink to the dozen or so guests. "You haven't lost anybody important, I hope?"

"Only a few minor staff," Alija replied. "What about you?"

"Oh, it's been awful," Marla exclaimed. "Besides a husband, I've lost three kitchen slaves, a doorman and now even Elezaar's gone missing."

Alija had been playing this game a long time, so nothing of her feelings reflected on her face, but she was shocked that Marla would mention the dwarf so carelessly. Not after what he'd done.

"The Fool is missing?"

Marla swirled the wine in her glass, staring at the deep red liquid as if it fascinated her. "I sent him out for wine and he never came back. That was two, no . . . nearly three weeks ago, now. I've almost given him up for dead. I can't imagine he'd be out there and not come home unless something terrible had happened to him."

"No, I'm sure you're right."

"I miss him so much, too," the princess admitted with a sigh.

"It must be a devastating loss for you."

"It is," Marla agreed. "I hope you never lose Tarkyn Lye, Alija, and find out how painful it can be."

"I'll make sure he stays safe," Alija agreed warily. *Is she playing with me? Does she know what happened or did the dwarf really disappear after Tarkyn spoke with him?* It made sense that the Fool had vanished, when she thought about it. He'd betrayed his mistress. In his place, Alija wouldn't have gone home, either. "Can I get you some refreshment, Marla?"

"More wine would be lovely, thank you," Marla replied, looking around the room at the other guests. "Surely this isn't everyone you invited?"

"I thought it prudent to keep the numbers down," Alija explained, signalling a slave forward with a tray of wine served in fine crystal goblets. "We're not out of the woods yet with this damned disease."

"True," Marla agreed, selecting a new glass from the tray.

"Still, it looks to be on the wane. I must encourage Lernen to reward Bruno Sanval for his discovery of how to control the outbreak, once we're in a position to hold such a public ceremony again. I admit, I seem to have been quite wrong about him. Thank the gods you didn't listen to me all those years ago, when I asked you to block his promotion to Lower Arrion."

It never occurred to Alija, until that moment, just what a brilliant actress Marla was. She knew now, that the only reason Marla had ever mentioned Bruno to her—back before Tesha Zorell retired—was because he was the candidate she wanted promoted. Bruno Sanval wasn't a Patriot sympathiser. The man barely cared what day of the week it was, let alone which faction his colleagues in the Sorcerers' Collective belonged to. *I thought I was being so clever*, Alija recalled. *And I wound up doing exactly what you wanted, didn't I, Marla?* The princess had played a stunning game of double-think and Alija had fallen for it because it didn't seem possible that such treachery could lurk behind such a guileless façade.

"Well, I'm glad his promotion worked out so fortuitously for all of us," Alija agreed, wishing she could find a polite way of excusing herself. She wanted to scream. She wanted to grab Marla by the hair and shake the devious little bitch until her ears bled, and it astonished Alija how much self-control it was taking to prevent her doing just that. "Have you heard from your children?" she asked, looking for a safe subject.

"Narvell is in Byamor with his grandfather, and the rest of them are out of harm's way with Mahkas in Krakandar," Marla replied. "Thank the gods."

"Indeed," Alija agreed. "It would be most unfortunate if anything was to happen to our precious heir."

Marla smiled. "Nothing will happen to him, my lady. Damin will be High Prince when the time comes."

"Of course," Alija agreed tonelessly.

"And your boys?"

"Safe in Dregian Castle. It's set apart from the main

population centres in the province and can be resupplied by sea, so they're quite comfortable."

"That must be such a relief to you."

"More than you know." Alija forced a polite smile, wishing they weren't in such a public place and that circumstances hadn't conspired to make it so vital that she appear ignorant of Marla's true nature. But it was time to get away from her. Alija wasn't sure how much longer she could maintain this outward veneer of poise. "I don't mean to be impolite, but would you excuse me, Marla?"

"Is something wrong?"

"Of course not," she assured the princess. "But Lord Marsh's wife is looking very lost and alone, and I did promise to introduce her around."

Marla glanced across the room to where the young woman in question was standing by the window, fidgeting awkwardly, while her husband, Lord Marsh, Galon Miar and most of Alija's other male guests stood in a group by the balcony doors, discussing horseracing.

"Go to her," Marla urged, placing her hand on Alija's arm, as if she wasn't fully aware the contact meant Alija could scan her mind as soon as they touched.

Alija didn't even waste her time trying. *You know there's nothing there for me to find, don't you, Marla? Wrayan Lightfinger has shielded your mind.*

"I can amuse myself," Marla was saying. "And I remember what it was like to be sixteen and married to a complete stranger twice your age."

"Maybe you should speak to her, then," Alija suggested. *Anything to get you out of my way for a while, Marla Wolfblade.*

"Would you mind?"

"Be my guest."

Marla handed her untouched wine to Alija. "It was nice of you to invite her tonight. What's her name?"

"Acora. She's from Pentamor, originally. The younger daughter of Lord Buckman."

"I met him once. Quite a disagreeable man, as I recall."

You mean he's a Patriot, Alija corrected silently. But she smiled and stepped back to let the princess pass. "I'm sure Lady Acora will appreciate making the acquaintance of the High Prince's sister. It will increase her social standing a great deal, if you single her out."

Marla raised an eyebrow. "And get her invited to more gatherings like this? Lucky girl."

The princess moved off towards Acora Marsh before Alija could respond. The High Arrion let out a breath she hadn't realised she was holding and glanced around the room. The low hum of conversation and the generally convivial atmosphere of the small gathering was very encouraging.

In fact, the only sour note Alija could find all evening was the speculative look on Galon Miar's face as he pretended interest in whatever Lord Marsh was saying while he followed Marla Wolfblade across the room with his eyes.

chapter 10

A cora Marsh was a plain-looking girl, pale and plump, squeezed into the latest fashion of tight bodices and wide skirts which did nothing but draw attention to her bulk. She looked desperately unhappy, obviously suffering from being newly wed to a man she barely knew and trapped in a plague-ridden city far from home.

Even though she'd offered to speak to the child simply as an excuse to get away from Alija, Marla's heart went out to her. It was unlikely Acora had had the benefit of someone like Jeryma Ravenspear to take her aside on her wedding day, as Marla had, to tell her she was special. More likely her father was glad to be rid of her. A youngest daughter wasn't easy to dispose of, particularly when she didn't have any outstanding beauty or wealth to recommend her. Julyen

Marsh would have seemed a godsend to Acora's father. He was wealthy, anxious to bolster his family's name by linking it with an old, if somewhat impoverished, line and willing to take the plain youngest daughter off Lord Buckman's hands.

Nobody, Marla was quite certain, would have bothered to consult Acora about the transaction.

The girl blushed crimson as Marla approached and dropped into an awkward curtsey. "Your highness!"

"Please, Acora, there's no need to be so formal in a gathering like this."

"I'm sorry, your highness," the poor child gushed, her eyes filling with tears. "I didn't mean to offend you."

Marla took her by the arm to help her up and smiled encouragingly. "You've done nothing of the sort, my dear. Please, don't be frightened. I don't bite, you know."

The young woman glanced nervously past Marla at the group of men where her husband was talking with the others. "Julyen, I mean, my husband . . . he said I wasn't to speak to you, your highness, unless he was with me."

"Why not?"

Acora looked away uncomfortably. "He was afraid I'd say something that might embarrass him, I think."

That amused Marla so much, she forgot about Alija for a moment. "And what terrible utterance are you likely to make, Lady Acora, that you can't be trusted alone with me?"

"It's nothing really, your highness."

"I seriously doubt it's nothing. Does your husband consider you an imbecile, Acora, or do you hold opinions likely to offend the crown?"

Inexplicably, Acora smiled. It changed her whole appearance. "To be honest, your highness, it's probably a little bit of both."

For no reason she could explain, Marla decided she liked this girl. And her curiosity had been piqued, wondering what Acora must have said to her husband that would have prompted him to forbid her to speak to Marla unsupervised. She was not going to find out this evening, however. Lord

Marsh must have seen who his wife was talking to, and hurried over to intervene before Acora could say anything more.

"Your highness! What a pleasure to see you again! And looking so well." He was a thin man with wispy hair that he parted just above his left ear and combed over his shiny pate in a vain attempt to disguise his baldness.

"As are you, Lord Marsh," Marla replied. "I was just getting to know your new wife."

He took Acora's arm and squeezed it, but the gesture appeared more threatening than affectionate. "Your generosity is commendable, your highness, but really, you don't have to bother yourself. Acora is very shy, and doesn't like to mix much."

"Then we'll have to do something about that," Marla announced, annoyed by the way he was trying to dictate to his young wife. "I was just inviting her to lunch tomorrow at my townhouse. You will make sure she gets there on time, won't you? At noon?"

To refuse would be to gravely insult the High Prince's sister and—Patriot sympathiser or not—Julyen Marsh wasn't certain enough of himself to risk doing that. He bowed in reluctant acquiescence, his smile forced. "Of course, your highness. My wife would be delighted and honoured to join you."

"Excellent, I shall see you tomorrow then, Acora, and we'll finish our conversation."

Lord Marsh bustled Acora away before she could say anything more, which left Marla smiling faintly at the notion that she may have struck a blow—however slight—for the cause of female emancipation in Hythria.

"You do like to stir the pot, don't you, your highness?" a voice remarked behind her.

Marla turned to find herself face to face with Galon Miar. Alija was nowhere to be seen.

"It's rude to eavesdrop, Master Miar."

"I'm only a common man, your highness. I was never groomed in the social niceties of the highborn."

Marla took a step back, feigning disdain to cover her uneasiness. She wasn't sure why Galon Miar made her feel so uncomfortable, but whatever the reason, she certainly didn't like it. "In my experience, Master Miar, good manners and a sense of nobility are inherent qualities in all good men, and not restricted to those of high birth."

The assassin smiled. "Surely you're not mistaking *me* for a good man, your highness?"

"Well, you apparently keep Alija satisfied," she replied dismissively. "So you must be good at something."

He leaned a little closer. "Care to find out?"

Marla was shocked, not because he had made such a suggestion, but that he dared it here, under Alija's roof, with his lover very probably in the next room. She shook her head, taking another step back, aware he had effectively cornered her and she had nowhere else to go. "Loyalty's not really your strong suit, is it, Master Miar?"

"I'm loyal enough to those who pay me."

"Alija's not getting her money's worth, I'd say."

"But then, she's not paying me."

Marla laughed, hoping her scorn would wound this man's impossibly high opinion of himself. "You're here out of real affection, I suppose? How quaint. How romantic even, that a man like Galon Miar desires a well-worn woman, more than ten years his senior, like Alija Eaglespike. You *have* been blessed by Kalianah, sir."

If he was insulted, Galon gave no indication. If anything, he seemed amused. "You know, for two women who claim to be friends, you say rather unflattering things about each other."

"Is that right?"

"You call her well worn. She calls you cold as a blue-finned arlen. Strange, don't you think? For friends, I mean."

Marla refused to be drawn. "Why don't you ask your lover?"

"I'm having rather more fun asking you."

She smiled, in spite of herself. "You like to live dangerously, don't you, Master Miar?"

"Call me Galon."

"And you may call me your royal highness."

He laughed. "You know, you may actually be as tough as your reputation suggests, your royal *highness*."

"Continue to irritate me, *Galon*. I'm sure you'll find out."

The assassin bowed and took Marla's hand, kissing her palm. "There's a great deal I'd like to find out about you."

"And absolutely nothing I care to know about you," she replied, extricating her hand quite deliberately from his grasp and making a point of wiping it on her skirt. He didn't miss the gesture. While Marla was quite certain Galon Miar had some terribly witty comeback on the tip of his tongue, fortunately she was saved from having to think up a response by Alija's steward stepping into the room to announce dinner was served.

Before the steward had even finished speaking, old Lord Axfardar, her dinner escort this evening, hurried over to her side, his cane tapping on the tiles impatiently. He pushed himself between Marla and Galon, rudely moving the assassin out of the way, and offered Marla his arm, completely ignoring the younger man. "Come, come, your highness, they're seating us for dinner. I'm starving and Alija tells me I mustn't let you out of my sight if I'm to be a gentleman."

"The gracious hostess, as always," Galon remarked, stepping back. "My lord. Your highness." He bowed to Lord Axfardar and Marla, then turned and walked away, no doubt to find Alija so he could escort her to the table.

Marla took Lord Axfardar's arm and with painstaking slowness—Axfardar was ninety, if he was a day—they headed for the dining room. The old lord glared at Galon's retreating back as his cane tapped out their progress, shaking his white head. "I don't know what the world's coming to, your highness. Common assassins mingling with the highborn as if they were equals! It's all your fault."

"My fault?" Marla asked in surprise.

"You married that damned sailor and then you married a wretched shopkeeper afterwards. Now every woman in Greenharbour thinks *she* should have a commoner as an accessory, too. They're popping up everywhere. Can't even go to a dinner party these days without having to rub shoulders with one of them."

"Maybe if the highborn men of Greenharbour hadn't so bravely fled the city to avoid the plague, my lord, the women wouldn't need to look elsewhere for companionship."

"We have *court'esa* if they want companionship, your highness. This is all about keeping up with the Wolfblades. Promise me you'll set things to right. Promise me your next husband will be a man of impeccable character."

Marla squeezed the old man's arm affectionately. "By all means, Lord Axfardar. Find me a man, highborn or low, of *impeccable* character and I'll marry him tomorrow."

"Don't patronise me, young lady. Other women look to you to set the fashion. I expect you to take that responsibility seriously."

Marla smiled. Her eldest son was almost twenty-five. It was a long time since she'd been called "young lady." "Perhaps *you* would consider remarrying, my lord?" she teased.

Axfardar looked at her and grinned suddenly, exposing his toothless gums. "I've worn out eight wives already. I doubt you could keep up."

"Then I shall just have to remain a poor widow until I meet a man who can compare with you, my lord," she declared with a woeful sigh. "I'm going to die alone, I'm sure of it."

He patted her hand with a fatherly smile. "You're a sweet girl, your highness, to humour an old man. But I'm only half joking. You will have to marry again. For your sake—and Hythria's sake—be careful who you choose."

"I'm always careful, my lord," Marla assured him as they took their places for dinner. "Hythria can't afford me to be anything else."

chapter 11

The exact position of the border between Elasapine Province and Krakandar Province was anybody's guess, so Narvell Hawksword chose to position his forces well inside his own border, across the entrance to a wide ravine on the western side of the village of Zadenka. Positioned just on the other side of the three-sided intersection on the main road that led through the narrow cutting to Byamor in the west, Zadenka Manor to the north and Krakandar in the east, the site offered protection from any flanking manoeuvres but enough room to move if it came down to close-quarter fighting. Lining the top of the steep sides of the ravine on both sides were Elasapine archers overlooking the village and the crossroads; Narvell's cavalry was arrayed across the narrowest part of the road behind a hedge of long, sharp pikes, held by his regular infantrymen.

Damin surveyed the disposition of his brother's troops from horseback on a small rise leading down into the village, cursing softly. This late in the afternoon, the sun was behind his brother's forces, sitting on the edge of the distant Sunrise Mountains, making Damin squint. Captain Almodavar rode up beside him, as puzzled as Damin was about this strange turn of events.

Tejay Lionsclaw and Adham Tirstone had a different take on the problem. They seemed to think the idea that any of his brothers would seriously declare war on him quite the most implausible thing they'd ever heard and were convinced this was Narvell's idea of a practical joke.

"Well, somebody was a good boy and paid attention to his lessons on battle tactics, I'd say," Tejay remarked cheerfully, looking down over the battleground. "And right by an inn, too," she noted, where a small crowd of nervous villagers had gathered outside the substantial roadhouse to watch the opposing armies converge on each other. "It's always nice to have somewhere to retire for a drink after a long day's carnage."

"Narvell *had* to pay attention to his lessons on *everything*, my lady," Adham informed her, sounding highly amused. Like Tejay, he seemed to think this whole situation was terribly funny, Damin noted with a scowl. "It was the only way to stay one step ahead of Kalan."

Damin glared at his stepbrother, but said nothing. For once, he was having difficulty finding any humour in the situation.

Smiling broadly, Tejay nodded in agreement with Adham. "Pity she's not here now. I'm sure she'd march right down there, box Narvell's ears, tell him to get out of her way—"

"After reminding him that she is twenty whole minutes older than he is," Adham interjected.

"Naturally," she agreed. "And that would be the end of it."

"Well, she's not here," Damin pointed out. "So do either of you jolly little souls have something constructive to offer, or are you just going to sit there and make fun of this mess?"

Adham and Tejay looked at each other questioningly, before Adham turned to Damin with a cheerful grin. "No, I think we're just going to sit here and make fun of it."

"Go down and talk to him, Damin," Almodavar advised, shaking his head at Adham's frivolous reply. "Something's going on, but I doubt Narvell will have you shot before he has a chance to explain."

"You *doubt* it?"

Almodavar shrugged. Even the old captain seemed to be biting back a smile. "You can never tell, my lord. He could be down there on Charel Hawksword's orders, or it might be something more personal. Have you done anything to upset your brother lately?"

"I haven't even seen him in six months."

"Well, then!" Tejay declared. "Off you go! You trot down there and find out what's going on and we'll wait here to see if Narvell orders one of his lads to take a shot at you. That should give us a good indication of how serious he is about blocking our progress into Elasapine."

Damin gathered up his reins and glared at his companions. "You think this is funny, don't you?"

"Not at all," Adham assured him. "We're all desperately worried for you, Damin. Really." He leaned across and nudged Tejay. "Aren't we, Lady Lionsclaw?"

"Oh! Absolutely!" Tejay agreed.

Damin swore under his breath and kicked his mount into a canter, heading down the road to where the Elasapine forces were arrayed, cursing all relatives in general, but his brothers in particular. As he approached the Elasapine forces, a single horseman broke away and rode out to meet him. Damin breathed a sigh of relief when he realised it was his younger brother.

"Narvell!" Damin greeted him, as they moved close enough to speak without being overheard by their forces. "What in the name of the gods do you think you're doing here blocking my way?"

Narvell glanced over his shoulder to survey his troops as he reined in and then turned to Damin, grinning proudly. "Pretty impressive, don't you think?"

"Pretty stupid was my first impression, actually," Damin retorted.

"Aw, come on, Damin, don't be angry with me," Narvell pleaded with an ingenuous smile. "This wasn't my idea."

"Whose idea was it?"

"My grandfather's."

"Charel *Hawksword* sent you out here to declare war on me?" Damin shook his head in disbelief. Narvell was his half-brother and the Hawksword family was probably the Wolfblade family's closest and most trusted ally. "What did I ever do to upset your grandfather?"

"Well . . . nothing, really . . ."

"Then why the hell are you declaring war on me?"

"You're so damn touchy, Damin. It's nothing personal. And stop exaggerating. I'm not declaring war on you. I'm making a stand."

"Is this because you're afraid we're bringing the plague with us?"

"It's because Grandpa thinks if I just let you march your army into Elasapine without raising a finger to object, for the rest of my life," Narvell explained, "people will be whispering that Narvell Hawksword is afraid of his big brother. It may not mean much now, but someday, when I'm Warlord of Elasapine and you're the High Prince . . ."

"You *cannot* be serious! I'm here to protect Hythria, not challenge you! Hablet's massing for an invasion, for pity's sake!"

"We don't know that for certain."

Damin looked at his brother, suddenly suspicious. "I know what's going on here. Charel's lost his mind, hasn't he? And you're covering for him."

"He's got a valid point, Damin."

"He's senile."

"Not *my* grandfather," Narvell chuckled. "He said to say hello, by the way. He's looking forward to seeing you again when we get to Byamor."

Damin scowled at his brother. "That's rather moot, don't you think, given you're blocking my way with an army."

Narvell shrugged, unconcerned. "I suppose he meant *after* I beat you."

"Beat *me*?" he asked. "Now I *know* you're joking."

Narvell sighed. "Can't you do me a favour, just this once? We can have a bit of a skirmish, I'll kick your royal rear enough to make it look convincing and then in a magnanimous act of nobility, I'll invite you into Elasapine to show there're no hard feelings. Nothing could be simpler!"

Damin let out an exasperated sigh, convinced he'd never heard anything more preposterous in his entire life. "Except that if I let you beat me, Narvell, for the rest of *my* life, people will be saying that Damin Wolfblade is afraid of his little brother."

Narvell studied him hopefully. "Well . . . aren't you?"

"Don't be ridiculous!"

"Not even a little bit?"

"Even if I was afraid of you," Damin replied, "which I'm *not* . . . I'm not going to risk the lives of my Raiders fighting yours when I need your men *and* mine, fit and ready to fight Hablet."

"Fine," Narvell agreed with a shrug. "Let's do it the old-fashioned way, then. Single combat."

Damin peered at his brother closely. "You've been waiting out in the sun too long, old boy. It's starting to affect your judgment."

"I'm serious!"

"I know you are," Damin agreed.

Narvell's good humour suddenly faded, as if he knew what his brother was thinking. "You think I can't win, don't you?"

"I think if you're trying to prove something to your grandfather, little brother, you need to pick a fight you *can* win."

"I *will* beat you, Damin."

"No," he replied confidently. "You won't. Not even if I let you choose the weapons. You've never been able to beat me, Narvell."

"I've learned a few tricks since we were children."

"And I grew four inches taller and forty pounds heavier than you. Still," Damin added, with a resigned sigh as he swung his leg over the pommel of his saddle. "If we're going to do this, we might as well get it over with." He jumped to the ground, pulled off his riding gloves and began to unbuckle his breastplate.

Narvell looked at him in confusion. "*Now?*"

"Waiting isn't going to make a difference."

Narvell thought about it, shrugged, and then jumped to the ground. "Damn right! Let's do it now. Choose your weapon!"

"No weapons," Damin told him. "Somebody might get hurt."

Amused, his brother began to remove his armour. "You don't have to worry about me, Damin."

"I'm not," he replied, lifting the breastplate over his head.

"This is a new shirt. I don't want you getting in a lucky strike and tearing it."

Narvell grinned. "Whatever you have to tell yourself, Damin. Just let's do it quickly, eh? The light's fading and I'm hungry. Once we're done we can retire back to Zadenka Manor for dinner and . . ." He stopped fiddling with the buckles on his shoulder and glanced past Damin to where the others were supposed to be waiting on the hill. "Is that Adham up there with Almodavar?"

"Ah, yes," Damin said, glancing back toward the rest of his forces. Seeing their prince dismount, they must have decided to find out what was going on and the three of them were trotting past the inn toward the brothers, an act that prompted several officers from Narvell's waiting cavalry to do likewise. Behind them, the troops began to move forward, down toward the village. "The gang's all here."

"Lady Lionsclaw!" Narvell cried delightedly, when he realised who rode beside Adham. "What a pleasant surprise!"

"Hello, Narvell," she replied cheerfully as she reined in her mare. Tejay glanced over his troops and then looked back at the young man. "I see Charel gave you an army for your birthday."

"Well, what else do you give a man who's got everything?" Adham joked, reaching down to shake Narvell's hand.

"Is Kalan with you?" Narvell asked, looking back over the advancing force hopefully as he shook the sorcerer's hand. Although he'd never admit it (nor would Kalan, Damin knew) the twins missed each other desperately when they were separated for too long.

"She's headed back to Greenharbour with Wrayan," Tejay told him with a frown. She glanced at the prince. "Didn't Damin tell you about . . ."

"We haven't actually got to that bit," Damin announced, as he tossed his greaves aside and began rolling up his sleeves. "First, we have to let my little brother prove his manhood."

Tejay looked at Damin in surprise. "You're going to fight Narvell?"

"No, I thought I'd tickle him to death," Damin retorted impatiently.

The Warlord's wife nodded in understanding. "Charel's concerned the people of Elasapine won't think you independent of your brother's influence once you're a Warlord," she surmised. "He's right, Narvell. You should fight Damin. And beat him."

"Tejay!" Damin objected. "Don't encourage him!"

In reply, Tejay moved her mount around, placing the bulk of the horse between Damin and Narvell. She leaned over, placed a hand on his shoulder and drew him even further away from the others. When she spoke, it was in a low, urgent voice that seemed at odds with everyone else's jovial demeanour. "Do you remember that conversation we had about you being intolerably competitive, Damin?"

"What of it?"

"Try to control it. Narvell needs to win this fight. Or at least give a good account of himself."

"Tejay . . ."

"I mean it, Damin. Charel's right to be concerned. His heir needs to prove he can stand up to you. Charel needs to believe he can do it, his men need to see that he can do it, and perhaps, most importantly, Narvell needs to believe he can, too."

"You want me to let him win?" Damin found the idea almost impossible to contemplate. He shook his head emphatically. "No way."

"I want you to let him keep his honour," she corrected. "You're bigger, stronger and a whole lot meaner than you used to be. I know everyone's joking and laughing about this, but it's far more serious than you realise, Damin. You run the risk of making a friend or an enemy in the next few minutes. Don't get it wrong."

Damin was sceptical, certain she was reading far more into this silly challenge than the situation warranted. "We're already friends, Tejay. He's my brother."

"And you think a brother can't turn on you, some day?"

"I think he *won't* turn on me," Damin countered.

A little annoyed at him, Tejay straightened in the saddle and shrugged. "Fine. Do whatever you think is best, your highness. What would a simple woman know? But if you imagine you can walk out there and knock your brother unconscious in under a minute in front of his own troops and not have him resent you for it for the rest of his life, then that damned dwarf didn't teach you anything."

Put like that, Damin had a sneaking suspicion she might be right. He was loath to admit it though. Glancing over the back of Tejay's horse he noticed Narvell was rid of his armour and almost ready to fight. He reached up and grabbed her bridle to prevent her turning away. "What am I supposed to do, Tejay? He's the one who wants to fight. And for the same reason he needs to win, so do I."

"I know," she agreed, glancing over her shoulder at his brother. "And I'm not telling you to lose, Damin. I'm telling you not to humiliate him. Let Narvell walk away from this fight with everyone thinking he could have taken you down. Believe me, his honour and your throne will greatly appreciate the gesture some day."

Damin looked up at her with a thin smile. "Were you always this wise?"

"Yes."

"How come I never noticed it before?"

"Because you're a man, Damin, and men don't see anything in a woman that doesn't eventually lead to sex."

"Ah, now the cynical Tejay I remember."

She smiled at him. "Do the right thing, Damin."

"Don't I always?"

"So far," she conceded.

"Your confidence in me is overwhelming, my lady."

"Then don't let me down, Damin Wolfblade," she warned. "Because, trust me, the bitterly-disappointed-in-you Tejay is one you don't want to meet."

chapter 12

As soon as it became obvious the heir to Elasapine and his royal half-brother planned to resolve this awkward impasse by the time-honoured tradition of slugging it out like a couple of common tavern roughs, the whole mood of the gathered forces changed. What could have been a tinderbox waiting on a single spark to ignite it suddenly took on a carnival atmosphere. The archers lining the ridges relaxed their bows and sat down to watch, laughing and joking among themselves. The pikemen ranked across the ravine lowered their lances and the cavalry dismounted.

Squinting against the setting sun, Tejay Lionsclaw glanced over her shoulder, as the bulk of the Krakandar troops gathered behind them, cursing all men and their childish need to constantly prove themselves to each other.

She wasn't unsympathetic. Tejay had been raised in an all-male household; she had four small sons of her own. She knew what men were like, and even empathised with their need to continually establish their supremacy over their foes. But that didn't mean she wasn't annoyed by it. Or that she didn't mean to put an end to this awkward situation with as little loss of honour to both the combatants, as fast as she could possibly manage it.

Dismounting, Tejay led her mare over to where Adham Tirstone stood by his horse watching the unfolding scene with rather a bemused expression. Adham wasn't quite so dedicated to honouring Zegarnald as Damin Wolfblade and his half-brother. He was his father's son, a trader at heart who fought only to protect his investments.

"Are they really going to do this?" Adham asked as Tejay walked up beside him.

"Never underestimate the capacity of noble young men to

do incredibly foolish things for perfectly good reasons," she replied with an impatient sigh.

The trader smiled. "That sounds like something my father might say." Then his smile faded and he corrected himself. "*Would* have said. Were you trying to talk Damin out of fighting, my lady?"

She shook her head. "There'd be no point. I was asking him to let Narvell win."

Adham laughed at the very idea. "You're an optimistic woman, Lady Lionsclaw, I'll grant you that."

"I think I managed to convince him to at least let Narvell get a few hits in before he destroys him," she informed Adham.

Before he could reply, Narvell Hawksword charged at his brother with a bloodcurdling yell and the fight was on. Tejay turned to watch as the gathered soldiers roared their encouragement, certain that no matter how necessary, this could only end in disaster if Damin's temper got the better of him. It was a valid fear. She'd been there when he maimed his uncle, crushing Mahkas Damaran's throat with a single, furious blow.

There seemed no danger of that happening at the moment. At first, it was obvious neither brother was very serious about harming his opponent, which was a good thing, given their difference in size. Narvell Hawksword was an accomplished fighter, slender and wiry. He'd inherited more from his fine-boned mother than his burly grandfather. Damin Wolfblade, however, had inherited only his colouring from Marla Wolfblade. Physically, he was pure Krakenshield—over six feet tall, athletic and powerfully built. Additionally, Tejay thought worriedly as she watched the two combatants feel each other out with tentative, probing blows to the encouraging cheers of their large audience, Damin had been tested in a way his easygoing younger brother had never been tested. Leila's suicide, Starros's torture and his confrontation with Mahkas had left an indelible mark on Damin Wolfblade, even if it was only visible to those who knew him well.

And Tejay did know him well. From the first time she'd watched him racing Starros, Kalan and Narvell through the broad halls of Krakandar Palace when he was a small child, shouting gleefully at the top of his voice that he'd beat everyone to the dining room, to the brash young man who had spent his formative years under her father's stern and watchful eye, she'd always suspected there was more to him than he let on. But she'd never realised just how shrewd he really was until that awful business in Krakandar. It wasn't that he'd almost killed Mahkas. It wasn't even that he stopped himself from killing a man who so patently deserved it. She'd seen Damin Wolfblade display a capacity for rage that was frightening to behold, but what impressed her was *why* he contained it. It was pragmatism, not mercy, that stayed his hand. Damin stopped himself from killing his uncle because he could see the bigger picture, which was all very well, she mused, but not likely to save anybody here.

Narvell needed to prove himself and Damin hated to lose. It might take as little as one lucky blow on Narvell's part to inadvertently trigger Damin's rage. Tejay knew well that once exposed to the light, such a fury took a long time to settle again. It was simmering below the surface, waiting for a crack in the fragile shell Damin had built to hold it back. If that brittle barrier crumbled, Damin Wolfblade wouldn't care about the big picture. He wouldn't care about his younger brother's future as the Warlord of Elasapine. In a moment of blind rage, he could easily decide his own need to win outweighed everything else.

With the chill of the coming night closing in on them, Tejay watched the fight, chewing on her bottom lip, waiting for Damin to make his move, wondering how she was going to be able to stop this fight with the honour of both men still intact. Fortunately, Damin appeared to have heeded her advice and there was no need to intervene just yet. The brothers seemed quite evenly matched, in fact, which clearly wasn't the case, but it meant Damin was letting Narvell get past his guard just enough to make it look convincing.

She wasn't the only one who realised Damin was fighting

below par. A few paces away, Geri Almodavar wore a disgusted look and when Narvell managed to bloody Damin's lip with a particularly lucky blow, he started yelling advice, although to which one of the brothers, Tejay wasn't really sure.

"Adham," Tejay said in a low voice. "Be a pet, would you, and sidle up to Captain Almodavar and tell him if he keeps on coaching those boys from the sidelines, I'll arrange to have his intestines relocated to the outside of his body as soon as we get to Byamor."

Adham looked at her askance and did as she asked without comment. She turned back to the fight and glared at Damin with an impatient frown. "You'll be considering the most artistic way to arrange your internal organs on the ground next to your corpse too, young man," she muttered to herself, "if you don't put an end to this, shortly."

But just as Damin seemed about to abandon all common sense and do exactly what she'd advised him not to, she heard a ruckus to her right and turned in time to see the soldiers blocking the road from Zadenka Manor suddenly fall silent as they hastily stepped aside to make way for a trio of charging horses that ploughed through the circle of gathered men with little care for anybody's safety.

Tejay was stunned to realise two of the riders were Rorin and the scout Damin had sent with the sorcerer yesterday to speak to Narvell at Zadenka Manor. Astride the mare in the lead was a dishevelled young woman, her long dark hair streaming out behind her. In hot pursuit of the trio was a troop of Raiders led by a grey-haired, middle-aged man who wore the same look of fury Tejay had feared she might see on Damin's face.

The horses skidded to a halt in a shower of loose gravel, sending Damin and Narvell diving out of their way to avoid being barrelled over. With a desperate sob, the young woman flew from the saddle and into Narvell's arms just as the other horsemen caught up with them.

The fight clearly no longer Narvell's concern, Damin hurriedly stepped back, watching this strange turn of events with a puzzled look. Narvell, on the other hand, obviously knew the girl. His brother forgotten, he put his arms around her and held her close briefly, and then pushed her behind him as the newcomers rode into the circle of troops, putting himself protectively between the desperate young woman and her pursuers.

"Well done!" Tejay said with an approving nod as Rorin dismounted hurriedly beside her, pushing his horse clear.

He turned to her in confusion. "My lady?"

"Turns out you really are a sorcerer, aren't you? A proper one, I mean, not one of those Greenharbour fools who buys his way into the Sorcerers' Collective and likes to think he's performed magic if he manages to melt snow over an open flame."

Rorin frowned, panting heavily from his ride, watching the other riders dismount, rather than paying Tejay much attention. "What do you mean, my lady?"

She patted him on the shoulder. "I was hoping someone would break this up before it got out of hand. I wasn't expecting magic, though. Impressive, lad. Not to mention quite original and totally unexpected. You've done very well."

Rorin glanced at her and shook his head as the man leading the troop of mounted Raiders jumped from his horse and advanced on Narvell threateningly, his hand on his sword hilt. "I'm not here to break anything up, my lady," he warned. "If anything, my arrival is going to make things a whole lot worse."

"You mean this isn't divine intervention? Because I tell you, Rorin, you couldn't have picked a better moment to appear if you'd actually cast a spell to *find* the most appropriate time."

"Get your hands off my wife!" the older man bellowed at Narvell while Tejay and Rorin were talking. The girl cowered behind her protector, who was—rather inconveniently— unarmed.

Tejay turned from Rorin and took in the scene with a glance. She sighed, shaking her head at the newcomers. "Maybe I was a bit hasty, thanking you for arriving at such an opportune time."

"There wasn't much else I could do, my lady." Rorin shrugged apologetically. "Under the circumstances."

Before Rorin could stop her, Tejay stepped forward, putting herself between Narvell and the young woman's irate husband. "Is that any way to address a member of your ruling family?" she demanded, guessing this man wasn't used to anybody standing up to him, particularly a woman.

He halted in surprise and then roughly shoved Tejay aside. "Out of my way, woman! This is between me and that treacherous little Hawksword bastard."

Tejay stumbled backwards but thankfully Rorin caught her before she fell. The girl Narvell was shielding whimpered in fear as her husband moved closer. Fortunately, the troop accompanying the man remained mounted and made no move to intervene, acutely aware they were surrounded by several thousand troops who didn't appear very sympathetic to their lord's cause.

But that was the least of her concerns. In a heartbeat the situation had changed and they were back in the tinderbox. The whole bizarre interruption had taken only a minute or two and Damin looked decidedly unhappy at the way this stranger was treating his brother and his friends.

"Almodavar!"

The captain had his sword out and tossed it to his prince, almost before Damin had finished speaking. The prince snatched the blade out of the air, took a step forward and pressed the point against the older man's throat, preventing him moving any closer to Narvell or his terrified wife.

"That 'treacherous little Hawksword bastard' is my brother," he informed the man coldly. "The lady you're pushing around is a very dear friend and the men you rode here in pursuit of are mine. Give me one good reason why I shouldn't just run *you* through, right here and now."

"Who the hell are you?" the man asked disparagingly, glancing down at the blade Damin held to his throat as if it was nothing more than a minor irritation.

"Damin Wolfblade," he replied. "Who the hell are *you*?"

The man hesitated. It probably wasn't fear that gave him

pause. Damin's reputation was quite deliberately that of a foolish young man with little to recommend him and the news of the events in Krakandar and Damin's attack on his uncle wasn't likely to have reached much beyond the walls of the city yet. But even an angry provincial lord thought twice before making an enemy of the next High Prince.

"I am Stefan Warhaft, the Baron of Zadenka," the man replied, taking his hand from his sword hilt. "And I demand satisfaction!"

"For what?" Damin asked. (Rather unnecessarily, Tejay thought; a blind man could see what was happening here.)

Lord Warhaft drew himself up self-righteously and pointed at Narvell and the woman using the young man as a shield against her husband's wrath.

"For that!" he announced loudly. "I want satisfaction because your brother accepted my hospitality and then the ungrateful little bastard stole my wife!"

chapter 13

It was after dark before Damin was able to make sense out of anything going on between Narvell, Lord Warhaft and his errant young wife, Kendra.

With the challenge between the two brothers no longer an issue in light of these new developments, Damin had arranged for Tejay to watch over the young woman and tend her cuts and bruises. He then commandeered the village inn while he tried to sort everything out. Almodavar and Adham were taking care of both the Krakandar and Elasapine troops, but he'd kept Rorin close by. As a member of the Sorcerers' Collective, he made an impeccable witness and Damin had a bad feeling he'd need an impartial point of view before this was done with.

Listening to Lord Warhaft's pompous recital of his woes, however, Damin began to wish he'd flattened his younger brother when he had the chance. If Stefan Warhaft was to be believed, Narvell certainly deserved it.

The trouble started some months ago, according to Warhaft, when Charel Hawksword sent his grandson to Zadenka to keep him safe from the plague that was ravaging Byamor, as it was every other city in Hythria except Krakandar. Stefan was a distant cousin of the Hawksword family and more than happy to do his liege lord a favour by offering the heir to Elasapine sanctuary in his isolated manor house on the border of the two provinces until the danger was past. Narvell had arrived in Zadenka with as many troops as Charel dared spare from the city. He was a wily old warrior, Charel Hawksword, Damin thought, obviously determined to protect more than his grandson. Once this crisis was past, the strongest Warlords would be those who still had some sort of army intact.

Narvell and Kendra had known each other since they were fifteen when Kendra was sent to court by her parents, looking for a suitable husband. She'd spent a summer in Byamor before Stefan made an offer for her hand and the following winter, when she turned sixteen, she'd been married to the Baron of Zadenka, a man thirty years her senior, and brought here to Zadenka to live. She had borne him a daughter a bare nine months after the wedding and then a son two years later.

Unconcerned, at first, about his wife renewing her acquaintanceship with the young heir to Elasapine, Lord Warhaft had seen little danger in their friendship. But it became clear, over time, that his wife and Lord Hawksword were sharing much more than old memories. The situation had come to a head, so Warhaft informed Damin, when Narvell left the manor two days ago with his troops to intercept his brother's forces coming in from Krakandar. Damin had sent a letter to Charel Hawksword before they left, advising him of the situation with Fardohnya. Charel, in turn, had written to Narvell and told him to take this opportunity to publicly establish who was going to be calling the shots in Elasapine, once the old man was dead.

It was that letter which had brought Narvell to this place, and his absence that gave Stefan Warhaft the opportunity to beat the truth out of his errant wife. He'd locked her up two days ago, he told Damin, obviously expecting sympathy for his plight, after chastising her severely for her infidelity with a horsewhip.

Kendra, however, wasn't nearly as chastened as Stefan believed. The moment his back was turned, she'd broken a window, climbed a trellis two storeys down to the ground, stolen a horse from her husband's stables and fled the manor, hoping she'd find Narvell before her husband found her.

Unfortunately for Kendra, her husband got to her first. He'd dragged her back to the manor in the early hours of this morning, ready to do his worst, only to find he had a visitor from the Sorcerers' Collective waiting for him, looking for Narvell Hawksword. Figuring she had nothing left to lose, the young woman had thrown herself on Rorin Mariner's mercy and begged him to protect her.

At this point, their stories diverged. If Warhaft was to be believed, Rorin began throwing his weight around like he owned the place, demanded Kendra be turned over to him and rode out of Zadenka Manor with Kendra at his side, gloating over his prize. Warhaft had naturally followed them, with the perfectly understandable desire to retrieve his wife.

According to Rorin, he'd done nothing of the kind. He claimed he'd made a point of not getting involved in the Warhafts' domestic dispute. It was only when Warhaft struck Kendra with a horsewhip in his presence that he'd decided to intervene. His idea of intervention was to get the poor woman out of the manor until her husband calmed down. Warhaft had given chase, so Rorin claimed, which had resulted in their rather dramatic arrival at the village and the end to any argument Damin and Narvell might be having over who was subordinate to whom.

Given the manner of their arrival, Damin was inclined to believe Rorin's version of events over Stefan Warhaft's.

"So you see, your highness," Lord Warhaft declared as he finished his version of the tale, "your brother has acted most shamelessly in this matter. And that Sorcerers' Collective lackey you sent to my house had no right to steal my wife from me."

"Sounds to me like she was running away, Lord Warhaft, not being stolen from you."

"A situation that would never have arisen, but for your brother's reprehensible behaviour! I demand my honour be restored!"

Damin shook his head. This fool had picked the wrong time to proudly announce he'd beaten his wife into submission with a horsewhip and expect any sympathy from Damin Wolfblade.

"And how do you propose to have your honour restored, my lord?" Damin enquired, his voice flat.

Warhaft didn't know him well enough to recognise the danger signs, but Rorin certainly did. "Perhaps we can discuss that later," the young sorcerer suggested, looking pointedly at Damin. "*After* you've spoken to Lord Hawksword, your highness?"

I must have really frightened Rorin in Krakandar, Damin thought, as he met his friend's eye. *He looks like he's afraid I'm going to run Warhaft through.*

"Perhaps you're right," Damin agreed, more to reassure Rorin he wasn't on the verge of uncontrollable rage than any desire to see justice done.

"I demand satisfaction!" Warhaft called after him.

Damin slammed the door, cutting off the irate voice, without bothering to answer.

Narvell was in a room down the dingy hall, watching over Kendra while Tejay tended her wounds. He opened the roughly finished door when Damin knocked and slipped outside into the hall, leaving the women alone.

"How is she?" Damin asked, catching only a candlelit glimpse of the two women as Narvell pulled the door shut behind him.

Narvell's voice was choked with barely contained fury. "He horsewhipped her, Damin."

"I know."

"I'm going to kill him," Narvell announced, turning toward the taproom where Rorin waited with Stefan Warhaft.

Damin blocked his way. "No, you're not."

"You're *defending* him?"

"Of course not."

Narvell seemed unconvinced. "Do you have any idea how much damage a man can do to a defenceless woman with a horsewhip?"

"More than you realise," Damin assured him bleakly. "Let's go outside. I need some fresh air."

Reluctantly, Narvell agreed and followed Damin down the gloomy hall. They stepped out into a crisp night, the stars lighting the small yard at the back of the inn with faint, pearly light.

"Is what Warhaft told me true?" Damin asked, as Narvell took a seat on an upturned keg by the woodshed.

"I don't know," Narvell shrugged. "What's he telling you?"

"That you came here to wait out the plague and decided to amuse yourself with his wife."

Narvell laughed sourly. "Well, I suppose he would see it like that."

"This is serious, Narvell."

"That's an odd thing for you to say," his brother remarked, looking at him curiously. "What happened to the man who refused to take anything seriously?"

"I buried him in Krakandar," Damin replied grimly. "Alongside Leila."

Narvell's expression darkened. "Tejay told me what happened. I can't believe Leila's dead. Or that you didn't kill Mahkas."

"It doesn't suit me for him to die right now," Damin

informed his brother. "It doesn't suit me for Warhaft to die, either."

"It'd suit me just fine."

Damin sighed. "If you had to fall in love, Narvell, couldn't you have found somebody less dangerous than another man's wife?"

"When I fell in love with Kendra, she wasn't another man's wife, Damin. She wasn't anybody's wife."

"Warhaft said something about you knowing her before they married."

The young man's eyes glazed over in remembrance. "She came to Byamor when I was fifteen. The first time I saw her, I couldn't breathe."

Having never been in love, Damin wasn't all that sympathetic, given the trouble his brother's love affair was likely to cause at a time when they could least afford the distraction. "I suppose she feels the same way?"

"We're soul mates, Damin. Two sides of the same coin."

And a pair of hopeless romantics, he amended silently. "Why didn't you say something to Charel? If Kendra was sent to Byamor to find a husband, surely the Warlord's heir would have been good enough for her parents?"

"I did talk to my grandfather," Narvell replied. "I begged him to let me marry her. He laughed at me. He said I was only a child so I couldn't possibly know what it meant to be in love. A month later he gave permission for Warhaft to marry Kendra and she was shipped off to Zadenka. I never even got a chance to say goodbye."

"And seven years later Charel just happens to send you here to wait out the plague?"

Narvell smiled faintly. "Actually, he wanted to send me to Krakandar. I convinced him I needed to be closer. Zadenka was as far as I could get from the plague in Byamor and still be in Elasapine Province."

"Well, that turned out to be a capital idea, didn't it?"

"You'd have done exactly the same thing in my place, Damin."

Damin found himself losing patience with his younger

brother. "I'd never be stupid enough to sleep with another man's wife, Narvell. They're not worth the trouble."

His brother looked unimpressed by Damin's naïve declaration. "You say that now. But you'll meet a woman someday, Damin, who'll steal your breath away. And you won't care who she is or who she belongs to. Then you won't be nearly so damned self-righteous."

"I'm not being self-righteous. I'm being practical." He smiled sourly. "Anyway, it's not like I'm going to have a choice: Any woman I marry is going to have to get past Marla first, and meet her exacting standards of what constitutes a suitable consort for a High Prince. As that narrows the field down to nobody who actually exists, I figure I'm not going to have to worry about it for a long time yet."

Narvell grimaced sympathetically. "You may have a point, brother."

Damin sighed, wishing he had some idea of how to handle this mess. "What am I supposed to do about this woman of yours?"

"She's not going back to him, Damin. I won't allow it."

"It's not your decision."

"I've made it mine, nonetheless. Anyway, I can't believe you'd let that savage bastard near her again, given what you did to Mahkas after he whipped Leila."

"I loved Leila like a sister, Narvell," he pointed out. "I don't know this Kendra of yours enough to care."

"Then do it for me."

"Do *what*, exactly?"

"Speak to Uncle Lernen. Ask him to annul Kendra's marriage."

"On what grounds?"

"Warhaft beat her like a dog!"

"Which is appalling," Damin agreed, "but not against the law. A woman is a possession, Narvell. A man can do what he wants to her. It might be barbaric, but it's not grounds to annul a marriage that's lasted seven-odd years and produced two children."

Narvell glared at him. "I dare you to repeat *that* little pearl of wisdom in front of our mother."

"It was Marla who pointed it out to me." He smiled thinly. "It's on that secret list she insists she doesn't have."

"What secret list?"

"The list of things she expects me to fix when I'm High Prince."

Narvell didn't seem to get what Damin was talking about. Neither was he interested in anything not directly related to Kendra's plight. "You have to help me, Damin."

"Why don't you ask Lernen yourself? You're his nephew, too."

"But you're his favourite. You're his heir. He listens to you."

"Only when he's in the mood."

"Then *ask* him when he's in the right mood."

Damin wished he could make Narvell understand that it wasn't as simple as he wanted it to be. "Even if I do speak to him, it doesn't solve the immediate problem of what to do with Kendra Warhaft. It might be months before I see Lernen again. What do you propose to do with your beloved in the meantime?"

"She can stay with me."

"Warhaft's going to *love* that idea. I can't wait to hear what Charel has to say about it, too. And what of Kendra's children? Is she prepared to abandon them for you?"

"They're not here. They're in the north with Kendra's parents. The children were visiting their grandparents when the plague struck and everyone agreed it would be safer to leave them there."

Damin was unconvinced. "Still, even if Lernen grants her an annulment, a man has a right to claim his heir. Staying with you might cost your lover her children, Narvell. You might want to make certain she's prepared to pay that price before I go back in there and announce that far from giving her husband the satisfaction he's expecting, I'm going to allow you to ride off into the sunset with his wife."

"You make it sound like I'm in the wrong!" Narvell objected, jumping to his feet.

"That's because legally, you are."

Narvell studied his older brother sceptically. "When did you become such a paragon of virtue?"

"I'm not being virtuous. I need you, Narvell, and every man Charel can muster. I don't have time for you to get caught up in a dispute over some woman."

"She's not just some woman . . ."

"I'm sure she's Kalianah made flesh," Damin agreed impatiently. "But that doesn't alter the fact that she's another man's wife."

"You claim you need me, Damin," Narvell pointed out, crossing his arms defensively. "Order Kendra back to her husband and you can go to hell, for all I care."

Damin stared at him in shock, Tejay's words earlier about Narvell turning on him suddenly coming back to haunt him. "You can't be serious!"

"Try me."

"Hablet is massing for an invasion, for the gods' sake!"

Narvell shrugged, apparently unconcerned. "He'll be after Greenharbour first, not Byamor. He'll come through Highcastle, or the Widowmaker, and head straight for the coast. Chances are, Hablet won't care about what's north of him until he's secured the capital. We've got enough troops left to defend Elasapine if need be."

"Charel Hawksword would never agree to sit back and do nothing while Hythria was being invaded," Damin declared, certain Narvell couldn't mean what he said.

"You think I can't convince him?" Narvell dared. "You might have the High Prince's ear, brother, but the Warlord of Elasapine is *my* grandfather and he'll listen to me before he'll follow you. Hell, all I have to do is tell him what you did to Mahkas to make him start to wonder about you."

Damin was flabbergasted. "You'd really do that? Choose some girl over your own family, your own country?"

"I think he's asking you not to make him choose at all."

Damin turned to find Tejay had let herself out into the yard. She was wiping her hands on a small towel and had obviously overheard enough of their conversation to glean the gist of it.

"Just exactly whose side are you on?" he asked the Warlord's wife impatiently.

"The side of a terrified young woman who faces a fate far worse than any death you could devise, Damin Wolfblade, if you send her back to that animal."

Damin threw his hands up impatiently. "Look, I'm not happy about this either, but—"

"Then don't do it," Tejay cut in. "Whether you've officially come of age or not, you outrank everybody here, Damin, so you're the only one who can make a decree about the fate of Kendra Warhaft and have any hope of making it stick."

"I'm actually more concerned about the fate of Hythria, at the moment," he snapped, annoyed at her for siding with Narvell. "The fate of one errant wife, even if she's in love with my brother, is hardly the point."

Tejay shook her head. "She's exactly the point. Hythria isn't just a geographical location, Damin. Hythria is its people. If you can't spare a thought for even one of your people, what's the point in trying to protect your nation from someone else who wants to possess it? You might as well let Hablet have the whole damned country. You obviously don't care about it that much."

Narvell smiled at Tejay. "I'm glad you're on my side."

Wounded by her accusation, Damin looked at the pair of them, shaking his head in disbelief. "He takes another man's wife and suddenly *I'm* the one in the wrong?"

"Life is very unfair like that sometimes, Damin," Tejay replied.

"What am I supposed to tell Stefan Warhaft?"

Tejay smiled. "I'm sure you'll think of something. But do it quickly, would you? Poor Kendra's exhausted but she's not going to rest while the threat of being returned to Zadenka is hanging over her head."

Realising he could only win this argument at the risk of losing the whole damned war, Damin glared at his brother. "You're going to owe me for this, Narvell."

His brother reached out and placed his hand on Damin's shoulder reassuringly. "Do this for me, Damin, and I swear you'll never have any need to doubt my loyalty to you or your throne again."

"If I do this for you, Narvell, the chances are good I'll never see any damned throne. If Warhaft doesn't kill me, Charel Hawksword probably will. Or Marla. Or Lernen . . ."

Tejay punched his shoulder impatiently. "Don't be such a coward, Damin. Go in there and strike a blow for Hythrun womanhood! Make a stand! If you won't do it for Kendra, then do it for Leila's memory. Let the men of this nation learn they can't treat their women worse than slaves and expect to get away with it any longer."

"You've seen that damned list Marla's got, haven't you?" he accused, peering at her closely in the darkness.

"What list?"

"My brother is of the opinion our mother has a secret list of things she expects him to change when he becomes High Prince," Narvell explained. "The plight of highborn Hythrun women seems to be relatively high on her agenda."

"As it should be," Tejay agreed. "I have a list like that, myself."

Damin ran his hands through his hair and glared at the pair of them. "This is going to cause a stink you'll be able to smell back in Greenharbour."

Tejay shrugged. "Don't worry about it, Damin. Nobody's going to smell anything over the reek of that cesspit. And you might be surprised by the people who back you in this. Not every man in Hythria is a brutal pig who thinks women don't deserve respect."

"No," Damin agreed. "Just the one you want me to tell he can't have his wife back."

"It's the right thing to do, Damin," Narvell assured him.

"So was not killing Mahkas Damaran," Damin replied

heavily. "But that doesn't mean it felt any better than this does."

Neither Tejay nor Narvell had an answer to that so Damin left them in the tavern's yard and went to look for Almodavar and Adham, in the vain hope the logistics of settling more than five thousand men around a village of a few hundred people would provide a welcome distraction to the other problems plaguing him this night.

chapter 14

By pushing their horses for as long as they dared each day, Kalan and Wrayan made excellent time. By the end of their first week on the road, they'd covered the better part of three hundred miles and were close to the border of Pentamor. Kalan was saddle sore, weary and had never been happier.

She and Wrayan travelled well together. Wrayan seemed to have forgotten she was anything other than his equal. That was an important milestone for Kalan. She had worshipped Wrayan Lightfinger for as long as she could remember, but she knew the fact that he'd known her since she was a baby might prove an impediment to their relationship. It was a foolish concern on his part, Kalan had decided for him. Wrayan Lightfinger was part Harshini, so the normal rules simply didn't apply to him. The thief was, Kalan knew, close to fifty years old, but at an inn a few days ago, the tavern keeper had assumed he was her brother. He looked to be in his late twenties, perhaps thirty at the most. But neither Wrayan's age, appearance, nor his profession concerned Kalan Hawksword.

True love, she was quite certain, could rise above all these minor impediments.

"We should stop soon," Wrayan advised, jerking Kalan out of her daydream.

"What?"

"I said we should probably stop soon. We're only about three miles from the village of Tallant Moor. It's a pretty rough place so I'd rather avoid it, if we can."

"If you want," she agreed absently.

He looked at her curiously. "Is something wrong?"

"No, of course not. I was just lost in thought."

He smiled. "Anything you'd care to share?"

"Can't you read my mind?"

"Your mind is shielded."

"You put the shield there, Wrayan. You can take it away, can't you?"

"I could," he agreed, "but that rather defeats the purpose of putting it there in the first place."

"It must be strange, being able to read people's innermost thoughts at will."

"I try not to, most of the time."

She glanced at him in surprise. "Why not? If I could read minds I wouldn't be able to resist it."

He frowned at her ignorance. "Believe me, Kalan, most people's innermost thoughts are pretty murky. I'll probe someone's mind out of necessity. I certainly don't do it for a bit of light entertainment."

"You're so frustrating, sometimes, Wrayan," she complained. "I mean, here you are, about the most powerful sorcerer alive, and yet you barely even use your power. And here *I* am, a full member of the Sorcerers' Collective, and I can't even light a fire without a flint."

Wrayan shook his head. "For one thing, I'm not the most powerful sorcerer alive by any stretch of the imagination, Kalan. Even if you discount the Harshini still living in Sanctuary, next to the Halfbreed, I'm almost powerless."

"Yes, but—"

"As for *you* being powerless," he cut in before she could add anything further, "your mother effectively runs the whole damn country, your twin brother is going to be a Warlord and your half-brother will eventually be High Prince of Hythria. Your stepsister owns half of Hythria's shipping fleet and your stepbrothers control the most comprehensive intelligence network in four nations, alongside a goodly portion of the spice trade. And let's not forget your uncle is the current High Prince. On your family connections alone, you'll wind up High Arrion someday, Kalan. Talk to Alija Eaglespike if you don't think that isn't power to burn."

"That's not what I meant . . ."

"I know," he said, smiling at her paternally. "I just don't want you to envy me for something you don't understand."

Having Wrayan look at her like that was the last thing Kalan wanted, so she decided to change the subject. "Didn't you say we should find somewhere to stop for the night?"

"I was hoping we'd find shelter, actually," he said, glancing up at the heavy clouds. "So we wouldn't have to stop in the village. But I don't like our chances."

Kalan looked around, silently agreeing shelter was a very optimistic hope. The sun had almost set and in the chilly twilight the countryside around Tallant Moor seemed uniformly bleak. To their right, a small treeless hill fell away to a steep valley. In the distance, some way down the slope, Kalan spied a flickering light. "What about down there?"

Wrayan glanced in the direction of her pointing finger, frowning. "Looks like a farmhouse."

Kalan smiled. "I can see why the Halfbreed accuses you of having a talent for stating the obvious, Wrayan Lightfinger."

"I can see I'm going to have to stop telling you any more anecdotes about him," he grumbled.

Kalan laughed. "Shall we check it out, do you think? Or is it too risky? There may be plague around."

Wrayan shrugged. "I'll scan the minds of the occupants from here. That should tell us if it's safe."

"I thought you didn't like doing that?"

"I also said I'd probe someone's mind out of necessity. This is a necessity, don't you agree?"

"Shall we tell them who we are or make up a story?"

"Is who we are a secret?" he enquired curiously.

"The closer we get to Greenharbour, the more it should be," she suggested. "Alija still thinks you're dead. I don't see any reason why we should disillusion her just yet."

Wrayan considered her suggestion. "You might have a point. What shall we tell our hosts, then?"

"We could pose as husband and wife," she said, glad her mind was shielded and Wrayan couldn't read her enthusiasm for the idea.

"Why not brother and sister?" he asked. "Or cousins?"

"Because if there's only shelter available in the barn," she explained, as if he was just a little bit thick for not having worked this out for himself, "and they think we're siblings, the chances are good you'll wind up sleeping out in the hayloft with the husband, and I'll end up being eaten alive by the bedbugs, sharing a pallet in the house with the wife. If we pose as a married couple, they'll offer us shelter in the barn and we can be clean *and* warm and not have to worry about anything or any*body* else."

"You really do think these things through, don't you?"

"One of us has to."

Wrayan didn't answer her, his attention obviously elsewhere. When he looked at her his eyes were black, the whites of his eyes completely consumed by the darkness, a sure sign he was drawing on his power.

"What can you see?" she asked, a little in awe of seeing him like this.

"They're a young couple," he told her. "No older than you, either of them. They're still grieving a child lost to the plague, but it's been safe here for some time now. They're fighting, actually."

"About what?"

"About whether or not to have another child. He wants to start a family again straight away. She's still grieving her lost child and can't bring herself to contemplate the idea."

The thought of walking into such a fraught situation and interrupting it, just for the sake of a roof over their heads for the night, suddenly didn't seem such an attractive idea. "Maybe we should push on, Wrayan."

"There's not much else out here. And it's going to rain again soon."

"I know, but these people don't need us intruding on their grief."

"Any more than you or I need pneumonia."

"Can't you make it better for them?"

"How?"

"You're obviously inside their minds. Can't you simply make one of them give in to the other one?"

"Which one? The randy husband or the grieving wife?"

Kalan had the decency to look away, feeling more than a little shamefaced. "All right, so that wasn't such a brilliant idea."

"Interfering in other people's lives is never as simple as it seems, Kalan."

"Honestly, I'm beginning to wonder if this magic of yours has any practical purpose," she complained. "I mean, if you can't actually use it to do anything useful . . ."

"Define useful."

"I don't know," she shrugged. "Bending the world to your will, I suppose."

Wrayan laughed. "You are *definitely* your mother's daughter, Kalan Hawksword."

Kalan wasn't sure she liked the way Wrayan was laughing at her. She tossed her head indignantly and tugged on the packhorse's lead rein, trotting on ahead until she spied a rutted wagon track further along, leading down to the faint light at the foot of the slope.

Without waiting to see if Wrayan was following, she turned onto the track and headed for the little farmhouse, wondering what was so wrong about wanting to bend the world to your will, anyway.

chapter 15

I've come to a decision," Damin told everyone, a few hours later. It was very late, but they were all gathered in the cosy taproom of the tavern which had been closed to the local villagers (at an exorbitant cost) while the heir to Hythria and his entourage were in the village.

His announcement got everyone's attention. Narvell was sitting by the door, glaring at Stefan Warhaft who sat near the fire nursing a tankard of ale and a foul mood. Tejay and Kendra sat at another table near Narvell. This was the first good look Rorin had got at the love of Narvell's life. Up until now, things had been moving too fast to consider her objectively. She was a little thin for Rorin's taste, and her skin seemed too pale for her dark hair. But she was pretty enough, he supposed. And she certainly had spirit. Only a brave woman or a very foolish one would defy a man like Stefan Warhaft more than once.

Flanking Damin was his stepbrother, Adham Tirstone, and Geri Almodavar. Rorin stood beside Almodavar. Damin had spoken to them privately before the meeting and they were ready for any trouble with either Lord Warhaft or Narvell, should either man object to their solution to the awkward problem of what to do with Kendra Warhaft.

"Then my wife and I will be leaving for Zadenka Manor at once," Warhaft announced, rising to his feet. "Thank you, your highness, for coming to the right decision."

"I haven't actually said what it was, yet."

"Well, yes, but I'm assuming . . ."

"Then you assume wrong, my lord."

"Thank you, Damin . . ." Narvell began, smiling with relief.

"I suggest you wait until you've heard my decision, too, Narvell, before you start thanking me for it."

His younger brother's expression darkened. "What do you mean?"

"I mean that while I agree Lord Warhaft has demonstrated he doesn't deserve to own a pack of dogs, let alone a wife, I'm not going to flout the law and allow you to run off with her, just because you're my brother."

"Don't do this, Damin," Narvell warned, rising to his feet. Rorin glanced at Damin, wondering if the fight he'd interrupted earlier was about to start again, this time for much more personal reasons.

"Don't threaten me, Narvell," the prince warned. "I don't like ultimatums and I'm not going to be dictated to by Elasapine, any more than I'd allow Cyrus Eaglespike to tell me what colour coat I should wear to the Feast of Kaelarn Ball."

"Then what have you decided?" Tejay asked impatiently, glaring at the men around her as if they were all fools.

"I've decided I don't have the authority to grant either Lord Warhaft's request, or Narvell's. The only one who can adjudicate on this matter is the High Prince."

"Damn right!" Warhaft agreed.

"Shut up, fool!" Adham snapped at the baron impatiently, shoving him back into his seat.

Damin ignored the interruption. "On the other hand, it is the duty of all Hythrun warriors to protect our women and I'm quite sure if I allow Lady Kendra to return to her husband, I would be putting her very life in danger, so I'm not prepared to do that, either."

"Then what are you going to do?" Narvell demanded.

"I'm going to leave her in the custody of the Sorcerers' Collective."

Narvell's gaze fixed on Rorin suspiciously. "You think *Rorin* can protect her?"

"I think the Sorcerers' Collective can," Damin corrected. "Despite what Lord Warhaft believes, traditionally, in the custody of a member of the Sorcerers' Collective, Kendra is inviolate, and if you want to put *that* theory to the test, be my guest. Take on the High Arrion with my blessing. I hear Alija Eaglespike likes a good bloodbath."

As Rorin knew he would be, Warhaft was furious. "But how do I get my wife back?"

"You can appeal to the High Prince."

"That could take months!"

"Now isn't that a damn shame?" Adham remarked with a grin.

"What happens in the meantime?" Narvell asked, smart enough not to question his good fortune. Warhaft had right on his side and it was only Rorin's knowledge of Collective law that had given Damin a graceful exit from this impossible dilemma.

"Kendra must remain in Rorin's custody until we can get to Greenharbour to sort this out. As Rorin is one of my aides, she'll have to stay with my entourage until then. I assume you've got no objection to accompanying me to Byamor now, Lord Hawksword?"

"None at all!" Narvell agreed, a little too quickly.

"Then I'm coming, too!" Warhaft announced, rising to his feet again, although he did make a point of staying well out of Adham's reach this time. "I am a vassal of Elasapine, and if her troops are being called up to defend the province, then I must do my duty to my Warlord."

Damin didn't seem very happy at that idea. "Do you doubt my word, Lord Warhaft? Or the integrity of a member of the Sorcerers' Collective?"

"Why should I trust any of you? Narvell Hawksword is your half-brother and you've just handed my wife over to the custody of a complete stranger who walked into my home and kidnapped my wife out from under me. He's not wearing the robes of his brotherhood. How do I know this pet wizard of yours is really even a member of the Sorcerers' Collective?"

A score of explanations flashed through Rorin's mind, but none of them seemed adequate. Apparently, Damin thought the same. With a sigh, the prince turned to Rorin. "Show him, Rory."

He wasn't expecting that. "Here? *Now*?"

"Sometimes, it's just better to show than tell."

"If you insist." He shrugged. Rorin turned to face Stefan Warhaft. The baron glared at him sceptically, an expression that slowly changed to abject terror as Rorin's eyes began to darken. About the same time Warhaft's feet lifted off the floor and he found himself floating up toward the ceiling. Kendra gasped, but nobody else in the room seemed surprised.

With his hands on his hips, Damin looked up at Warhaft, who was pushed up against the rafters, held there by nothing more than Rorin's will. "So, Lord Warhaft, are we satisfied now that Master Mariner is a real sorcerer?"

The baron nodded in wordless horror. Rorin saw the look on his face and decided he wouldn't be much trouble from now on.

"Good." Damin turned to Rorin. "Let him down."

Rorin did exactly as Damin asked. With a thud, Stefan Warhaft crashed to the floor, face first, and lay there bellowing in pain.

Kendra had covered her mouth with her hands. Narvell was grinning like a fool. Even Tejay was smiling.

"Oops," Rorin said.

Damin glared at him.

"Captain?" the prince said, turning to Almodavar. Even the old Raider seemed amused. "Escort Lord Warhaft to his men and inform them he's returning to his manor tonight."

"I said I'm coming with you!" Warhaft insisted as he painfully pushed himself up onto his hands and knees.

"Then I suggest you take this opportunity to go home and settle your affairs, my lord. We're going to war, after all. You can follow us in a day or two. Given we're travelling along the main highway into Elasapine with a combined force of more than five thousand men, I'm sure even you'll be able to follow our trail."

The baron staggered to his feet and glared at Damin. "You think you're so damned smart, don't you?"

"Perhaps," Damin retorted. "But at least I don't think beating a defenceless woman with a horsewhip makes me a man."

Warhaft grunted something unintelligible that Rorin suspected was a curse and limped from the taproom with Almodavar close on his heels. As soon as he was gone, everyone relaxed. Narvell stepped closer to Kendra and put his arm around her shoulder.

"Thanks, Damin."

"Don't thank me, Narvell. I meant what I said. Kendra is now Rorin's responsibility. You can't have her any more than Warhaft can, until we present her case to Lernen and get him to make a ruling on the matter."

Rorin expected Narvell to object, but he didn't. Instead, he glanced down at Kendra, squeezed her shoulder encouragingly, accepting the inevitable. "I still owe you my thanks. And you too, Rory. You probably saved Kendra's life."

It occurred to Rorin, at that moment, Narvell really did love this girl, if he was willing to forgo her company simply to keep her safe from the brute to whom she was married. Suddenly, he was glad he'd had to interfere. He looked at Tejay and noted she was nodding her approval.

Damin turned to the Warlord's wife then and asked, "My lady, I know Rorin's technically responsible for her, but would you take Lady Kendra into your care, at least until we reach Byamor?"

"Of course."

Rorin glanced at Kendra, wondering what she thought of all this. She'd had surprisingly little to say up until this point.

"I hope you find these arrangements satisfactory, my lady?" the prince enquired.

"Yes, your highness," she replied, her hands clasped demurely in her lap. Kendra was sitting with her back in an unnaturally straight position, no doubt out of care for her injuries. "And I thank you. It was never my intention to be the cause of so much trouble."

"If I thought it was, my lady, you'd be on the way back to Zadenka with your husband."

"Damin!" Narvell objected, putting himself protectively between his brother and his lover.

"Oh, settle down, little brother," Damin advised. "I'm kidding."

"Fine time you pick to discover your lost sense of humour."

"I got mine back about the time Warhaft broke his fall with his face," Adham chuckled, winking at Rorin.

"Which brings me to you, Rorin Mariner," Damin said, turning on him with a disapproving frown. "While I empathise with the desire of every person in this room to beat that fool into a bloody pulp, it didn't help matters to drop him on his head like that. No matter how much he deserved it."

Rorin faced him, feigning innocence. "It was an accident, Damin! Honestly! I slipped."

"You were using magic, not holding him up with brute force. How could you slip?"

Rorin glanced past Damin and winked at the others. "Well, if you don't know, I'm certainly not about to explain it to you."

"Oh, leave him alone, Damin," Tejay laughed. "And don't be such a hypocrite. You wanted that animal to fall on his face as much as the rest of us."

"True," the prince admitted with some reluctance, much to Rorin's relief. Having seen what he was capable of, Rorin didn't really fancy being on the receiving end of Damin Wolfblade's rage. "But I was trying very hard to give the impression I was the noble statesman here. Having one of my aides drop the Baron of Zadenka on his head demonstrates a distinct lack of class."

Tejay was still laughing. It relieved Rorin to see her so amused. There were few people in this world whose good opinion Damin actively sought. Tejay Lionsclaw was one of them and if she was smiling, the chances were good that everyone else would follow her lead.

"I'm sure you'll get plenty more chances to play noble statesman that don't involve having your aides throw people around the room," she assured Damin.

He turned to Rorin. "I'm relying on you to keep Lady Kendra safe."

"You know I will."

Damin turned back to Narvell again. "Friends?"

Narvell nodded. "Friends."

"Good," Damin said. "Because if you ever challenge me publicly again, little brother, I'll crush you like a bug."

Narvell thought about it and then shrugged. "Fair enough."

Damin smiled and offered Narvell his hand.

As they shook on it, Tejay Lionsclaw rolled her eyes, muttering something Rorin didn't quite catch, but it sounded like she was complaining about men and their foolish, immature, endlessly frustrating male pride.

chapter 16

The farmer and his wife were poor, but not desperately so. They welcomed the supplies that Wrayan and Kalan offered in return for shelter, and although there was obviously tension between them, they'd put aside their argument while there were visitors in the house. It was quite late when Wrayan and Kalan retired to the barn, but clearly, the presence of strangers had diffused the argument. Perhaps the young couple had had enough shouting for one day. Kalan was glad of that. She hated to see two people so obviously in pain unable to resolve their differences.

The night was cold and as Wrayan had predicted, the rain started bucketing down a little after dinner. They snuggled close together for warmth, two blankets better than one, the heat of their bodies the only source of warmth in the draughty hayloft.

"Are you warm enough?" Wrayan asked, as Kalan pressed her back into his warm embrace.

"Actually, I'm freezing," she admitted, pulling the blankets up under her chin. "But I'm thinking a fire in the hayloft to address the situation might not be such a brilliant idea."

Wrayan chuckled softly as he settled in beside her and pulled her closer. "I've heard farmers take a dim view of passing travellers burning their barns down, regardless of how cold it gets."

"No sense of humour," Kalan remarked. "That's their problem."

She felt, rather than saw, Wrayan smiling in the darkness, wishing she could see his face, but with her back to him, she could only imagine his expression. This close to him, with his arms around her to conserve what warmth they could, Kalan could imagine quite a few other (much less innocent) things she'd like to do with Wrayan, but she was acutely aware that handled incorrectly, any chance she had of a relationship with him would be ruined.

The biggest problem, Kalan readily admitted to herself as she lay in the darkness listening to Wrayan's deep, even breathing, was getting him to see her as someone other than her mother's daughter. Wrayan had known her mother since before even Damin was born and he had an infuriating tendency to look upon all Marla's children with the same affection as might a benevolent uncle. As far as Kalan was concerned, he could be an uncle to her brothers all he wanted. But to have him smile at her indulgently wasn't what she wanted.

Kalan wanted Wrayan to *want* her. She wanted him to lust after her.

She sighed, wishing she could find a way to make him see how much she desired him without attracting either his contempt or his ridicule. She was pretty enough, she decided. Although not the rare beauty her mother was, Kalan was confident she'd matured into a presentable young woman. Her mother still got offers for her hand in marriage on a regular basis, but Kalan knew those proposals were prompted by political expedience, not her radiant beauty.

She was the future High Prince's sister, after all.

Still, Kalan knew she wasn't unattractive. She also knew, without vanity, that she was intelligent, perceptive and well educated and while some men appeared intimidated by such a female, Wrayan Lightfinger wasn't one of them. No man lucky enough to count himself a part of Princess Marla's inner circle (with the possible exception of Mahkas Damaran) was under any illusions about the ability of women to hold their own in a world dominated by men.

But knowing all of this did little to help Kalan unravel the puzzle that was Wrayan Lightfinger. She knew he wasn't celibate (Fee could attest to that—she seemed able to name every woman who had ever crossed the threshold of Wrayan's room at the Pickpocket's Retreat). But neither had he ever been in love that Kalan knew about. In fact, it was doubtful any relationship he'd been involved in had lasted much past two or three days. This disturbed Kalan a great deal. What was Wrayan looking for? She knew him too well to consider him simply selfish or uncaring of the feelings of the women he took to his bed. It was the reason, she suspected, that Wrayan limited his attention to *court'esa* and never attempted to woo a woman who might expect some sort of commitment. Whatever it was that stopped Wrayan from becoming involved with a lover on more than the most superficial level was something from his past, she reasoned. Something Kalan needed to discover before she attempted to act on her desires, otherwise she would wind up just another notch on Wrayan Lightfinger's belt, or worse, looking like a complete fool.

"Wrayan?" she ventured softly in the darkness, wondering if he was asleep yet.

"Mmm?" He was awake but didn't sound far from sleep. Maybe now was the time to question him, when he was off-guard and at his most vulnerable.

"Have you ever been in love?"

He hesitated before he answered. "Once."

"What happened?"

Again Wrayan hesitated, as if debating the advisability of sharing his secrets with her. "She was . . . *is* . . . way out of my reach."

Kalan was silent for a time, a little surprised he'd volunteered even that much information. "Did she love you?"

"I suppose. In her own way."

"But not enough to stay with you?"

"Things are never that simple, Kalan," he replied. She couldn't see his face but she got the impression he was smiling.

"Do you still miss her?"

"Every day of my life."

Kalan was almost afraid to ask the next question. "Do you think that maybe . . . someday . . . you and her . . . ?"

She felt him shaking his head. "There's no chance of a happy ending, Kal. We're too different. Now shut up and go to sleep."

"I'm sorry."

"So am I."

Kalan felt silent, wondering who he spoke of with such painful longing. Was it the Harshini princess he'd mentioned the first day they were on the road together, or someone much closer to home? The mystery frustrated and infuriated Kalan. She didn't mind a flesh and blood rival for Wrayan's affections. One could do something about a real adversary. But there was no way to compete with a ghost.

"Wrayan . . ."

"Go to sleep, Kalan."

"I really am sorry."

"Just drop it."

There was an edge of impatience to his voice that warned her she was on the brink of pushing him too far. Kalan closed her eyes and settled down to sleep with the musty smell of hay and the tattoo of rain upon the roof, content that for the time being at least, regardless of who her mysterious rival was, right now she was the one sleeping with Wrayan's arms around her.

The rest of their journey to Greenharbour was uneventful, except for one incident that reminded Kalan sharply that the man of her dreams was no ordinary man.

It happened almost a week after they'd stopped at the isolated farmhouse. They were riding at a walk as Wrayan continued telling her the story he'd begun several days ago about his exploits as a burglar in Greenharbour during his youth, when he was known as Wrayan the Wraith.

Kalan wasn't sure she believed half of what he was telling her. The stories seemed a little far-fetched, even for Wrayan. His narration disturbed her a little, too. While she appreciated the entertainment, she had a bad feeling Wrayan was telling her stories to keep her amused, the way he had when she was a small child. That didn't augur well for her plans to change Wrayan's opinion about her. One told amusing anecdotes to children on a long journey to stop them from becoming fractious, not because this was a woman one was hoping to seduce.

And then Wrayan stopped, mid-sentence, and hauled his mount to a stop. Standing on the road in front of them was a boy of about fourteen or fifteen, dressed in a most remarkable collection of cast-off clothing that appeared to represent almost every fashion trend of the last millennia.

"Divine One!" Wrayan exclaimed in surprise.

Kalan stared at him in astonishment and then studied the boy on the road. "*Divine* One?"

The thief looked at Kalan in surprise. "You can *see* him?"

"The child blocking our path? Yes. I can see him. Why wouldn't I be able to see him?"

"Why are you letting her see you?" he asked the child.

The boy shrugged. "She might think you're crazy if you suddenly start talking to thin air." The boy stepped closer and stared up at them with an ingenuous grin. "Aren't you going to introduce me?"

Wrayan looked at her uncertainly. "Um . . . sure . . . Kalan Hawksword, meet . . . Dacendaran, the God of Thieves."

Kalan nearly fell off her horse. "Divine One!" She hurriedly dismounted and fell to her knees in front of the god. "Forgive me for not recognising you, Divine One!"

The boy-god leaned forward. He took her elbow gently,

urging her to stand, and then looked up at Wrayan. "You see? That's how *nice* people greet their gods. And she's not even one of my disciples." He turned his attention to Kalan then, eyeing her speculatively. "You could be a thief, you know. You look like a thief."

"I'm . . . flattered, Divine One," she stammered. "But I'm a member of the Sorcerers' Collective. I'm sworn to worship all gods equally."

The god squinted a little, studying her closely, clearly puzzled by what he found. "But you can't wield magic. How can you belong to the Sorcerers' Collective?"

"The ability to wield magic is no longer an admission requirement to the Sorcerers' Collective," Wrayan informed him. "Hasn't been much of a priority since the Harshini went into hiding."

"Well . . . that's just silly," the god said with a frown. "Who ever heard of anything so odd? Mind you," he added, winking at Wrayan, "it could explain why they chucked you out."

"They didn't chuck me out," Wrayan corrected. "Someone tried to kill me."

"Same difference." He turned his attention back to Kalan. "Are you sure you wouldn't like to be a thief? I'm a very generous god, you know. I don't make my disciples worship in a temple, or insist they hold those long, boring services on Restdays. No rites. No sacrifices. Just steal the odd trinket every now and then and I'll watch over you until Death comes knocking on your door. Even then, if I like you, I can speak to the old boy about taking you as painlessly as possible."

Kalan glanced up at Wrayan, wondering how she was supposed to respond to such an offer. He shook his head at the god and frowned. "Come on, Dace, you know you're not supposed to recruit humans already in the service of the Sorcerers' Collective."

"Who told you that?"

"Brakandaran."

"He's a fine one to talk about breaking the rules."

Kalan looked from Wrayan to Dace in confusion. "Hang on. If you're not allowed to recruit members of the Sorcerers' Collective, why did you make a deal with Wrayan to save my mother?"

The god looked at her closely and then laughed. "*Your* mother? *She* was the one I released from that time spell? Are you sure? You don't look much like her. And you seem quite a bit older than she was."

"You saved her before I was born, Divine One." It made Kalan cringe to remind Wrayan of that after all her hard work playing down the difference in their ages.

"Was it *so* long ago?"

"More than twenty-five years," Wrayan confirmed.

"Fancy that!" the god laughed. "Well, just goes to show what a good judge of character I am, doesn't it? Are you sure you don't want to be a thief?"

"I'm sorry, Divine One."

Dacendaran shrugged. "At least you're not following one of the others, I suppose. Not like they need any help, at the moment, mind you. Between Zeggie's war and Cheltaran's pesky little ailment . . ."

"You mean the plague?" Kalan asked in surprise. "You're not suggesting the God of Healing set the plague among us deliberately, are you?"

"Don't be stupid. He fixes things, he doesn't break them. It was probably Voden."

"Why would the God of Green Life set the plague among us?" Wrayan asked, apparently just as confused as Kalan.

"Why not?" Dace shrugged. "You're all just little bits and pieces on a game board to Voden. He doesn't think human life is any more valuable than some itty-bitty little bug he's decided needs a chance to thrive for a while."

"But that's appalling!" Kalan gasped.

"Only if you're human." The god shrugged.

"But what about Cheltaran?" Wrayan asked.

Dacendaran's expression grew rather smug. "Ah, now

that's where you get lucky, Wrayan. After you suggested I speak to which ever one of my siblings was causing this little illness that seems to bother you all so much, I had a chat with my brother, Chellie."

"*Chellie*?" Kalan repeated incredulously. She'd never imagined anybody could refer to Cheltaran, the noble God of Healing, as "Chellie."

"Anyway, I pointed out that instead of just sitting on his hands waiting for Voden to get bored with his new friends, he should take this opportunity to do something useful, particularly as Zeggie's getting so full of himself with half of Fardohnya waiting over the border to invade you, so I—"

"Hang on!" Kalan interrupted, forgetting for a moment that she was in the presence of a god. "Half of Fardohnya is waiting over the border to *invade* us?"

"Well . . . maybe not half," Dace conceded. "But there *are* a lot of them. Brak said there was some way of working it out by counting fires, but—"

"You spoke to Brak?" Wrayan cut in. "When? Where? Is he all right?"

"If you'd let me *finish*," Dace retorted impatiently. "Maybe I'll get around to telling you."

"Sorry," they both muttered contritely.

"As I was saying, before I was so *rudely* interrupted," the god continued, "I spoke to Chellie and pointed out he'd have a lot more fun if he helped the whole healing thing along instead of just waiting for nature to take its course, and how Death was run off his feet, and Zeggie was just being a pain, and even Kali was feeling it with people too afraid to touch each other for fear of dropping dead or something, and how the whole world just generally reeked at the moment, and how all of us could get back to normal if things settled down a bit, and he said yes."

"He said yes to what?" Kalan asked, thoroughly confused.

"To stopping this plague thing you're all so upset about, of course. There's hardly been a death from it in weeks now. I would have told you the other day when we healed your friend, Wrayan, but I was so excited over you finding me another soul, I forgot all about it."

"Do you mean the plague is over?" Kalan gasped.

"Of course not!" The god sighed, rolling his eyes at her ignorance. "You can't just stop a thing like that dead in its tracks. People would get suspicious."

"Yeah," Wrayan agreed wryly. "They might think their prayers had been answered."

Dace took a step back in alarm. "Good grief, man! Do you have any idea what would happen if we started actually *answering* prayers?"

"More people might believe in you, Divine One," Kalan suggested.

"Which is all well and good," the god agreed. "But you've no idea what the world would be like. We know humans. Nobody would do anything! You'd just sit down, say a prayer and wait for one of us to do it."

"So the gods' willingness to sit back and let untold pain and suffering torment the mortals of this world is really just your way of demonstrating your selfless concern for our well-being?" Wrayan asked.

"Exactly!" Dacendaran agreed.

The thief stared at his god in amazement.

"So many things Brak told me when I was in Sanctuary suddenly begin to make sense," Wrayan said, turning to Kalan.

For her part, Kalan was dumbfounded, but she wasn't sure if it was this god's bizarre logic or merely the fact she was standing here talking to one that left her so bemused.

"Anyway," Dace said, "I just thought I'd drop by and let you know that I've fixed your little problem so now you can fix mine."

"What problem?" Wrayan asked suspiciously.

"Does the phrase *greatest thief in all of Hythria* ring a bell?"

Wrayan sighed. "Things have been rather difficult lately, Divine One . . ."

"And I've just put an end to all that," Dace reminded him.

"So I expect to see some action soon, Lightfinger, or we'll be having a discussion about what happens when you break a pact you made with a god."

"What's to steal out here?" Wrayan asked, looking around the empty rolling grasslands flanking the gravelled road.

"You'll be in Greenharbour in a matter of days. I'm sure there's something *there* that's not nailed down."

"I'm supposed to be helping Princess Marla."

"Help her all you want." Dacendaran shrugged. "Just don't forget to steal something in my honour every now and then."

"Every now and *then*?" Wrayan echoed doubtfully.

"Oh, all right . . . you know I meant every chance you get. I was trying to be nice."

"And I appreciate your forbearance, Divine One."

"Don't get smart with me, boy," he warned, which sounded odd coming from a creature that looked like a child.

Then Dace turned to Kalan. "You could steal something too, if you like."

"I'll honour you in my prayers, Divine One."

"I'd rather you stole something."

"I'll see what I can do."

That seemed to make Dacendaran happy. Smiling, he turned on Wrayan and pointed at him. "Greatest thief in all of Hythria, Wrayan Lightfinger. I haven't forgotten."

He was gone even before his words had faded into the hazy sunshine, leaving Kalan and Wrayan staring at the empty space in the road.

After a long, astonished silence, she looked up at Wrayan, shaking her head in wonder. "So, that was the God of Thieves . . ."

"Yes."

"He's . . . not what I expected."

"No."

"Is he likely to come back?"

Wrayan shrugged. "How should I know?"

She gathered up her reins and remounted her horse. "Greatest thief in all of Hythria, eh?"

"Don't start."

Kalan bit back her amusement, and said nothing further, convinced her strange and unexpected encounter with a god was simply more proof Wrayan Lightfinger was destined to be by her side.

Kalan Hawksword had plans, after all, to be High Arrion someday. Who better as a consort for the High Arrion of the Sorcerers' Collective than a man who could put her directly in touch with the gods?

chapter 17

arla Wolfblade's plans to destroy Alija Eaglespike involved more than simply having her killed. That was far too simple, far too easy and far too quick. *Alija is going to suffer,* she decided, *as much as I have.* Marla intended to play with Alija the same way a cat played with its prey before it killed. The High Arrion would experience the same pain and anguish she had caused Marla. She would suffer as Marla had suffered. Feel the loss Marla felt. Shed the same river of tears.

The most obvious target was Alija's son, Cyrus, but even if the notion of killing a ruling Warlord wasn't politically unwise, he wasn't in the city at present and therefore was out of Marla's reach. But Tarkyn Lye was here and he was the one responsible for tormenting Elezaar into betraying Marla. His death would not only hurt Alija, it would avenge poor Elezaar at the same time.

Two for the price of one. Revenge doesn't come much better than that.

There was no question, however, of Marla being seen to be

directly involved in his death. She wanted vengeance, not open warfare, and would reveal her part in his downfall when it suited her own agenda. So Marla did what any respectable Hythrun did when they wanted an enemy taken care of.

She hired the Assassins' Guild.

The Raven himself came to call on her, after Marla had asked Rodja to let it be known she was once again interested in employing the guild to take care of a small problem for her. The Raven was an old man now. Quite a remarkable feat for someone in his line of work and probably the reason the speculation was so rife about his successor. Marla greeted him cordially, showing him into the main reception hall of her townhouse, inviting him to join her in a light supper. The old assassin lowered himself to the cushions carefully and accepted the glass of wine she poured with her own hand.

"It's been a long time since we've done business together, your highness," the Raven remarked, as he took a sip of the wine, nodding appreciatively at the fine vintage. He knew enough about wine to understand Marla was treating him as an equal by serving the best. That's what Ruxton always advised. *Serve the commoners the good stuff, Marla, and they'll follow you anywhere.*

"I'm a woman, Master Raven," she said, taking a sip of wine. "I tend to find other ways of dealing with my problems than just having them killed."

"But not this time?" he asked with a raised brow.

"Not this time," she agreed.

"So who is this miscreant who has incurred the wrath of Hythria's most tolerant princess?"

"A *court'esa.*"

"You don't need my guild for that, your highness. You're well within your rights to kill your own slave."

"He's not my slave."

"Ah, yes, well that does complicate matters, somewhat." He took another generous mouthful of wine. "Still, a slave, even a *court'esa,* is easy enough to dispose of, and not even against the law, should your involvement become public knowledge. It shouldn't cost much."

"What if he belongs to the High Arrion?"

The Raven studied her, looking a little doubtful. He knew as well as Marla there was only one *court'esa* in the employ of Alija Eaglespike. "I've no wish to buy into anything political, your highness. You know how we feel about interfering in things that might bring the guild unwanted attention."

"Then why have you done nothing about Galon Miar?"

The Raven put down his wine and stared at her. "What do you mean?"

"He's openly flaunting himself as the High Arrion's lover. You might find that amusing, but I believe it seriously undermines your guild's credibility."

"Who Galon Miar sleeps with is his own business. I don't believe he's betraying our guild. Or bringing it into disrepute." He smiled knowingly. "Are you sure you're not jealous?"

"*Jealous?*"

"Galon's an attractive man, your highness, and closer to your age than Alija Eaglespike's. Women have done far worse than order a slave killed to get his attention."

"And you think that's why I want this done? To get a man's attention?"

"Stranger things have been known to happen."

Marla spoke with all the withering scorn she could muster. "Alija Eaglespike is an Innate magician, Master Raven. That is common knowledge. She can read minds. She can read your precious Galon Miar's mind. Instead of worrying about *my* motives, perhaps you should be worrying about how many of your secrets she's siphoned out of your lieutenant's memory in the last couple of months."

The Raven frowned. "You impugn the honour of one of my most trusted men."

"I'm more concerned that he's not compromising mine."

He smiled reassuringly, leaning forward to pick up his wine again. "Only you and I know the details of our previous arrangement, your highness."

"You sent Galon Miar here to remind me of that obligation."

"But he doesn't know the details."

"He knows I've used your guild in the past," Marla pointed out. "All I need is for Alija to learn that from Galon Miar's mind and the next thing you know she'll be trying to find out why. In light of whom I had killed, and the reason for it, I doubt it would take any giant leap of intuition to work out the identity of my victim."

"These are the risks one takes when one arranges an assassination, your highness."

"I'm prepared for the risks. For that matter, I'm prepared to stand up publicly and defend what I did. But logic and emotion are two entirely different things, sir. The man I paid you to eliminate was the father of two of my children and the only son of my closest ally. I'm not about to jeopardise those relationships just because Galon Miar can't keep his trousers on."

The Raven frowned. "Is this an opening gambit, your highness?"

"An opening gambit?"

"Are you trying to renegotiate our arrangement?"

"Not at all, Master. I'm trying to protect myself from your uncharacteristic sentimentality when it comes to your deputy."

"What exactly did you want of me?"

"I want Tarkyn Lye killed," Marla informed the head of the Assassins' Guild. "And I want Galon Miar to do it and I want him to know who ordered the job."

The Raven was silent for a moment. "Why Galon?"

"Firstly, because I want proof my secrets are safe with your guild, Master Raven. But mostly, because he has access to Alija's household and can probably do the job with a minimum of fuss."

The Raven sipped his wine thoughtfully. "How we perform a job is not usually the concern of our clients, your highness. I have any number of men who could move in and out of the Sorcerers' Palace, or Lady Eaglespike's private residence for that matter, without being detected. And if what you say about the High Arrion's ability to read minds is true, Galon would be in extreme danger if she was to learn of his deed."

"That would be a tragedy, wouldn't it," Marla agreed.

"I don't imagine she'll be very pleased with you, either, should she learn of your involvement in this affair."

"And how will the High Arrion learn of it, Master Raven? You seem fairly certain your secrets are safe in the hands of Galon Miar. Of course, should she find out who killed her favourite slave, I imagine that will put a swift end to their affair."

The old man scratched his chin thoughtfully. "I see. This has more to do with some problem between you and Lady Alija than the death of a slave or getting Galon's attention, I daresay."

"I don't enquire into your affairs, Master Raven. I'd appreciate you not enquiring into mine."

"In that case, your highness, you need to just accept that certain men among us are possessed of . . . *skills* . . . that make their minds impervious to casual scrutiny, and leave it at that."

"You expect me to believe that old wives' tale about assassins who can control their thoughts well enough to stop the Harshini reading them?"

"It worked well enough when the Harshini were around, your highness."

Marla was unconvinced. "How would you know? You haven't seen a Harshini in your lifetime to put your theory to the test."

"Then accept that despite how many times the High Arrion has made physical contact with my deputy, she's done nothing to indicate she's learned anything from him other than a few interesting new positions for making love." He smiled and added, "Trust me, given the guild secrets Galon Miar is privy to, we'd know about it pretty damn quickly if he'd been compromised."

Marla wasn't completely persuaded, but neither was this

an argument she was going to win. She shrugged, and let the matter drop. "How much to remove Tarkyn Lye?"

The Raven nodded his agreement. "Ten thousand gold rivets."

She was shocked. "For the death of a *slave*? He probably didn't cost that much when Alija bought him in the prime of life."

"You require one of my most valuable men to risk his life."

"Every one of your assassins risks his life on a regular basis," she reminded him. "This is no different. Let him use his much-vaunted mental skills to protect himself from his lover's wrath."

"I'm not sure Galon will see it that way."

"That's his problem, Master Raven. Not mine."

"And what of our original agreement?"

"What of it?"

"You owe us an apprentice, your highness. I see no sign of one on the horizon."

"I've been a widow for little more than two months, Master Raven. Surely I'm allowed some time to grieve before I start seeking a new husband with a child suitable for your needs?" She smiled then, aware she couldn't afford to make an enemy of this man while her agreement remained unfulfilled. "It should make for some interesting pillow talk on my next wedding night, don't you think? *Thanks for the lovely wedding, dearest, and did I mention I've promised your son to the Assassins' Guild?*"

The Raven didn't seem impressed with her attempt at levity. "If you are planning to marry a man with a suitable child for us to recruit, make sure the boy is no older than eleven or twelve. They're too old, after that, to undertake the training with any degree of success."

"I shall add that to my list."

The Raven's eyes narrowed slyly. "Perhaps I could aid you, your highness, by providing a list of suitable candidates?"

Marla's eyes widened in surprise. "Do you have a sideline in matchmaking, Master Raven?"

He shrugged. "A natural consequence of being responsible for creating so many widows and widowers, when you think about it."

"I suppose it is." There was something very disturbing about the idea, she thought, but decided not to pursue the matter. After leaning forward to ring the bell to order supper brought in, she picked up the decanter and offered more wine. "And I thank you for the offer, Master Raven," Marla added, as she refilled his glass, "but I think I can manage. I've done well enough so far, finding husbands, without the help of the Assassins' Guild."

It was three hours after the Raven left that Galon Miar banged noisily on the front door of Marla's townhouse. Just enough time, Marla calculated, for the Raven to return to his guild headquarters, inform his lieutenant of Marla's request, and for Galon to ride here in a fury.

Cadella, accompanied by two palace guards, opened the door to his insistent banging. Galon pushed his way in as soon as the door was unlocked, looking around impatiently.

"I want to see the princess!"

Waiting out of sight, just inside the main reception room, Marla watched the commotion in the foyer with interest.

"Her highness doesn't see anybody this late," Cadella scolded. "And you've no right to be here banging on decent people's doors like that in the middle of the night."

"Decent people don't hire assassins," he pointed out furiously. "Where is she? I demand to see her!"

Cadella waved the two guards forward, obviously intending to have Galon thrown back out into the street. Marla almost let them try, but reconsidered. Galon Miar was an assassin, and these men were palace guards, not seasoned Raiders trained by Geri Almodavar; it was debatable if either

man was a match for him. They certainly didn't deserve to
die over something as trivial as this.

"It's all right, Cadella," Marla said, stepping into the hall.
"You can let Master Miar in."

Clearly unhappy at the notion, the housekeeper took a
step backwards. "As you wish, your highness."

Galon turned on Marla angrily. "You've got a damn
nerve!"

"*I* have a nerve?" she repeated, raising an elegant brow.
"I'm not the one barging into people's houses in the middle
of the night, yelling at the top of my voice."

"You know *exactly* why I'm here . . ." He took a threatening step closer, which prompted her guards to reach for their
swords.

Marla waved them away. "There's no need for weapons,
gentlemen. I'm not in any danger. Master Miar isn't here to
kill me. Just to rant at me, I suspect. Cadella, have some
wine brought in, would you? Fortified, I think. Our guest
looks like he could use a drink."

Marla stood back to let Galon enter the hall. He stormed
past her as Marla nodded reassuringly to her housekeeper
and then waved the guards to her. "Wait here," she ordered
in a low voice. "If I call you, he doesn't leave the house
alive, understand?"

The men saluted solemnly and took post on either side of
the door. Marla closed it and turned to face her guest. He
was pacing the rug near the cushions like a caged animal.

"Is there something I can do for you, Master Miar?" she
asked, leaning against the doors.

"You can tell me why!" he demanded, turning on her furiously.

"I assume you're referring to the commercial arrangement I entered into with your superior earlier this evening?" She pushed off the door and walked a little further
into the room, feigning indifference to his anger, although
she surreptitiously made sure she was in shouting distance
of the guards. *This was the part of vengeance nobody*

warned you about. Her lack of concern was simply an act. Inside, Marla was quietly terrified of what she may have unleashed.

Galon glared at her. "Don't play with me! Just tell me why you insisted that I kill Tarkyn Lye, and why you made the Raven tell me who commissioned the kill."

"You have access to Alija's household."

"So do a score of other people."

"You're the only assassin among them, I'm guessing."

"Why do you want him dead?"

"Tarkyn Lye? That's none of your business."

"Neither is it any of my business who pays for the assassinations I perform."

"I merely wanted you to know who you were dealing with, sir. Nobody is asking you to make the information public."

"If I kill Tarkyn Lye for you, the High Arrion will know about it the first time she touches me, and when she learns the truth, she'll have *me* killed because she'll think I'm in league with you."

"Now *why* would she think that?" Marla asked, feigning ignorance.

"Assassins are never told who orders a kill. Ignorance of that fact is often our only protection."

"The Raven assures me you have other resources to call on, Master Miar. Aren't you one of those rare few who can consciously block their thoughts?"

He stared at her, obviously surprised. "The *Raven* told you that?"

"He was trying to assure me you could be trusted. I wasn't convinced then and I'm still not. If you kill Tarkyn Lye and Alija doesn't learn it was you who wielded the blade, however, I will be satisfied."

"You just don't get it, do you? The ability to consciously block your mind isn't a skill one can turn on and off like a stopcock. I'm no sorcerer. For us mortals it takes hours of meditation and days of preparation, none of which I have time for. If Alija reads my mind, she'll assume I'm working on my own because if it was a legitimate kill, I wouldn't have any idea who I was working for."

Marla smiled. "Gracious! You do have a problem, don't you?"

Galon wasn't amused. "I think I have a right to know why you're so anxious to have me die."

"Your concern she'll learn the truth if she touches you seems easy enough to deal with," Marla suggested with a shrug. "Don't let Alija touch you."

"And you think that won't make her just as suspicious?"

"How many people have you killed, Galon Miar?"

"*What*?"

"How many? A dozen? Two score or more?"

"I don't keep count," he replied, obviously puzzled by the question. "Why?"

"How many of your previous employers have you burst in on, in the middle of the night, demanding a reason for their actions?"

"You're the first employer who wanted me to know who hired me. You asked for me specifically. Have I done something to offend you?"

"You're the one who brags about how good he is, Galon Miar. Am I to be held accountable if I believe the stories you spread about yourself? If you're afraid, refuse the job," she suggested. "You have that option, don't you? Oh, wait a minute . . . this is the Assassins' Guild we're talking about, isn't it? Refusal means death, as I recall. Or is that just one of those nasty little rumours you people spread about yourselves to make you all sound rough, tough and manly?"

He let out a low, appreciative whistle. "Gods, I thought Alija was a manipulative bitch. She's a real amateur compared to you."

"Maybe you should have considered that before aligning yourself with the House of Eaglespike."

He looked quite shocked. "Is that what this is all about?" he demanded. "You think *I'm* a Patriot?"

"Are you?"

"Of course not!"

"Do you know what a Patriot is, Master Miar?"

He was almost grinding his teeth in anger. "I'm sure you're going to tell me, your highness."

"A Patriot is nothing more than the dupe of traitors, a fool who can't see the bigger picture because he's too busy glorying in his own self-righteous delusions of grandeur."

"Is that what you think of me?"

"Only when I'm feeling generous."

He shook his head, denying her charge. "I'm no Patriot sympathiser."

"I don't care what you are, Master Miar. What I care about is that you—the gods forbid—may be the next Raven and by your actions you risk aligning the entire Assassins' Guild with enemies of my brother's throne. I will not tolerate such a thing happening. Now, or at any time in the future."

Strangely, by the shocked and offended look on his face, Marla decided he was more insulted by the accusation he might oppose the crown, than any suggestion he might be endangering the neutrality of the Assassins' Guild.

"I'm no traitor to Hythria, your highness," he repeated. "Or her High Prince."

"Then kill Tarkyn Lye for me and prove it."

"What you're asking of me is a death sentence, either way," he pointed out. "I can't refuse the commission and if I carry it out, Alija will kill me when she learns what I've done."

"Only if you continue to count yourself a member of her household," Marla replied. "Maybe you should find yourself a less perilous lover."

His eyes narrowed dangerously. "You have no right to dictate who I sleep with."

Marla shrugged. "Sleep with whomever you please, sir. I am interested only in preserving my son's throne against the day he is ready to take it. *Your* actions are threatening that, so *I* am taking the actions I deem necessary to correct the situation. If, in the process, I happen to rid the world of a slave who's offended me . . . well, so be it."

"And how do you intend to protect yourself from Alija's wrath, your highness?"

"I'm better at that than anybody else in Hythria," she assured the assassin. "Trust me, I've had more practice than you know."

Galon visibly forced himself to calm down. He was no longer ranting as he had been when he first arrived, but somehow, it made him seem more terrifying. He took a step closer to her and she reacted instinctively by stepping back.

He noticed the movement and seemed genuinely amused. "You're afraid of me."

"I'm afraid of an egotistical fool who imagines he's being so terribly clever because he has the High Arrion in his pocket. I'm afraid of a man who doesn't realise he risks plunging us into chaos because he can't see past his own list of conquests. I've spent the better part of my adult life trying to put an end to the Patriots, Galon Miar. I will not have them thinking they've gained a new lease on life because they believe you've delivered the Assassins' Guild to them."

He hesitated, looking at her in surprise, as if coming to a sudden realisation about something. "You genuinely believe that, don't you?"

"You sound surprised. Did I look like I was kidding?"

"No . . . it's just . . ."

"What?"

"It's nothing, your highness," he said, all trace of his fury apparently under control. He bowed politely. "I apologise for my rudeness. You're right—I shouldn't have come here so hastily, and so belligerently. I apologise if my actions have offended you. It's late, and I'm obviously keeping you from your bed. If you will excuse me?"

Baffled by his sudden capitulation, Marla rose to her feet. "Goodnight, Master Miar."

"Goodnight, your highness."

He turned on his heel and left the hall, leaving Marla staring after him in confusion. Galon even bowed politely to Cadella on his way out, as she entered the room carrying a tray and a glass of fortified wine.

"He's leaving?"

Marla didn't bother to answer such an absurd observation.

"I have his wine . . ." Cadella looked a little put out that she'd gone to the trouble of pouring the assassin a drink and he didn't even have the good manners to stay long enough for her to serve it.

"Bring it here, Cadella."

The old woman did as Marla ordered. The princess took the wine from the tray and downed it in a gulp.

"Are you all right, my lady?"

"I'll be fine."

"He's a dangerous piece of work, that one."

"Thank you, Cadella. But I had noticed."

"Would you like another wine, your highness?"

Marla shook her head. Wine wasn't the answer to her problem. She wasn't sure what the answer was, but she was fairly certain she wouldn't find it at the bottom of a decanter. "No. Just tell Elezaar . . . I mean, just have my bed turned down, would you?"

"Of course, your highness."

Cadella scurried away to do her bidding, leaving Marla to ponder two things of equal concern: if Cadella had noticed her moment of weakness when she asked for Elezaar to attend her.

And why the heat seemed to have gone out of the room with the departure of Galon Miar.

Despite the fact he'd ordered his grandson to stop Damin on the border and challenge him, Charel Hawksword greeted Damin like a long-lost son when they finally reached Byamor some two weeks after the altercation at Zadenka. As Damin suspected, Charel had ordered the challenge for the sake of his grandson's future rule of the province. He had no personal gripe against Damin; if anything, he was rather more complimentary than usual, particularly about the way Damin had handled the problem with Kendra Warhaft.

"She was such a pretty little thing when she first came to court," Charel told Damin as he pushed the old Warlord's chair along the corridor toward the great hall. "I remember thinking when I gave permission for her to marry him, that Warhaft was a brute, too."

"So why did you agree to it?"

"Don't be so naïve, Damin. Why do you think I agreed?"

"Seems a high price to pay to keep a man like Warhaft on your side."

Charel glanced over his shoulder at Damin. "Wait till you're High Prince, lad, then you tell me what you'd do when you have to make a choice between strengthening an alliance with a fractious border baron against the potential unhappiness of sixteen-year-old girl."

"Narvell says he told you how he felt about her."

"He was a boy. He didn't know what he was feeling."

"He's not a boy now, Charel. And he's pretty damn sure about what he's feeling."

The old Warlord wasn't impressed. "He's still acting like a moonstruck boy from where I'm sitting, Damin, even if he doesn't look it. Still, you handled the situation better than I could have hoped. I'd never have thought of putting the girl in the care of the Sorcerers' Collective."

"Actually, it was Rorin Mariner who thought of it."

"Don't do that!" the old man snapped.

"Don't do what?"

"Don't ever refuse the credit for something people think is your doing. Damn it, boy, how do you think I got such a brilliant reputation?"

"I thought it was because you *were* brilliant, Charel," Damin said, as he pushed the chair over the rough, unfinished flagstones of the long, chilly passage. "That's what you've been telling me and Narvell since we were boys, anyway."

"And you believed me!" Charel pointed out. "The fact is, I'm not responsible for half the things I'm credited with. But it suits me to let people think I am. My theory is this: if I'm smart enough to surround myself with clever people, why shouldn't I take the credit for their successes?"

"What if one of these clever people you've surrounded yourself with does something really awful?"

"Then it's even better," Charel chuckled. "You get all the benefits of a reputation for being an evil bastard and none of the effort that goes into gaining it."

"You're a sneaky old rascal, Charel Hawksword," Damin laughed as they reached the great hall.

As they approached the tall, carved doors, a slave pushed them open to allow them entrance. Since Charel had suffered a stroke three years ago, he'd been confined to the special wheeled chair he'd had built to help him get around. His right side was paralysed by the stroke and his speech was often slurred as he forced his words past his uncooperative lips, but only a fool mistook his painful enunciation as a sign of fading intelligence.

Tejay, Adham and Rorin were waiting for them, sitting at the end of a table just below the High Table where Charel conducted the formal business of his province. The massive beams of the ceiling that supported the vaulted roof were decked with the flags of every noble house in Elasapine. The effect was colourful, but did little to ease the oppressive solidity of the castle. Byamor was a fortress, older even than Krakandar. It lacked the grace and symmetry of Damin's ancestral home. Neither had it ever benefited from the impeccable good taste of a mistress like Marla Wolfblade. The furniture was heavy and masculine and always reminded Damin of a well-appointed war-camp.

Adham and Rorin stood as they entered, bowing respectfully to the old Warlord as Damin parked the chair beside the bench where Tejay was sitting. Charel greeted the young men and then turned to Tejay with a crooked smile. "Lady Lionsclaw! I swear you grow lovelier with every passing year."

"And your eyesight obviously gets worse," she replied, leaning forward to kiss the old man's cheek. "You're looking very chipper, my lord."

"And you claim *my* eyesight is failing?" he chuckled. "It's good to see you again, Adham," he remarked, turning his attention to his other guests. "How's your father?"

"The plague in Greenharbour took him some time ago, my lord."

"I'm sorry to hear that, lad. Ruxton Tirstone was a good man." He turned his gaze on Rorin and examined him for a moment before nodding his approval. "Lord Wolfblade tells me good things about you, young Mariner."

"I'm sure he exaggerates, my lord."

"Then be grateful for it, lad. It's not often one gets unasked-for praise and if he follows my advice, you won't be getting it again."

"Are you trying to corrupt our future High Prince, you old fox?" Tejay asked.

"I think if he was corruptible, Lernen would have managed it long before now, lass." He glanced around the table and suddenly frowned. "Is this a dry argument? Bring wine!" he bellowed to nobody in particular. At the back of the hall a slave hurried to comply and moments later a tray with five goblets and a decanter of wine was sitting on the table in front of Tejay.

"You can pour," he informed Tejay with another crooked smile.

Tejay did as he asked and placed the cup in his left hand. He was shaking as he raised it to his lips and a trickle of wine dribbled out of the paralysed right side of his mouth as he drank.

"Is Narvell not joining us?" Adham asked.

"I sent him out to keep an eye on the troops," Charel said, wiping his mouth awkwardly on his sleeve. The army Damin had brought to Elasapine and the soldiers Narvell had with him on the border were camped some ten miles south of the city, both to protect the troops from plague in the city and the city from five thousand bored and lonely Raiders looking for entertainment. "The men needed somebody visibly in charge and with Warhaft on the warpath, I thought it might be prudent to keep my grandson and the lovely Kendra apart."

"I'm going out to meet him later today," Damin told them. "I'll let him know what we've decided then."

"What's to decide?" the young trader asked. "Isn't the point here to gather up every man in Hythria who can hold a sword and march him to the border to stop Hablet?"

"Put in its most simplistic terms, yes," Charel agreed. "What we really need to consider, though, is how to deal with Hablet if he breaks through."

"Do you think that's possible, my lord?" Rorin asked.

"Anything's possible." The old man shrugged with his one good shoulder.

"It would help if we knew who was going to be leading his forces, too," Damin said, thinking back to Zegarnald's warning that the leader of the Fardohnyan forces was both intelligent and experienced. "Until we know that, there's not much point in discussing tactics."

"On the bright side," the Warlord said, "you've got one thing going for *you*."

"Youth and inexperience?" Damin joked.

"Exactly," Charel agreed.

"How is that good?" Rorin asked.

"What Charel's trying to say, Rory, is that if I do anything unusual, Hablet will probably assume it's because I don't know any better."

"Which gives him more freedom of movement than any of you appreciate," Charel told them.

"I don't understand," Rorin admitted, the least knowledgeable about warfare among them. "How does that help?"

"If I was leading this war, Rorin," the Warlord explained, "Hablet and his generals would be studying every battle, every skirmish, every tavern brawl in which I've ever taken part, until they know my mind better than I do. There wouldn't be a tactic I could try they wouldn't anticipate. But they don't know anything about Damin, other than he's Lernen's nephew. If our boy here is in command and he does anything out of the ordinary, Hablet is just as likely to assume his decisions are motivated by ignorance as anything else."

"Which means we can lure the Fardohnyans into our trap," Damin informed his companions smugly.

"If only we had one," Adham added.

Tejay shook her head in disagreement. "There's no need for a trap. We can keep the Fardohnyans bottled up in the passes indefinitely."

"Maybe," Charel conceded. "But even with Elasapine and Krakandar troops to aid you, Lady Lionsclaw, how long can Sunrise keep it up?"

"All of Hythria will come to Sunrise's aid if Hablet attacks us," Tejay declared confidently.

"They may not, my lady," Rorin warned thoughtfully. "If they believe, as you do, that the Fardohnyans can be held off indefinitely in the mountain passes, they may be willing to play a 'wait and see' game."

"The lad's right, I fear," Charel agreed. "The only way to guarantee all the Warlords come to Sunrise's aid may be to actually suffer the invasion."

"That's a huge gamble," Adham remarked.

Damin couldn't help but agree, appalled at the very idea of allowing Hablet past their first and most effective line of defence just to get Hythria's Warlords off their collective backsides. He nodded grimly. "Well, the plan has one advantage. Letting him past Winternest without a fight should go a long way to convincing Hablet I have no idea what I'm doing."

"Just remember," Charel reminded them. "Superior weapons, superior numbers, even superior generals count for less and less the closer the troops get to each other."

"Then we bring the fight to Hablet," Damin said. "We make him take Hythria one step at a time. One man at a time."

"But first we have to close the passes," Adham suggested.

Damin shook his head. "No. First we need to know what we're facing. That doesn't require a battle. It requires intelligence."

"A foray into the Widowmaker?" Adham asked with a hopeful grin.

"And the Highcastle Pass. Hablet won't make the mistake of attacking on only one front. If he's serious about this he'll attack through both passes simultaneously."

"Toss you for it," Adham said, pulling a copper rivet from his pocket. "Heads I take Highcastle, tails, the Widowmaker." The coin spun in midair before Adham caught it and held it out for the others to see. "Tails," he told them. "Looks like I'm heading for Winternest."

"And poor Damin gets to visit his dear old cousin Braun, the Lord of Highcastle," Tejay said sympathetically.

Damin grimaced at the thought. Braun Branador was an idiot. "We'll see you safely to Cabradell first, my lady. I want to speak to Terin, in any case. He should have some idea of what's happening on the other side of his borders."

"Don't count on it," Tejay muttered.

Damin looked at her with a frown. These off-handed comments about Terin were very unsettling. It wasn't going to make it any easier to fight Hablet, if he had to waste time worrying about a man who should have been one of his closest allies.

"I've got a better idea," he said, changing his mind. "You take Highcastle, Adham. Your father has been trading through there for decades. You know Braun and he trusts your father, so he's likely to be much more cooperative if you ask him for help."

"He's *your* cousin, Damin."

"Second cousin," Damin corrected. "And he despises me because I'm Marla's son. Don't ask me to explain it. It's something to do with Marla and all her cousins at Highcastle, particularly Braun's sister, Ninane. Apparently, they've hated each other since they were children. You, on the other hand, have helped him get rich. Trust me, you'll get a lot more out of him than I will."

"What about Winternest?"

"Rorin can take the Widowmaker."

The sorcerer's head jerked up in alarm. "When did I become a spy?"

"Right now. I need intelligence I can trust. And you've been through the Widowmaker before, haven't you?"

"I was twelve at the time," Rorin reminded him. "And unconscious."

"You know Westbrook, though," Damin said. "And you're Fardohnyan. You've got a better chance than the rest of us of finding out what's going on over the border."

"The only part of Westbrook I'm closely acquainted with is its dungeons, Damin," he replied. Then he shrugged. "But, what the hell . . . there's already a price on my head in Fardohnya for murder and probably another one for escaping lawful custody. Adding spying for a foreign power to the list won't make it any worse, I suppose."

Tejay smiled. "They can only hang you once, Rorin."

"Once is actually one time too many, my lady."

"You're a magician, aren't you?" Charel asked.

"Yes."

"Then what are *you* worried about? You've got an advantage some men would kill for. The rest of us have to muddle through the hard way, son."

"I'll go," Rorin hastened to assure them, but he still

seemed very uncertain. "I'm just not sure I'm the right person for the job, my lord."

"The right person for any job is the one who gets it done," Charel Hawksword informed him gruffly. "And that's usually," he added, holding his cup out to Tejay for a refill, "some poor sod in the wrong place at the wrong time who gets left with no other option than to be a hero."

Chapter 19

Brakandaran the Halfbreed shivered a little as the sun slipped down into the shadows behind them. It had been a cold day; spring merely a distant hope here in the foothills of the Sunrise Mountains. He hadn't been much past Winternest in the last twelve years and it seemed strange to be walking the roads of Hythria again, particularly as he was here as a Fardohnyan spy.

Brak had always liked the Hythrun people, and it concerned him a little to think he was aiding a tyrant like Hablet of Fardohnya to overrun their country. But despots come and go, he knew. In the long run, Hythria would benefit much more by not losing what remained of this devastated generation to a useless war that would do nothing but entertain and empower the God of War.

Such dark thoughts plagued Brak as he walked. They were heading toward the village of Urso, some eighty miles from Cabradell. The capital of Sunrise Province was surely the most logical place to muster their troops if the Hythrun knew anything of Hablet's invasion and they were planning to defend their border. Brak's travelling companion was a young man named Ollie Kantel. Nineteen years old, swarthy and well-muscled, he was one of Chyler's countless nephews who'd grown up in the Sunrise Mountains around Westbrook.

Like Brak, he'd made the journey over the mountains into Hythria numerous times. This was the first time, however, he had ventured so far east.

They stopped on a small rise overlooking the village, a picture-perfect little hamlet nestled among the tall mountains. With roofs steeply sloped to shed the winter snows and smoke rising out of the chimneys making the air taste faintly of wood smoke, it seemed hard to believe plague or pestilence of any kind had ever blighted this land.

"Do you think there's much chance the Hythrun know we're planning to invade them?" Ollie asked, shifting his pack to the other shoulder.

"Not by the look of Urso," Brak replied, casting his gaze over the sleepy little hamlet. He adjusted his own pack a little and moved on, heading down the deserted road. "Still, we'll find out soon enough, I suppose."

"How?" Ollie asked, hurrying to catch him.

"We'll stop at the local inn tonight."

"Is that a good idea?"

Brak glanced at him curiously. "Why wouldn't it be a good idea?"

"Well, we're spies . . ."

"Say it a little louder, son. I don't think they heard you down in the village."

The lad let out an exasperated sigh. "You know what I mean! Shouldn't we be sneaking around, listening at keyholes? Stuff like that?"

"Ah!" Brak said. "You mean shouldn't we act suspiciously so everyone will know we're Fardohnyan spies, instead of acting like two simple travellers who have nothing to hide and need information about the road ahead?"

Ollie stopped and frowned. "Oh. I hadn't actually thought of it like that."

Brak kept on walking. "Which is why they hired me to do the thinking and you to do the leg work, Ollie, my lad."

Obviously concerned, the boy hurried after him again. "So what are we going to tell people in the village, then? About who we are?"

"We'll say we're two simple travellers who need information about the road ahead."

"Won't it look suspicious? Us coming from the border, I mean? With it being closed and all?"

Brak shrugged. "We'll tell them we got sick of waiting at Winternest for the border to reopen and decided to take the long way home."

Ollie's eyes lit up approvingly. "That's a really good story, Brak. Have you done this sort of thing before?"

"There's not much I haven't done, Ollie," he told his young companion. "Just lots of things I'd rather not remember doing."

And with that cryptic comment, Brak left Ollie staring after him with a puzzled expression as he continued on down the road into the peaceful village of Urso.

Maybe Patanan, the God of Good Fortune, was looking out for them, because when the two spies arrived they discovered a travelling apothecary in town, with the unlikely name of Kelman Welman, who'd recently come from Cabradell. With only one tavern in the small village and only one meal served nightly to all the patrons who frequented the inn, Brak and Ollie found themselves seated at the long table in the taproom, several hours later, opposite the garrulous old man who seemed determined to provide them with all the intelligence they wanted, for nothing more than the pleasure of an audience who hadn't heard all of his tales at least three times already. The table was lit by several fat candles and his old face looked quite flushed in their flickering light.

"Is there much plague in Cabradell?" Ollie asked when he learned the man had arrived from there recently. The boy wasn't the least bit frightened by the notion of being hanged as a spy, but he was terrified of catching the plague.

"It seems to be on the wane wherever I go," the old man replied. "No doubt they've taken my cure and now find themselves immune to the pestilence."

"You have a tonic that provides immunity?" Ollie gasped.

"Actually, young man, I do. It's made of—"

"Horse shit," Brak cut in.

"I beg your pardon!" Kelman demanded, hugely offended.

"Horse shit," Brak repeated, taking a mouthful of stew. "If your tonic's as effective as you claim, then it's probably made of horse shit."

"*Brak . . .*" Ollie gasped, appalled at his bad manners.

"I'm not trying to insult the man, Ollie," Brak explained. "I'm just stating a fact. The plague is carried by fleas and fleas hate anything to do with horses. It's quite simple, really. You smell like a horse, the flea'll jump on someone else. The Harshini have known that for thousands of years."

Kelman Welman smiled indulgently at Brak. "You shouldn't fill the lad's head with fairy stories about creatures of myth, sir. Your tales of the Harshini are more romantic than the science of my cures, I don't doubt, but far less effective."

"The Harshini didn't think so."

"And you, I suppose, are some sort of authority on the Harshini?"

Brak shrugged. "I've studied them a little."

"Well *I*, young man, have studied them extensively and my tonic is a direct result of that research. I won't go into specifics—you wouldn't understand them—but I can tell you it involves achieving a delicate balance of the four humours to enable the body to fight off infection."

"I'm sure you must be doing a roaring trade," Brak agreed. "In fact, I'm curious about what you're doing here in Urso, Master Welman. Surely, with a cure for this blight at hand, you'd be better off in a larger town? Perhaps even Cabradell itself?"

Kelman shrugged selflessly. "I believe all people should be allowed access to my cures."

"But Brak's right!" Ollie gasped, eagerly swallowing every word this old charlatan uttered. "People would be throwing gold at you, surely, if they knew of your cure!"

"I'm a modest man, Ollie. I have no need for great wealth,

only the joy I gain from helping people wherever I can. Besides," he added, reaching for a trencher of bread, "there're too many people in Cabradell these days for my liking. Particularly since the prince arrived."

"The prince?" Brak enquired, between mouthfuls of the surprisingly good stew.

"Lernen's heir, young Damin Wolfblade," Kelman explained. "He arrived a bit over a week ago with his brother, the Hawksword boy, five thousand of their troops and some wild tale of a Fardohnyan invasion. It's nonsense, of course, but with the High Prince's heir in the city, the authorities were less tolerant of those of us who honour the gods using . . . unconventional . . . healing methods."

Loosely translated, Brak guessed the old man had been either run out of the city or had fled before his lies about a plague cure were exposed. Still, it was interesting news about Lernen's heir. *So much for the Hythrun not putting up a fight.*

"Five thousand men, you say?" Brak asked. "Hardly an overwhelming force."

"That's what I thought," Kelman agreed. "Hell! It could have been his entourage, for all I know! He's Lernen Wolfblade's nephew, after all. *There's* a family who knows the meaning of excess."

"Then the stories about the perversion and debauchery of the Hythrun court are true?" Ollie asked, more than a little scandalised at the notion.

"The wildest stories you've heard, lad, probably aren't even the half of it," Kelman told him with the relish of a man who loves to gossip. "Why even on their way to Cabradell they say the Wolfblade heir saw another man's wife, took a fancy to her, and had her kidnapped right out of her husband's castle."

"Surely *not*!"

"It's true, I tell you!" the old man confirmed. "Lady Kendra Warhaft is her name! A rare beauty, I hear she is, too. They say Wolfblade hasn't spared her from his foul lechery for a single night since stealing her from her husband.

And poor Lord Warhaft is forced to ride with the prince's company in a vain attempt to rescue his wife, but to no avail. Rumour has it Wolfblade's placed her in the care of an evil black sorcerer, and cast a spell on her so she'll look at no other man."

"An evil *black* sorcerer?" Brak asked. "What the hell is that?"

"A sorcerer who practises the dark arts," Kelman informed them, lowering his voice ominously.

"There are no *dark arts*," Brak pointed out, irritated at the way these rumours got out of hand so easily. "Just idiots who believe in *fairy* stories about creatures of myth."

The apothecary bowed his head in acknowledgment of Brak's wisdom. "I take your point, Master Andaran. You are correct, of course. If there are no creatures of myth, there can be no black sorcerers, either."

"Which means Wolfblade probably didn't kidnap anybody's wife."

"Ah, now in that, I beg to disagree, sir. Lady Kendra and her husband are most definitely in Cabradell, and Lady Kendra travels with Lord Wolfblade's entourage. As did Lady Lionsclaw, too, I hear, after leaving her husband and running straight to the arms of her young lover in Krakandar."

"Sounds like this young Wolfblade prince of yours is going to be far too busy having his way with the entire female population of Hythria to have time to do anything about a Fardohnyan invasion," Brak remarked. "Imaginary or otherwise."

Kelman shrugged. "I can do no more than report on what I know, Master Andaran."

If he confined himself to just reporting on what he actually knew, Brak thought, *Kelman Welman's tales wouldn't be nearly so entertaining.*

"Well, when we get to Cabradell, Master Welman, we shall make a point of checking on this dissolute prince of yours and ascertain for ourselves if he matches your dire description of his character."

"We're going to Cabradell?" Ollie asked in surprise.

Brak gave the young man a look that spoke volumes. "If we're going to try and get back to Fardohnya, young cousin, by travelling overland through Hythria and catching a ship in Bordertown, then it's on our way."

"Oh," Ollie said. "I forgot about that."

Brak covered his annoyance at Ollie's clumsy earnestness with another mouthful of the delicious stew and wondered what small grain of truth lay at the core of the apothecary's wild tales.

He wondered too, how the Hythrun had learned of Hablet's plans for them. And what would be worse for Hythria—an army led by her useless High Prince or his young and inexperienced nephew.

CHAPTER 20

For King Hablet of Fardohnya, departing the Summer Palace in Talabar was never easy, particularly if one was going off to war. There was all that gnashing of teeth, and wailing and breast beating—and that was just his chamberlain. The women of his harem were a thousand times worse. They jockeyed for position among themselves, turned on each other and betrayed their best friends over the most minor infractions, all to bring their names to the king's attention and get themselves invited to the Winter Palace in Qorinipor. They all wanted out of the harem, even for a few months, and every one of those silly bitches in the harem was doing whatever they thought they had to, to achieve that aim.

Everyone, that is, except Adrina.

Hablet's eldest daughter seemed to be quite content at the notion she would be left behind in the Summer Palace. She hadn't once asked her father to take her with him. She hadn't tried to bribe anybody; she hadn't even thrown a tantrum. All she'd done was smile at the antics of her stepmothers and her siblings and make subtle enquiries she didn't think her father knew about, regarding how long he was likely to be out of Talabar.

The certainty she was up to something was so strong even Lecter Turon was more nervous than usual, probably because he couldn't work out what she was scheming. After several nervous nights, tossing and turning, imagining all manner of trouble she could cause in his absence, Hablet decided there was only one thing for it. He called his daughter before him and informed her she would be joining him at the Winter Palace for the duration of the Hythrun campaign and there was nothing she could do to change his mind. Although she tried to hide it, she was bitterly disappointed, which reinforced the king's opinion she was planning something deceitful the minute his back was turned and that it was a damn good thing he was taking her out of the capital and removing the devious little minx to a place she could do no harm.

It wasn't until they reached Qorinipor that Hablet realised how skilfully he'd been duped. The moment she stepped out of the carriage, Adrina's bad mood vanished. Her sour disappointment at being taken against her will from the Summer Palace miraculously turned into unabashed delight at her escape from the harem. As Adrina watched them unloading her trunks, she began issuing instructions to her slave, Tamylan, regarding her plans to go sailing on the lake, hunting in the foothills of the Sunrise Mountains and even hinted a shopping expedition into the markets of the city might be on the cards.

Lecter Turon was furious, Hablet noted. He kept glaring in the direction of the princess as their large entourage milled about in confusion on the delightful chequerboard paving of the Winter Palace's inner courtyard. Finally, the eunuch issued orders to move the luggage inside, and put another two underlings in charge of getting everyone settled. Then he sidled up to Hablet.

"You've been had, your majesty," he pointed out crossly.

Hablet glanced at his daughter, smiling proudly. "Rather expertly, Lecter. Damn, she would have made a fine son, don't you think?"

"You should send her back to Talabar immediately."

"Why?" Hablet asked.

"She's made a fool of you, sire."

"She's made a fool of all those women back in the Summer Palace who promised me the soul of their firstborn child in order to escape the harem for a few months," he chuckled.

"What is one supposed to do with that, do you think?"

He looked at Lecter in confusion. "What?"

"A soul, your majesty. What is one supposed to do with a soul, if one is lucky enough to secure it? I mean, does one put it on a shelf somewhere, and bring it out on special occasions? For that matter, how does one extract a soul . . . ?"

"Have you been drinking, Lecter?"

"No, sire," the eunuch sighed. "Just considering the logistics of the problem so the next time you're given a choice between the Princess Adrina's company and the soul of someone's firstborn child, I'll be ready to aid you in the latter so we might be spared the former."

Hablet laughed. "Admit it, Lecter, you're just vexed because you've been outfoxed by a girl."

"She outfoxed you too, your majesty."

"And I'm actually quite proud of her for that. Which reminds me of something else. She's not to have any sort of contact with Axelle Regis while she's here."

"I wasn't aware Her Serene Highness and General Regis were acquainted."

"They're not," Hablet assured him. "And I'd like it to stay that way."

"Do you doubt Lord Regis's loyalty, sire?"

"Not at all," Hablet said. "But all the qualities that make Regis a good general are all the reasons I don't want him for a son-in-law."

"He's made an *offer* for the princess?" Lecter gasped in shock, no doubt furious at the thought he hadn't received a kickback from the transaction.

The king shook his head. "I wouldn't have put him in charge of a detail digging latrines if he had. The problem is *what* he is, Lecter, not anything he's done."

Lecter smiled slyly as he realised what his king was implying. "You mean he's rich, ambitious, intelligent and unmarried. All the things you fear the Princess Adrina is looking for in a husband."

"Exactly. Until I have a legitimate heir, any man with those qualities allied with my eldest daughter could easily threaten my throne. So let's just avoid the issue and make sure they never meet, eh?"

The eunuch bowed, delighted by the prospect of foiling any sort of plans the young princess had made, even those she may not have thought of yet. "As you wish, your majesty."

"And send a message to Regis. Tell him I'd like him to join me for dinner."

"If he's near the front lines, that may not be possible, your highness. A messenger would take the better part of a day just to find him."

"At his earliest convenience, then." Hablet shrugged, turning for the broad steps that led into the palace. "Just make sure that whatever day he gets here, it's the day Adrina decides to take her meals in her room."

It was nearly a week before Axelle Regis appeared at the Winter Palace in response to his king's summons. The general arrived with only a small guard in tow, just before lunch, fortunately while Adrina was out on the lake.

Hablet greeted him warmly. The king of Fardohnya valued genuine talent—while doing his best to make sure it never got too close to him—and he'd always had a soft spot for Lord Regis. It was just the danger to his throne that a man like him represented that worried the king. It was the constant torment of all rulers, Hablet lamented. *You need men like Regis to get the job done, but afterwards, it's always better if they're remembered as dead heroes rather*

than live focal points for those disaffected subjects who think
a change of leadership might be in order.

After a sumptuous lunch of boar's ribs, fowl dressed with spiced maize flour and delicate little fish-pasties followed by an elaborate starch pastry served with fresh fruit, Hablet and the general took a turn through the carefully manicured gardens that stretched down to the edge of the lake to aid their digestion. The lake's choppy surface was a brilliant shade of sapphire in the clear mountain air, shimmering in the crisp breeze coming off the tall Sunrise Mountains in the east.

"So everything is ready for the invasion?" Hablet asked.

"As ready as I can be without better intelligence," Regis agreed. "I've recruited some bandits who used to make their living in the Widowmaker Pass and sent them across the border to see what we're facing. My preliminary reports are all good. It seems the Hythrun have no idea we're coming."

Hablet nodded approvingly. "What about Highcastle?"

"We'll make the first feint through there to throw the Hythrun off our main objective," Regis confirmed. "But realistically, despite the advantage of being able to disembark troops at Tambay's Seat from the sea, the southern pass is too narrow to move troops into Hythria in any useful number. If I recall my history lessons correctly, Laran Krakenshield blocked the pass with a simple avalanche once, didn't he, which effectively sealed the border well into the following spring?"

Hablet scowled at the reminder. "So your main attack will be through the Widowmaker? How do you intend to get past Winternest? The place is impregnable."

"And terrified by the fear of plague," Regis reminded him. "My information is that on Chaine Lionsclaw's orders the fortress was sealed against refugees fleeing the plague into Fardohnya months ago, even before you closed the border, and nobody's thought to countermand the order since. Winternest is rapidly running out of food and morale."

"They're still not going to take kindly to an army marching past their front gate."

"Which is why, as soon as I have confirmed the location

of Hythria's forces," Regis told him, "I'm sending the Plenipotentiary of Westbrook through the pass with a small delegation and several wagonloads of supplies to relieve their suffering."

Hablet smiled at the deviousness of the plan. "How thoughtful of you, Axelle. I never realised what a humanitarian you were."

"Once we have people inside the fortress, your majesty, it will be a simple matter to open the gates to our forces. With a foothold established at Winternest, Hythria will be ours for the taking."

"Bring me the heads of Damin Wolfblade and Narvell Hawksword, Lord Regis, and I'll see you get what you deserve," Hablet promised.

Regis bowed to his king. "I live only to serve, your majesty."

Hablet was considering the unfortunate prospect that Axelle Regis might have to die to serve him, too, when he spotted someone heading along the path toward them from the direction of the lake. With the sun reflecting off the bright water, he had to squint to see who it was.

It was too late, by the time he realised it was Adrina, to avoid her.

"Hello, Daddy," she said as she reached them, eyeing his companion with open curiosity. She looked stunning—windswept and flushed from sailing on the lake, her skirts blown against her body, outlining every tempting curve, and those dangerous emerald eyes. Her whole being radiated a sort of raw vitality that Hablet had no doubt Axelle Regis would find very beguiling.

"Adrina."

She waited expectantly. There was no way the king could avoid an introduction without offending Lord Regis, and right now, he needed him too much to risk offence.

"This is Axelle Regis," he told her with extreme reluctance. "Lord Regis, this is Her Serene Highness, the Princess Adrina. My eldest daughter."

Axelle bowed with courtly grace and took the hand Adrina offered him, kissing her palm in a perfectly proper manner. "Your highness."

"So you're father's latest general, are you?" she asked.

"I have that honour, yes."

"You must be very competent," she remarked, looking him up and down speculatively, the way one might examine a naked *court'esa* they were looking to purchase in the slave markets. "Or you've paid Lecter Turon a fortune."

Regis seemed a little unsettled by her forthright manner. "I . . . I'd like to think it's the former, your highness."

"For the sake of every man under your command, I'd like to think so, too," she replied. "Will you be joining us for dinner, my lord?"

Regis looked at his king questioningly. Hablet shrugged, giving no indication that in reality, he would very much like to strangle his daughter for leaving him no alternative but to invite the general to share another meal with them. "Of course he will, my dear. Will *you* be joining us?"

"Naturally."

"I thought perhaps, after a morning on the lake, you might be too tired . . ."

Adrina smiled brightly. "It's all right, Daddy. I've never felt more invigorated." Then she turned to Regis and lowered her eyes demurely. "I will look forward to speaking with you at greater length over dinner, Lord Regis."

"As will I, your highness."

The princess leaned forward to kiss her father's cheek. "Thank you so much, Daddy, for bringing me to Qorinipor so I can meet all these really *fascinating* people."

The king and Lord Regis stood back to let her pass. Adrina gathered up her skirts and continued on the path back toward the palace. Regis followed her with his eyes, his gaze openly admiring.

"The stories I've heard about your daughter don't do her justice, your majesty," he remarked. "She seems quite charming."

"You mean the ones about her being a screaming shrew?" he asked, annoyed at the way Adrina had once again outsmarted him. "Oh, they're true enough. I had her mother beheaded, you know. She tried to murder a *court'esa* and one of my other children. Do you suppose that sort of inclination runs in families?"

A little taken aback, Regis frowned. "I couldn't really say, your majesty."

"Well, before you get too enchanted with my daughter, Lord Regis," he suggested, "you might want to find out."

"Sire . . . I didn't mean to imply . . ."

"It's all right, Axelle, I know what you meant."

"I would never behave improperly toward your daughter, your majesty. You must know that!"

I'm more worried about her behaving improperly toward you, Hablet thought, but didn't say it aloud. Let Regis think he'd crossed the line. It always paid to keep a man like him on his toes.

"I hope you mean that, son, because Adrina means more to me than my own life. If I ever had reason to suspect anything . . ."

"I understand, your majesty."

Hablet clapped him on the shoulder in a fatherly manner. "Good. And now that's cleared up, let's go find ourselves a drink and you can tell me about the rest of your plans for my invasion of Hythria."

PART TWO

TRAITORS, TRICKS AND TREACHERY

chapter 21

It was only a matter of days after Damin Wolfblade left Krakandar that Luciena Taranger began to regret her husband's hasty decision to stay here and keep an eye on things until his cousin returned.

And all of her concerns began and ended with Xanda's uncle, Mahkas Damaran.

At first, with Mahkas still in shock over the death of his daughter and his serious injuries, it wasn't too bad. Although the whole city was in mourning for Leila, Luciena had her hands full with her own three children as well as Tejay Lionsclaw's four young sons, whom the Warlord's wife had left in Krakandar to keep safe from the plague, while she accompanied Damin back to Cabradell. With the funeral to arrange and Lady Bylinda incapacitated by grief, it had been easy for Luciena and Xanda to fool themselves into believing that all would be well. But as the weeks progressed and Mahkas regained his strength, it became clear that things were far from normal.

Unfortunately, the only one who could do anything about it was her husband, Xanda.

Damin had done one very useful thing before he left, which was probably the only thing keeping Xanda's head on his shoulders, because every time her husband disagreed with his uncle, the old man flew into a rage. Damin had taken aside Orleon, Raek Harlen and the other captains he was leaving in Krakandar and quietly explained to them, in no uncertain terms, that he would be back as soon as this problem with Fardohnya was sorted out, and when he did come back, the chances were good he would be removing Mahkas Damaran from his position as regent. If it came to a question of whom the Raiders should follow and they wanted any sort of long-term future in Krakandar, they would do well to remember Xanda Taranger was here at their prince's request, and acting with his full authority.

As a consequence the palace had fallen into a strange routine that involved Xanda giving an order, Mahkas overruling it, everyone apologising profusely, bowing to the regent's wishes, and then going off and quietly doing exactly what Xanda had asked them to do in the first place.

Mahkas was up and about again, but Damin's attack on him—or maybe it was Leila's suicide—had left him a changed man. It was as if someone had scraped away the veneer of sanity and exposed the madman underneath. He could speak only in a painful, hoarse whisper, which meant he yelled a lot to make himself understood, but because of his damaged throat it often proved futile. It also gave everyone the perfect excuse to ignore him, either on the grounds they hadn't understood him, or simply hadn't heard him issue the order in the first place.

Even with such a bizarre arrangement in place, it wasn't always successful. When Raek Harlen tried to leave the city with the other two and a half thousand troops Damin was expecting as reinforcements on the border, Mahkas threatened to hang Raek and flog any man who attempted to follow the captain out of the city. In a show of loyalty to his prince that left Luciena breathless, Raek had ignored Mahkas's orders, gathered his troops and marched them toward the inner gate of the city, in preparation for their departure. Furious, and shouting after the captain in a rasping whisper, the regent had run on ahead of the departing Raiders, taken the steps to the wall-walk two at a time, grabbed a crossbow from the first sentry he came to, and shot Raek Harlen clean through the chest ten feet from the inner gate.

There was no question, after that, of any more Krakandar troops going to Damin's aid.

Luciena lived in mortal fear of what might happen next. It wasn't herself she feared for. Luciena couldn't be intimidated by Mahkas the way Leila had been. But she feared for the children—her own and Tejay's—afraid Mahkas might decide to vent his barely concealed rage on those least able to defend themselves against it.

Her fear made her afraid to leave the palace, even afraid to leave the nursery some days, which just made things worse, because she desperately wanted to speak to Starros and assure herself he was all right. So she watched over the children and anxiously paced the nursery, wishing she could just gather them all up and flee this place. Wishing she had somewhere else to go.

Luciena glanced out of the window. It was midafternoon and gloomily overcast and she hadn't seen Xanda since breakfast. He'd been planning to approach Mahkas about opening the city up again. His reasoning was that since the expected wave of refugees had not eventuated, the city was suffering from its self-imposed isolation. Privately, Luciena knew, Xanda wanted the city unsealed so anybody who wanted to flee had the chance to do so while they still could. With the city gates open, Luciena could take the children to Xanda's brother Travin in Walsark, where they'd be safe from Mahkas's wrath, if nothing else.

Pacing up and down in front of the hearth, Luciena was nauseous with worry. Mahkas had killed Raek Harlen for defying him without stopping to think about it. He'd tortured Starros, beaten Leila like a dog . . . his capacity for cruelty was staggering and there was no telling how he would take Xanda's suggestion they unseal the city. He might think it a brilliant idea, or he might run his nephew through for having the temerity to suggest such a thing.

There was just no way to know.

To distract herself, Luciena picked up the little porcelain horse with its proud blue knight from the mantle. The knight's lance had a broken tip, but was otherwise unmarked. The figurine had belonged to Xanda when he was a boy, shattered when his mother committed suicide in the castle at Winternest. In an act of rare generosity, Mahkas had retrieved all the pieces except one and glued it back together for the distraught little boy. There was no sign of the joins now, though. The day he arrived in Krakandar, Rorin had magically sealed the breaks while attempting to show his new cousins that he really did have magical talent.

It was a pity, Luciena lamented, *that Rory's magical talent couldn't heal a few of the other gaping wounds in this family that Leila's death has exposed.*

"Mama?"

Luciena looked down at Emilie. "Yes?"

"Is something wrong?"

She forced a smile and put the little horse and rider back on the mantle. "Of course not, darling, what makes you say that?"

"You look sad."

"I was just thinking about poor cousin Leila." Emilie was old enough to understand Leila was dead, although not the reasons why.

The little girl inclined her head solemnly. "Leila was a nice person, so Death would have taken her to a good place," she assured her mother. "Uncle Rorin says not all the seven hells are bad."

Luciena smiled thinly. "And when were you discussing theology with Uncle Rorin?"

"The last time he came to visit us in Greenharbour. He was telling us about the Harshini. He says they're not really dead. Just in hiding."

"Well, if anybody would know for certain," Luciena agreed, "Uncle Rorin would."

"Can we go outside and play?"

Luciena was on the verge of saying no, when the nursery door opened and, to her vast relief, Xanda stepped into the room.

"Of course you can," she told her daughter. "It will do you

good to get some fresh air. Aleesha, take the children out into the gardens, would you? They could do with the exercise." .

The slave did as she was bid and herded all the children outside as Xanda approached, his expression grim.

Luciena eyed him up and down warily as he stopped in front of her.

"What's wrong?" he asked, puzzled by her close examination of him.

"Just looking for stab wounds."

Xanda smiled grimly. "No blood. Not even any visible bruises."

Hoped surged in her. "Then he's going to unseal the city?"

Her husband shook his head. "No. But he did tell me he's planning a monument to Leila in the main plaza. He wanted to know what I thought she should be wearing when he has her immortalised in marble."

"Has he completely lost his mind?"

"I don't know," Xanda said, taking her in his arms. He knew how crushed she was by the news she was trapped here for the gods knew how long.

She clung to him, needing his embrace to remind her she was safe and warm and that Xanda would never let any harm come to her. Then another thought occurred to her and Luciena leaned back in his arms, her fear surging back with a vengeance. "Xanda, suppose Damin doesn't come back?"

"What do you mean, *suppose Damin doesn't come back*? He won't forget what he's left behind here, Luci. There's no danger of that."

"But he's gone off to fight a war, Xanda. Suppose something happens to him?"

"Rorin won't leave his side," he assured her. "If Damin is wounded, your cousin can heal him. That was the whole point of him joining the expedition, remember?"

"Rorin can work magic, Xanda, not miracles. Suppose Damin is wounded beyond Rorin's ability to heal him? Suppose the unthinkable happens and he's killed?"

"Then Tejay Lionsclaw would come. We have her children. And I doubt Marla will simply ignore Krakandar, once Kalan and Wrayan tell her what's been going on here."

She sighed. "I know. I'm being silly. I understand this is only temporary. But whenever I see Mahkas . . . whenever I think of the way he just shot down Raek Harlen in cold blood . . . what he did to his own daughter, to Starros. And then there's Bylinda . . . gods, have you seen her lately? She's like a walking ghost."

Xanda glanced around sorrowfully. "This is not the happy household I grew up in, I can tell you that."

"I just want to get the children away from here."

"I know," he said. "And as soon as we can get them to my brother in Walsark, we will. But in the meantime . . ."

"In the meantime, we just have to grin and bear it and pretend our lives aren't in the hands of a madman."

"He's sick with grief, Luci . . ."

Luciena pushed out of Xanda's embrace and stared at him in shock. "You're *defending* him?"

"Of course I'm not defending him! I'm just saying he's not himself." He looked at her with concern, and even a little hurt, when it became clear to him that Luciena didn't understand his position. "Mahkas raised me and Travin, Damin and Narvell and Kalan . . . this man . . . he's not the uncle I remember."

"He wasn't sick with grief when he whipped Leila," she accused. "He was angry. Did you take a close look at your cousin before they buried her? She was savaged! And he certainly wasn't grieving when he tortured Starros, either!"

"Still . . . this isn't like him . . ."

"Tell that to Leila or Starros, perhaps. Raek Harlen might not agree with you, either. Or if you want an objective opinion, maybe you should ask some of the farmsteaders over the border in Medalon what they think the Regent of Krakandar is like? You know—the ones he crucifies if they dare raise a hand in protest when he steals their cattle?"

"Now come on!" Xanda objected. "Stealing Medalonian cattle is a time-honoured tradition in Krakandar! You can't blame him for that."

"Crucifying farmsteaders was a refinement your uncle added. And I know you had concerns about it because you mentioned it to Marla when you heard what he was doing."

"And as Marla pointed out, he is regent here and entitled to take whatever action he sees fit to ensure the safety of Krakandar's borders."

Luciena shook her head, fully aware of the political motives that drove every single thing this family did. "You don't buy that excuse any more than Marla does. She just doesn't want to confront Mahkas until Damin's old enough to inherit the province," she pointed out. "Just like you don't want to confront your uncle, either."

Somewhat to her surprise, Xanda agreed with her. "And for the same reason, Luci. We can't allow Krakandar to fall under the control of the Sorcerers' Collective. Mahkas has to stay alive and remain in his position as regent here until Damin comes of age. If that means letting him flay Medalonian farmsteaders alive to keep himself amused, then I'll stand back and let him do it, because in the long run, that's less dangerous to Krakandar—and our family—than handing the province to Alija Eaglespike."

"And what if he chooses to flay one of *our* children alive to keep himself amused?" she asked. "Does your impressive loyalty to your family extend to your own children?"

He looked horrified. "How can you even *ask* me that?"

She sighed, instantly contrite. "I'm sorry, Xanda. You didn't deserve that. I know you'd die before you let anything happen to our children. I'm just so on edge . . . this place is a living nightmare."

He took her in his arms again and held her close. "I know, Luci. I know. And I swear, the moment I can get you and the children out of here, I will. Just don't be mad at me for doing what I promised Damin I'd do."

"I'm not mad at you, Xanda," she told him, resting her head on his shoulder. "I'm scared."

"So am I, Luciena," he admitted reluctantly as he held her close. "So am I."

chapter 22

The slaveways of Krakandar Palace were a labyrinth of hidden paths, all of which led to the heart of power in Krakandar Province. Starros knew them better than any man alive. He'd grown up here in the palace and roamed them freely when he was a boy. As an adult, in his role of Assistant Chief Steward, he'd discovered even more offshoots and isolated nooks and crannies that gave access to the service areas of the palace as well as the more public areas he'd been familiar with as a child.

It seemed surreal, to be walking the slaveways again. This time, if he was caught, it wouldn't be Damin, or Narvell or one of the Tirstone boys leaping out of the shadows to surprise him. It was more likely to be a slave or a member of the family taking a shortcut through the hidden passages. Regardless, they'd know he no longer belonged here. They'd know he was up to no good.

Starros had gained entry to the palace through the fens. Like the slaveways, he'd roamed the myriad trails through the swampy water-park with Damin and the others as a child and was one of the few who could find his way unerringly through the dangerous pools to the path that led to the palace gate. In an appalling breach of security that would have had Almodavar lopping off heads if he'd known of it, the gate to the palace remained unlocked. The chances were good nobody had been through the gate since the night Damin had gone down to the fens to seek some much needed solitude after he almost killed his uncle.

Whatever the reason, as Starros had hoped, the gate remained unlocked and he had been able to slip inside the inner wall of the city and gain access to the palace where he was free to roam the slaveways at will.

He was cautious in the beginning, fearful of discovery. But

this was his third visit, and each time he grew bolder. He wasn't just strolling through the slaveways for old times' sake. Starros was looking for something; something that would give him unlimited access to every room in Krakandar Palace.

He was looking for the master key he and Damin had pilfered and copied when they were boys.

The key had sat—for as long as Starros could remember—on the lintel above the entrance to Damin's room. When he searched for it, however, it was gone. Somebody had moved it. Unfortunately, the only people who even knew the key existed were no longer in the city, so he couldn't ask anyone why it had been moved, or to where. He had to guess what might have happened, perhaps even relive that last dreadful night in the palace when Leila died, in the hope of finding what had become of it.

A noise further along the hall sent him diving for cover. He held his breath and waited in the shadows for the footsteps to pass him by. He risked a glance as the figure moved past the narrow alcove. It was a slave carrying a tray loaded with empty dishes. He waited until the slave's scuffing footsteps had faded completely before he moved again. It was risky to be in this wing of the palace. In this wing the family suites were located. On his right was the door to what had once been Marla's room when they were very small. A little further along the torch-lit corridor was the Blue Room, the room reserved for the most honoured guests.

The door past that was Leila's room.

Starros hesitated, not sure if he had the courage to go on. He didn't want to enter the room. He needed to find the key, and if he remembered what Kalan had told him of that last awful night of Leila's, her mother had entered the room from the slaveways, using the master key the boys had created all those years before, to tend her poor savaged and brutalised child.

That's when she'd discovered Leila, floating facedown in the bath, her wrists slashed, her blood washed away by the tepid bath water. Leila had gone to meet him, Starros knew.

She thought he was dead and had gone to join him in the afterlife.

Starros wished he had the courage to do the same.

He approached Leila's room with caution, his heart pounding. It wasn't fear of discovery that made his blood race. It was an odd mix of guilt for not being there to help the woman he loved when she needed him most, and anger at the man who had kept them apart. He hesitated a dangerously long time, and then cursed his own cowardice, before stepping forward and reaching up to run his hand along the dusty lintel. It was empty.

"Looking for this?"

Starros nearly jumped out of his skin with fright. He spun around to find Leila's mother standing behind him holding a single candle in one hand and the missing master key in the other.

"My . . . my lady . . ." Starros stammered, wondering how far he'd get before Bylinda raised the alarm. He looked over her shoulder but there was no sign of any guards yet. Starros quickly assessed his escape routes and the conclusion he came to wasn't good. He didn't want to hurt Bylinda, but she was standing between him and the quickest way out of the slaveways. And he had to run. Starros was under no illusions about his fate if Mahkas Damaran got his hands on him a second time.

"I knew you'd come back," Bylinda said.

Lady Bylinda seemed thinner than he remembered, pale and washed out, as if she'd not seen the sun for months. Starros studied her with concern. This woman was the closest thing he had known to a mother and he couldn't think of a single person in the world he had less desire to harm.

"Are you all right, my lady?" he asked, momentarily forgetting the peril he faced. To see her so frail, so delicate, alarmed him a great deal.

"She went to meet you," Bylinda said, as if he hadn't spoken. She wasn't even looking at him, just some vague point over his shoulder.

"Lady Bylinda . . . you must believe me . . . if there was any way I could have prevented . . ."

Bylinda shook her head and forced her eyes to focus on him. "It wasn't your fault, Starros. You have to understand that. Leila always loved you, even when you were small children. You looked after her. You loved her for being Leila. She just wanted to be safe. Safe with you."

Starros didn't know what to say. He'd thought his own grief was intolerable, but Bylinda's pain was like staring into an open, gaping wound.

"I swear, I never meant to hurt her . . ."

"None of us did, Starros." She glanced down at the key and then held it out to him. "You might as well have this. I don't need it any more."

He stared at the key cautiously. The suspicious part of him wondered if this was a trap. Perhaps she was setting him up by making sure he was carrying something incriminating when they captured him. But then he decided it was nothing of the sort. Bylinda seemed lost in her own private hell of grief and recrimination. There was no room for thoughts of vengeance.

Besides, if Mahkas caught him again, evidence or the lack of it wouldn't matter. There would be no pretence of justice involved. Starros would be dead as soon as Mahkas could get his hands on a blade.

"You shouldn't come here again, Starros. It's not safe for you in the palace now." Bylinda looked him over and then smiled ever so faintly. "I'm glad he didn't hurt you."

She meant Mahkas, Starros guessed. She would have no way of knowing he'd been beaten almost to death by her husband and it was only the intervention of a god that saved him.

"I guess I was the lucky one."

He couldn't keep the touch of irony from his voice, but it was doubtful she noticed it because Bylinda's eyes suddenly glistened with tears. "Do you think she's happy now?"

Starros wished the floor would open up and swallow him. He had no idea how to deal with Bylinda's sorrow, no way of offering her comfort. And no time, in any case. Any minute now, anyone—from another slave clearing dishes to Mahkas himself—might stumble across them.

He took the key and pocketed it, wishing he knew something to say that might ease her heartache. "My lady . . . if there's some way I can make amends . . ."

She shook her head desolately. "It's not your job to make amends, Starros, because it's not your fault. Don't worry. I'm going to take care of it."

He wasn't sure what she meant by that and didn't wait around to find out. At the first sound of the scraping of metal on metal a little further up the hall, he bolted, squeezing past Bylinda, heading for the only corridor in this wing that would lead him safely outside and away from the unbearable torment in Bylinda Damaran's eyes.

Back in the Pickpocket's Retreat, Starros dropped the master key on the table in front of Luc North. The forger had taken over Wrayan's favourite haunt while his boss was away and was having a high old time ordering Fee around and playing King of the Hill while he dealt with the guild's business each evening.

"What's this?" Luc asked, looking up at Starros.

"The master key to every room in Krakandar Palace."

Luc stared at the key in amazement and then looked up at Starros with a broad grin. "You're really starting to take your devotion to the God of Thieves seriously, aren't you, son?"

Starros shrugged. "Wrayan said I should steal everything I could from Mahkas. I thought this would be a good start."

"How the hell did you get this?"

"Bylinda Damaran gave it to me."

"Yeah . . . right," Luc agreed sceptically. "Still, I suppose I shouldn't really ask. What are you going to do with it?"

"Rob the palace, of course."

Luc thought about that and then indicated his approval with a nod. "You do realise that with the city sealed, it'll be impossible to fence anything you get away with? Nobody in

Krakandar is going to be foolish enough to handle stolen goods from the palace. Not the way things are at the moment."

"I'm not doing this for the money, Luc."

The forger laughed. "There's an attitude that'll change the first time you go hungry, I'll warrant."

"You know what I mean."

"Aye, I do. Did you want some help?"

"Maybe later, when I get to the bigger stuff. I thought I'd just start small. I am new to this whole burglary thing, you know."

"That's why you decided to start with something small, like a palace, I suppose?" he chuckled. "Still, you're always better off working in familiar territory. Aren't you worried about getting caught?"

"Do *you* worry about it?"

"Not really."

"Then why should I?"

"Well, for one thing," the forger said, "if I get caught doing something . . . awkward, I'm likely to get nothing more painful than a lashing. If you get caught, my friend, the Regent of Krakandar is probably going to flay you alive, stake you out naked over an anthill and then piss in your eye sockets after they've been picked clean by the ravens, all of which he'll do *before* he kills you."

Starros smiled grimly. "That's a picture I could've done without, Luc."

"Just trying to help, lad," the older man chuckled. "You let me know if there's anything I can do, won't you?"

"I will."

Starros left the table and headed out the back (he never used the front door for fear of being recognised), wondering why he was so keen to risk his neck. He couldn't explain it, any more than he could explain this sudden urge to empty the Krakandar Palace of as much contraband as he could get away with. Perhaps it had something to do with the fact that his soul now belonged to the God of Thieves. Perhaps it was his way of seeking vengeance.

The scariest thing of all—and the most substantial difference Starros had noticed in himself since his soul was traded without his consent—was the notion that more than anything else, stealing anything from Krakandar Palace would probably be, well, fun.

Chapter 23

Tejay Lionsclaw had never been under any illusions about her role as a wife and mother of the next generation of Hythria's ruling class. As she paced the rug beside her bed dressed in nothing but a sleeveless silk nightdress, her feet freezing whenever she stepped off the rug onto the icy tiles, she tried to recall a time when she hadn't done the right thing. Until she'd fled Cabradell, she couldn't name a single incident. Her responsibilities as a Hythrun noblewoman had been drummed into her from an early age and even though she railed a little at the unfairness of it all, she had never attempted to defy her father, her husband or the society into which she had been born until the Karien, Renulus, had come into her life.

She'd warned Damin while they were still on the road to Byamor to be wary of her husband's seneschal, but it wasn't until they were back in Cabradell that Tejay truly began to wish she'd carved her initials on his spleen before she'd left. The man's very presence set her teeth on edge.

It was the effect he had on her husband. Terin wasn't really a bad man, just a foolish one. He keenly felt his low birth, even though his father had been a Warlord in his own right for more than two decades before he died, and Terin had inherited his title and his province with all the rights and privileges that went with it. But Terin remembered his childhood here in Cabradell. He remembered being taunted about his father. He remembered other children teasing him, because his grandfather was supposed to be Glenadal Ravenspear, yet the old Warlord had never done much more than nod in Terin's direction when he passed him in the hall.

Tejay didn't blame Lord Ravenspear. No Warlord with any sense singled out his bastard, or his bastard's offspring, unless he was planning to acknowledge the man and make him his heir. Old Ravenspear had had bigger plans for Hythria and they involved creating an heir for the Hythrun throne. His own province he left in the hands of Laran Krakenshield, Marla's first husband—and significantly, Damin Wolfblade's father—and trusted fate would take care of the rest of his family.

Fate hadn't quite worked the way anybody expected. Glenadal's only daughter—and arguably, his legitimate heir—Riika Ravenspear had been killed by the Fardohnyans when she was barely sixteen. Laran Krakenshield had died in a Medalonian cattle raid less than two years later, and Marla had prevailed upon her brother, the High Prince, to appoint Chaine Lionsclaw the Warlord of Sunrise Province.

Lernen had done what Marla asked of him, but he'd made Chaine a Warlord in his own right, not granted him legitimacy, or acknowledged him as a member of the Ravenspear family. Terin believed he still carried the stigma of his father's baseborn status and thought his wife—the last of a line of Warlords stretching back to the very foundation of Hythria—looked down on him because of it.

In truth, Tejay couldn't have cared less. What she cared about was Terin's foolishness, not his family tree. It had taken her a long time to realise that made no difference to her husband; a long, painful time in which all her attempts to aid him in ruling his province were either misconstrued as criticism or rejected outright as interference. If she made any suggestion, he thought she was implying he wasn't capable as a ruler since his father had been nothing more than a bastard captain elevated to Warlord because he just happened to be acquainted with the High Prince's sister.

In the early days of their marriage, Tejay had racked her

brain trying to think of what she'd done to make her husband believe she thought that way about him. By the time she gave birth to her fourth son (Tejay was too well versed in her duties as a wife to think of refusing him her bed) she'd resigned herself to the knowledge that it didn't matter what she did. Terin believed what he wanted to believe and nothing she could do or say was ever going to alter it.

And then Renulus had come to Cabradell.

The Karien was a big man, his bulk the result of good living rather than muscle. He was well educated—his credentials were the reason Chaine Lionsclaw hired him tó conduct a census in the first place—but he was sly, ingratiating and rabidly misogynistic. He fed Terin's insecurities with frightening proficiency. Before Renulus came to Cabradell, Terin had been an impractical but not inconsiderate man. After the Karien arrived, he grew more and more opinionated, more sensitive to any slight, real or imagined, and much more aggressive until finally, after one disagreement too many, the day after Chaine died (and at Renulus's urging, Tejay was certain) Terin had unwisely attempted to beat his wife into submission for disagreeing with him in public.

Tejay won the fight—she'd been taught to defend herself by far better men than Terin Lionsclaw, and husband or not, nobody laid a hand on the daughter of Rogan Bearbow in anger and walked away unscathed. It should have been Renulus she flattened, Tejay thought afterward. Terin would never have attempted anything so foolish without the Karien's encouragement.

Regardless of who was to blame, Lady Lionsclaw had left her husband on the floor of her bedroom nursing a black eye, a fat lip and two broken ribs, gathered up her children, written her husband a scathing letter of condemnation, and then headed for her father's home in Natalandar, the capital of Izcomdar Province, without so much as a backward glance.

Tejay hadn't counted on the plague, however, or her father's death preventing her reaching her childhood home. When she got to the border of Izcomdar and received her brother's message, she couldn't go on, nor was going back an option. After assaulting Terin, she couldn't return to Cabradell without losing her children and possibly endangering her life.

Tejay had been on the verge of desperation when she heard the news Damin Wolfblade was in residence in Krakandar. With the sure knowledge she would be both welcomed and protected in her foster-brother's city, Tejay Lionsclaw had headed north, only to ride into the tragedy that was Leila and Starros's doomed love affair.

Tejay's return to Cabradell some two months later flanked by Damin Wolfblade and Narvell Hawksword, and accompanied by five thousand of her foster-brothers' Raiders, had prevented Terin from doing anything rash to his wife. He was livid when he discovered Tejay had left the children in Krakandar under the protection of Luciena and Xanda Taranger, and although he began a tirade about his children—a Warlord's heirs, no less—being placed in the dubious care of a common merchant and his wife, Tejay knew he was posturing for appearance's sake. Terin was angry certainly, but not so foolish as to attempt to harm her with Damin standing there, glowering at him. He continued his embarrassing rant, however, until Damin was forced to remind him Xanda Taranger was his cousin and Luciena was his adopted sister and did Lord Lionsclaw have some sort of problem with the pedigree of the High Prince's family not being good enough for a Lionsclaw?

Terin had stammered out an apology, fearful he may have offended the High Prince's heir, but it did little to ease the simmering tension in the palace.

And the Cabradell palace was in chaos. As if her own problems with Terin weren't enough, Tejay arrived home to find Prince Lunar Shadow Kraig of the House of the Rising Moon, heir to the throne of Denika—whom Marla had sent secretly to Sunrise Province months ago in the hope Chaine could get him over the border and on a boat back to Denika through Tambay's Seat—was still languishing in the palace, disguised as a slave. Chaine had dispatched the young man to Highcastle too late to get him over the border and they'd been forced to turn back. As only Chaine and Tejay knew the true identity of the prince, and Chaine was dead and Tejay gone by the time he returned to Cabradell, he'd been sent to the slave quarters and left there to rot.

The Denikans weren't going to take very kindly to the treatment their scion had received as a guest of the High Prince of Hythria.

She needed to enlist Damin's help, Tejay knew that. But she didn't want to add to his problems. He was already furious that Terin had made no attempt to gather any sort of intelligence since Hablet had closed the border and was busy trying to get Rorin and Adham organised and provisioned for such an urgent undertaking with Renulus blocking him at every turn. Narvell was no help. He spent most of his time searching for reasons to be alone with Kendra Warhaft while Kendra's husband, Stefan Warhaft—who'd invited himself along for the ride—spent most of *his* time trying to *catch* Narvell Hawksword alone with his wife so he could call him out in a duel.

Tejay shared Damin's frustration. Sunrise Province should have known everything that was happening over their border with Fardohnya. They should have had an army in excess of twenty thousand men to call up, but between the plague and Terin's mismanagement, there were barely a tenth of that left. To further add to Damin's woes, there was no sign yet of Raek Harlen and the additional Krakandar Raiders he should be bringing with him.

And to top it all off, Tejay mused, pacing her room angrily, her husband had now decided she was having an affair with Damin Wolfblade.

This latest problem had started a few days after she arrived back in Cabradell. Furious with his wife for leaving him, Terin had made the mistake of berating her over dinner in the full view of every guest present. Naturally, Damin had come to her defence and because he was a prince and Terin merely a Warlord, there was nothing her husband could do but apologise for his rudeness to both his wife and his prince in front of the entire Cabradell court.

That public humiliation had turned what little like or respect Terin may have had for Damin into open loathing, and because Damin was young, and good-looking and extremely protective of his foster-sister, Terin immediately jumped to the conclusion that it was because the two of them were lovers.

Tejay didn't know what to do. If she told Damin that Terin suspected him of being her paramour, he might laugh at the very notion, or he might—given his present frustration with her husband—decide to call him out. She couldn't risk that happening, but neither could she risk Damin hearing the rumour from another source. And it would get about. Renulus would see to that.

Tejay shivered a little in her nightgown. She crossed her arms and rubbed them, thinking she'd be better served stoking the fire. Or going to bed. But there wasn't much point in trying to sleep. All it meant was a long sleepless night, staring into the darkness, wishing she had an answer for even half her problems.

Without warning, the candle guttered in a sudden draught. She stopped her pacing to find Terin standing at the door of her bedroom with a determined look on his face.

"What do you want?"

"What everyone else seems to be getting a piece of lately."

"Find your own bed, Terin. I'm not in the mood."

"You're my wife," he reminded her, stepping into the room and closing the door. "Your mood is of no consequence to me."

Tejay glared at him. "Do you remember the last time you tried to lay a hand on me, uninvited?"

"I remember. And you'll pay for that, too."

"And who's going to *make* me pay, Terin? *You?*"

"Perhaps I'll make your lover pay," he suggested, as he approached her. "Maybe I'll write to the High Prince. I'm sure he'd be interested in learning what his nephew's been doing with another man's wife."

He stopped in front of her, but she wasn't afraid of him. Not physically. The only thing she feared about this man was that he had the power to take her children from her, but even then, she'd done what she could to protect them. She had possession of them, out of his reach, and the High Prince's heir on her side. The rest was up to the gods.

Tejay shook her head, amused at the notion. "You're going to be sorely disappointed, Terin, if you're relying on Lernen Wolfblade's moral compass to serve your own private agenda."

Her husband grabbed her by the arms and pulled her to him. He tried to kiss her but she turned her face away, making it clear what she thought of his touch.

What happened, she wondered, as Terin's stubbled chin scratched at her face, *to the girl who was prepared to lie down and take whatever she must for the sake of her family, her province, her nation?*

She's had enough, another silent voice answered.

Terin's grasp was bruising her arms, his breath smelled of wine and he was furious she refused to respond to him. This wasn't about desire, she knew. This was Terin trying to prove he had power over her.

"Get your hands off me, Terin Lionsclaw," she told him calmly. "Or I will break your neck."

Angrily, Terin pushed her away. "Whore! You'll give it up for a princeling, but your own husband isn't good enough for you, is he?"

"I will tell you this one more time, Terin," she told him in a level voice, clenching her fists by her side to stop herself from strangling him. *One Warlord,* she reminded herself, in a chilling echo of Rorin's words in Krakandar. *We're one dead Warlord away from disaster.* "I am not now, nor have I been at any time in the past, Damin Wolfblade's lover. I been can't help it if you don't believe me. I do suggest, however, that you think very hard before accusing my alleged paramour of something you can't substantiate. No doubt you've heard what happened in Krakandar to Mahkas Damaran. He was family. I doubt my foster-brother will be quite so gentle with you if you make him lose his temper."

Terin was a little drunk, but he wasn't so far gone that he failed to heed Tejay's warning. He'd tried to bully her once before and come off second best. And he feared Damin for any number of reasons, but mostly because he was physically bigger and politically more powerful. Terin was intimidated by things like that.

"If I catch you with him, you'll both die!" he threatened, determined to get the last word in.

"Fine," she said with a shrug. "Are we done now?"

Terin glared at her. "Whore!"

"You said that already."

When Terin couldn't think of an answer, he turned on his heel and stormed out of her room, slamming the door behind him. Tejay stared after him, shaking her head at the foolishness of all men and with nothing resolved and a long night ahead of her trying to figure it out, she resumed her restless pacing.

chapter 24

Damin trained each morning with Narvell, Almodavar and their senior officers, as well as those Sunrise officers who wished to take part in the bouts. It was a habit drilled into the young prince from an early age by the old captain and a much needed release for his pent-up frustration. Mindful of the reason Charel Hawksword had sent Narvell out to challenge him on the border, Damin made a point of letting his younger brother win, every now and then. This morning, however, Narvell hadn't come down to the yards and as Damin was feeling particularly restless, he trained with Almodavar instead.

Although well into his fifties, there was no other man in his service Damin trusted as much. Almodavar was the only man Damin wasn't afraid of injuring seriously if he didn't hold back. If anything, he knew he'd find himself in trouble if he gave the fight anything less than his all.

Almodavar, after all, had punished Damin as a child for failing to kill him when he had the chance.

"Damin!"

He turned at the call to find Narvell hurrying along the vine-covered walkway behind him. Damin was heading back to his rooms in the sprawling Cabradell Palace to clean up after his training bout before confronting whatever round of fresh calamities were likely to find him this day. He was sweaty and dusty and bleeding from several small nicks Almodavar had inflicted on him when he foolishly let his guard down. The wind was chilly on his bare flesh as it whistled off the distant snow-capped Sunrise Mountains in the west, down through the Cabradell Valley and along the open walkways of the palace. Damin hadn't wanted to get blood on his shirt, so he carried it in his left hand, leaving his nicks and bruises for all the world to see.

Narvell stopped when he caught up with his brother and eyed him curiously. "Was there a war this morning and I missed it?" he asked.

"I trained with Almodavar."

"It looks like he tried to kill you."

Damin shrugged. "He looks worse. Where were you this morning?"

"I had . . . something else to do."

"Did that *something else* involve Kendra Warhaft?"

Narvell avoided meeting his eye. "You're going to get mad at me if I say yes, aren't you?"

Damin sighed at his brother's recklessness. "She's supposed to be under the protection of the Sorcerers' Collective. If Warhaft catches you two . . ."

"He won't," Narvell promised.

"Famous last words, Narvell. Can't you just let things be until we speak to Lernen?"

"That could be months from now!"

"Deal with it, little brother," Damin told him unsympathetically. "I've stretched the limits of my power about as far as they'll go to keep her away from her husband for you. I can't do anything more to protect her—or you—if Warhaft finds you breaking our agreement."

"We'll be careful . . ."

Damin frowned, thinking if Narvell understood the meaning of the word *careful*, he wouldn't be trying to sneak time alone with Kendra in the first place. "Where was Rorin while you two were so blithely courting disaster?"

"He was there . . . sort of."

"Define *sort of*."

"He was in the next room."

"Right after we have a little chat about the definition of *careful*, I'm going to have a talk with my pet sorcerer about the meaning of the word *chaperone*."

"It wasn't his fault . . ." Narvell hesitated at the sound of footsteps, glanced past Damin to see who approached and then warmly greeted Lady Lionsclaw.

"Tejay!"

Damin turned to find the lady of the house walking toward them, dressed in a sleeveless blue gown, her thick blond hair arranged to perfection, a slave at her side taking notes as she issued orders about the daily running of the vast Cabradell Palace, the very picture of the perfect Warlord's wife. She stopped when she saw the two of them, pulling her shawl around her bare arms against the cold, dismissed the slave and then, as Narvell had, eyed Damin's battered body curiously.

"Have fun working out this morning, did we, your highness?"

"I trained with Almodavar. There's no better sparring partner when one is looking for something to hit, so one doesn't fall for the temptation of venting their frustration on one's host."

She smiled. "Have you considered the possibility, Damin, that Almodavar really *does* want to kill you?"

"Actually, the thought has crossed my mind on more than one occasion," he laughed, and then he glanced down at the bruises on Tejay's upper arms which she was trying to hide with her shawl and his smile faded into a scowl. "What's your excuse?"

Puzzled, she looked at him oddly. "What do you mean?"

He took her arm, pushed the shawl aside and held it up so she could see the bruises. "Who's been trying to kill *you*?"

Tejay impatiently shook her arm free. "It's nothing, Damin. I was just clumsy, that's all."

"But those bruises look like handprints," Narvell pointed out with concern. "Did someone attack you, my lady?"

The Warlord's wife laughed at the very notion, but it was forced and Damin could tell she was lying. "Don't be foolish, Narvell. I can fight better than most of Sunrise's Raiders. What man would be foolish enough to—?"

"I can think of one," Damin cut in ominously.

She shook her head at him. "This is none of your business, Damin."

"The hell it isn't."

Tejay put a restraining hand on his arm. "I can deal with it, Damin. I don't need a protector."

"Well, you've got one, my lady," he informed her, shaking off her touch as he changed his mind about returning to his room. "Whether you want it or not."

Terin was in the main hall holding court when Damin found him. The doors banged open as the prince pushed his way into the hall, his anger controlled but no less dangerous for that.

One unexpected outcome of his altercation with Mahkas was that Damin had acquired a reputation for being unpredictable when enraged. People who had heard the story and didn't know him well now treated him with a degree of cautious fear he'd never encountered before, particularly if they thought he was angry. At first it amused him, and then it began to irritate him. Right now, it seemed a rather useful reputation to have acquired. People scurried out of his way as he approached the business end of the hall, their eyes full of apprehension.

Renulus stood at his lord's right hand, whispering something to his master. Damin pushed his way through the petitioners until he was standing in front of the podium that held Terin's throne. The throne and the elaborate silk banner on the wall behind it bearing the lion's head escutcheon of the Lionsclaw House were new, Damin thought. Terin's father, Chaine Lionsclaw—the baseborn son of a nobleman who rose to the rank of Warlord—had never felt the need to rule his province from a throne.

Sensing Damin's mood, Renulus stepped between the prince and his lord, drawing himself up pompously. "I'm sorry, your highness, but we're in session here and you don't have an appointment."

Damin replied by belting the fool in the mouth. It wasn't much, just a short, sharp jab, but it had the desired effect. Howling in pain, Renulus dropped to the floor at Damin's feet, nursing a split and swollen lip.

Interestingly, only one of the guards flanking Terin made a move to intervene.

Damin glared at him. "Back off."

The guard stepped smartly back into place, stood at attention and didn't move another muscle.

Wiping the blood from his mouth, and blubbering in protest, Renulus began to climb to his feet. With his foot, Damin shoved the Karien backwards. "I'll tell you when you can get up."

The Karien thought about it for a moment, and then wisely

stayed on the floor, muttering unhappily about uncontrollable brutes while dabbing at his bruised and still-bleeding lip.

On the throne, Terin glanced down at his seneschal's bloody mouth and then leaned back against the cushions and began to applaud slowly. "Behold the mighty Damin Wolfblade," he mocked. "Is this how you intend to rule us when you're High Prince, your highness? By throwing your royal fist around?"

"You'd know all about throwing your fist around, wouldn't you, Terin?"

"I'm sure I've no idea what you're talking about."

"I'm talking about your wife."

The Warlord smiled. "Why? Do you think you have some claim on my wife?" Then his eyes narrowed suspiciously. "Ah. I see what this is about. Surely you're not going to get all hot and bothered over a few bruises acquired during a . . . *conjugal engagement* . . . between a husband and his wife, are you? Besides demonstrating a rather squeamish side to your character, your highness, it's not really any of your business."

Damin stepped up to Terin's throne, grabbed him by his shirt and pulled him out of his seat with one hand, holding him a few inches from his own face.

"I'm *making* it my business," he warned with a snarl, watching Terin shrink back from him in fear. "And if I ever see so much as a hair out of place on Tejay's head again, I will break your spine into so many pieces your children will be able to use it to play knucklebones." He shook Terin's limp form to emphasise his point. "Do you understand that, or are you too *stupid*?"

"How dare you stand in my own hall and tell everyone I'm stupid!" Terin gasped in a show of defiant bravado.

Damin let him go with a shove. "I'm sorry, I didn't realise it was a secret."

He turned on his heel and headed toward the door. It was only as an afterthought that he glanced over his shoulder at Renulus, still cowering on the floor.

"You can get up now," he said and then pushed through to the doors at the end of the hall and headed back to his suite to wash away the blood and the dust from his body, wishing there was some way of washing away the sour taste in his mouth that seemed to develop every time he had to deal with Terin Lionsclaw.

chapter 25

By the time they reached Greenharbour, Kalan and Wrayan were saddle sore, weary, mightily sick of travelling, and a little surprised to find the city gates open when they arrived. The High Prince had ordered them opened only the day before, one of the sentries on the gate informed them, when they stopped to learn what news they could about the state of affairs inside Greenharbour's walls. The plague appeared to be on the wane, the guard told them, and the High Prince was anxious to get rid of the bodies before another batch of diseases had time to incubate as a result of all those rotting cadavers lying about the city.

As they pushed through the crowded streets, they passed scores of work crews wearing rags tied across their faces against the smell, loading dead bodies in various stages of putrefaction onto wagons to be taken outside the city and disposed of in the mass graves they'd passed on the way in. Wrayan gagged at the smell, wishing they could ride faster to escape the stench of death and decay, but there was no easy way to push through the streets without trampling scores of people with stunned, grief-stricken eyes who seemed to be roaming Greenharbour without purpose or hope.

It took several hours before they reached Marla's townhouse. When Marla's housekeeper opened the door to them, they were so travel-stained and weary she almost refused them entry until she realised it was her mistress's own daughter standing on the threshold.

"I'm so sorry, my lady," the housekeeper gushed, standing back to let them into the foyer before dropping into a deep curtsey when she realised who it was. "I wasn't expecting you and we've been having some rather strange guests of late."

"It's all right, Cadella. Is my mother home?"

"No, my lady. She's at the palace. I'm expecting her back shortly, though."

"This is Master Lightfinger," Kalan told the slave. "Could you arrange for rooms to be made ready for us? And a bath. I doubt I'll ever be able to wash away the stink of this city, but I'd certainly like to try."

"Aye, it's bad out there at the moment, my lady. Can I get you some refreshment?"

"Thank you, Cadella. We'll take it in the hall."

Cadella bowed again and hurried away to tend her visitors. Wrayan followed Kalan into the hall, looking around with interest. He'd only seen Marla's private palace once before, many years ago, when Kalan was just a toddler. That was the night he arranged the introduction between Princess Marla and the Raven, the head of the Hythrun Assassins' Guild. He'd not had time that night to study the place in detail, but he was fairly certain the room had changed.

The last time Wrayan had been here, Marla was the wife of Nash Hawksword and the decor reflected his taste as much as hers. Now it was all Marla, from the carefully placed knick-knacks on the shelves down to the scattered, multicoloured cushions that seemed to pick up every hue woven into the expensive, imported Fardohnyan rugs.

"Oh, gods! No!"

Wrayan looked around and discovered Kalan had wandered out through the tall open windows and onto the terrace and the small walled garden beyond. He hurried out after her and found her standing on the lawn, looking down at two fresh graves. He slowed as he neared them, reading the headstones curiously. One of the graves—not surprisingly—was Ruxton Tirstone's final resting place. The other had simply one name carved into the wooden marker. *Elezaar*.

"Not Elezaar, too," he sighed, when he read it. "The plague must have taken him."

"Not the plague, Master Lightfinger," Cadella informed them.

They both turned to look at the housekeeper curiously. She placed the tray she was carrying on a small table by the door and stepped out onto the terrace.

"What happened, Cadella?" Kalan asked.

"Can't say for certain, my lady." The housekeeper shrugged. "He disappeared a few weeks ago. We'd just about given him up for dead when he came back all grubby and dishevelled, like. He walked in, sat down, talked to the princess for ten minutes or so and then keeled over. I didn't even realise there was anything amiss until Master Rodja came by to speak to your mother about an hour later and he opened the door and found her holding the dwarf's poor dead body, sobbing like a child."

Kalan looked at Wrayan with concern. "Mother must be devastated. She relied on Elezaar for everything."

"She's not herself," Cadella agreed. "And it doesn't help having the Assassins' Guild around here every five minutes, banging the door down and making a scene."

"The *Assassins'* Guild?" Wrayan asked, wondering what Marla had done to incur their wrath.

Cadella glared at him suspiciously.

"It's all right, Cadella," Kalan assured the slave. "Wrayan is a trusted friend."

The slave seemed unconvinced. "I'm sure you think so, my lady, and I know it's not really my place to say so, but perhaps this isn't the right time to be bringing your gentlemen friends home to meet your mother."

Kalan glanced at Wrayan, amused by the slave's assumption he was her boyfriend. "Actually, Cadella, Wrayan is also my mother's friend."

"In fact, Mistress Cadella, we've met before," he added,

deciding to put an end to any foolish speculation about where he fitted into the general scheme of things.

"I don't remember you," she said, squinting at him short-sightedly.

"It was just after Kalan's father, Lord Hawksword, died," he reminded her. "I was here with Princess Marla."

She stared at him, clearly unconvinced. "You'd have been a mere boy then," she declared, obviously judging his age at no more than thirty, which (by her calculation) would have made him only ten or twelve when Kalan's father died. "I don't recall seeing you before. Were you here for Lord Hawksword's funeral?"

No, he wanted to answer, *I was here to introduce your mistress to the head of the Assassins' Guild and to put a mind shield on you and every other member of the household.* But on reflection, perhaps that wasn't such a good idea. Nor did he have the heart to tell her that her estimate of his age was off by a good fifteen years.

"There were so many people coming and going, you probably don't remember," he agreed. "But rest assured, I am a loyal friend of the family."

"Tell me what's going on with the Assassins' Guild," Kalan demanded of the slave. "Has someone taken a contract out on my mother?"

"Not that I'm aware of," the housekeeper assured her. "But she seems to be doing an awful lot of business with them lately, if you take my meaning."

"Actually, Cadella, just exactly what *is* your meaning?"

The slave spun around at the sound of her mistress's voice. Marla was standing in the doorway, her expression grim. She was dressed in widow's white, which made her seem almost ethereal.

"Your highness!" the slave gasped guiltily.

"Mother!" Kalan flew across the lawn and into her mother's embrace.

"Might be a good time to make a strategic exit," Wrayan suggested in a low voice to the slave. Cadella fled before she was forced to offer any excuse for being caught gossiping about the princess's business.

Marla let the slave go without comment, hugging Kalan tightly until she realised who else was standing by the graves. "*Wrayan?*"

"Your highness," he replied with a bow. "It's good to see you well."

"What, in the name of all the Primal Gods, are you doing in Greenharbour?"

"It's a long story, Mother," Kalan said. "And a painful one. Can we clean up first? We've been on the road for weeks." She glanced over her shoulder at Elezaar's small grave. "And you've your own tales to tell, too, I suspect."

Marla nodded. "We'll meet for dinner." Impulsively, she hugged Kalan again and added, "You've no idea how good it is to see you, darling. Both of you, in fact."

"Something's wrong, isn't it?" Kalan asked, eyeing her mother warily.

"We'll talk at dinner, Kalan. In the meantime, go soak in a nice warm bath for a while. I'm sure you'll feel better for it."

Kalan kissed her mother's cheek and walked inside, leaving Marla standing at the door, staring thoughtfully at Wrayan.

"Should I not have come?" he asked, curious about her silence.

"No, you couldn't have picked a better time, actually." The princess smiled thinly. "Do you remember once offering to kill Alija for me?"

"The offer still stands, your highness."

"Then I'm very glad you're here, Wrayan."

He nodded in understanding. "You've finally tired of Alija?"

"I've finally tired of Alija," she agreed.

"I can tell you one thing that might help bring her down."

Wrayan was bathed and clean and sharing a wine with the

princess while they waited for Kalan to finish her ablutions. It was dark outside. Marla stood by the window, framed by the darkness. In the candlelight and her sleeveless white gown she looked even more delicate than she had when Wrayan had first seen her in the garden earlier today. She was pale, too, and she looked tired. Although Marla was unlikely to admit it, the loss of Ruxton and Elezaar, so close to one another, had obviously hit her hard.

"You know something I can use?"

"Tarkyn Lye fathered her children, not Barnardo Eaglespike."

Marla shook her head. She seemed unsurprised. "Don't even think about going there, Wrayan."

He was shocked at her quiet acceptance of his news. "What do you mean, *don't even think of it*? She's trying to pass off a couple of slave's bastards as descendants of the royal family."

"Just as I would have sworn by every Primal God I could name that Kalan and Narvell were Laran Krakenshield's children, had Nash Hawksword refused to claim them."

He looked at her in surprise. "*You*?"

The princess smiled. "Don't look so shocked. I'm not above swearing a false oath if it will save my family. Few women are. Just as few women are willing to take the risk of not producing an heir."

"I'm not sure I understand what this has to do with the fact Cyrus and Serrin Eaglespike are actually the sons of Tarkyn Lye."

"If we were to expose Alija's deception in this matter," Marla replied, "every noblewoman in Hythria would be suspect. Do you imagine Alija's sons are the only children fathered by slaves? The practice is rampant. But it's never spoken about. And for damn good reason. Expose Alija and you endanger every mother in the country, even those whose children are quite legitimately the sons and daughters of their fathers."

"You condone her lies."

"I condone the need for them," Marla corrected. "And much as I'd like to bring Alija down, it won't be that way. If I make public the news that a woman of Alija's status bore her *court'esa* two sons and passed them off as her husband's heirs, how many other husbands will look at their children and start to wonder if they've also been duped? At best, it will cause dissension in countless previously happy homes. At worst, innocent women will die. I won't go there, Wrayan. Not even for Alija."

"I admit, I never thought about it like that."

"That's because you're a man, Wrayan. You don't have to worry about losing your children. The law in Hythria favours fathers over mothers."

He finished his wine and walked to the small table near the window where Marla was standing, to help himself to a refill. "You always manage to make being a woman in Hythria sound something akin to one of the seven hells."

"Try it sometime," she suggested grimly. "You might be surprised."

Wrayan turned to the princess and looked at her curiously. "Are you all right, your highness?"

"Are you reading my mind, Wrayan?"

"No."

"Then I'm not the clever actress I thought I was." She handed him her glass for a refill. "To be honest, I don't think I've ever felt so lost. You can't know what it meant to lose Elezaar."

"I think I can guess."

She shook her head. "No. Unless I open my mind to you and let you see the wounds for yourself, you will never understand." Marla's eyes filled with unwanted tears. "She took him from me, Wrayan. And she forced him to betray me. I think that's what I hate her for most." She brushed away the tears impatiently. "Isn't that odd? She stole Nash from me. She's tried to kill Damin the gods know how many times. And yet the thing I really despise her for is that she made Elezaar fear me."

"That's understandable."

Marla turned to face him, her eyes glistening. "I've been putting on such a brave face, pretending I don't know what's happened to him. Pretending it doesn't hurt that he's gone. Pretending I don't care what he did . . ." She sniffed and wiped her eyes, squaring her shoulders. "I'm sorry. I don't mean to blubber like a child. It's just you're the only person in Hythria I can't lie to, Wrayan, so you're the unfortunate recipient of my maudlin self-pity."

"I don't think you're being maudlin, your highness. Or self-pitying."

The princess shrugged, feigning indifference with little success. "He was just a slave. We highborn aren't supposed to get emotional about our slaves. It's unseemly."

Because of the mind shield Wrayan couldn't read her thoughts, but he could easily feel her pain. Her bottom lip trembled as she spoke; it was an effort for her to hold back the grief she'd been working so hard to contain. Without thinking, he held his hand out to her. Marla turned to him and let the tears flow as he took her in his arms and comforted her the same way he'd comforted Kalan after Leila died.

Wrayan let her cry on his shoulder and said nothing. There was nothing he could say. Marla Wolfblade was probably the strongest person Wrayan had ever met, and it pained him to see her suffering, but even with the ability to wield magic there was nothing Wrayan could do to ease her pain except give the princess—quite literally—a shoulder to cry on.

Marla was still sobbing quietly in his arms when Wrayan glanced up and discovered Kalan standing in the doorway, staring at them with a thunderous expression as if she'd burst into the room and discovered Wrayan and her mother doing something indecent.

chapter 26

I'm not interrupting anything important, I hope?"

Marla looked up and stepped back out of Wrayan's embrace, wiping her eyes. "I'm sorry, darling. You've caught me in a rare moment of weakness. Wrayan was kind enough to loan me a shoulder to cry on."

"Well, aren't we lucky Wrayan's here?"

"Luckier than you know," her mother agreed. "Shall we talk over dinner? Cadella has everything ready in the dining room. We were just waiting for you to finish your bath."

"And to think, I was worried I might have arrived too soon for you."

The thief looked at her strangely, but Marla didn't seem to notice her daughter's sarcasm. They walked through to the dining room, took their places at one end of the long banquet table and talked of inconsequential things as Cadella supervised the slaves serving the first course.

Kalan sat on her mother's right, Wrayan on Marla's left. She watched the two of them intently, so many things suddenly making sense to her now, the memory of her conversation with Wrayan back in the barn of that isolated farmhouse a few days ago aching like an open wound.

"Have you ever been in love?"

"Once."

"What happened?"

"She was . . . is . . . way out of my reach."

Kalan picked up her spoon and stared determinedly at her bowl. *Of course she's way out of his reach,* she realised now. *He's a thief pining for a princess.* A woman whose station in life was so far above his that it was astonishing he would even consider such a relationship possible.

And what of you, Mother? Kalan looked up and studied

her out of the corner of her eye, wondering if Marla reciprocated Wrayan's feelings.

"Did she love you?"

"I suppose. In her own way."

"But not enough to stay with you?"

"Things are never that simple, Kalan."

No, Kalan mused. *Things are never that simple. Marla is the High Prince's sister.* When Alija plotted to kill Damin the first time—when Kalan herself was merely a baby—it was Wrayan, she knew, who uncovered the plot and risked the wrath of the Thieves' Guild to tell her mother of it. It was enough to make them allies, certainly, but Kalan never dreamed it might be enough to bring them even closer.

"Do you still miss her?"

"Every day of my life."

Kalan had no reason to doubt they'd been friends before her father died. But how long had they been lovers? How long had Wrayan and her mother kept their tawdry little secret . . . ?

"Kalan?"

She looked up in surprise. Her soup bowl was empty and Cadella was clearing away the dishes in preparation for the next course. She didn't recall swallowing any of it.

"Sorry, Mother. I must have been daydreaming. Did you say something?"

"This business with Leila and Starros," Marla said sadly, obviously taken aback by the news of her niece's suicide and Starros's brutal torture. "I can't believe Mahkas would do such a thing."

"Oh, he did it, all right," she confirmed, her own woes fading at the reminder of her cousin's fate. "It was the worst thing I ever saw. You can't imagine how bad it was."

"Did nobody try to stop him?"

"Nobody could." Kalan shrugged. "With Damin away in Medalon—"

"What was your brother doing in Medalon?"

Kalan was surprised her mother would need to ask. "Raiding cattle, of course. What else would he be doing there?"

"And your uncle approved of this?"

"I don't think Damin left him much choice. But there was nothing to worry about. Geri Almodavar and Raek Harlen were with him."

"Damin's father had a whole squad of Raiders with him when he was killed raiding cattle in Medalon, too," Marla pointed out, unimpressed, as Cadella wheeled in a small trolley with the next course. "It didn't do him any good."

"Damin is fine, Mother," Kalan assured her impatiently.

"Although in hindsight," Wrayan added, "it might have been better if he'd stayed home. Maybe then, Mahkas wouldn't have found them . . ."

Marla shook her head sorrowfully, as the slaves began to lay out the main course. It was ham, boiled with figs and bay leaves, rubbed with honey, baked to golden-brown perfection in a pastry crust. Even in the midst of a plague, Marla managed to set an impressive table. The effort was lost on Kalan, however. She was too concerned with the deception that had apparently been going on under her very nose her whole life to care how inventive Marla's kitchen slaves were.

"I can't say I'm the least bit surprised Leila and Starros were lovers," Marla told Wrayan, "but I'm still in shock over what you tell me about Mahkas's reaction to it."

"He crucifies innocent farmsteaders in Medalon whenever they dare resist him," Kalan reminded her, feeling argumentative. "Why are you acting so surprised that he's proved himself capable of being just as cruel to a member of his own family?"

Marla looked a little bewildered by Kalan's question. "I'm not *acting* surprised, Kalan. I *am* surprised. Your uncle doted on Leila. His daughter meant the world to him."

"The world he feared losing if you didn't allow her to marry Damin," Wrayan pointed out. "Finding her in bed with Starros was akin to slapping him in the face with a reality he didn't want to contemplate. And he didn't take kindly to it."

Marla shook her head in disbelief. "But Damin must have

said something to him to dissuade him from that belief, surely? He wrote me asking permission to set Mahkas straight on the issue of their betrothal—or the lack of it— weeks ago. I sent a letter as soon as I could, stating in no un- certain terms that while I loved her like a daughter, I did not consider Leila a suitable consort for Damin."

With the main course served, Cadella tactfully shooed the slaves out of the room, leaving them alone.

"Your letter arrived the day after Leila killed herself," Kalan said, as she heard the door close. "Brilliant timing, Mother."

"Kalan!" Wrayan exclaimed in surprise.

Marla was just as shocked at her daughter's sarcasm. "You think this was *my* fault, somehow?"

"You could have put Leila out of her misery when we were children, Mother," she accused. "But you're too fond of playing politics."

The princess shook her head in denial. "If I thought my si- lence might cost Leila her life someday, or harm Starros in any way, I would have shouted it from the rooftops, Kalan. You must know that."

Kalan shrugged, picking up her fork and turning it over and over in her hand. "I don't know what to believe any more." Wrayan was studying her with concern. Feeling his eyes on her, she glared at him. "*What?*"

"What's the matter with you, Kalan?"

"Nothing."

"You're spoiling for a fight."

"What would you know?"

"Kalan!" Marla scolded, shocked by her daughter's bel- ligerent tone. "Wrayan's right. What is wrong with you this evening? You sound like you're *looking* for somebody to ar- gue with you."

"Maybe I'm just sick of all the pretence."

"What pretence would that be?"

"Why don't you tell me, Mother?" she suggested, rising to her feet. Kalan tossed her fork down and shoved her plate aside. "You're the one with all the secrets."

With that pain-filled declaration, Kalan pushed her chair back and stormed out of the dining room, unable to bear the sight of the two of them sitting there so cosily together, leaving them staring after her in surprise.

"Kalan!"

Ignoring the call, Kalan tucked her knees under her chin, and stared out into the darkness. The windows were open and she could smell the sharp salt air of the harbour, the fresh breeze blowing away the rank smell of the city. The door shook as Wrayan impatiently tried the lock and then a moment later it opened.

She turned to look at him as he stepped into the room. "Your talent is supposed to be for reading minds, not opening doors."

He held up a small key. "I'm pretty good at getting what I want out of people, even without resorting to magic."

Kalan scowled at him. "Cadella's master key, I suppose?"

He shrugged. "What can I say? She likes me."

Kalan looked back out over the small garden with its two fresh graves. "Cadella's not the only one in this house who likes you, apparently."

Wrayan placed the key on the small table by the door, before closing it behind him. "And just exactly what is that supposed to mean?"

"You don't need me to explain it, Wrayan."

"I think your mother might like an explanation. You owe her an apology, too. Your behaviour at dinner was appalling."

Kalan turned back to glare at him. "Don't you dare lecture me on my manners!"

Wrayan crossed the room, stopping by the bed. He leaned against the bedpost and studied her curiously. "Have I done something to upset you?"

"Of course not!" she exclaimed. "I'm just being childish, aren't I? Isn't that why you're here? To scold me for my appalling etiquette? Do you think sleeping with my mother gives you the right to act like my father?"

Wrayan was silent. If Kalan hadn't known better, she might have thought he was shocked by the accusation. Maybe he *was* shocked, but only because he believed nobody would ever learn the truth.

"I see," he said after a time. "You thought what you saw down in the hall earlier was proof your mother and I are lovers?"

Kalan glared at him. Far from being offended or guilty, he sounded amused.

"I'm not stupid, Wrayan."

"Up until just now, I probably would have agreed with you, Kalan."

She was staggered by his denial. "You as good as admitted it to me!"

"If you're talking about the conversation we had on the way to Greenharbour about whether or not I've ever been in love, Kalan Hawksword, I don't believe your mother actually rated a mention."

"You said the woman you loved was way out of your reach."

He smiled. "And you think the only woman in the world who falls into that category is your mother? I'm truly flattered by your high opinion of me, Kalan."

"Don't you dare patronise me!"

"Then don't behave like a child."

Kalan looked away, determined not to let him see her pain. "I know what I saw, Wrayan."

"You saw me comforting a friend, Kalan. That's all it was. Your mother's lost a good husband and her closest friend within weeks of each other and if you'd hung around a bit longer at dinner, you would have found out Elezaar's parting gift to his beloved mistress was to blab every secret he knew about the Wolfblades to Alija Eaglespike's favourite lackey, Tarkyn Lye, right before poisoning himself and dying in your mother's arms."

Kalan stared at him in shock. "But that's not possible! Elezaar would never betray us!"

"This really is your night for badly misjudging people, isn't it?"

Kalan swung her feet around and stood up from the window seat, not sure what concerned her the most, Elezaar's betrayal or the idea she might have misread what she saw in the hall and made a complete fool of herself. "Is my mother all right?"

"Of course she's not *all right*, Kalan. She's devastated. And what's more, she needs your help to fight Alija. If you ever get over this little jealousy tantrum you appear to be having, you might realise that."

"I'm not jealous!" she gasped, horrified to think she'd been so transparent. Afraid he could tell what she was thinking—even if he wasn't actually reading her mind— Kalan tried to put some distance between them but Wrayan caught her arm as she passed him and stopped her.

"Your mind is shielded, Kalan, your emotions aren't."

"Let go of me."

"It would never work, you and I."

"Because I'm too young for you, I suppose?" she asked. "Well, you're right, Wrayan. You should probably only get involved with women your own age. So tell me. What are you planning to do when you're two hundred years old and still look thirty? Only court two-hundred-year-old women?"

He sighed. "It's not that simple, Kalan."

"That excuse is starting to wear a little thin, Wrayan."

"Then be practical," he suggested. "Even if we ignore the inconvenient reality that I'm twice your age, despite the fact I don't look it; even if we discount the possibility of your mother sending an assassin after me if she thought I'd laid a hand on her daughter, I can't give you what you want, Kalan. I'm not in love with you and the cruel reality is, I'm never going to be."

"What's her name?" Kalan asked, pulling her arm free. Her anger was fading in light of his honesty. She hadn't expected such candour from him.

"Shananara."

"The Harshini princess?"

He nodded.

"Way out of your reach, eh? I guess you weren't kidding."

Wrayan smiled apologetically. "On the bright side, she is over two hundred years old . . ."

"Is she beautiful?"

"Indescribably. But it's not just about physical beauty, Kalan."

"You told me the Harshini may never emerge from hiding again," she reminded him, not prepared to give up her dreams without a fight. "Certainly not in my lifetime and probably not in yours. Don't you think it's foolish to deny yourself any chance of happiness on the off-chance the Harshini may come back, some day?"

"You think I'm deliberately masochistic? I want to be happy as much as any man. And that's the problem. Even if she came back tomorrow, it wouldn't make any difference. There's no happy-ever-after waiting for me. I'll be lucky if she remembers my name in another ten years. Shananara is Harshini. They don't look at the world the way you and I do. They're not even capable of loving the way humans understand it. But they have this gift . . . this way of . . . I can't explain it really; it's something you can't appreciate unless you've experienced it. The Harshini even have a name for it."

"Kalianah's curse," Kalan said softly, beginning to understand. "It's what happens when a mortal falls in love with a Harshini. I've heard of it. But Wrayan, it's not as if we couldn't . . ."

He put his finger on her lips to stop her protests. "Don't, Kal . . . there's no point."

Her eyes glistened with unshed tears, as the logical part of Kalan understood what he was telling her, even while her heart was shattering into a million little pieces at his touch. "So that's it? *I can't ever love you, Kalan, so let's just be friends?*"

"Given the family you come from," he remarked dryly, "I certainly don't want to be your enemy."

She sniffed back her tears and drew herself up proudly, determined to preserve what little dignity she had left. "So you're telling me to grin and bear it? That I'm doomed to go through life suffering the pain of an unrequited love?"

Wrayan shrugged.

"Welcome to my world," he said.

chapter 27

Of all the wounds Mahkas Damaran had received at the hands of his ungrateful nephew, the most inconvenient was the fact he could no longer command authority simply by speaking his will. Damin's rage-driven fist had severed his vocal cords and only Rorin Mariner's ability as a magical healer had saved Mahkas's life and stopped him bleeding to death where he fell. But the young man was not skilled enough, it seemed, to save his voice.

Mahkas had his suspicions about that. Although he'd heard Rorin pleading with Damin to spare his uncle's life, his reasons were political not personal. Rorin Mariner couldn't have cared less about Mahkas Damaran. What he cared about was the political make-up of the Convocation of Warlords. That preserving one meant saving the other, was purely incidental.

Perhaps, Mahkas mused, *it wasn't a lack of skill, after all, that prevented the young sorcerer from repairing my throat, but a lack of will.*

He paced his office impatiently, rubbing at the sore spot on his arm as he worried about it, working himself into another frenzy. The lump in his arm was swollen and painful. He'd barely left it alone since Damin attacked him.

"Did you hear me, Uncle Mahkas?"

He looked up in surprise. With all this worrying, he'd

forgotten Xanda was in the room. He'd forgotten what they were talking about, too.

"Of course I heard you!" he snapped in a hoarse whisper.

"Then you don't mind if I issue the order to unseal the city?"

"Why?" Mahkas demanded anxiously. Unsealing the city meant letting strangers in. Worse, it meant letting Damin back in.

"Because . . . as we were just discussing . . . the threat of the plague seems to be waning," Xanda explained patiently. "We're not surrounded by refugees fleeing the southern provinces as we feared we might be. There hasn't been a new case of the plague reported in weeks. And the issue of food is becoming critical. We can avoid most of *those* problems right now by simply throwing open the gates."

"Throw open the gates," Mahkas muttered, pacing up and down behind the desk. "He's probably just waiting for me to do that."

Xanda strained to hear him. "Who's waiting for what?"

"Your damned cousin," he rasped, pointing to his ruined throat. "The bastard who did this to me!"

"Damin is in Cabradell," Xanda reminded him.

"He *says* he's in Cabradell," he exclaimed, his scorn actually causing him physical pain. "Who can believe a word that treacherous bastard says? For all I know he's sitting at the Walsark Crossroads with an army—*my* army, mind you—just waiting for me to open the gates. Just waiting for me to let down my guard." He rubbed furiously at the sore spot on his arm again. "He's already tried to get the rest of them, you know. Tried smuggling them out of the city under the pretext of a Fardohnyan invasion. But I put a stop to that, quick smart. There weren't many men anxious to join that smug little bastard once I put an arrow through Raek Harlan's chest, let me tell you."

"I was there, Uncle," Xanda said in an odd tone. "I saw what happened."

Mahkas chose to take Xanda's flat voice as a favourable sign. At least he didn't fly into a rage over the smallest little things like his cousin. "He's out there, Xanda. You mark my words."

"If you fear that, Uncle, let me send someone out to check," his nephew offered.

He kept shaking his head, back and forth, like a dog worrying at a bone. "They might not come back. Whoever I send might desert us. Or Damin would kill him. Yes, that's what would happen, Damin would kill him. Like he tried to kill me. And to think, I was almost going to let him marry my daughter!" He coughed painfully, alarmed to find his spittle flecked with blood. Rorin had warned him not to overdo it, but it was hard. So very, very hard.

Particularly when he had so much to say.

The door opened while he was still recovering from his coughing fit. It was Bylinda, all pale and pathetic in her mourning white. She never bothered to knock these days. Nobody did. There was no point. They couldn't hear him calling permission to enter.

She smiled wanly at Xanda. "Good morning, Xanda."

"Aunt Bylinda."

"Will you and Luciena be joining us for dinner this evening?"

Mahkas glared at her. There were more important things going on here than her bloody social arrangements.

"Do you mind!" he tried to shout, but she ignored him, pretending she didn't hear his hoarse yelling.

"Actually, my lady, Luciena and I thought we should join the children in the nursery for dinner. Lady Lionsclaw's boys are feeling a little homesick and they miss their mother. She feels they need the company."

Bylinda touched his arm, her grip fragile. "You're very good to those children, Xanda. And a good father to your own children, too. You don't see that too often, these days."

She curtseyed to her nephew and, without even acknowledging her husband, turned and drifted out of the room, off to do the gods knew what. She'd been like that a lot, lately. Vague, detached . . . her eyes, on the rare occasion Mahkas could get her to look at him, full of grief. Full of pain.

And full of accusation.

"It's her own fault, you know," Mahkas rasped.

Xanda looked at him. "Pardon?"

"What happened to Leila," he explained. "It's Bylinda's fault."

Xanda actually looked surprised. *Young men . . . they just don't get it*, Mahkas lamented silently. *They splash their seed around and sire a few brats and think fatherhood gives them some sort of insight into human nature.*

"Women are weak," he explained to his nephew, glad of the opportunity to impart some of his own wisdom to the young man. "They need to be disciplined. That's why Leila was so easily corrupted. I let Bylinda take care of the discipline when she was younger and it clearly wasn't enough . . ." He coughed again, the pain in his ravaged throat getting worse with every word he uttered.

Xanda rushed to his side and helped him into his seat. "You need to stop talking, Uncle. You need to rest. Trust me, you've said quite enough for one day."

Mahkas nodded wordlessly. It hurt too much to speak.

"I'll take care of things here," Xanda promised. "You should go back to bed and take something for the pain."

He's such a good lad, Xanda Taranger.

Living proof of Mahkas's theory about women and discipline, too. Mahkas had removed the irritation of Xanda's mother, Darilyn, from the boy's life when he was only six years old and look how well he'd turned out without a woman to corrupt him.

"Just one thing," Mahkas managed, as Xanda helped him to his feet and gave him an arm to lean on as they walked across the rug to the door.

"What's that, Uncle?"

"Unseal the city without my authority," he gasped painfully, "and I'll have you hanged for treason."

Xanda didn't react immediately to his threat. He hesitated just long enough for Mahkas to be certain that's exactly what his nephew had been planning to do as soon as he had his back turned.

"As you wish, Uncle," he said eventually, opening the door.

Xanda beckoned one of the guards waiting outside to help his lord to his room. Mahkas winced as he accepted the soldier's support, but was satisfied he could sleep now, and wake to find he still had a city under his control.

He smiled at his nephew, just to let him know he knew what he'd been thinking, but he didn't hold it against him. He was a bigger man than that. "Just so long as we understand each other, Xanda."

"I understand, Uncle," Xanda replied. "Better than you think."

"Then there won't be any problems, will there?"

"No, my lord."

Mahkas patted his arm encouragingly. "There's a good lad."

And then he turned and let the guards help him back down the long corridor, leaving Xanda Taranger staring after him thoughtfully and in no doubt about who was really in control of Krakandar Province.

chapter 28

Marla was working at her desk when the door opened and Kalan let herself into the study.

"Good afternoon, Kalan." She hadn't seen her daughter since she'd stormed out of dinner the evening before.

"Mother."

"Is there something I can do for you? As you can see, I'm rather busy."

"I came to say I'm sorry."

Marla put down her quill and studied her daughter

thoughtfully. "Is that because you *are* sorry, or because Wrayan told you to apologise?"

"Both, actually," Kalan admitted as she took a seat on the other side of the desk. "He told me about Elezaar, too."

Marla shrugged. "It's a done deed now. No point in losing sleep over it."

"I can't believe you're taking it so calmly."

"I'm not. I'm just better than you at hiding my feelings."

Kalan had the decency to look away guiltily. Marla's heart went out to her. She knew what Kalan's tantrum had been about, just as she knew that despite everything she'd done to discourage it, Kalan had doted on Wrayan since she was a small child. Her fantasy must have seemed so real, so achievable, Marla thought. Here was a man who hadn't visibly aged in thirty years. To a young girl with a hopeless crush it must have seemed as if the gods had stopped time for Wrayan, to allow her a chance to catch up. What Kalan didn't understand—and there had never been any reason until now to explain it to her—was that the two years Wrayan spent among the Harshini had done more than teach him to wield magic proficiently. He'd been one of them. Lived with them. Loved with them. Such a rare opportunity was a double-edged sword. They'd saved his life, given him a chance to live the long life his distant Harshini ancestry would allow, but it came at a cost.

Wrayan was in love with a Harshini.

The Sisters of the Blade in Medalon had set out to destroy their entire race because of what that could do to a human.

"Did I act like a complete fool last night?" she asked.

"Yes," her mother replied bluntly. Then she smiled. "But I wouldn't worry about it, darling. Wrayan doesn't think any less of you for it."

"What about you?"

"I've been in love just as desperately, Kalan," Marla told her daughter. "And for a while, I was the happiest I've ever been in my entire life. But it also caused me the most intense pain I've ever experienced. Worse, even, than childbirth."

Kalan frowned. "I thought childbirth was supposed to be a wonderful and moving time for a woman?"

"That's a lie men spread about to convince us we should keep having babies for them," Marla grumbled. "Don't believe a word of it. Childbirth hurts like hell."

Kalan smiled faintly, but her amusement soon faded in the face of their more serious problems. "What are you going to do about Alija?"

"Destroy her."

Kalan wasn't even a little surprised. "That's a given, I would have thought. But how are you going to do it? You can't just have the High Arrion killed. That would destabilise the whole damn country at a time we can least afford it."

"No," Marla agreed. "But I can have that slimy little sightless ground-slug, Tarkyn Lye, taken care of any time I want. In fact I've already arranged it with the Assassins' Guild."

"And then what? If something happens to Tarkyn Lye, isn't she going to suspect it was you behind the attack?"

"That doesn't bother me."

"She'll retaliate."

"Also a given," Marla agreed. "Our job is to find a way to see that whatever Alija does, it discredits her, rather than bolsters her cause."

Kalan stood up and walked to the window to look down over the garden. "She couldn't have picked a worse time. We're about to be invaded. How are we going to get the troops belonging to the provinces under the Sorcerers' Collective control to the border if Alija's out for vengeance? Then there's the risk she'll see this as an opportunity to finally be rid of Damin. If he's killed in battle, she can hardly be blamed for it."

"Unless his death is a direct result of her failure to send the troops Hythria needs to defend itself," Marla pointed out. "But you're right, of course. We need the Collective supporting the throne, not actively working against it. Which brings up another issue. What do you think of Damin's plan?"

Kalan glanced over her shoulder at her mother. "The one that has him leading our armies to war or the one that lowers the age of majority?"

"Both."

She shrugged and sat down on the window seat. "The first one's easy, Mother. Damin's trained for this all his life. He'll make a fine general."

"And reducing the age of majority?"

"That's the one that really surprises me," Kalan admitted. "I never thought my brother smart enough to come up with an idea like that on his own. But then, as Wrayan pointed out to me last night, I'm compiling a fairly impressive list of people I've misjudged lately."

"From what Wrayan tells me, your brother comported himself with remarkable restraint after Leila died."

Kalan seemed amused at the assessment. "Remarkable is a good word. The man who was bossing everybody around in Krakandar wasn't the Damin I know."

"Then I'll speak to Lernen about it. Hopefully, there won't be a problem getting him to agree to either suggestion."

"Do you think he'll object?" Kalan asked in surprise. "I was under the impression Uncle Lernen signed anything you put in front of him."

"Ah, the good old days," Marla sighed wistfully, leaning back in her chair. "Your uncle is a sick man, Kalan. The gods alone know how he avoided falling victim to the plague. But along with the sores and infections he suffers comes a level of paranoia that is truly frightening to behold."

"What do you mean? Is he insane?"

"That's something I've been trying to decide for twenty-five years." Marla shrugged. "This is more like unreasonable fear. He thinks everyone's out to get him."

Kalan chuckled softly. "Well, if you think about it, Mother, he's not that far off the mark. A lot of people *are* out to get him."

Marla frowned. "I'd probably find humour in the situation too, if his delusions didn't include even me, on occasion."

Kalan rose to her feet. "Did you want me to come along? Maybe, if I was there to support you . . . ?"

Marla shook her head. "If he's in one of his moods, it will just convince him we're ganging up on him. No, I'll speak to him and we'll get Damin the command he needs. And the authority to use it. After that, we'll just have to leave the fate of Hythria in your brother's hands for a while, because you and I, Kalan, will be too busy destroying Alija Eaglespike to worry about it."

When Marla arrived at the palace the following day, Corian Burl was waiting for her. The old chamberlain bowed as deeply as his weary bones would allow and smiled at the princess as she entered the palace. "You're early today, your highness."

"I wanted to see my brother before he gets too engrossed in his latest entertainment," Marla explained as she walked across the tiled great hall toward her office with the chamberlain at her side. "What is he currently occupied with? Or would I be better off not knowing?"

The old man shrugged. "Surprisingly, his highness's amusements have been quite dull of late, madam. He has decided the garden on the roof of the west wing contains too many advantageous places of concealment for assassins. He actually hasn't left his room for the past three days. He informs me he's officially in hiding."

Marla sighed. "Perhaps I should go and speak to him first."

"That might be a good idea, your highness. He's been asking where you are."

Marla turned for the stairs, wondering what sort of mood she'd find her brother in. The news he'd been hiding from assassins for the past three days wasn't good. It meant he was probably in the full throes of a paranoia attack, which, if it was bad enough, might mean he feared his only sister had turned on him as well. If that was the case, Marla knew she would get nothing useful done until he was over it.

When she arrived outside the magnificent doors of the High Prince's suite with its gilded wolf's head escutcheon, she hesitated, took a deep breath, and then motioned the guards on duty to admit her. The soldiers did so without question. Inside, the suite was dark, the heavy drapes drawn and the candles extinguished. When the guards closed the doors behind her she could hardly see anything at all.

"Lernen?"

There was no answer. The rooms smelled musty. In Greenharbour's humid climate, it was never a good idea to seal rooms up like this. They needed fresh air and light or, before you knew it, there were things growing off the walls. She walked to the window and threw back the drapes before opening the windows to let in some air.

"Lernen? It's me, Marla!"

"Are you alone?"

She looked around, wondering where he was hiding.

"Yes, dearest. I'm alone."

"They're gone then?" the disembodied voice asked fearfully.

"Who?" she asked, walking toward the sofa.

"The assassins the Patriots sent after me. Are they gone?"

"There's nobody in the palace who looks anything like an assassin," she assured him. Marla knelt on the seat of the sofa and looked over the back. Hythria's High Prince was curled into a foetal position on the floor behind the couch. "They're all gone, Lernen. You can come out now."

Hesitantly, her brother pushed himself up onto his hands and knees and looked up at her. "Are you sure?"

"I made it here alive," Marla pointed out.

That seemed to satisfy the old man. He climbed painfully to his feet. "You're very brave to roam the halls of the palace alone, Marla. They're everywhere, you know."

She patted his arm reassuringly. "I've had Corian Burl order a sweep of the palace. They'll find any assassins lurking around and have them killed."

"Bah!" he spat. "Corian Burl is probably one of them."

"Then I'll have him killed too," she promised. "Come sit by me, dearest. We need to talk."

Lernen walked around the sofa and took a seat beside her. He wore only a thin loose shirt that he obviously hadn't changed in days, his spindly legs bare and grubby underneath it. When he got like this, even the slave boys he normally surrounded himself with were banished from his presence. Because of that, he hadn't bathed for some time, either, she guessed, steeling herself against the smell of his unwashed body. The High Prince of Hythria was apparently incapable of taking a bath without a score of attendants to help him.

Lernen sat himself down beside her. "Have you news for me?" he asked hopefully. "Good news?"

Marla wasn't sure what her brother considered good news, but it certainly wasn't what she'd come to deliver. She shook her head. "Quite the opposite, I'm afraid. I bring the saddest news of all. Leila Damaran is dead."

"Little Leila?" Lernen gasped. "Mahkas Damaran's girl? She's quite the sweetest creature I ever met. Was it Patriot assassins?"

"She took her own life when her father wouldn't let her marry the man she loved."

"Why, that's appalling!" the High Prince declared. "Did you want me to order Mahkas killed?" He leant forward and added in a low voice, "I can do that, you know. I'm the High Prince."

Marla nodded solemnly. "I think Damin would like to take care of it himself."

At the mention of his heir, Lernen smiled proudly. "He'd do it, too, that boy. Will he kill him very slowly, do you think?"

"He can't afford to, Lernen. If Mahkas dies before Damin comes of age, then Krakandar Province will fall under the protection of the Sorcerers' Collective and that would mean handing it to the Patriots. Of course . . . if he was of age already . . ."

"Then we must do something!" Lernen insisted, his fear

of the Patriots apparently the order of the day. Tomorrow he might be frightened just as easily by a teapot. "We can't let something like this go unavenged."

"I couldn't agree more, brother, but unless you did something like lowering the age of majority to twenty-five so if Mahkas dies, Damin can inherit Krakandar immediately," she sighed mournfully, "I don't see how we can risk doing anything at all."

He looked at her curiously. "Lower the age of majority? Can I do that?"

"You *are* the High Prince," she reminded him.

He slapped the sofa cushions determinedly. "Then we'll have to lower the age of majority, by the gods! Damin must be free to take vengeance! Leila's death deserves nothing less."

"I'm so glad you thought of doing such a brave thing, Lernen," Marla told him, squeezing his hand affectionately. "I'd never have come up with such an inspired solution on my own. And I promise, Damin won't—"

"Damin won't what?" he asked, suddenly suspicious.

"I was going to say he won't let you down," Marla assured him, patting his hand comfortingly.

"No, you weren't!" the High Prince accused, snatching his hand away. "You were going to say something else! This is a plot, isn't it? If I lower the age of majority, he'll be able to take my throne!"

"Your throne is perfectly safe, Lernen," she assured him, wishing she could slap her brother for being such a fool. It would only make matters worse, she knew, but it was so very tempting . . . "Very well," she conceded, knowing the more she pushed on the subject, the more likely he was to dig his heels in. She took a deep breath. "Forget the age of majority. Why not keep Damin too busy to threaten you, Lernen? Give him something to keep him occupied and out of your hair until he does come of age."

"Keep him busy how?"

"I don't know . . . perhaps a role in the military . . . something to let him know how much you appreciate his loyalty, along with too much responsibility to leave him any time to plot against you."

"Damin would never plot against me!" Lernen exclaimed, in a complete reversal of his position of a moment ago. "The boy dotes on me. You've told me that any number of times."

"And he does, dearest," Marla assured him hurriedly. "But isn't it nice to do something unexpected for those we love, every now and then. Just because we can?"

"I suppose." Lernen shrugged. "But what role could I give him?"

"Hmmm . . ." Marla said, as if trying to think of something suitable. "Why not Lord Admiral of Hythria's Navy?"

"We don't really have a navy," Lernen pointed out with a frown. Then he brightened suddenly. "I know! What about Lord of the Northern Marshes? That would keep him out of my hair in the north, wouldn't it?"

"You awarded him that title when he turned eighteen," Marla said. "And it's a meaningless one, dear. There's nobody to fight in the Northern Marshes."

"Ah . . . well, what about . . . Lord Commander of Hythria's Army?"

Marla thought about it for a moment. "I suppose. Although unless you were to call up the combined armies of Hythria—which hasn't happened in a millennium—it's rather an empty title, and it wouldn't give him that much to do."

Lernen patted her hand and winked at her. "Empty titles are always the best ones to hand out as gestures, Marla. Can't have the boy getting too full of himself now, can we? He'll be busy enough, I think. They have lots of parades."

"Of course," Marla agreed, rising to her feet. "You're very wise, brother. I shall have the papers drawn up immediately and you can sign them this afternoon. Shall I send someone in to run your bath?"

Before he could answer, the door flew open and Alija strode into the room, followed by Corian Burl (objecting loudly to the intrusion) and the two soldiers who were supposed to be guarding the door outside. The men seemed unsure if their duties included manhandling the High Arrion to prevent her entering the High Prince's chambers.

Lernen squealed like a girl when he saw Alija and hid behind Marla, who had jumped to her feet when they were disturbed.

"She's one of them!" Lernen screeched, pointing at Alija. "Kill her! Kill her now!"

For a precious moment Marla hesitated, wishing the guards would do as her brother ordered, but they weren't about to cut down a woman in cold blood, particularly not the High Arrion of the Sorcerers' Collective.

"Belay that," Marla sighed, making no attempt to disguise the reluctance in her voice. "And leave us."

Bowing as they backed out of the room and looking more than a little concerned, Corian Burl and the two guards closed the doors behind them.

Alija glared at her. "Smart move, Marla."

That's debatable, Marla replied silently.

"What's she doing here?" Lernen demanded, tugging on Marla's skirt. "She's a Patriot. She's one of them. She's the one who sent the assassins after me."

Alija rolled her eyes impatiently. "For the gods' sake, Lernen, if I wanted you dead, I'd have done it long before now. As it happens, I'm here to report on some disturbing news about your nephew."

Marla's eyes narrowed dangerously. "Which nephew?"

"Why our precious heir, of course," Alija replied. "I have news that he's in Cabradell with an army, preparing to invade Fardohnya."

"Are we invading Fardohnya, Marla?" Lernen asked.

"It's more like he's protecting us from the Fardohnyans, dearest," Marla told her brother soothingly, wishing she hadn't so hastily belayed that order to kill Alija.

"Then the rumours I've heard about Hablet gathering his army over the border are true?" Alija enquired. She directed the question to Lernen but she was looking straight at Marla. "We face an invasion from Fardohnya and all we have to protect us is a handful of cattle thieves led by an inexperienced boy not yet come of age?"

"That's all right. I've taken care of that," Lernen announced.

Marla could have cheerfully throttled him. Even though Lernen had refused her request today, he might just as easily grant it tomorrow. If Alija learned of her plans to lower the age of majority before Lernen signed the decree, Marla was sure she'd find a way to talk him out of it. In her own way, Alija was just as proficient at playing on Lernen's fears as Marla.

"Taken care of what?"

"Damin," Lernen told her. "Him being too young. Found a way to keep him busy. I'm giving him a new title. Lord Commander of Hythria's Army."

Alija glared at Marla as she realised the magnitude of Lernen's gift (even if he didn't) and then smiled sweetly at Lernen. "That's remarkably generous of you, your highness. There aren't many sovereigns who would pass up an opportunity for fame and glory in favour of their heir."

Lernen stared at her, obviously puzzled. "Fame and glory?"

"I would have expected *you* to lead Hythria's combined forces, your highness. It was very courageous of you to award your nephew the honour."

"*Me*? Lead a *real* army?"

"Naturally. I mean, isn't that why we have a High Prince?"

To Marla's horror, she realised her brother was seriously contemplating the idea.

"You have matters of state to attend to here in Greenharbour," she reminded him. "We don't even know if there's an invasion coming. Let Damin play with his soldiers in Cabradell while you remain here, Lernen. Keeping us safe from the Patriots," she added, staring pointedly at Alija.

"Marla!" Alija exclaimed, quick as a rodent. "It's not like

you to be so selfish. Surely you can muddle through with things here in the palace while our High Prince is fulfilling his sacred role as Hythria's defender?"

"She has a point, Marla," Lernen mused. "That is *my* role, you know. Hythria's defender."

Marla stared at her brother, standing there with his grubby shirt and his skinny legs. *The gods help us,* she thought, *if you're defending Hythria.*

"You will need to call up the reserves of all the provinces to defend us, your highness," Alija reminded him, ignoring Marla completely. "With so many under the control of the Sorcerers' Collective, it is my duty as High Arrion to provide the throne with the support it needs to defeat this threat, and while I have no doubts about *your* ability to lead our forces into war, sire . . . I'd be reluctant to do the same if I thought command of our forces was in the hands of an inexperienced boy."

You conniving bitch! Marla wanted to shout, as she saw what Alija was doing. By refusing to release the troops under the Sorcerers' Collective's command unless Lernen led the army, she was making it his fault if Hythria fell to the Fardohnyans. And forcing Marla's hand. There was almost no chance Lernen was going to be able to deny Alija now.

"You are needed here in Greenharbour, Lernen," Marla insisted, even though she knew she was fighting a losing battle. "This city has been devastated by the plague. If you leave now, people might think you've abandoned them in their hour of need."

"Of course, if he left now, the chances of our beloved High Prince catching the plague would be significantly reduced," Alija pointed out, strengthening her hand by playing on Lernen's fear of the deadly disease. "As for people thinking he's abandoned them, Marla . . . you'd be better served wondering what people will say about Lernen Wolfblade when Hablet of Fardohnya is sitting on Hythria's throne."

"That barbarian will never take my throne!" Lernen declared, stamping his foot like a child. "You are right, Lady

Alija! I am Hythria's High Prince! It is my sacred duty to lead our forces into battle!"

"Good for you, your highness!"

"Lernen, I think we should talk about this . . ."

"What's to talk about, Marla? The High Arrion is right. Hythria needs her High Prince on the front lines, not cowering in his palace hundreds of miles from the battle. You may send a message to my nephew, sister, and inform him Lernen Wolfblade, High Prince of Hythria, will assume command of our combined forces immediately!"

"Might I suggest you appoint an experienced officer as your second-in-command, your highness?" Alija added. "My son, Cyrus—"

Oh no you don't! Marla fumed silently. "But Cyrus is in Dregian Province, my lady," she cut in before the High Arrion could finish her sales pitch. "It would take far too long for him to get here. And besides, as you've already reminded us, my dear, your son has plenty of experience in command. Lernen needs an opportunity to test the mettle of his heir, and what better place to do that than in a battle? I'm sure if Damin proves less than able, the High Prince will know he can call on Cyrus for aid."

Alija smiled at her with all the warmth of a predator eyeing its prey. "I shall send for Cyrus in any case," she said. "He will insist on leading Dregian's forces."

"Then let him lead them all the way to the Fardohnyan border, my lady!" Lernen declared. He turned to Marla, his earlier paranoia forgotten, his face flushed with excitement. "And now we've settled the fate of Hythria," he added, "I think I'll take that bath."

chapter 29

ow the *hell* did she know about the Fardohnyans?"
Marla demanded.

The princess was pacing the main hall in the townhouse and looked ready to kill something. Kalan and
Marla's stepson, Rodja Tirstone, were sitting opposite
each other on the cushions around the low table. Wrayan
stood by the doors leading out onto the terrace. It was hot
and humid and he was vainly hoping for a breeze from the
harbour to relieve the heat.

"An army's not an easy thing to hide, your highness."

"That might explain how Alija knew Damin was in
Cabradell," Rodja said, sipping his wine. "It doesn't explain
where she got her intelligence about the Fardohnyans."

"I'm still reeling from the news she actually convinced
Lernen he should lead the army," Kalan said, shaking her
head in disbelief. "And I can tell you one thing for certain.
Damin's not going to be happy about it."

"Name one single warrior in Hythria, even among the
Royalists, who *will* be happy about it," Rodja challenged. He
looked up at Marla, shaking his head in disbelief, just as
Kalan had. "This is bizarre. I mean, surely Alija must know
what a disaster this is."

"Maybe she does," Wrayan suggested.

They all turned to look at him.

"You're not suggesting she wants us to lose this war, are
you, Wrayan?" Marla asked.

"Why not? It's patently clear she doesn't have the support
to unseat Lernen on her own. You've made sure of that, your
highness. But if our esteemed High Prince leads us to war
and stuffs it up? What could be better for her? Maybe she'll
get really lucky and both Damin and Narvell will be killed in
a battle, too. For that matter, if Hablet invades Hythria and

wins the war, he's not going to govern us from Greenharbour. He'll need some sort of administrator to rule in his stead when he goes back to Talabar. Who better than a disgruntled highborn Hythrun who's conveniently changed sides at the last moment?"

"That's it," Kalan said.

Marla looked at her daughter curiously. "What's it, Kalan?"

"The way to destroy Alija," Kalan said. "Expose her as a Fardohnyan collaborator."

"What's to expose?" Rodja asked. "Wrayan's simply speculating, not stating any provable facts."

"But it's a plausible scenario."

"There's a world of difference between a plausible scenario and the truth, Kalan," Wrayan warned. "Who'd seriously believe the High Arrion of the Sorcerers' Collective was collaborating with the Fardohnyans?"

"Anybody we want," Marla suggested. "If it's handled correctly."

Wrayan shook his head. "Even if you could somehow manage to concoct such a far-fetched state of affairs, your highness, it wouldn't actually help us. Collaboration might be despicable, but it's treason that's the capital crime and you can't prove that."

"You're missing the point," Kalan said. "The idea isn't to make everyone else believe we have proof. Only Alija has to believe it." When they all looked at her in confusion, she sighed impatiently, as if she couldn't understand why they didn't see what she did. Wrayan had a bad feeling he knew what she was driving at, but he remained silent, waiting for Kalan to explain before he voiced his objections.

"Alija Eaglespike would kill herself before she did anything to jeopardise her sons or what she believes is Cyrus's chance at the throne."

"So . . . what are you proposing, Kalan?" Rodja asked. "That we somehow manage to convince the High Arrion she's turned into a collaborator and hope she falls on her sword to save her sons from the disgrace?"

"That's exactly what I'm suggesting."

Rodja disagreed. "You can't make her believe something so patently untrue."

"No," Marla conceded. Then she turned and looked at Wrayan thoughtfully. "But Wrayan could."

"You don't know what you're asking."

"I'm asking you to repay twenty years of friendship."

"I've repaid your friendship plenty, your highness," he replied, refusing to be manipulated so blatantly. "But what you're asking for isn't possible. You can't make somebody believe something they fundamentally disagree with, and hope to make it stick. Even the Harshini wouldn't try it."

"But we're not," Kalan said, truly warming to the idea. Her eyes were alight and he could almost see the cogs of her devious little mind ticking over as she worked out the plan in her head.

Like mother, like daughter, Wrayan thought.

"Alija is a Patriot," he reminded her. "And their entire manifesto is based on preserving the sovereignty of Hythria from the ravages of what they see as a corrupt and worthless dynasty. Even if I was a Patriot, you're not going to convince me—and you're certainly never going to convince Alija—that Hythria's best interests lie in aiding a foreign power to invade us."

"But if she believed someone . . . another Patriot perhaps . . . was willing to smooth the way for her son to become High Prince, she'd jump at the chance like a drowning man reaching for a lifeline. You just have to get her to take the bait."

"Set her up, you mean?" Rodja asked. "With a false agent?"

"Exactly. Give her what she wants. Give her someone who offers to do precisely what she's hoping for. Have him promise he can dispose of all the Wolfblade males in one fell swoop during battle, in a way that leaves the Eaglespikes and the Patriots blameless . . ."

"And then, when she's taken the bait, you expose her co-conspirator as a Fardohnyan," Marla concluded. "Kalan's right. It doesn't need to go any further if Alija thinks we have proof she's a traitor, even inadvertently."

"Just watch how fast she falls on her sword then," Kalan suggested, with unaccustomed savagery, "if she thinks her precious sons might suffer from the stigma of having a traitor for a mother."

"Alija would never fall for anything so blatant," Wrayan warned. "She'd smell a trap a mile away."

"Not if you're there to smooth over her doubts," Kalan pointed out.

Wrayan wished that damn breeze would pick up. He was sweating like a pig but he wasn't certain, any longer, if it was just the muggy evening that made him so uncomfortable. "That's coercion, Kalan. I won't do it. For that matter, I'm not even sure I *can* do it."

"But isn't coercion making someone believe something they fundamentally disagree with?" Marla asked. "Kalan's right. This would be giving Alija exactly what she wants, what she's prayed for. She may even consider it a gift from the gods."

"And anybody with half a brain knows what a gift from the gods is worth."

"Your irreverent blasphemy aside, Wrayan," Marla said, "this idea may actually have a chance of succeeding. It's certainly the best plan I've heard so far."

"It's actually the only plan you've heard so far."

"Then come up with a better one," Kalan challenged. "We can't kill the High Arrion outright. Even if it didn't mean losing the support of the Sorcerers' Collective as a whole, we can't risk the Wolfblades being seen to be the cause of her downfall or we'll be guilty of the very thing the Patriots accuse us of and we'll drive even our most forgiving allies straight into the arms of our enemies. Nor can we risk destroying her House completely for the same reason—much as it pains me to admit it. We need to cut Alija out like a tumour. Remove her from Hythria's body without damaging any of the surrounding organs. The only way to do that is to have her perform the surgery on herself."

"And who's going to prompt her into this remarkable act of self-mutilation?" Wrayan asked. "It's not as if one of us can walk up, knock on the door of the Sorcerers' Palace and tell the High Arrion we've got a great idea about how she can arrange for her son to inherit the throne."

"I might have someone," Rodja volunteered. The news didn't surprise Wrayan. Rodja's father had made his fortune trading information as much as spices. For every legitimate business associate the Tirstone brothers had, there was a shadier one lurking in the shadows.

"What about you, Wrayan?" Marla asked.

He hesitated, wondering if he should refuse. Coercion was right up there with murder, according to the Harshini. On the other hand, Kalan was right, loath though Wrayan was to admit it. Convincing Alija there was a chance to remove Lernen, Damin and Narvell in a way that left her blameless was something she probably prayed for on a daily basis. There would be no coercion involved.

He shrugged. "I suppose."

"Your enthusiastic commitment to our cause is overwhelming, sir," Kalan remarked sourly. She still sounded a little hurt, but he was fairly certain she'd get over it. Kalan was young and resilient, and would survive a broken heart. She'd probably forget all about him as soon as something better came along.

Marla looked at him curiously too, a little concerned by his response. "Are you afraid, Wrayan?"

He didn't take offence at the question. He knew Marla wasn't trying to goad his male ego into action. She was genuinely concerned.

"Not for the reason you think, your highness. This isn't about how much power either of us has. I know I'm stronger than Alija. The fact she's never been able to detect any mind shield I've created since I came back from Sanctuary is proof enough of that. If you want me to make sure she has no doubts your agent is genuine, I can arrange it. But this . . . it involves more than just the people in this room. This man Rodja's offering to bring on board, for instance. How are you going to silence him afterwards? Have him killed, too?" When none of them was able to offer an answer, he added, "I'm not afraid of Alija, I'm afraid of what this makes us. There's no glory in victory if the casual observer can't tell the difference between your particular brand of tyranny and your enemy's."

"So now we're *evil*?" Kalan snapped. "Funny how that hasn't bothered you up until now."

"You offered to kill Alija yourself, Wrayan," Marla reminded him. "Isn't that just as evil?"

"I suggested a clean kill, your highness. You're suggesting luring an innocent woman into a trap and then driving her to suicide through guilt."

"Alija may be many things, Wrayan," Rodja pointed out, "but innocent isn't one of them."

"You don't have to convince me of that," he said. "I've been affected by Alija's pernicious ambition more directly than any other person in this room, including you, your highness," he added to Marla. "But don't we hold the moral high ground here? Are you willing to surrender that just for vengeance?"

Marla glanced at Rodja and Kalan before answering. "Absolutely."

"I'm sorry if that shatters your illusions about the noble character of the Wolfblades," Kalan added with an edge of bitterness.

"I think it shatters a fair few of the noble illusions I had about my own character, Kalan." He smiled faintly as a peace gesture. He didn't want to fight Kalan or her mother about this. It just made him uneasy to witness how quickly they'd come up with this plan. And how eager he was to abuse his own magical gifts to aid the Wolfblades in bringing down his nemesis. "It's a brilliant plan," he added to Kalan. "And it'll work. Frighteningly well, I suspect."

Marla turned to her stepson. "Then it's agreed. When can we speak to this man of yours, Rodja?"

"It may take me a day or so to find him, but I'm not sure you *should* speak to him, Marla. Wrayan brought up a very good point about what we're supposed to do with him later. Perhaps I should deal with him alone. That way, there's no need for him to know you've got anything to do with this. And it's probably safer if he doesn't, anyway. If Alija reads his mind, the last thing you want her to discover is that he's been given his instructions by her good friend, Princess Marla."

"I hadn't thought of that," Marla said. "You'll take care of it then, Rodja?"

"The man I have in mind is such a good liar he ought to be Jakerlon's high priest," Rodja assured the princess. "And he doesn't know my real name, either—just that I'm willing to pay for accurate information when he has it."

"Accurate information about what?" Kalan asked curiously.

Rodja shrugged. "Just . . . things."

Marla nodded. "That's it, then. Rodja can speak to his man and when he's been briefed we can discuss the most effective way to make contact with Alija, at which point, Wrayan can make sure any doubts Alija has are quashed before they get a chance to take hold of her."

"And the irony," Rodja added, climbing to his feet, "is that by sending Cyrus off to war with Lernen, the only person she'd dare share her plans with for the destruction of the Wolfblades won't be there to question her good fortune."

"I must be slipping," Marla remarked with a smile. "I hadn't thought of that either."

"It must be the first sign of impending senility, I'm sure," Rodja joked. "And on that note, I really must be getting home. If I'm a minute later than I promised, Selena will immediately assume the worst and start arranging my funeral."

Wrayan smiled. "I hear congratulations are in order, Rodja. Her highness tells me you have a new son."

He made no attempt to hide his pride. "He was born a few days before you and Kalan arrived. We named him Ruxton. After my father."

"I shall have to come and visit my new nephew," Kalan added. "Is Selena well?"

"She's fine. Mother and son are both thriving, actually."

"I wish my own sons were as eager to give me grandchildren," Marla sighed.

Kalan laughed at the very idea. "You wish nothing of the sort, Mother. Give Selena my love, won't you, Rodja? Tell her I'll be around to visit as soon as I can."

"I will," he promised. "Good night, Marla. Kalan."

"I'll walk you to the door," Wrayan offered, wondering if the air in the street was any less humid than the heavily scented air of Marla's small garden.

He pushed off the door frame and fell in beside Rodja as the two of them left the hall. Once they were safely out of earshot, Wrayan turned to Rodja. "This man you're planning to use. I'll need to read his mind. And shield it. It's the only way to protect him."

"I'll send word once I find him," he agreed. "What about you?"

"What about me?"

"Are you going to let Franz Gillam know you're back in Greenharbour?"

Wrayan looked at Rodja Tirstone in surprise. "You know the head of the Greenharbour Thieves' Guild?"

"Our paths have crossed." Rodja shrugged. "On occasion."

Wrayan smiled. "Sometimes, Rodja, I get the feeling your father was a bigger crook than all the thieves in my guild put together. And you seem very comfortable following in his footsteps."

"Our business interests are . . . diverse," Rodja agreed.

"Diverse enough to include the Thieves' Guild? Never mind, you don't have to answer that. I suppose I should send word to Franz though. He won't be happy if he finds out the head of another city's guild is in town and didn't have the courtesy to advise him. We thieves can be very territorial, you know."

"I can let him know if you want." They reached the door and opened it. Outside, Rodja's carriage waited. His coachman hurriedly sat up straighter as his master approached. Rodja offered Wrayan his hand and shook it warmly. "I'm glad you're here, Wrayan. Marla could do with a friend right now."

"I don't know how much I can do. Those two in there seem to get along just fine without any help from anyone."

"I'm just glad they're on our side," he agreed. "Good night, Wrayan."

"Good night, Rodja."

Wrayan waited as the young man climbed into his carriage and the vehicle moved off, heading down the quiet street, before he turned and headed back into the house.

chapter 30

A week or so after Mahkas refused—yet again—to unseal the city, Krakandar Palace had settled into a strange state of anticipation. It was almost as if everyone in the palace was holding their breath, waiting for something terrible to happen. The children could feel it, the slaves were so jumpy they were dropping things, and Luciena was starting to wonder if she was going crazy because of it.

Her latest problem seemed to be that she was losing her mind. Or her memory. Things were missing she could have sworn she'd seen only the day before. Nothing so large it was noticeable, but odd things, like the silver tray that sat on the sideboard in the dining room that seemed to be there one day and gone the next. Or the silver figurine depicting Kalianah, the Goddess of Love, that was on the mantle in her bedroom last week and now was nowhere to be found. And now, just as the light began to fade, when she'd reached for the candelabra that normally sat on the side table in the morning room, she discovered it wasn't there. In fact, there wasn't a candlestick to be had anywhere in the room.

"Orleon, have you done something with the silverware?" she called, emerging from the morning room into the main foyer of the palace in search of some light. The grand staircase sweeping up toward the upper storeys was already shadowed by the gathering gloom.

The Chief Steward stopped and turned to look at her. "No, my lady. Why do you ask?"

"There're no candles in the morning room."

"I'll see to it at once, my lady," he said with an apologetic bow. The old steward snapped his fingers at a nearby slave who was lighting the lamps in the foyer and ordered him to see to the morning room first. "The problem will be rectified immediately."

"Thank you, Orleon. I swear they were there last night before I went to dinner. Every time I turn around lately, there seems to be something missing." She hesitated a moment, before asking, "Have you ever had a problem with pilfering among the staff?"

He shook his head, a little offended by the question. "The vast majority of the servants and slaves in Krakandar Palace have been with the family for years, Lady Taranger. If there is a problem with thievery, it's only started since you arrived."

She smiled at his thinly veiled insinuation. "I'm not even sure if there is a problem, Orleon. This isn't my home and I don't really know what's what. I might simply be imagining things."

"I can order a full inventory to be taken, my lady, if you so desire. Just to be certain nothing is missing."

Luciena frowned. Such a move might unsettle the already nervous staff. On the other hand, it might give them something to worry about, other than the possibility of Mahkas exploding unexpectedly and ordering them all lashed to death, a fear—her slave, Aleesha, had informed her anxiously—that was the prime topic of conversation below stairs these days.

"Perhaps we should look into it," she agreed. "But let's do it discreetly. I've no wish to pour oil on a simmering tinderbox at a time like this."

The Chief Steward bowed in acknowledgment of her wisdom. "As you wish, Lady Taranger."

The old man turned and continued on his way, leaving her standing in the vast entrance hall, wondering if perhaps the insanity of this place really was starting to get to her. She hoped she was wrong. Given the mood of the palace, if one of the staff was discovered stealing, the fear of being lashed or beaten to death by Krakandar's regent was quite a reasonable one.

"It can't be that bad."

Luciena started a little and turned to find her husband standing behind her. "What do you mean?"

"You've been standing here in the foyer, just staring off into space, looking like you have the weight of the entire world on your shoulders, Luci. It can't be that bad, can it?"

"You've just come from Mahkas," she replied, tartly. "You tell me."

"He's not too bad today," Xanda replied uncomfortably. The topic of Mahkas Damaran was not a happy one between them.

"As opposed to yesterday?" she asked. "When he ordered a man hanged for complaining he was hungry?"

Xanda was obviously pained by her interpretation of events. "The man was standing on a box in the marketplace, suggesting the people of the city rise up and slaughter the Regent of Krakandar," he reminded her. "And everybody else in the palace, incidentally. Including you and our children."

"Because he was hungry," Luciena retorted.

Xanda sighed heavily. "I'm trying my hardest to fix this, you know."

"You're trying your hardest only so far as it doesn't rock the boat," she corrected.

"Which is precisely what Damin asked me to do."

"Don't try shifting the blame onto your cousin, just because he's not here to disagree with you. Damin wouldn't put up with what's happening here, Xanda, and you know it. He'd have openly challenged Mahkas weeks ago."

"Which is just fine for Damin Wolfblade, my love, because he's actually the heir to this province and has the legal right to do something about the way it's being managed. I'm only his cousin and my authority to do *anything* in Krakandar is strictly limited. You know that."

She shook her head, unwilling to acknowledge their helplessness. "You have to make him unseal the city, Xanda. People are getting very, *very* hungry out there and there's no good reason to keep them confined any longer. That poor man Mahkas condemned yesterday was only the beginning. More and more people are going to start complaining and the louder they get, the more they'll start to wonder why Mahkas Damaran is keeping them virtual prisoners in their own city. He can't hang every soul in Krakandar who disagrees with him."

"It won't come to that . . ."

"Xanda! Open your eyes! You can't really think he's doing this for any other reason than fear, surely?"

Her husband shrugged. "He wouldn't be the first man in history to make a foolish decision out of fear of the plague, Luci."

"I'm not talking about the plague. I'm talking about Damin. Mahkas is terrified of losing Krakandar."

"Damin's not even here . . ."

"And if he was, he'd be camped outside the walls, unable to get back in," she pointed out bluntly. "Think about *that*, my love, the next time you stand by and do nothing to stop your precious uncle from butchering innocent people."

He grabbed her arm and pulled her closer, aware that the main foyer of the palace was the last place they should be having a discussion like this. "Don't you think I want to see an end to this insanity?"

"Xanda . . ."

"Do you have any idea what it's like for me?" he hissed impatiently, lowering his voice as a slave hurried by, heading for the kitchens. "This man raised me. He's like a father to me."

"He lashed your cousin to within an inch of her life, drove

her to suicide and then beat one of your best friends into a bloody pulp. Oh, did I mention he killed Raek Harlen in cold blood? He was a friend of yours too, wasn't he? Exactly what part of your idyllic childhood does *his* death evoke fond memories of, Xanda?"

He let her go, clearly wounded by her lack of sympathy. "I'm doing what I can, Luciena, to keep you, our children, the Lionsclaw children, and the rest of the city safe. I'm also trying to ensure my cousin has a city to come home to. I'm sorry if you don't like the way I'm going about it, but I can't help that."

Luciena sighed apologetically, feeling a little guilty for attacking him so harshly. "I'm sorry, Xanda. You didn't deserve that. I know you're doing what you can. I just worry about the children, that's all."

"We're all worried, Luci," Xanda agreed, his expression grim. "You don't have a monopoly on that."

"Then I should . . ." Her voice faltered as she noticed Bylinda Damaran walking in their direction. "We should talk about this later."

Wondering at her warning tone, Xanda glanced over his shoulder. Bylinda was walking slowly across the foyer dressed in her nightgown, even though it was just on sunset, smiling vaguely, as if something only she could see amused her. Luciena wondered if she'd even bothered to dress this morning.

"Aunt Bylinda?" Xanda said warily. "Is everything all right?"

"Hello Xanda," she replied distantly. "Luciena."

"My lady," she replied, with a small curtsey. "You're still in your nightgown. Are you unwell?"

"Not particularly."

She glanced at Xanda with concern before asking, "Would you like me to see you back to your room?"

"Where are the children?"

"In the day nursery, my lady," Luciena told her. "Given the hour, they're probably having dinner. Perhaps you'd like to visit them?"

It might help, she hoped. Bylinda's grief over Leila's death had destroyed her. The woman who wandered so aimlessly through the palace corridors these days, looking for something only she knew how to find, was a pale echo of the Bylinda Damaran that Luciena had met the first time she came to Krakandar. His aunt's descent into inconsolable grief had been even harder for Xanda to witness. If Mahkas Damaran had been the father Xanda never knew, Bylinda had been his mother, the woman who had taken him and his brother, Travin, to her heart after their mother hanged herself with a harp wire in the fortress at Winternest when Xanda was barely six years old.

"Watch over Emilie, Luciena," Bylinda advised, reaching up to touch her face gently. "You never know when she's going to be taken from you."

Bylinda's hand was icy against her cheek. Luciena glanced at Xanda in concern before she answered. "Is there some particular reason I need to watch over my daughter, my lady?"

"*Because* she's your daughter," Xanda's aunt advised, her empty eyes blazing with passion for a rare moment. "Daughters are precious commodities, Luciena. They sell precious commodities, don't you know? Trade them. Barter them. And sometimes they destroy them." She smiled and the passion faded, to be replaced by the familiar hollow emptiness. "But then . . . you're in trade, aren't you dear. You'd know that already."

"I'd never let anybody hurt my daughter, my lady," Luciena assured her. "Nor would her father."

Xanda, who was standing right beside Luciena, nodded in agreement. "Luci's right, Aunt Bylinda. I swear, nobody will ever hurt my daughter and live to tell about it."

Bylinda Damaran's smile faded. She fixed her eyes on Luciena. "Don't make the mistake of believing their lies. That's what my husband said about his daughter, Luciena. I'm still waiting for him to keep his oath."

Without another word, Bylinda wandered off, leaving Luciena and Xanda staring after her with concern.

"What do you suppose she means," Xanda asked after a long silence, "by Mahkas fulfilling his oath?"

"I'm almost afraid to ask," Luciena replied, more disturbed by Bylinda's strange words than she cared to admit.

chapter 31

With only himself to worry about and the furthest distance to travel, Adham Tirstone was able to get away from Byamor and head straight for the pass at Highcastle to see what he could learn about Fardohnya's troop movements with little or no fuss. Getting Rorin dispatched from Cabradell to investigate Winternest for the same reason proved much more problematic. Not only did Damin have to contend with the dilemma of what to do with Kendra Warhaft while Rorin was gone, Terin Lionsclaw had decided the Widowmaker was *his* pass and Winternest was *his* fortress, and if anybody was going to find out what was happening over the border, then it ought to be Sunrise Province's Warlord.

"You can't let him come, Damin!" Rorin begged, when Terin made his announcement. "Please!"

The Warlord was hugely offended by the young sorcerer's reaction to his suggestion he should be in charge of the intelligence-gathering mission. "I beg your pardon, sir?"

Rorin ignored him. "Spying on the Fardohnyans requires subtlety, Damin, not a bloody military parade."

Damin was inclined to agree. But Terin's suggestion had one undeniable advantage. It meant he'd be rid of Tejay's husband for a couple of weeks at least, maybe longer. That was almost too good an offer to refuse.

"I suppose Lord Lionsclaw could accompany you as far as Winternest," Damin mused. "And then you could check out the actual pass and the border on your own."

"Please, Damin," Rorin pleaded. "I thought you were my friend."

"I don't like what you're implying, sir," Terin bristled.

"He's not implying anything," Damin said. "Rorin's merely concerned for your safety."

"Actually, Damin, it's my own safety I'm worried about," Rorin corrected. "Lord Lionsclaw can look after himself."

"I will not be insulted in my own palace in such a manner!" Terin declared, slamming his wine glass down on the table and splashing the map beneath it.

Damin winced at his carelessness. The maps they were studying had been hand drawn in excruciating detail in the time of Terin's grandfather, Glenadal Ravenspear. They were priceless.

"Rorin's not insulting you, my lord," Damin assured him. "He's just used to working alone."

"I demand an apology!"

"Say sorry, Rorin."

"But Damin . . ."

"I said, say you're sorry," he repeated, warning the young sorcerer with a look.

Rorin knew what Damin's glare meant. He backed down unhappily. "I'm sorry, Lord Lionsclaw. I didn't mean to offend you."

"There, you see? We're all friends again. My lord, I think it's an excellent idea that you accompany Rorin Mariner to the border."

"You do?" Terin asked, suddenly suspicious. "Why?"

"Because you know Winternest better than anybody else. Isn't that what you just claimed?"

"Well . . . yes . . . but . . ."

Damin smiled as he realised Terin's offer hadn't been a serious one and now he was trapped by his own posturing. "Is there a problem?"

Terin's eyes narrowed suspiciously. "My wife will have to come with me."

"Don't be absurd! The front lines are no place for a woman."

"I see," the Warlord said, his eyes narrowing suspiciously. "You'd rather send me to the front and keep my wife here with you, eh?"

Damin shrugged. "You volunteered, my lord."

"Do you deny you prefer my wife's company?" Terin demanded.

Damin looked at him oddly. "To yours? Count on it."

"That's *not* what I mean, your highness."

Damin gripped the edge of the table, his knuckles white, and made a great show of studying the map. "I know what you mean, my lord. And unless you want to have a discussion with me about it involving naked steel, I suggest you drop the subject."

There was a moment of tense silence and then Terin turned on his heel and stormed out of the room. When Damin heard the door slam, he relaxed and then looked up and grinned evilly at Rorin. "Have fun."

"I hate you for this, Damin Wolfblade. You know that, don't you?"

"You'll get over it."

The sorcerer shook his head unhappily. "No, I won't. I'll probably have to join the Patriots and devote my life to destroying you for inflicting him on me."

"Fine," he said. "Just do it after you've found out what Hablet's up to at Westbrook, would you?"

Rorin sighed. "How come nobody quakes in their boots when I threaten them, Damin? You seem to have it down to a fine art."

"I think you need to rip somebody's throat out first."

"I'll bear that in mind. Would you be terribly upset if I dropped Terin Lionsclaw off a cliff along the way?"

"Not personally," Damin said. "But we still have that pesky one-dead-Warlord-away-from-Alija-having-control-of-the-Convocation problem hanging over our heads."

"Ah well, I can dream about it, I suppose."

Before Damin could offer Rorin his sympathy, the door opened. He looked up and found Tejay standing at the door, looking uncharacteristically nervous about something.

"Damin, can you spare me a moment?"

"Of course. What's wrong?"

"I've been thinking about what Charel Hawksword said in Byamor," she told him, walking into the office, but leaving the door open. "About Hablet knowing nothing about you other than you being Lernen's nephew."

"So he thinks I'm a lecherous fool with nothing other than my own pleasure on my mind. I could be accused of worse things, I suppose."

"Such a misconception is not a bad thing, if you're planning to trick him."

"Assuming we *can* trick him," Rorin said. He bowed politely to the Warlord's wife. "Would you excuse me, Lady Lionsclaw? I have to go and write my will. I'm planning to kill myself later today, and I'd like everything to be in order."

"Kill yourself?" Tejay asked curiously.

"His royal highness—my *former* good friend, here—is sending me to Winternest with your husband, my lady. I'm thinking suicide might achieve the same end result and be marginally less painful."

"Keep that up and you won't have to kill yourself, Rorin," Damin offered. "I'll do it for you."

Tejay smiled sympathetically. "I'm sure you'll manage."

"Rorin, get out of here," Damin ordered. "And stay out of Terin's way. You've offended him enough for one day."

Rorin bowed to Tejay. "My lady."

She waited until Rorin had left and then turned to Damin. "I like Rorin. He's very . . . sure of himself."

"I would be too if I could throw people around the room just by wishing for it. Is something the matter?"

"I'm worried about Hablet."

Damin's brow furrowed. "Aren't we all?"

"I'm serious, Damin. You can't risk him realising your potential."

"What do you mean?"

"He's bound to have spies in your camp. Unless you comport yourself in a manner consistent with the reputation you're hoping to establish, Hablet will be suspicious of any tactic you employ."

Damin leaned against the table and studied her curiously. "And how exactly do you define 'comporting myself in a manner consistent with the reputation I'm hoping to establish'?"

"You need to take a few *court'esa* to war with you, for one thing."

"War is no place for *court'esa*."

"I agree, but that's the opinion of a sane and rational man."

"And I'm supposed to be an inexperienced, lecherous fool?"

"Precisely."

"I've got a bad feeling I'm not going to like where this is leading, Tejay," Damin sighed, crossing his arms with a frown.

"But you do understand the problem."

"I suppose."

"Then you will accept the gift I'm going to give you without complaint."

"Tejay . . ." Damin began, but she ignored him, turning to snap her fingers in the direction of the door.

At her command, three *court'esa* entered the room. In the centre of the trio was a young man with a physique that looked as if he'd been carved out of a single block of rich dark wood by a Harshini artisan hoping to depict a god. He had long dark hair threaded with tiny gold beads reaching almost to his waist and an expression of arrogant condescension. The women were of equally impressive beauty and just as disdainful. Both were dark-skinned and dark-haired and of similar statuesque proportions.

Damin looked at them in surprise and then turned to Tejay. "*Denikans*?"

"This is Lyrian," she told him, pointing to the stunning,

dark-eyed young woman on the left. "And the other young woman is Barlaina."

"And him?"

"This is Kraig."

"I thought all Denikans died within a few months if you tried to enslave them?" Damin asked in surprise.

"Most of us do," the man replied in a deep and surprisingly cultured voice. "So it's a good thing we're not actually slaves."

Damin looked at Tejay in confusion. "Free *court'esa*? Now there's a novel concept."

"The *court'esa* collars are merely a disguise, Damin," she said. "A necessary one."

"Are you going to tell me exactly what's going on here?"

She pointed in the direction of the cushions around the low table in the centre of the room and then looked up at the male *court'esa*. "Would you like to join us, Kraig?"

Tejay sat down as Barlaina closed the door. The man said something in his own language to his companions before taking his place beside Tejay as if he was her equal, not her slave. The two Denikan women moved to stand behind him in a manner that reminded Damin more of sentinels than servants.

As Damin joined them on the cushions around the low table, Tejay introduced them formally. "Damin Wolfblade, heir to the throne and Prince of Hythria, allow me to introduce Prince Lunar Shadow Kraig of the House of the Rising Moon, heir to the throne of Denika."

Damin studied the Denikan in shock then looked at Tejay. "This is a joke, right?"

"Do you consider it a joke that a slave could be a prince, your highness?" Kraig asked in his deep, measured voice. He spoke without accent but carefully enunciated each word, making it clear Hythrun was not his native language. "Or is it the idea a nation as barbarous as you perceive Denika to be has any notion of what it means to be ruled by kings or princes that you find so humorous?"

Damin stared at the young man warily. "Neither, your *highness*. I was merely referring to Lady Lionsclaw's apparent belief she could hide someone as important as the heir to the Denikan throne by disguising him as a *court'esa* and expecting me to take him to war." He glanced up at the two women who were glaring at Damin threateningly. "Your *court'esa*, I suppose?"

"My bodyguards."

"I see. How long have you been here?"

"I've been in Hythria since just after the plague began," Kraig told him. "I came to your country in response to a request from your High Prince to negotiate a treaty between our two nations. When I got here, I discovered your people beating my people to death in the streets."

"I imagine that put paid to the treaty negotiations."

Tejay didn't appreciate his attempt at levity. "Enough, Damin."

"Sorry," he said. "Old habits die hard. How did you finish up in Cabradell, your highness?"

"With emotions running so high—and the danger of the plague—Princess Marla thought it unwise to let us remain in Greenharbour," the Denikan prince explained.

"By then all the Denikan ships had fled in fear of their lives. So she sent him here," Tejay continued, "in the hope Chaine could get him over the border at Highcastle and then onto a ship bound for Denika out of Tambay's Seat."

"But Hablet closed the borders before you could get out of Hythria," Damin concluded, beginning to understand the problem. "And now you're stranded here in Cabradell. I can understand you fleeing Greenharbour, but why the disguise?"

"People believe it was the Denikans who started the plague, Damin," Tejay reminded him. "They were ready to stone any free Denikan they found walking the streets of Greenharbour. *Court'esa*, on the other hand, are property, therefore much less obvious targets."

"And what does Terin think of all this?"

"He doesn't know," Tejay replied. "He thinks your mother bought Kraig and the girls at the slave markets in Greenharbour just before they closed, as a gift to Chaine. He believes Kraig is a Loronged *court'esa* and that Lyrian and Barlaina are simply a passing fad his father was going through."

Damin admired the two statuesque young women, thinking he could easily indulge in a passing fad like that given slightly different circumstances. Then he cursed himself for a damned fool, and turned to Tejay.

"Then why do you need my help? You seem to have everything under control."

"Chaine is dead, Damin, and sooner or later it's going to occur to Terin that his father's *court'esa* are still in the slave quarters and that they're not earning their keep. He'll either decide to sell them for a profit or worse, decide to make use of them."

"Neither scenario is particularly desirable," Kraig remarked.

Damin sympathised with their plight, but wasn't sure what he was supposed to do about it. "And just exactly what do you expect *me* to do with your Denikan visitors?"

Tejay glanced at Kraig before she spoke. "I want you to take Kraig with you, Damin, and Lyrian and Barlaina, too. The only way to get them home now is to take them back through Greenharbour."

"But I'm going to war, Tejay, not Greenharbour."

"I know, but you will get back to the city eventually and when you do, you can arrange for Kraig to get home on one of Luciena's ships. In the meantime, Kraig and the women can provide you with the cover you need by pretending to be your *court'esa*."

"They can, can they?"

She looked a little annoyed he hadn't immediately fallen in with her clever plan. "It all works perfectly, don't you see? I'll tell Terin you spied the Denikans in the *court'esa* quarters and expressed your curiosity, so I gifted them to you to keep you happy. He'd never dare ask for them back because of the huge insult to ask the High Prince's heir to return a gift. Their identity remains a secret. Better yet, word will get back to Hablet that you have *court'esa* in the battle camp with you, *court'esa* of *both* sexes, which means the Fardohnyans will quickly jump to the conclusion you're just as wanton as your uncle, and therefore just as foolish. They'll fall for whatever trap you devise, you will defeat the Fardohnyans, and then after the war is done, you can get Kraig back home without him being stoned to death on the streets of Greenharbour for bringing the plague down on us."

"You make it sound far too easy, Tejay." Damin studied the Denikan prince doubtfully. "And what do you think of this, your highness? Are you really willing to pretend to be my slaves . . . my *sex* slaves . . . on the off-chance I can get you home?"

For the first time, the Denikan prince cracked the faintest hint of a smile, folding his perfectly sculpted arms across his massive chest. "*Pretend* is the operative word here, Prince Damin."

Damin grinned. "I'm glad you feel that way, your highness, because I have to say, you're really not my inclination."

Kraig stared at Damin in silence.

"That was a joke."

"I know," the Denikan prince replied unsmilingly.   .

"Good thing you'll be posing as my *court'esa*," Damin remarked. "You'd have a hard job convincing anyone I'd taken you on as my court jester."

"Damin, behave," Tejay warned. She turned to the Denikan prince apologetically. "You'll have to forgive my foster-brother, Kraig. He's got a bad habit of not taking anything seriously."

"I can see that."

There was a hint of condescension in the Denikan's tone that Damin didn't much care for, but he had no chance to respond to it. The door opened without warning and Rorin burst into the room, breathing heavily, as if he'd run all the way here.

"Sorry to interrupt, but I just snatched this out of the hands of that nosy little Karien friend of Terin's." He crossed the room and handed a crumpled letter to Damin that bore the Hythrun royal seal. "A messenger just arrived from Greenharbour. Renulus got to him first and was apparently planning to read the royal dispatches before passing them on, so I took the liberty of delivering them myself."

Damin was less concerned about Renulus than about what the letter might contain. He tore it open expectantly. Hopefully, it was the commission he'd been waiting for, awarding him command of Hythria's combined army. And news Lernen had agreed to lower the age of majority.

Damin read the letter and then read it again in growing disbelief, his eyes widening in horror as he realised the disaster they were suddenly facing.

"What's wrong?" Tejay asked in concern.

He read the letter twice more, not sure he believed his own eyes.

"Damin?"

Finally, he looked up. "You're not going to believe this."

"Has something happened to your uncle?"

"Apparently he's lost his mind."

"What's it say?" Rorin asked.

"It says we have our general."

"He's given you command?" Tejay asked.

Damin handed her the letter, certain she wouldn't believe it either until she'd read it herself. "No, he hasn't, Lady Lionsclaw. My uncle has decided to lead us into the fray himself. The new commander of Hythria's combined armies is the High Prince of Hythria, Lernen Wolfblade."

CHAPTER 32

Marla was at the palace going through the day's correspondence when Corian Burl announced she had a visitor. She'd been burying herself in mundane tasks in the hope that if she didn't think about it consciously, her distraction would magically produce a solution to the problem of her brother's intention to lead their troops to war.

It hadn't happened yet, but she did get a lot of work done this way.

She looked up curiously, glad of the new distraction. "Who is it?"

"He refuses to give his name, your highness."

Marla sighed. "Show him in."

"But your highness . . ."

"It's all right, Corian. I know who it is."

Unhappily, the slave bowed and did as she bid. A moment later Galon Miar stepped into the room. The assassin bowed politely and looked around at the erotic murals with interest.

"Fascinating taste you have in art, your highness," he remarked, tilting his head to the side to study one couple engaged in a particularly optimistic position. "How ever do you get any work done in here?"

"By ignoring them," she replied. "What are you doing at the palace?"

"I brought you a gift." He reached into his vest and produced a flat, silk-wrapped parcel. The pale blue silk was stained with blood.

"What's this?"

"Tarkyn Lye's slave collar. I tossed up the idea of bringing you his head as a token of my loyal service, but decapitations are so damned messy and one tends to get odd looks from passersby when one walks the streets of Greenharbour carrying a disembodied head."

"You mock me at your peril, Master Miar."

"I think if I was worried about peril, your highness, I might have chosen another line of work."

Marla studied him curiously, wondering if it was a personality trait that allowed men like Galon Miar to kill so easily, or simply the training he'd received as a boy. Maybe it was a little bit of both.

"Does it bother you?"

"That I just killed someone?" He shrugged. "It's my job."

"You seem so . . . unaffected."

"*You* ordered the killing, your highness," he reminded her. "I'm just the tool you used to do the job. In the eyes of the law, I'm no more guilty than the blade I used to slit his throat. I don't see *you* falling apart with remorse and guilt."

"You think I have no conscience?"

"Not a shred," he replied. "It's probably what I find most alluring about you."

She didn't like it when he smiled at her like that. A change of subject was definitely in order. "So, does Alija suspect you of Tarkyn Lye's assassination?"

"I don't know. She probably doesn't even know he's dead yet. I'm not all that inclined to be around when she finds out, either."

"I'm sorry," Marla said insincerely. "Has my involvement in this affair cost you a lover? Imagine how devastated I must be at the very idea."

Galon didn't rise to the bait. "What did Alija Eaglespike do to you, Marla Wolfblade, to make you hate her so much?"

"That's none of your business."

"Actually, it is," Galon corrected. "You made it my business when you asked the Raven to tell me who commissioned the kill on Tarkyn Lye."

"Then content yourself with the knowledge that her crimes against me and those I care for are numerous and heinous and leave it at that."

"It can't be just because she's a Patriot," he speculated, as if she hadn't spoken. He was moving around the room slowly, studying the murals as he went. "If you were in the habit of assassinating people just because they're Patriot sympathisers, a good third of the highborn families in Hythria would have been wiped out by now and I'd be a very rich man. I suspect it's personal."

He continued to work his way around the walls, examining Lernen's explicit murals as if they were the most absorbing thing in the room. "Does your hatred of Alija have something to do with your missing dwarf?"

Marla looked up, instantly on the defensive, but he had his back to her and she couldn't read his expression. "What do you know about Elezaar?"

"Only that he's missing." Galon shrugged. "And that Alija seems desperate to find him and you don't—which would seem to imply *you* know where he is and she doesn't."

"Elezaar is dead."

Galon glanced over his shoulder at her. "Did Alija kill him?"

"I did." It wasn't actually a lie. Elezaar's fear of Marla's reaction to his betrayal was the reason he took his own life. She was just as responsible for his death as Alija.

"And I thought you were merciless when it came to your *enemies*."

She glared at him. "Is there something you want, Galon Miar? Or did you just come here to aggravate me?"

"Ah, now that's a little complicated," he said.

His study of the murals had taken him around the room until he was on the same side of the long table as Marla. She debated standing up from her chair, to enable her to escape him more quickly if the need arose, but if she moved he would know she feared his proximity and she was in no mood to give this man any sort of power over her.

"It's a simple enough question."

"But a very complex answer."

He moved even closer. Marla tensed, wondering if she was about to die. Perhaps she'd misjudged his affection for Alija. Perhaps the thought that he could never touch Alija again without the High Arrion discovering he was Tarkyn Lye's murderer was enough to make him break the cardinal rule of his profession: *never undertake a kill not sanctioned by the guild.* Maybe Alija had actually ordered a kill on Marla and she'd just welcomed her own assassin into her private sanctum, thinking she was the clever one . . .

He was right behind her, so close her spine tingled. Before Marla could move, Galon leaned over her, placing a hand on either side of her on the table, effectively trapping Marla in her seat.

His lips were next to her ear. "I want what you have," he breathed softly.

"I'm sure I don't know what you mean."

"I think you do."

Marla was rigid but it wasn't out of fear. Galon's hot breath on her exposed neck disturbed her in a way that was both thrilling and alarming. The goosebumps that prickled her spine were caused by emotions dangerously out of place in a situation as fraught with peril as this.

"You see, Marla, I'm not the second most powerful man in the Assassins' Guild just because of my good looks and winning personality," he whispered. "Yet you managed to set me up, and you did it brilliantly. There aren't many men in this world who've done that, so I actually admire you for it."

"I have no idea what you're talking about . . ."

"Oh, yes, you do, my sweet," he purred softly. "You knew that by commissioning a kill on Tarkyn Lye and making sure I carried it out, I'd never be able to go near Alija again, unless my mind was shielded. But even more puzzling—you had the Raven tell me it was *you* who ordered the job. So I started to wonder why you weren't afraid of Alija's mind-reading abilities yourself. Now, I'm no expert on Innate magicians, but she doesn't need an embrace to read your thoughts, does she? Just a touch. It set me thinking. This trouble between you and her goes way back, I suspect, yet you're not in the least bit worried about what she'll take from your mind."

"Maybe I'm just very careful about letting her touch me," Marla suggested stiffly, wishing Galon Miar had found a less distracting way of confronting her. It was all part of his game, she knew; all part of his strategy to rattle her.

Unfortunately, it was working.

"Nonsense!" he breathed, as seductively as any lover, his lips burning the flesh of her earlobe. "I've seen you two embrace like old friends. No, Marla, my precious, you don't care if Alija touches your mind because she *can't* read it, can she? You've found a way to stop her and I'm guessing it's a whole lot more effective than any assassin mind-trick. Not to mention a lot less effort to maintain."

Marla was finding it hard to breathe. "Even if you're right, why . . . should I share my discovery with you?"

"Because you need me."

"Do I?" Marla managed a thin smile, her eyes fixed determinedly forward. "Give me one reason why I need you and I may not have you cut down where you stand for being so presumptuous."

She could feel his lips against her skin. "Let's start with your unfulfilled bargain with the Assassins' Guild. Has the Raven explained to you yet exactly what happens when we decide you've reneged on our deal?"

Marla wished she could see his eyes, but he was still behind her, almost on top of her, and moving her head would place her lips much too close to his for comfort. "That is between me and the Raven."

"Not if I'm the one who has to carry out the punishment."

His empty threat made Marla smile. "You wouldn't risk harming me, Galon Miar. And neither would the Raven."

"But you promised the guild a son, your highness. We intend to get paid. If you can't provide a live one, a dead son will do just as well."

His threat broke the spell. She jumped to her feet angrily, pushing him away. "Don't you dare threaten my family! I swear, if anything happens to one of my children . . ."

"You'll what?" he asked. "Send an assassin after me?"

"Get out!"

"You haven't heard my proposal yet."

"I'm not interested in anything further you have to say to me, Galon Miar."

He made no move to leave. "Did I mention the Raven has left it up to me to decide when to declare your debt to the Assassins' Guild forfeit?"

Marla glared at him, wishing she had never made such a foolish bargain. It had seemed so distant, so harmless a promise back then . . .

And now this man held the lives of her family in his hands. She knew the Assassins' Guild wouldn't launch a bloodbath to satisfy their debt; nor would they dare hurt Damin or Narvell, both of whom were too important in their own right for the guild to risk harming them. It was her extended family who was in danger. Luciena and Xanda's sons, who were up in Krakandar with no way to warn them of the threat. Rielle and Darvad's children in Dylan Pass. Rodja and Selena's precious newborn son. They were all close enough to Marla to discharge the debt, but unimportant enough not to raise comment.

With more courage than she thought she owned, Marla stood her ground as the assassin approached her. "What do you want?"

"I have a business proposition for you."

"I don't deal with blackmailers."

"I must be far less scrupulous than you, your highness. I'm more than happy to do business with a bad debtor."

"Just tell me what you're proposing and be gone," she demanded.

"Well . . . you see, that's it . . . I'm proposing."

Marla stared at him in stunned disbelief and then burst out laughing. She couldn't help herself. "*What*?"

"I think you should make me your next husband."

"Are you *insane*?"

"Quite the opposite. I'm offering you the opportunity of a lifetime."

"And how exactly am I supposed to benefit from this . . . *opportunity*?"

"Well, for a start, I have a son already apprenticed to the Assassins' Guild. That would solve your biggest problem at the moment."

She was breathless, marvelling at his conceit. "You have no concept of the problems I face at the moment, Galon Miar. Callous as it may sound, saving the lives of my stepchildren's sons is actually the least of them."

He didn't seem perturbed by her scorn. "This proposal's not as crazy as it sounds, Marla. What you said the other day about my involvement with Alija sending the wrong message to the Patriots is very true. You may not believe this, but I'm Royalist enough that such a thought disturbs me. Marry me and it would send the Patriots reeling."

"I am the sister of the High Prince of Hythria and you'll be the Raven of the Hythrun Assassins' Guild in the not too distant future," she pointed out. "Such a union would be unconscionable."

"I'm happy to make it a condition of the agreement that we divorce the day I become Raven," he said. "I'd rather not have to defend the guild from accusations that we're answerable to the High Prince, in any case." And then he eyed her up and down suggestively. "My reasons for this marriage aren't all altruism and loyalty to the throne, you know."

"Which brings up another pertinent question," she said, refusing to be seduced by him. "What do you possibly think I could do for you?"

"Well, for one thing, you'll promise to give me access to the protection against having my mind read that you have," he told her. "And you'll treat my children with the same generosity and favour you've shown Luciena Mariner and the Tirstone children."

She shook her head, still unable to believe she was hearing this. "Even if I thought this idea had one iota of merit, how could I possibly trust a man like you to keep up his end of the bargain?"

"If you've found a way to stop Alija reading your mind, you've probably got your own magician out there somewhere, is my guess. He can probe my mind and tell you if I'm lying, can't he? If I can be trusted?"

He'll be doing that anyway, Marla told him silently, wishing Wrayan was here now. *You can count on that.*

"And that's all you want?" she asked. "A wedding, a mind shield and access into highborn society for your children?"

"Isn't that enough?"

"For you, perhaps," she said. "You certainly haven't convinced me it's worth *my* while."

"Well, in addition to not killing one of your stepgrandsons, there's the effect our wedding would have on Alija to consider," he reminded her. "If you're out to destroy a woman and rub her nose in the fact, stealing her lover and marrying him is a fairly low blow."

"Assuming she cares enough about you to even notice you're gone," Marla remarked coolly. She was faking it, though. Of all the reasons Galon had offered to support his bizarre proposal, humiliating Alija was the one that appealed to her most.

"You assume so much about me," he said. "And yet you know so little. How do you know I wasn't simply trying to ingratiate myself into Alija's household for my own devious purposes?"

She laughed at the very idea. "Is that your story now? You've got an ulterior motive? I'll bet it's a good one, too."

"The very best," he assured her.

"But one you're conveniently not at liberty to divulge, I suppose."

"How did you guess?"

She shook her head. "You are so full of hot air, Galon Miar, I'm surprised you don't wear weights in your boots to stop you floating away on the morning breeze."

He moved closer. "That's as may be, your highness, but even if you think I'm the worst liar in the world, you're ignoring the most compelling reason of all."

Marla held her ground, refusing to be intimidated. "Which is?"

Before she could pull away, Galon took her face in his

hands and drew her to him until his lips hovered over hers. Shocked, horrified and unaccountably thrilled all at the same time, Marla froze, unsure how to react to such blatant seduction. She couldn't bear to look at him. She closed her eyes . . . waiting for his lips to touch hers. The anticipation was torture, the temptation so exquisitely dangerous . . .

The moment seemed to last forever . . .

"You might actually enjoy it," he whispered.

And then he let her go, bowed politely while Marla was still reeling, and left her alone with her thumping pulse and the certain knowledge she'd been played like an untrained virgin on her first night with a new *court'esa*.

chapter 33

Fresh from his bath following another vigorous workout with Almodavar, Damin was pulling a clean shirt over his head when he heard the bedroom door open and close behind him. Wondering who would dare enter his room without announcing themselves, he turned to discover his new *court'esa,* Prince Lunar Shadow Kraig of the House of the Rising Moon, entering the room carrying a tray with a number of small bowls, two larger bowls and what looked suspiciously like a pile of apple pips. The prince ignored Damin, walked across the room, the beads in his long hair tinkling faintly as he walked, and placed the tray on the table by the window and then finally turned to face his supposed master.

"Good morning, your highness."

"Good morning, Kraig," Damin replied a little warily as he tucked in his shirt, wondering what was going on and the significance of the tray. "Is there something I can do for you?"

The Denikan crossed his intimidatingly well-formed arms

across his massive chest and stared at Damin. He was dressed as a *court'esa* in a sleeveless embroidered vest, loose linen trousers and a jewelled slave collar, but still managed to give the impression he was the master and not the slave here.

"I wish to discuss our arrangement."

"Is there something about it that doesn't please you?" Damin asked. He couldn't imagine what the Denikan's complaint might be. Kraig and his bodyguards were accommodated in the *court'esa* quarters of Cabradell Palace in quite decadent luxury and had been left in peace since Tejay had arranged their transfer into Damin's care, in no danger of being forced to prove they were actually *court'esa*. In fact, he'd barely spared any of them a thought since Tejay had suggested her plan to hide Kraig in Damin's entourage more than two weeks ago.

"Yes, there is something that does not please me."

"What's the problem?"

"You."

"*Me*?" Damin said, quite taken aback. "What have I done?"

"Nothing," Kraig informed him quite crossly, "which is precisely my complaint. The success of this deception requires everyone to play their part, your highness. You are not pulling your weight and your reluctance—for whatever reason—is endangering us all."

"Hang on!" Damin said in confusion. "Let me get this straight. You're here posing as my *court'esa* and I'm in trouble for not calling on your services?"

"The reason for this charade," the Denikan prince reminded him, "is to conceal my identity and the identity of my companions until we can secure safe passage home, while at the same time, deceiving your enemies into believing you and your uncle share a similarly foolish and venal nature."

"I know, but—"

"It may inconvenience you, Damin Wolfblade," the prince continued, allowing Damin no chance to defend himself, "to have your people realise you are not what you seem, but it will cost me and my companions our lives if the same becomes true for us. For whatever reason, you have chosen not to do what Lady Lionsclaw asked of you. Be it some misguided sense of propriety or simply squeamishness on your part, your reluctance to make use of such a valuable gift—as we Denikans so obviously are in your culture—is to both demean us and to cast doubt on the veracity of our arrangement. You ignore us at your peril."

Damin reluctantly conceded that Kraig had a point. "I didn't really think about it like that, to tell the truth."

"That is abundantly clear," the prince agreed. "Which is why I have taken matters into my own hands."

"*You've* taken matters into your own hands?"

Kraig nodded decisively. "As of tonight, Lyrian and Barlaina will take turns coming to your room. I am sending Lyrian to you first because apparently she considers you . . . not unattractive. If you treat her well, she will report this to Barlaina and she should give you only a little trouble when it is her turn."

"Only a *little* trouble?"

Kraig hesitated and then squared his shoulders manfully, as if he was about to make a confession. "I fear I might have misled you, your highness, when I described my companions as bodyguards. They are, in fact, members of the Denikan Warrior Caste, noblewomen in their own right and used to being treated as such. It is a little hard to explain what this means to one not of our . . . society. Suffice to say, it would be more accurate to compare Lyrian and Barlaina to members of your Assassins' Guild rather than your Raiders."

"Oh . . ." Damin said, unsure how to respond to such a revelation.

That answer seemed enough for Kraig. "Lyrian, being the younger, is slightly more tolerant of foreigners. Barlaina, on the other hand, is highly critical of many Hythrun customs. In particular, she disdains your need for *court'esa* and believes you treat your womenfolk like breeding cattle."

Damin smiled. He couldn't help himself. "I can assure

you, Kraig, the *last* thing that leaps to mind when I think of Lyrian or Barlaina is the word *cow*."

Kraig wasn't amused. "Can we consider the matter settled?"

"I suppose. But what about you?" he asked curiously, wondering how far Kraig intended to take this charade. "When shall I send for you, *slave*?"

"I am here now."

That caught Damin off guard. "Ah . . . I see . . ."

"Clearly, you do *not* see," Kraig told him impatiently. "You and I will spend time together playing."

"Playing what, exactly?"

"I will teach you the seed game," the Denikan announced. He spoke as if it was some great favour only bestowed on someone blessed by the gods.

"Sounds . . . riveting . . ." Damin replied, not wishing to offend him.

"It is riveting. We teach the seed game to young children in Denika to promote strategic thinking and forward planning. It takes a moment to learn and a lifetime to master." Kraig uncrossed his arms and turned to the tray he'd brought with him and began to arrange the bowls on the table. "In Denika, I am considered a master."

"What about the meeting I have this morning?" Damin asked, thinking Kraig had a lot to learn about the nature of the relationship between a slave and his master if he expected to carry off his disguise, particularly given his disapproval of Damin's behaviour. "In about three minutes, I'm supposed to be meeting with the senior officers of our combined forces to discuss the logistics of moving the army west once we find out what Hablet is up to."

"Make them wait."

"What shall I tell them?"

"That you're playing with your *court'esa*."

Damin grinned. "You know, I think underneath that stern and implacable snarl you wear all the time, Kraig, you have quite a sense of humour."

The Denikan smiled briefly. "In my own country, I am

also considered something of a wit." He pulled out the chair and sat down. "Sit," he commanded, indicating the chair opposite.

Damin did as Kraig commanded. "I guess the Denikan sense of humour is different than ours."

"Not at all, your highness. Many things you do amuse me. I am simply too polite to laugh at a fellow prince."

"I'm not," Damin chuckled, and then looked down at the table. "So, what're the rules of this seed game of yours?"

Kraig had arranged the small bowls so there were six on each side of the table with a larger bowl at either end. He was counting the seeds into each of the small bowls. "You own the six bowls nearest you. Your aim is to fill the large bowl at the end with seeds. The one on your right is your bowl. The one on my right is mine. This game is an ancient tradition in Denika, although in my country, when we play, we use gemstones or coloured beads instead of seeds."

"That's all I have to do? Move the seeds?"

"We begin with four seeds in every bowl," the prince explained. "You may choose to start in any bowl on your side of the table you wish and sow the seeds, one at a time, in each bowl in this direction. When you come to your own large bowl, you may place a seed in it. When you come to my large bowl, you jump over it. When you run out of seeds it is my turn. We continue like this, turn about, until all the seeds are gone or you have no seeds in your small bowls. The winner is the one with the greatest number of seeds in their large bowl at the end of the game."

Damin nodded slowly, thinking he could probably master this seed game of Kraig's quite easily. *How hard could it be to place a handful of seeds in a line of ceramic bowls?*

"You must accustom yourself to defeat," Kraig warned. "I am an expert at this game and will, of course, defeat you soundly. However, if you pay attention and listen to my advice, you may, after a time, become a tolerable opponent. Or at least one who keeps me occupied."

"I may, may I?"

"I do not mean to insult you, your highness. I simply refer

to both your youth and inexperience, neither of which are your fault. I will be patient with you."

Damin couldn't help his smile. He'd never met anybody quite so arrogantly condescending as Prince Lunar Shadow Kraig of the House of the Rising Moon. Or anybody who seemed less aware of it. "Tell you what, let's throw in a small wager on the outcome?"

"You wish to wager something? Even though I have warned you I am a master?"

"I do have to keep up the useless wastrel image, you know . . ."

Kraig inclined his head in agreement. "You are correct. What do you wish to wager?"

"How about Medalon?"

Kraig frowned. "Medalon is an independent nation to the north of Hythria, is it not? One you do not actually own?"

Damin shrugged. "Mere detail."

Kraig allowed himself another brief smile. "Very well, your highness. I accept your wager of Medalon and offer you the Principality of Rostinelle in return."

"The Principality of Rostinelle?" Damin asked. "Never heard of it."

"It is a smallish nation on the western border of Denika," Kraig explained. "It is peopled by a race of barbarians with little to recommend them other than their numerous emerald deposits. Even calling it a principality may be a little optimistic, given the brutal nature of its citizenry, but I don't think 'thugipality' is a word in either your language or mine."

Damin grinned. "The same could be said for the Sisters of the Blade in Medalon, your highness. Who goes first?"

"It doesn't matter. I will beat you either way."

"Really?"

"As I said, I am a master."

"You seem to be a master of a lot of things, Kraig."

The Denikan nodded solemnly. "I am."

There wasn't much he could say to that so Damin scooped up the seeds from the bowl closest to him and began to distribute them according to Kraig's instructions, wondering how long it would be before Narvell sent somebody looking for him.

And what the reaction was going to be when he sent back a message saying he was too busy to attend the meeting because he was playing with his *court'esa*.

CHAPTER 34

F inding intelligence about the Hythrun wasn't as simple as Brak had hoped. There was as much rumour doing the rounds in Cabradell as there was useful information and no way to tell the difference. It wasn't troop numbers they were after. Any man with ten fingers and ten toes could count the troops massing around Cabradell well enough to report back to Axelle Regis. Real intelligence involved things that were *going* to happen, not things that already had.

Such information wasn't easy to come by, however. Since arriving in Cabradell they'd drunk in so many taverns as they listened to one useless rumour after another that Brak was starting to fear he might inadvertently turn poor Ollie into a drunkard. He was tempted to make his way up to the palace, sit himself down under a nice shady tree somewhere and scan the minds of anybody he could reach, to find out for certain what was happening. Brak was reluctant to cheat like that, though. For one thing, he would never be able to explain the source of his intelligence without admitting how he got it, which also meant admitting who he was. The other reason was simply pig-headedness. This was a human war and nobody, particularly Hablet of Fardohnya, deserved an unfair advantage.

Zegarnald was obviously going to get his war, but Brak had no intention of making it easier for him.

And then, just when they were on the verge of returning to Fardohnya empty-handed, they stumbled upon a man who was in a position to give them real information, not just speculation or wild guesses. Brak met him in a tavern not far from the north gate of the city, the gate closest to the palace. The palace itself was located about a half mile outside the city walls on a small hill overlooking the Cabradell Valley.

He was a nobleman. An officer under Lord Hawksword's command with the Elasapine troops and his name was Stefan Warhaft.

Lord Warhaft, it seemed, had good cause to drown his sorrows. This was the man the old apothecary in Urso had spoken of. The man whose wife had caught the eye of the High Prince's heir and had her stolen from him without so much as a by-your-leave. The man was depressed, angry and anxious to tell his tale to any soul willing to listen. Brak and Ollie bought him ale and offered a sympathetic ear. That was all Warhaft was looking for.

According to Warhaft, it wasn't just Damin Wolfblade at fault, it was his half-brother, Narvell Hawksword, who started it all.

If Warhaft was to be believed, the Hawksword boy had arrived in Zadenka some months ago to wait out the plague and—being a typical descendant of that useless pervert, Lernen Wolfblade—decided to relieve his boredom with Warhaft's wife. When Lord Warhaft learned of the affair, he was justifiably outraged and took it upon himself to correct his wife's foolish ways which, Brak assumed, meant that he'd beaten the poor girl senseless. Aided by some renegade member of the Sorcerers' Collective, she'd run away (understandably, in Brak's opinion), straight into the arms of her lover, who unfortunately was in the company of his older brother—the High Prince's heir—by the time Warhaft caught up with her.

Warhaft gripped his tankard until his knuckles turned white as he related his tale.

"What happened then?" Brak asked.

"Well, his royal bloody highness gets involved, of course!" Warhaft growled, taking a good swallow of his ale. "And who do you think he sided with? The cheating slut's husband? Her rightful master? Or his slimy, two-faced, wife-stealing brother?"

"I'm guessing the slimy, two-faced, wife-stealing brother."

"The *bastard*!" Ollie exclaimed in disgust.

Brak frowned at the lad, wishing he'd either leave, have a bath, or move downwind. The young bandit had taken his advice about horses and the plague quite literally. In his desperation to avoid the disease, he'd taken to smearing horse dung on his bare arms when they first arrived in the city.

Brak had convinced him eventually that it was the general smell of horses and not necessarily their excrement that deterred the fleas, so now he wore an old horse blanket he'd traded for his warm fur coat, preferring to be cold rather than infected. But he still wore the unmistakable aroma of a stable about him, which was rather unpleasant, particularly if one was trying to eat.

Warhaft didn't seem to notice the smell, though, so Brak said nothing and turned his attention back to the unhappy nobleman.

"But surely even a prince couldn't just take your wife from you like that?" Brak asked.

"Oh, no, he's too sly to openly flout the law. He dug up some thousand-year-old statute that allows him to place my wife in the custody of the bloody Sorcerers' Collective until the High Prince makes a ruling, can you believe it?" The man emptied his tankard in a swallow and slammed it down on the table. "And of course, the bastard who stole her from my house just happens to be another Wolfblade cousin-by-marriage apparently, who conveniently just happens to belong to the Sorcerers' Collective. So now I'm stuck in the war camp and my whore of a wife is strutting about the Cabradell palace like she owns it, probably spreading her favours around between both the Wolfblade brothers and all their damned cousins, for all I know."

"That's appalling!" Ollie agreed. "More ale?"

Warhaft thrust his tankard forward. Ollie filled it from the jug on the table and then waved to the barkeep to bring more. Brak wondered what sort of nightmare offspring Lernen Wolfblade was planning to unleash on the world. Having heard Wrayan Lightfinger go on endlessly about what a fine job Marla was doing raising her sons a few years ago, he reasoned either Warhaft was lying or Wrayan was blind.

"A man shouldn't have to go to war with something like that hanging over him," Brak sympathised.

"War? What bloody war?" he complained. "It's not going to be much of a war with Lernen Wolfblade in command. That's assuming these rumours about the Fardohnyans massing for an invasion aren't just an excuse young Wolfblade thought up to gather up his army and go whoring around the countryside. Did you hear what he did in Krakandar?"

"No."

"Ripped his uncle's throat out with his bare hands and left him for dead, they say. It's a miracle the man is still alive."

"Surely not!" Ollie gasped.

Warhaft nodded eagerly, warming to his attentive audience. "They had an argument over another girl, I hear. Young Wolfblade has a temper you wouldn't credit. The man's an animal when he's enraged. Which is why I didn't call him out over Kendra," he added hastily.

"Perfectly understandable!" Ollie agreed.

I'm going to have to talk to this boy about accepting everything he hears without question, Brak decided. He didn't doubt for a moment there was a kernel of truth in Stefan Warhaft's tale, but he could read between the lines well enough to appreciate that it wasn't quite so black and white as the man would have them believe.

"You said *Lernen* Wolfblade was in command?" Brak reminded him, hoping to get the conversation back where he wanted it. "Is the High Prince here in Cabradell, too?"

"He's on his way," Warhaft confirmed. "We got the news a few days ago that he'd decided to lead the troops himself. And he's bringing the rest of our forces from the southern provinces with him, according to Damin Wolfblade."

Brak forced himself not to smile. Zegarnald wasn't going to get much of a war with that idiot Lernen Wolfblade in charge of the Hythrun defences.

Warhaft chuckled nastily and added, "The only *good* thing about that useless prick Lernen Wolfblade being on his way was his nephew's reaction to the news. Apparently, he was ropable." The man smiled unpleasantly. "I'd have paid good money to see that."

"Do you think he'll make trouble?" Ollie asked.

"He certainly objected loudly enough, I'm told!" Warhaft laughed. "Not that it'll do him any good. He's too young to lead us anyway. Not even twenty-five until the end of summer. To be honest, I'll follow Lernen Wolfblade to the very gates of the deepest of the seven hells if it means I get to watch that arrogant, jumped-up nephew of his grinding his teeth in frustration over it."

Why bother with an invasion, Zegarnald? Brak wondered silently. *At this rate they'll tear themselves to pieces. You don't need Hablet for the job.*

"Is he bringing many troops?" Brak enquired.

Warhaft shrugged disinterestedly. "A couple of thousand from Pentamor and Greenharbour, I hear. And Cyrus Eaglespike is right behind him with another three thousand from Dregian. Lady Lionsclaw's brother is supposed to be sending us reinforcements from Izcomdar, too, and Wolfblade claims he had another twenty-five centuries of Raiders on their way from Krakandar, but we've seen no sign of them yet."

Brak did a quick mental calculation. With the five thousand troops already here in Cabradell, maybe half that many again from Sunrise added to the mix, only another five thousand on the way and the vague possibility of reinforcements from Izcomdar and Krakandar, it meant the Hythrun had been able to muster less than fifteen thousand men. For the first time, Brak began to fully appreciate the effect the plague must have had on Hythria. Each province should have been able to muster twenty thousand men on its own.

Even more concerning was the thought Hablet had already gathered twice that number in Qorinipor, nearly two months ago. There was no telling what the final number was by now, or what he'd mustered on the coast at Tambay's Seat in the interim.

"Well," Brak said, topping up Warhaft's tankard, "this whole ridiculous rumour about the Fardohnyans invading Hythria is probably a load of horseshit, anyway. By the sound of it, I reckon you were right the first time, my lord. It's just young Wolfblade looking for an excuse to go whoring around the countryside, throwing his weight around."

"Aye," the disgruntled nobleman agreed. "Has a taste for the high life, does Lernen's heir, just like his uncle. Still it's all right if you know how to pander to him. Lady Lionsclaw just gave him a gift to keep him occupied, did you hear? Three . . . *three*, mind you . . . Denikan *court'esa*. A matched trio they are—a man and two women. They're priceless. I'll give Tejay Lionsclaw one thing—she knows how to stay in his good graces. Still, I suppose that's because he was fostered with her father as a boy. She probably learned how to manage him then." Warhaft took another long swallow and then stared at the bottom of his tankard with a frown when he realised it was empty. "Anyway, I doubt we'll have to worry about him too much when we finally engage the enemy. I hear he's planning to take his *court'esa* with him when we move out. No doubt he'll be too busy with them and that whoring wife of mine to actually contribute anything useful to the battle."

Brak refilled his tankard, shaking his head sympathetically. "Sounds truly dreadful."

"You've no idea what it's like having a Wolfblade in command."

"It must be terrible," Ollie agreed. "But what sort of things does he do?"

Brak sighed. *Don't be subtle about it, Ollie,* he lamented silently. *Come right out and tell the man we're pumping him for information.*

Fortunately, Warhaft didn't seem to notice. "I'll give you a good example," he offered drunkenly. "Called us all to a meeting the other day, he did, and then kept us all waiting for an hour or more. And do you know *why*?"

"Why?" Ollie asked breathlessly.

"I'll tell you why! The stupid prick was fooling around with his new toys! Arrogant little bastard even sent a message back telling us to wait for him. Said he was 'playing' with his *court'esa* and we'd just have to wait until he was done."

Ollie was disgusted. "That's just . . . *wrong*."

Brak looked at the lad askance, wondering if perhaps it wasn't high time he took him aside and explained a few home truths about Hablet to the young man. The Wolfblades might be a degenerate lot, but there was probably much less blood on their hands than on the hands of Ollie's precious Fardohnyan king.

"It's a truly sad state of affairs," Brak agreed, emptying the jug into Warhaft's tankard. "It's a good thing we're headed in the opposite direction."

"I wouldn't worry too much, my friend," Warhaft predicted grimly. "With a Wolfblade in command of Hythria's defence, we'll all be kissing the hem of Hablet's cloak before the end of summer. You mark my words."

"Did you hear what Warhaft said?" Ollie gushed as they headed back to their lodgings later that evening. The young Fardohnyan was fairly bouncing up and down with the news the Hythrun baron had shared with them.

"I heard."

"Should we send a message home? Let them know what we've learned?"

"That's what we came here for."

"When do we leave?"

"*You* can leave in the morning."

Ollie stopped and stared at Brak with concern. "What about you?"

"I think I'll hang around until Lernen gets here and then follow you later. General Regis would probably appreciate final numbers once they're all mustered."

The lad thought about Brak's suggestion and then nodded. "That's probably a good idea. What shall I tell him?"

"That the Hythrun know he's coming. That they've been able to muster less than fifteen thousand men. And that the High Prince of Hythria is in command of their army, assisted by his nephew, who doesn't appear to be much more sensible than his uncle."

Ollie grinned. "It's going to be a pushover, this war, isn't it?"

"War is never a pushover, Ollie," Brak told him as he turned into the street where their lodgings were located. "And I hope you never have to find that out the hard way."

chapter 35

arla returned from the palace quite late and sent for Wrayan almost as soon as she got home. Kalan had gone to visit Rodja and Selena, so except for the slaves, they were effectively alone in the house. Once she realised there was little chance of Kalan walking in on them by accident again (however innocently they were behaving) the princess seemed to relax a little. She offered Wrayan a seat on the cushions but remained standing, pacing the room as if she was too restless to stand still.

"I had a visitor today at the palace."

Wrayan poured wine for himself and Marla and handed her a cup. She accepted it absently, as she continued to pace the tiles. "Anyone I know?"

"I'm not certain."

He waited expectantly.

"Galon Miar," the princess said, after a long moment.

Wrayan frowned as he realised where he'd heard of him. "I know that name."

"I thought you might."

Unlike the Thieves' Guild, which tended to have its own independent chapter in every city of note in the same way the other trade guilds did, the Assassins' Guild had only one chapter based here in the capital with tentacles that reached into every strata of Hythrun society. Despite his relative isolation in Krakandar these past twenty years, even Wrayan knew of Galon Miar.

"I hope you know what you're doing, your highness. Not even you should play games with the Assassins' Guild."

She shrugged and sipped her cup of wine. "Galon Miar strikes me as nothing more than an over-confident, ambitious social climber trying to sleep his way to power."

"That man is a trained killer, your highness, and far smarter than you give him credit for. He was being spoken of as the next Raven long before he hopped into Alija Eaglespike's bed. I'd be very, *very* careful, if I were you. Particularly if he's wrapped up in Alija's schemes."

"Do you think a man like that might actually feel something for Alija?"

Wrayan shook his head. "I know his type. He likes powerful women and he likes beautiful women, but the Galon Miars of this world would never risk falling in love with either one of them. It compromises his professional ethics to do anything so human. But that doesn't stop him from lusting after women like her. Or you for that matter."

Marla suddenly coughed, choking on her wine, and then stared at him so hard, Wrayan wondered if he'd inadvertently stumbled onto something the princess hadn't been planning to share with him.

"Don't be ridiculous!" Marla sounded as if she was trying to convince herself as much as Wrayan. "I've barely spared the man a civil word the whole time I've known him."

"Which probably makes you all the more attractive to him." Wrayan sipped his wine thoughtfully. "Sort of leaves you wondering why he set his cap at Alija, rather than you, come to think of it."

Marla was silent for an awkwardly long time then she suddenly turned and stared at Wrayan. "What would you say if I told you he has?"

"Set his cap at you?" he asked, and then added without hesitation, "I'd suggest that you run like hell."

"You never complained when I told you I was thinking of marrying a common spice merchant."

"Ruxton Tirstone didn't kill people for a living."

Marla smiled. "You've obviously never spoken to any of his competitors."

"I'm serious, your highness."

"So am I." She put down her cup on the side table. "But you can relax, Wrayan. I'm not going to play that game. I'm quite aware how dangerous Galon Miar is. As soon as I conclude my business with the guild, I'll have nothing more to do with him."

"Can you be sure of that?"

"We have a barely civil relationship based on some unfinished business I have with his guild and a mutual acquaintance in the High Arrion." Then she smiled deviously, as another thought occurred to her. "I can't imagine Alija will be too pleased, though, to learn her lover has a wandering eye."

"Assuming she knows."

"Given Galon Miar's open flirtation every time I set eyes on him, I'm fairly certain she would have some idea."

"Then you're right. She'd be furious. Alija already thinks

you've robbed her of Hythria's throne. The idea you'd stolen her lover as well would be like rubbing salt into an open wound."

Marla laughed humourlessly. "It's almost tempting, just to see her squirm. And the irony is," she added, obviously amused by the thought, "she can't say anything to Galon without betraying the fact that every time he touches her, she can read his thoughts."

"More fool him then."

"He's many things, Wrayan, but I doubt a fool is one of them. What do you suppose she'd do?"

Wrayan looked at her blankly. "What would who do?"

"Alija? If I stole her lover from her?"

"You can't be serious!"

"I was just wondering . . ."

Wrayan put down his wine and stared at her in concern. "Please, your highness, don't wonder about it. Not even in jest."

Marla laughed. "Look at you, Wrayan. I swear, you've gone quite pale."

"Because I can't decide which would be more dangerous— challenging Alija so openly, or inviting a viper like Galon Miar into your bed."

"Given that we are actively plotting to destroy the High Arrion, Wrayan, I think it's a bit late to start worrying about challenging her. As for Galon . . . are you suggesting I couldn't handle him?"

"I'm suggesting you don't even try."

"Perhaps we should discover what is in Master Miar's mind, then, before we involve ourselves with him," the princess suggested.

Wrayan looked at her suspiciously. "What exactly do you mean by *we*?"

Marla hesitated and then walked to the sideboard to refill her cup.

"I want you to read his mind, Wrayan, and tell me if I can trust him," she said, her back to him quite deliberately so he couldn't see her expression.

"You can't trust him," he stated emphatically.

Marla turned before she replied. "Do you know this for a fact?"

"He's an *assassin*, your highness. You do *know* what that means, don't you?"

"Gracious, *no!*" Marla exclaimed with mock astonishment. "Perhaps you should explain it to me, Wrayan."

"Your highness," he sighed. "I'm not trying to insult you. I just want you to be very sure you know what you're dealing with. Assassins take an oath, binding until death, which places loyalty to their guild above loyalty to everything and *everybody* else. Even if you could trust Galon Miar, you could only trust him up to the point where the Assassins' Guild invoked his bond to that oath. After that, he has no choice. There's a reason they have that old saying about thieves and assassins knowing no borders."

Marla looked down at him apologetically. "I know you have my best interests at heart, Wrayan, and believe me, the issue of whether or not I trust Galon Miar goes to the heart of that interest. I made a deal with the Assassins' Guild, you might recall, a long time ago. In hindsight, I realise I wasn't thinking all that clearly. The cost of that . . . *incident* . . . involved more than just an exchange of money. And now that deal has come back to bite me. It's a problem I could well do without and Galon Miar has suggested a . . . somewhat radical . . . solution. I need to know if it's an option."

Wrayan stared at her curiously.

"What did you do?" he joked. "Promise the Raven the soul of your firstborn child, or something?"

"You would be horrified to learn how close to the truth you are, Wrayan."

Suddenly, Marla's willingness to deal with a man like Galon Miar made sense.

"You promised the guild a son." It wasn't a question.

"Are you reading my mind?" she asked in alarm.

He shook his head. "It's a common practice in the Assassins' Guild. Part of the reason they're so successful is their ability to infiltrate every level of society, from slave to high-born. Whenever the opportunity comes along, they ask for a son in addition to the payment. They don't need the children to bolster their numbers. It's more about the network they build up in the process. And for a man with three or four spare heirs, it's a useful way to take care of a younger son. It gives the guild access to places they wouldn't normally be able to recruit from, and it's a pretty good way of making sure they stay in business."

"How do you mean?"

"With almost every noble house in Hythria having some sort of connection to the Assassins' Guild, however vague, they're not likely to be shut down without a protest." He smiled wistfully and added, "I'd do the same thing in the Thieves' Guild if I thought anybody was frightened enough of our wrath to agree to handing over their sons and daughters to become disciples of Dacendaran."

Marla shook her head in amazement. "And all this time I thought your only use to me, Wrayan, was your magical ability to shield and read minds. I never knew you were such an authority on the Assassins' Guild."

"Our territories cross fairly frequently, your highness. It's a bit difficult to avoid the assassins completely when you're a thief. I suppose they're calling in the debt?"

"Not yet," she said. "I have it on good authority, however, that my time is running out. It also appears I didn't hear the bit about taking a son meant just that—taking a son. Dead or alive."

"Your eldest son is the High Prince's heir," he assured her. "Your second son is the heir to Elasapine. The Assassins' Guild wouldn't risk harming either one of them over something like this."

"Of course not," Marla agreed. "But it was pointed out to me, in no uncertain terms, that I have stepchildren, and some of them have children of their own. Apparently the guild isn't too fussy about the bond being one of blood."

He nodded in understanding. "Then you really do have a problem, your highness. What can I do to help?"

"Tell me about Galon Miar," Marla said, as if she could shrug off the seriousness of her dilemma. "Is he some nobleman's third son, apprenticed to the guild in return for a favour? Or does he just act as if he's highborn because it amuses him?"

"I don't know," Wrayan told her. "But I can probably find out."

"I'd appreciate that."

Sensing the audience was over, he rose to his feet and bowed. "It may take a day or two."

"Just let me know when you have something useful. In the meantime, I'll arrange for Master Miar to pay us a visit so you can examine his mind and tell me how far he can be trusted."

"As you wish, your highness."

"Goodnight, Wrayan."

"Goodnight, your highness."

He turned for the door but Marla stopped him dead in his tracks when she remarked casually, "Did I mention that Tarkyn Lye is dead?"

Wrayan spun around to stare at her. "When did *that* happen?"

"Yesterday sometime, I believe."

"How did he die?"

"Someone slit his throat," she informed him calmly. "Right in the middle of Alija's bed, I hear."

He stared at the princess. "Did it cost you much?"

Marla smiled coldly. "Not as much as it's going to cost Alija," she said.

entlemen, I have a proposition for you."

The gathering turned to look at Starros, their expressions hard to read in the flickering lamplight. They were ensconced in the back room of the Pickpocket's Retreat, a place, Starros had recently learned, where most of Wrayan Lightfinger's more underhanded transactions were carried out.

He'd been a little surprised to learn about this room. Starros had always had a vaguely noble picture of Wrayan as gentleman thief, settled into his own private corner of the taproom, dispensing wisdom and stolen property with equal panache. He forgot, sometimes, that the Thieves' Guild was no place for the faint-hearted and that the reason Wrayan Lightfinger was considered one of the greatest thieves in all of Hythria was that when it came to his honouring the God of Thieves, he was unrelenting. And he wasn't in the least bit squeamish about it either, Starros guessed, eyeing a few of the stains on the long wooden table that looked more like blood than beer.

Like Starros, Wrayan had sold his soul to a god. It was sobering, sometimes, to realise what that meant.

"You found something worth stealing?" The man asking the question was Kylo Korenne, a pickpocket who worked the markets in the central ring near the palace. A slender little man with lightning-quick reflexes, he was one of the four men Wrayan had appointed to his informal council of thieves. In his absence, no significant business in the guild's name took place without the council's approval, which was why Starros was here tonight. Sick of pilfering small items from the palace, he'd come up with something much more ambitious; something that would require the approval of the Thieves' Guild council.

"People."

Medin Crow, a thin-faced burglar who worked the more salubrious part of town, took a swallow of ale before announcing, "People ain't worth stealing . . . unless they're slaves or hostages."

"They are if you're stealing them out from under the nose of the very person trying to keep them confined."

"What do you mean?" the third man in the council asked. His name was Vale Granger and he was rather cagey about exactly what he did. The fourth member of the council, Luc North, sat opposite Starros at the other end of the long table listening to them, but saying little.

"I mean, gentlemen, that if the Regent of Krakandar won't unseal the city, we will. We're going to open up a route out of the city. And charge for it."

"Strictly speaking," Luc North mused, "that's extortion, not theft."

"If Mahkas Damaran finds out about it, I'm not sure he'll care too much about the distinction," Starros said.

"Get them out how?" Vale asked.

"The same way we do when we don't want to be seen."

"But to do that, we'd have to reveal the routes through the sewers to outsiders."

"Only one," Starros said. "And if we choose it carefully, we can make sure it doesn't intersect with any of the other routes."

"And if the Raiders catch us . . . hell, Lord Damaran hanged poor old Umbrose for just complaining out loud about the city still being sealed. I hate to think what they'd do to us if they caught us selling passage out of the city. Defying the Regent is treason, you know."

"I have a plan for that, too," Starros announced.

Medin Crow scowled at him. "Been a thief for ten bloody minutes and now he has a *plan*. This ought to be a good'un."

Starros ignored the man's derision. "I think I can arrange for the palace guards to turn a blind eye to our activities."

"How?"

"Xanda Taranger is currently in the palace, and he has

some influence over the guards. He can't do it officially, but he can whisper in the right ears. More importantly, he'll know the *right* ears to whisper into."

"Nice plan, Starros, but how the hell are you going to get into the palace to speak to Xanda Taranger? And what's to stop him having you arrested the moment he lays eyes on you? You're not exactly welcome up at the big house these days, I hear."

"Don't worry about the how," Luc advised the men. "Starros can come and go as he pleases to the palace. But Kylo does have a point, lad. Are you *certain* he won't have you arrested on sight? Word is he's mightily close to his uncle these days."

"Only because Damin asked him to stay here in the city and watch over things until he returns. I'd bet my life on Xanda not betraying me to Mahkas."

"You *will* be betting your life on it, my friend," Luc pointed out. "But if you think it's worth the risk of making contact with him, then do it. Knowing the palace guard isn't going to make a surprise appearance every time we escort a group of people through the sewers will make it easier to co-ordinate. And don't think it won't take a lot of work to open a route, Starros. To get out of the city through the sewers, even from the Beggars' Quarter, is going to take a lot of negotiation. The shortest route crosses the territory of a half dozen different thieves and none of them is going to be thrilled by the idea of exposing their secrets, even for a profit."

"And it's not going to be the shortest route you want," another man added, "but the safest."

"And the least strenuous," Starros added. "Some of these people will have children with them."

"Which raises an interesting point," Kylo remarked. "Why should we just help the rich get free? Don't seem right opening up a route and only letting out them what can pay for it."

Luc smiled. "Why Kylo, I do believe you're getting sentimental in your old age."

"Well . . . I was just thinking, that's all. There's a profit to be made here for certain, but admit it. What we'd all *really* like to see is that bastard Mahkas Damaran suffering a whole world of grief. I don't know about you, but I'd like to see his little empire come crashing down on top of him." A series of nods around the room indicated their agreement. "So let's do what the lad says. Let's steal his people."

"All of them?" Starros asked in astonishment.

"All of them," the old thief agreed. "Let's honour Dacendaran and pull off the greatest heist in history! Let's rob an entire city of its people."

"It would take an unprecedented level of cooperation," Starros mused. "You'd need to involve every guild in the city."

"Why the other guilds?" Luc asked.

"Because knocking on someone's door in the middle of the night without warning and suggesting they come with us to the sewers isn't going to wash with the vast majority of people. There are more than twenty thousand people in the city. To move them quietly, we'll need the guilds to disseminate the information and coordinate the exodus. We're not going to get all the people out in one night. That would be physically impossible. We're going to have to do it over a period of days, so we need to make it happen around a Restday."

"Why Restday?"

"So it's not immediately obvious a goodly portion of the city's workforce is nowhere to be found."

"And we need somewhere for them to go," Vale added, warming to the idea. "You can't just get them out of the city and have them milling about outside the walls, waving at the guards, waiting for someone to take a shot at them."

"Walsark would be the nearest safe place," Starros said. "The Lord of Walsark is Xanda Taranger's brother. I'm certain he'll shelter our people, temporarily at least."

"You're still relying on the cooperation of Mahkas Damaran's own nephews to make this work," Kylo warned. "That's more risk than I like on a job."

"Damin Wolfblade is Mahkas Damaran's nephew,"

Starros reminded him. "You don't seem to have a problem with him."

"Our prince is Laran Krakenshield's son."

"Travin and Xanda Taranger are Laran Krakenshield's nephews, too. I know them. They can be trusted."

"Wrayan trusts Starros, Starros trusts the Taranger brothers, and we trust Wrayan," Luc North pointed out. "If we're going to honour Dacendaran in such a spectacular fashion, there's got to be a risk, or it's no honour at all. And like Kylo says . . . think about the effect this is going to have on Mahkas Damaran."

Vale nodded. "Aye. Lady Leila was the most precious jewel in Krakandar's crown. After what that mongrel did to her . . ."

The other thieves indicated their agreement, which still left Starros shaking his head in bemusement, even though he'd encountered dozens of thieves since joining the Thieves' Guild who behaved as if his loss was theirs as well.

Most of these men had never even seen Leila, except from a distance, and they'd certainly never met her, yet her beating and her suicide had affected the whole city. To Starros, it seemed as if the entire Thieves' Guild thought of Leila as some kind of delicate piece of artwork that had belonged to the whole of Krakandar and her death was like having their precious painting stolen from them. They were more than happy to aid in taking vengeance on the man they considered her thief.

"It's settled then," Luc announced, looking around the room at the others for their agreement. "We steal Krakandar's people." He glanced up at Starros. "When Wrayan told you to steal something of value from Mahkas Damaran, lad, you really took him literally, didn't you?"

Starros smiled. "Blame it on Orleon. He always claimed a job worth doing was worth doing properly."

"Then take a seat, lad," Kylo advised. "We've got a long night ahead of us."

The discussion after that turned to the practicalities of

evacuating the entire population of Krakandar out from under the nose of her regent, the work to be done and who they needed to bring in on the plan in the early stages.

Starros took a seat between Vale and Medin, thinking that if this actually worked, he might really be able to claim he was a criminal mastermind after all.

chapter 37

lija Eaglespike had faced more than her share of hard decisions during her life. She'd ordered the deaths of every man, woman and child in Ronan Dell's household and never lost a moment's sleep over it. When she was being honest with herself, Alija was even prepared to acknowledge she'd been responsible for more people dying than she could count with her decision to unleash the plague on Greenharbour in the hope it would strike down a few Wolfblades as it ravaged the city. She'd arranged for others to die more directly, too. And at last count, she'd been responsible for at least six direct attacks on Damin Wolfblade over the past twenty-four years, never mind the other deaths she had so calmly arranged.

Not once, in all that time, had Alija felt a moment of remorse, or experienced even a whisper of guilt.

Until she walked into her bedroom and found Tarkyn Lye splayed across the covers with his throat cut.

Alija knew it was her fault. He had died because of her. Without her, Tarkyn was nothing more than an old, blind slave who'd long outlived his usefulness as a *court'esa*. It was his relationship with the High Arrion of the Sorcerers' Collective that gave the man standing.

And his relationship with Alija had cost him his life.

She was paralysed with grief for the first few days after it happened, unable to think straight. Unable to eat. Unable to stop blubbering. Nothing made sense and even Tressa, the slave who had been with her for the last two decades, could do nothing to console her mistress. Alija had wept an ocean of tears. It was days before she was thinking clearly enough to even consider vengeance.

Once she was able to think about it, however, her first thought was the Assassins' Guild. Someone had obviously paid to have Tarkyn killed. His slave collar was missing, probably souvenired by the assassin as proof of the kill. And the cut had been a clean one; a simple and effective slice, almost certainly done from behind. That fact alone made it a certainty the Assassins' Guild had been responsible.

Tarkyn was blind. His other senses were sharper to compensate. Nobody sneaked up on Tarkyn Lye.

Nobody except a trained assassin, perhaps.

"My lady?"

Alija looked up anxiously. She was sitting in front of her dressing table, which was unfortunate. When she caught her reflection she was horrified. She looked old and haggard. And alone.

"Is he here?"

Tressa shook her head. "I'm sorry, my lady. There's still been no word from Master Miar. It's Princess Marla."

"What about her?"

"She's here, my lady."

Alija sat up straighter in astonishment. "Marla's *here*? In my house?"

"Downstairs, my lady."

"Did she say what she wants?"

"Only that she wishes to speak with you, my lady."

Alija looked at herself in the mirror again, wondering if Marla had come to see how she was coping. *Has she come here to gloat, to see how Tarkyn's death has affected me?*

Then again, unless she'd had something to do with it, how would Marla even know Tarkyn was dead?

Which set Alija wondering. Perhaps the princess had

some idea of what had happened to the dwarf and had killed Tarkyn in retaliation. Who else had the coin to waste hiring an assassin to kill a slave?

"Serve her highness with refreshments and tell her I will be down shortly," she ordered the slave.

"Yes, my lady."

"And Tressa . . ."

"My lady?"

"Say nothing else to her," she commanded. "Do you understand? Not a word. Don't even talk about the weather."

"Yes, my lady," Tressa agreed, then she curtseyed and hurried away to do her mistress's bidding while Alija turned back to her mirror and began brushing out her hair.

"Marla!" Alija gushed with vast insincerity as she strolled into the morning room almost an hour later. "Please forgive me for keeping you waiting. You quite caught me unawares."

"I'm not interrupting anything, am I?" Marla asked with a slightly raised brow. Dressed in mourning white, she was standing by the window, framed by the sunlight, which gave her an unexpected aura of ethereal, almost mystical light. Alija wondered if she had chosen to stand there deliberately. Whether she had or not, this was one morning Alija didn't need reminding of Marla's legendary beauty.

"Of course you didn't disturb me! To be honest, I was just having a lie-in. It's not often one gets to relax these days. I didn't have much on this morning, so I thought I'd take the opportunity to laze around the house for a few hours before I have to tackle the problems of the day."

"How lucky you can afford the time, Alija. With the High Prince departing for war, I thought you'd have a great deal to do. Particularly as it was you who put the idea into his head in the first place."

Alija found herself unable to completely hide her pleasure at how much it had irked Marla when she'd done that. "Are you angry at me, dear?"

Marla shrugged. "Why would I be angry at you, cousin?

You've provided my brother with an opportunity to carve his name into the annals of history. I'm just amazed I didn't think of it first."

Alija was sceptical. "I'm sure if you'd thought Lernen was going to carve his name with distinction in anything, Marla, you *would* have thought of it first."

"And you seem fairly confident he won't. Isn't that why you wanted Cyrus appointed as his second-in-command?"

"We'll see," she replied, refusing to be drawn. "Is that what you wanted to see me about?"

"No," Marla replied brightly. "Actually, I have a gift for you."

"A gift?"

"I know, there's not really an occasion," the princess said, holding out a small parcel wrapped in blue silk and tied with a silver ribbon. It was about the size of a small plate. Alija couldn't imagine what it might be, or why Marla was offering it to her. "But I just felt it was time I gave you a token of my appreciation," Marla told her, "for all the years of faithful service you've shown me and the High Prince. I can't imagine what life would have been like without you, Alija, and then I saw this . . . and it just said it all . . . so much better than words could ever do . . ."

Curiously, Alija unwrapped the gift. As the bloodstained silk fell away and she realised what it was, she dropped the silver slave collar in horror and jumped back from it.

"Does it not please you?" Marla asked with venomous sweetness.

"You evil bitch!" Alija hissed, unable to take her eyes from the slave collar on the floor. Tarkyn Lye's collar. "*Why?*"

"*Why?*" Marla repeated with an incredulous laugh. "Surely you don't have to ask."

"I can't believe you did this!"

"Then you have fatally underestimated me, my lady. You might find that something of a problem in the days and weeks to come."

She tore her eyes from the bloodstained collar and stared at Marla. "What are you talking about?"

"The days and weeks between now and when I'm able to spit on your corpse," the princess replied pleasantly. "I'm sorry, did I forget to mention that part?"

Alija thought she might be sick, but it wasn't the blood on Tarkyn's collar making her queasy. It was Marla's cold-blooded, triumphant expression that nauseated her. This was Marla letting her know she was wise to her. This was an open declaration of war.

"How . . . how did you get the Assassins' Guild to . . . ?"

"To kill Tarkyn Lye when you so obviously had the guild in your pocket?" Marla finished for her. "Ah, that would be part of the whole 'fatally underestimating me' problem you have, Alija." The princess made a great pretence of looking around the room for something. "Where is your handsome younger lover, by the way? Not here consoling you in your hour of need? What sort of fair-weather friend is he?"

Alija had to force herself not to scream. She clenched her fists by her side and fought to remain calm. "I will destroy you for this, Marla Wolfblade."

Marla didn't seem the least bit intimidated by her threats. "You had your chance to destroy me, Alija. You let it slip you by. Now it's my turn."

The High Arrion shook her head, not sure if it was denial or disbelief that prompted it. "You haven't got the guts for this fight, Marla. You're too practiced at avoiding confrontation."

Marla seemed amused. "We just keep coming back to that little 'underestimating me' problem, don't we? Do give Galon my regards when you see him, won't you?"

She's gotten to Galon, Alija realised with despair. *Dear gods, how did she manage that?* But Marla wasn't going to just walk out of here looking so smug and superior, Alija decided. Not while she still held the trump card.

"Fool! Do you really think you can fight *me*?" Alija asked. "Do you think you have any secrets from me, you perfidious little bitch? I know everything! The Fool betrayed you! I know about Wrayan. About Luciena. And Rorin Mariner. I know about the mind shields . . ."

Marla stopped and turned to look at her serenely, apparently unsurprised by the news of the Fool's betrayal. "Did Elezaar mention that Wrayan's actually here in Greenharbour at the moment?" she asked. "Ah, no, he wouldn't have known that when he spoke to Tarkyn, would he? Perhaps you should have waited a few more days, Alija, before suborning him. He would have had so much more to tell you, if you had. In fact, I'm willing to bet that until the day you die—a happy occasion which I can assure you is significantly closer than you appreciate—you're going to wonder how much of what Elezaar told you is true and how much is merely what I wanted you to hear."

She stared at Marla in shock. "You knew."

"Of course I knew."

Alija wasn't going to let such a triumphant smirk go unchallenged. "And what do you think you can do about it?"

Marla pointed to a folded document lying on the table next to the fruit platter. "Perhaps you should read that."

Alija looked at the document, obviously puzzled. "What is it?"

Marla waited until Alija had picked up the document and unfolded it before she answered, "You have a little problem, my lady."

She opened it, glanced over it, and then looked up at Marla in confusion. "It's the decree granting my son interim status as the Warlord of Dregian after his father died in the plague, until it can be confirmed by the Convocation. What's the problem? Cyrus was of age and the legitimate heir when I signed that, and in case you hadn't noticed, it's been co-signed by the High Prince. That decision can't be overturned."

"It can if I prove the confirmation was made under false pretences."

"What false pretences?"

"It says Cyrus is Barnardo Eaglespike's son," Marla

pointed out. "But we know that's not true, don't we? Tarkyn Lye fathered both your sons."

Alija was almost amused by Marla's clumsy attempts to blackmail her. "Is that your plan to bring me down, Marla? I'd like to see you prove it."

"Wrayan is willing to testify that he took the information from Tarkyn Lye's mind. And yours."

"Nobody would believe him," she predicted.

"Oh . . . I think they might. Given the right incentives."

Alija stared at Marla, confident this was a bluff. "You'd never support exposing the truth about my sons, Marla. Not even to bring me down. It would threaten every woman in Hythria if the men of this country had any idea how many of their sons were fathered by slaves and lovers."

"I would prefer not to," Marla agreed, "but you're sadly mistaken if you think I wouldn't."

"What are you suggesting, then?" Alija asked, curious to see how far Marla was prepared to go.

"Your life in return for your sons' futures," Marla informed her calmly.

Alija stared at her in surprise. She hadn't expected that. "My *life*?"

"I'm tired of you, Alija. I don't want you around for another twenty minutes, let alone another twenty years. I want you gone and if you had any care for the Eaglespike name you would commit suicide now, and save your sons the pain of your coming downfall."

Alija shook her head, wondering if Marla had been drinking. Or maybe Tarkyn's murder had emboldened her so much she was becoming reckless. "You're deluded, Marla. You can't bring me or my House down. Nobody will ever question my son's right to inherit Dregian Province."

"Trust me, they'll question it, Alija. All it would take is a few words in the right ear. And Wrayan testifying about how you lied regarding your sons' parentage. This document clearly states that Cyrus, son of Barnardo, is the legal heir to his father's province. Now, I'm guessing that's not the case because in order for Cyrus to be your husband's heir, he would have to have been legally adopted by Barnardo, but to do *that*, you would have had to confess about him not being Cyrus's father, wouldn't you?" When Alija didn't answer, she smiled. "So . . . without legal status as Barnardo's heir, my brother, the High Prince—you remember Lernen, don't you, Alija? He's the one you're always trying to unseat—he'll call the Convocation together as soon as I bring your little indiscretion to his attention. I think it would be an interesting debate, don't you? The legality of a slave's son posing as an heir and then being appointed Warlord under false pretences. Oh, and the best part?" Marla added, gleefully twisting the knife. "Thanks to your endless urge to tell anybody who will listen that your late husband was a member of the Wolfblade family, the only logical heir to Dregian Province if your sons are exposed as frauds would be one of *my* sons. Now isn't *that* just deliciously ironic?"

Alija stared at her in disbelief. The picture Marla had painted was a very believable one. But highly improbable for all that. The woman's gall was breathtaking. "And to avoid all this, you want me to commit *suicide*?"

Marla nodded. She didn't seem to find anything about this bizarre proposal the least bit extraordinary. "My daughter suggests you would kill yourself before you did anything to jeopardise your sons or what you believed was Cyrus's chance at the throne. I'm gambling on that holding true for him simply hanging on to Dregian Province."

Alija had had enough of this game. "Don't take that tone with me, Marla Wolfblade."

The princess looked at her innocently. "I beg your pardon?"

"That holier-than-thou attitude you're so fond of. That noble 'I'm only doing this for Hythria' act you've played so well all these years. It doesn't impress me. And it certainly isn't going to drive me to suicide."

"I thought perhaps your concern for Cyrus and Serrin might." Marla picked up the document and folded the decree with a shrug. "Still, if you want them to remember you as a stain on the Eaglespike name, the woman who broke a once-great House out of stubbornness, rather than the woman who selflessly took her own life to spare her sons the embarrassment of her dishonour, that's entirely up to you."

Marla turned away, her contempt obvious.

"Wait!" Alija called, as Marla headed for the door. "How do I know you'd even keep your word?"

The princess hesitated, and then turned to face Alija. "You mean what's to stop me standing over you while you fall on your sword, and then have Cyrus tossed out of Dregian, anyway, as soon as you're dead?"

"That's exactly what I mean."

Marla considered her answer carefully. "Actually, there's nothing stopping me, Alija. Except for two things. One, I would give you my word, which you may or may not accept, and two, it would be stupid of me to do it. We both know the consequences of advertising how many supposedly legitimate heirs are really the spawn of favoured *court'esa*. If I no longer have to worry about you, then I'm not going to worry about your son. He can be Warlord of Dregian if he wants. But if he wants my brother's throne he'll have to find a way to take it himself, without any help from you or the Sorcerers' Collective."

Alija knew that suicide—under the right circumstances—was considered a noble, if somewhat archaic tradition in Hythria. The ultimate sacrifice to the God of War to redress a wrong and restore honour to one's House. But if Marla Wolfblade thought she was going to win this conflict by threats of some vague accusation she couldn't prove, then perhaps she wasn't the clever politician Alija feared. Maybe it had been the dwarf who owned all the political acumen and now that she had lost him, Marla was floundering.

She looked down at the decree the princess was holding, as if she was actually contemplating the idea. "If I . . . if I did this? You'd guarantee my sons' safety?"

"Your eldest son is a Warlord now, Alija. I don't know I'd

be able to guarantee his safety, but I could guarantee nobody would challenge his right to rule Dregian Province."

Alija savoured the moment, watching Marla thinking she might win, and then shook her head, smiling coldly. "This is just another one of your twisted schemes to cover your brother's incompetence. Did you really come here thinking you could make me do such a thing?"

Marla shrugged. "It was worth a try, don't you think? And I did so want to see the look on your face when I gave you your present."

Sheer force of will was the only thing holding back Alija's fury. She wished for the power she'd had that day long ago, when she'd used the Harshini enhancement spell and burned out Wrayan Lightfinger's mind. She'd have done it now to Marla, except for that damnable shield. "I think you have no idea who you're dealing with, Marla."

"Nor do you," Marla replied. "But I will give you one little bit of advice. Some of what Elezaar told Tarkyn Lye really is true and some of it was a complete fabrication. I'll leave it to you to figure out which is which." The princess frowned, then added with concern, "Do sit down, Alija. You're looking quite peaked. I can see myself out."

Marla gathered up her skirts and sailed serenely from the room, leaving Alija staring after her in speechless rage. It didn't seem possible Marla would challenge her so openly. Marla was the Queen of Avoidance. She had made a career of never rocking the boat. In Alija's opinion, that's all she'd ever been good for. She didn't have the brains or the wit to deceive someone like Alija Eaglespike so completely . . .

And then she remembered something else Marla had said. *Did Elezaar mention that Wrayan's actually here in Greenharbour at the moment?*

That was the name of her nemesis.

Wrayan Lightfinger.

chapter 38

The temple devoted to the God of War in Cabradell was far less pretentious than the temple in Greenharbour. At this late hour it was deserted, lit only by a single candle burning on the altar at the far end of the hall. Near the doors were two tall pillars covered with spikes to allow worshippers a chance to prick a finger on their way out of the temple, leaving a blood sacrifice—however symbolic—for their god.

Brak wasn't sure what had brought him here tonight. He certainly had no intention of offering the God of War a sacrifice. As far as he was concerned, Zegarnald was getting plenty of satisfaction from the war currently brewing between Fardohnya and Hythria. He didn't need any of Brak's blood spilt to add to his joy.

Maybe he missed Ollie's company, he wondered, walking further into the temple. Piled in front of the altar were a number of dead animals, ranging from cats and dogs to a newborn kid, left by petitioners seeking more than a simple blessing from their deity. The young Fardohnyan bandit had driven Brak insane on their journey here with his credulous, wide-eyed acceptance of everything he heard, and his foolish, romantic notions about being a spy. But he'd been company of sorts and Brak hated being alone with his thoughts. Ollie kept his mind on other things and in that regard, he missed the young man sorely.

Stepping up to the altar, Brak saw that scratched on the wall, like some sort of chaotic abstract mural, were the names of generation after generation of firstborn sons offered to Zegarnald by their fathers the night of their birth. That custom, along with the Hythrun propensity to solve most of their problems by fighting about them, had a lot to do with the God of War's fondness for these people.

The Halfbreed was intrigued by what the War God was really up to, and although he tried hard to convince himself it was none of his business, Brak knew, in his heart, that if he could do anything to foil Zegarnald's plans, he'd probably do it. The gods didn't often directly interfere with the mortal world. The results were never what they hoped and often catastrophic. If the God of War was meddling now, then he had a reason, and Brak would dearly like to know what it was.

So he had come here tonight, it dawned on Brak at that moment, to ask the god outright what he was up to, and be done with it.

"Zegarnald!"

Brak waited a moment and then called again.

"Zegarnald!"

"Well, well," the god remarked, appearing before Brak in a blaze of light. "Lord Brakandaran té Carn in my temple. And without being invited. Or dragged here against his will."

"Do you mind?" Brak complained, raising his arm and averting his eyes. Zegarnald was almost too bright to look upon, his golden armour emitting a light of its own. It wasn't necessary. It was an affectation, Zegarnald glorying in his growing power. And gloating about it.

"What can I do for you, Brakandaran?" the god asked curiously, as he faded to a more tolerable luminescence. "Can I assume that now you have abandoned your foolish dalliance with the followers of Dacendaran, you have come to beg my forgiveness? And perhaps ask for my patronage?"

Brak lowered his arm now he no longer needed to shield his eyes, amused by the very idea. "Now why would I want *your* patronage, Zegarnald? You're far too demanding a god for my liking. At least Dace just wants his followers to steal something. And he doesn't ask for blood, either, even a symbolic amount."

"If you do not seek my patronage, Brakandaran, what are you doing in my temple? Why did you summon me?"

"Maybe I just wanted to talk."

"In seven hundred years you have never *just wanted to talk*, Brakandaran."

"There's a first time for everything."

Zegarnald glared at him. "I have not the time to waste, while you entertain yourself with riddles at my expense. Why did you summon me?"

To ask you what the hell you're playing at, was Brak's first thought, but he was too familiar with the gods to expect an answer to such a direct question. Getting anything out of a god required subtlety. "Actually, I came to congratulate you, Divine One. You may have finally arranged things so that Hablet of Fardohnya will achieve what no Fardohnyan king has ever managed to do before—reclaim Hythria and unite the two kingdoms for the first time since Greneth the Elder divided Greater Fardohnya and awarded it, and his twin sister, to Jaycon Wolfblade twelve hundred years ago."

"Was it really so long ago?" Zegarnald asked. "It's so hard to keep track of these things." The god hesitated, frowning. "What do you mean, Hablet will reclaim Hythria? I've arranged no such thing. I expect the Hythrun to resist the Fardohnyan invasion with every man they can muster. It will be a glorious and epic struggle that will go on for years and be honoured by generations of my followers."

"I have no doubt that was your intention," Brak agreed. "But you messed up somewhere. Not only has Voden's little dalliance with the plague cost you tens of thousands of believers, it devastated Hythria's militia. They're down to a fraction of the numbers they could muster before the epidemic. And just to make it really interesting, what's left of your Hythrun army of desperate defenders is going to be led by that well-known disciple of mediocrity, Lernen Wolfblade. Somehow, I think Hablet might prevail a little more quickly than you planned, don't you?"

Zegarnald was obviously confused. "Is not the Wolfblade scion leading the Hythrun forces?"

"From what I hear, it wouldn't help your cause much if he did. He's a regular chip off the old block, by all accounts."

"You are mistaken, Brakandaran. I have taken some pains to ensure the Wolfblade heir is a worthy successor to the throne. And a devout follower of his god. He seemed most anxious to honour me when I spoke to him."

Brak was shocked. "You *appeared* to Damin Wolfblade? In person?"

"I can appear to anybody I please."

"Isn't that crossing the line? I mean, it's one thing to arrange circumstances to suit your agenda, Divine One, but if you start sticking your nose in too closely, won't the other gods think they can do the same?" Brak's brow creased in concern at the thought. "I can just imagine what Kalianah would do if she thought she had a free hand to make people fall in love on her whim. You might find your armies otherwise engaged when you sound the battle cry if the Goddess of Love had been let loose among your followers with the idea that it's open season on your believers."

He watched the apprehension grow on the War God's face. Long experience had taught Brak that the easiest way to upset him was to suggest the Goddess of Love was trying to encroach on his territory.

Zegarnald shook his head in denial. "You are wrong, Brakandaran. Kalianah would not dare interfere with my war. Even she knows what is at stake here."

"We are talking about the *same* Kalianah, aren't we?" Brak enquired with a raised brow.

The God of War thought it over for a little longer, clearly not pleased. "Have you been speaking to her?" he demanded. "Putting ideas in her head?"

"Of course not, Divine One!" Brak assured him. "You know me. I never get involved in your business if I can avoid it."

"So you claim."

"So how did he take it?"

"How did who take what?" the god asked in confusion.

"The Wolfblade lad. When you appeared to him."

"He was honoured. Naturally."

Brak eyed the god doubtfully. "Well, you *would* think that, wouldn't you? What did you tell him?"

"Just that I supported his endeavours."

Brak swore under his breath. "Oh? Is *that* all?"

Zegarnald drew himself up self-righteously. "I have not interfered in another god's domain, Brakandaran," the god insisted. "I don't know why you're so upset. The lad was quite moved to meet his god."

"I'll bet he was," Brak agreed sourly. "So moved, he'll probably lead every man under his command to their deaths in your honour, because he thinks you're on his side."

"I am not unaware of the risk. In fact, I have provided him with a mentor to ensure he puts up a decent fight. As you say, it would be a pity if the conflict ended too soon."

Brak stared at him suspiciously. There was something else going on here, more than just the God of War playing games to bolster his disciples. "What's the real reason for this war, Divine One?"

"I need Hythria and Fardohnya, both, ready to tackle the real enemy."

"Who?"

"Xaphista."

For once, Brak was stunned into silence. Of all the motives he'd imagined Zegarnald had for stirring up this conflict, the god of the Kariens was the last thing he'd have thought of.

"There will be a confrontation, Brakandaran," the War God continued. "It will not happen for a time yet, but there *will* be a confrontation, and when it comes, the fate of every nation on this continent will hang in the balance. Already, plans to deal with the threat of Xaphista are in motion. You've even had a hand in them, unwittingly."

That sounded ominous. "*I've* had a hand in them?"

"Indirectly," the god agreed.

Brak wasn't sure he wanted to know what that meant. "And how exactly is a war between Fardohnya and Hythria supposed to weaken Xaphista? If they wipe each other out, you've just handed the Overlord the whole continent on a platter."

"No human has fought a proper war in more than a generation. The nations of the south have grown lax. Their devotion wavers and their warriors grow fat. To face the final battle, they will need experience."

That Zegarnald was probably right about the Hythrun and the Fardohnyans lacking real experience in battle didn't make his actions any easier to live with.

"There's a name for this inconvenient state of affairs, you know," Brak reminded him. "It's called peace."

"It is not *peace*," the God of War corrected, almost choking on the word. "It is complacency."

"Well, I hate to be the bearer of bad news, Zegarnald, but your timing's a little off. Your precious, well-trained scion isn't old enough to lead anybody anywhere. His uncle is in charge, and Hablet of Fardohnya will walk all over Lernen Wolfblade like a well-worn doormat. Between Lernen and all those fat warriors, this little war you've stirred up will be lucky if it lasts a month."

The God of War didn't appear amused. "A situation you would find to your liking, I suspect, Brakandaran," he accused.

Brak couldn't help himself. He smiled. "You know me, Divine One. I find the machinations of the gods an endless source of entertainment."

"Then perhaps," the god suggested, clearly irritated by his smirk, "I should find something else to keep you amused."

In the blink of an eye the walls around Brak faded, replaced by tall, snow-tipped pines. A bitter chill sharpened the air and his breath frosted as he exhaled in surprise.

Below him, a white palace rested on a small island near the edge of a lake, the water reflecting the torchlit palace in its obsidian surface so perfectly it appeared as if the lake itself was on fire. Dotting the plain surrounding the lake and the nearby town were countless camp fires, stretching into the distance as far as the eye could see.

Brak knew immediately where he was. That was the Winter Palace down there and near it the city of Qorinipor. The camp fires were Hablet's army, gathering for the invasion.

He was back in Fardohnya.

CHAPTER 39

D
espite all his best efforts, Hablet of Fardohnya and his trusty eunuch, Lecter Turon, had little success in keeping his daughter away from Axelle Regis. With uncanny accuracy, every time the general even looked like visiting the palace, Adrina was there, fluttering her eyes coyly at Lord Regis as if he was the only man in Fardohnya worthy of her attention.

Hablet knew exactly how she did it. Adrina might be a shrew among her peers but she was very careful of her slaves. And remarkably considerate of them. Consequently, she had access to palace gossip that would not normally reach the ears of the highborn. Because of her generosity and consideration and because she championed the cause of any lesser creature she considered mistreated, the palace slaves quickly became Adrina's co-conspirators as much as her lackeys. If the cooks were ordered to prepare an extra place for dinner, Adrina knew about it before the dining room staff had a chance to rearrange the seating. If a groom met Lord Regis at the palace steps and led his horse away to be rubbed down and fed, Adrina was descending the staircase—a vision of loveliness—greeting him with those devastating green eyes, before any slave out in the stables had the time to take so much as a currycomb to the beast.

It was yet another sign of her astuteness, the king knew. Confined to the harem and informed only of what her father wished her to know, the young princess had found a way to get information independent of official channels and used her advantage every chance she could.

Not for the first time, Hablet lamented the capricious will of the gods that had given him a firstborn with all the qualities he wished for in a son and then deposited them—most inconsiderately—in a daughter.

And this evening—yet again—Adrina had foiled all his efforts to exclude her. She sat opposite Axelle Regis, flirting with him so openly Hablet wondered why she didn't just shove the silverware aside, throw herself at the young man and suggest he take her, right here on the dinner table.

Even more troubling was Axelle Regis's reaction to Adrina's open flirtation. He responded just enough not to offend the princess, but was very guarded in the presence of the king. That indicated the general was in possession of a disturbing degree of political acumen. *Just the sort of thing a king wants in a general, but damned inconvenient when your eldest daughter is looking at him with those dangerous bedroom eyes.*

Hablet would have been happier if Axelle had responded to Adrina the way any red-blooded man should have, or better yet, if he'd run like hell at the first hint the king's daughter was interested in him. Either would have left Hablet certain where Regis stood on the matter. Unfortunately, Axelle Regis did neither, which immediately made the king suspicious and that meant Lord Regis's career was likely to be a glorious but short one, which was a shame really, because Hablet genuinely liked the general. But the King of Fardohnya would tolerate no rivals and a man of Axelle's obvious ability aligned with the eldest daughter of a king with no male heir was a temptation too rich for most men.

"What do you think, Daddy?"

Adrina's question jerked Hablet out of his disturbing train of thought. "What?"

"Lord Regis and I were discussing hunting, Daddy," she explained. "Weren't you listening? He was telling me he thinks the chase is better than the kill. Whereas I think the kill is the best part . . ." Her voice dropped to a low purr and although she was supposed to be speaking to her father, Adrina's eyes were firmly fixed on Regis. "You know what I mean . . . when you're all hot and sweaty and breathing hard and you've finally cornered your quarry and you can see the fear . . . the excitement in their eyes . . . taste the blood . . ." Adrina ran her hand over her neck as she spoke, as if in the cool depths of the Winter Palace, she could feel the heat of the image she'd evoked and was obviously aroused by it.

Hablet silently cursed the custom that gave daughters like Adrina access to *court'esa*. She was dangerous enough without professional instruction on the art of seduction.

"So what do you think, Daddy?" she repeated, after running her tongue over her lips to moisten them. "What do you enjoy most? The chase? Or the kill?"

Before the king could answer, the door opened and one of Lord Regis's lieutenants entered the dining room. Bowing to the king and then hurrying to his general's side, he leaned over and whispered something into Axelle's ear.

Lord Regis rose to his feet as soon as the young man had finished speaking. "I must beg to be excused, your majesty. I have word of a spy who has just returned from across the border. I'd like to interview him immediately."

"Surely it can wait, Lord Regis?" Adrina asked, disappointed. "You haven't finished your dessert."

"Unfortunately, it can't wait, your highness," Regis replied apologetically. "This is one of the bandits we recruited from the mountains around Westbrook and he's been all the way to Cabradell. He has the first accurate assessment of Hythrun troop numbers and composition."

"Then you'll want to hear about it too, won't you, Daddy?" she asked. "Why not just have him brought in here? That way you can interrogate him and I won't have to be deprived of your company. Or yours either, Daddy," she added with an innocent glance in the king's direction.

"Have him brought in." Hablet shrugged when Regis looked to him for guidance. It didn't really matter, the king supposed, what Adrina learned about the Hythrun. It wasn't likely to do her any good and while, like Regis, he was anxious to hear what the spy had to say, she was right. He hadn't finished his dessert.

Regis ordered his lieutenant to bring the man to them and resumed his seat. A few moments later the officer returned with a nervous young man in tow who looked about him in open awe, and then dropped to his knees and placed his forehead on the floor when he realised he was in the presence of his king.

Hablet smiled. Abject abasement was always a good way to open a discussion with the King of Fardohnya.

"Get up, lad," the king ordered indulgently. "I hear you bring us vital news of the enemy."

"I do, your majesty, I do!" the young man gushed.

"What's your name?" Regis asked.

"Ollie Kantel, my lord. I went into Hythria with Master Andaran."

"I remember him," the general replied. "Very experienced but rather arrogant fellow, as I recall. Is he not with you?"

Ollie shook his head. "He's still in Cabradell, my lord. He was waiting for the rest of the Hythrun armies to arrive. So he could report on their final numbers."

"And what estimates do you have of their current numbers?"

"There are about five thousand troops in Cabradell from Krakandar and Elasapine, your majesty," the lad told him. "Because of the plague, Sunrise will be hard-pressed to match that number when they're finally mustered."

"Less than ten thousand men?" Hablet exclaimed. "Why, that's excellent news!"

"What of the other provinces?" Regis asked, not quite so enchanted with the report. "Have they not sent troops as well?"

"Our informant claimed Pentamor and Greenharbour were sending troops and Dregian Province is supposed to be sending another three thousand men, but they wouldn't know for certain until the High Prince arrived in Cabradell. That's what Brak was waiting around for."

"The High Prince?" Adrina echoed curiously. "Surely he's not in command of the Hythrun defences?"

"That's what Lord Warhaft told us, your highness."

"Who is Lord Warhaft?" Regis asked.

"He's an officer in Lord Hawksword's Elasapine contingent, sire," the young spy answered.

"You actually spoke to a Hythrun officer?" Regis said doubtfully. "Is that where your information comes from?"

The lad nodded. "Brak found him crying into his beer in a tavern just near the temple of Zegarnald in Cabradell. He was very upset, my lord. His wife had been taken from him by Lord Hawksword and then when he appealed to Lord Narvell's brother, the High Prince's heir, he took a fancy to her too, and now she's part of his entourage. The man had no great love of the Wolfblades, that's for certain, and with just cause once you'd heard his tale. He was happy to tell us what he knew."

"So the nephews are cut from the same cloth as the uncle?" Adrina remarked sourly, almost as keen as her father to see the end of the Hythrun royal line, although for quite different reasons—Hablet fervently hoped—than his own. "I almost feel sorry for the Hythrun."

"Aye," Ollie agreed. "You should hear the stories we heard about the High Prince's heir, your highness. Tales of orgies with his Denikan *court'esa*. How he makes his officers wait on his pleasure, sometimes for hours at a time. And then—"

"But you say *Lernen* Wolfblade is on his way to lead their troops against us?" Hablet cut in, impatient with Adrina's unhealthy interest in the lad's gossip about the decadent goings-on in the Hythrun court. "Are you certain?"

"Quite certain, your majesty," the boy confirmed. "Nobody was very happy about it, either."

Hablet glanced at Axelle Regis. "I would have thought he'd send someone like Rogan Bearbow, at the very least. Or Charel Hawksword, perhaps?"

"He had a stroke."

Both the king and the general turned to look at Adrina.

"Charel Hawksword," she explained. "He had a stroke. About three years ago. He's paralysed down one side of his body. He can barely sit a horse, let alone lead troops into battle."

This is why she's dangerous, Hablet thought. *She makes it her business to know these things.*

"Perhaps the plague took out more key men than we've heard about yet," Axelle suggested. "I heard Barnardo Eaglespike of Dregian Province was taken in the early days of the epidemic, but who's to say how many more Warlords Hythria has lost that we've yet to hear about?"

"Are you suggesting Lernen's leading his troops because there's nobody else?" Hablet laughed. "Oh . . . that's just too precious for words!"

Adrina looked hopefully at her father. "Can I be High Princess of Hythria after it's been conquered, Daddy?"

"Don't be ridiculous," he told her, patting her hand affectionately. "I'd never let you get even a *smell* of that much power, my sweet. You know that."   ·

"I'd be very loyal, Daddy," she promised.

"Yes, I'm sure you would, petal," he said, privately alarmed at the thought that she actually meant it. "And the Harshini are going to magically reappear tomorrow, too, I suppose?"

Adrina laughed dismissively, but Hablet wasn't convinced. It would be just like his daughter to want the Hythrun throne. For that reason—among many others— he'd gone to great lengths to keep Adrina in the dark about his problem with the distant Wolfblade cousins being in line for the Fardohnyan throne if he failed to get an heir. Adrina was nobody's fool and it wouldn't take her long to realise even the notoriously patriarchal Fardohnyans might be persuaded that the unthinkable notion of a Fardohnyan queen was preferable to the unconscionable notion of a Hythrun king.

Yet another reason to ensure her relationship with Regis never progresses any further than flirting across the dinner table.

"Well, I say we've waited around long enough," he declared, anxious to divert his daughter's alarming train of thought from the idea that she was fit to rule anything. "What say we move these boys out, Regis? By the sound of it, Lernen is waiting for us. Time to show the old pervert who the gods truly favour, eh?"

Lord Regis rose to his feet and bowed. "As you wish, your majesty. I will issue the appropriate orders tonight and we can begin moving the troops through the Widowmaker immediately."

The King of Fardohnya nodded his approval and with those few words the invasion of Hythria had begun.

PART THREE

WAR GAMES

chapter 40

As dawn crept across the Cabradell Valley, Damin climbed out of his bed. He had dreamed again of his meeting with the God of War, and it had unsettled him. Careful not to disturb Lyrian, he padded barefoot to the table by the window to study the game in progress, hoping for a distraction. He'd still told nobody of his meeting, more than a little afraid of the reaction if he announced he'd started seeing the gods. Rorin may have been sympathetic, but Damin wasn't sure about how others might view his revelation. He could risk no hint of anything that might indicate he was as crazy as his uncle. But he desperately wished Wrayan was here. He'd seen the gods. He'd spoken to them.

He'd know if Damin's vision was real or just wishful thinking.

Damin fixed his attention on the ceramic bowls on the table, pushed all thoughts of gods from his mind. By the time Lernen Wolfblade had arrived in Cabradell several days ago, Damin had lost Medalon, Karien and a good portion of Fardohnya to Prince Lunar Shadow Kraig of the House of the Rising Moon, all because of his stupid seed game and the fact that Damin was becoming obsessed by it.

Tejay's accusation that he was intolerably competitive was proving truer than he'd imagined. Until now, Damin never fully appreciated how much he hated losing, compounded by the fact that for the first time in his life, he was confronted by something he couldn't master easily. Kraig's smug condescension every time he won wasn't helping much either. The seed game, so simple in theory and so complex in its execution, was proving a challenge the young prince was obsessively determined to conquer.

"Come back to bed," Lyrian complained, pulling up the covers to compensate for being robbed of the warmth of Damin's body.

"Do you know how to play this damn game?" he asked, without looking up from the table.

"Every child in Denika learns it," she told him sleepily. When she got no further response from him, the Denikan warrior turned on her side, resting her head on her hand as she watched the young prince. "But I'm not very good at it. I don't have the patience to become a master. Not like Kraig."

Damin frowned at the seed bowls before he turned to look at her with a thin smile. "Ah, yes . . . his royal smugness, Prince Lunar Shadow Kraig. I'd like to get him down in the training yards for an hour or so. I may not be able to take him in this game but I could beat him with a quarterstaff. In fact, I think I'd rather enjoy beating him with a quarterstaff."

"Kraig is a master of many weapons," Lyrian informed him confidently. "In my country he is thought of most highly as a warrior."

"Now why doesn't *that* surprise me?"

"So why don't you?"

"Why don't I what?"

"Why don't you and Kraig go down to the training yards together? He could teach you a great deal."

Damin smiled and reached for his shirt. It was officially spring, but the air was crisp so close to dawn. "For one thing, Lyrian, despite the insufferably high opinion you and Barlaina have of your prince—and for that matter the insufferably high opinion he has of himself—I think I can manage to find my way around a quarterstaff without any help from his royal highness, the Crown Prince of Superiority. And secondly, Kraig is posing as a slave. If I was caught arming him, even in a training yard, every slave owner in Hythria would be howling for my blood."

Lyrian frowned. "If you are afraid of your slaves, Damin Wolfblade, perhaps you shouldn't keep them."

"I'm not afraid of them." He pulled the shirt over his head and walked back to the bed, where he sat down to pull on his trousers.

"You're afraid to arm them," she accused.

"That's not fear, that's pragmatism."

"It is fear," she corrected. "Your slaves outnumber you in this country . . . what . . . three or four to one? If they staged an armed uprising, you would be annihilated."

"Which is why any slave owner with half a brain treats his slaves as if they're members of his own family," Damin informed her. "I haven't noticed you complaining about the harsh treatment you're suffering as one of my chattels."

"People don't sell off members of their own families like cattle," she pointed out. "Your argument is flawed."

"I suggest you speak to Lady Lionsclaw. Or Kendra Warhaft. Ask them if they think we don't sell members of our own families off like cattle. Barlaina can be rather vocal on the issue, too. I believe your friend thinks we're all barbarians with no morals and only barely tolerable table manners."

Lyrian smiled at the mention of Barlaina. "My companion is not as tolerant of foreigners as I am."

"No, *really*?"

The first night Barlaina had come to his room—on Kraig's orders and clearly under protest—she had presented herself just as Damin was getting ready for bed. Standing at the foot of his bed, her hands on her hips, Barlaina had calmly informed the heir to the Hythrun throne that if he attempted to lay so much as a finger on her, she would break every bone in his hands, followed by his arms, followed by his collarbone, and so on, until he either got the message or was incapable of acting on his desires. She had then climbed into bed, pulled the covers up under her chin, turned over and promptly gone to sleep.

Not surprisingly, Damin didn't rest much when Barlaina was in his bed.

Lyrian, on the other hand, was making the most of this rare opportunity to experience Hythria like a Hythrun, even if it was as a *court'esa*. They'd had a number of interesting discussions in the middle of the night about the differences between their cultures. The Hythrun and Fardohnyan custom of keeping *court'esa* was a particular bone of contention. The Denikans considered the practice both barbaric and immoral, and nothing Damin said was likely to convince them otherwise. In their view, one honoured the Goddess of Love by treating her favours as precious gifts, unlike the Hythrun and the Fardohnyans who believed one couldn't honour Kalianah in the manner she deserved unless one was trained from the age of sixteen to use what the goddess had given them to the best of their ability.

Barlaina would have none of it. The much more openminded Lyrian, however, insisted she was selflessly learning what she could of Hythrun customs—for purely diplomatic reasons—and was therefore required to suffer the full indignity of her position, a role she undertook at every opportunity with rather more enthusiasm than one might have expected from a woman who professed abhorrence of the whole concept of keeping sex slaves.

There was little Damin could do under the circumstances, he consoled himself, but show Lyrian what she seemed determined to learn—for the same purely diplomatic reasons, of course, that she used to justify her actions. He was very careful of her feelings, however, partly because he liked her, and partly because he had a sneaking suspicion Barlaina was planning to crush his testicles with her bare hands if he upset her friend even a little.

There was a fine line, Damin had discovered, between diplomacy and disaster.

Fortunately, he was saved from having to defend the structure of Hythrun society further by the door opening.

Expecting a slave come to see if he wanted breakfast brought to his room this morning, Damin was surprised to find Tejay standing in the door.

"You're up already," she noted with relief.

"What's wrong?" There was no reason for Tejay to be here at this hour for anything other than bad news.

"Adham's back from Highcastle," she informed him grimly. "And you'd better come quickly, Damin, because there's a good chance he's dying."

"A damn tavern brawl!" Adham called out to Damin painfully when the wounded young man spied his step-brother hurrying across the hall to greet him. He was laid out on the cushions surrounding the low table in Tejay's main reception hall, looking very pale and rather peeved by the whole situation. "Can you believe it? The bastard pulled a knife on me and I didn't even see it until he was slicing my guts open with the wretched thing."

Damin squatted down beside Adham, whose face was sheened with sweat. Across his abdomen was a bloody bandage that Tejay's physician was gingerly trying to peel away from the wound.

"When did it happen?"

"Last night. In Staunton."

"Why did you ride all the way back to Cabradell?" Damin asked, puzzled by Adham's risky journey in such a perilous condition. "Staunton's only twenty miles from here. Why didn't you send word? I would have come to you."

"That's not what I heard," Adham told him, wincing. "And I thought about staying in the village, but the physic there was drunker than I was, so I figured I was better off coming back here." He jerked in pain and grabbed Tejay's physician by his shirt, pulling the man to him with a snarl. "Do you mind?" he gasped. "That's my guts you're trying to spill all over the carpet."

"Leave him alone, Adham," Tejay scolded. "He's only trying to help."

"Then tell him to do it a little less enthusiastically." Ignoring the hapless physician, Adham turned back to Damin, obviously in agony. "From what I hear, brother, you've precious little time for anyone besides yourself these days."

"Where did you hear that?"

"The rumours are everywhere," Adham said. "I got this hole in my gut defending you from them. You should have heard what this stupid bastard was claiming you were up to! I couldn't stand by and let it go unchallenged. Mind you, don't tell Almodavar I got caught out by a drunk with a skinning knife, will you? He'd never let me live it down."

"You didn't have to defend me, Adham."

"I shouldn't have *had* to . . . OW!" he yelped, and the last of the bandages were lifted from his wound, which seemed to be just above his navel. From what Damin could see of it, the cut looked clean, but he understood now why Tejay feared Adham may be dying. Even a small nick in his intestines could easily turn septic and such a wound was invariably fatal. "I'm warning you!" he growled at the physician. "Do that again, and I'll disembowel *you*, little man."

The old slave rose to his feet and looked to his mistress helplessly, wiping his hands on a towel. "The wound seems fairly straightforward, my lady, but I cannot do anything for him here. And I certainly could do with some cooperation from the patient if I'm to have any hope of treating him."

Tejay nodded. "We'll move him to one of the guest rooms," she agreed. "As for you," she added, looking down at the young trader, "I know you're in pain, Adham, but Caranth Roe is the best physician in Cabradell and as I have no intention of allowing you to die under my roof, if you don't start letting him do his job I'll knock you unconscious myself, so he can work uninterrupted."

Without waiting for Adham to respond, she turned away, issuing orders to her slaves to make the arrangements to have the spice trader moved.

"You'd think *she* was the damned Warlord around here,"

Adham complained in a low voice to Damin. "She ought to be, the way she bosses everyone around."

He smiled sympathetically. "She means well."

"I don't suppose Rorin's back from Winternest?" his stepbrother asked hopefully. "I could do with a bit of magical healing, right about now. I don't care what Tejay says about her physician. The man's a butcher."

"Haven't heard from Rory or Terin, I'm afraid." Then he added, "Uncle Lernen's here though. He arrived a few days ago. And he's going to lead us to victory against the Fardohnyans."

"I noticed." Adham groaned as another wave of pain washed over him. "At least I'm assuming the bright red pavilion roughly about the size of the Greenharbour palace I saw from the road on the way in was his personal accommodation."

"Yes, that's Lernen's accommodation," Damin sighed.

"In keeping with his well-known preference for subtle austerity, I see." Adham grimaced. He knew Lernen almost as well as Damin did. "I wish I was the bearer of better news then."

Before Damin could ask about Adham's news, Tejay returned with two more slaves carrying a stretcher. "There he is, lads," she told the stretcher-bearers. "Be firm but gentle with him. And don't listen to a single word he says. Or to any of his empty threats. This is my palace and regardless of what Master Tirstone claims, I won't allow anybody to be beheaded on his whim."

"That's hardly fair, my lady!" Adham objected. "I'm seriously injured!"

"I know you are," Tejay agreed unsympathetically. "But you're also bleeding all over my good cushions."

"A moment, my lady?" he asked. "Please?"

"*One* moment," Tejay agreed reluctantly.

Adham turned to Damin. "Just in case this heavy-handed butcher botches things up and kills me, I better tell you what's going on in Highcastle."

"What *is* going on in Highcastle?"

"Nothing," Adham said. "Hablet's got less than three thousand troops mustered at Tambay's Seat."

"Are you certain?"

He nodded painfully. It was obviously costing him a lot to keep the agony at bay. "We went right through the pass into Fardohnya."

"So there's no invasion?"

He shook his head, grimacing at even the slightest movement. "Never fear, you'll get your invasion, but it's coming through the Widowmaker, brother, not Highcastle."

Damin rose to his feet and stepped back to let the slaves lift Adham onto the stretcher. The trader cried out as they moved him. Caranth Roe fussed over him as the slaves picked up the stretcher, but Adham yelled at them to stop, turning to look at Damin as they tried to take him away. "One last thing. I found out who's leading Hablet's troops."

"Who?"

"Axelle Regis."

"Thanks." That news wasn't good. Damin had heard of Lord Regis.

"Enough stalling, Adham!" Tejay declared. "Get him out of here."

The slaves obeyed their mistress and hurried from the hall with their patient, the physician following close behind. Damin watched them leave, shaking his head.

"Don't, Damin."

He glanced at Tejay. "Don't what?"

"Don't start blaming yourself."

"You heard what he said, Tejay. He was stabbed defending me from the dreadful reputation you and that damned Denikan have had me spending so much time creating. How can you say I'm not responsible?"

"It's *not* your fault, Damin. Adham looks for trouble. If he hadn't been fighting over you, he would have found something else. You know that. So stop blaming yourself. You've got other things to worry about."

Damin sighed reluctantly in agreement, thinking nobody had quite the same gift for putting things into perspective as his foster-sister.

Adham's right, he thought as his stepbrother was hurried away to be treated for a wound that might prove fatal simply because he had felt the need to defend Damin's reputation. *It really is a pity that Terin and not Tejay Lionsclaw is Warlord of Sunrise Province.*

cbapter 41

The High Prince of Hythria was taking his role as commander-in-chief of Hythria's combined armies very seriously. A few hours later, when Damin and Kraig arrived at his massive pavilion located on a small rise overlooking the city, Lernen was prancing around the main chamber of the tent in an elaborate, gilded suit of armour inlaid with gemstones, the likes of which Damin hadn't seen outside of an ancient Harshini mural in the Temple of Zegarnald in Greenharbour.

"What do you think?" the High Prince demanded as his nephew and the *court'esa* were admitted into his presence. There were several other slaves, all young, half-naked and beautiful, spaced around the main chamber of the pavilion holding up full-length mirrors up so Lernen could admire himself from every possible angle. "Don't I look fearsome?"

Damin studied him warily, acutely aware of his mother's inviolate rules when dealing with the High Prince: *Never lie to him. Never judge him. Never betray him.*

"It's very impressive," he agreed. "Did you have it made specially for the battle?"

"It was a gift," he explained, preening like a young girl in front of the mirrors. "From the High Arrion." Lernen looked over his shoulder and motioned one of the slaves to move the mirror a fraction so he could see what he looked like from behind. "Apparently, she's starting to see the light."

Damin raised his brow. "See the light, eh?"

"The Patriots are a spent force, Damin. Alija explained it all to me. She realises that I am the only rightful ruler of Hythria and has finally given up trying to put a member of her own family on the throne."

Damin never ceased to be amazed by Lernen's gullibility. "She told you that herself, did she?"

He turned to examine his profile from the other direction. "She did. When she gave me the armour. It was her way of apologising, you see."

"Alija Eaglespike actually apologised to you?"

"Well . . . not in so many words . . . but it was her idea I lead our troops to war, you know. That says something, don't you think?"

Damin frowned. It certainly did say something, but not what his uncle thought. "You didn't consider the possibility she sent you here in such distinctive armour, I suppose, because it would make you a better target?"

The High Prince's brows knitted together in concern. He obviously hadn't considered that. "Do you think so?"

"It seems more logical to believe that, Uncle Lernen," he suggested, crossing his arms, "than accept the idea Alija Eaglespike has suddenly abandoned her lifelong quest to remove you from the throne."

Lernen lifted the impressively plumed helmet from his head and stared at Damin suspiciously. "Isn't that what *you're* after, nephew?"

"*Me?*"

"Your mother told me about your grandiose plans to have me lower the age of majority." The prince's eyes narrowed. "Getting a little impatient, are we? Got your eye on my seat a little sooner than I'd like?"

"I have no wish to be High Prince a moment sooner than I

have to, Uncle Lernen," Damin assured him, not offended by the accusation. He was used to Lernen's irrational bouts of insecurity and knew arguing with him about it only made things worse. "I want you to lower the age of majority so I can go back to Krakandar after we've dealt with Hablet and do something about Mahkas Damaran."

Lernen seemed unconvinced. "Your mother used to sing his praises all the time."

"My mother and I have a somewhat different view of things these days," Damin replied, not wishing to get into specifics.

Marla had written and told him that Lernen knew about Leila and Starros, but she'd given no indication of his uncle's feelings on the subject. Damin didn't want to talk about it anyway, particularly not with Lernen. It was a very fine line he walked with his uncle. A glance in the wrong direction could send the old man into a frenzy. He couldn't risk Lernen getting a fix on the notion that Damin wanted his throne and that lowering the age of majority was his way of achieving it.

"I told her I wouldn't do it. You're going to have to wait for my throne, nephew, like all the other vultures."

"I know."

"Are you mad at me?"

"Would there be any point?"

Inexplicably, Lernen smiled. "You're a good lad, Damin. I like that you don't get angry at me when I don't let you have your own way. Did you really get so angry at Mahkas that you cut his throat?"

"Sort of," Damin replied uncomfortably.

"Did he bleed much?" Lernen asked, his eyes alight with anticipation of his nephew's answer. Lernen liked blood. Other people's blood. By all accounts he got hysterical if he thought it was his own.

Damin shrugged, wishing he could find a polite way to change the subject. "I didn't wait around to find out. Anyway, Rorin healed him before he bled to death, so I suppose there couldn't have been that much splashed around."

"You didn't hit an artery, then," Lernen concluded. "Blood sprays like a geyser when you hit an artery, did you know that?"

"Yes, Uncle, I knew that."

Lernen's gaze suddenly shifted to Kraig, who was waiting patiently by the entrance. "Who's that?"

Damin beckoned Kraig closer. "Don't you remember?"

It was a vital question. The only person in Hythria, besides Tejay, Marla and Damin, who knew the true identity of Kraig and his companions was the High Prince, who'd met the Denikans in Greenharbour when they first arrived in Hythria. Damin needed to establish if his uncle remembered who Kraig was, and if he didn't, to make certain it stayed that way.

The prince frowned and leaned closer to his nephew. "Am I supposed to know him?" he asked in a loud whisper. "He looks vaguely familiar, but Denikans all look the same to me."

"You may have seen him before, Uncle," Damin agreed. "In Greenharbour. Mother sent this one and two female *court'esa* to Cabradell as a gift for Lady Lionsclaw, don't you remember?"

Lernen was fairly susceptible to suggestion, and it wasn't actually a lie. Marla really had sent Kraig, Lyrian and Barlaina to Tejay disguised as *court'esa*. What they were anxious to avoid at all costs, however, was the High Prince remembering the real reason at an inappropriate time.

"I think I remember something about that," Lernen said, obviously struggling to recall the incident. "Was I pleased about this gift?"

"I believe you thought it a marvellous idea, Uncle."

Lernen shrugged uncertainly. "Well then, I suppose I must remember him. Why is he here?"

The Denikan stepped forward and bowed respectfully to the High Prince. "I asked Prince Damin if I might be allowed to pay my respects to you, your highness," Kraig answered before Damin could stop him.

Damin cringed in anticipation of Lernen's reaction. Kraig really didn't understand what it meant to be a slave in the presence of the High Prince.

"He spoke to me!" Lernen gasped, jumping back from the big Denikan in alarm.

"Don't worry, Uncle," Damin assured him, with a warning glare at Kraig. "I won't let him address you directly again unless you want it."

Lernen shrank back from them both, alarmed that the slave had uttered a word in his presence without permission. "He's awfully large, isn't he? How can you be sure he's tame?"

"He's quite tame," Damin told his uncle, wondering what Kraig must be thinking right now. Fortunately, the Denikan's expression was inscrutable at the best of times, so Lernen couldn't detect anything of the prince's true feelings. "I just thought you'd like to meet him again . . . perhaps you might enjoy his company . . ."

"No!" Lernen screeched. "Keep him away from me! In fact, I don't wish to see him. Never again! Not ever, do you hear?"

"As you wish, Uncle."

"Take him away!"

"Shall I come back later?"

"If you want; just don't come back with him," the prince insisted. He turned to one of his patiently waiting slaves, still holding the mirrors in place for their prince. "I'm not in the mood to be a warrior anymore. Get this thing off me."

Damin motioned Kraig to leave, stepping outside a moment later to the sound of Lernen complaining about the weight of his damned armour and how Lady Eaglespike had probably only given it to him so he'd stand out on the battlefield, making it easier for an enemy arrow to find him.

Damin stopped outside the pavilion, squinting a little in the bright sun. Kraig was waiting for him. For a moment, the prince said nothing, content to stand beside Damin and survey the chaotic war camp laid out before them and in the distance, the sprawling city that was Cabradell.

"It occurs to me," the Denikan observed after a time, "that your High Prince is not entirely sane, Damin Wolfblade."

"Ah," Damin replied. "You noticed that."

"It also occurs to me," Kraig added, "that if you played the seed game even half as well as you played your uncle just now, you would soon be considered a master."

Damin glanced at the Denikan, not sure if Kraig was complimenting him or censuring him. "I just arranged for you to stay out of Lernen's way for the duration of the campaign," he pointed out. "I thought you'd be grateful."

"I am grateful," Kraig assured him. "I am just not used to being surprised, that's all. You have depths I did not previously suspect, your highness. I must take this into consideration, or risk losing all I have won from you."

Damin looked at him askance. "You do know we're only joking about winning the continent from me, Kraig. Don't you?"

"*Were* we?" the Denikan asked with a raised brow.

Damin wasn't amused. "You really do think you're rather funny, don't you?"

Kraig smiled thinly. "Don't *you*?"

Damin didn't answer him, distracted by the sight of Almodavar hurrying through the camp toward them.

"Lady Lionsclaw told me I'd find you here," the captain said, as he approached. He saluted Damin but pointedly ignored Kraig. Even in the normal course of events, as far as Almodavar was concerned, the Denikan was a *court'esa* and beneath the notice of a Raider in the service of any Warlord. Given Damin's behaviour of late, which the captain apparently blamed on his fascination for his new Denikan slaves, the old man was even less inclined to acknowledge Kraig's presence.

"Is it Adham?" Damin asked, fearful Tejay had sent Almodavar after him to deliver even more bad news.

Almodavar shook his head. "Worse, I'm afraid."

"How could it be *worse*?"

"One of the scouts just rode in to let me know the troops

from Dregian, Greenharbour and Pentamor Provinces have been spotted on the main road from Warrinhaven. They'll arrive by midday."

"Wonderful," Damin said, rolling his eyes. "That's all I need."

"Does the arrival of more men not please you?" Kraig asked curiously.

"It's not the troops, Kraig," Damin explained with a sigh. "Those I welcome with open arms."

"Then what's the problem?"

"It's their Warlords," he replied, thinking the day had just gone from bad to infinitely worse. "My *extremely* distant cousin, Lord Cyrus Eaglespike, the Warlord of Dregian Province, and no doubt his good friend and constant shadow, Toren Foxtalon, the Warlord of Pentamor, are about to grace us with their noble presence."

"This is not a good thing, I gather?"

Almodavar rolled his eyes contemptuously. Damin wasn't sure if it was because of Cyrus Eaglespike's impending arrival or the fact his prince felt the need to explain anything to a slave.

Damin ignored the captain's obvious displeasure and glanced at Kraig. "I think you'll find Almodavar would rather have another visit from the plague. For myself, I just think Cyrus is a pompous pain in the backside, and his little friend, Toren Foxtalon, isn't much better."

Kraig nodded in understanding. "We have a saying in my country: Dead enemies are far easier to live with than live ones. Perhaps this war will be kind to you, your highness, and they will be taken honourably in battle."

The old captain eyed the slave suspiciously. "That's an odd attitude for a slave."

"I am an odd slave," the Denikan replied with a perfectly straight face.

It's time, Damin decided, watching the Denikan and the old Raider captain size each other up, *to let Almodavar know who Kraig really is*. There would be hell to pay, he guessed, if he didn't do something to explain his strange behaviour to Almodavar, and soon. And with Cyrus Eaglespike in the camp, things were likely to get even more tense. He couldn't afford to lose Almodavar to some stupid brawl, defending his prince's honour.

After what happened to Adham, Damin was acutely aware of the possibility.

"Let's ride out to meet them," Damin announced. "All three of us. I'm sure Cyrus will appreciate the gesture. Conin Falconlance is probably with them, too. Conin I can put up with for short bursts if he doesn't agree with Cyrus too often."

"You really are starting to lose your mind, aren't you, your *highness*?" Almodavar remarked sourly.

"Riding out to meet them will give us a chance to talk," Damin added. "Without being overheard."

The old captain studied Damin for a moment then turned his curious gaze on the Denikan.

"I think," the old warrior said slowly, "that sounds like a grand idea."

Damin turned to Kraig. "Do you ride?"

"In my country, I am considered—"

"Let me guess—an expert horseman," Damin finished for him. "Now why am I *not* surprised to hear that?"

The Denikan prince cracked a rare smile. "Perhaps you are beginning to fully appreciate my worth, your highness."

"*He* might be," Almodavar remarked, "but I'm certainly none the wiser."

"Then let's go somewhere we can talk," Damin suggested. "There are a few things I need to explain about my new slaves, Almodavar."

The old captain eyed him warily. "There're more than a few things you need to explain, my lad. And the explanations," he added ominously, "had better be good ones."

chapter 42

Wrayan waited with Marla for several hours before concluding that Galon Miar had ignored her invitation to her townhouse to discuss his proposal. Wrayan wasn't even sure what the "proposal" was, only that Marla seemed uncommonly anxious to learn what was really going on in the mind of the assassin and was more than a little peeved he had dared to refuse her summons.

Irritated and severely put out by the assassin's rudeness, Marla retired an hour or so before midnight. Wrayan wasn't nearly so upset at the assassin's failure to appear. To get involved with a man like Galon Miar was dicing with disaster and in his opinion, Marla's ongoing dealings with the Assassins' Guild were fraught with danger. Besides, her departure left Wrayan free to attend his own business; business he should have taken care of as soon as he arrived in the city.

It was time, Wrayan knew, to pay a visit to Franz Gillam and the Greenharbour Thieves' Guild.

He let himself out of the house a little before midnight and headed through the lamp-lit streets of the better part of Greenharbour on foot towards the darker, seedier part of town. The night was still and humid, the air thick with the rancid and unmistakable aroma of the Greenharbour docks when Wrayan arrived at his destination.

The Doorman waited outside the Thieves' Guild headquarters as if he hadn't moved since the last time Wrayan had visited this place some twenty years ago. A little thicker around the girth and a little greyer at the temples, the big man seemed otherwise unchanged. Nor had his temper improved, Wrayan discovered, as the Doorman moved to block his way as the thief approached the entrance.

"I'm here to see Franz Gillam," Wrayan explained, when it became obvious the Doorman didn't intend to let him pass.

"Why would he want to see you?"

"Professional courtesy," Wrayan replied. "I am Wrayan Lightfinger, the head of the Krakandar Thieves' Guild."

The big man squinted at him suspiciously. "Sorry, but I've met the Wraith before, lad. And you ain't him."

"Well, actually, I *am* Wrayan the Wraith, as I'm sure Franz will tell you once he's—"

"I met the Wraith a good twenty years ago, boy," the Doorman said. "Back before you were old enough to know what a thief is. So why don't you run along, eh? And next time you want to honour the God of Liars, pick someone your own age to impersonate."

Wrayan stared at the man, startled to realise he hadn't been recognised because of his youthful appearance. Wrayan knew his Harshini ancestry meant he didn't age like other men, but it never occurred to him he hadn't aged at all. Nobody mentioned it in Krakandar. Maybe, because they saw him every day, they didn't notice time had been kinder to him than it was to other men. But here in Greenharbour, where he hadn't been seen for twenty years, the difference between Wrayan Lightfinger and ordinary mortals was patently obvious. And a lot harder to explain away.

He debated arguing with the Doorman and then shrugged. "Very well."

Turning away, Wrayan headed down the street, mostly to shield his eyes from the Doorman so he wouldn't see him drawing his power. As soon as he rounded the corner, Wrayan drew a glamour to himself that would make the Doorman's eyes slide right over him without noticing he was there, and then he walked back down the street, past the Doorman and—without so much as a whimper of protest from the guild's most fierce and loyal protector—let himself into the headquarters of the Greenharbour Thieves' Guild.

Wrayan might not have aged much, but Franz Gillam had been ravaged by time. When Wrayan opened the door to the old man's office, he was confronted by a shrivelled, wrinkled little figure who seemed to be huddling inside someone else's skin, and it didn't fit him well. The room was lit with several guttering candles and had an air of musty decay about it, much the same as the wizened figure behind the desk.

The old man looked up when he heard the door, smiling serenely. "Have I died?"

"Not that I know of," Wrayan replied, a little confused. "Why?"

"I'm seeing ghosts from the past. I thought maybe it meant I'd finally slipped away." Franz Gillam shifted a little in his chair, grimacing. "No, it still hurts like hell, so I must be alive. You're definitely a ghost from the past though."

"You know who I am?"

"Wrayan the Wraith. The Greatest Thief in all of Hythria."

Wrayan smiled and closed the door behind him. "Dacendaran will be very happy to hear you say that, Franz."

"I do what I can to appease my god," the old man replied. "I thought you were running things in Krakandar these days?"

"I was . . . or still am, actually. I'm only visiting Greenharbour."

"Pity," Franz sighed. "How did you get past the Doorman?"

"Magic."

The old man smiled, assuming Wrayan was joking, and pointed to the decanter on the bureau by the door. "Pour me a drink, eh, lad? For old times' sake?"

Wrayan did as he asked and then took a seat on the overstuffed sofa opposite Gillam.

"This damn plague has gutted our ranks," Franz remarked, taking an appreciative sip of brandy. "Three of my best men were taken in the first month, including the man I had marked as my successor. Damned if I know how *I* managed to survive."

"Death has enough trouble running the seven hells, I

would imagine," Wrayan suggested. "He probably doesn't want you down there complicating things."

Franz chuckled. "You don't believe all those rumours about me being a tyrant, do you, Wrayan?"

"Are they only rumours? I thought they were well-established facts."

Amused, perhaps even a little proud of his vicious reputation, the old man's gap-toothed smile widened. "You flatter an old man."

"Then my work here is done."

Franz grinned even wider and took another sip of brandy. "You're looking well, Wrayan Lightfinger, I have to say. I swear you haven't aged a day since I saw you last."

"Just lucky, I suppose." He shrugged.

If Franz thought there was another reason for Wrayan's lack of visible aging, he gave no sign of it. "What can I do for you, Wrayan?"

"Nothing much," the thief told him. "I just thought I'd drop by and let you know I was in town."

"You've been in town for a couple of weeks. And staying at Princess Marla's townhouse, I hear."

Wrayan wasn't surprised to learn Franz already knew of his presence in Greenharbour. Not much got past the old rogue. He shrugged again, as if there was nothing out of the ordinary about a thief being a guest in the home of a princess. "You know how it is."

"Actually, with you, Lightfinger, I'm not really sure *how* it is. You never did tell me how you came to be such a close confidant of the High Prince's sister."

"No," Wrayan agreed. "I never did, did I?"

The old man sighed. "And you're never going to either, I suspect. Are you sure there's nothing I can do for you? I like the idea of a man in your position owing me a favour."

"There might be one thing," Wrayan replied.

"Name it."

"What can you tell me about Galon Miar?"

Franz Gillam took a long time before answering.

"He's—" Wrayan began, thinking perhaps that Franz didn't know who he was.

"I know who he is. How do you know him?"

"I don't know him. He's . . . the friend of a friend."

"He's nobody's *friend*, Wrayan."

"You do know him, then?"

The old man drained the last of his brandy. "Known him since he was a lad. His father placed him with the Assassins' Guild when he was just a boy, maybe nine or ten. A gifted student who exceeded everyone's expectations, to hear the Raven tell it."

"Who's his father?"

"You don't know?" Franz slid his glass across the desk for a refill. "His father is . . . or rather was . . . Ronan Dell."

That news left Wrayan speechless. He filled the glass from the decanter and slid it back to Franz.

"He's a bastard, of course—in the quite literal sense, as well as any other way you care to name. I think his mother was a *court'esa*. One of the few slaves that deviant monster, Ronan Dell, didn't manage to kill. Or maybe he did kill her, come to think of it. Just not in his usual manner. She was barely thirteen when she gave birth, I hear. She didn't survive the experience."

"What did he do with the boy?"

"Took the child in and raised him in his palace as if he was his legal-born heir, as far as I recall. He doted on the child. Trouble was, you can't flaunt your bastard too openly when you're hoping to make a match with a respectable family, and Dell would have married the High Prince's own sister if he could have got away with it. He might have, too, except old Kagan Palenovar talked Lernen into doing a deal with Fardohnya instead."

"A deal the High Prince also reneged on."

"Who can trust the highborn to keep their word on anything?" The old thief shrugged. "Anyway, as soon as the boy turned nine, Ronan apprenticed Galon to the Assassins' Guild. I don't know who he arranged to have killed, but the guild usually only accepts highborn bastards in payment for services rendered, so I suppose he had someone disposed of. It wasn't as if Ronan Dell lacked for enemies."

"Then Galon Miar's not likely to be a Patriot," Wrayan speculated.

"Miar! A *Patriot*? If that man had his way, he'd slit the throat of every soul in Greenharbour who dared to even *think* like a Patriot, Wrayan. That's common knowledge."

"It's unusual, isn't it, for any assassin to express a political opinion?"

"Understandable, though," Franz replied. "It was young Galon who discovered his father's household had been massacred and raised the alarm a few hours after it happened. Walking into that bloodbath is going to leave a mark on any sixteen-year-old boy, even one training to be an assassin."

And now, twenty-five years later, he's courting the woman who ordered the assassination of his own father, Wrayan thought, frowning. "I heard he was romantically involved with Alija Eaglespike."

Does she know who he is? Wrayan wondered. *Does Alija know she's sleeping with the son of a man she had killed? And if Galon Miar knew it was Alija who murdered his father, how would he have kept his knowledge from her?*

Like any thief, Wrayan knew the rumours claiming the Assassins' Guild had long ago developed techniques involving mental discipline that enabled an assassin to shield his mind. The stories were as old as the Assassins' Guild itself, a remnant of a time when the Harshini roamed the world at will. According to the legends, when an assassin was caught killing a man, it had been a simple matter for the Harshini to read his mind and learn the name of the man who had commissioned the crime. Under Harshini law the one who ordered the kill was the guilty party, not the assassin who wielded the blade. An assassin they considered nothing more than a tool in the hand of the real killer.

To counter the Harshini mind-readers and protect the identity of their clients, the Assassins' Guild had sought a way to make their assassins impervious to Harshini interference and had—according to legend, at least—come up with a way of blocking certain unwanted (and incriminating) memories from the reach of a probing Harshini mind, through a series of mental exercises that took years to master. It was fear of the Harshini exposing them that also gave rise to the practice of keeping assassins ignorant of anything other than the name of their intended victim. Over time, ignorance proved just as effective as discipline. Brilliant mental control or not, even the Harshini couldn't take information from an assassin's mind that wasn't actually there.

But that gave rise to another question. Did Galon Miar have that sort of mental discipline? Or was he playing a different game? One that meant it mattered little if Alija discovered he was Ronan Dell's bastard.

"Galon Miar's love affairs are often common knowledge," Franz said dismissively, forcing Wrayan to abandon his unsettling train of thought to concentrate on what the old man was saying. "He's a real charmer. Should have been a *court'esa,* not an assassin. Women trip over each other trying to climb into his bed. It's this whole *dangerous assassin* allure, I think. He's a good-looking man and some women like the menace he represents."

"Still, sleeping with the woman who orchestrated his father's murder? Hardly the actions of a dedicated Royalist."

"Which just proves how far he's willing to go, to achieve whatever it is he's after. Galon Miar is working to his own agenda, Wrayan. Take my advice and don't get involved."

Wrayan frowned, wondering if Galon Miar's interest in Princess Marla was also part of his private agenda. If it was, then he should warn the princess. Marla was probably the most careful person Wrayan knew, but she was grieving and vulnerable at the moment. There was always a chance she could be seduced by a charming smile and the thought of something so forbidden that just thinking about it was an aphrodisiac. He knew exactly how that felt.

Swallowing the last of his brandy, Wrayan rose to his feet. "I'll tell my friend to be careful. Thanks for the drink."

"You planning anything while you're here?"

"Nothing at the moment," he assured the guild head, understanding that Franz was asking about his larcenous plans, not his social calendar. "But you never know when an opportunity will present itself. And I do have Dacendaran dogging my heels, making sure I earn my 'greatest thief' title."

The old thief smiled. "That's one thing I've always liked about you, Wrayan. You really are a true believer."

"Do you doubt the God of Thieves exists?" Wrayan asked, a little surprised to hear such an admission from the head of a Thieves' Guild. He forgot sometimes that the Harshini were long gone and the gods didn't appear to others the way Dace appeared to him. When one had proof of the gods' existence, it seemed strange to confront someone forced to rely on faith.

The old thief shook his head ruefully. "If he does, with your devotion, you're far more likely to run into him than I am, son."

"Shall I tell Dacendaran you're expecting a visit from him when I see him next?"

"You do that, Wrayan," Franz chuckled. "I'm an old man, and I'll die someday soon. It'd be nice to know—*before* I go—that I devoted my life to an entity who actually exists."

"Dacendaran exists, Franz. You have my word on it."

"You say that with such sincerity, I almost believe you."

"Believe it, Franz," he assured the old man. "And be grateful he's not in the habit of dropping in on you. He can be a little . . . trying."

Franz looked surprised to hear Wrayan admit such a thing. "And here, all this time, I thought you worshipped our god unconditionally."

"I believe in him, Franz. And I honour him every chance I get. But *worship* . . . ? As a good friend of mine is fond of saying—*nobody knows better than I that the gods exist. Whether I believe them worthy of adoration is an entirely different matter.*"

"And which good friend would that be?"

His hand on the door, Wrayan smiled cryptically at the old

thief as he pulled it open. "You wouldn't believe me if I told you."

"You have too many secrets, Wrayan Lightfinger."

"As do you, old man."

"True, but mine won't get me killed."

Wrayan looked at him curiously. "What makes you think mine will?"

Franz Gillam eyed him up and down. "You come here in the dead of night, looking no older than you did two decades ago. You're in Greenharbour as a guest of the most powerful woman in Hythria and you're here asking about the most dangerous assassin in the country. That's more secrets in one day than I deal with in a year."

"Don't worry about me, Franz. I can take care of myself."

"I'm not worried about *you*," the old thief told him. "Nor am I a fool. You're not visiting a city recovering from the plague out of concern for your health, my old friend. You're up to something, Wrayan Lightfinger, and if it involves Galon Miar and Marla Wolfblade, it's the rest of Hythria I fear for."

chapter 43

Furious her summons had been ignored, Marla paced her room for a good hour before she felt settled enough to attempt sleep. She was unaccustomed to such rudeness, even among her peers. To be treated in such a cavalier manner by a common-born assassin was more than she could tolerate.

You are a damned fool, she told herself, as she began to undress. She had dismissed her slaves when she retired, not wishing them to witness her agitation. As usual, the night was heavy with moisture, but the breeze was cool on Marla's clammy skin. Tugging on the laces of her bodice, she pulled it off impatiently and tossed it on the floor, wondering how much of her anger was really just irrational disappointment. Marla was honest enough with herself to recognise her emotions for what they were. She knew she'd been waiting for Galon Miar to arrive with something akin to giddy anticipation, which was ridiculous, because Marla also knew that's exactly what the assassin was trying to make her feel, so she should know better than to fall for his barefaced manipulation.

Unfortunately, knowing about a disease didn't make one immune to it.

Perhaps that's why she'd been waiting for him so anxiously, Marla consoled herself, as she dropped her skirt on the floor and stepped out of her undershift. If he'd shown up when he was supposed to, Wrayan would have read Galon Miar's mind and exposed his treacherous motives, which were undoubtedly some sort of dire plot against the throne and she'd be over this idiotic obsession with a man so inherently dangerous, that just thinking about him as anything other than an enemy was probably suicidal.

"Gods, Marla!" she told her reflection as she slipped the cool silk of her dressing gown over her bare shoulders. "Get a grip on yourself, girl! You're starting to sound as crazy as Lernen!"

"Talking to yourself isn't a terribly encouraging sign either, your highness."

Marla squealed in fright and spun around to find Galon Miar reclining on the windowsill of her open bedroom window. She had no idea how long he'd been there. Or how he'd gotten there. She certainly hadn't heard him coming through the second-floor window, nor had he betrayed his presence with any unexpected movement.

A thousand reactions to his appearance raced through her mind, but oddly, not one of them involved calling for the guards. Marla knew she was in danger from this man, but it wasn't physical danger. It was something far more insidious. And far more seductive.

She took a deep breath, her inner turmoil something she wasn't planning to share with anybody, least of all the man who was causing most of it.

"What are *you* doing here?" she asked calmly, pulling the robe closed.

Galon jumped down from the windowsill, landing silently on the rug. Dressed in black from head to toe, he moved like a cat, which was an apt description, Marla thought, because that's what he was—a predator. A very dangerous predator.

"You invited me."

"I invited you to come through my front door at a reasonable hour, Master Miar, not through my bedroom window in the dead of night."

He smiled. "But it's so much more romantic this way. And if we're to be married . . ."

"I have agreed to nothing of the kind," she informed him, turning back to the mirror, and more importantly, turning her back on the intruder as a sign of her contempt.

"But you will," he told her confidently. "Eventually."

She picked up her brush and began to stroke her shoulder-length fair hair. Marla was damned if she was going to let this man think he could intimidate her. "Get out of my house."

Galon didn't seem to hear her. He moved closer, right behind her, staring at her reflection with eyes that saw far too much.

"Why don't you scream?" he asked, picking up a strand of her hair and running it over his lips as if the mere smell of it aroused him. "You've got enough guards in this house to cut me down before I get back to the window."

Marla met his eyes in the mirror and shrugged carelessly. "Screaming would imply I'm afraid of you, Galon Miar. I'm not afraid of you."

"You should be," he warned softly, stepping so close she could feel his hot breath on her neck.

Marla didn't break the rhythm of her brushing. Galon let the strand of hair fall as she continued her slow, deliberate strokes. She could sense the danger, even if she couldn't see it directly. She was feigning indifference but was aware of the nearness of him like a blind man stepping too close to an inferno. "Why should I fear you? You're just a man, Galon Miar, and I don't fear *any* man."

"But I'm not *any* man." He put his hands on her shoulders and began to massage them gently, making her spine tingle. He leaned forward and breathed into her ear, watching her in the mirror. "I can make you forget yourself, Marla Wolfblade. I can take you somewhere you're afraid to go. I can make your blood sing."

"You can't *make* me do anything," she insisted, as he gently eased the edge of her robe from her shoulders. She thought about pulling away from him; about turning around and slapping his insolent face . . .

But that was all she did—thought about it.

"I can make your heart race," he assured her softly, as his hands caressed her neck and began to work their way down toward her breast. She closed her eyes for a moment, almost gave in to the sensation . . .

Then she realised what she was doing and her eyes snapped open. Marla shook off his hands and turned to face him, deciding this had gone far enough.

"My pulse will race just as merrily watching you bleed to death at my feet," she pointed out with all the icy dignity she could muster. "A situation I could easily arrange, simply by screaming."

"If you scream because of me, your highness," he predicted with a wicked little smile, as she pulled the robe back up around her shoulders, "you'll be screaming for more, not for help."

The man's arrogance was breathtaking. Marla looked down her nose at him, wondering if contempt would work where disdain had failed. "You really do think you're Kalianah's gift to women, don't you, Galon Miar?"

"You mean I'm *not*?" he asked, in mock horror.

"Sadly for you, no. Nor are you particularly creative," she added. "Do you think I'm so starved for human contact

I'll welcome an assassin into my bed, or worse, marry one? If I want sex, Galon, I can send for a *court'esa* any time I please."

"Your *court'esa* is dead, your highness. You told me that, yourself. And you never seem to have acquired any others, oddly enough. Why is that, I wonder?"

"Whatever the reason, Galon, it's none of your business." She turned back to the mirror and resumed brushing her hair. "Now, if you don't mind, you've had your fun and I'd like to go to bed."

He grinned mischievously at her reflection. "The two aren't mutually exclusive, you know."

Despite herself, Marla smiled at him. It was difficult to maintain her icy demeanour in the face of such a blatant invitation. "You really should leave now, before I decide to have you run through."

He seemed confident she was bluffing. "You'd have called your guards long ago if you seriously meant me harm," he told her. "Or if you thought I meant you harm."

"You think you know me that well?"

"I think I'd have a great deal of fun getting to know you better."

Putting down the brush, she turned to face him again, amazed by his persistence. "Have you no shame?"

"Not a lot." He glanced down at her robe, which had fallen open, and studied her appreciatively. "Nor do you, your highness," he added.

Quite deliberately, Marla pulled it closed, her actions robbed of a little of their disdain when she realised she was blushing.

"You've married four men for political and financial gain, Marla Wolfblade," he said, watching her closely. "You can't possibly be embarrassed by the thought of a man seeing you naked."

"I'll have you know," Marla replied stiffly, lifting her chin, "I only married *three* men for political or financial gain. One of them I actually loved."

"Which one?" he asked.

"That's none of your business."

He stared at her for a long moment. "You were wasted on all of them. I doubt any one of them appreciated you."

"Oh, and you do, I suppose?" she asked.

Galon crooked his finger at her and beckoned her nearer. "Come here," he taunted, "and I'll show you."

Marla glanced at the small empty space between them, shaking her head. "I don't think so."

"Afraid?"

"Not tempted enough," she lied, aware this game was stupid, dangerous and worst of all, easily stopped. She only needed to call out and that would be the brutal and bloody end of any man who dared sneak into her room in the small hours of the night, hoping to seduce the High Prince's sister.

Galon Miar seemed able to read her intentions, if not her thoughts. But if Marla wasn't ready to cross the space between them, he certainly was. Without waiting for her answer, the assassin reached for her hand and drew her to him until his lips hovered over hers. He waited for a fraction of a second, as if he expected her to pull away, and then he kissed her.

When Marla didn't respond, Galon raised his lips from hers and looked at her oddly. His genuine surprise that she hadn't melted at his touch was quite gratifying.

"What? You think one blazing kiss and I'm yours? You do have a high opinion of yourself, don't you?"

Galon studied her expression as if he didn't believe a word she was saying and then he took her face in his hands and slowly, with agonising tenderness, he kissed her again.

For a moment, Marla surrendered to the sensation. She hadn't been kissed like that since Nash had made love to her in Kalianah's grotto in Krakandar Palace when she was a girl. But that sort of familiarity was far too tempting and ultimately futile. She'd ended up having Nash assassinated. Soft lips, a hard body and too much raging lust weren't the basis for anything but trouble. Marla knew that for a fact.

She pushed him away, marvelling at her own strength. Galon Miar was far closer to winning this confrontation than he knew.

"What part of 'I have no interest in you' are you having trouble understanding?" she asked coolly.

Her question seemed to amuse him. "You're *court'esa* trained, aren't you?"

"Of course," she replied, puzzled by the question.

"Then you should know better than to lie about what you're feeling."

"I am not lying about anything. I don't like you, I don't want you, and you're completely insane if you think I'm going to marry you."

"Really?" he asked, gently brushing the hair off her face. "Didn't your *court'esa* tell you about the physiological changes that happen when you're aroused, your highness? You must remember. It's pretty much the first thing you would have learned. You know, all those little telltale signs: ragged breathing, galloping heart rate, pupils dilating, and," he added, looking down, "a few other . . . miscellaneous symptoms . . ."

Offended by his brazen gall, Marla raised her hand to slap him, but he caught her wrist and held it fast. "Now you've got your breathing under control, but your pulse is racing, princess," he said, glancing at her raised hand he held fast around the wrist, "and your eyes are so wide I could drown in them. Tell me you don't like how I dress. Tell me you don't like what I do for a living, but don't tell me that right at this moment, you don't want me just as much as I want you."

Marla struggled to free her hand from his grasp, but he had no intention of letting her go. She raised her other hand, but he caught that, too, and she was effectively trapped in his embrace. He wasn't hurting her, but neither was he giving an inch.

Call the guards, she told herself sternly. *Stop playing games with this man and call for help.*

The trouble was that Marla didn't really want help.

What she wanted here was victory.

And to win, she realised in a sudden flash of insight, she was going to have to lose. "Very well, then I admit it. I want you."

Galon was so stunned by her sudden surrender that he let her go. *"What?"*

"You're right, Galon," she sighed, sliding her arms around his neck. "I want you. You make me feel things I haven't felt for years. You're a very attractive man—unfortunately, you know that, which makes you a little obnoxious—and I'm a living, breathing woman, no more immune to your charms than any other. Take me."

He lifted her arms away and studied her suspiciously. "A minute ago you were fantasising about me bleeding to death at your feet . . ."

"We all have different things that arouse us," Marla observed. "That's *court'esa* lesson number two, isn't it?"

Now he was really starting to worry. Marla was delighted. In a heartbeat she had turned the tables on her adversary and suddenly held the upper hand. Galon Miar was no longer anywhere near as sure of himself. Now he doubted her motives, was suspicious of her inexplicable capitulation, certain there was something sinister in her intentions.

"What are you up to?"

"I'm surrendering," she told him, breathless as a lovelorn girl.

He wasn't convinced. "Surrendering? Why? So you can call your guards and claim I took you by force?"

"If you weren't prepared to risk that fate, Galon, you wouldn't have come through my window." She deliberately let the robe fall open and moved closer to him. "Isn't that what you wanted, darling? Marla Wolfblade throwing herself at you, desperate for your touch, your kiss, your caress?

So take me, Galon. Take me hard. Show me what I've been missing out on. Ravish me. I'm yours."

He actually took a step backward and Marla knew she'd won. She studied him triumphantly and stepped back, once again full of icy dignity.

"Now who's afraid of whom?" she said, tying the robe closed. Then she walked to the centre of the room and turned to face him. Her eyes never left his face as she called out, "Guards!"

At her summons, the door flew open and two palace guards burst into the room. When they realised their princess was not alone, the men drew their swords and turned on the intruder. Galon stared at her in shock, but was smart enough to make no threatening moves other than to raise his hands to show the soldiers he wasn't planning to resist.

"Your highness?" the more senior of the two guards asked in confusion, staring at the assassin. "Are you all right?"

They'd been on duty outside since she'd retired and had let nobody past her door. The unsuspected presence of a strange man in their mistress's bedroom had her guards looking almost as stunned as Galon.

"Master Miar was just leaving," she told the guards. "Be so kind as to escort him off the premises, please."

She turned to look at him. To his credit, he recovered quickly. He lowered his hands, bowed with genuine respect. "It's been a pleasure, your highness. I expect we'll resume our . . . *conversation* . . . sometime soon?"

"Don't hold your breath," Marla advised.

"It'll be soon enough," he predicted with an insolent wink, already back to the Galon she knew. "You need me." And then he grinned at her. "Almost as much as you want me."

Marla allowed herself a small smile. "I wouldn't bet the family fortune on it if I were you, Galon."

For once, he didn't seem to have a clever comeback. Marla watched as the guards escorted him from her room and down the hall toward the stairs.

Once he was out of sight she closed the door and leaned against it, her breathing ragged, wondering why, of all of the emotions she was battling with right now, the hardest to deal with seemed to be the urge to run down that hall after Galon and call him back to her room.

chapter 44

As it turned out, the most difficult part of Starros's grand plan to honour Dacendaran by robbing Krakandar of its entire population was finding a way to speak to Xanda Taranger without bringing the wrath of Mahkas Damaran down on all of them. Damin's commission to his cousin had been to keep an eye on Mahkas, which meant even with uninhibited access to the slaveways, there weren't many opportunities to find Xanda alone in the palace.

Krakandar Palace probably wasn't the safest place for such a potentially dangerous meeting to take place, in any case. After days of mulling over the problem, Starros decided to take a more direct approach. With Luc North's assistance, he arranged for Wrayan's Thieves' Guild henchmen to kidnap Xanda Taranger off the streets of the city in broad daylight.

Their mission was made easier by Xanda himself. He made a point of inspecting the city two or three times a week to see how things were going, to talk to the people, reassure them, gauge their mood, and generally try to put a good face on things. Because he was here as a guest and actually held no formal position in Krakandar's court, he was able to do this without fanfare and usually accomplished his inspection with no more than a single guard accompanying him.

Wrayan's men ambushed Xanda and his guard as he entered the narrow streets of the Beggars' Quarter, a few blocks from the Pickpocket's Retreat. They overwhelmed them and bundled the two men away, trussed up like chickens on their way to market, not removing the ropes or the sacks thrown over their heads until they were behind closed doors in the safe house.

"What the hell . . ." Xanda began, struggling as his kidnappers freed him. His voice faltered as the sack was pulled from his head and he found himself face to face with Starros.

"Hello, Xanda."

"*Starros*? For pity's sake, man!" he complained, shaking free of the ropes that had bound him, while he glared at the men who'd taken him prisoner. "Couldn't you have found a less dramatic way of getting me to your . . ." he glanced around and then shrugged, ". . . your *lair*?"

"Believe me, Xanda, if there'd been an easier way to do this, I would have used it." He glanced at the men still holding Xanda's accompanying guard, tied and blindfolded. "Let him go."

Luc's men did as Starros ordered. As soon as the man's hands were free he pulled the sack from his head and stared at Starros in shock.

"I thought you'd be dead by now, lad."

Starros smiled gratefully. "Thanks to you, Sergeant Clayne, I survived."

His thanks were heartfelt and genuine. Clayne was the man in charge of the palace cells the night Damin returned to Krakandar. This was the man who'd stood aside to allow Damin to come to his aid.

The big man was clearly disturbed by Starros's miraculous recovery. He eyed him up and down, his expression grim. "You shouldn't have survived, lad. You surely shouldn't have walked away from it without a mark on you."

"I had help of a sort you couldn't imagine, Sergeant."

The man looked around the room with a frown. "And now you've fallen in with criminals, I see."

"I don't know if he's fallen, so much as been given an almighty shove," Xanda remarked, rubbing his chafed wrists. "Is there anything to drink around here, or are you lot planning to torture me, as well as tromp all over my dignity?"

"Get him something to drink," Starros ordered the man standing closest to the door. "And take Sergeant Clayne into the next room. I'm sure he'd appreciate an ale or two."

"I'm not going anywhere," Clayne announced belligerently. "My job is to watch over Lord Taranger."

"And I swear no harm will come to him. I'm asking you to leave for your own protection, Sergeant," Starros explained. "You did me a favour once, and now I'm returning it. What I have to say to Xanda could be considered treason. You've risked a charge of treason once before on my behalf. I'm not going to implicate you, even by association, a second time."

Clayne thought about it and then held up his hands to indicate he would offer no further resistance. "Very well."

Starros waited until the others had escorted Clayne from the dingy room and then turned to look at Xanda once they were alone.

"Noble of you to care so much about Clayne's neck, while you're endangering mine without a second thought."

"Oh, we'd thought of that," Starros assured him. "We're going to beat you senseless after we finish our meeting and leave you for dead in an alley somewhere. Just to make it look good."

"There's the mark of a true friend."

Starros smiled. "I like to help where I can. How have you been, Xanda? You look tired."

"I'm all right, I suppose." He sank down on the bench beside the fireplace. "As right as any man can be, living in an insane asylum, at any rate." Xanda jerked his head in the direction the others had disappeared. "You seem to be fitting in with your new friends rather nicely."

"I've been touched by Dacendaran," Starros reminded him, taking the seat opposite. "That makes me something of a celebrity in the Thieves' Guild. Didn't you notice? I even have my very own henchmen now, ready to do my criminal bidding."

"Yes, I noticed that."

"In truth, they're not really mine, they're only on loan from Wrayan while he's away, but they do the job and they look at me like I know what I'm doing, so I suppose that means something."

The conversation halted when the man Starros had sent for ale returned with a jug and poured one for Xanda, and then let himself into the other room where they were holding Clayne. Xanda took a long swallow before fixing his gaze on Starros. "So, what is this treasonous plot you wish to implicate me in, old friend?"

"I want to evacuate Krakandar."

"Wouldn't we all," Xanda agreed sourly.

"I'm serious. Mahkas Damaran stole the thing I loved most in this world, Xanda. I want vengeance. Real vengeance, not some token of it. So I plan to take away the thing he loves most."

"I'm not sure he actually loves the people of Krakandar, Starros. Come to think of it, I'm not sure he actually loves anybody."

"He loves the power the people of this city represent."

"True enough."

"Then you'll help me?"

Xanda rubbed his chin thoughtfully. "I'd love to. But what exactly do you expect *me* to do? If you want me to unseal the city, you're wasting your time. Luciena would have nagged me into it weeks ago, if it was even remotely possible. Every time I suggest it, Mahkas gets more obstinate about it."

"We don't need to unseal the city," Starros assured him. "The Thieves' Guild has other ways to get past the walls."

"They *do*?"

"Don't ask me for details, Xanda, you're better off not knowing."

He took another swallow of ale. "I don't doubt that. Are you going to tell me how you plan to get the people out?"

"That's something else you'd be better off not knowing."

Xanda looked at him curiously. "Then why exactly did you bring me here? To brag about it?"

"I need to make certain we're not interfered with; that the soldiers in the city don't start looking into anything out of the ordinary. I don't want them tipping off Mahkas to our plans."

Xanda raised a brow at him. "You want me to quietly put it about that the Krakandar Raiders should turn a blind eye to your criminal activities?"

"Exactly."

"You don't want much, do you?"

"Only vengeance," Starros replied.

Xanda barely hesitated before agreeing to grant the favour Starros asked for. "I can probably do what you ask, but I have a condition of my own."

"Name it."

"Among the first people you smuggle out of the city will be my wife, my children, and the Lionsclaw boys. Promise you'll get them to my brother in Walsark and I'll burn down the damned palace myself as a diversion, if need be."

"I'm not sure we need anything quite so drastic. I do appreciate the offer though. But you have my word that Luciena and the children will be among the first to leave the city. Do you think Travin will mind twenty thousand-odd refugees in his borough?"

Xanda smiled thinly. "Not if you promise to make them all buy at least one piece of his wretched porcelain."

The young thief was mightily relieved. "I'll make it a condition of every citizen's exit from the city. And thank you. I thought it would take hours to convince you of the cleverness of my diabolical scheme."

"Nothing's too much trouble for an old friend," Xanda said, draining the last of his ale. "You really are taking this whole Thieves' Guild engagement rather seriously, aren't you?"

"Not really my choice, Xanda. Damin traded my soul to

the God of Thieves when he should have let me die. I'm stuck with this."

"And you're too well brought up to do a sloppy job on anything," Xanda noted wryly. "I wonder what Almodavar will make of the new Starros when he gets back."

"I dread to think," he said. "Can't imagine he'll be too impressed by my change of circumstances. On the other hand, it's hard to tell with Almodavar, and there's no proof he's actually my father, you know."

"No proof he isn't, either." Xanda put his tankard on the seat beside him and looked across at Starros. "I'll need to be getting back soon or they'll come looking for me. There's really no need for the whole beating-me-senseless charade, you know. I can fake it."

"If Mahkas suspected for a minute . . ."

"I can deal with Mahkas," Xanda assured him. "You take care of your end of things and let me deal with the maniac."

Starros was surprised at the sudden feeling of melancholy that washed over him. "I remember a time when we all thought Mahkas Damaran was the most wonderful man we knew."

"That's the worst thing about childhood illusions," Xanda agreed. "They really hurt when you discover how wrong they are."

The pain in Xanda's voice surprised Starros. He'd thought he was the only one suffering intolerable grief. "Just how bad is it up there?"

"You can't begin to imagine," Xanda sighed. "Mahkas can only speak in a hoarse whisper, even when he's yelling. It drives him crazy. He thinks everyone is secretly plotting to bring Damin back to unseat him. It's most of the reason he won't open the city gates. Nothing anybody says will convince him Damin rode off to war against Fardohnya. Mahkas is convinced Damin merely stopped out of sight at the Walsark Crossroads and is waiting for his opportunity to come back and take the city by force."

"Has it occurred to Mahkas that Damin was in the city not

so long ago and could have taken over any time he pleased, if that was his intention?"

"Ah, now that sort of conclusion requires a degree of rational thought. Mahkas isn't real big on rational, right now."

"What about Bylinda?"

Xanda shook his head in sorrow. "She's the hardest one to watch. Leila's death has destroyed her."

Starros wasn't surprised to hear Xanda's news. "I know what you mean. I saw her a few weeks ago. In the slaveways."

Xanda looked at him in alarm. "In the *slaveways*? Do I want to know what you were doing in the slaveways, Starros?"

"Probably not. But I do understand what you mean about Bylinda being destroyed by grief. She looked like a wraith when I spoke to her."

"That's a pretty fair description, actually," Xanda agreed unhappily. "Luciena's desperately worried about her. We all are, for that matter."

"Well, I'd offer to help, but I don't think my presence in the palace would do anything to ease matters."

Xanda forced a weary smile. "There's an understatement if ever I heard one. But I'm glad you survived this, Starros. There's been enough death in this family to last a lifetime. And you appear to be adapting remarkably well to your sudden change in circumstances, even if your life is turning in a direction you didn't anticipate."

"I still haven't convinced myself this whole 'let's sell Starros's soul to the God of Thieves' plan isn't Damin's idea of a sick joke."

Xanda looked around the small main room of the safe house, nodding with approval. "Well, you're on your way to a fine career as a thief, I'd say. Your own minions. A nice lair. What more could a thief want? You'll be giving Wrayan a run for his money soon, won't you? How long before you're the head of the Krakandar Thieves' Guild?"

"Never," Starros said and then, before he could stop himself, he burst out laughing as something else occurred to him, something so ironic it was almost painful.

Given the serious nature of their conversation only a few moments ago, Xanda wasn't nearly so amused. "I don't get the joke, I'm afraid."

"It just occurred to me—I used to complain Orleon would live forever and I'd never get to be Chief Steward of Krakandar Palace."

"Oh, yes, I can see how you'd think that was hysterically funny."

"Don't you see the irony?" Starros laughed, unable to help himself. "Even if I wanted Wrayan's job, it wouldn't make any difference. I've sold my soul to a god and I'm still no better off than I was in the palace."

"I don't get the joke."

"Wrayan's part Harshini, Xanda," he reminded him. "There's a good chance he really *will* live forever."

Xanda smiled. "That is kind of funny, when you think about it."

Starros wiped his eyes and forced his laughter under control. "I'm sorry. You're right, it's not that funny. I don't know what . . . you know, I think that's the first time I've laughed since Leila . . . since she died."

"I think it's the first genuine laugh I've heard since then, myself," Xanda replied. "Don't feel guilty for being alive, Starros."

"I don't . . ."

"Yes, you do," the older man scolded. "You think it's not fair that you're still here and she's gone. And maybe you're right, given the manner in which you were saved. But you can't live like that, Starros. I know. After my mother died, I spent months thinking she'd hanged herself because of something I did. Absurd, I know, but I was only six at the time. I used to walk around clutching that damned ceramic horse and knight Mahkas mended for me, reliving those last few moments in my mother's room before our uncle sent me and Travin out, wondering what I'd done to make her so upset she'd kill herself."

"I'm not six years old, Xanda."

"I know. But the guilt is still there, no matter how old you are, or how hard you try to deny it. All suicides are the same, Starros. It's the ultimate act of selfishness. Suicide offers a release to the one who dies and a lifetime of grief and pain to those who have to go on."

"Leila wasn't being selfish," he objected, a little surprised to hear Xanda say such a harsh thing about his own cousin. "She was the most unselfish person I knew."

"She killed herself to get back at her father, Starros," Xanda reminded him. "I know you loved her, but you need to remember that. And someday you'll get over your grief, too. And you need to accept it'll happen and not feel guilty about that, either."

Starros rose to his feet, uncomfortable discussing anything so intensely personal, even with an old friend, particularly with his grief still so raw. "I appreciate the advice, Xanda, but really, I can deal with this on my own."

"Vengeance won't make the pain go away."

"I don't want the pain to go away," Starros told him. "Because when it does . . . then she'll truly be gone, Xanda, and I'll finally have to accept that no matter how hard I wish for it, Leila is never coming back."

CHAPTER 45

Nobody was more surprised to see Brakandaran the Halfbreed than Chyler Kantel and the Fardohnyan bandits hiding in the Sunrise Mountains, where Brak had spent much of the last twelve years keeping Dacendaran happy.

He arrived at the bandit camp high in the mountains a bit over a week after Zegarnald had so inconsiderately dumped him back in Fardohnya, figuring there wasn't much point in reporting to Axelle Regis, as the general was probably already on his way through the Widowmaker Pass (if not already well into Hythria) by the time Brak arrived in Westbrook.

Still cold enough at this altitude to make his breath frost as he trudged upward toward the light, it was quite late when he found the thieves' camp. He didn't mean to frighten anyone, but his sudden appearance out of the darkness had the bandits gathered around the small camp fire hastily reaching for their weapons until they realised who the intruder was. Chyler seemed the most shocked of all and after a brief round of greetings to his old compatriots, she bundled Brak away to her tent, to find out what he'd been up to since he left.

Sitting cross-legged in her small tent, his head brushing the steeply sloped hide roof, Brak sipped the hot herbal tea Chyler made for him and told her about his expedition into Hythria, how he'd sent Ollie back to Qorinipor and exactly how he'd arrived back in Fardohnya. Chyler was a good listener and interrupted little as he related his tale, but her expression was grim, and by the time he was finished, more than a little confused.

"You mean the God of War just picked you up and carried you back here magically?" she asked, her eyes wide with the notion Brak had been transported anywhere by the God of War.

"It was a little more immediate than that, but it's basically what happened."

"But . . . even after everything you've just told me, I still don't understand why."

"I irritate him." Brak shrugged. "I tend to do that a lot."

"But why is the God of War mad at you? You told me you had no interest in this war. Didn't you tell him the same thing?"

"I really *don't* have an interest in this particular conflict," he agreed. "It means nothing to me that Hythria and Fardohnya are fighting again. They've been doing it on and off for the past thousand years. Life just wouldn't be the same if it didn't include at least one Hythrun-Fardohnyan skirmish every century or so."

"But . . ." she prompted.

"He's interfering a little too directly," Brak told her. "Not enough to annoy the other gods yet, but more than enough to get up my nose."

Chyler smiled, amused, it seemed, by his annoyance with the immortals. "And just exactly how does a god manage to get up your nose, Lord Brakandaran?"

"By making sure the Hythrun put up a decent fight."

"Wouldn't they do that anyway?" she asked with a puzzled look. "I mean, the Hythrun teach small children how to hold a weapon. I can't see the world's most dedicated followers of the War God suffering an invasion from anybody without objecting to it."

"But they've been decimated by the plague," he reminded her. "If things were left to progress naturally, Axelle Regis would be lucky if he encountered even a token resistance between here and Greenharbour. The end result would change the political climate of the whole continent, but the cost in lives would be negligible."

"And now?"

"The God of War is stacking the odds. He tells me he's taken a personal interest in the Hythrun leadership and is crowing about it as if it were a grand idea. I suppose to him it is. If the Hythrun manage to rally themselves and put up an effective defence, there'll be a bloodbath and the more blood the better as far as Zegarnald's concerned."

Chyler still didn't see the problem. "Will it make that much difference, though? Hablet's amassed a force of over eighty thousand men. Even a brilliant and experienced general would have trouble making much of a dent in our forces with fewer than fifteen thousand to throw against us."

Brak shook his head. "Actually, a brilliant strategist and fifteen thousand men could cause untold damage, given the right circumstances. And that's exactly what Zegarnald is banking on. To put up any sort of effective resistance, the Hythrun are going to have to decimate the Fardohnyans every chance they get, preferably with minimal casualties on their side. The only thing holding up this massacre he's arranged to keep himself amused is the insanity of Lernen Wolfblade, who's decided to lead the Hythrun forces himself."

"How does that help?"

Brak smiled grimly. "Ollie could probably mount a successful campaign against the High Prince of Hythria."

"Then you have nothing to worry about, do you?"

"Zegarnald won't allow such a situation to last," he assured her, shaking his head. "Lernen's just bought us some time. Sooner or later, Zegarnald will get impatient and he'll intervene, either directly or indirectly, and then we'll have our massacre. Count on it."

Chyler frowned. "I think I'm beginning to understand. You're not worried about the Hythrun so much as all the Fardohnyans who are going to die in this conflict, are you?"

"I'm half Harshini, Chyler. I have this unfortunate tendency to despise the futile waste of human life."

"But I've seen you kill without hesitating."

"I said *futile* waste. I don't have a problem with the necessary stuff."

She leaned forward to top up his tea from the pot sitting over the tiny stove she used to warm her tent. "I know this is going to be hard for you, Brak, but I really think you need to accept that you can't fight the will of the gods."

He looked at her in surprise. "Who says I can't fight the will of the gods? I do it all the time."

Chyler was unimpressed by his boast. "So what are you going to do? General Regis has shifted a good thirty thousand men through the pass in the last month alone. Winternest is in Fardohnyan hands for the first time since it was built. The behemoth is on the move. Even someone with your talents is going to have trouble stopping it."

She was right, of course, which didn't make Brak feel any better. But he was convinced of one thing. Even if he couldn't stop the war—which seemed unlikely now—he was determined to do something to limit the damage. Every life saved was one less Zegarnald could feed on.

"I don't know." He shrugged. "I suppose the only way to

slow this down now is to find a way to even the odds a little. If the Hythrun aren't confronted with overwhelming numbers, they're more likely to fight a traditional war, rather than go looking for new and creative ways to annihilate large numbers of their enemy in one fell swoop."

"You can't do that unless you can convince Hablet to stop sending his troops through the Widowmaker."

"Should I ride down to the Winter Palace, do you think?" Brak suggested. "And inform his majesty that I'm the fabled Brakandaran the Halfbreed and I'd very much like him to stop invading Hythria, please, because I'm having a disagreement with the God of War?"

Chyler laughed. "Oh, definitely! That's bound to work."

Brak smiled. "And to think I thought stopping this wretched war was going to be a problem."

"Well, if anybody can find a solution, Brak, I'm sure it will be you."

He studied her in the flickering light of the small lamp. "I thought you'd be violently opposed to me doing anything to aid the Hythrun."

"You're not really aiding them, though, are you? You're trying to find a way to limit the number of Fardohnyan casualties. Besides," she added with a scowl, "this damned interruption to trade between Hythria and Fardohnya is costing me a lot of business. With all these troops on the move, we haven't been able to rob a decent caravan travelling through the Widowmaker in months."

"How awful for Dacendaran."

"I'm not worried about the God of Thieves, Brak. My people are starving. If you're planning to do something to put an end to this insanity, I'm right there with you."

He swirled the tea around in his cup while he thought about it. Chyler waited impatiently for a time, but clearly, she expected him to have the answer at his fingertips.

"So," she asked, when the silence dragged on too long for her liking. She was glaring at him as if he already knew the answer to the problem and was just waiting for the most dramatic time to announce it. "How are we going to stop another fifty thousand-odd young, innocent Fardohnyans from marching through the Widowmaker to almost certain doom in Hythria?"

"We have to block the pass," Brak replied thoughtfully, wondering if it could even be done. Since the Widowmaker had been paved it was much wider than it once was. A simple rock fall wouldn't be enough and it was too late in the year, and not enough snow left, to trigger a decent avalanche.

"How?" Chyler asked, obviously thinking the same thing.

"We're going to have to blow it up, I suppose."

The bandit stared at him. "*What*?"

"You know. An explosion. Big boom. Lots of smoke and noise. I hear they're quite common in Fardohnya, particularly since Hablet's had them trying to perfect his cannon. Impressive they are. If we pick the right spot there'll be rocks flying everywhere—but significantly downward—conveniently coming to rest somewhere it'll take 'em six months to clear . . ."

She rolled her eyes at him. "I know what an explosion is, Brak. What I don't know is how you're going to make it happen. Unless you're planning to attack a column of heavily guarded artillery and steal their ammunition when they finally come through the pass, you have nothing to work with. The recipe for making the explosive powders they used when they constructed the pass—and presumably the same recipe is used in the cannon—is the best kept secret in Fardohnya. Hablet would line his daughters up and shoot an arrow through each one of them himself, before he allowed that information to fall into the wrong hands. And you have to admit, given what you're planning, you do qualify as the wrong hands."

"I don't need Hablet's damned explosives."

"Then how are you going to blow up the Widowmaker?" When he didn't answer her immediately, her eyes widened in shock. "You're going to use *magic*?"

"Aren't you the one who's always telling me you *want* to see some real magic at work?"

"Well, yes . . . but . . . can you do something like that?"

"You'd be amazed by some of the things I can do, Chyler."

Her eyes narrowed suspiciously as she studied him in the golden lamplight. "Why now?"

"What do you mean?"

"I've known you for twelve years, Brak. You've never once done anything even remotely magical. Why now?"

Brak shrugged and drank down the last of his tea.

"Now I have a reason," he said.

ChAPTER 46

Not since he was twelve years old had Rorin Mariner spent so much time dodging large numbers of Fardohnyan soldiers who would cheerfully hang him as a Hythrun spy if they caught him. He wouldn't be dodging them now, he knew, if not for the rank stupidity of Terin Lionsclaw.

The trip to Winternest had been bad enough. Terin brought along a small army of retainers, suffering under the sorry delusion that a large entourage somehow made him look more important. Nothing Rorin said seemed to convince the man this excursion behind enemy lines was to gather intelligence, rather than impress people. Terin was a Warlord and Rorin was simply a commoner, the Warlord pointed out tersely, even if he was a member of the Sorcerers' Collective. In the end Rorin gave up trying. There was nothing he could do or say that was going to change such a vain man's mind.

He'd had one small win, however, which had led Rorin to this rock he was hiding behind this night, as yet another troop of Fardohnyan soldiers in their blue and grey livery marched through the Widowmaker Pass. Terin Lionsclaw crouched beside him, glaring at the soldiers as if the presence of every single man was a personal affront to his lordship over Sunrise Province. Rorin silently prayed he'd remain quiet until they passed. They were barely a mile beyond Winternest and it was a minor miracle they hadn't been spotted heading into the pass, only the darkness and the confusion of a fortress overwhelmed by too many troops to feed and house providing cover for them to slip through the darkness and into the Widowmaker itself.

"How many do you think there are?" Terin hissed as the troops filed past in a seemingly endless line.

"At least two hundred in this lot," Rorin replied softly, wishing Terin would just shut up and wait until the danger was past before he started with the questions. They were very close to the road. It would take little more than a snapped twig and one alert Fardohnyan for them to be discovered.

"I mean all up," the Warlord corrected. "How many troops do you think they've gotten into Hythria so far?"

That was a much more difficult question to answer. In the past couple of weeks Rorin had almost lost count of the Fardohnyans he had seen as they dodged and weaved and dived off the road into the bushes more times than he could recall. The enemy were well past Winternest and gathering on the slopes of the Twin River Valley a few miles to the southeast of Winternest—a narrow stretch of fertile farmland flanked by the foothills of the forested Sunrise Mountains in the west, the Saltan River to the north and the Norsell River to the south. Strategically, it was a brilliant place to muster. There was ample food, lots of water, and no way to sneak around behind the invaders or cut off their supply lines to the west. Rorin didn't know who had command of the Fardohnyans, but whoever it was, he was nobody's fool.

"Hard to say," Rorin whispered. "Twenty, maybe thirty thousand." He watched the troops marching past. "And they seem to just keep on coming."

This lot, he guessed, were the last contingent sent through the pass this morning from Westbrook, hence the reason they were still marching after dark. He turned to look at Terin, hoping he was finally in a mood to be reasoned with. "We need to get this information back to Prince Damin, my lord, don't you agree?"

"Your precious prince will have a much better chance of winning this war if we have an accurate assessment of the final numbers Hablet is likely to throw at us," Terin hissed, repeating a phrase so well worn now that Rorin could have answered his own question.

At the outset, he didn't know why Terin was set on this suicidal notion of sneaking through the Widowmaker into Fardohnya to report on troop numbers. Given the Fardohnyans were making no secret of their location, it would have been (and still was) a simple matter of placing scouts in the hills around the Twin River Valley, to watch from there. They weren't likely to make a move until all their troops were through the pass, so there was plenty of time.

But Terin had insisted on this mission and finally Rorin had agreed to come along, mostly because he didn't want to face Tejay Lionsclaw and explain to her how he lost her husband (although he suspected if he did lose him, her period of mourning would be mercifully brief). He'd managed to convince Terin to send the rest of his entourage down to the Twin River Valley to set up an observation post to report on the troop numbers from there while the two of them made this insanely dangerous foray into Fardohnya.

When Terin readily agreed to that idea, Rorin finally worked out what was going on. Terin wanted to be a hero and heroes did brave and noble things, usually alone and always against incredible odds. Sneaking into Fardohnya might not help their cause much, but it was far more dashing than sitting on a hillside counting camp fires.

Rorin, who was quite content with the notion that he didn't have a single heroic bone in his entire body, had regretted agreeing to Terin's ludicrous suggestion from the moment Winternest came into sight just before sunset earlier today and nothing had happened in the intervening hours to change his opinion.

Finally, the last Fardohnyan trooper marched past. They waited a few moments longer to ensure there were no stragglers before emerging from behind the rocks that had concealed them from the enemy.

"My lord," Rorin said softly while they waited, hoping he might yet change Terin's mind. "We'd be far better served by getting this information back to Cabradell."

"If you've not the stomach for this, sorcerer, go back."

Terin truly had no concept of the danger he was courting, Rorin realised.

The Warlord squared his shoulders manfully and rose to his feet, his expression determined. "We'll see who's the bigger man."

Rorin had a strong suspicion the Warlord wasn't referring to him. He watched as Lord Lionsclaw pushed past him, convinced he was being a hero. Rorin studied his retreating back, thinking if he had any brains, he'd turn around right now and head back through the pass while it was still dark and he had some hope of slipping past Winternest without being detected. But if he did that and something happened to Terin, he'd have to explain it to Damin—and worse, to Lady Lionsclaw. Neither of them would be terribly happy if the only thing Rorin Mariner had to report on his return to Cabradell was the capture or death of Sunrise Province's Warlord.

With a sigh, Rorin glanced over his shoulder to be certain none of the Fardohnyans were heading back their way, and then stepped out from behind the rocks to follow Terin. He could hear nothing in the darkness that might indicate they were not alone.

He'd barely taken a step, however, before he froze, stunned at the sudden appearance of something he hadn't seen since he was twelve years old.

In front of him, perched on a rock a few feet away, was a little grey creature with huge black eyes and drooping ears, staring at him with interest.

"Hello, Rory."

"Lady *Elarnymire*?"

"How many other demons are you on first-name terms with?" the little demon asked, blinking her liquid black eyes at him.

"What . . . what . . . are *you* doing here?"

"I don't have time to explain."

"Then what the . . . ?"

"Run away."

"*What*?"

"Run away, Rory. Right now."

"But I . . ."

"Don't argue with me, boy," the demon commanded crossly. "Just do as you're told. Turn around and run away, as fast as you can."

Only in times of the direst need had the demon Elarnymire appeared to Rorin. The last time he'd laid eyes on her was more than twelve years ago, at the other end of this very pass, when she'd talked him into surrendering to the Fardohnyan authorities in Westbrook, while he waited to be rescued by Wrayan. For her to suddenly materialise now meant the danger must be dire, indeed.

And immediate. Rorin hesitated only a moment, before doing what the demon ordered. He'd only taken three steps, however, before he stopped and turned back, cursing savagely.

"*Now* what?" Elarnymire demanded impatiently.

"My companion . . . Lord Lionsclaw . . . I have to . . ."

"You don't have time, and from what I've seen, he's probably not worth it. Get away from here, Rory, this minute, or you will die."

No sooner had Elarnymire spoken than a low rumble reverberated through the pass. Almost simultaneously Rorin felt his skin prickle. Somebody was using Harshini magic in the vicinity, which probably accounted for the demon's unexpected presence here in the Widowmaker. Rorin couldn't imagine who it would be. As far as he knew, the only other soul alive capable of wielding Harshini magic besides himself was Wrayan Lightfinger and he was a thousand miles from here, with Kalan and Princess Marla in Greenharbour.

"Who's doing this?" he asked the demon, stumbling as the ground began to tilt. The only other distant possibility, excluding the Harshini, was Brakandaran the Halfbreed and even Wrayan wasn't completely convinced he was still alive.

"Run away and you might live to find out, someday," Elarnymire suggested.

Rorin hesitated a moment longer, his skin beginning to burn as the intensity of the magic increased. Whoever was making this happen was drawing far more magic than Rorin or Wrayan could manage. But he didn't have time to figure out who was causing the earth to shake, any more than he had time to go after Terin, assuming the demon would even allow him to take another step further. The ground was trembling even harder and loose rocks were beginning to tumble down the steep walls of the pass.

"Can you find my friend and warn him?" he asked the demon, not wishing to simply abandon Terin to his fate, no matter how tempting the notion might have been ten minutes ago.

"Only if you promise to turn around, run away as fast as you can, and not look back."

"I promise."

"I'll see what I can do." The demon shrugged, and then she vanished into thin air.

Rorin turned and ran. Sending Elarnymire to look for Terin was the best he could do, he assured himself, dodging larger rocks the ground tremor had worked loose higher up the slopes. As he rounded the bend, a deep boom rolled over the mountains and echoed through the pass, the terrifying sound amplified by the steep rock walls. It was followed a moment later by a deafening crash as tons of rock and debris smashed together and fell down into the Widowmaker.

A massive dust cloud, thicker than a Karien fog, billowed out of the darkness, choking Rorin. Going flat out now, his eyes watering as he ran, he managed to stay a few steps in front of the avalanche of rocks and trees tumbling into the pass. Coughing to clear his tortured lungs, Rorin knew he wasn't going to make it through without help. Urgently, he grabbed for the source and felt the magic infuse his body. With his eyes as black as the surrounding night, he jumped fallen trees and dodged falling rocks, using his ability to move things magically to clear a path for himself and prevent some of the larger falling objects from crushing him.

Rorin didn't know how long he ran. The only thing he knew was that eventually the tall towers of Winternest appeared out of the choking dust, the road clogged with both Fardohnyan soldiers and Hythrun captives drawn out by the massive explosion in the pass. He dodged them, too. Drawing every ounce of power he could manage, it was no trouble to add a glamour that made him effectively invisible to a casual glance.

But as he stumbled past the spectators, he wondered·why he'd bothered. Nobody was looking at Rorin Mariner. They all stared into the pass, their mouths open, stunned by the realisation that the Widowmaker Pass was no longer there.

chapter 47

Not surprisingly, the presence of Cyrus Eaglespike in the war camp sent the High Prince into a frenzy. Forgetting all about Alija's recent assurance the Patriots had abandoned their quest to unseat him, he was torn between the notion that Alija had sent Cyrus to kill him or that he was a Patriot spy sent to threaten his throne. The two fears were one and the same to Damin—he couldn't quite see the distinction—and there was nothing anybody could say that would change Lernen's mind about the Dregian Warlord.

Damin didn't think his distant cousin was plotting against the High Prince. At least not directly. Cyrus tended to follow his mother's lead and Alija was back in Greenharbour. Without someone to do his plotting for him, Cyrus was just a monumental pain in the backside, in Damin's opinion, rather than a murderous one.

To add to his growing list of woes, Lernen was also convinced—at least for the past week—that if he didn't come up with a brilliant tactical plan to defeat the invaders, people might suspect he wasn't a very good general. Damin didn't have the heart to tell him there wasn't a soul in Hythria who thought he was any sort of general, let alone a good one.

The High Prince had taken to sitting up half the night, working on his plans, and then summoning his nephews the following morning to explain his ideas and get either Damin or Narvell's seal of approval. Narvell begged off as often as he could. Unlike Damin, he found it hard to keep a straight face when Lernen started explaining his plans and didn't want to offend his uncle by laughing out loud at some of his more outrageous suggestions.

Damin, being Lernen's heir, didn't have that luxury. When Lernen called, Damin answered. That was the way of things and they would stay that way until his uncle died and he became High Prince.

It was in response to such a summons that Damin and Kraig had come to visit the High Prince this morning. In the middle of the night, Lernen had gotten the notion that the Fardohnyans were afraid of fire and that the obvious solution to their invasion was wait until the summer months and the warmer weather arrived, and then set fire to the slopes of the Sunrise Mountains and drive the Fardohnyans back across their own borders where they belonged.

"Such a fire would be uncontrollable," Damin pointed out, after Lernen proudly finished explaining his latest strategy. "Not to mention hideously expensive."

"Why expensive?" the High Prince asked. "How much can a few torches cost?"

"I was referring to the timber we'd lose. Some of those forests have stood since the Harshini were here and a good half of Sunrise Province's population earns their living, either directly or indirectly, from logging. And there's no guarantee the prevailing winds would favour us on the day. Cabradell Valley acts like a funnel for the wind coming off the mountains at the best of times. Set loose a wildfire and you may well kill the city and everyone in it, instead of driving the enemy back, which is kind of doing the Fardohnyans' job for them, don't you think?"

Lernen glanced down at the map table with intense disappointment. "So you don't think it's a good idea, then?"

Damin shook his head. "I'm sure you'll come up with something much more inspired soon, Uncle."

The High Prince frowned but before he could actually come up with something more inspired, one of his slaves appeared from behind the screen that led to the private areas of the massive pavilion to inform his master that his bath was ready. Without a word to his nephew, Lernen hurried off to take advantage of his bath while it was still hot, almost as if he'd forgotten Damin was there.

Damin watched him leave, and then turned to Kraig, who was waiting patiently by the door. Lernen seemed to have forgotten his initial fear of the big Denikan by the following morning, so Damin often brought Kraig to Lernen's tent these days, partly because it enhanced the reputation he was trying to foster and partly because, much to Damin's delight, Cyrus Eaglespike was almost as intimidated by the Denikan as the High Prince and if he tried to ingratiate his way into Damin's private daily meetings with his uncle, Kraig's presence actually scared him off.

With a sigh, Damin glanced down at the map. "You know, the Harshini have an old saying," he remarked as he began pinching out the candles Lernen had placed on it to indicate his great plans for a wildfire. *"War is the easiest hell to get into and the hardest to escape."*

"Not an inaccurate assessment," Kraig agreed.

Damin glanced at him over his shoulder. "I think the first part of that saying has been lost over the eons. I suspect it used to be: *When being led by a fool, war is the easiest hell to get into and the hardest to escape."*

"I would agree your uncle is not a . . . military man," Kraig remarked tactfully.

"Really?" Damin gasped in amazement. "What*ever* gave you that idea?"

Kraig smiled, which was a rare thing for the Denikan. "You, on the other hand, I sense . . . have been trained with just such a conflict in mind. And your uncle's incompetence frustrates you enormously."

"Well, all that brilliant training doesn't do me a whole lot of good with him in charge."

The Denikan walked to the map and looked down at it thoughtfully. "There are four things that always affect a battle," he noted. "They are immutable and, if you understand them, the key to winning any conflict."

A little fed up with the Denikan's insistence that he was an expert in everything, Damin's first reaction was to ignore his advice. But something Zegarnald had said to him stuck in his mind. *I ask nothing of you that you are not capable of,* his god had assured him. *And I will see you have what assistance you need.*

The Denikan prince spoke with an air of authority Damin had rarely heard from anybody but Almodavar. Perhaps this was the assistant Zegarnald promised. He certainly couldn't think of any other reason why the gods might have thrown these Denikans across his path.

"What four things?"

"The first is how you move your men," Kraig explained, leaning on the edge of the table to get a closer look. "Your ability to put them where you want them, have them hold as long as you need them, and have them respond to changes as quickly as you need them to." Kraig studied the map closely as he spoke. "The second is your ability to be flexible. Victory always falls to the leader who can change his strategy when it's clear the planned one isn't working."

"I wouldn't argue with that."

"The third quality is a leader's ability to innovate. It's all well and good to study the history of other men's battles, but the *reason* you study them is because they were the first to think of a particular manoeuvre or strategy." He glanced at Damin and added, "Which is usually *why* they won the battle you end up reading about."

Damin nodded in agreement. "And the fourth?"

"Ah, that is something much less tangible but no less important. You must claim victory over men's minds before you can take it from their bodies."

"Do you mean the army's morale?"

Kraig shook his head. "It's more than that. And it's not just your own men. Certainly, you need them to believe you can win, but you need your opposition to suspect you can, too." He shrugged and stood up straighter. "Still, in that, at least, you have the advantage. Men fighting for their own land always have a lot more to lose than the men invading it."

"Have you been in many battles?" Damin asked curiously.

"A few."

"Did you win?"

"In Denika, we don't take prisoners. I am here discussing the matter with you, your highness. You can, therefore, safely assume I was victorious."

Damin smiled, wondering if Kraig was trying to be humorous, or if it was just his intense seriousness that always struck Damin as funny. "So what do you advise, Kraig? If you were fighting this battle for the House of the Rising Moon?"

Kraig barely even hesitated before pointing to the map. "I would force my enemy to confront me here, at this place you call Farwell."

Damin glanced down at the map. "That's right between the Saltan and Norsell rivers. If they muster there we're in trouble. There's no way to get around behind them and no way to cut off their supply lines."

"But if you owned this crossing on the Saltan and that bridge on the Norsell, you could draw the invaders down into the far end of this valley, come in behind them and trap your enemy with the rivers on either side of them and your forces in front and behind them. You would control the battle-ground."

"That'd be useful."

"And necessary," Kraig agreed. "Given the enemy will probably outnumber you significantly. If I was in command, I would play on their assumption of superiority and let them break through the centre of my lines. It would then appear to the attacking forces that they have managed a rout. Even better, I would have my flanks withdraw in as much chaos as I could manage. My enemy would taste the victory, and keep pushing on toward the hills here at Lasting Drift . . ."

"Where you'd have the rest of your forces waiting on the other side of the rivers," Damin finished for him, seeing immediately where the Denikan was going with this. "That might actually work."

"You sound surprised."

"You want to see surprised? Come talk to me *after* we've won."

"Excuse me, your highness."

Damin turned to find one of Tejay's house slaves standing near the entrance to the pavilion, clutching a small folded note. "Yes?"

"Lady Lionsclaw bade me deliver this, your highness."

Damin accepted the note, opening it curiously. It was unlike Tejay to interrupt him when he was meeting with the High Prince and once again, he feared it might mean the worst for Adham, who still teetered on the brink of real danger with his slow-healing belly wound.

"What is it?" Kraig asked, as Damin read the note.

"Tell Lady Lionsclaw I'm on my way," he ordered the slave. As soon as the young man was gone, he turned back to the Denikan prince. "We have to get back to the palace."

"Is there a problem with your brother?"

"Rorin's back," Damin told him. "And according to Tejay's note, he's come back without Terin."

CHAPTER 48

By the time Damin arrived back at the palace with Kraig, Tejay had heard most of Rorin's story for herself. She was still trying to decide how she felt about the unexpected news that Terin might be dead.

A part of her was sorry, a part of her relieved. But mostly she was worried, and not for her own fate. They couldn't afford another Warlord's death. Not now. With Cyrus Eaglespike here in Cabradell, the news Terin was missing and probably dead would get back to Alija faster than the speed of gossip and she would immediately move to have her son appointed guardian of Sunrise Province in the name of the Sorcerers' Collective, and could do it quite legally because Terin's heir, Valorian, was only five years old.

Thank the gods, she thought as she paced, *it was Rorin Mariner who brought back the news.* And that he'd had the sense to share it with nobody else before he could inform Tejay and Damin of this disastrous development.

"What happened?" Damin asked by way of greeting as soon as he'd closed the door of her husband's study behind him. Kraig was with him, Tejay was relieved to see. Besides being rather pleasant to look at, she thought irreverently, the big Denikan was a master tactician, which had proved a totally unexpected bonus when she placed him in Damin's care. Tejay never doubted that Damin had potential, but neither did she forget he hadn't yet turned twenty-five. Even the greatest leaders needed to be pointed in the right direction occasionally.

Rorin stood up wearily. "I'm sorry, Damin. I lost Terin in the Widowmaker."

"Lost him?" Damin said. "How do you lose a whole person?"

"There was an avalanche," the young sorcerer explained. "He was ahead of me . . . I barely made it out, and I was using magic. I can't see how he would have survived."

"Isn't it a bit late in the year for an avalanche?" the prince asked. "I wouldn't have thought there was that much snow left."

"Strictly speaking, it was an explosion, I think. I'm not really sure. One minute we were hiding from Fardohnyan troops, the next thing Lady Elarnymire is warning me to get the hell out of there and it's raining rocks."

"Who is Lady Elarnymire?" Tejay asked in confusion. Rorin hadn't mentioned anything about having a woman with him in the Widowmaker Pass.

"She's a demon," Rorin explained.

"You didn't mention anything about demons the first time you told your tale."

The young sorcerer shrugged. "I thought you'd think I was crazy."

"I'm not sure I don't. What happened to your escort?"

"We sent them on ahead to the Twin River Valley to do a head count of the troops already through the pass. Only Terin and I tried to slip past Winternest."

"So nobody else can verify your account of what happened, can they?"

"No, my lady."

Tejay paced the rug for a moment before turning to Damin. "Is there a chance your friend here is lying?"

"I trust Rory completely."

"Do you believe he speaks to demons?"

Damin agreed without hesitation. "According to Wrayan, they're as thick as flies in Sanctuary."

"Ah, yes," Tejay said, unconvinced. "Wrayan Lightfinger. The fellow from the Thieves' Guild."

Damin shrugged, not sure how to explain away either Wrayan or Rorin. "It's complicated, Tejay."

"I can see that. And even if I accept you were just strolling along the Widowmaker, Rorin, when a demon popped up and warned you to get out of there, why didn't you try to save my husband?"

"He was too far ahead of me by then, my lady. Elarnymire promised she'd try to help him, but there wasn't much time. Whoever was working the magic that closed the pass, he wasn't fooling about."

"Hang on a minute," Damin exclaimed, obviously shocked by Rorin's casual remark about magic. "What do you mean, 'whoever was working the magic'? Are you telling me some-one destroyed the pass deliberately? Using magic?"

"I don't know for certain," Rorin said. "All I know is that I felt someone drawing on the source, someone much more powerful than me or Wrayan, and then the world went mad."

"Who could it have been?" Tejay asked, just as stunned by the implications of such an event. "The Harshini are gone . . ."

"Actually, they're only in hiding, my lady," Rorin cor-rected. "But if I had to make a guess, the only other person I know of with that sort of power, who isn't tucked away in Sanctuary, is the Halfbreed."

"He's just a legend," Tejay reminded them, shaking her head. She crossed her arms and walked to the window. She wondered if these men thought her callous or brave because she wasn't grieving over her husband's death.

"Wrayan's met the Halfbreed," Damin informed her, which had Rorin nodding in agreement. "He says he's real."

"Your *thief*?" She turned and studied the two young men closely. "I've heard insanity can be contagious but I didn't think it happened quite so quickly."

"My lady, even in Denika we have heard of Brakandaran the Halfbreed."

"Which just proves my point about him being nothing more than a myth, your highness," she replied.

Rorin looked at Kraig oddly. "Your *highness*?"

Tejay cursed under her breath. She'd forgotten Rorin wasn't in on the secret about Kraig and his companions. "It's a long story, Rorin. Get Damin to explain it later." She turned and looked at the Denikan prince. "You don't believe this nonsense about mythical magicians and demons, too, do you?"

"If I believe in the gods, Lady Lionsclaw, it would follow that I must believe in everything that goes with them, including demons, the Harshini and the Halfbreed."

Tejay decided arguing theology with a Denikan was probably a very foolish thing to do. "All right then, explain this to me. Why, in the name of all the gods, would the Halfbreed want to destroy the Widowmaker Pass?"

"He didn't actually destroy it," Rorin told them. "He sealed it. It'll be months before it can be cleared, and even then it'll take a mammoth effort on both the part of us and the Fardohnyans to reopen it."

"Perhaps he's on our side?" Damin suggested.

Tejay shook her head, highly suspicious of the whole bizarre situation. "And I'm the demon child."

Damin smiled thinly. "Yes, well . . . that would account for a few things."

"Grow up, Damin."

"Sorry."

She turned to Rorin, still shaking her head in disbelief. But the Widowmaker wasn't her concern right now. She had a province to fight for and nobody was going to take it from her if she had anything to say about it. "Do you know for certain that Terin is dead?"

Rorin shrugged. "Not for certain, my lady. But if he was caught in the rockslide . . ."

"Then we don't need to tell anybody," she announced.

"Not *tell* anybody?" Damin gasped. "How can we not tell anybody the Warlord of Sunrise is missing, Tejay? We're in his province, for the gods' sake! This is his damned palace! We're going to war with his troops making up a significant part of our forces, in case you'd forgotten. We can't just pretend he's not here. Who's going to lead his men?"

"In Denika, if a husband falls, it is the wife's duty to take his place," Kraig informed them.

"Unfortunately, this isn't Denika," Damin snapped. "And I've got enough trouble with Lernen trying to be a general,

Narvell trying to get himself killed by Stefan Warhaft every time he glances at Kendra, I'm hiding the damned heir to the Denikan throne disguised as a slave and trying very hard to keep a lid on all of this, so that Cyrus Eaglespike doesn't even get a whisper there's anything amiss. And now you want to pretend Terin's still alive? Great plan, Tejay. Even if it had a glimmer of hope, you'd never be able to stop that Karien worm, Renulus, from exposing you the moment he got wind of his beloved lord's highly suspicious fate."

"I can take care of Renulus," Rorin volunteered. "It'd be no trouble. Really."

"Fine! Take care of him! It doesn't alter the fact that putting a woman in charge of a province—or that province's army—is out of the question."

Tejay could see he was unhappy with the situation, but that didn't alleviate the pain she felt to hear Damin, of all people, scorn her gender so bluntly.

"Don't you dare stand there and tell me I don't know how to lead or manage this province just because I'm a woman, Damin Wolfblade. I can do it better than Terin. I can probably do it better than *you*, and what hurts the most is that you know it, yet you're still going to adhere to a tradition that's likely to hand everything I have over to the Sorcerers' Collective, rather than entertain any idea that might dent the legendary male pride of Hythria."

Damin seemed surprised that she had taken his rejection so personally. "I don't think you're incapable, Tejay. I think you're one of the smartest people I know. And one of the best fighters, too. It's just that putting a woman in charge of a province . . . it's . . . well, it's against the law."

"You don't have any trouble changing other laws that don't suit you," she pointed out.

"Trying to change the age of majority is different," he objected. "That was—still is, actually—a necessity to protect the Convocation of Warlords from majority control by the Sorcerers' Collective."

"And how is this situation any different?"

"She has a point, your highness," Kraig remarked, throwing his weight behind Tejay's argument, which might not actually help her cause, she lamented, if Damin thought they were ganging up on him.

"Thanks," Damin replied sourly, "but when I want to hear from the Master of Absolutely Everything, I'll let you know."

"Damin!" Tejay scolded, shocked at the insult. "That was uncalled for."

He sighed heavily. "I know. I'm sorry, Kraig, I didn't mean to malign you, or the House of the Rising Moon. But we can't do this, Tejay. We have to find someone else."

"There is no one else," she said. "Nobody you can trust, at any rate."

"There is no way the other Warlords will agree to any woman taking charge of a province, even temporarily, Tejay. You know that as well as I do."

"Then don't tell them," Rorin suggested.

"We just had this discussion."

"No, we didn't," the sorcerer corrected. "Tejay suggested it and you dismissed her out of hand. That's not actually a discussion, Damin."

"Then, by all means, let's discuss it," he said. "I'm all ears. Explain to me how you intend to make everyone believe the Warlord of Sunrise is still here and in command of his province, and not buried under a few hundred tons of rock in the Widowmaker Pass. And when you've finished with that miracle, we can talk about how the whole 'leading his troops into battle' illusion is going to work."

"The first part is easy," Tejay said, more than a little annoyed with Damin's intransigence. "We just get rid of Renulus and appoint someone else as Terin's seneschal and use him to relay Terin's orders. My husband often ruled by decree, rather than in person, particularly when he thought the whole world just wanted to mock his low birth. It will barely raise an eyebrow if he's heard from but not seen."

"Which brings us to how he's going to manage to lead his troops into battle if he's locked himself in his room, sulking."

"He needs your uncle's suit of armour," Kraig suggested.

They all looked at the Denikan. "What are you talking about?"

"The first day I went to meet him, your uncle was parading around in a jewelled suit of armour; one—as you so rightly pointed out—that could be recognised anywhere, even on a battlefield."

"But what use is the High Prince's armour?" Tejay asked.

"This pass that is now blocked . . . its closure means you now have a fighting chance of winning this war, yes?"

"Yes," Damin agreed warily.

"Then the man responsible for its closure should be rewarded."

"The *Halfbreed*?" Rorin asked in confusion.

Kraig shook his head. "If the story gets about it was Terin Lionsclaw who blocked the pass, it would not be unremarkable for the High Prince to reward such bravery, would it?"

"And if he rewarded him with a unique and conspicuously gaudy suit of armour . . ." Damin mused.

"*Huh*?" Rorin said, looking at the two princes. "I don't get it."

Tejay smiled in understanding. "What they mean, Rorin, is that if the High Prince rewards Terin's bravery with a suit of armour so distinctive that every man in Hythria knows who owns it, they'll also assume it's him wearing it in battle, too."

The sorcerer rubbed his chin thoughtfully. "One problem though, my lady . . . how does the High Prince present a reward to someone who isn't actually here?"

Damin glanced at Tejay. "That's a good point."

"How well does the High Prince know your husband?" Kraig asked.

"They've met a few times. Terin didn't like Greenharbour much so we didn't go there often. Not unless we really had to. Why?"

"Prince Damin introduced me to the High Prince recently, claiming I was a slave. Only a few months before that, we met in Greenharbour where I was introduced as a prince.

The man made no connection between the two events because he wasn't expecting it. If you hold the ceremony in private, present him with someone who looks something like your husband and acts as if the man truly is a Warlord, I suspect your High Prince will accept whatever you tell him without question."

Tejay looked to Damin. Nobody knew Lernen better. He would know if such a ruse were possible. After a long silence, Damin shrugged. "It might work."

"Does this mean I get to do something about Renulus?" Rorin asked hopefully.

Tejay looked to Damin before she answered. It was up to him. Without his support, this clever plan wasn't even a slim probability.

Damin studied her carefully for a long moment. "Can you do this, Tejay?"

"I should slap you for even asking."

"You know what I mean."

She nodded. "I have four sons to keep safe, Damin. Even if I didn't give a wooden rivet about your problems with the Patriots, and the Fardohnyans, I wouldn't do anything that might jeopardise their future."

"You mean if there was any man in Hythria you considered as good as you, you'd let him have your province?"

She grinned suddenly. "Well, as there probably isn't any man in Hythria as good as me, that's not really the issue, is it?"

"You lose this battle on me, Tejay, and you'll be wishing you died in it."

"You're all talk, Damin . . ." she sighed dismissively, privately delighted at her unexpected victory, as she turned to face Rorin. "And just how do you intend to get rid of Renulus, my lad? Kill him?"

The young man frowned. "I'm not a killer, my lady. I don't know if I could kill someone, even if I tried. But I do know how to get rid of Renulus."

"How?" Damin asked curiously.

"He's a devoted Karien, a follower of the Overlord. I'm a wicked part-Harshini sorcerer. It's simple," the young man explained. "I'll just draw on the source and show him my evil black eyes. That'll scare the living daylights out of him."

"You mean show him what you are?" Damin asked, a little concerned. "Is that a good idea?"

"Why is it a bad one?"

"Well . . . I kind of like the idea of having a sorcerer as my secret weapon against the Fardohnyans. Sort of ruins it if you start going around flashing your big evil black eyes at all and sundry."

Rorin was adamant. "Trust me, if he thinks the wicked Harshini are still among us, Renulus will scuttle back to Karien so fast wanting to let his precious priesthood know about it, you won't see him for the dust."

"Won't that just bring the wrath of the Kariens down on us?"

"Possibly," Rorin agreed. "But they'd have to go through Medalon first to get here. You'd have years before it's a problem."

"Oh, well that's all right then," Damin replied sourly.

Tejay, on the other hand, was quite impressed with Rorin's solution. He seemed to have a knack for coming up with solutions to seemingly insurmountable problems that didn't involve bloodshed. She was becoming rather fond of the young sorcerer for that. "Rorin's right, Damin, and I don't think Renulus will be a problem, either, provided we convince him to leave."

Damin didn't seem convinced. "It'd be easier to just kill him."

Tejay sighed. She loved Damin like a brother and he'd just given her an unheard-of opportunity, one she never thought she'd have in a thousand lifetimes, but that didn't alter the fact that in some things—somewhat like her late and unlamented husband—he was such a *boy*. "You see, that's why they shouldn't let men rule the world, Damin. You just want to kill things."

Her comment produced puzzled looks from both Damin

and Kraig. "What's wrong with that?" Damin asked, with a wounded look.

"When you work that out, my dears," she told them, "there really might be a man in this world who can measure up to me, after all."

chapter 49

Taking care of Renulus was something that couldn't wait. Very few people in Cabradell knew Rorin was back, or that he had returned alone, and something had to be done about the Karien seneschal before he realised his Warlord was missing and started making a fuss about it.

As he hurried along the covered walkway to the Karien's room, Rorin wished he was as confident of scaring off Renulus as he'd assured Damin and Lady Tejay he was. It had sounded great in theory, but as he neared the man's room his confidence began to waver. Three pillars away from Renulus's door, he stopped completely, torn with indecision.

Suppose it doesn't work? Suppose Renulus just laughs at me? The torch by his head spluttered and hissed as he fretted, the silence complete except for his racing heart and his chaotic, panicked thoughts. *Suppose I just . . .*

"Is there a problem?"

"*Agghhh!*" Rorin exclaimed, jumping with fright. He turned to find the big dark Denikan *court'esa* standing behind him. "Don't *do* that!"

"Do what?"

"Sneak up on me like that. You scared me half to death."

"Is it not your intention to scare the Karien half to death?"

"Well . . . yes."

"Then you should try to calm yourself, sorcerer," he suggested. "Scaring a man enough to make him run away requires your victim to be more frightened than you are."

"Oh, that was very droll," Rorin replied, annoyed the Denikan could see through him so easily. Rorin squared his shoulders manfully, as if he was in no doubt about his purpose. "What are you doing here, anyway?"

"I thought you might want some help." Kraig shrugged, and then added with a perfectly straight face, "Scaring people."

Rorin studied him curiously. "Are you really a Denikan prince?"

"Don't I look like one?"

"You look like a slave," Rorin told him. "A really, *really* big slave, granted, but a slave, nonetheless. It's probably the slave collar. Sort of gives that impression."

"You judge me only by what I wear?"

"Don't *you* judge people by what they wear?"

The Denikan nodded. "I must admit, I do on occasion. Like now, for instance."

"*Now?*"

"You stand before the door of a man you are hoping to intimidate, Master Mariner, dressed like a farm boy headed for a night on the town. Where are your robes, sorcerer? Your badge of office?"

"Ah," Rorin said, thinking Kraig might have a point. "Perhaps I should get changed first."

"There is no time," Kraig replied. "This Karien might be minutes away from learning you have returned without his Warlord. There is not a moment to waste. You work your fearful magic, sorcerer. I will take care of the intimidation."

Rorin warily eyed the big Denikan up and down. "I believe you will, Kraig. Does Damin know you're here?"

"He is engaged in . . . diplomatic negotiations . . . with my companion, Lyrian. I thought it best not to disturb him."

"Will he mind?"

"Only if someone comes along and finds us standing here

openly discussing the very thing he wishes to remain secret."

"Good point," Rorin agreed, turning to look at Renulus's door. "Do you think we should knock?"

The Denikan walked up to Renulus's door, calmly raised his booted foot and kicked the door, splintering the wood around the lock with an ear-splitting crack.

"I think he now knows he has visitors," the slave-prince remarked, as he stood back to let Rorin enter.

Rorin stared at the Denikan and then the shattered door, shaking his head. "You're going to have to explain that to Lady Lionsclaw, you know."

That threat didn't seem to worry Kraig. "Call up your magic, sorcerer," he commanded. "You have work to do."

Not surprisingly, Renulus leapt out of bed when Kraig so rudely opened the door with his boot, spluttering angrily at the intrusion.

"What is the meaning of this?" Renulus demanded, striking a flint with shaking hands to light the room. As soon as it was lit, the Karien held up his candle and squinted at them. "What do you want?"

Rorin entered with a commanding stride, thinking the man looked vaguely ridiculous in his nightshirt.

"You and I need to have a chat," Rorin said, opening himself up to the source. He felt the magic infuse his body, knew his eyes were darkening as he spoke, simply from the horrified expression that slowly crept over the Karien's face as he watched the change happen.

"*Demon!*" the man gasped, taking a step backwards. He put the candlestick on the night table and made some symbol with his hands, no doubt trying to ward off evil spirits, or some such thing.

"Don't be stupid. I look nothing like a demon."

"You are one of them!" He kept backing away until he was pushed up against the bed.

"One of *what?*"

"An evil creature of the night!"

Rorin grinned, unable to maintain his menacing expression in the face of such an absurd accusation. But he hurriedly pushed the smile away. He was here to intimidate this man.

"Harshini *mongrel*!" the Karien spat, trying to back away from him even further, but with the bed at his back, all it did was land him on his behind on the mattress. Renulus glanced around, as if searching for something to use as a weapon, and then glared at Rorin with contempt when he couldn't find one. "You are an abomination. Just like the Halfbreed. A mixed-blood sin against the Overlord."

Rorin was having a hard time keeping a straight face. Nobody had ever accused him of anything nearly so illustrious before. To be put in the same class as Brakandaran was a compliment he never expected. Not that the Karien meant it as a compliment, of course. But it was hard not to smile, and right now, Rorin's job was to do something about removing this fool from the palace. Still . . . fully aware he was probably the least powerful sorcerer alive, it was nice to think *somebody* thought he was dangerous.

"Abomination I may be," he snarled impressively, advancing on the terrified Karien. "But right now, I'm your worst nightmare come to life. Any particular preference for the way you'd like to die?"

"You can't harm me, sorcerer!"

Rorin did smile this time and held out his arm, mostly for dramatic effect, and the Karien began to rise from the floor. With a screech of despair, Renulus flailed around like a speared fish as he drifted up towards the ceiling.

"What do you think, Kraig?" Rorin asked the slave, who'd stood behind him silently, watching the exchange. "Should I kill this Karien worm here or let him run home to his Overlord and tell his priests the Harshini are still among us?"

"If you kill him here," Kraig pointed out, "you will have to explain the blood on the rug as well as the broken lock to Lady Lionsclaw."

"True," Rorin agreed, holding Renulus by the rafters with

casual disinterest as he discussed the problem with his companion. "But strictly speaking, you're the one who has to explain the broken lock. I don't think she'd mind the blood so much. Not if it was his."

"You may be right, Master Mariner," Kraig agreed. "Of course, you could hold him up there while I fetch a towel."

"Let me down!" Renulus screeched. "When Lord Lionsclaw hears of this . . ."

"Sadly, Renulus, Lord Lionsclaw had a change of heart about you, while he was away," Rorin informed the seneschal. "He's decided you're not worth feeding any more, but he didn't really have the heart to tell you your services were no longer required. Now Kraig here, he volunteered to break your neck—to save Terin the trouble of dismissing you—but I thought it would be more fun to just throw you around the room a bit until you offered to resign." He sighed regretfully. "But now . . . I fear Lord Lionsclaw was right. You're never going to accept your dismissal gracefully and leave the palace without a fuss, are you? I suppose we're going to have to kill you, after all."

The Karien was pretty sure of himself. Even suspended in midair, he still managed to sound superior. "I don't believe you! Lord Lionsclaw would never dismiss me! And when he hears about this, I'll make certain you suffer torment beyond description before you die, you Harshini gutter-scum."

Rorin stared up at him with his black-on-black eyes, guessing his gaze alone was almost enough to unman a Karien fearful for his soul. "You're not really in a position to threaten me with anything." Just to make his point, he let the man drop sharply. It was only a few feet, but it was enough to make the Karien break into a sweat. "Any luck finding a towel yet, Kraig?"

"No!" Renulus screeched as he dropped. "Wait! I'll go!"

Rorin looked at Kraig in surprise and then stared up at Renulus. "You *will*?"

He nodded vigorously. "Let me down. I'll leave the palace. I swear. You're right . . . it's more important I inform my people that an abomination such as you still walks the land, than staying here helping some fool of a Hythrun run a province that's about to be overrun by the Fardohnyans, in any case."

His capitulation was far too quick to be genuine, but it was costing Rorin more effort than he was willing to let on to hold Renulus against the ceiling and maintain a normal conversation. He let the man drop, breathing a sigh of relief.

Renulus landed heavily, and then pushed himself up onto his hands and knees. "Thank you."

"Don't mention it. Get up."

Painfully, the Karien did as Rorin ordered, climbing to his feet.

"You've got about a minute to gather your things before we escort you out of Cabradell."

Suspiciously acquiescent, Renulus hurried to the long trunk at the foot of his bed and dropped to his knees after he opened it. He tossed a few garments aside and then reached in for something at the bottom.

A moment later he rose to his feet, all sign of his previous subservience gone. In his hand he held a staff, a black metal shaft topped by golden star intersected with a silver lightning bolt and embedded with crystals, including a large one set in the centre. He held it out in front of himself, as if it was a shield.

Rorin hesitated. The sight of the staff dragged another one of those seemingly endless snippets of information that Shananara had planted in his mind to the surface. Instinctively, he knew he couldn't touch it without pain. He just didn't understand why.

"Nice little trinket you've got there," Rorin observed, eyeing the staff warily as the Harshini memories flooded through him. "Not something you see every day. At least, not outside of a Karien temple devoted to Xaphista the Overlord."

"Touch me again with your heathen sorcery and you will die!" Renulus announced, holding the staff out before him.

Rorin wasn't entirely certain Renulus was bluffing. He knew what the staff was, although he'd never expected to see one in his lifetime. He also knew only a priest of Xaphista would be carrying such a weapon. The question of what a Karien priest was doing acting as an adviser to a Hythrun Warlord put a whole different light on the situation.

"Kraig, can you get that thing off him?" he asked, studying the staff cautiously.

"If you wish it."

"Believe me, I wish it."

Without hesitating, the Denikan moved towards Renulus, but he was quicker than either Kraig or Rorin anticipated. The Karien thrust the staff forward before Rorin could dodge it, connecting with his shoulder.

In agony, Rorin screamed and dropped to his knees as if he'd been branded with a white-hot sword. An instant later, Kraig was on the priest. He tore the staff from Renulus's hands, and then swung it upwards, connecting with the older man's chin. The Karien's head snapped backward sharply, and he fell back against the trunk, dazed and limp. The big Denikan tossed the staff aside and took Renulus by the throat.

"Don't . . . don't kill him . . ." Rorin gasped from the floor.

"Why not?"

The pain scorching through Rorin was indescribable. His shoulder burned like someone had poured acid on his bare skin. The Harshini magic he was channelling, normally so sweet, burned through his veins as if it had been set on fire. "He's . . . a Karien . . . priest."

"Then I suspect his death is no great loss to anyone in Hythria."

Rorin blinked, battling to stay conscious. "Damin . . . want . . . know . . . what . . ."

He'd been meaning to say: *Damin will want to know what a Karien priest is doing here in Hythria*, but the agony was too intense and Rorin didn't have the strength to get the words out.

His eyes watering with the pain, Rorin collapsed onto the floor. His last memory before he lost consciousness was of Kraig holding Renulus by the throat, waiting for a reasonable explanation as to why he shouldn't kill him.

CHAPTER 50

odja's contact, the one Marla had been planning to use to lure Alija into her trap, had—rather inconveniently—died in the plague about a month before Wrayan and Kalan arrived in Greenharbour. The news left them floundering a little about exactly who should make contact with the High Arrion. The list of likely candidates was depressingly short and there was one name on the list which in Wrayan's opinion shouldn't have been there at all.

"You can't be serious about involving Galon Miar," he said, when the princess suggested it. They were once more gathered in Marla's reception hall—Marla, Kalan, Rodja and Wrayan—which Wrayan was coming to think of as their unofficial war room.

"Do you think he can't be trusted, Wrayan?"

"He's an assassin, your highness. It goes without saying."

"I disagree," Kalan said, partly, Wrayan suspected, because she enjoyed disagreeing with him. "You told us he was Ronan Dell's bastard, that it was Galon Miar who discovered his father's massacre when he was merely a youth. Surely it means he has more reason than most to want Alija Eaglespike brought down?"

"He's sleeping with her, Kalan."

"Was," Marla corrected. "I think you'll find that's one love affair that's come to an abrupt end."

"Anyway, Wrayan, for all you know, he was sleeping with her for his own ends. If it was me, I'd do anything—sleep with anybody—if that's what it was going to take to get vengeance on the woman who killed *my* father."

Wrayan glanced at Marla, wondering if she could see the irony, but the princess was far too disciplined to let any emotion show on her face that she didn't want broadcast.

"Perhaps you and I need to sit down and have a chat about the kind of sick monster Ronan Dell was, Kalan," he suggested. "Believe me, holding up Miar's parentage as proof of his reliability is no way to convince anybody who remembers the father that the son can be trusted."

"The Raven trusts him," Marla pointed out.

"The Raven is also an assassin, your highness. They tend to stick together."

Marla smiled at him. Apparently his intransigence on the topic of Galon Miar amused her. "There are plenty of people who believe I shouldn't trust you, Wrayan Lightfinger. You are a thief, after all."

"The Greatest Thief in all of Hythria, no less," Kalan added.

"Mock away, Kalan, you won't change my mind."

"What a shame, Master Lightfinger," Galon Miar announced from the door. "And I *so* hunger for the trust and respect of the Thieves' Guild, too."

Wrayan spun around, staring at the assassin in shock, and then he turned to the princess. "What's *he* doing here?"

"I invited him."

"The last time you invited him, he didn't bother to show up."

"Oh, but I did, Wrayan," Galon assured him, walking into the room as if he owned it. "Just not when I was expected. Or where." The assassin turned his gaze on the princess who, somewhat to Wrayan's astonishment, actually looked away first. Then he looked at the thief again. "I can call you Wrayan, can't I?"

"How do you know who I am?"

"You checked up on me. Surely I'm allowed to return the favour?"

Franz Gillam had told him then. Or the Doorman. It didn't

really matter which. The end result was the same. Wrayan glanced at the princess, shaking his head. "You have no idea if you can trust this man, your highness."

"I know that, Wrayan," she agreed. "You, however, *can* look into his mind and tell me if he can be trusted. That's why Master Miar is here. He's agreed to prove his loyalty to the throne, even to your satisfaction."

"Ah!" Galon exclaimed, studying Wrayan with open curiosity. "So you're Princess Marla's secret sorcerer. That explains a few things. I'm interested though, how you started out in the Sorcerers' Collective and finished up in the Thieves' Guild."

"Mother . . ." Kalan ventured cautiously. "Should we be discussing this so . . . openly? In front of strangers?"

The princess smiled confidently at her daughter. "There's no danger, Kalan. Master Miar is on our side."

"How do you know?"

"Because he told me he is."

"Funny," Galon remarked, looking at her curiously. "I didn't think you believed me the last time we spoke."

"Actually, I didn't then, and I don't now, but on the off-chance you are likely to be of some use to me, I thought it worth taking the time to find out."

"By having someone read my mind?"

"It was you who suggested it, Galon," the princess retorted, walking to the sideboard for more wine. There were no slaves present to wait on Marla and her guests. Marla was too smart to let this business become gossip in the servants' quarters. She took her time refilling her cup and then turned to face the assassin with an elegantly raised brow. "Rather suspicious of you to back out now, don't you think, when you discover I really can do what you only suspected I might be able to do?" Marla turned and added calmly to her daughter, "There's really nothing to be worried about, Kalan. If Galon submits to having his mind read, we'll know for certain whose side he's on. Either way, we have nothing to fear from him. If he's trustworthy, Wrayan will know soon enough. If he tries to block Wrayan's probe, even slightly,

Wrayan will kill him while he's still in Master Galon's mind. It's all quite simple. And it doesn't even involve any blood."

Wrayan wondered when Marla had been planning to share this little modification in her plans with him, or if it had been her intention all along to spring it on him when it was too late for him to back out. The assassin seemed just as uncertain. But he thought about it for barely more than a moment and then shrugged.

"As you wish, your highness." He turned to Wrayan. "Go ahead. Read my mind, thief. Tell me what a bad boy I've been."

"Drop the shield."

Galon glanced at Marla. "Ah, she told you about that too, did she?"

"Princess Marla hasn't told me anything. If you've touched Alija and she didn't read your mind, you've shielded it somehow."

"Aren't we the clever one?" Galon replied. He hesitated and then turned to Wrayan. "Go ahead, thief. Do your worst."

Until he began to draw on his power and his eyes darkened, Wrayan suspected Galon Miar didn't really think anybody was actually going to probe his mind. The assassin's eyes, which had been so confident a moment ago, began to fill with uncertainty.

"What the . . ." He took an involuntary step backwards.

From across the room Wrayan sought out the assassin's mind, but once he got past the turmoil of Galon's surface thoughts he ran into a wall. And it was—quite literally—a wall, as if someone had spent hours weaving individual strands of thought together so tightly they couldn't be penetrated. He examined the barrier curiously, marvelling at the effort that had gone into constructing such a defence. It was nothing like the smooth, undetectable surface of a Harshini mind shield. Nor did it make any pretence of being anything other than an unscaleable barricade. Nor could he knock it down without causing immeasurable harm. The Assassins' Guild of old had needed a way to stop the Harshini reading their minds and they'd found it, sure enough. But it must take years of training, Wrayan thought, to master such mental discipline. It was no wonder they began training their apprentices as young as nine or ten.

"I told you to drop the shield."

Galon stared at him, more than a little disconcerted. It was probably at that moment the assassin realised Wrayan really *could* read his thoughts. "If I do that, I'm defenceless against Alija. Against anybody who can read my mind, for that matter."

"If you *don't* do it, I'll assume you have something to hide from Princess Marla and I'll kill you."

Galon stared at him oddly. "You're not an Innate like Alija, are you? You must be part Harshini."

"So?"

"Don't the Harshini have inviolate rules regarding killing people?"

"I find them much less specific on the subject of castration," Wrayan assured him. "I think you'll find I've got plenty of room to manoeuvre if it comes to dispensing a bit of rough justice, Galon Miar."

Wrayan could feel the assassin's confidence surging again, even if he couldn't read his actual thoughts through the barrier. "You think you could take me, thief?"

"I think I could slip into your mind and make you cut your own balls off, *assassin*," he lied.

"Excuse me," Kalan interrupted, a little impatiently. "But if you two madmen are through deciding who's the toughest, can we get on with this?"

Wrayan glanced at her. She was standing beside her mother, her arms folded, tapping her foot on the tiles, as if she was annoyed about how long this was taking. Rodja Tirstone—who'd done nothing but observe the whole exchange with interest—sat on the cushions near the table, doing his best to empty the fruit platter. Marla, curiously enough, was watching Galon Miar expectantly, almost as if she wanted Wrayan to be proved wrong. He couldn't understand her attitude, either.

"We can do this as soon as he drops his mind shield."

Even under the threat of grievous bodily harm, Galon was more than a little reluctant to let the shield go. "It's not magic, you know. I just can't turn it on and off like you probably can."

"You can let it go," Wrayan guessed. "And if you're that scared of Alija, I'll put it back again when we're done. Assuming you survive the experience, of course."

Galon looked at Marla, almost as if he was pleading for her help, but her expression remained implacable.

"Your highness, I know what I said . . . but is this *really* necessary . . . ?"

"You want a ticket into my world, Galon. This is the price of admission."

The assassin stared at the princess for a long moment. "I think I'd better sit down."

"Be my guest," Marla said graciously, offering him a place on the cushions near Rodja with a sweep of her arm.

Galon lowered himself onto the cushions, made himself comfortable and then glanced up at Wrayan. "Do you actually know how to do this without cracking my head open?"

"Yes."

He frowned. "I have information . . . things I know . . . secrets belonging to the Assassins' Guild. They are nothing to do with you, thief. Don't go seeking them out. And if you ever use anything you learn in my mind tonight to betray my guild, I will hunt you down and kill you. Count on it."

"Wrayan will do what he must to ascertain your trustworthiness," Marla assured him. "Nothing more. Do you understand that, Wrayan?"

"Yes, your highness."

Satisfied with her assurance, Galon took a deep breath and closed his eyes. "Then do your worst, thief."

As he spoke, Wrayan sensed the strands that made up the wall begin to unravel. It was slow at first but as the weave loosened, they separated more quickly until finally the barrier disintegrated and Wrayan Lightfinger was able to step into the swirling darkness of Galon Miar's mind.

eeling any better?"

"*Damin?*"

Rorin blinked a few times, and looked around the room blankly. He was back in his own room in Cabradell Palace, daylight streaming through the windows. At first glance, the bedroom seemed to be full of people, although when he managed to focus his eyes a little better he realised it was just the prince and Lady Lionsclaw standing on either side of the bed. His agonizing encounter with a Karien priest seemed like a distant memory, something out of a nightmare he couldn't quite recall. He struggled to sit up, collapsing with a yelp of pain as soon as he tried to put any pressure on his left shoulder.

Damin winced sympathetically. "You might want to wait a bit before you try that again, Rory. That's a pretty nasty burn you've got there."

Rorin frowned, wondering how he'd gotten burned, and then he realised the whole sorry business with Kraig and Renulus and that damned Staff of Xaphista hadn't been a dream, after all.

"What happened?"

"You passed out."

"That much I get. What happened to Renulus? Did Kraig kill him?"

Damin smiled. "I gather he was sorely tempted, but he managed to contain himself."

"He's a Karien priest, Damin."

"No, actually he's a Denikan prince."

"I meant Renulus."

Damin smiled. "I know. And I believe you. I saw the staff. And what it did to your shoulder. How come it didn't harm Kraig?"

"It only works on those who can channel Harshini magic."
Rorin turned his head and looked up at Lady Lionsclaw, who
was standing on the other side of the bed looking down on
him with concern. "And he hit me with it when I was channelling, which would have amplified the effect a thousand-
fold. Did you have any idea what Renulus was, my lady?"

"He'd have been dead long ago, if I had," Tejay assured
them. "I'm fairly certain Terin had no idea he was a priest of
Xaphista, either. My late husband was many things I didn't
admire, but a follower of the Overlord wasn't one of them."

"What do you suppose he's doing here?" Damin asked.

Lady Lionsclaw shrugged. "I have no idea. And no idea if
I should be worried about it, either."

He tried to smile reassuringly. "Maybe there's nothing to
be concerned about. His presence in Cabradell could be as
innocuous as one curious Karien wanting to see how the
other half lived."

"Or as sinister as a spy sent here by the Church of
Xaphista the Overlord for some nefarious reason we know
nothing of," Damin suggested. "I suppose we'll find out
when we question him."

"Don't get your hopes up," Rorin warned. "If he's a
Karien priest then he's a fanatic and fanatics tend to enjoy
suffering. It makes them think they're earning a place at the
Overlord's table in the afterlife." He yawned and shifted on
the bed a little, grimacing with pain. "I'm sorry, Damin," he
added, feeling guilty that he'd brought down even more trouble
on his friends at a time when they could least afford it. "I was
just trying to help."

"You've nothing to apologise for," Damin assured him.
"You exposed a spy in our midst and if nothing else, gave me
a perfectly good excuse to keep him locked up for the duration of the campaign, which means we've got a much better
chance of convincing everyone Terin is still alive. Which
brings me to my next problem." He glanced across at Tejay.
"It seems the Lionsclaw family has a vacancy for a seneschal,
and I've volunteered you to fill it."

"Kalan ordered me to stay by *your* side."

"Do you always do what Kalan wants?"

"Hardly ever, now you come to mention it."

"Then consider yourself the new seneschal to the Warlord of Sunrise Province, Rorin Mariner." Damin glanced over the bed at Tejay. "Or War*lady*, as the case may be."

"I don't think there's such a word, Damin," Tejay said.

"There will be if word gets out about what we're up to here. Are you sure you'll be all right, Rorin?"

"I'll be fine. Truly."

"Can you heal yourself?" Tejay asked.

"Not as well as I can heal others, but even a little bit of Harshini blood means I'll heal faster than most."

"Well, do what you can to get well," she ordered. "Because as soon as you're up to it, we have another patient who needs your attention."

"Another patient? Who?"

"Adham," Damin told him, his good humour fading a little. "He took a knife in the belly a few weeks ago in a brawl over my honour. It's not getting any better."

Rorin frowned. "I'll do what I can, Damin . . . but it might be a day or so . . . that damned staff . . . it's like it sucked the life out of me."

"I had my physician, Caranth Roe, administer a draught to ease your pain," Lady Lionsclaw informed him. "Some of your fatigue may be the effects of the drug, rather than the residual effects of the staff."

"I hope so, my lady," Rorin agreed.

"I thought it was just legend, all that stuff Wrayan told us about Karien priests and the Staff of Xaphista when we were boys," Damin said. "Guess that was another one of his tall tales that turned out to be true, eh?"

"Most assuredly," Rorin replied, his shoulder throbbing in time with his pulse. Whatever Caranth Roe had given him, other than making him drowsy, it didn't seem to be having much of an effect on the pain. "Orleon would be most put out to learn of it. What are you going to do with Renulus?"

Damin sat down on the bed, his expression grim. "I'd really, *really* like to kill him, but with every damned Warlord in Hythria converging on this place, I don't want it getting back to anybody in the war camp that we might have uncovered a Karien spy in our midst. That's just giving Cyrus Eaglespike way too much rope to hang us with."

"Will he care?" Rorin asked. "We're at war with Fardohnya, not Karien."

"You know Alija better even than I do," Damin reminded him. "She'd find a way to turn it against us. Or against the Lionsclaw family because they've always been Wolfblade allies. I'd rather not give Cyrus, or his mother, the opportunity, if I can avoid it."

"He's going to be suspicious when I suddenly start acting as Terin's seneschal, isn't he?"

"I doubt it," Tejay assured him. "For one thing, it's not uncommon for members of the Sorcerers' Collective to act as stewards and seneschals for highborn Houses. It happens quite frequently. For another, Cyrus never met Renulus and because Terin was convinced the entire Eaglespike family looked down on him more than most, their dealings with his family were pretty much confined to the Convocation."

"And there hasn't been a Convocation since Cyrus inherited his father's province," Damin reminded him.

Rorin felt a little better for hearing that. "Poor Terin. Knowing what an arrogant ass Cyrus Eaglespike can be, for once, he may have been right about the highborn looking down on him." He turned to look at Tejay, wondering how she was dealing with the notion that her husband was probably dead. She didn't seem to be debilitated by her grief. In fact, she hardly seemed to be grieving at all. "I can't apologise enough for not being able to save your husband, my lady."

Tejay patted his hand with a comforting smile. "Don't worry about it, Rorin. I'm sure I'll manage to get by."

"You don't seem very upset."

"Which is a damned good thing, don't you think? We'd never be able to pull off this dangerous little escapade if I was moping about the palace, weeping and wailing for my long-lost husband like a silly girl."

"I guess not."

"You go back to sleep, Rorin," she advised. "Concentrate on getting better and regaining your strength so you can help Adham. Let me and Damin worry about the rest of it, all right?"

He nodded, thinking more sleep would be nice. The draught was making him lethargic and at the very least, solitude would help. He couldn't concentrate on easing the pain or doing anything to magically speed up the healing process with an anxious audience looking on.

"I'll be up and about soon, my lady. I promise."

"I know you will," she agreed. Then she turned to Damin and pointed to the door. "You. Out."

"I was just . . ."

"Let the man rest, Damin."

"Call if you need anything," Damin said, rising to his feet.

"I will."

"And thanks."

"For what?"

"For being there when we needed you."

"It was nothing." Rorin shrugged, wincing with pain at such a foolish impulse. "I face down evil, staff-wielding Karien priests all the time."

"Of course you do," Damin agreed. "You're a real hero, Rory. I'm sure Kalan will be very impressed."

The comment left him a little confused. "Huh? . . . Oh, I see . . . Well, despite what *you* think, your highness, I'm not in the least bit interested in impressing your sister."

"Good," Damin said. "Because you know I'd have to kill you if you ever laid a hand on her."

"You don't scare me, Damin Wolfblade," he replied with a hazy smile, as the draught pulled him down towards sleep. "I survived the Staff of Xaphista."

Rorin heard Damin laugh softly, heard Tejay urging him to let the patient sleep, their retreating footsteps and then faintly registered the door opening and closing as the effects of Canath Roe's drug overtook him. He drifted off to sleep, the pain in his shoulder fading to a dull ache in the distance, his dreams filled with visions of heroic sorcerers, evil, staff-wielding Karien priests, large, intimidating Denikan princes, and being comforted in the unlikely arms of Lady Kalan Hawksword.

chapter 52

The final meeting of Hythria's generals in Cabradell happened the day after Rorin returned from the Widowmaker. With Renulus in the dungeons and nobody else in the palace aware that the young sorcerer had returned alone, Damin was able to pass on his apologies for Terin's absence and nobody thought anything more about it.

Tejay's brother, Rogan Bearbow, had finally arrived, the last of the Warlords to answer the call to arms. His late arrival had much to do with the distance he had to travel from Natalandar; the capital of Izcomdar, which was located in the far east of the province on the other side of the country.

Rogan was a few years older than Damin, and he came with some two thousand infantry, and more importantly, another thousand light cavalry. The problem with Rogan was that, like Damin, he wasn't actually old enough to inherit his province yet, and strictly speaking he had no authority to bring his troops to war, and no right to expect them to follow his orders.

The reality, however, was that Hythria was torn apart by plague. There had been nobody else to step up and take charge of Izcomdar Province when his father died. The Sorcerers' Collective—the traditional trustee of all provinces that find themselves without a Warlord—had been in no position to send an administrator to Natalandar to counter Rogan's orders, and facing a choice between waiting on the pleasure of the Sorcerers' Collective or racing to the aid of his only sister, there really wasn't much question of which way Rogan was going to go.

But his arrival in Cabradell without the sanction of the Sorcerers' Collective did cause a fuss, particularly when Cyrus Eaglespike started complaining about the legality of an under-age heir having command of his late father's forces with no Sorcerers' Collective–appointed guardian to watch over him. The Warlord of Dregian even went so far as to suggest the High Prince appoint *him* as Rogan's interim guardian in lieu of the Sorcerers' Collective, a suggestion that so offended the younger Warlord, he and Cyrus almost came to blows over it.

Damin managed to thwart Cyrus's manoeuvring by convincing Lernen he should take direct command of the Izcomdar troops himself, and then had him appoint Rogan Bearbow as his second-in-command over the province's forces. As Lernen Wolfblade had no intention of going anywhere near the actual battle himself, the move effectively handed command back to Rogan and circumvented the Sorcerers' Collective entirely. It was a smart move politically, too. Rogan and Damin had always been civil acquaintances, but Rogan had been away for much of the time Damin spent in Izcomdar as a fosterling, so they'd never really been friends. Once Damin prevented Cyrus Eaglespike or the Sorcerers' Collective from getting their hands on Izcomdar's army, Damin knew he'd made an ally for life.

They had gathered for this meeting in Terin's study in Cabradell Palace at Damin's suggestion. The reason he gave for moving the meeting from the camp outside the city to the palace was that the Warlord of Sunrise had the best and most accurate maps of his province, therefore any discussion about strategy should take place with those maps within easy reach. The reality, however, was that holding the meeting in the palace was the only way Tejay could legitimately attend. She was the hostess here in her husband's home and nobody would pay any attention to her presence in the room, assuming she was there to supervise the slaves responsible for delivering refreshments.

Lernen attended the meeting, arriving at the palace with great pomp and ceremony and a half-dozen retainers who did nothing but get in the way. In addition to Rogan, Narvell was representing Elasapine. He had command of his grandfather's forces because Charel had awarded authority to him directly and there was nothing Cyrus could do about that. Damin represented Krakandar (Cyrus never thought to question the legitimacy of Damin's authority over Krakandar's forces, fortunately), and of course, there was Cyrus Eaglespike himself. The forces he wielded were considerable. In addition to the Dregian troops he commanded, his mother, in the name of the Sorcerers' Collective, had given him command over Conin Falconlance's Greenharbour forces. With his good friend, Toren Foxtalon, nodding agreement to every word he uttered, he had effective control over the Pentamor troops as well, which meant he had direct control over more than a third of their combined forces.

It might have been a little less than that, had the reinforcements arrived from Krakandar, but Damin had heard nothing from Xanda or Mahkas and the troops had never appeared. He didn't want to think too hard about what that might mean, simply praying that whatever was happening in Krakandar in his absence, Xanda and Luciena were able to keep things under control until he got back.

"If Hablet comes through both passes simultaneously, we're done for," Narvell remarked, as he studied the map laid out on the table, dragging Damin's attention back to the meeting.

Rogan nodded in agreement. "We're the weakest we've been in three generations. The only hope we have to fend off the Fardohnyans is to avoid an all-out conflict."

"That's not going to be easy," Narvell mused. "We should

be able to hold Highcastle—it's too narrow to allow a force through in any dangerous numbers unchallenged—but if we can't hold them at Winternest, we'll have our all-out conflict, whether we want it or not."

"We must force them down onto the plains," Rogan suggested. "Perhaps that way, we might be in command of any battle."

Damin wished he'd had time to take Narvell and Rogan aside before the meeting and tell them the news Rorin had brought back from the border. He'd tried to find them, but Rogan was late getting to the palace and Narvell was getting rather good at not being found when he didn't want to be—absences that coincided rather conveniently with the absence of Lady Kendra Warhaft. Still, Damin supposed, he could tell them later Winternest was already in the hands of the Fardohnyans and the Widowmaker was blocked and all the Fardohnyans they were going to be facing for the foreseeable future were already in Hythria.

"Frankly, I don't see how we're going to stop Hablet pouring his troops into Sunrise Province at his own pace," Cyrus complained. "You've already admitted Winternest is woefully undermanned."

"I think you'll find the gods favour us more than you imagine," Damin said to Cyrus.

The Warlord wasn't impressed with Damin's faith. "You might want to rely on divine intervention, Prince Damin. I'd rather we came up with a plan."

"We have a plan." Damin pointed to a place on the map between two small rivers. "We'll create a front here, at Farwell, between the Saltan River on the right and the Norsell River on the left. We'll bait the trap with Sunrise troops and reinforce the flanks with infantry from Krakandar and Elasapine, leaving your Dregian light cavalry and Sunrise infantry in the centre here, the most vulnerable part of the line. If we throw in the banners of the other provinces, General Regis should believe that's all the support we've been able to muster."

Narvell pointed to the narrow wedge of land in question

on the map. "With the rivers on either side of him, there's few other places he can go, anyway."

Damin was relieved there was someone else in the room who'd been taught tactics and military history by Geri Almodavar and Elezaar the Fool.

Rogan could also see the merit in Damin's tactics. "With luck, the Fardohnyans will see the weakness in the centre and break through here."

"Exactly! When the lines collapse, there'll be a rout and the flanks can withdraw. Regis will force our troops back, pushing on toward the hills here at Lasting Drift, past the two river crossings, where we'll have the rest of the forces from Pentamor and Greenharbour, in addition to Rogan's Izcomdar cavalry, waiting for him. The flanks will cross the rivers and close in from behind, cutting off his supplies, his retreat and any hope of reprieve. After that, gentlemen, it should be like spearing fish in a barrel."

"Regis is no fool," Rogan warned. "There's no guarantee he'll fall for this."

"He'll come to us," Damin replied confidently. "Because we're certainly not going to move any closer up the valley, where he might gain the advantage. Our supply lines are more secure than his. We can afford to wait. He can't."

Cyrus Eaglespike considered the plan and then turned to Lernen, who was sitting at the head of the table pretending he had some idea of what was going on. "And what is *your* plan, your highness?" Then he added with a condescending smile at Damin, "Now that we've heard from the boy."

"Um . . ." Lernen stammered, unprepared for the question. "What he said."

"What?"

"What my nephew said," Lernen decreed. "That's my plan." He leaned back in his chair and waved his arm over the table. "I explained my plans to Damin earlier and he's covered my intentions well enough."

Cyrus glanced at Damin, waiting for him to object to Lernen claiming credit for what everybody in the room knew must be his work, but Damin said nothing. He wasn't about to humiliate Lernen with Cyrus Eaglespike watching, or give the Dregian Warlord the slightest opportunity to drive a wedge between them.

"Well, what about the archers?" Cyrus demanded, when it was clear Damin wasn't going to contradict the High Prince. "If you're basing your strategy on them, we're doomed. I've seen what you call the Sunrise light infantry, these days. There's barely an experienced man left among them and their Warlord isn't even back from his excursion into the mountains to lead them. They're nothing more than reckless farm boys looking for a bit of adventure."

"They're farm boys defending their homes, my lord," Narvell corrected. "And I'm sure Terin Lionsclaw will be back in time."

Cyrus was unimpressed. "Leaderless, untrained rabble likely to break at the first sign of trouble."

Damin nodded absently, as he recalled a conversation he'd had with Kraig. *There are four things that always affect a battle*, the Denikan prince had told him. *They are immutable and, if you understand them, the key to winning any conflict . . . you must claim victory over men's minds before you can take it from their bodies . . . you need them to believe you can win . . .*

"Then that's what we'll tell them to do."

"What do you mean?"

"The High Prince's plan is to make Axelle Regis think our lines have collapsed. Peasants running away screaming couldn't help us more if they tried. But we'll control it. We'll order each man to shoot three arrows and then retreat." He glanced across the room at Tejay, who was pretending to supervise the slaves laying out the buffet on the side table. She met his eye, inclining her head imperceptibly to let him know she agreed with his suggestion, and then turned back to chastise a careless slave for spilling the soup.

Damin turned his gaze on Cyrus. "If they only have to face the enemy for a short time, and if our *untrained rabble* believes they're retreating under orders, rather than running away, I guarantee we'll get those three arrows out of every man there. The rout won't happen too quickly, that way. The Fardohnyans will think we're putting up some sort of a fight before falling apart and we can draw them down into our trap at Lasting Drift in numbers we can deal with."

"I think it'll work," Narvell said, and then smiled at the High Prince. "In fact, I'm certain it will. Well done, Uncle. It's an excellent strategy."

Damin glanced across at Cyrus Eaglespike. There wasn't a man in the room who seriously believed Lernen Wolfblade had anything to do with this plan, but that his nephews apparently showed no resentment about letting him take the glory for it had Cyrus gnashing his teeth with frustration.

"Lunch is ready, my lords," Tejay announced before Cyrus could say anything. Her announcement effectively put an end to the discussion for the time being. Muttering to himself, Cyrus turned away from the table and went to inspect the buffet.

"Damin!"

"Yes, Uncle?"

"Might we have a word?" the High Prince asked, rising to his feet.

It was unlike Lernen to be so tactful. Leaving the others to their lunch, Damin followed his uncle out into the hall.

"Is something wrong?" he asked, when they were out of earshot of the rest of the Warlords.

Lernen was wringing his hands worriedly. "You had plenty of opportunity to make me look like a fool just now; plenty of opportunity to promote yourself as a better general of our armies than me. You didn't. Instead, you made me look like a statesman. Why? Are you up to something?"

Although he sounded lucid enough, the madman, Damin feared, wasn't far away. "I would never have embarrassed you in public, Uncle. You're family."

Lernen glared at him suspiciously for a moment and then lowered his voice, looking over his shoulder furtively. "I know I'm not always an easy man, Damin. It's good your mother raised you and your brother to be so loyal."

The admission was a rare thing indeed from the High Prince, and proof, Damin suspected, the old man wasn't yet completely lost to the sickness that ravaged his mind and his body. Such a moment wasn't to be wasted, however. "Then would you do something for me, Uncle?"

Lernen was instantly suspicious. "What do you want?"

"I'm not actually interested in becoming High Prince any time soon so get rid of that damned armour, would you? As a favour to me."

"It was a gift."

"It was given to you by your enemies to make you vulnerable, Uncle. A target. Don't fall into their trap. For my sake, if not your own," he added.

Lernen threw his hands up helplessly. "How can I dispose of it without offending the High Arrion? If I don't wear it in battle, she'll know. Even if I don't finish up with an arrow through me, that slimy son of hers will report it straight back to her and then she'll start yelling at me . . . and asking me why and . . . well, I just don't like it when she yells at me."

"You could give it away," Damin suggested, not bothering to point out that Alija wasn't here to yell at anybody. Lernen was probably right about Cyrus reporting it back to his mother, though.

"To whom?"

"How about someone who does something very brave? Alija can't fault you for rewarding great valour with something so precious."

"Do we have anybody who's done something brave?"

"I'm sure we will have soon, Uncle Lernen. We're going to war, after all."

Lernen smiled. "You find someone to give it to, Damin, and it will be his."

"Thank you, Uncle."

"Thank *you*, nephew. I'm lucky to have people like you and your mother looking out for me."

You're lucky to have people like me and my mother to do your thinking for you, Damin corrected silently, but he was too polite to say such a thing out loud. Instead he bowed and opened the door for the High Prince so they could have some lunch before continuing their council of war.

ChAPTER 53

Alija took her time getting ready when Tressa informed her Galon Miar was waiting downstairs to see her. It was important, she felt, to appear at her best. And her most controlled. Nobody would ever learn of the depth of her grief for her *court'esa*. Not only was it unseemly to feel so deeply for a slave, her grief exposed a weakness she had no wish to reveal. So Alija took her time and made herself beautiful, the cosmetics and her robes of office surrounding her like a shield designed to protect her from her own vulnerability.

She'd not seen the assassin since before Tarkyn Lye's murder. The coincidence was not lost on Alija and she wondered as she descended the stairs if Galon had stayed away because he knew something that would incriminate the Assassins' Guild and was afraid to share it with her. That Marla Wolfblade had hired the guild to murder Tarkyn Lye was a foregone conclusion. There was no way the princess was going to sully her own delicate little hands with the blood of a slave. Given his rank in the Assassins' Guild, the chances that Galon knew the identity of the assassin were high. He might also know who commissioned the job. He certainly had the resources to find out.

And as proof of his loyalty to her, Alija had every intention of *making* him find out.

"Alija," he said, as she entered the hall, smiling at her warmly. "You're looking particularly lovely this afternoon."

He didn't seem uncertain, or the slightest bit nervous. Perhaps he didn't know anything about Tarkyn's murder, after all. There was no need to let him know how much his absence had worried her, though. She lifted her chin, eyeing him with disdain. "How thoughtful of you, Galon, to squeeze me into your busy social calendar."

"Don't be like that," he said, crossing the room to her. He took her hands in his and kissed her—significantly, on each cheek rather than the mouth. She didn't have time to wonder what that meant. While he held her hands she quickly scanned his thoughts. As usual, there was nothing untoward she could detect, but it was never easy to tell with Galon. He was one of those rare assassins who had mastered the mental discipline required to construct a mind shield. Although she couldn't actually feel it, she knew it was there because there was information in his mind she had never been able to find, things he should have known about the Assassins' Guild that simply weren't there. The only thing she did know for certain was that even the best assassin couldn't just hide his most recent thoughts away. It took hours, sometimes days of concentrated meditation to consciously create a mind shield, and assassins usually left the city to do it. The guild had some hidden retreat not far out of Naribra, Alija knew, which was where most of the advanced training for assassins took place. Galon hadn't had time to get to Naribra and back since she'd seen him last.

"Where have you been?" she demanded, still holding his hands. If she couldn't read his every thought, she could certainly tell when he was lying.

Galon smiled. "Plotting your demise with your nemesis."

Alija snatched her hands away, taking a step back from him. He wasn't lying.

"You've been plotting with Marla Wolfblade?"

"She really does have a set against you, doesn't she?" Galon seemed to find the idea quite amusing.

"I hope you're joking."

"You know I'm not."

"Then you'd better explain yourself, Galon Miar."

"Marla thinks she's found a way to bring you down. Using me."

His candour didn't surprise her. Galon knew Alija could tell if he was lying, so there was no point in trying to deceive her. His willingness to play along with Marla's schemes disturbed her a little, though.

"You mean her absurd plot to expose my sons as slave's bastards? I'd not lose too much sleep over that, if I were you. She's bluffing."

"No, I believe her latest plan involves convincing you to send an assassin to the front to arrange for both Damin Wolfblade and Narvell Hawksword to be killed in a battle."

She smiled. "Don't think I haven't fantasised about such a thing. But that's almost as ridiculous as her plan to expose my sons. And hardly reason to involve you. You're too well known to send on such a mission. She must know I would never be so blatant. Or so easily manipulated."

"I think she's a little desperate."

Alija doubted that. The woman who had waltzed in here clutching Tarkyn's bloodied slave collar was anything but desperate. More likely she was lost without Elezaar's guidance as these increasingly absurd plots to destroy her seemed to indicate.

"Marla's getting anxious," he explained, confirming at least one of her suspicions. "The army we've been able to raise is woefully outnumbered by the Fardohnyans and—thanks to you—it's under the command of an incompetent fool. What really has her frightened is the possibility that Hablet will actually win, and if he does, there's no place in this world for the Wolfblades."

"A thought which is almost enough to make me like Hablet."

"That's what Marla fears most. If Hablet wins this war, he won't stay in Greenharbour long. After he's killed every member of Marla's family he can find, he'll appoint a governor to rule the country, head back to Talabar and simply bleed Hythria dry. And he'll need someone who knows Hythria well to do the bloodletting."

Alija stared at him in shock. "And she thinks I would collaborate with a Fardohnyan in this?"

"She thinks you'd do anything to see your son on the throne."

"If Hablet wins," Alija pointed out, "there won't actually be a throne."

"Not for a while," Galon agreed. "But we'll recover from the plague eventually, and from an invasion. At some point in the future, there'll be a High Prince of Hythria again."

"But if her line is obliterated by Hablet, it won't be a Wolfblade," Alija concluded. She studied him curiously. "I find it remarkable that she confided all this in you."

"I have an honest face."

Alija wasn't amused by his flippancy. "Don't waste my time, Galon. What did you have to do to gain this remarkable intelligence from Princess Marla? Sleep with her?"

"No," he assured her. Then he added with a grin, "Although not for lack of trying on my part."

"You find her attractive?"

"You know I do."

She walked around the desk to put some distance between them. It wouldn't do to let him know how much his admiration for Marla's great beauty irritated her. "So . . . what . . . she invited you to tea and just blurted out all her plans to you?"

"She thinks she can trust me."

"Really? Now why would that be?"

"She had someone read my mind."

Alija's head jerked up. "Who?"

The assassin shrugged. "You probably don't know him. He's a thief. A man named Wrayan Lightfinger."

Alija gripped the edge of the table in shock. "You've actually spoken to Wrayan?"

"You *do* know him? Fancy that. Cocky sort of chap, isn't he? Calls himself the greatest thief in all of Hythria."

"Wrayan actually read your mind?" she gasped. "And you let him?"

He shrugged, apparently unconcerned. "The mind shield assassins learn to create was designed to stop the Harshini, Alija. You don't seriously think some distant descendant of their race would be able to crack what a full Harshini couldn't, do you? You have nothing to fear. Trust me, Lightfinger took nothing from my mind I didn't willingly let him have."

This was too much to take in, all at once. She sank down in her chair. "I don't understand."

"It's quite simple. Marla Wolfblade made contact with me because she knows about our relationship. She's trying to subvert me to her cause. She's out to destroy you and she's prepared to use anything or any*body* to do it."

"Why didn't you just tell her to go to hell?"

"That wouldn't have helped you much. This way, I'll know her plans and I can keep you apprised of them."

"Take my hand," she commanded.

Galon did as she asked, reaching across the desk, unconcerned that she might doubt him or that she had the means to tell if he was being untruthful.

"Have you slept with Marla?"

"No."

It was the truth, Alija discovered with relief. "Did you really allow Wrayan Lightfinger to read your mind?"

Galon didn't even hesitate. "Yes."

Also the truth. "Did he break through your shield?"

"No, he didn't break it."

Again, Galon spoke truthfully. Relieved beyond measure, she let his hand drop.

He sank down into the chair opposite the desk. "Does this mean you believe me? That you trust me?"

"I believe you, Galon. I'm not at all sure I trust you. What exactly are you supposed to do, to lure me into this trap of Marla Wolfblade's?"

"I'm supposed to subtly let it slip I can put you in touch

with someone who can get a message through to Hablet, telling him you're willing to do a deal about the administration of Hythria after he's won the battle, and that to prove your good intentions, you'll arrange to have the Wolfblade line destroyed so there is no focus for opposition against his rule."

"How?"

He smiled. "Thieves and assassins know no borders, you know."

Alija shook her head. Such a plan seemed pointless and unworkable. "What makes her think Hablet would have any interest in dealing with me? I'm High Arrion of the Sorcerers' Collective. He despises the Collective just on principle."

Galon leaned back in his chair. "Princess Marla was of the opinion that if you let it be known it was *you* who manipulated Lernen Wolfblade into taking command of Hythria's army, it will more than adequately prove your change of allegiance to King Hablet."

Alija couldn't help but smile. "I imagine she would see things that way. And when I make contact, Marla exposes me as a Fardohnyan traitor, is that the plan?"

"I believe so."

She shook her head in wonder. "Her gall appears to be boundless."

"I don't know," Galon remarked, sounding suspiciously admiring of Marla's schemes. "It's a pretty slick arrangement, actually. Or it would be, if I wasn't playing for the wrong side."

"Don't you mean the *right* side?"

"Depends on where you're standing, I suppose."

Alija frowned, but knew he was baiting her, so she didn't react. "This contact of Marla's . . . is he really a Fardohnyan agent? He would almost have to be if she seriously thought I would fall for this absurdity."

"I couldn't say. Despite what it looks like, Alija, I wasn't actually given every little detail of the plan. All I know is I was supposed to come here, pretend everything is fine, and then convince you that your best hope of ever seeing your son ruling Hythria someday is to do a deal with Hablet *before* he's won the war, rather than after, when he's in no mood to deal with anybody."

Alija rose to her feet and paced the floor thoughtfully, wondering if there was a way she could turn this around; if there was a way to trap Marla in her own schemes.

"Given her connections," she mused, "it's not hard to imagine Marla has extensive contacts in Fardohnya, either through the Tirstone brothers, or Luciena Taranger. I suppose it wouldn't be that hard for her to arrange to get a message to Hablet. But would she really risk exposing herself like that, just to get at me?"

"You'd know that better than I, Alija."

The High Arrion nodded grimly. "Then the answer is probably yes. Tell her I'll meet him."

Galon looked at her in genuine surprise. "*What?*"

"Tell Marla I'll meet with this Fardohnyan agent she's lined up. Tell her you succeeded in convincing me my only hope of seeing an end to her line is to ally myself with Hablet. How does the old saying go? The enemy of my enemy is my friend?"

"You can't be serious!" he exclaimed. "She's trying to trap you into proving you're in league with Hablet. That's high treason."

"I know that."

"So you're going to foil her plans by meeting with a Fardohnyan agent? There's a *grand* idea."

She smiled confidently. "I'm going to turn the tables on her, Galon."

"How?"

Alija was surprised someone as astute as Galon Miar couldn't see what she was driving at. "In order for this plan to proceed, Marla, or one of her stepchildren—and I'm assuming it will be Rodja Tirstone—will have to make contact with this Fardohnyan agent first. And he will have to be genuine. She knows I can read his mind. Any hint he's not what he claims, and her scheme will be exposed. All *I* need to do is prove Marla is conducting business with our enemies and the entire Wolfblade family will fall."

"And how are you going to prove it?"

"I'm not. You are."

"*Me?*"

"You obviously have her confidence. Tell her I agreed. Get the time and the place for this meeting and when we arrive, I will scan his thoughts. It will take me a matter of minutes to establish he was at the meeting at the behest of Rodja Tirstone, or someone else connected to Marla. Once we have proof, I will call in the Sorcerers' Collective Guard. You will testify that she set the meeting up, and there you have it. All the evidence we need to prove the High Prince's sister is a traitor to Hythria. Marla tied up in knots, using the very noose she set to hang me. There's a rather delicious irony in that, don't you think?

"I think you're insane, actually."

"It is insane," Alija agreed. "Which is why this will work. Tell me one thing, though. Why did you bring this plan to me? You could have taken Marla's side. She's wealthier than a god. And I know you think she's beautiful. Why not just fall in with her plans and reap the rewards? It's not as if you love me, Galon."

The assassin rose to his feet and walked to her. With heartbreaking tenderness, he took her hands in his, a gesture she knew was designed to ease her fears. "Alija, I swear to you, my feelings for you have never changed since we first met. Nothing Marla Wolfblade has said or ever will say is going to alter that."

Even if she hadn't known for certain he was telling the truth because of their physical contact, his demeanour was so intense, she would have believed him. Still holding her hands, he kissed her, this time on the mouth. And then he let her go. "I can't stay much longer. I have to report my progress to my co-conspirators."

"Let me know how it goes."

"I will." He let her go reluctantly and then turned and headed for the door.

"One other thing," she called after him.

"Yes?"

"I want you to find out who ordered the kill on Tarkyn Lye."

Galon hesitated before he answered. "You want me to break my oath to the guild by giving you the name of a client?"

Significantly, he didn't sound surprised to learn Tarkyn was dead. That, in itself, told Alija a great deal. "Yes. I do."

"I can't."

"But you do know who ordered it, don't you?"

He nodded reluctantly. "And I really can't tell you who it was, Alija. Much as I'd like to."

"Then tell me this much. Did Tarkyn's death affect your decision to remain loyal to me?"

"In more ways than I can ever explain," he replied with total conviction.

Alija crossed her arms with a look of satisfaction. *He knows it was Marla who ordered Tarkyn killed. And clearly, the notion disturbs him.*

It seemed odd for an assassin to be unsettled about the idea of a woman hiring the Assassins' Guild to remove an enemy. Perhaps it was because this wasn't just any woman. This was the High Prince's sister. No guild wanted to become the private army of a despot, so they determinedly stayed out of politics. Just as the Assassins' Guild refrained from taking jobs that might affect the succession, they were, historically, just as reluctant to accept commissions from those in positions of ultimate power. Learning Marla Wolfblade had hired his guild to take care of an enemy—even if it was only a slave—would have had ramifications even the princess hadn't considered.

"I'll see you again soon?"

"As soon as I can arrange it," he promised, and then he was gone, leaving Alija alone, the faint taste of his kiss still lingering on her lips. She revelled in the sensation and then called for Tressa.

"My lady?"

"Send a message to the Sorcerers' Palace," she ordered, thinking that even if it took an inordinate amount of double dealing to bring Marla Wolfblade down, Wrayan Lightfinger was much more easily dealt with. "I've just heard there is a notorious thief in the city looting the houses of the dead. I need to speak to the Captain of the Guard."

chapter 54

The second time Galon Miar came through her window, Marla was expecting him. She was sitting at her dressing table, fully dressed this time, brushing out her hair. It didn't need brushing, but it gave her something to do with her hands while she waited.

As soon as she heard the window open, she looked up and watched him in the mirror, climbing through her window. He turned and closed it carefully behind him before acknowledging her presence.

"Your highness."

"Do you have some sort of problem with using a door, Galon?"

"How come you never call the guards when I sneak through your window? By the way, you're starting to make a habit of that," he said, walking up behind her.

"Not calling the guards?"

"Calling me by my first name."

She turned to face him directly. "That's only because I'm too much of a lady to call you a lowlife gutter-scum to your face. You've been to see Alija, I take it?"

"Oh, yes."

"And how did she take the news all her dreams are about to come true?"

"Pretty much how you'd expect her to take it. She wanted to know if I was sleeping with you."

"What did you tell her?"

"Not yet."

Marla couldn't help herself. She laughed out loud. "You're an optimist, Galon. I'll grant you that much."

"You will accept my offer eventually, your highness. Remember, there's still the issue of your agreement with the Assassins' Guild to take care of."

"I could walk down to the Slave Quarter and find some abandoned child on the street tonight, legally adopt him tomorrow and then hand him over to the Assassins' Guild the day after, Galon. Your plan isn't nearly so clever as you think it is."

"Don't get too excited about *your* clever little plan to circumvent guild law, your highness," he warned. "I'm the one responsible for deciding when you've fulfilled your obligation to the guild. Trust me, you could adopt every homeless child in Greenharbour and it won't be good enough for me."

"So now you're *telling* me which child it has to be? And conveniently it's one *you* fathered?" She shook her head. "It would seem in the matter of honour, you really are your father's son."

The insult didn't seem to faze him. "Actually, I'm not my father's son at all. My *real* father was another slave, a *court'esa*. My mother told Ronan Dell I was his son to protect me from him. Pretty smart move for a terrified thirteen-year-old girl, when you think about it. It saved her any further suffering at his hands and it had the added bonus of setting me free. A slave's bastard grows up to be a slave, you know. But a highborn bastard . . . that's a whole different pile of horse dung. Highborn bastards are looked after. Fed. Clothed. Well educated. Almost treated like real people. I was probably the only child to ever walk the halls of Ronan Dell's palace without fear."

"I was told your mother died giving birth."

"She did. But my father lived to the ripe old age of thirty-six," he replied. "He was a linguist. A damn good one, too. Ronan Dell's wealth came from precious metals. His family had mines all over Hythria and interests in more than a few other countries, as well. He did a lot of business with the Far-dohnyans and even the Medalonians and Kariens so he kept my father around as an interpreter. Until Alija Eaglespike sent her henchmen through Ronan Dell's palace on a killing spree, that is. I found him out in the courtyard, you know. He'd just been sitting there in the sun, reading a book, when some Dregian thug sneaked up on him and cleaved his head in two from behind."

"I'm sorry. I didn't know."

He shrugged. "No reason you should. And I'm not telling you this to get your sympathy. I mention it only so you don't make the mistake of thinking I'm anything like that monster you mistakenly believe gave me life. The massacre at Ronan Dell's palace took place over twenty-five years ago. I've pretty much come to terms with it."

"Yet you want me to believe you're still burning with the need for vengeance?"

"I'm burning with a need, your highness," he agreed, squatting down in front of her to brush the hair gently from her face. "But right now, it's not vengeance."

She ignored his unsubtle hint and pushed his hand away impatiently. "On consideration, your guild's vengeance for reneging on an agreement might be slightly less harrowing than the reaction of my children, were I to tell them my next husband was going to be an assassin."

Galon smiled and stood up again. "So you *have* been considering my offer?"

"Only when I feel the need for a bit of light entertainment."

"But you *are* considering it," he pointed out. He was awfully close. Perhaps because he knew how much it unsettled her. "That's a step in the right direction."

"You've met my stepson, Rodja, and my daughter, Kalan, but you've never met my other sons, have you?"

"I've seen your eldest son around town on occasion. He likes the taverns, I hear. And the races."

"Don't be fooled by his affable manner. Damin could take down a grown man by the time he was twelve."

The assassin seemed rather amused. "Are you trying to scare me, Marla?"

"I just mention it in passing."

"You're not threatening to set your boys on to me, then?"

"The Wolfblades are a *ruling* family, Galon. By definition that means we delegate." She rose to her feet and walked across to the window, throwing it open. She took a deep breath of the damp night air, hoping the faint breeze would cool her clammy skin, and then turned to look at him. "People like *us* hire people like *you* to do our dirty work."

He looked at her oddly. "People like *us*?"

Marla looked down her nose at him. "Feel free to leave the same way you came in, Galon. I'm actually starting to think rather fondly of this window as the tradesmen's entrance."

He crossed the room to the window and looked out over the rooftops of the palace. Marla was a tiny bit disappointed. She thought he'd put up more of a fight before she tossed him out.

Finally he turned to look at her. "So, tell me, your highness, do people like *you* ever spare a thought to what your lifestyle costs people like me?"

Marla rolled her eyes. "Oh, gods, spare me! Just when I thought I had you all figured out, it turns out that at heart you're really a noble champion of social justice."

He smiled at the very suggestion. "Not me, your highness. I want *in* to your world. I'm not interested in tearing it down."

"Here's a little tip, then, Galon," she told him softly, reaching up to pat his face like a mother chastising a spoilt child. "Learn to use the door."

He caught her wrist and held it fast. No longer in charge of this dangerous exchange, Marla struggled to free it. "Let me *go*!"

"Here's a tip for *you*, your highness," he breathed, pulling her to him. "People like me don't pay a whole lot of attention to people like you when they're behaving like spoilt, condescending little bitches."

"Get your hands off me!"

"Or you'll scream?" he asked, pushing her back against the curtains. "You threaten that a lot, your highness, but you never seem to actually do it."

"I'm warning you . . ."

"And now I'm *really* scared, because when people like you warn people like me, we'd better pay attention, hadn't we?"

"Stop saying that!" she ordered. "You're completely misinterpreting what I meant."

"I'm pretty sure I know what you mean, Marla Wolfblade, which begs a rather interesting question." He held her against the curtains, her wrist held fast, his body pressed against hers. "What does it take, I wonder, for people like me to make people like you scream anyway?"

Bereft of her senses, let alone a comprehensible answer, Marla turned her face away, but all it did was give him unhindered access to the hypersensitive skin just below her ear. His lips trailed fire down her neck, deliberately tormenting, torturously delightful.

"Stop it," she commanded without conviction.

"Stop what?" he asked, as his lips burned their way across her throat. "This?" He waited and when she didn't answer, he added with a wicked little smile. "Or this?"

"Galon . . ." she breathed helplessly.

Her whispered call was all he seemed to be waiting for. He kissed her then, and Marla forgot everything. Galon let go of her wrist and pulled her closer. Marla gripped the curtain and let him, wishing there was some way to make this feeling last forever. This was raw animal lust, pure and simple—the *court'esa*-trained part of her knew that. That didn't make the experience any less intense. If anything, it sharpened the need, the hunger. This wasn't logical, or sensible, she knew. It was something that only happened on that rare occasion when two people, against all logic and common sense, wanted each other so badly they were prepared to throw caution to the wind and give in to that part of them they normally kept hidden in the darkest recesses of their souls.

When she was younger she might have called it love, but she was older now and far more cynical.

The savagery of her desire shocked Marla a little. She barely noticed when the curtains came crashing down as Galon lifted her into his arms and carried her to the bed, didn't hear the table fall or the vase by the bed shatter to the floor as they bumped it on their way past. Marla was lost completely to her hunger, his touch, oblivious to anything else but her desire . . .

Until Galon cried out in pain and suddenly slumped on top of her on the bed and Marla looked up to discover her guards standing over them, one of them wiping the blood from the blade he had just used to run Galon Miar through.

CHAPTER 55

It wasn't until Aleesha reported to her mistress that Emilie wasn't anywhere to be found that Luciena really started to worry. Nor was she entirely certain that "nowhere to be found" was an accurate statement. Krakandar Palace was a huge place riddled with hidden nooks and crannies a ten-year-old might hide in, not to mention the labyrinthine slave-ways which it would take days to search, if they were really serious about it.

No, Emilie had found entertainment somewhere else in the palace and had given Aleesha the slip long enough to find it. It was up to the adults to find Emilie, because until she was ready, she probably didn't want to be found.

"Did she say anything to you before she left the nursery?" Luciena demanded of her slave.

"Not a word, my lady. Not really."

"What exactly does *not really* mean?"

"Well, she was talking about a promise her father made to take her riding later today . . . I don't know . . . maybe she went looking for him?"

"Didn't *you* check?"

"Your husband is with Lord Damaran, my lady," the slave replied. "I'm not about to knock on his door. Besides, I didn't think she'd go . . ."

Luciena cursed under her breath, not waiting to hear the rest of Aleesha's explanation. She hurried out of the nursery, across the foyer and along the broad east wing corridor where Mahkas's office was located. Taking a deep breath, she knocked on the door when she reached it, and then opened it cautiously, dreading what she might find inside. If Mahkas was feeling fractious and didn't want to be disturbed, who knew how he'd react to this unwelcome interruption.

"Luciena!" Xanda was alone in the study, working on the accounts by the look of it. He looked up in surprise when the door opened. "What are you doing here?"

"Looking for Emilie. She's been missing for nearly two hours from the nursery. Aleesha thought she might have come looking for you. Have you seen her?"

He shook his head, apparently unconcerned. "Not for a while. I promised her we'd go riding as soon as I was finished here and she said she'd wait for me. I assumed she meant in the nursery."

"Never assume anything with that girl," Luciena warned in exasperation. "I'll bet you anything you care to name that she's *waiting* for you down in the stables, hoping she doesn't get caught."

He smiled. "Well, I'm nearly done here. Did you want me to go and find her?"

"I'll come with you. We need to have a talk to that girl about the meaning of the rule *no roaming around the palace unaccompanied*."

Xanda closed the ledger he'd been reading and rose to his feet. "I can't say I blame her, though. This palace is wonderful for a child. Or at least it used to be."

Luciena frowned. "Ah yes, the good old days. I remember some of those wonderful things you and your cousins got up to as children. Wasn't sneaking out onto a second-storey roof and drinking yourselves into oblivion with a stolen wineskin one of your favourite pastimes?"

"You make it sound so unromantic, Luciena."

"I recall it being perilously dangerous. You haven't been filling Emilie's head with your wild childhood reminiscences, I hope?"

"Gods no!" Xanda exclaimed in alarm. "I don't want my child doing even half the things I got up to as a boy."

"I'm very relieved to hear it. You don't think they would have let her go riding on her own, do you?"

"Unless she's bullied one of the stable boys into saddling a horse for her, I doubt it. I don't think she's tall enough to saddle a Raider's mount on her own."

"Let's just go down to the stables and find out for certain," Luciena suggested, a little impatiently. Xanda's words had left her feeling even more nervous. Emilie wouldn't think twice before trying to bully a stable boy.

Xanda followed Luciena's impatient steps through the palace and out through the solar into the garden that led down to the corrals. When they arrived at the stables, the warm summer air was buzzing with the sound of flies and thick with the smell of horse manure but there was no sign of Emilie, which relieved Luciena no end. If her daughter had found mischief to get into, obviously she'd found it elsewhere.

"Jendar, have you seen my daughter this morning?" Xanda asked one of the stable boys mucking out an empty stall near the entrance.

The lad stopped his shovelling long enough to point in the direction of the yards. "She's with Lord Damaran, sir. Down in the round yard, I think."

"Lord *Damaran*?" Luciena exclaimed in alarm. "What's she doing with him?"

The young slave shrugged, the goings-on among the high-born obviously something he cared little about. "She was hanging around here for a while, getting underfoot, when Lord Damaran came down to check on Brehn's Pride. She got to talking with him about you taking her out this afternoon, my lord, so he saddled the bad-tempered brute and took her down to the round yard for a ride."

"Who are you calling a bad-tempered brute?" she asked distractedly, looking around for Emilie.

"That stallion of his, Brehn's Pride," the slave replied, shaking his head. "Mean-spirited thing it is. Even Lord Damaran can't control him half the time."

"And he took my daughter riding on this beast?"

"Hang on a minute!" Xanda said, grabbing her arm before she could storm off in the direction of the round yard.

She shook free of him impatiently. "*Xanda*! That maniac has my daughter! And he's put her on a damned stallion! Even if it wasn't this brute his slaves claim, she's barely mastered her pony . . ."

"If they're in the round yard, she's not likely to hurt herself. Mahkas wouldn't let her come to any harm . . ."

"Ah, yes!" she agreed. "The great Mahkas Damaran! The well-known Regent of Krakandar, renowned throughout the land for *not* hurting people!"

Xanda glanced around at the slaves who'd stopped working to watch this interesting altercation between two of their ruling family. He took Luciena's arm and led her out of the stables, and out of earshot—provided they didn't shout—of their audience.

"Calm down, Luciena."

"Calm *down*?" she hissed furiously. "How can you tell me to calm down? He's got Emilie . . ."

"And I will go and get her," he promised. "Let me handle this. You'll just make things worse."

"Xanda, have you forgotten Leila already?"

"Of course not! But this isn't the same thing. However twisted, Mahkas had a reason for what he did to Leila . . ."

"By the gods, Xanda! You're *defending* him again!"

"I'm doing nothing of the kind. Now please, Luci, let me deal with this."

Luciena wanted to scream at him. *Don't you understand!* This place was dangerous and her children were in the most danger of all. They were living under the roof of a madman, at the mercy of his fickle moods, and her husband, the father of those same children, seemed reluctant to do anything to protect them.

She searched his face, wondering why he couldn't—or wouldn't—see what was so clear to her. "The biggest mistake I ever made was agreeing to stay here when Damin left the city. I should have got out—with my children—while I still had the chance."

Xanda sighed wearily, as if he was tired of hearing her complain about it. "I'm doing what I can, Luci. More than you realise. But it's important . . . no, it's *critical* . . . that you do nothing to upset my uncle at the moment. Chief among the things *likely* to set him off, incidentally, is you marching down to the round yard to deliver a scathingly indignant lecture on his total lack of common sense and responsibility."

She scorned his excuses, sick of his insistence that doing nothing equated with doing something. "You're not doing a damned thing to help us, Xanda, except defending that monster at every turn."

"Luci, trust me on this," he pleaded, lowering his voice. "I can't tell you why, certainly not standing here in the stables, but I'm doing far more than you realise to get you and our children out of danger. *Please* don't jeopardise my efforts for the sake of a silly argument."

Luciena's eyes narrowed suspiciously. "What are you talking about?"

Xanda hesitated for a moment, glancing over his shoulder before he replied. "If I promise to tell you later, will you promise to turn around, go back to the palace, and let me fetch Emilie?"

Luciena debated the issue silently, not at all happy about the idea, but conceding, however reluctantly, that Xanda was making sense. "You'll bring her straight back?"

"I'll be back before you can say *Xanda, where the hell have you been?* I promise."

"And you'll tell me what's really going on?"

"I swear."

Luciena nodded grudgingly. "You have to say something to him, Xanda. We can't have him taking Emilie riding every time he's feeling—"

"Go, Luci! I said I'd deal with it."

With a great deal of reluctance, Luciena did as her husband asked. She turned her back on the stables, the flies, and the rank smell of the manure and made her way back to the palace, trying to imagine what plans Xanda might have up his sleeve. It disturbed her to think he was plotting against Mahkas without telling her about it, almost as much as the idea that others might be plotting with him.

Luciena had no problem overthrowing Mahkas Damaran. But if she was going to be tainted by a plot and possibly condemned by it if it failed—which, if her husband was a key player, was unavoidable—if she was going to risk her children, she wanted to know the details.

chapter 56

You're still alive, I see."

Kalan Hawksword stared down at the figure lying on the bed, without compassion. Galon Miar looked around the room, blinking owlishly, as if his eyes were having trouble focusing.

"Lady *Kalan* . . . um . . . where am I?"

"In my mother's bed," Kalan informed him coldly. "This is her room, in case you're wondering, but then, you probably wouldn't recognise it, I suppose. I don't believe you've seen it in daylight."

He grimaced at her tone. "You're mad at me about something, aren't you?"

"You really are very good at reading people. Do they teach you that in assassin school?"

"Apparently they don't teach manners in sorcerer school," he retorted. "What happened to me? And why can't I feel anything below my waist?"

Kalan smiled nastily. "After the guards ran you through and then knocked you unconscious when they found you trying to rape my mother, I gave you something for the pain. They tell me it's quite agonising when you castrate someone."

Galon was silent while her words sank in and then, with a panicked cry, he threw the covers back to check the damage for himself. There was a bandage around his chest, but he was wearing nothing else.

Hastily he covered himself again, and glared at her. Kalan burst out laughing.

"That was cruel, Kalan," her mother scolded, entering the room with a slave behind her carrying a tray.

"But you should have seen the look on his face, Mother. It was priceless."

The assassin looked up at the princess, not in the least bit amused. "Your daughter is *sick*, your highness."

"And yet we feed her anyway," Marla replied. "How are you feeling?"

"Like my head's been cleaved in two and some bastard stabbed me in the back. How bad is it?"

"Better than you deserve," Kalan informed him. "But you were lucky. You weren't actually run through. The guard who stabbed you hit a rib and the blade slid off your left side, so it's really only a flesh wound, albeit a rather long and impressive one."

Galon turned to her mother with a frown. "You need to do something about your guards."

"I'm not going to chastise them for trying to protect me, Galon."

"I wasn't going to suggest you do, your highness. But if they seriously thought I was raping you, they should have killed me, not left me with a flesh wound. And for that matter, running a sword into me when I was on top of you was insanely dangerous. If my rib hadn't deflected it, the blade might have gone right through me and into you, as well."

"You? On top of my mother?" Kalan remarked. "There's an image I could have done without." Having the guards burst into a room in response to the sounds of a struggle, only to find her mother in the grip of unbridled passion with a lover—one who had actually sneaked in through her bedroom window—was a little more than Kalan was ready to deal with at the moment.

It was almost as bad, she mused, *as when I thought Wrayan and Mother were more than just good friends.*

Frowning, Kalan watched her mother chatting affably with Galon Miar as the slave placed the breakfast tray on the bed. She knew Marla was probably already looking for another husband, but after sixteen years of Ruxton Tirstone, who was pleasant and unobtrusive, Kalan wasn't sure she was prepared to welcome a man like Galon Miar into the family. In her mind, ideally, Marla's next husband should be someone very old and preferably bedridden;

someone willing to let her mother control his political power and his wealth and not actually make any demands on Marla or her family. Galon Miar was far too full of life (and obviously lust) for Kalan's comfort.

"Will you be needing me any further this morning, Mother?" she asked. Kalan had her own part to play in their complex plan to bring Alija down and she was anxious to get on with it.

"No, thank you, Kalan," her mother replied. "Once the draught has worn off, I'm sure Galon will be able to find his way home without any further assistance."

"See that you *do* go home," Kalan advised the assassin, then turned on her heel and stalked out of the room, leaving her mother alone with him. She'd barely closed the door, however, before her mother followed her into the hall.

"Kalan!"

She impatiently turned and looked at her mother. "What?"

Marla closed the bedroom door before she answered. "That last remark was uncalled for."

"I'm sorry. Did I hurt your precious lover's feelings?"

"Galon Miar is not my lover."

"Then why is he still breathing, Mother?"

Marla sighed. "The situation is complicated, Kalan."

"*Bizarre* is the word *I* was leaning towards."

"Galon Miar is in a position to do me a very useful service."

"So is any *court'esa* worth the price of his collar."

"I wasn't referring to that kind of service," her mother explained patiently, walking toward her. "There are other things afoot, things you don't know about. Even more delicate than this business with Alija . . ."

Kalan took a step back. She wasn't in the mood to hug and make up. "You don't have to justify yourself to me, Mother. I don't really care who you sleep with. I just think you should be a little more cautious, that's all. You don't know anything about that man."

"Wrayan says he can be trusted."

"Wrayan said Galon Miar can probably be trusted not to

betray us to the Patriots. That's not the same thing as trusting the man in your bed."

Marla sighed. "I didn't invite him in, you know."

"You seem to have a rather unconventional method of throwing him out."

"It's not what you think. He does it to rattle me, that's all."

Kalan was unconvinced. "Don't try and fool yourself, Mother. I was watching him the other night when he was here. He never takes his eyes off you. I swear he counts your heartbeats. Are you in love with him?"

"The only man I have ever truly loved was your father, Kalan."

"Didn't you love Damin's father, too?"

She shook her head. "I respected him. Liked him, even. But I never loved him. Love isn't required to produce an heir to the throne, you know, just the willingness of both parties to do what's required of them."

Kalan was so much luckier than her mother, she often thought. "I should thank you more often, you know, for letting me find a way to escape your fate."

"Speaking of which," her mother remarked, eyeing the itchy black robes Kalan was wearing. "Given your formal attire, I gather you're on your way to the Sorcerers' Palace?"

Kalan nodded. "I'm going to visit Bruno. He's a traditionalist. Or he doesn't recognise me if I'm not wearing my robes. I've never been really able to work out which it was, actually. Whatever the reason, we need Bruno Sanval on our side. He'll have to be ready to step up and take over when Alija's gone. And it will be up to him to appoint a new Lower Arrion, as well, and that's a decision we need to have some control over. There are more peripheral consequences to this plot than you realise, Mother."

"You sound as if you enjoy the politics of it all."

"What can I say?" She shrugged. "I am my mother's daughter."

Marla had no answer for that. "Be careful."

Kalan stared at her, a little offended by the warning.

"There's an assassin in your bed, Mother, and you're telling *me* to be careful?"

"The irony is not lost on me, darling."

"Well, I'll promise to be careful, if you promise me you'll do the same."

Her mother seemed satisfied with that. "A fair exchange."

"Then be careful, Mother."

"I'm always careful, Kalan, that's why we're all still here."

The Chief Librarian of the Sorcerers' Collective library was a man named Dikorian Frye. At first glance, he seemed an odd choice for librarian. He was a big, muscular man who seemed more at home with physical labour than the intellectual pursuits of a scholar. But he was a cheerful soul and Kalan had always got along with him. He was also the only person in the Sorcerers' Collective likely to know the whereabouts of the Lower Arrion, Bruno Sanval.

"Kalan Hawksword!" the big librarian exclaimed when he saw her enter through the large carved doors of the labyrinthine library. "I thought you were lost in the north of Pentamor somewhere, hiding from the plague!"

"I was in Krakandar, actually. I got back a few weeks ago," she told him, standing on her toes to kiss his cheek. "I'm glad to see you survived the troubles, Dikorian."

"Only because no self-respecting rat would be seen down here in the bowels of the Sorcerers' Collective," he chuckled. "What are you doing here, anyway? Didn't I hear you swear at your graduation that you weren't planning to open another book until you turned thirty? Or was it young Rorin who said that? Might have been him. He never was one for studying, much."

"It was probably Rory," she agreed with a laugh. "And it's an oath I can vouch that he's keeping religiously."

"Then what can I do for you, my dear?"

"I was looking for the Lower Arrion. Is he down here?"

"When *isn't* he down here?" Dikorian asked. "You'll find

him in the Harshini archives. Down one level, third door on the left."

"Thanks."

"Come see me before you go!" he called after her.

"I will," she promised over her shoulder as she headed down the stairs that would take her into the lower levels of the vast Greenharbour library.

When Kalan first came to the Sorcerers' Collective as an eleven-year-old, she'd expected the lower levels of the library to be a dank, dark place, lit by flickering torches, cluttered with several thousand years of accumulated dust, rotting books and fragile scrolls. To her surprise, it was quite the opposite. There was no dust to speak of, and certainly no damp. The information stored here was far too precious to allow it to be consumed by mould. To reduce the risk of fire, the passageways were well lit with glass-shielded oil lamps designed to discourage people bringing candles or torches down there; the corridors were wide and the small rooms that led off them clearly marked with their particular area of interest.

It was clean and well ventilated and never allowed to degenerate. The Harshini would come back someday, the Sorcerers' Collective believed. When they returned, they would find their library just as they'd left it.

The room where the Lower Arrion was ensconced had a small brass plaque attached to the wall by the door, which announced *Harshini: Xaphista to Sisters of the Blade*. Kalan wasn't surprised to find him here. Bruno's obsession was to discover the location of Sanctuary (or even confirm that it really existed) and if he had to read every single word in the archives to find it, then he was quite prepared to do it.

She knocked on the door and then opened it. The old man was hunched over an ancient scroll, examining the faded text with a small magnifying glass.

"Bruno?"

"Hmmm?" he replied without looking up.

"It's me. Kalan Hawksword."

He spared her a brief glance and went back to examining his scroll. "Thought you died in the plague."

"It would seem not."

"Pass me that."

"What?" she asked, looking around.

"That!" he told her impatiently, waving in the general direction of the end of the long table near where she stood. Kalan looked around and guessed he meant the small open notebook beside the inkwell. She picked it up and walked the length of the long bench to hand it to him.

He accepted it without looking up and began flicking through the pages until he found what he was looking for. Brushing his long white hair out of his face, he laid the notebook down next to the scroll and began moving the magnifying glass from one to the other, comparing the text of the scroll and the notebook, making strange little noises that sounded as if he'd discovered something momentous.

"Have you found it?" She wasn't asking out of idle curiosity. Her whole plan hinged on Bruno *not* having reached his life's goal to find the hidden Harshini settlement.

He scratched his chin thoughtfully. "The writings of Balankanan the Minstrel clearly refer to his intention to stay for some time in a place north of a small human village in the Sanctuary Mountains named Hayden, while he mastered the remaining Songs of Gimlorie, and he uses the word *sanctuary* on a number of occasions, but not in the titular context. Paranasien, some two hundred years later, however, says the Harshini who came to his aid took him back to . . ." he referred to his notes, ". . . *a white fortress of inestimable beauty hidden high in the mountains* . . . which was much farther north, according to his diaries."

"Who's Paranasien?"

"A Medalonian villager trapped in the mountains after a logging accident. The Harshini found him in the forest and took him back to Sanctuary to heal him, so he claims. It's supposed to have happened about three hundred years before the Sisters of the Blade came along."

"Why *supposed* to have happened? Do you doubt his story?"

"There are other accounts dated around the same time which claim Paranasien was on the run from an irate father expecting him to wed the daughter he'd dishonoured just before he vanished into the mountains. By the time Paranasien returned to civilisation two years later without so much as a mark on him, the daughter was wed to another man . . ."

"And Paranasien was off the hook," Kalan finished with a smile.

"Hence the doubt about the veracity of his account," he agreed. "Thank you for the notebook, you can go now."

"Actually, I came to see you."

"Which you have done," the old man pointed out, a little impatiently. "Now be a good girl and run along, Kalan. I'm busy."

"I know where Sanctuary is."

"Yes, yes, I'm sure you do." He shrugged dismissively.

"I know someone who's been there."

Bruno looked up at her with a shake of his head. "You should stay out of taverns, Kalan. And not listen to the drunks who frequent them."

"He gave me this." She reached into her pocket and retrieved the tiny crystal cube suspended on a chain that Wrayan had given her to prove her story, holding it out for Bruno to see.

He glanced at the necklace without really seeing what it was, then he looked at it a second time. This time he cried out in shock and snatched it from her hand.

Anxiously, he studied it under the magnifying glass, making more of those funny little noises, before he looked up at her, clearly shocked. "By the gods, girl! Do you know what this is?"

"It's a *couremor*, isn't it?"

"A lover's link," Bruno breathed in awe as he held it up to the light to examine the tiny dragon magically etched inside the crystal. "The Harshini would infuse these with magic and leave them with their human lovers so they could call them. There hasn't been one of these found in more than a hundred years. How did you *get* this?"

"My friend gave it to me." And then she added with a smug little smile, "The one who knows where Sanctuary is."

This time the Lower Arrion didn't dismiss her claim quite so quickly. "Who is this friend? I must meet him."

"I can probably arrange that."

"You *must* arrange it, girl!" he ordered excitedly. "At once, do you hear! At once! This is the most remarkable discovery since . . . since . . . the last . . . I don't know . . . the last . . . remarkable discovery!"

Kalan smiled at his blubbering excitement. "I appreciate your enthusiasm, Bruno, but my friend is very shy. Not to mention he's been sworn to secrecy by the Harshini."

"If he's been sworn to secrecy, why did he tell you about it?"

"He told me that he'd been there. Not where it is. He swore not to reveal the location of Sanctuary unless there was a dire need."

"But . . . but . . ." Bruno stammered impatiently. "I've been searching for this all my life. Your friend's need might not be dire, young lady, but mine certainly is!"

"There *might* be a way I could convince him to talk with you," she said, thoughtfully. "But you'd probably have to do something first. Something to prove you can be trusted with such knowledge."

"I'm the Lower Arrion of the Sorcerers' Collective!" he barked at her, quite offended by the implication that he was anything less than totally trustworthy. "What makes you think I can't be trusted?"

"It's not you, Bruno. It's the High Arrion who has my friend worried. She's already tried to kill him once. He's afraid if he comes forward now, you'll reveal his secret and because she's in league with Hythria's enemies, by sharing anything with you, he'd be bringing about the ruin of the last of the Harshini."

"What do you mean, she's in league with Hythria's enemies?" he demanded. "What nonsense are you babbling, girl?"

"She's doing a deal with the Fardohnyans, Bruno, even as we speak. Alija is arranging for her son to be appointed governor by Hablet when he overruns us. I thought you knew all this?"

"I've never even heard of such a plot. How do *you* know of it?"

"I'm the High Prince's niece. How do you *think* I know?"

Bruno looked on the verge of tears. "This cannot be."

Kalan leaned forward and took the *couremor* from him, replacing it in her pocket. He reached for the necklace anxiously, as she took it from him, but Kalan was too quick for him. "I'll tell my friend you can't meet with him. I'm sorry."

"No! Wait! You just can't take it away like that! I have to study it . . . hold it . . ."

"I have to give it back, Bruno."

"But can't I just . . ."

She looked down on him sadly. "I'm sorry. My friend won't come near the Sorcerers' Collective unless he thinks it's safe, and until someone is willing to expose Alija . . . well, look at it this way, Bruno. At least now you know Sanctuary is real."

Kalan turned and walked toward the door. She had barely reached the end of the table before he called her back.

"What do you want of me?" His tone was resigned, almost defeated. Bruno Sanval had spent the last twelve years as Lower Arrion trying to stay clear of the politics of the Sorcerers' Collective. It obviously pained him to realise that in order to achieve his lifelong ambition, he was going to have to step up and be counted.

"I want you to do nothing more than come with me, Bruno," she said, turning back to face him. "I'll tell you the time and place when I know the details myself. I want you to listen, that's all. You can make your own mind up about Alija, after that."

"Is that all?"

"Do this for me and I'll arrange a meeting with my friend. He'll tell you anything you want to know about Sanctuary and the Harshini."

He agreed unhappily. "Very well."

"You mustn't tell anybody about this, Bruno. One word and my friend and his *couremor* are gone forever."

"I understand," he agreed.

She smiled. "I knew you would. I'll be in touch." Kalan turned back to the door, and then hesitated on the threshold. "Oh, there was one other thing you could do for me."

"Name it."

"When you've discovered for yourself what Alija is up to and publicly denounced her as a traitor, we're going to have to remove her. That makes you the High Arrion until a permanent one can be appointed."

"Who did you have in mind?"

"Why you, of course, Bruno," she told him brightly. "What makes you think I'd try to influence who got *that* job?"

"Then what is the favour you want of me, child?"

"I want *your* job," she told him. "When Alija Eaglespike is removed and you are High Arrion, I want you to appoint me Lower Arrion."

"Out of the question! You are far too young."

"Alija was elected High Arrion when she was only twenty-six. And you're not getting any younger, Bruno, my old friend. Deny me if you want, but I'm the only person in the world who can hand you the answer to your quest. Surely you're not going to pass up a chance like that because I'm only twenty-three?"

He stared at her for a long moment, his expression pained. "Perhaps I *should* appoint you," he told her with a heavy sigh. "You're obviously a damn sight better at this sort of underhanded double-dealing than I am."

She preened at the compliment. "Why thank you, Bruno. You say the nicest things when you're cornered."

The old man treated her to a rare smile. "The Sorcerers' Collective hasn't been the same since they let you in, Kalan Hawksword."

"Then you should be grateful I'm on your side, old man."

"You're on your own side, Kalan," the Lower Arrion replied. "And whose side that is, is anybody's guess."

chapter 57

News that the Widowmaker Pass had been destroyed arrived at the Winter Palace more than a week after it happened. The news was delivered by the young bandit-turned-spy Ollie Kantel, and left the King of Fardohnya more than a little put out to hear his plans had been foiled by something as unexpected as a rockfall.

He was suspicious, of course, about what might have caused the disaster, but he was sceptical about the reports of an explosion. Nobody Hablet didn't own body and soul knew how to make the explosive powders his engineers had mastered nearly two decades ago when they first opened up the Widowmaker. Hablet had slit throats and cut out tongues to make certain things remained that way.

But whatever the cause of the avalanche, King Hablet of Fardohnya had a much more pressing problem. He had fifty thousand troops stranded on the wrong side of the Widowmaker and an army of thirty thousand trapped in Hythria with no way to support it. There would be no point in Axelle Regis carving his way in glorious battle to Greenharbour now, Hablet knew, because there would be nobody following behind to hold any territorial gains.

And to further add to his woes, Adrina was with him

when the fool blurted out this depressing snippet of intelligence. Hablet didn't like to have anybody see his weakness, particularly not someone who might one day use those weaknesses against him. His daughter remained remarkably demure, however, as young Ollie delivered the news, so in the end Hablet had decided to let her stay. Adrina had seen his weakness. Let her now observe her father demonstrate his strength.

"How could you let this happen, Lecter?" he demanded peevishly of his chamberlain.

"*Me*, sire? How is this calamity my fault?"

"I pay you to keep an eye on this sort of thing."

"I'm a slave, your majesty. You don't pay me at all, hence my reliance on whatever small recompense I can eke out of your subjects."

"*Small* recompense?" the king sneered. "You're probably richer than I am, you've extorted so much money out of *my* subjects."

The eunuch shrugged. "I can't help it if I'm good at what I do."

"Well you're not very good at this. I've got fifty thousand men sitting out there on the plains, picking their noses, while my only practicable route into Hythria has been destroyed by what? The act of a capricious god?"

"It would seem so, your majesty."

"Then find out *which* god did this to me, damn it! And tell him to fix it!"

"If Lecter Turon could talk to the gods, Daddy," Adrina remarked from her seat by the window, obviously relishing the slave's discomfort, "I'm sure you'd have a legitimate son by now. Isn't that right, Lecter?"

The slave glared at her but offered no reply.

"Exactly how bad is it?" Hablet demanded of the spy. "Can we clear the obstruction?"

"Eventually, I suppose, your majesty," the young man concluded. "But it's going to take a lot of manpower. There's a good half-mile of the pass buried under all the rocks and debris."

"We'll just have to divert the troops through Highcastle then," the king announced. "How long will it take to move them south, Lecter?"

"Two, maybe three months."

"I don't have three months, fool! In three months summer will be over and the weather will turn against us. In three months the troops stranded in Hythria will have starved to death, assuming the Hythrun don't wipe them out first."

"Why don't you just cut your losses and give up the idea of invading Hythria at all, Daddy?"

He glared at his daughter. "*What?*"

"Give it up," she replied with a shrug. "As you say, we don't have three months; we don't even have three weeks. If you can't find a way to send reinforcements through the Widowmaker to General Regis in the next few days, he might as well throw himself on the mercy of the Hythrun."

"I can't just give it up!"

"Why not?" Adrina asked, uncurling her legs and putting aside the book she'd been reading. "You certainly can't clear the pass in time to do any good here, and even if you could, how long is it going to take to clear half a mile of rubble? Probably longer than shipping the troops south to Highcastle, is my guess. And even if you could manage to get your army to the coast before the winter snows set in, the reason you decided to invade through the Widowmaker in the first place was because Highcastle is so narrow in places, the Hythrun would be able to sit comfortably on the high ground and pick us off at their leisure while we're traversing the pass. Your alternative is to keep that army out there waiting around until next spring, I suppose, while your engineers clear the Widowmaker, which won't help General Regis much, but if you forget about him, that's thirty thousand men you don't have to pay, which should go some way to offsetting the cost of paying the other fifty thousand who'll be sitting around here for the better part of a year, picking their noses."

Hablet stared at his daughter worriedly. *This*, he lamented, *is what happens when you let a woman learn to read.*

He turned to Lecter Turon. The bald eunuch appeared almost as disturbed as Hablet by his daughter's alarmingly accurate analysis of the situation. "Much as it pains me to agree with Her Serene Highness, sire, she has summed up the situation fairly succinctly."

But the king wasn't willing to give up his dearly held dream of adding the wealth of Hythria to his treasury quite so readily. Not to mention the opportunity to wipe out the Wolfblades, once and for all. Impatiently, he turned to the young spy. "What about you?"

The lad jumped, startled by his sudden inclusion in the conversation. "Sire?"

"You come and go into Hythria as you please, don't you?"

"Well . . . yes . . ."

"Then my army will use your route through the mountains!" he declared. "We don't need the damned Widowmaker. We'll find another way through."

Ollie looked down at his boots uncertainly. "Um . . . it's . . . well . . ."

"Don't stammer at me, boy! What?"

"Well, sire, you won't . . . you can't . . . there are no roads, you see," he told the king. "Your soldiers wouldn't be able to take their supply wagons by our route."

Hablet shrugged, unconcerned. "Each man can carry his own supplies."

"There's a lot of climbing . . . they'll need ropes."

"And you won't be able to send your artillery across the mountains, either," Adrina surmised, stating aloud what the bandit was obviously too terrified to tell his king. She smiled encouragingly at the nervous lad. "How long does it take you and your friends to get across the mountains?"

"Two of us who know the route, travelling light, assuming no accidents and that the weather holds?" He shrugged. "From Westbrook to Winternest . . . four, maybe five days, I suppose."

Adrina looked up at her father. "Well, given our men are neither mountain climbers nor know anything about this secret route the bandits favour, you can multiply *that* time by a factor of at least ten," she estimated. "And it will get you what, Daddy? A line of men in single file, trickling into Hythria, one at a time? That's going to scare the Hythrun witless, I'm sure."

"Your highness, you speak as if you have no wish to see your father's campaign succeed," Lecter sneered, no doubt hoping to undermine her remarkably astute observations by implying she was less than supportive of the king's endeavours.

Adrina smiled venomously at the eunuch. "I think it's a waste of money, Lecter. If Daddy wants to throw millions of rivets away on something frivolous, I'd rather he spent it on me."

Before he could stop himself, Hablet laughed aloud. "You want me to cancel the war so you can go shopping, Adrina?"

"But, your majesty!" the eunuch complained. "She's accusing your righteous campaign to reclaim Hythria and rid the world of the Wolfblades of being frivolous!"

"I'm accusing him of nothing of the kind," the princess countered, rising to her feet. "I think the Wolfblades are a perverted, deviant family of monsters, and that the nicest thing we could do for the Hythrun people would be to free them from their tyranny. But I also believe the window of opportunity is lost. The plague only weakened Hythria temporarily and if we could have sent enough men through the pass in time, we might have walked in and taken the country with barely a fight. But that's not going to happen now, is it, Lecter? At best, even if Lord Regis manages to establish a foothold and can keep it until we can get a few reinforcements through to him, every day we delay is a day longer the Hythrun have to gather their strength." She turned to her father, her emerald eyes blazing with conviction. "You know I'm right, Daddy. If you want to own Hythria and destroy the

Wolfblades, you're going to have to find another way across their borders, because this isn't it."

He frowned, disturbed to realise she might be right. "If I follow *your* line of reasoning, Adrina, I must abandon Regis and his men in Hythria."

"Unfortunately," she agreed with a total lack of sentimentality.

"I thought you fancied him."

"One can't be swayed by personal likes or dislikes when making hard decisions," she reminded the king. "Isn't that what you're always telling me?"

"Sire!" Lecter cried, when he realised Hablet was seriously considering his daughter's suggestion. "I must object!"

"Don't *object*, Lecter," Adrina advised. "Tell us *your* plans. If you don't like the idea of calling off the war, please enlighten my father as to how you think he can successfully prosecute it . . . with us having no way to get our troops or artillery onto the battlefield, and all . . ."

The eunuch glared at the princess, before turning to the king. "Your majesty, we need to think this through more carefully . . . consider all our options . . ."

"What options?"

"I'm sure, once we've had time to look at the situation objectively . . ."

"Objectively," the king concluded, "we're in serious trouble."

"But sire, if nothing else, think of the humiliation! You gathered an army of eighty thousand men to invade your sworn enemy and at the first hurdle you're going to run away?"

"A half a mile of fallen rock is quite a hurdle, Lecter," he retorted. "And it's not running away if you achieve something useful, even if it's not everything you hoped for."

"And what exactly have we achieved thus far, your majesty, other than to make fools of ourselves if we back down the moment the going gets tough?"

"I want to be rid of the Wolfblades, Lecter, and right now, I've every Wolfblade male alive under the command of the biggest fool of them all, facing the considerable army I *do* have in Hythria. Regis is a smart lad and he has almost twice the number Lernen has been able to muster. I might not get the whole country, but the chances are still very good I'll get the Wolfblades before Regis is forced to surrender."

"And how are you going to break it to Lord Regis that you're cutting him adrift in a foreign country with no support, no supplies and no hope of reinforcements?"

Hablet turned to the young bandit who had listened to the entire exchange with a startled look on his face. "You! What's your name again?"

"Ollie Kantel, your majesty."

"Well, Ollie Kantel, I have another mission for you."

"Of course, sire."

"I want you to use your secret route to slip back into Hythria. I want you to find my army and deliver a message to General Regis for me."

"What shall I tell him, sire?"

"Tell him . . ." the king announced, turning to stare at his daughter. She might have demonstrated a disturbingly acute military mind, but he didn't intend to let her get away with it. "Tell him my daughter, Her Serene Highness, the Princess Adrina of Fardohnya, doesn't think he's worth saving. Tell him that at *her* suggestion, we're going to abandon him and his men to their fates. Tell him, at my daughter's behest, we are leaving him to do what he can against the Hythrun for the greater glory of his king and his family name, but there will be no further support from Fardohnya."

Adrina stared at him in shock. "You're blaming this disaster on *me*?"

"There is always a scapegoat in times of trouble, your highness," Lecter informed her gleefully.

Adrina turned on the slave angrily. "And how exactly does it become *my* fault, slave?"

"You're in the room," the eunuch smirked. "That's usually enough."

"*Daddy!*"

Hablet shrugged helplessly. "I only take the credit for the things that work, petal. Defeat is never, *ever* my fault. I'm the king."

PART FOUR

FOR PRIDE AND GLORY . . . AND THE TRUTH

cbapτεr 58

L uciena Taranger stared at her husband in shock. They were alone in their bedroom in the guest wing of Krakandar Palace, but that didn't seem to ease her husband's mind as he furtively outlined the plans he'd been making behind her back with Starros and the Thieves' Guild.

"You've arranged to do *what*?"

"Not so loudly!" Xanda exclaimed, looking around the room.

"*When*?" she demanded, albeit in a significantly lower voice.

"Soon," he informed her. "Maybe a couple of weeks. We figured if we do it the evening before a Restday, it won't be quite as obvious."

"And you're planning to evacuate the *whole* city?" she gasped. "In one night?"

He shook his head. "It'll take all night, all day and all the next night, I suspect, and even then I'll be surprised if we get everyone away. But even if we don't manage to get everybody through the sewers, with so many people out of the city, it'll mean those who are left will have much less chance of starving to death before help arrives."

"By help, I assume you mean Damin coming home?"

"That would be useful."

"But we have no way of knowing how the war's going," she reminded him. "For all you know, he's lying dead on a battlefield somewhere."

Xanda put his hands on her shoulders and looked at her. "I know you're normally the pessimistic one, Luci, but could you try *not* to think the worst, every once in a while. For me?"

"I'm sorry," she said, putting her head on his shoulder. "I really don't mean to be the harbinger of doom all the time. It's just . . . it's a very ambitious plan, Xanda. If Mahkas got wind of it . . ."

"We'd all be doomed," he finished for her, holding her close. "I do understand that, my love. But we *have* to do something."

She leaned back in his arms and looked at him. "So you recruited the *Thieves'* Guild to your cause? Not quite what I had in mind, dear."

"Actually, it was the other way around. They recruited me. And it's not just the Thieves' Guild. There's a lot of empty bellies out there. We've got most of the other guilds working with us now. They're all willing to help get their people to safety."

"And what prompted this remarkable act of civic generosity by the guilds? Are you sure this isn't an elaborate ruse to empty the city so the Thieves' Guild has a free hand emptying all those soon-to-be-abandoned houses of their valuables?"

He shrugged. "It has something to do with Starros being healed by the God of Thieves after Mahkas tortured him. Apparently he's now required to honour his god in a fairly substantial way to return the favour."

She raised a suspicious brow at him. "Emptying all those soon-to-be-abandoned houses of their valuables would achieve that goal rather impressively, don't you think?"

"It's not like that, Luci. I've spoken to Starros a number of times. He's not planning anything underhanded."

"He's joined the Thieves' Guild, Xanda. By definition, *any* plan they come up with is going to be underhanded. But even if I believe Starros is driven by the noblest of motives, evacuating Krakandar honours Dacendaran how, exactly?"

He grinned at her. "By stealing the population from Mahkas."

Luciena thought about it and then shrugged, thinking there was actually a twisted sort of logic in there somewhere. "I see. And while you and Starros are stealing the population of Krakandar for the greater glory of the God of Thieves, what will I be doing?"

"You'll be among the first out through the sewers," he informed her in that tone he used when he wasn't willing to negotiate. "You, our children, the Lionsclaw boys, Aleesha, and whatever help you need getting them out of the city. We've already had Thieves' Guild messengers going through the tunnels carrying dispatches and checking the route. Not that he can do much if he's in the middle of a war, but I've sent word to Damin about what's happening, and to my brother in Walsark. Travin's with us. He'll be waiting for you on the other side. Once the children are safe, you'll need his help to get the rest of the people away."

"And you?"

"I'm staying here to help organise the evacuation."

"What happens if the Raiders try to stop you?"

"More than half the troops in the city are with us, Luciena. The rest of them . . . well . . . we've made arrangements . . ."

She frowned. "What does *that* mean? You're not going to kill them, are you?"

"Not if we can avoid it. But they will need to be confined. We can't risk Mahkas discovering what's going on and having him call up the remaining loyal troops to put a stop to it."

"Loyal?" Luciena wondered grimly. "Or afraid of him?"

Her husband shrugged. "If the end result is the same, what difference does it make?"

"This is absurdly dangerous, Xanda."

"So is every day we spend in this palace," he pointed out. "As you so frequently remind me."

Luciena brushed the hair from his forehead. "So you decided to do something insanely heroic to stop me nagging you? Is that what you're telling me?"

Xanda kissed her lightly. "Greater deeds have been done for lesser reason, you know."

"I can't think of any off the top of my head," she replied. "And I'm not leaving you here to face that maniac alone when he realises what's happened, either. You must come with us, Xanda. Mahkas will kill you."

"Why would Uncle Mahkas kill Papa?"

Both Luciena and Xanda jumped with fright.

"Emilie!" Luciena scolded, her heart pounding, as she wondered how much her daughter had overheard. "How did you get in here?"

"Through the slaveways," she informed them, her face creased with concern. "Is Uncle Mahkas mad at Papa about something?"

"No, darling," she assured the child. "Of course not. What do you want?"

"But you just said—"

"What do you *want*, Emilie?" Luciena cut in. "Your father and I are busy."

"Um . . ." Emilie stammered, her confidence waning in the face of her mother's growing impatience. "I've just been to visit Uncle Mahkas . . ."

"I thought we told you to leave Uncle Mahkas alone?" Xanda reminded her. He let Luciena go and squatted down in front of their daughter, his expression serious. Luciena marvelled at Xanda's patience with their children. She wasn't nearly so tolerant when they defied her. "Uncle Mahkas isn't well, Em," he explained. "You know that. You really should leave him alone so he can get better."

"But he says he likes having me around. He says I remind him of Leila."

Before she could utter a sound, Xanda turned to glare at Luciena, warning her to silence. He then turned back to his daughter. "I'm sure you do remind him of Leila, sweetheart, but that's part of the problem. Leila's death still hurts Uncle Mahkas a great deal. Sometimes it's painful to remind somebody of people they're still grieving for."

"But I feel so sorry for him, Papa. His eyes are so sad. And he's really sick."

"Out of the mouths of babes," Luciena muttered. She understood why Xanda was dealing with Emilie this way. At the same time, she wished she could just yell and scream and confine the child to her room in order to keep her safe from her dangerously insane uncle.

"I know, Em," Xanda agreed, "But in time . . ."

"No," Emilie objected. "I mean he's *really* sick. That's what I came to tell you. He's in his office and he's all hot and sweaty and mumbling stuff I don't understand and his arm's all swollen and burning . . ."

Xanda glanced up at Luciena. "Don't look at me. I have no idea what she's talking about."

"I tried telling Aunt Bylinda, Mama," Emilie added, "but she just said something about the gods and about making people keep their oaths. I didn't really understand what she was saying, either. But Uncle Mahkas is really sick, Papa. I think he needs a physician."

Xanda nodded and stood up. "And we'll see he gets one, Em. Now how about you get back to the nursery, eh? Aleesha will be panicking about you being lost again. Don't you worry about anything. Your mother and I will see to Uncle Mahkas."

"He's not going to die, is he?"

"Probably not," Luciena assured her daughter. Then she added sourly under her breath, "More's the pity."

Emilie looked up at her curiously. "What do you mean, Mama?"

"Your mother doesn't mean anything," Xanda assured her, with a look of stern disapproval in Luciena's direction. "Now back to the nursery with you, my girl, so we can see to Uncle Mahkas."

Without any further objections, Emilie did as her father ordered, leaving Luciena and Xanda alone again. He turned to Luciena with a frown. "You shouldn't be so hard on her."

"You shouldn't be so lenient. Do you think Mahkas is really ill?"

He shrugged. "It wouldn't surprise me. He's been complaining about his arm being sore for years and he worries at it like a dog with a rag doll when he's upset. Maybe it's infected. I suppose we'd better check on him."

Luciena sighed wistfully. "Sure you don't want to wait a little while? You know . . . until it's too late to save him?"

"You don't mean that."

"Yes, I do," she assured him with conviction.

He pulled her close, offering her what comfort he could in his arms. "It'll all be over soon, Luciena, I promise."

"I've heard *that* before."

"When?"

She looked up at him. "Our wedding night?"

He frowned at her. "You really think you're hilarious, don't you?"

"I'm teetering on the very edge of hysteria here, Xanda. Allow me a little leeway."

He hugged her even tighter. "You'll be safe soon, Luciena, I promise."

"But what about you?"

He kissed the top of her head. "I spent two years in the High Prince's Palace Guard with Cyrus Eaglespike as my captain. If I can survive that, I can survive anything." He held her for a moment or two longer and then gently pushed her away. "I'd better check on Mahkas."

Luciena slid her arm around his neck again and kissed him soundly, while her other hand ventured further south. "Are you *sure* you wouldn't stay here with me for a while longer?" she teased.

Xanda pushed her away again, smiling at her suggestion. "You are shameless, Luciena. Unfair delaying tactics aren't going to work on me."

"Go then," she ordered, feigning disdain. "See to your precious uncle. I'll just have to find a *court'esa* to keep me entertained while you're gone, if you're too busy to do your husbandly duty."

"You do that," he said. He leaned forward and kissed her cheek again, and promised, "I'll let you know what's happening as soon as I know."

Luciena nodded to reassure him she understood, watching him leave the bedroom with a heavy heart. She wished he had stayed and made love to her almost as much as she wished they didn't have to keep Mahkas alive.

"I'm not shameless, Xanda," she murmured as he closed the door behind him. "I'm afraid."

chapter 59

D amin broke the news about the destruction of the Widowmaker two days after Rorin Mariner returned to Cabradell. By then Renulus was safely tucked away in a dungeon and the various conspirators in their dangerous plan had had time to get their stories straight.

As far as everyone was concerned, Lord Terin Lionsclaw was back from Winternest but had been wounded in the rock fall that closed the Widowmaker and only his remarkable bravery had allowed the intelligence to get through to Cabradell. Everyone believed he was being attended by his wife and would join the other Warlords as soon as he was sufficiently recovered.

At his nephew's prompting, Lernen announced he would reward the Warlord of Sunrise's valour with a prize of inestimable value, and in a private ceremony, with Tejay's physician, Canath Roe, posing as the wounded (and heavily bandaged) Warlord, Lernen Wolfblade made a florid speech and, more importantly, a gift of the High Prince's distinctive jewelled and gilded armour to the man he assumed was Terin Lionsclaw.

Other than the physician, the only other new conspirators now privy to Damin's ruse were his brother, Narvell Hawksword, Tejay's brother, Rogan Bearbow, and oddly enough, Kendra Warhaft. Damin had been loudly opposed to bringing her into the fold, until Narvell pointed out that trying to fool everyone into believing Terin was alive simply wasn't enough. They also needed to convince everyone that Lady Lionsclaw was acting no differently from any other Warlord's wife. Lady Kendra would be invaluable when it came to keeping up the illusion that Lady Tejay was back in her tent attending to her embroidery, when in fact she was out fighting a battle.

Damin had been reluctant in the extreme to trust such a secret to someone he barely knew, but Narvell trusted her and as Rorin pointed out, technically she was still under the Sorcerers' Collective's protection until Lernen gave them an answer—something he'd shown no inclination to do thus far—and would have to accompany Rorin to the front in any case until the matter was settled. It was easier to have her helping them keep the secret than have her discover it.

With the news the Widowmaker was blocked, the mood of the army improved noticeably. When Damin finally gave the order—in Lernen's name—to move from Cabradell to the hills surrounding the chosen battlefield at Lasting Drift, it was with a sense of excitement and anticipation that the Warlords broke camp and turned their armies south. For the first time since the news had filtered through from Fardohnya that Hablet intended to invade, there was some hope they might prevail. They were outnumbered two to one, admittedly, but that news didn't bother the Hythrun. A hard-fought victory was always better than an easy one and a much better way to honour the God of War.

Besides, with the Widowmaker closed, a victory for the Fardohnyans would be a hollow one. Lord Regis and his invading army couldn't take Hythria with thirty thousand men, and even if—by some miracle—they managed to prevail, they couldn't hold on to it.

But neither could they turn around and go home. Realising this, the biggest fear many of the Hythrun warriors held now was that Axelle Regis would recognise the bitter truth and order his army to throw down their weapons, avoiding unnecessary bloodshed. Damin thought it unlikely, however. Although Lord Regis had very few options open to him now, giving up wasn't likely to be high on the list. And Damin didn't really blame him. In his place, Damin thought he'd probably seek a glorious death in battle, too, rather than the ignominy of surrender, being held for ransom and eventually being sent home in disgrace.

"Your highness?"

He glanced up from the map table to find Kendra Warhaft standing at the entrance of the tent. She smiled at him nervously—apparently he scared her a little, according to Narvell—and curtseyed with unconscious court-bred grace.

"Lady Kendra! What can I do for you?"

"Good evening, your highness, my lords. Lady Lionsclaw sends her compliments, your highness, and requests you call on her and her husband in their tent at your earliest convenience."

Damin glanced across the table at Cyrus Eaglespike and Toren Foxtalon who were also studying the layout of the battlefield. Cyrus looked across at Kendra with a frown. "Is Terin Lionsclaw planning to join us at some point in this conflict, or is he going to let his underlings . . ." he asked with a scowl at Rorin Mariner, who was standing beside Conin Falconlance on the opposite side of the table, ". . . do all the work for him?"

"He's still not fully recovered from his injuries yet, my lord," Kendra lied smoothly. "I'm sure once he's well again, he'll be happy to join your council."

"The man's an idiot anyway," Conin complained. "I say we're better off without him. Show me again where you hope to conceal my cavalry, Damin."

"Here and here," Damin told him, pointing to the map. Then he glanced across at Kendra. "Tell Lord Lionsclaw I'll come by as soon as I'm able. And give Lady Lionsclaw my regards."

"Of course, my lord." She curtsied again and left the tent, leaving Cyrus shaking his head.

"A battlefield is no place for a woman," the Warlord of

Dregian grumbled. "We'll be wasting valuable men protecting them come the day of the engagement."

"Lady Kendra is here under the protection of the Sorcerers' Collective and Lady Lionsclaw is attending her husband until he recovers. Neither is in the war camp for frivolous reasons, Cyrus."

Toren Foxtalon, the Warlord of Pentamor, frowned at him. He was a close friend of Cyrus Eaglespike and the two of them together were about as much fun as a couple of dried-up old virgins at a *court'esa*'s picnic, Narvell had remarked to his brother only the day before. Since then, every time Damin had looked at the two of them standing side by side, he'd wanted to burst out laughing, which wasn't helping his battle planning.

"A man who brings *court'esa* to the front with him to keep himself amused is hardly in a position to judge what might be frivolous, your highness."

Damin grinned at Toren's censorious tone. "Sure you're not just annoyed that you forgot to bring your own?"

Cyrus Eaglespike was not amused either. "If we lose this battle, Damin Wolfblade, and your *court'esa* end up raped, beaten and rendered completely worthless by the Fardohnyans, you may not think the idea quite so entertaining."

"I'm curious. What concerns you most? That they might be raped and beaten, or that they'll be damaged goods and I might lose money on them?"

"I'm sure your first consideration is their value," the Dregian Warlord replied. "You Wolfblades aren't renowned for caring about the physical welfare of your slaves. And I hear you take after your uncle in that regard."

Damin wondered, for a wistful moment, if relocating Cyrus Eaglespike's face to the other side of his head with something blunt and heavy would feel anywhere near as satisfying as he hoped it might. Even as a child—when Damin was little more than a toddler, Cyrus in his early youth—and Alija had brought her sons to Marla's house to play, he'd disliked him. That feeling had hardly altered at all in the intervening twenty years. Cyrus was still an arrogant mummy's boy. He'd not made a move since he learned to walk, in Damin's opinion, that he hadn't consulted Alija about first. What made him dangerous was the temptation to think that also made him a fool. Cyrus wasn't a fool and Damin had to keep reminding himself that any man well past the age of majority still following the advice of his mother was nothing to be sneered at if the mother was someone as treacherous as Alija Eaglespike.

"What I do with my *court'esa* is actually none of your business, my lords," he said, turning his attention back to the map. Perhaps only Rorin guessed how close Damin was to giving in to the temptation to rearrange the Warlord of Dregian's face.

"I suspect the details would turn our stomachs, in any case," Toren Foxtalon remarked, determined to get the last word in.

"Your highness, did you say you wanted the Sunrise archers here or here?" Rorin asked, giving Damin a graceful way to ignore the taunt. "I want there to be no mistake when I relay your instructions back to Lord Lionsclaw."

"We want them across here," Damin explained, turning his back on Cyrus and Toren. "You'll have to make certain they understand their mission is to put up a token resistance and then run, but they're to regroup back here, so we have them in reserve if we need them."

Rorin looked around the table at the Warlords. "In view of my lord's incapacity at present, perhaps one of you gentlemen should address his troops?"

Damin looked at Rorin in surprise. This wasn't part of their agreed strategy. The plan, as far as Damin knew, was to keep the other Warlords away from the Sunrise Raiders. It certainly wasn't to invite one of them to speak to the men.

"Can't Terin see to his own troops?" Cyrus asked. "Or do we have to do *that* for him, too?"

"Lord Lionsclaw is still not well, my lord," Rorin explained apologetically. "If one of you doesn't think it would help to address his troops before the battle, I might be able to prevail upon Lady Lionsclaw to do so in her husband's stead."

"Don't be ridiculous!" Toren exclaimed. "Who ever heard of anything so absurd?"

"I'll talk to Terin about it," Damin volunteered, giving Rorin a look that spoke volumes. "If he's well enough to fight, he'll be well enough to address his troops before the battle."

The Warlord of Dregian eyed Damin scornfully. "Why don't *you* do it, your highness? I'm sure being addressed by the High Prince's heir will inspire them to remarkable feats of courage on the day."

Damin forced a smile, thinking a closed fist right between the man's eyes would have been so much easier. "Why, Cyrus. Do you think I have a way with leaderless rabble?"

"I don't doubt *your* ability to relate to the leaderless rabble, cousin," the Warlord replied in a tone that was anything but complimentary.

"Then, if we're done here, I shall retire," Rorin announced, interrupting the brewing argument. "If my lords will permit? I have a lot to tell Lord Lionsclaw."

"I'll come with you," Damin said, deciding it might be prudent to retreat before he gave in to temptation. "I want to see if he feels well enough to join us yet."

"He's only got a day or so left to recuperate," Rogan warned, playing along with their subterfuge with remarkable willingness. Damin supposed he shouldn't be surprised. Rogan knew what was at stake. And he knew what his sister was capable of. Given a choice between handing the command of yet another province to the Sorcerers' Collective (which effectively meant handing command to Cyrus Eaglespike), or letting a woman lead his brother-in-law's army into battle, taking his sister's side might well appear to be the lesser of two evils. "The Fardohnyan scouts have spotted us by now, for certain. As we speak, Regis is sitting further up the valley, trying to make up his mind whether or not he should come down to meet us."

"Suppose Regis decides to wait for us to come to him?" Toren asked.

"He hasn't got the supplies to wait," Rogan told him. "We've been here for five days already and it'll soon be clear we're not moving any further. Any day now, he's going to come to the same conclusion and decide he has no choice but to come down to meet us or stay put and starve."

"He may take weeks to come to that conclusion," Cyrus suggested.

Conin Falconlance shook his head. "He doesn't have that much time. I agree with Damin and Rogan. I'd be surprised if the Fardohnyans weren't already running low on supplies. The Widowmaker's been cut off for the better part of three weeks now. If they attack, it'll be sooner rather than later."

"Then you'd better tell your lord to get better, Master Mariner, *sooner* rather than later," Cyrus instructed the young sorcerer impatiently.

"I will pass on your message, my lord," Rorin agreed with a humble bow to his betters.

"You do that," Cyrus muttered in reply. "Because I'm damned if I'm going to war with anybody's *leaderless rabble* in the van of our attack."

"It won't happen, Cyrus," Damin assured him with a sudden grin, stepping back from the table. "The Dregian troops will be in the rear, not the van. You have nothing to worry about."

On that note, Damin escaped the command tent, Rorin hot on his heels, before Cyrus Eaglespike worked out the young prince had just insulted his troops, his province and probably his honour and he had the chance to call him out over it.

CHAPTER 60

The next time Alija saw Galon Miar, he came to visit her in the Sorcerers' Collective, a rare thing for him to do. He preferred, as a rule, to keep away from the Sorcerers' Palace. It didn't look good to have a man so highly placed in the Assassins' Guild be seen coming and going from the Collective. Such a thing caused people to ask questions neither the Collective nor the guild was particularly inclined to answer.

When he was shown into her office, Alija embraced him, surprised when he flinched from her touch.

"What's the matter?" she asked, stepping back from him.

"Had a little accident," he winced.

"On the job?" she asked in surprise.

"Not exactly. It happened in Marla Wolfblade's bedroom. I was trying to seduce her, actually. One of her damned guards ran me through. Or he tried to, at any rate."

Alija stared at him in shock, appalled by his admission. "You *admit* you've been with her?"

"Not much point in denying it, is there?" he said, taking a seat gingerly on the chair in front of her desk. "You can tell if I'm lying."

"You assured me you weren't sleeping with her."

"I'm not."

"Then what were you doing in her bedroom?"

"I also told you it wasn't for lack of trying," he reminded her with a pained expression. "I was trying."

"Why?"

"To keep up appearances, of course," he said, looking at her as if old age was starting to erode her wits. "Marla thinks I want her so badly I'd do anything for her—up to and including betraying you."

"Is that the truth?"

"That I want Marla so badly I'd do anything?" He laughed, and then winced as the movement obviously pulled at his fresh stitches. "Oh, absolutely. That's why I keep coming back here. So you'll find out I'm deceiving you and punish me for it."

"Some men like to be punished. They find it quite . . . stimulating."

Galon seemed amused. "I think you'll find the men who like to be punished also like to be around to enjoy themselves at the end of it. I have a feeling your punishments are a little bit too final for my taste, Lady Eaglespike."

"What are you really doing here, Galon?"

He carefully settled back into the chair. "I have another message for you. From the Fardohnyan agent you're supposed to be conspiring with. You know, the one Marla has hired to trap you, the same poor dupe that you're planning to use to trap her?"

Alija raised a brow at him. "And both of us fools for thinking we can trust you?"

He laughed. "Ah, now you see, that's the biggest difference between you and Marla, my sweet. She just *thinks* she can trust me. You know you can."

Alija wished she was as sure of that as Galon seemed. "What's the message?"

"They want your proposal in writing."

Alija laughed aloud and walked back around the desk. "Out of the question!"

"No document, no meeting," Galon informed her with a shrug. "That's the deal. I'm supposed to tell you the Fardohnyan won't even consider going back to Hablet with your offer unless he can prove it comes from you."

"And the moment I commit to parchment the suggestion that I can arrange to have the High Prince and his heirs killed in battle in return for granting my son the governorship of Hythria, I have committed treason."

"You're committing treason now, just by talking about it."

"That's a whole world away from putting it in writing," she pointed out. "Does Marla think I'm a fool?"

"Far from it," he replied. "If anything, it's because she knows she can't condemn you without proof that she's insisting on this."

"And you think I should write it?"

"Absolutely not!" he advised. "I think you'd be putting your head in a noose to even consider it."

"Then you may tell your fellow conspirators that I am nobody's fool and that I refuse to put anything in writing. If they want to condemn me, they'll have to use a little more imagination."

He rose to his feet, wincing a little with the pain. "I'd best be off then."

She looked up at him in surprise. "But you just got here. Where are you going?"

"To call the whole thing off," he explained, looking a little puzzled. "Isn't that what you just told me to do?"

"I told you I wasn't going to commit anything treasonous to writing, Galon. Nothing else has changed."

"But without that document there is no plan," he warned. "If you don't want to provide it, that's fine, but nothing more is going to come of this without it."

She frowned, annoyed to think her clever scheme to confound Marla might be halted by something so mundane. Alija was days away from proving the High Prince's sister guilty of treason. She didn't intend to let it finish here. "You must speak to this Fardohnyan yourself, then. Arrange a meeting with him. If I'm going to turn this plan to disgrace me back on her, *I* need proof that Marla is in contact with the Fardohnyans, Galon."

Galon shook his head helplessly. "I have no idea who he is. I'm not even sure Marla knows, either. I think the agent is someone Rodja Tirstone has arranged."

"Can't you find out who it is?"

"Not without giving away the fact that I'm working for the wrong side."

She smiled coldly. "Not even with Marla convinced you're so very desperately in love with her?"

"If I go back to Marla and tell her you refused to put your proposal in writing, she'll do exactly what you *should* be doing, Alija—calling the whole damned thing off. She knows she can't implicate you without proof, and I'm fairly certain she's not going to try."

Alija shook her head. She wasn't about to give in on this. She hadn't remained High Arrion of the Sorcerers' Collective for twenty years by being reckless. "If you think I'm going to hand over a document like that to a perfect stranger, without being certain they're not part of this trap set by Marla Wolfblade to discredit me, then you are as insane as she is."

"Don't hand it over, then."

"What do you mean?"

"What if I just tell Marla you've agreed to write it? Then we could still set up the meeting."

"That doesn't help. If this Fardohnyan is working for Marla, he'll be under instructions to do nothing until they're sure I've implicated myself in treason. He'll insist on seeing it."

Galon rubbed his chin thoughtfully. "How about this for a plan, then? Write the letter and show it to the agent without handing it over."

"It might help Marla's cause. I can't see that it would do me a lot of good."

"What if I was there?"

Alija stared at him suspiciously. "*You?*"

"If I come to the meeting with you, I could make sure the document didn't fall into the wrong hands."

She shook her head doubtfully. "How? By killing Marla's agent? For one thing, you're not supposed to undertake uncontracted kills. For another, a dead Fardohnyan doesn't help implicate Marla in anything."

He gave her a wounded look. "Why do you automatically assume I'm planning to kill him?"

"You're an assassin, Galon. It's not an unreasonable assumption."

"We can do this, Alija," he insisted. "Please. Write the letter and I'll tell Marla you'll only attend the meeting if I'm there to protect you. I won't let that letter be used for any other reason than its intended purpose, I swear."

She believed him. Galon didn't lie to her. It was possible he was planning to cheat on her, but his word was something she didn't doubt. And he was right. If she refused to keep playing the game, it wouldn't be a win for anyone; it would be the end of it. Once the plague settled down and the war really began to impact on people, who knew when she'd get another chance like this?

But there was one contingency they hadn't covered and until she knew what was going on there, she wasn't prepared to take another step.

"What about Wrayan Lightfinger? Where does he fit into all this?"

"I'm not sure," Galon said, his brows knitting together as if he was puzzled by the thief. "He wasn't at the house the last time I visited."

"The visit where Marla's guards stabbed you?"

"Hmmm . . . can't really figure out what's going on with him. You said you knew him, didn't you? From years ago."

She nodded. "He was the former High Arrion's apprentice."

"Strange. He doesn't look old enough."

"What are you talking about?"

"Wrayan Lightfinger. The man who tried to read my mind. I'd put him at thirty, thirty-three at the most. Shouldn't he be about your vintage?"

Alija wasn't sure she liked the way he phrased that, but she chose to ignore it. "You never mentioned anything about this before."

"It only just occurred to me . . ." He laughed suddenly. "*No* . . . it couldn't be . . ."

"What are you on about, Galon?"

"I was just thinking . . . suppose this Wrayan Lightfinger isn't the real thing?"

"He's the real thing, Galon. Believe me. I've felt his magic."

"I'm not saying he doesn't exist. I'm just wondering if the man Marla is parading around Greenharbour as her pet magician is the real thing. For all we know, the Wrayan Lightfinger you knew is long dead, or he refused to leave Krakandar . . . there could be any number of reasons he's not here. It's obvious she had some relationship with the real one at some point, so it's possible she knows of your past history with him. Maybe she's just found a suitable dupe and is using him to threaten you."

Was it possible? Could Marla be so devious? The mere fact that she was contemplating the question seemed answer enough for Alija. It could also account for why her attempts to have him found and arrested by the Sorcerers' Collective guards had been singularly unsuccessful to date. "It would account for why I've not felt anybody working Harshini magic since he allegedly arrived in the city."

"Well, that puts a whole different light on things, doesn't it?"

Alija paused for a moment. If what Galon was suggesting was true, then it certainly did put a whole different light on the situation, one that favoured her enormously. "It would account for why he had no luck breaking your mind shield," she mused. "Of course, if Marla really has brought an impostor to town, she would know your mind hadn't been read. That would also seem to imply she might not trust you quite as much as you imagine."

"Hence the reason I'm pursuing her so relentlessly. Love is blind, you know."

"For your sake, I hope it's deaf and dumb, as well. I want to see him."

"See who?"

"This man calling himself Wrayan Lightfinger."

"I doubt he'd agree to a meeting."

"I don't want a meeting. I just want a good look at him. Find out where he's going to be and when, and then let me know. I wish to see this pretender for myself." *I should have done this weeks ago,* she realised, mentally kicking herself for being so stupid.

Galon nodded. "I can probably manage that much. Shall I tell Marla you're prepared to write the letter?"

Alija hesitated. "If I stall, she may begin to suspect I'm on to her. Tell her I'll write the letter. Let her get her hopes up. Have them set up the meeting with this Fardohnyan agent of theirs. The sooner this is done with, the better."

The assassin bowed to her and turned for the door.

"Galon."

His hand on the door, he stopped to look at her. "Yes?"

"Haven't you forgotten something?"

The assassin smiled disarmingly. "I can't kiss you good-bye. I'm on my way over to Marla's. If she smells your perfume on me, she'll be suspicious."

You always have an answer for everything, don't you, Galon?

"Be careful, then."

"Of Marla?" he asked. "She's not the one to worry about, I suspect. She's a kitten compared to the daughter, actually."

"Kalan?" Alija asked in surprise. "I didn't know she was back in the city. You really *have* been taken into the fold, haven't you?"

Galon shrugged as he opened the door. "I keep telling you, Alija, I have an honest face."

Before she could disagree with him he was gone, leaving Alija with the uneasy feeling this scheme was becoming so complex it could only result in disaster. But then the idea she might get even with Marla for twenty years of deception, twenty years of being made to look a fool ... the unforgivable murder of Tarkyn Lye ...

Well, this sort of thing didn't come without a risk, and the sort of men willing to take such risks were the Galon Miars of this world, and they didn't come without their own unique set of dangers.

That's what made them so enticing.

And why Alija was so certain she would win.

chapter 61

Mother of the gods, boy! Where the hell does this bit go?"

"Here," Rorin told Tejay calmly, pushing her hand away. "It joins that bit there in the back."

Impatiently, Tejay let the young sorcerer fix the buckles on the shoulder of her gilded armour, cursing under her breath in several languages when she ran out of all the words she knew in Hythrun.

"I swear, Tejay, you know curses I've never even heard before."

She looked up to find Damin ducking under the tent flap, dressed for battle, wearing the same metal gauntlets he had used to rob Mahkas of his windpipe. It was just on dawn and the whole camp was roused. Thunder rumbled distantly across the hills and the occasional flash of lightning blanketed the overcast sky. For the past two days as the storm built up, the Fardohnyans had been moving down the valley and it seemed they had arrived together. It had all been terribly civilised, too. Envoys had been exchanged, the peace offerings dutifully rejected. All the forms of war had been adhered to. Now they were down to the fighting.

She glared at the young prince, thunder rattling dramatically in the background. "Make one more smart-mouthed comment, my lad, and you'll find I do a *lot* of things better than you besides cursing."

"I wouldn't dream of it," Damin assured her. "I must say, you do look very . . . decorative."

She tugged on the uncomfortable breastplate and scowled. "I look like a galloping great fool."

"Which will simply reinforce everyone's opinion that it really is Terin inside this thing," Rorin remarked. "Hold still, my lady."

"Gods! I spent less time getting dressed for the Feast of Kaelarn ball in Greenharbour," she complained.

"You probably moved around a lot less, too," Rorin protested. "Please, my lady, we're almost done."

"Is he always like this?" she asked Damin grumpily.

Damin sympathised with her discomfort, but there wasn't much he could do about it. "Are you sure you know what you have to do today?"

Still suffering Rorin's ministrations, Tejay rolled her eyes. "Hold the line long enough to draw them in, collapse it, bit by bit, so we can encircle them, and then fake a rout, leading the enemy too far in to retreat when the flanks close in behind them. I'm not stupid, Damin."

"I never meant to imply that you were, Tejay. I asked Rogan, Conin and Narvell the same question."

"What about Cyrus and Toren?"

"Didn't get a chance. They took off for the command post at Lasting Drift before I could speak to either of them."

"Now why doesn't that surprise me? *Ow*!" She glared at Rorin. "Just watch how tight you're pulling that strap, young man. There's a healthy bosom under there that's fed four children, you know. It wasn't meant to be squashed into a steel bucket."

"I'm sorry, my lady, but this armour was designed for a man. We always knew the fit was going to be a bit dicey."

"Which brings up another point nobody seems to have mentioned," she declared, turning to look at Damin. "What happens if I want to pee?"

"*What*?"

"Don't look at me like that. It's a perfectly reasonable question. How does one pee in a suit of armour?"

"Um . . ." Damin said uncomfortably. "Well . . . I know how *I* would do it . . ."

"Thanks, Damin, you're a real big help." She turned to Rorin. "Do you know?"

Rorin looked at her helplessly. "If I had to hazard a guess, I'd say very carefully."

"Wonderful! Just what I need. Another fool who thinks he's a wit!"

"In all fairness, Tejay," Damin pointed out, "they don't make these things for women, as a rule. I don't suppose anyone's given the matter a great deal of thought."

"I can imagine I will have remedied *that* little problem by this evening. Are you sure this looks convincing?"

"You look like a galloping great fool."

"Thank you, your highness. I feel so much better now."

"Well, that's my job, you know. Keeping up morale. You'll make sure you keep that damned helmet on, won't you?"

She glared at him.

"I'm just offering a bit of useful advice."

Tejay sighed. "What do you really want, Damin?"

"Cyrus Eaglespike's naked body smeared with honey and staked out over an anthill." Then he thought about it a little longer, adding, "And the news Hablet of Fardohnya has died a gruesome and painful death in a manner that can't be traced back to anybody in my family."

She tossed one of her gauntlets at him. "Get out of here, you fool. And take Rorin with you."

Damin's smile faded. "He's staying with you, Tejay. I won't have you arguing with me about it, either."

"Rorin's a healer, Damin. He needs to be by *your* side."

"I don't intend to get hurt."

"Neither do I," she retorted, "and what's more, I'm wearing armour, so I'm far less likely to. You need him. I'll be fine."

Damin was adamant. "He stays with you. If anything happens . . ."

"It won't."

"I *meant*," he repeated, a little annoyed she had interrupted him, "that if anything happens and you're knocked off your horse or otherwise incapacitated, I want Rorin in a position to get you off the field before anybody realises there's a healthy and impressive bosom under that breastplate, and not the Warlord of Sunrise Province."

"He's right, my lady," Rorin agreed. "I really should stay with you."

"Armour or not, Tejay, you'll be right there in the front lines in the thick of battle," Damin reminded her. "I would never forgive myself if anything happened to you."

"Damin, if you don't want people getting killed, you really should rethink this whole worshipping the God of War philosophy, you know. It's been my observation that people quite often come to harm when you throw them all on a field together, arm them with sharp implements, and tell them to hit each other until there's nobody left standing."

Damin smiled at her. "Rorin stays."

"Bully. What happens afterwards?"

"What do you mean?"

"After the battle? Do I just go back to my embroidery and await some man to come and tell me what's best for me and my province once you have no further use for my military skills?"

Damin frowned, as if the question had caught him off guard. "To be perfectly honest, Tejay, I haven't thought that far ahead yet. I'll owe you a big favour though, once this is over, I know that much."

"Well, don't think about it for too long, will you? This battle is likely to be decided, one way or the other, by the end of the day. Assuming I'm still around at the end of it, I want to know if I have to start looking for another husband."

"Do you *want* another husband?" Rorin asked curiously.

"I didn't even want the first one," she informed him with a grimace, picking up her helmet. "But there's no other way to hold on to Sunrise Province except find a semi-decent husband and have him appointed my son's regent. There's a reason your mother's been married four times, you know, Damin, and it isn't her great love of being a wife."

The prince seemed sympathetic to her plight even if, as a man, he didn't fully grasp the gravity of her situation. "I know how you must feel, Tejay . . ."

"No, you don't," she declared, settling the helmet on her

head. It was a little loose, but her long blond hair was gathered up in a bun and served as extra padding, which stopped the helmet moving around too much. "You haven't got the slightest notion of what it's like to be dictated to by someone you know you're smarter than, having to watch them make stupid decisions, knowing you could have done better . . . and then having to lay down and open your legs to him, just because the law gives him the right to have you any time he pleases. If you want to do me a favour, Damin Wolfblade, find a way for me to avoid that fate. How do I look?"

Damin nodded approvingly. "Like a Warlord," he said.

Which is all well and good, Tejay lamented silently, as Rorin helped her buckle on her sword. *But regardless of what happens on the battlefield today, come tomorrow I'll still be a mere woman and you'll be the lords and masters.*

Worst of all, she knew, by tomorrow these men would have forgotten that in the heat of battle, for a short time at least, they couldn't tell the difference.

CHAPTER 62

Damin had one more stop to make before he took up his position for the battle, and to the rumble of distant thunder, he made his way through the busy camp to the command tent which was the front section of Lernen's huge, multiroomed red silk pavilion. He glanced at the sky, wondering if the rain would favour their side or the Fardohnyans. It was hard to say, but deep down, Damin had a good feeling about this fight. The Hythrun were defending their homeland and the God of War was on their side. Zegarnald had told Damin as much in person.

The Fardohnyans were fighting only to save face. The collapse of the Widowmaker had handed Damin's forces that indefinable advantage Kraig warned him about. The moral high ground; the *morale* high ground, too. According to Kraig, the enemy had to believe he could win, as much as their own troops. With no chance of reinforcements and the Fardohnyans forced to fight out of hunger as much as territorial ambition, provided nobody made any monumental blunders, Hythria would win this day and win it soundly, regardless of the enemy's superior numbers.

When he arrived at Lernen's tent, the High Prince was nowhere to be found. Damin had expected him to be giddy with excitement at the prospect of leading a battle, even if it was by proxy. But the High Prince was still abed, one of his slaves informed Damin when he asked after his uncle, and was anxious to see his nephew as soon as possible.

The slave gave no other hint as to his master's state of mind, so with a great deal of trepidation, Damin followed him into the back of the pavilion, thinking that of all the times Lernen had chosen to have a relapse, the day they were going into battle was probably the worst time to do it.

"You wanted to see me, Uncle Lernen?"

The High Prince's room was dark, even though dawn was all but past. The drapes were pulled tight against the light and the room was uncomfortably warm. On the nightstand were the remains of a sleeping draught. This end of the pavilion reeked of opium and stale incense.

"Damin? Is that you?"

"Yes. It's me."

"Are you alone?"

"Of course."

Lernen struggled to sit up, studying Damin with rheumy eyes. He seemed to be partially dressed, as if he'd climbed out of bed and then changed his mind halfway through dressing and retreated under the covers. "Come. Sit by me," he ordered, patting the side of the bed.

Damin did as his uncle asked, wondering what was bothering the old man. And why he'd chosen today of all days to be bothered by it.

"I don't have long," he warned, as he sat down. "We're

expecting the Fardohnyans to move as soon as it's fully light. I need to get into position."

"Should I be out there, do you think?" the High Prince asked. "You know . . . leading . . . ?"

"It probably wouldn't hurt. You being the High Prince and General of the Combined Hythrun Armies, and all . . ."

Lernen pulled the covers up to his chin. "They'll all know it's a joke. They'll know I'm not really a general. I should have listened to your mother. Alija did this to me on purpose. I don't know how to fight. Tell me the truth, Damin . . . I'm the laughingstock of every Warlord in Hythria, aren't I?"

"Is that why you're still in bed? Hiding?" he asked, neatly avoiding having to answer the question.

Lernen's eyes filled with fear. "If we lose, Damin . . . do you know what they'll do to me?"

"We're not going to lose, Uncle Lernen."

"How can you be sure of that?"

Damin smiled. "Because I won't allow it."

"You're too much like your damned father," Lernen complained. "He said much the same thing."

"He did?" Damin asked curiously. In all the time he'd known his uncle, this was the first time he'd ever mentioned Laran Krakenshield.

"When he made the offer for your mother. I tried telling him then, that Hablet would go to war with us over it. He said he wouldn't allow it, too. And that if Hablet did declare war on us, we'd beat him."

"And he was right, wasn't he?"

"That just makes it more irritating, Damin."

"Well, I don't mean to irritate you, Uncle, but I will win this for you. I can't inherit Hythria when you're gone if I let Hablet take it from you now, can I?"

Lernen patted Damin's hand as if he was a small child. "Win this war for me and you can have your decree, nephew."

"My decree?"

"About lowering the age of majority. Tell your mother I'll sign it. After we've won."

Damin looked at him in surprise. The only time they'd

spoken about it, his uncle had been vehemently opposed to the idea. "What changed your mind?"

Lernen shrugged. "A lot of things. It wasn't anything you said."

"I don't understand."

Lernen leaned back against his pillows. "When your mother first came to me and suggested I should lower the age of majority, and that it was all your idea, I feared you were making a push for my throne."

"But, I never . . ."

"I know," Lernen agreed. "And I know I'm not a great High Prince. Kagan Palenovar kept me on the throne for years and your mother has held the country together in my name since he died, with little help or thanks from me. I'm not ignorant of her efforts, Damin, or ungrateful. But I'm a sick old man subject to bouts of deep insecurity. I thought maybe you'd gotten impatient. I thought signing that decree might be as good as signing my own death warrant."

"I might have wished you lived differently at times, Uncle Lernen, but I've never wished you any harm."

"I know that. And I wanted you to *know* that I know it. *Before* you go to war. If we lose this fight and you die today, Damin, I wanted you to die thinking well of me."

"I will," Damin promised. "Although your pep talks leave a lot to be desired."

Lernen looked about the darkened room, as if he was expecting to see someone else present, and then lowered his voice to just above a whisper. "Do you want me to give you command of the army today, nephew?"

Damin thought about it and then shook his head. "The orders are issued, the battle all but begun. There's no time to advise everyone of the change in command."

Faced with the enormity of the task before him, Lernen shrank back under the covers again. "But I know nothing about war. People will be looking to me to lead them. Suppose someone has to make a decision? Stay with me today, Damin. *Please?* I don't care that people think I'm a fool. I'll ruin everything for certain."

Never have you spoken a truer word, Damin thought, realising Lernen's offer was more about shifting the responsibility from his own shoulders than any particular trust he had in his heir. And the offer was a tempting one. A chance to control the battle from a distance, to move the pieces around like a game of chess . . . but Damin wanted to fight too, and he had a particular mission in mind—one that might have a decisive effect on the battle—and it left no room for playing general.

"How about I give you someone to help?" he suggested, thinking of the perfect solution. "Someone nobody will even suspect of being an advisor. He can watch over the battle with you, tell you what you must do to deal with problems as they crop up, how and where to move the troops . . . all you'd have to do is issue the actual orders. That way, nobody will ever know it wasn't you responsible for victory this day. All of Hythria will think you a hero."

"What advisor?" the High Prince asked, emerging from under the covers, his curiosity piqued.

"One of my *court'esa*. The Denikan. Kraig."

"The large terrifying one?"

Damin smiled. "Yes, Uncle, the large terrifying one."

"Didn't I tell you not to bring him near me?"

"He's been at every meeting we've had since you got here, Uncle. I keep him around because he frightens Cyrus even more than you."

Lernen grinned. Anything that might keep Cyrus Eaglespike at arm's length was a wonderful idea in the High Prince's book. "Does he know anything useful, this *court'esa* of yours?"

Damin nodded. "He used to be a warrior in his own country. He'll advise you well. And nobody will think anything odd about it other than your taste in *court'esa* has changed."

Lernen thought on that, studying his nephew warily. "You're nearly as clever as your mother, aren't you?"

"Very nearly."

"I'm glad I changed my mind about you."

"So am I," Damin agreed, rising to his feet. "Stay well,

Uncle. I'm really not ready to become High Prince yet. Shall I send your slaves back and tell them you're ready to get dressed now?"

The High Prince grabbed at his arm to prevent him leaving. "Don't die today, Damin, if you can manage it. I've not the energy left to go looking for another heir."

"I'll do my best," he promised.

On his way out of the pavilion, Damin ordered the High Prince's slaves back into the bedchamber, and instructed them to get their master dressed and ready for the battle. Once that was taken care of, Damin went looking for Prince Lunar Shadow Kraig of the House of the Rising Moon to inform him he was about to become—albeit unofficially, and only for a single day—General of the Combined Armies of Hythria.

chapter 63

To the sound of distant thunder, Rorin Mariner rode out at Tejay Lionsclaw's side, just as the last of the Sunrise archers was settling into place. Feeling awkward in the unaccustomed weight of the borrowed breastplate he wore, he followed Tejay in her magnificent jewelled and gilded armour, wondering why he was the only one who didn't realise at first glance that the armoured figure cantering to the head of the lines wasn't Terin Lionsclaw.

Even wearing a suit of archaic armour, Tejay rode better than her husband. She was far more confident in the saddle, far more anxious to lead from the front. Rorin hurried to keep up with her. It was important any final orders be relayed through him. The armour might fool everyone into believing the Warlord of Sunrise was recovered enough to take the field, but one word from Tejay would give the game away.

The officers saluted their Warlord as he rode past, but made no attempt to address their liege lord. Their orders had been relayed the night before by Rorin, who had addressed the officers and made certain they were fully briefed on today's strategy. There'd been a few discontented rumblings about why the troops were getting their orders from their Warlord's new seneschal, rather than their Warlord, most of the complaints coming (not surprisingly) from Stefan Warhaft, heading up the small contingent of Elasapine cavalry. They were to cover the right flank, mostly because Damin didn't want him anywhere near Narvell while he was carrying a weapon. Rorin had handled the questions well and eventually, even the most disgruntled man was forced to accept their orders came from the High Prince and through Terin Lionsclaw, and the seneschal was merely here to fill them in because their lord was still too unwell to do it himself.

The plan they had was quite specific and had been worked out in minute detail by Damin, Narvell, Almodavar, Kraig and Lady Lionsclaw over many late nights in the darkness of Tejay's tent, talking in whispers as they tried to second-guess every possible contingency.

The purpose of Tejay being here this morning was twofold. The first was to rally the inexperienced Sunrise archers, to ensure they got away those critical few arrows before they retreated, and the second was to make certain everybody believed Terin Lionsclaw was alive and well and in command of his Raiders. Rorin was under strict instructions to accompany Lady Lionsclaw through those first vital moments of the engagement and then make certain she retreated with the archers, leaving the infantry battle in the hands of the more experienced officers of Greenharbour and Pentamor Provinces, who made up the bulk of the first wave.

The air was heavy with impending rain, the sky low and overcast. Rorin could actually feel the mood of the men—an odd mixture of excitement and apprehension—even though he had no telepathic ability to speak of.

His palms moist with anticipation, Rorin heard the Fardohnyans long before he saw them. Banging their spears against their tall wooden shields, the enemy advanced in a disciplined formation, their interlocked shields presenting an impenetrable wall that moved with the slow and merciless force of a lava flow. He watched with growing apprehension as the enemy filled the field of battle from the bank of the muddy Norsell to the fast-flowing Saltan River on the other side, assuming (not incorrectly) that the Hythrun would be unable to flank them with the rivers blocking the way. Of course, they didn't know this wasn't really the chosen battlefield; that they would be drawn much further down the valley before the day was done, down to the foothills around Lasting Drift, past the only two river crossings in this part of the country, where the massed cavalry of Dregian, Elasapine and Krakandar awaited them.

As the Fardohnyans moved into view, the unrelenting thumping pounded against the ground so hard the earth throbbed in time with the beat. More than a little anxious himself, Rorin leaned forward to calm his skittish gelding and glanced at Lady Lionsclaw. She sat upright and unflinching in the saddle, as if the sight of the seemingly endless Fardohnyans was nothing to be concerned about.

"Ye gods," Rorin breathed in awe. "Is there no end to them?"

"*We* are the end of them," Tejay replied simply. Then she turned to look at him through the narrow eye slits of her jewelled helmet. "Can you actually use that sword you're wearing?"

Rorin glanced down at the borrowed weapon she'd found for him last night. "Not really."

"Then use magic to protect yourself, Rorin. I can't watch over you every minute."

Rorin thought that was probably a very good idea, even though he was supposedly watching over Tejay. Deflecting a killing blow magically was a far safer bet than trying to be a hero with a blade he'd probably drop out of fatigue ten minutes after picking it up. And it would also allow him to extend that magical protection to cover his companion. But it didn't seem fair to be the only one using magic.

"Isn't that cheating? Using magic?"

"If it means you're still alive at the end of the day, will you care?"

"Well . . . no, I suppose not."

"Then do it, lad, and don't argue with me about it. I'm your Warlord."

Rorin couldn't argue with that. He closed his eyes briefly, drawing the magic to him. When he opened them again, his eyes were as black as his gelding, the Fardohnyans had finally stopped moving and Tejay Lionsclaw had raised her arm to give the signal that would start the war.

There was a pause, a pregnant moment of anticipation as the Fardohnyans settled into place and the Hythrun faced them across the field. A breathless, silent moment, long enough for men to realise they were about to die, but not nearly long enough to ponder why. As soon as Lady Lionsclaw dropped her arm, the air hissed with the flight of several thousand arrows arcing overhead and there was no turning back.

Many of the Fardohnyans recognised the sound and had the wit to raise their heavy shields against the deadly rain. Others did nothing—too close to their comrades to be able to lift anything, even if they recognised the danger. Either that or they were contemptuous of their enemy's efforts to halt them. It was a foolish attitude and a costly one, Rorin thought. Even inexperienced fools will hit something if enough of them simultaneously shoot into a mass of closely packed bodies.

Rorin's horse reared, a little unnerved by the noise and the sporadic lightning streaking the horizon. Horns rang out across the valley and the Fardohnyans began to move forward in a tight and disciplined formation, the sky behind them black with the advancing storm and almost keeping pace with them. Tejay raised her arm a second time, but held it there for what seemed like an eternity before she finally gave the command. Rorin flinched as the sky darkened with arrows a second time. Again, rank upon rank of the Fardohnyans fell, but their companions simply stepped over the dead and wounded, moving up to fill the gaps caused by the men who had fallen. His heart in his mouth, Rorin watched the advance, wondering why nobody was taking a shot at him or at Tejay dressed in her tempting jewelled armour. Wondering if Sunrise Province's inexperienced archers would stand long enough to deliver the third volley they needed. Wondering what had possessed him to think there was any glory in battle. He wouldn't blame the archers if they ran away. It was certainly what every instinct Rorin owned was telling him to do.

"Any minute now," Tejay remarked, "they'll let loose their own . . ." She ducked intuitively as a shower of arrows suddenly arced overhead from the Fardohnyan side and sliced into the ranks of archers behind them. "That's the trouble with the enemy being in range. It means we're in range of them, too."

Arrows ploughed into the ground around them. Two or three bounced off Tejay's armour. Frantically, Rorin extended the magical shield over both of them and watched in awe as the sky rained deadly missiles. He could barely hear Tejay over the cries of the men caught by the Fardohnyan volley. Screams filled the air, punctuated by thunder as the storm and the Fardohnyans moved closer.

The God of War might be Hythria's god, Rorin thought, *but it seems as if the God of Storms is on the side of Fardohnya.*

Forcing her excited horse under control, Tejay raised her arm again. "We need to get that last volley away and those men out of here," she told Rorin, yelling to be heard over the advancing infantry and the screams of their own wounded. "Once that rain sets in, this place is going to turn into a quagmire and we won't be drawing anybody anywhere."

Decisively she dropped her arm and another volley followed, this one much less certain than the others, a little more sporadic, a lot less confident. As soon as the arrows whooshed overhead, Tejay pulled her sword from its scabbard and raised it high—the pre-arranged signal for the Sunrise archers to retreat.

Seeing at least some of the enemy running from them, the inexorable Fardohnyan advance surged forward, the lead group laughing and calling insults to the retreating men as the Sunrise Raiders fled.

"My lady . . ." Rorin warned, with concern. She was facing the oncoming army as if she intended to take them on single-handed and was too tempting a target out here in front of her men in that damned jewelled armour. "Please! We need to fall back."

Tejay hesitated and then wheeled her mount around, barely fifty paces ahead of the advancing Fardohnyans. As they galloped toward their own lines, Rorin noticed the Izcomdar and Elasapine light cavalry forming on their flanks. Despite there only being two provinces represented among the cavalry, to the casual observer it looked as if every province was in attendance. Riders carried the banners of each province spread out among the Raiders, to give the impression this was all they'd been able to muster of Hythria's once formidable strength.

Ten thousand men facing a force of close to thirty thousand and right now, Rorin thought, *Axelle Regis probably thinks he can win.*

Another volley arced overhead from the Fardohnyan archers, this one peppering the ground around them. Protected by Rorin's magical shield, they were invulnerable to the deadly missile shower, but the fleeing archers surrounding them weren't nearly as lucky. Either side of them, terrified men screamed and fell as the Fardohnyan arrows rained down on them.

Then ahead of Tejay's horse, another young man took a tumble, a blue-fletched arrow in his shoulder. The war horse reared at the sudden obstacle. She fought the beast down and turned it sharply, while Rorin's mount charged ahead. A moment later, when he realised she was no longer by his side, Rorin turned to discover Tejay had jumped from her horse and was dragging the wounded young Raider to his feet.

Cursing, Rorin turned his mount, attempting to reach them, but the tide of frightened, retreating soldiers pursued by the deadly rain of Fardohnyan arrows pushed him back, even further out of reach. He could see Tejay, her arm around the lad, trying to lift the wounded boy into the saddle, while behind them the advancing horde of Fardohnyans, screaming some unintelligible war cry, thundered down the valley. Tejay had only moments until she was overrun. Rorin stretched out with his shield to protect her, knowing how useless a gesture it was. His magic could deflect arrows, toss a man across a room and maybe push aside falling rocks, as it had in the Widowmaker, but he couldn't build a wall that would hold back an entire attacking army.

Desperate and helpless, he watched Tejay glance over her shoulder at the oncoming army. It was obvious she was aware of the danger, just as it was obvious she had no intention of abandoning the young man she'd stopped to rescue. The Fardohnyans were less than fifty paces away, their blood-curdling screams so loud Rorin could barely hear his own thoughts. Tejay struggled with the Raider, but the boy was fading fast and even though she was a fit and healthy woman, Tejay lacked the physical strength to lift a full-grown man wearing armour onto the back of a horse.

Rorin suddenly cursed his own stupidity for not thinking of the solution sooner. Taking a risk that Tejay's armour would protect her, he dropped the shield, reached out with his magic and picked up the young Raider, depositing him bodily across the saddle. Tejay jumped back, startled by the miraculous relocation of her burden, and then glanced across the field in Rorin's direction when she realised such a thing could not have happened without some sort of magical intervention. He waved her forward, wishing he had Wrayan's ability to communicate mentally and tell her to get the hell out of there . . .

He didn't need to, however. It took Lady Lionsclaw a split second to work out Rorin had helped her, and another split second to realise she was out of time and—wearing metal armour—had no hope of remounting her husband's big war-horse unaided.

With the Fardohnyans almost on top of Tejay, Rorin urged his horse forward against the tide of fleeing men, trying to reach her. With her sword in her right hand, Tejay had grabbed the horse by the bridle and with her wounded passenger draped across the saddle, she forced the beast across the arrow-littered field toward the Hythrun lines, no more able to run in Lernen's decorative armour than she was able to mount a horse wearing it. Desperately, Rorin extended the shield again, hoping it was enough to reach her. He actually wasn't quite sure where the outer edges were, and could only hope that it was enough to keep her safe.

It wasn't, he discovered a moment later. Still frustratingly close, but desperately far from help, Tejay stumbled and fell, an arrow protruding from her left leg, embedded in the gap in her armour that allowed her knees to move.

Rorin cried out as she was knocked down. The last of the archers were running past him, many of them dragging their wounded companions. Desperate to reach her, he still wasn't clear to go to Tejay's aid, when the sound of horns split the thundery morning. Although he was only vaguely aware of it, behind him the much better disciplined Pentamor and Greenharbour infantry moved up to take their place.

Tejay was still closer to the Fardohnyans than her own lines when the first of the Fardohnyans caught up with her. Tejay must have heard the man approach. She staggered to her feet, turning just as the Fardohnyan raised his arm to strike her with his war axe. Almost casually, and despite the fact she was wounded, alone and had the whole Fardohnyan army bearing down on top of her, she ran her assailant through without flinching, and then grabbed the reins of her horse again and resumed her desperate bid for safety, slashing wildly at another Fardohnyan as he tried to prevent her reaching her own lines.

Sick with fear, Rorin was seriously contemplating picking her up and moving her bodily out of the fray when rescue appeared in the shape of a Pentamor captain Rorin didn't even know. The officer must have also seen the danger to the Warlord of Sunrise. Before Rorin even thought of asking for help, the man shouted something behind him and a squad was rushing forward to surround the Warlord. The Fardohnyans overtook them just as the Raiders reached Tejay and her companion, but the Pentamor men were prepared for the attack and retreated in a much more orderly fashion than the Sunrise Raiders had, fighting off the Fardohnyans as they went with the wounded Raider and Warlord in their midst. Tejay stumbled along in the middle of them with the arrow still sticking out of her calf.

They caught up with Rorin a few moments later, a hair's breadth ahead of the Fardohnyans. The men parted for them as they stumbled through to the safety of their own lines. Rorin flew from the saddle and caught Tejay as she staggered and fell again, crying out in agony as someone behind her bumped the arrow protruding from the back of her leg.

They made it through just as the two armies crashed into one another and the din left him speechless. It didn't sound like men. The battle was a constant roar made of screams and cries and curses that all blended together to create a wall of intolerable noise. He shuddered and looked down at Lady Lionsclaw.

"My la—lord!" he cried over the unbearable cacophony, as he lowered her to the ground. "Can you make it a bit further? You *have* to make it a bit further."

Tejay glared at him through the narrow slit in her helmet. She was not in so much pain that she'd forgotten the danger of answering him where they could be overheard, although given the battle noise surrounding them it was unlikely. She tried to stand up, but she wasn't able to put any weight on the leg. With the battle behind their position now, Rorin dropped the magic shield again and wrapped his will around her, using it to lift her onto his own horse. Desperate to put the roar of the battle behind them, Rorin picked up the reins of her horse. Leading Tejay's mount and the wounded soldier she'd rescued, Rorin pushed his way back through the attacking troops toward the position on the rise overlooking the field of conflict where the High Prince was waiting with his entourage.

It took quite some time to get off the field, but finally he got his two wounded charges clear of the melee. When he looked up at the pavilion, somewhat to Rorin's surprise the Denikan prince-in-disguise, Prince Lunar Shadow Kraig of the House of the Rising Moon, was standing at the very front of the tent, watching over the battle with a brass telescope.

Rorin glanced over his shoulder, shaking from the narrowness of their escape. Fortunately, there was little chance they'd be caught up in it further. From now on the main battle was in the hands of the officers and men of Pentamor and Greenharbour.

Tejay glanced up at the command tent and then looked down at Rorin. "Get that damned thing out of my leg."

He eyed the arrow warily. "Are you sure?"

"Yes, I'm sure," she said with a grimace. "It's really just a flesh wound . . ."

"I can heal it," he offered.

"No wonder Damin puts up with you." He couldn't see her expression because of the helmet, but she sounded impressed. "Do it then, lad. Before someone comes down to enquire what we're doing."

Taking a deep breath, Rorin gripped the shaft of the arrow and pulled. It came away easily. Tejay didn't so much as whimper as he did it, and she was right, it was little more than a flesh wound, slicing into the muscle of her calf, one of the few places she was unprotected by the decorative jewelled armour she wore.

He placed his hand over the bleeding gash and drew on his magic, feeling the flesh knit as it healed. A few moments later he opened his eyes and looked up at her. He couldn't read her face, but the set of her shoulders was visibly more relaxed.

"You really are a handy lad to know, aren't you?" Tejay

sounded as if she'd just come from ordering an inventory of
the cellars, not narrowly escaping a battle with her life.
Rorin was amazed. He was trembling like a leaf.

"I do have my uses, my . . . lord. Did you want me to heal
your young friend there, too?"

Tejay shook her head and gathered up her reins. "I'll take
him to the medics. It'll give me an excuse not to join Lernen
for a bit longer. You go up there and give the High Prince my
apologies. Tell him I'll be along presently."

A little bemused by her manner, Rorin left the Warlord of
Sunrise with the young Raider draped over her horse, and
headed up the short slope to the command pavilion.

"Rorin!" she called after him. He turned to look at her.
"Your eyes."

He stared at her blankly and then realised what she meant.
He was still drawing on the magic of the Harshini. His eyes
were still totally black and if he confronted the High Prince
like that, who knew what his reaction might be. Tejay's
poise wasn't an act at all, he decided. She was thinking
much more clearly than he was.

With a final wave to the brave young woman posing as the
Warlord of Sunrise Province, Rorin let the magic go, waiting
a moment for his eyes to return to normal before he scrambled up the slope to report to the High Prince.

chapter 64

Normally, the command pavilion should have been
jammed with men, but Damin had arranged for Lernen, Kraig and only a few of the High Prince's most
trusted slaves, dressed in armour to make them look
like officers from a distance, to be stationed in the
pavilion. The real battle would take place some miles from

here, further down the valley, but the absence of the High Prince and a pavilion over which to observe the battle would strike a warning note with any enemy general worthy of his command. Axelle Regis and his officers had to believe this was where they were making their stand and that the ten thousand men below were all they had to throw into the fight.

Rorin bowed as he entered the open pavilion and approached the prince. "Your highness, Lord Lionsclaw sent me to check if you have any further orders."

Lernen took his eyes off the battle long enough to glance down at Tejay, who was securing the wounded young soldier more safely to her saddle with her back to the tent. "Why doesn't he come here and ask me himself?"

"The Fardohnyans are overpowering the weaker cavalry on the right," Kraig informed them, saving Rorin from having to answer. Kraig had taken the news about his reassignment to the High Prince's entourage rather stoically, but as he took just about everything rather stoically, it was hard to tell what he really thought about it.

"Warhaft's men?" Rorin asked. He turned, shielding his eyes against the lightning, and stared down over the battlefield. "Already?"

"I know that name," Lernen mused, the battle momentarily forgotten. "Why do I know that name?"

"He's a vassal of Lord Hawksword's," Rorin reminded him. "His wife, Lady Kendra, has petitioned you, your highness."

"Why?"

"She wants you to grant her a divorce."

"Doesn't she like her husband?"

"She wants to marry your nephew Narvell, your highness."

"Hmmm . . ." Lernen replied thoughtfully. "It would really be much better for everyone if he died in battle then, wouldn't it? Much neater. Less argument."

"I . . . er . . ." Rorin replied, having no idea how to answer such a suggestion. "I suppose . . ."

"I tell you what," Lernen announced. "We'll let the gods

decide. If she's to be rid of this husband she no longer wants, let the gods take him in battle today. If he survives the day, obviously the gods think she should keep him."

"That's a very . . . *interesting* solution, your highness."

Lernen smiled. "I'm very wise. It's because I'm the High Prince, you know. What were we talking about?"

"Your *court'esa* was just noting that the Fardohnyans are overpowering the weaker cavalry on the right. Lord Warhaft's men."

"Well, there you go, then. The gods have . . ." In a sudden burst of panic, Lernen forgot all about the Lady Kendra and her marital problems and grabbed the big Denikan by the arm. "Hang on . . . does that mean . . . are we *losing*?"

"No, your highness," Kraig assured him. "This is as it is meant to be."

"Are you sure?" Lernen asked nervously. "It doesn't sound like we're winning. Doesn't the enemy overpowering us mean we're losing?"

"We want them to break through, your highness," Rorin reminded him. "This is just a feint, remember?"

"But that means they'll come this way, doesn't it?"

"We'll be long gone before the Fardohnyans reach us, your highness," Kraig assured the High Prince. "But your presence here is required to disguise the ruse, just as you fleeing at the right moment will reinforce the notion your forces have been routed and you believe they are defeated. This will draw the enemy into our trap."

"So . . . I'm doing something important, then?" Lernen asked, with sudden childlike excitement. "This whole battle, this clever ruse . . . it's all up to me?"

"Most assuredly," the Denikan replied solemnly.

"Well, in that case," the High Prince announced, squaring his shoulders manfully, "tell Lord Lionsclaw to get back out there and at least try to give the impression he's fighting this damned war! Off you go!"

Rorin glanced at the Denikan, rolled his eyes, and then bowed to the High Prince. "My lord is currently escorting a wounded Raider to the medical pavilion and was hoping, on his return, to have the honour of escorting you to the fallback position, your highness. Once you give the order, of course."

Lernen frowned and looked up at the Denikan slave. "Is that a good idea?"

"An excellent idea, your highness," the big man agreed.

"Oh, well . . . all right then, you may tell Terin Lionsclaw he can wait and escort me when the time comes." The prince turned to Kraig. "When will that be?"

"A good hour at least," Kraig predicted. "Any sooner and your enemy will smell the trap."

What followed was the most nerve-racking hour of Rorin's life. Miraculously, the rain held off while on the plain below both infantry masses were caught in a bloodbath that was part cut and slash and part pushing and shoving. The actual fighting was only going on between the first ten or so ranks of men. The rest of the battle seemed to be made up of the troops at the rear trying to push their way into the fight, even if it meant trampling their own dead and wounded to do it.

As Rorin watched, the Pentamor and Greenharbour infantry that made up Hythria's centre line slowly but inexorably yielded before the pressure of the numerically superior Fardohnyans, until they had pushed deep into the middle of the Hythrun troops. The flanks, made up of Izcomdar's light cavalry and a smattering of Elasapine horse, gave every indication it was barely holding on, but hold on they did, while more and more Fardohnyans poured into the funnel.

All we need to do now, Rorin thought, *is spring the trap before the Fardohnyans realise they're in it.*

"Your highness," Kraig suggested abruptly. "Now might be a good time to issue the order."

The High Prince looked at the Denikan blankly. An hour was a long time in Lernen Wolfblade's world. "What order?"

"The order to retreat, your highness. We must make the enemy think they have routed your army."

"But . . . isn't retreating . . . just . . . you know . . . running away?"

"This is not running away, your highness. Remember? This is withdrawing to a strategically superior position."

"No!" Lernen announced petulantly, crossing his arms like a defiant child. "I've been thinking about this. We're staying right here. The people of Hythria look up to me! The soldiers of Hythria need a leader! I will not be seen to do anything so cowardly!"

Kraig looked at Rorin with exasperation. The young sorcerer shrugged. He had no more idea than the Denikan as to how they should deal with Lernen Wolfblade in this mood. Damin was the expert when it came to handling the High Prince.

"*Rorin!*" an impatient voice hissed.

He turned to find Tejay Lionsclaw standing on the slope behind him, still disguised in her armour, waiting for Lernen to implement the next phase of their plan. She had been gone this whole time, and had returned leading both her and Rorin's horses. Presumably, the young man she'd risked her life to rescue was safe in the hands of the physicians now.

"*Tell him to give the order!*" she urged in a loud whisper, obviously having overheard Lernen's foolish declaration. "*Now!*"

Rorin shrugged helplessly and turned back to the High Prince. "Your highness, you *must* sound the retreat and then abandon this place," he begged as the noise of the battle grew even closer. "The Fardohnyans have to believe they've routed us, or they won't follow our troops into the ambush."

"An ambush is a cowardly way to win a war!" Lernen Wolfblade declared. "I'm not going anywhere."

"Oh! For pity's sake!" Tejay snapped. "An ambush is the *only* way to win a war when you're outnumbered two to one, you old fool."

Rorin debated trying to stop her, but Tejay was in no mood to allow anyone to stand in her way. She pushed past Rorin and planted herself in front of the High Prince, hands on her hips, glaring at him through the narrow eye-slits of her helmet.

"You give that order right this minute, Lernen Wolfblade, then get your arse out of here and back to the real command post, or so help me I'll put you over my knee as if you were one of my boys and slap some sense into you myself. We'll see how cowardly your pasty-white backside looks to the Fardohnyans then, eh?"

Lernen squinted at her in surprise. "*Lady* Lionsclaw?"

There being no further point in subterfuge, Tejay lifted the helmet from her head, letting her thick blond hair tumble out.

Lernen gasped in shock. "My lady! You're pretending to be a *Warlord*?"

"So are you, Lernen Wolfblade," she accused. "Now give the damned order!"

Lernen studied her fearfully and then nodded, as if too scared to defy such an angry woman. Relieved beyond measure, Rorin signalled to one of the waiting messengers to pass the order along. A few moments later the horns rang out, sounding the retreat.

The troops below, waiting for the command, immediately broke and ran in chaotic disarray. After a moment of stunned disbelief a cheer went up from the Fardohnyans as they realised the enemy was on the run, and then, just as they planned, the Fardohnyans followed.

"Axelle Regis has now lost control of the battle," Kraig remarked to Rorin, watching the retreat with satisfaction.

"How can you tell?"

"Because the Fardohnyans are following our soldiers without waiting for orders," Tejay answered for him. "Once men move as a group in a direction you haven't sent them, you no longer own the battlefield."

Kraig inclined his head in agreement. "We should leave now. Another few minutes and those soldiers will be on us. Your highness?"

Still staring at Tejay Lionsclaw in dismay, with hardly any resistance at all, Lernen let Kraig lead him to his waiting horse, where the big Denikan picked him up and sat him in his saddle like a father lifting his child onto a pony.

A few minutes later, the command pavilion abandoned, Rorin was mounted again, following Tejay Lionsclaw, the High Prince, Prince Lunar Shadow Kraig of the House of the Rising Moon and the few trusted retainers Damin had appointed to watch over his uncle as they cantered away from the scene of the first engagement.

"Where do you suppose the Fardohnyan cavalry are?" Rorin asked Kraig as they urged their horses toward Lasting Drift a few minutes ahead of the fleeing Hythrun and the advancing Fardohnyans.

"Gathering as we speak," the Denikan predicted grimly.

It was only as the rain started to hit Tejay's armour beside him with a metallic plinking sound—even before he felt the first drops on his face—it occurred to Rorin that even though he had sailed through this battle untouched, there were probably two or three thousand men on the field, from both sides, either dead or dying behind them.

And the tragedy of it, he knew, was that unknown to the Fardohnyans, whooping victoriously in the wake of the fleeing Hythrun, the worst was yet to come.

chapter 65

When the message arrived from Galon that the meeting with Marla's Fardohnyan agent was finally arranged, Alija couldn't help wondering if she was trying to be too clever by half. Although she knew Galon hadn't lied to her, the sting of discovering from Ruxton Tirstone's dying mind how she'd been duped so comprehensively by Marla in the past had eroded her confidence.

That she had received no communication from Cyrus was equally concerning. Surely, by now, he would have found the time to write? Of course, all the official dispatches went to the palace, which meant they went to Marla, but she should have received some word from her son by now about what was happening in Sunrise Province and the war with Fardohnya.

But she could worry about the war later, once Marla was taken care of. Once it fell to the High Arrion to govern the city in the absence of the High Prince and his advisors, which—if everything went according to plan—should be sometime this afternoon, she would have time to discover the truth about what was really happening at the front.

Forcing her concern about her son's fate to the back of her mind, Alija read through the letter once again. It was addressed to Hablet of Fardohnya and should have spelled out, in no uncertain terms, that the High Arrion of the Sorcerers' Collective expected him to win this battle and that in return for the obliteration of the Wolfblade line, she was prepared to guarantee the cooperation of the Eaglespike family, provided the King of Fardohnya recognised her son's claim to the Hythrun throne and accepted him in such a role—as a vassal of Fardohnya, of course.

But Alija was nobody's fool. The letter stated quite the opposite. It was nothing more than a declaration of her loyalty to Hythria and her High Prince once one got past the flowery introduction that went on for a page or more. She'd deliberately designed it that way. Alija needed to confront this Fardohnyan Marla had found to carry her message to the enemy and gain his trust sufficiently to touch him. While he was wading through the flowery prose—and before he got to the gist of the letter—she could get inside his head. Once she was in the Fardohnyan's thoughts, even if he didn't know Marla personally, Alija was quite certain she had the ability to make him testify that he did.

Let her squirm her way out of that one, Alija thought. Her supposedly incriminating letter would be destroyed as soon as it had served its purpose—Galon had promised her that.

Trust me, he'd assured her, as he took her hands in his, understanding that through the contact she would know if he was deceiving her. *I will not—under any circumstances—allow your letter to fall into the wrong hands.*

"And I do trust you, Galon," she murmured softly. "Up to a point."

"My lady?"

Alija looked up from the letter. "Yes, Tressa?"

"Master Miar is here."

"Send him in."

The slave bowed and backed out of the room. A few moments later, Galon walked into the High Arrion's office. He glanced down at the parchment she was holding. "All set?"

She rose to her feet. "Where is the meeting to be held?"

"In the Temple of the Gods."

"Here?" Alija asked in surprise. "In the Sorcerers' Collective? How did Marla arrange that?"

"Marla didn't," Galon told her. "It was Kalan's idea. Apparently there's some ancient notion of the Temple of the Gods and the Sorcerers' Palace being neutral ground?"

"Nobody's invoked that rule for a century or more."

He shrugged, unconcerned. "I gather this Fardohnyan we're going to meet is a tad skittish. Understandably, I suppose, given we're at war with them."

She didn't like this. And there was some other unfinished business she still wasn't happy about, either. "You were supposed to arrange for me to see this man calling himself Wrayan Lightfinger before the meeting," she reminded him.

"No need," the assassin replied. "He'll be there. Are you ready?"

Alija hesitated one last time, wondering if she was allowing her arrogance and her desire for vengeance to get the better of her. This was insanity, really, thinking she could pull this off. So many things could go wrong. The risk was unthinkable.

But worth it, she reminded herself, a vision of Marla standing in her parlour, gloating over Tarkyn Lye's blood-smeared collar suddenly filling her mind. *If it brings that bitch down, the destruction of my own world would almost be worth it.*

"I'm ready," she told Galon. "Are you?"

"I'll be right beside you the whole time, Alija."

She walked around the desk, folding the letter as she went, quite certain that he was telling her the truth. "I won't forget your assistance in this matter, Galon."

The assassin opened the door for her. "I don't doubt that, Alija. Shall we go and destroy an evil, twisted, bitter little woman with delusions of grandeur?"

Alija smiled at his description of Marla. "I'll bet you didn't whisper that juicy little sweet nothing in her ear when you were trying to seduce her."

"You've got that right," he chuckled, offering his arm. "My lady?"

Alija took his arm, searching his mind as her skin touched his. Galon's mind was full of hope, of anticipation and the excitement that came from knowing vengeance was finally within his grasp.

She understood exactly what he was feeling.

What she didn't understand, and what she intended to ask him later, once this was done, was why he was so eager to exact vengeance from Marla Wolfblade in the first place.

The Sorcerer's Palace sat high on a bluff overlooking everything in Greenharbour, even the Royal Palace. Although everyone called it the Sorcerers' Palace it was actually a complex of temples and residences, encircled by a thick white wall, constructed of stone quarried from the chalk cliffs west of the city, their fragile strength reinforced by ages-old Harshini magic. It had stood for over two thousand years, almost as long as the Citadel in Medalon. Old Bruno Sanval surmised the two complexes were very similar in design and was planning to undertake a study of the possibility, once he located Sanctuary. Alija couldn't have cared less. Although men like the Lower Arrion lived for the day the Harshini might return, she always considered the notion they might come back rather more of an inconvenience than an occasion to look forward to.

Alija climbed the steps of the Temple of the Gods with Galon at her side, the letter burning in her hand. She clung to it tightly, tight enough to turn her knuckles white.

The temple was almost empty, but for a solitary figure standing in front of the large crystal Seeing Stone. With Galon a pace behind her, Alija strode down the centre of the temple, her footfalls echoing loudly on the mosaic-tiled floor. The Seeing Stone in the Temple of the Gods—a solid lump of crystal as tall as a man mounted on a black marble base—loomed over the waiting figure. Candles set in solid silver sconces lit the altar, reflecting off the Stone with flickering rainbow light, shadowing the features of the man until she was right in front of him.

Alija stopped a few feet from the Seeing Stone and stared at the man waiting for her. This was no Fardohnyan agent.

"Alija."

For a moment, she was too surprised to speak. Galon hadn't lied when he said this man looked far too young to be the man she remembered, but neither could she deny the evidence of her own eyes. The young man who stood before her was undeniably Wrayan Lightfinger. Even if his physical appearance hadn't told her that, the fact that his eyes were as black as polished onyx would have given him away. He was channelling Harshini magic, not flirting with the edges of it, like Alija did, but actually channelling enough to affect his eyes.

"Wrayan Lightfinger."

She couldn't think of anything else to say. And it was merely a stalling tactic to give her time to reach for her own power. It was a risk. She no longer had the benefit of an enhancement spell to guarantee her success and it was clear that Wrayan had learned a great deal since she'd confronted him the last time, in this very temple.

"Galon," she ordered, her voice betraying no emotion. "Kill this man."

"Sorry, Alija," the assassin said, taking a step back from her. "But I don't do uncontracted kills."

"Then I'm contracting you to kill him!" she declared impatiently, glaring at him. "Whatever price you want. Just do it."

Galon appeared to consider her offer and then shook his head. "I don't think so, Alija."

"Why don't you kill me yourself, Alija?" Wrayan asked. "It's not like you haven't tried before."

"The next time, I won't fail," she snapped, turning to stare at Galon. "What do you think you're doing?"

The assassin shrugged. "What I said I was coming here to do, my lady. Destroy an evil, twisted, bitter little woman with delusions of grandeur."

It took Alija a moment to realise he was referring to her. She stared at him in shock, unable to believe he had deceived her so completely. She'd touched his mind. She'd read his thoughts. He'd sworn Wrayan hadn't been able to break his shield . . .

And then the truth dawned on her and she turned to face Wrayan again. "He let you."

"Pardon?"

"Galon *let* you into his mind, didn't he?" She laughed bitterly at her own stupidity. "By the gods . . . I should have known if you had the skill to shield the minds of Marla and all her family, reconstructing an assassin's shield would have been child's play. He wasn't even lying. He said you hadn't broken his shield. I never asked him if he'd lowered it voluntarily."

"More fool you," Wrayan replied.

"Why?" she asked, turning to the assassin.

"Master Lightfinger and I had an interesting discussion about the consequences of resisting his probe," Galon replied. "At one point there was a suggestion I might be forced to cut my own balls off. One does what one must to keep the family jewels intact, my lady. You'd understand that much better than I."

That he could be so glib about something so important was a telling sign, a terrifying indication of how little respect he had for her. It hurt Alija more than she cared to admit.

"That's not what I'm asking. Why betray me? I could have given you everything."

"Which wouldn't have come anywhere near making up for what you took from me, Alija."

She studied him in confusion. "What are you talking about?"

"Didn't you know?" Wrayan asked with a note of reproach. "I'm shocked, Alija."

"Know what?"

He pointed to Galon. "This is Ronan Dell's son. You remember Ronan Dell, don't you? You had him and his entire palace slaughtered a few years ago."

She shook her head in denial. "You couldn't possibly know that. Or prove it."

"Oh, but we can, Alija," Wrayan informed her. "We have the statement of Elezaar the Dwarf, who witnessed the entire attack. Ah, and then there's the blubbering confession of a certain slave trader by the name of Venira, whose memory of that night was magically restored when it was pointed out to him that incurring your wrath was one thing, but making an enemy of the next Raven of the Assassins' Guild was a different matter entirely. And then—most regrettably for you—there was the young man with a rare afternoon off from his guild training, who just happened to drop into home to visit his father . . . just as a troop of Dregian Raiders were making their escape over the back wall of Ronan Dell's palace."

"Very sloppy of you, by the way, to allow them to undertake such a grisly task wearing something identifiably Dregian." Galon was involved in this deception far more deeply than Alija had ever suspected and was delighting in her knowing it, too. "Was that a mistake, Alija, or just arrogance?"

She stared at him, horrified by his revelation. "You? *You're* Ronan Dell's bastard?"

"Actually, I'm not, but he died thinking I was. I suppose I should be grateful you relieved me of that burden. Can't say I'm willing to be so forgiving about the death of my real father, though. That was unnecessary, Alija, and I really do mean to see you pay for it."

Alija looked at them both, shaking her head when she realised that none of this mattered. Not really. They couldn't prove a word of it. She sneered at their amateurish attempt at revenge. "And this is your trap?" she asked, glancing around. "Your pitiful vengeance for something I did twenty-six years ago and haven't lost a night's sleep over since? Or is it the letter you were so insistent that I write, Galon? The one incriminating me as a traitor?"

"Either one will do."

"There's no Fardohnyan agent, either, I suppose?" she surmised, looking around the empty temple. "All this was just a ruse to get me to write that letter?"

Galon smiled at her. "Clever, don't you think?"

"You're fools!" she accused. "Both of you! And Marla as well! As if I would be foolish enough to commit something like that to parchment!" She tossed the letter onto the ground at Galon's feet. "Take it. There's not a word there you can use to condemn me."

"I would have been disappointed if there had been," Galon said, making no attempt to pick up the letter. "But confessing to the murder of Ronan Dell? That's a different kettle of broth, my lady."

"My *confession*, as you call it, is worth nothing if a dead man and an assassin are the only witnesses."

"Ah, but that's the beauty of this plan, my lady," Kalan Hawksword announced, stepping out from behind the Seeing Stone. "They're merely the players in this little theatrical act. Perhaps you'd like to meet the audience?"

Before Alija had a chance to react to the surprise appearance of Kalan Hawksword, the Lower Arrion, Bruno Sanval, and the Sorcerers' Collective's Chief Librarian, Dikorian Frye, emerged from their concealed hiding place behind the massive monolith, their expressions grave. She stared at them, realising what their discussion must have sounded like to these men.

These men whose integrity was beyond reproach.

These men who could impeach her.

"This is ludicrous!" she exclaimed, staring Kalan down. "You can't possibly imagine this little charade proves anything other than your mother's willingness to do anything to destroy me."

Bruno's brow furrowed. "Kalan's mother? The Princess Marla? This has nothing to do with her, Lady Alija."

Alija shook her head in disbelief. "Show yourself, Marla!" she shouted, her words echoing off the temple walls. "You've had your fun! Now come out here and face me!"

"My lady . . ." Dikorian began. "Really . . . there is nobody here but us."

"Have the guts to face me, you craven bitch!" she screeched to the empty hall.

There was no answer, of course. Marla wasn't there.

She didn't need to be, Alija realised with a sinking heart.

Was never going to be.

Once again, Alija had fallen into a trap set by Marla, this one disguised by another trap so devious nobody would think to look further for the real poison that lay at the heart of it.

Alija turned and faced her accusers. "This was never about the Fardohnyans, was it?"

"You must have thought us all deranged fools, my lady," Kalan replied, apparently quite amused by her gullibility. "Why would we bother to concoct such an absurdly complicated plot, when your own actions condemn you far more thoroughly than anything we could have thought up?" The young woman smiled even wider, unable to hide her glee. "I can't believe you actually fell for it." She glanced across at the assassin, and bowed in acknowledgment of his skill. "You're a better salesman than I suspected, Master Miar."

Kalan's smug superiority was enough to make Alija nauseous, but the assassin's betrayal was incomprehensible.

"What of you?" she demanded of Galon. "How long have you been part of this conspiracy?"

"Since the day I found my father's head cleaved in two by your henchmen, Alija."

"That was more than twenty-five years ago!"

"Timing is everything, don't you agree?"

"You lied to me!" she hissed.

"Never once," he told her. "You just never asked the right questions."

"And you?" she asked Wrayan, finally. "This is your idea of vengeance, I suppose?"

"Actually, I harbour much less angst toward you than you'd imagine," he told her with a shrug, his black eyes a constant reminder of her helplessness. "You did try to kill me, admittedly—the details of which I've been more than happy to apprise these gentlemen of—but thanks to you, I got to meet the Harshini. So I suppose, in a twisted sort of way, I should be grateful."

"He's been to Sanctuary," Bruno added, his voice filled with awe.

"And you *believe* such nonsense?" she asked, turning on the old man, recognising the light of fanaticism in his eyes. Wrayan must have spun quite a tale indeed to get Bruno on his side. "You're a senile fool, Bruno, who'll swallow anything that lets him think his lifelong quest hasn't been a complete waste of time! What's your excuse, Dikorian? Did I once run over your dog in my carriage, or are you Kagan Palenovar's long lost twin, emerging out of hiding after all these years to seek vengeance for his death, too?"

"You killed your predecessor, too?" the librarian gasped. The big man shook his head with a heavy sigh. "I thought I couldn't be any more surprised by your viciousness, my lady."

"My *viciousness*?" she demanded. "Everything I have done, I have done for my country!"

Dikorian was unmoved by her declaration. "You just admitted you killed the former High Arrion, Kagan Palenovar. You attempted to kill Wrayan Lightfinger, a member of the Sorcerers' Collective, my lady, and I just heard you confess you ordered the murder of over thirty other innocent souls, including a ruling lord, not to mention commissioning yet another murder in our presence only a few moments ago. I have no need of some vague notions of vengeance to recognise a homicidal tyrant when I see one."

She couldn't believe they were condemning her for things she had done to save Hythria from ruin. "I have done nothing but try to protect my nation from a despot! And you dare to call me *homicidal*? Have you done a head count of the palace slaves lately? How many has Lernen killed while you cheerfully turned a blind eye to his excesses?"

"Lernen Wolfblade has never killed anyone who wasn't his slave," Dikorian pointed out. "That is his right. However, nobody, not even the High Arrion, has the right to kill free men. Or to kill a man to open up an opportunity for promotion. If you think you can justify your actions, then by all means, do so. But you'll have to do it at your trial, my lady. It is the proper forum."

"A *trial*? Don't be ridiculous! Who will preside? The High *Prince*?"

"Uncle Lernen will like that," Kalan said with a smug little smile. "You know how he likes to dress up."

"You have no authority to do this to me!"

"A sorcerer may be accused and forced to answer to a trial by her peers," Bruno reminded her. "It is the law."

"I see only three of you."

"Wrayan Lightfinger never formally left the Sorcerers' Collective, my lady," Kalan pointed out. "He's still a member. That's the law, too. I looked it up."

Alija took a step back, gathering her power to her. "I will die before I allow you to dishonour me or my family name in this manner!"

"That can be arranged, my lady," Kalan offered. "In fact, it would be much cleaner for everyone if you just fell on your sword. Does anybody have a sword handy?"

"Behave, Kalan," Wrayan scolded. "We'll handle this the right way."

Dikorian took a step closer and raised his arm, indicating she should precede him out of the temple. "If you please, my lady. Let's not make this any more difficult than it already is."

"Make me!" she dared him defiantly.

"I will have you physically removed from the temple if you force us," Bruno assured her, his voice filled with regret. "I beg you, my lady, retain what dignity you have left. For your sons' sake, if not your own."

With a scream, Alija let out a burst of power that sent both Bruno Sanval and Dikorian Frye slamming into the Seeing Stone. Feeling Galon move behind her, she spun around and used another burst of power to toss him across the temple, his body sliding along the polished mosaic floor, until he came to rest against one of the decorated pillars that supported the high domed roof. Then she turned her attention to Kalan and Wrayan, who stood side by side, watching her fury but apparently unmoved by it.

"You're next!" she announced, pointing at Kalan. "Your mother seems to deal with losing husbands and slaves well enough. Let's see how she deals with losing a child."

Alija raised her hand, gathering what she had left of her power, aware that she was draining it faster than she could replenish it. It made no difference, she decided. She was done for, whatever happened. Besides, Wrayan—the only one here who could challenge her magically—was part Harshini. He might be more powerful than she was in theory, but he could do no harm, which was the only thing she could think of that would account for his lack of action thus far.

Or she might have been too quick for him. It had taken her only seconds to incapacitate her foes.

"I'm not going to let you hurt Kalan," Wrayan informed her calmly, stepping between Alija and her intended victim.

"Do you really think you can stop me?"

Wrayan didn't answer her verbally. He didn't have to. Almost before she'd finished speaking a headache of monumental proportions began building in her skull. Taken completely unawares by the sudden pain, Alija clutched at her head and collapsed to her knees.

Alija looked up at Wrayan, but his unnaturally youthful

face was expressionless. The pain kept on building in her head, the pressure beyond description. She felt a trickle coming from her nose and realised it was bleeding. There were tears in her eyes from the pain, but when she tried to wipe them away she realised they were tears of blood, not brine. With her brain feeling like it was set to explode, she cried out in agony as her eardrums splintered and blood began to spill from them, too. All the while, Wrayan watched her impassively, Kalan Hawksword standing just behind his shoulder, her expression just as distant. Just as unforgiving.

"No . . ." Alija gasped helplessly, doubled over with the agony. This was beyond torture, beyond pain. A red haze swam before her eyes, but she couldn't tell if it was blood or pain that caused it. "Stop . . ." she gasped. "*Mercy . . .*"

"Enough, Wrayan," she thought she heard Kalan say. "You're killing her."

"Isn't this what you wanted?"

Alija thought Wrayan said the words to Kalan, but then she realised the words came from inside her mind. *Isn't this what you crave, Alija? Access to the power of the Harshini?*

Wrayan had entered her mind, she realised, as effortlessly as a knife slicing through warm butter.

Panic filled her at the realisation that he could do such a thing so easily. *What have you done to me?*

I've done nothing, Alija, except open your mind to the possibilities. This is the power you wanted. Don't you recognise it? It's the same power you accessed the time you burned out my mind. Pity you're only an Innate, though, and don't have that spell to protect you from it this time. Didn't Brak tell you how dangerous it was, for a human Innate to attempt to access the power of the Harshini? It could kill you, you know.

Truly filled with fear for the first time since she discovered she was one of those rare humans who could skim the surface of Harshini magic, Alija tried to pull away. But it was too late. The power had a hold of her and it was drawing her down. She had no natural defences against it.

The pressure kept on building in her mind, blood vessels

bursting under the strain. Consciousness was slipping fast. It was all she could do to remain on her hands and knees. Her fingernails were bleeding now, too, and she had lost the power to speak, her mouth filled with the metallic taste of blood mixed with immeasurable terror.

I'll tell them you died in an magical accident, Wrayan's voice assured her. *That you tried to draw too much power to yourself. No need for anybody outside this temple to learn of your disgrace.*

Except Marla, came the unbidden thought. *She'll know.*

Yes, Wrayan agreed. *She'll know.*

The pain was so intense she wondered that she was still able to form a coherent thought. But she had room for one idea. One final wish.

Curse you, Wrayan Lightfinger. And a curse on the Wolf-blades, too. All of them.

CHAPTER 66

"Damn this rain!"

Already the sound of the approaching battle could be heard in the distance. Damin looked out over the rolling hills around Lasting Drift, frustrated that he had no way of knowing if everything was going according to plan. They were gathered on the knoll of a small hill just out of sight of the Norsell River, waiting for the signal that the Fardohnyans were moving into their trap, but it was a long and frustrating wait and Damin was going a little bit crazy with impatience. Thunder rolled off the distant hills and rain was spitting down in large, sporadic drops, a warning of what was yet to come.

"It's going to make it hard to see," Narvell agreed, looking up at his brother. The Elasapine heir was squatting beside

Almodavar, watching the wily old captain draw something in the dirt.

"Do you think it'll help them or us?"

"Neither," Almodavar concluded. Damin had thought he was doodling on the ground with a stick, but on second glance he realised he was drawing out a map of the battlefield. Damin glanced down at it, wondering what he was up to.

"How long do you think we have before they get here?"

The captain shrugged. "Not long. The scouts will let us know. The trick isn't them getting here, though. It will be getting across the bridges and closing the pincers behind them at the right time *after* they get here."

Damin smiled. "I remember Elezaar telling me once that the enemy invariably attacks on one of two occasions, when you're ready for him . . ."

"And when you're not ready for him," Narvell finished for him.

Damin studied the map in the dirt and then looked down at Almodavar. "Where do you suppose Regis is now?"

The old Raider looked up at Damin and pointed to the map he'd sketched in the dirt.

"You old fox," Damin chuckled, as he realised why Almodavar was so interested in his rough map of the surrounding terrain.

"What?" Narvell asked, a little confused.

"Unless Regis is one of those fools who likes to lead from the front and get himself killed in the first few moments of the fight, I'm guessing he's back here somewhere," Almodavar surmised, poking a stick at the location. "With his cavalry. He'll want to see how the battle goes before he commits them."

"Then our brilliant ambush may not be as brilliant as we'd like," Damin agreed, "if he's got another five or six thousand fresh troops who can come up behind us."

"You mean if he hesitates before he commits them?" Narvell asked.

Almodavar nodded. "When he sees our flanks that were

so easily broken in the earlier part of the attack suddenly starting to regroup, he's going to know what's going on."

"By then he may have no choice but to follow," Narvell suggested.

Damin shrugged. "Perhaps. His only other option will be to abandon his infantry and try to get away with his cavalry intact."

"A man who runs from a fight he can't win is a man still looking for a fight he can," Almodavar reminded them.

"So is Regis the type to cut his losses and run, or the sort who'll fight a glorious but futile battle to the bitter end?"

"I'm guessing the former," Almodavar said. "Hablet's a nasty piece of work, but he knows real talent when he sees it. If this man was smart enough to get command of Hablet's army for this campaign, he's not the selfless, self-sacrificing type. I suspect he'll cut and run in the hopes of either making it back to Fardohnya or making a last stand somewhere he can do some real damage."

"Back up the valley," Damin concluded. "There's nowhere else he can go but west."

The old captain looked up at Damin. "We probably should do something about that."

Damin grinned at the old man. "We probably should, shouldn't we?"

Narvell looked at his brother and then the captain, shaking his head as it dawned on him what the others were suggesting. "No way! You're not leaving me here to fight the battle while you two go off chasing rainbows!"

Because Damin had brought only cavalry with him from Krakandar, his troops and the remainder of Narvell's Elasapine light cavalry made up most of the left flank that would close in behind the Fardohnyans. Cyrus Eaglespike and his Dregian cavalry made up the right flank, while across the end of the valley at Lasting Drift, the remainder of the infantry—the most experienced men drawn from every province in Hythria—and the re-formed Sunrise archers waited for the oncoming army with growing impatience. Discipline held them in check, however, just as it would ensure they moved at the right time; of that Damin was quite certain.

They should have had another two or three thousand Raiders to deploy but there had been no sign of them, nor word from Krakandar about why they'd never arrived. It was a problem that niggled at the back of Damin's mind constantly, but one he couldn't spare the time to deal with right now. This battle had to be fought with what they had at hand, not what might have been.

"You can handle the left flank without my help, little brother," Damin assured him. "Think what Charel will say when he hears about your glorious victory!"

"Think what Cyrus Eaglespike will say when he finds out you ran away from the fight, Damin."

"Think what the fool will have to say when we capture the Fardohnyan general and his damned cavalry," Almodavar suggested.

Narvell glared at both of them. "You're as bad as he is, Almodavar."

Damin frowned, a little annoyed to think Narvell assumed he was suggesting this just for a bit of light entertainment. "I'm not just doing this for fun, you know, Narvell. If Regis gets away today with his cavalry intact, we're going to have to do this all over again, either tomorrow or a week from now, or a month from now. This damned war will drag on for ages. Let's be done with it, here and now."

"You *are* doing this for fun," Narvell accused. "I don't care how many clever ways you've come up with to rationalise it. And since when did you care if the war drags on for a bit, Damin? You like war."

"I like the idea of killing Mahkas better."

"What's Mahkas got to do with it?"

"The last discussion Mahkas and I had about Leila and Starros was interrupted by the unfortunate need to keep him alive. I believe we have some rather important unfinished business."

Narvell stared at his brother, and then turned to the captain.

"Don't look at me for help," Almodavar warned. "I think he's right."

"You're both mad," Narvell announced, rising to his feet. "How many men are you taking or do you think the two of you are enough?"

"No more than a dozen," Damin told him.

"You really are insane."

"I'm not trying to confront the Fardohnyan cavalry, Narvell, or capture them single-handedly. The idea is to find Regis and have him surrender them. A small band can move faster and has a much better chance of slipping through the enemy lines than a whole century of Raiders. Besides, you need them here."

"I need *you* here," his brother pointed out unhappily.

"No, you don't," he assured Narvell with an encouraging slap on the back. "Think of this as your opportunity to show the world what you're made of. One that doesn't involve you and I having to shed each other's blood at regular intervals."

"Cyrus is going to explode when he hears about this," Narvell warned.

"Only if we fail," Damin pointed out reasonably. "Think you can handle things here?"

Narvell sighed at his brother's folly, and then he seemed to change his mind after thinking about it for a time. He shrugged, perhaps accepting the futility of trying to dissuade Damin when Almodavar was supporting him. "You'd better be right about this, brother, or you're going to look like a coward *and* a fool."

"I am right," Damin promised. "And by this evening, we'll have the Fardohnyan surrender. You mark my words."

Skirting the thinly forested foothills of Lasting Drift, Damin, Almodavar and their handpicked men got a unique overview of the battle from the heights. For the average soldier in the thick of it, a man's view was rarely more than his own fight for survival and what was happening in the few feet surrounding him. The big picture was something he learned about afterward, something gleaned by anecdote and rumour, sitting around the camp fires after the day was won.

The view Damin received was vastly different as he watched the battle progress while they made their way northwest to where they assumed (and fervently hoped) Axelle Regis was directing the conflict.

As the enemy passed the river crossings and reached the ambush at Lasting Drift, the Hythrun mobilised the remaining cavalry and the pincers began to close, advancing against the Fardohnyan infantry on the wings which, until then, had only skirmished with the Izcomdar light horse. Attacked on both sides, the Fardohnyans were taken completely by surprise, their progress checked as soon as the echelons emerged from hiding.

By the time Damin and his handpicked squad turned toward the small valley where they figured Axelle was holding his cavalry in reserve, the Fardohnyans had been forced to a halt, fronting the enemy on all sides.

After that, it was—as Damin had predicted—like spearing fish in a barrel. The low foothills rang with the sounds of battle as the enemy was attacked every way they turned by the Hythrun infantry with short swords, by the cavalry with javelins and by the devastating accuracy of the mounted Hythrun short bows, the Raiders rarely missing in the densely packed mass.

"It'll be all over soon," Almodavar remarked, urging his mount up the slope beside Damin as they watched the Fardohnyans being pushed back, relentlessly crowded together. Without hope of relief, they probably expected death and fought as if their only hope of salvation was to honour the God of War before they died. The carnage sickened Damin a little. It was one thing to win a glorious victory, but there came a point when triumph moved to slaughter, then war no longer seemed quite as splendid as one imagined.

"We need Regis to surrender before this war is done. And we need to stop him sending in his reserves in a last-ditch attempt to save the day. He could still take this if he can move his cavalry up quickly enough."

"If he's watching this and has even the slightest humanity in him," Almodavar disagreed, "he'll already be considering surrender."

"Let's go make it easier for him, shall we?"

The old captain nodded and turned his horse away. Damin followed a few moments later, thinking how easily the shine came off a glorious victory once it became tarnished with blood.

chapter 67

Emilie's concern about Mahkas Damaran's condition proved well founded. The Regent of Krakandar appeared to be suffering from blood poisoning, a direct result of the infected and ulcerated sore on his right forearm. It was the physician's opinion that the scar Mahkas fiddled with so obsessively in times of stress harboured a tiny fragment of metal, a leftover from some long-forgotten skirmish, and it had worked its way to the surface, exacerbated by Mahkas's relentless worrying at it. Since his discovery of Leila and Starros and his descent into undisguised madness, he'd barely left the scar alone and it had eventually become infected. Unless the wound was lanced and cleaned of the poison, it was likely to kill him.

The palace physician, Darian Coe, who'd come to Krakandar some fifteen years ago when Damin's stepsister, Rielle Tirstone, was presented with her first *court'esa*, explained the situation to Luciena, Xanda, Bylinda and Emilie, after he'd tried unsuccessfully—yet again—to treat Mahkas's injury. The regent would have none of his ministrations, convinced Darian Coe was an assassin sent by his nephew, Damin Wolfblade, to have him killed.

"Is he really going to die, Mama?" Emilie asked with

concern. Luciena wasn't happy about Emilie being included in this meeting, but she'd been keeping Bylinda company when Darian arrived to inform Xanda and Luciena of the situation and they'd come to the Lady of Krakandar's room, not realising their daughter was here. Given the child's affection for Mahkas (misplaced though Luciena believed it was) and the fact Emilie was so worried about him, she decided to let the child stay.

"He should be all right if I can clean the wound, my lady," Darian assured the little girl. "But he won't even let me get a close look at it."

"Suppose we just do it by force?" Xanda suggested. "If I get enough men in there, we can hold him down while you cut this infection out."

The handsome former *court'esa* shook his head. "Given Lord Damaran's current state of mind, that would probably just make things worse."

"I agree with Darian," Luciena said. "He's likely to go crazy if he sees you marching into his room with a troop of burly Raiders, all there for the sole purpose of restraining him."

"We can't let him die from an infected arm, Luciena," Xanda reminded her.

"He has to keep his oath," Bylinda added. Nobody was really sure what she meant, but she talked a lot about keeping oaths these days. Suddenly she gripped Emilie by the hand. "Don't you listen to their lies, child. They swear they'll do it, but they don't. I'm still waiting for him to keep his oath."

With a grimace, Emilie extracted her hand from Bylinda's grasp. "I'll not listen to anybody's lies," she promised, clearly with no more idea than the adults what Bylinda was talking about. She frowned uncertainly and looked to her parents for help, but Bylinda's words meant nothing to them, either.

"Could *you* talk to him, Aunt Bylinda?" Xanda asked. "Perhaps he'll listen to you. You must press on him the importance of allowing a physician to treat him."

"I'm still waiting for him to keep his oath," she replied with such a vague expression on her face, Luciena wondered if she'd heard a word anybody had said.

"I could talk to him, Papa," Emilie volunteered.

"Out of the question!" Luciena declared.

"Now, now, Luci . . . let's not be hasty," Xanda cautioned, looking at their daughter curiously. "Why do you think Mahkas would listen to you, Em?"

"Because he likes me." She shrugged, as if the reason were self-evident. "I remind him of Leila."

Darian Coe seemed to be on Emilie's side. "The child speaks the truth, my lord. He often mistakes your daughter for his own."

"I hope your intention of telling us that, Darian Coe, wasn't to reassure us our child is in no danger from him," Luciena remarked with a worried expression.

"Of course not, my lady," the physician replied with an apologetic bow. "I merely make note of the fact in passing. But you have nothing to fear in any case. Mahkas Damaran is in no condition to hurt anybody but himself at the moment."

"So why don't we just wait until he falls unconscious and treat him then?" Xanda asked.

"By then it will probably be too late to save him, my lord."

"I'm still waiting for him to keep his oath," Bylinda said, as if she was taking part in another conversation none of the others was privy to.

"Please, Papa," Emilie begged. "Let me help. I can talk to Uncle Mahkas. I'll make him let Darian fix his arm."

With some reluctance, Xanda nodded in agreement. "Perhaps you should talk to him, sweetheart. Do you know what to say to him?"

Emilie nodded solemnly. She was a bright child, even if she did have a blind spot where Mahkas was concerned. But perhaps that was Luciena and Xanda's fault. They'd gone to great pains to keep what had happened in this place from their children. "I have to tell him what Darian just said. That his arm is making him sick and if the wound isn't cleaned and treated, he'll die from it."

"Do you think you can make him understand how important this is?"

"Yes, Papa."

"Xanda, you can't be serious about letting her . . ."

"We don't have a choice, Luciena. We can't let Mahkas die."

It was only the presence of Bylinda and Emilie that prevented Luciena from replying, *"Why the hell not?"*

Far from being repulsed by Mahkas's infected arm, Emilie Taranger was morbidly fascinated by it, a fact that left Luciena shaking her head in despair. It took the child less than an hour to convince Mahkas he should let Darian Coe treat his arm, although he did insist Emilie stay with him throughout the entire procedure, to keep him company.

Luciena wondered if Mahkas made Emilie's presence a condition of the treatment simply to bolster his own courage. Although she had no sympathy for him, she knew he was in unbearable pain. Perhaps, with Emilie there to be brave for, he'd have the nerve to suffer through Darian Coe slicing into his badly swollen and infected arm and digging around for the tiny shard causing him all this trouble.

Darian was still setting up when Luciena arrived. Emilie was sitting on Mahkas's bed, chatting to him as the physician arranged his tools. Mahkas was propped up on a mountain of pillows, his arm resting on another pillow. His face was strained and he was sweating profusely, clearly in agony.

A moment after Luciena arrived, Xanda appeared behind her with two large Raiders. Mahkas said something to Emilie they couldn't hear and then glared at his nephew, obviously displeased about something.

"Uncle Mahkas wants to know why the soldiers are here, Papa," Emilie asked from the bed. With his throat so damaged that he couldn't speak louder than a whisper, he needed Emilie to relay his messages.

"They're here in case you need help, Uncle," Xanda explained. "This is liable to be very painful, and—"

Mahkas's gesticulating cut Xanda off. He whispered something to Emilie and then pointed angrily toward the door.

"He says he doesn't need anybody to hold him down."

Xanda shrugged. "As you wish." He turned and ordered the guards to wait outside and then looked at Luciena helplessly.

"If we had any sense at all," she told him in a low voice, "we'd start the evacuation tonight. While he's too sick to notice what's happening."

"The thought had crossed my mind."

"But?"

· "We're not ready yet . . . and if he doesn't . . ." Xanda hesitated, unwilling to finish the sentence. "Well . . . there may not be a need."

She knew what her husband really meant was that if Mahkas died, there would be no need to evacuate the city. And much as she might hope for it, that outcome was a double-edged sword. Mahkas's death would relieve the immediate problems in Krakandar, but they would just make things worse in greater Hythria. Another province under the control of Alija Eaglespike was something Luciena was prepared to do almost anything to prevent. Even keeping Mahkas Damaran alive.

"Uncle Mahkas wants to know what you're whispering about," Emilie called.

Luciena turned toward the bed, smiling. "We were discussing your quite remarkable ability to avoid your lessons, young lady. Once this is over, I expect Uncle Mahkas will be sending you back to the nursery where you belong."

Emilie grinned at her mother and turned to Mahkas. "You're not going to send me back to the nursery, are you, Uncle Mahkas? It's full of horrible little boys."

Mahkas smiled, patting her arm reassuringly with a shake of his head.

"See! Uncle Mahkas says I'm not missing anything. Besides, I read better than Aleesha. She can't teach me anything."

Sadly, Emilie was probably correct. And in a way, Luciena didn't blame her daughter for constantly trying to escape the nursery. With her two brothers and the four young Lionsclaw children down there, it really was full of horrible little boys at the moment.

"I'm ready to start as soon as you are, my lady," Darian advised, finally happy with the arrangement of his scalpels.

Xanda leaned forward and kissed her cheek. "I'll see you when you're done then. I'm heading into the city to check on a few things." What Xanda neglected to mention was that he was taking this opportunity to meet with Starros and his friends to work on some last-minute details of their evacuation plan. He looked at Mahkas and smiled encouragingly. "I suppose this will all be over and you'll be fighting fit again by the time I get back, Uncle Mahkas."

His uncle nodded wanly and whispered something to Emilie.

"He says if you open the city gates while he's sick, he'll have you castrated. What does castrated mean, Papa?"

"Nothing you need bother yourself with, sweetheart," her father replied. He frowned at his uncle but said nothing further, leaving Luciena alone with Darian, Emilie and Mahkas.

After that, Darian Coe took over. He explained what he intended to do to both his patient and to Luciena, who had volunteered to assist him mostly so she could stay and keep an eye on Emilie. It sounded straightforward enough. Darian intended to slice into the centre of the infected area, clean it, and then hopefully find the metal fragment causing all this woe, remove it, debride the lesion of all the dead and dying tissue, flush the wound and then let the maggots do the rest, eating the diseased flesh and leaving a clean area he could stitch closed at a later time.

Once he finished his explanation, the former *court'esa* glanced down at his patient. "Are you sure you don't want anything to bite on, my lord? The draught I gave you will take the edge off the pain, but it's still going to hurt like hell."

"Just do it!" Mahkas rasped. With his left hand he took

Emilie's hand in his and smiled at the child. "Leila is here. She'll help me bear it."

"My name is Emilie, Uncle Mahkas."

"Yes . . . I know . . . Emilie . . ."

"What do you want me to do?" Luciena asked the slave.

"Pass me the instruments as I ask for them. And try to keep the wound clear of blood so I can see what I'm doing. That jug there is full of boiled water. I'll need you to wash the wound thoroughly before I release the maggots."

Darian picked up one of his scalpels laid out on the tray beside the bed and then turned to Mahkas. "Are you sure you're ready for this, my lord?"

"Do it," he croaked. His face sheened with sweat, Mahkas turned his face away, fixing his gaze on Emilie. A moment later, with infinite care and a sudden burst of foul air as the pus in the wound was released, Darian Coe sliced his way into Mahkas's infected arm.

Mahkas never uttered a sound as Darian worked, a fact that astonished Luciena. Just watching the physician at work was making her ill, but Mahkas bore the agony with stoic acceptance.

Perhaps it was something to do with his madness. Perhaps, along with his inability to comprehend emotional pain, the ability to feel physical pain had been affected, too. Luciena wasn't sure, but in a way she was glad. Emilie was watching with intense interest as her mother swabbed at the wound so Darian could find the tiny shard. She didn't seem to notice the foul smell, or be bothered by the blood and pus seeping from the dead and dying flesh of her uncle's forearm. Had Mahkas been thrashing around, screaming in agony, Luciena guessed, her daughter might not be nearly so enchanted with the whole disgusting spectacle.

"There it is!" Darian exclaimed.

Luciena and Emilie both leaned forward as Darian gently lifted a bloodied lump from the wound with a thin pair of tongs. To Luciena, the strange object looked too small to have caused so much trouble. In fact it looked like a bright blue thorn.

"What is it?"

"I have no idea," the *court'esa* shrugged. "I doubt it's metal, though. It shows no sign of rust or decay."

"So it's not the tip of an arrow or a spear, then?" Emilie asked. "Can I see it?"

She held out her hand. Darian dropped the bloodied little blue thorn into her palm. Emilie examined it curiously and then held it out to her uncle. "Did you want to see it, Uncle Mahkas?"

Mahkas shook his head and turned his face away.

"Emilie! Put that down. It's disgusting!"

"But don't you want to know what it is, Mama?"

"Whatever it is, it was in pretty deep," Darian remarked, as he started to cut away the dead flesh. "It's taken years to find its way out. You can see the track of scar tissue in the muscle where it's worked its way up."

"Really?" Emilie asked, thoroughly fascinated, still holding the bloodied shard. "Show me!"

"Don't be so morbid, Emilie," Luciena scolded. "And get rid of that thing."

"Can I keep it?"

"I suggest you wash it first," the slave recommended.

"Can I, Mama?"

"*Why*, for pity's sake?"

"As a souvenir," she announced. "I've decided I'm going to be a physician, too, and this will be a reminder of my very first operation."

Luciena despaired, convinced her only daughter was beyond redemption. "Keep it if you must," she sighed, not wishing to make an issue of it in front of Mahkas. "Just make sure you do what Darian says and wash it. Properly. And don't go around showing it to people. They'll think there's something wrong with you."

"More water, please, my lady."

Luciena washed the wound again as Emilie turned her attention back to her gruesome souvenir. It was then that Luciena noticed Mahkas's eyes were closed, his face relaxed. For a brief moment, she wondered if he was dead, but then she saw the gentle rise and fall of his chest and realised he had, regretfully, just passed out from the pain.

CHAPTER 68

T hey're here," the scout informed Damin, Almodavar and the rest of their small band, pointing to another rough map drawn in the mud a couple of hours later. The rain was pelting down relentlessly, smacking the oiled cape they were using for shelter during this brief halt in their pursuit of the Fardohnyan general and his missing cavalry. It was a bit more than two hours since the ambush closed around the Fardohnyans. Damin figured the death toll must already be in the thousands. If the man had any human feeling at all, getting Regis to surrender might be as easy as giving him the opportunity.

He turned to Almodavar. "You were wrong."

"How so?"

"You assumed they'd set up their command post here," he reminded him, pointing to another spot on the map a bare inch from where the scout had indicated. "You're out by a whole . . . hundred yards, I reckon."

Almodavar rolled his eyes and turned to the scout. "How many?"

"In the command tent? About half a dozen, including Lord Regis. Plus a constant stream of messengers."

"It's not going to be easy sneaking up on him," the old captain surmised. "He commands an almost three-hundred-and-sixty-degree view of the terrain. Where are the cavalry?"

"Back here," the scout replied, pointing to another small valley between two hills just to the north of the Fardohnyan command post. "I gather they're just waiting for the word to move."

"He won't give it," Damin predicted.

"Are you sure?" Almodavar asked.

Damin pointed further down the rough map. "They're too far back. The spot he's chosen would have been fine at the start of the day—I'd have chosen it too, if it were my decision—but his army's been drawn too far down the valley. He might have had a chance if he mobilised the moment our lines looked like breaking, but he's left it too late. If he sent out the cavalry now, we'd have a good half hour to mount a counterattack before they got to the actual battle."

The scout nodded in agreement. "He didn't sound like a man about to mobilise anything. Mostly he sounded as if he was trying to reduce the damage by getting the stragglers to pull back."

"How close were you able to get?"

"Close enough to hear them talking," the scout replied, squatting down to indicate his route on the map. "The only way to approach without being seen is along the northern ridge of the hill here. The overhang gives you protection from being spotted from above. After that, if you scale the cliff on the north western side of the hill, you can get close enough to hear what they're saying."

"And if we go over the cliff?"

"Then we could take them from behind," the scout suggested. "They won't even know we're there until we're running them through."

"We have to scale a cliff, though?" Almodavar asked doubtfully.

"It's not that high." The scout shrugged. "Forty, maybe fifty feet."

"You can stay and mind the horses if you're getting too old for this sort of thing, Almodavar," Damin offered.

The old man glared at him. "You worry about yourself, lad, and I'll worry about what I'm getting too old for."

Damin expected no other answer. He turned and looked around the circle of faces, all huddled under the oiled cape. "Let's do this, then," he declared. "And no unnecessary killing. Wound if you have to, but I don't want anybody accidentally killing Regis. He can't surrender his damned cavalry if he's dead. And given there's only fourteen of us, I'd rather we didn't have to capture them the hard way."

"Sire?" one of the men asked, obviously not sure what he meant.

"He means we might have a bit of a problem surrounding five thousand men and convincing them to throw down their arms," Almodavar explained.

"I don't know," the scout joked. "Fourteen Hythrun Raiders against five thousand Fardohnyan light horse? Seems a fairly even fight to me."

"If only your skill matched your ability to brag about it, Noran," Almodavar lamented, shaking his head at the young man's foolishness.

"How will we know which one is Lord Regis?" one of the others asked.

"We won't know," Damin said. "Hence the order to avoid unnecessary killing. Any questions?"

The silence that greeted his question was enough for Damin.

He smiled. "Let's go hunt Fardohnyan."

Scaling a steep rock face in the rain with no ropes while wearing full battle gear was, Damin Wolfblade decided about halfway up the cliff, an experience he could well have done without. It wasn't so much the height. Damin had spent enough nights as a boy watching the city lights of Krakandar while perched on the palace roof for the drop to hold no fear for him. And it was by no means a sheer cliff. Weathered and broken in places, it offered plenty of hand and footholds for the ambitious climber. No, what made it terrifying was the rain. The cliff was slimy. Tiny rivulets of water trickled down the rocks, merging in places to form full-blown waterfalls. It was perilously slippery and with the added weight of leather armour and his weapons, Damin was dangerously off-balance. He could appreciate why Regis had chosen this place as his command post. Only a madman would think climbing up the treacherous cliff behind him was a viable option.

A few feet from the top, Damin stopped and signalled his men to do likewise. The rain was starting to relent and he could just make out the enemy voices. They were speaking Fardohnyan and although he understood the language, he couldn't quite make out what they were saying.

Carefully, Damin moved a little further up. Any noise now would give them away and the rain, which up until a moment ago he'd been roundly cursing, was easing off and no longer offering them cover. As slowly as he dared, Damin raised his eyes over the rim of the cliff and then jerked his head back again as a pair of booted feet approached. Waving his men down, Damin froze against the muddy cliff face.

The boots stopped just above Damin's head.

He held his breath, praying to Zegarnald to protect them, wondering what had drawn the man out into the rain and over to the edge where one glance down would reveal the dozen or more Hythrun Raiders climbing up the cliff. A moment later, Damin had his answer when a thin stream of liquid shot over the side, mingling with the rain until it vanished below. He glanced across at the man beside him, the scout, Noran, who had already climbed this cliff once today. The man grinned and rolled his eyes and then pointed upward. A few moments later the stream stopped and presumably the urinating Fardohnyan had returned to the shelter of the command pavilion. Just to be certain, Damin silently counted to twenty in his head, and then once again inched his eyes over the edge of the cliff. This time the small plateau was clear, only the back of the pavilion visible.

With a final heave over the edge, Damin lay flat against the wet ground as the others moved up behind him. Glancing around, he did a quick count and discovered all twelve of his men and Almodavar, who looked no more bothered by the climb than the men half his age, were accounted for. He climbed to his feet, signalled his men to fan out to surround the pavilion, and then, just as the final raindrops fell, gave the order to attack.

The command pavilion was really just a large square tent with three sides rolled up to give a clear view of the countryside. Regis obviously wasn't a man concerned with aesthetics so much as practicality.

"Ollie, take word to Captain Jerris," Damin heard a man ordering as they closed in. "Tell him we're pulling back."

"Ollie," Damin suggested in Fardohnyan, as he and his Raiders surrounded the open pavilion with drawn swords, "how about you stay right where you are, my friend."

With no advance warning of their approach, the half-dozen Fardohnyans inside were taken completely by surprise. Almost before Damin had finished speaking, the officers were disarmed and on their knees, swords to their throats. Everyone, that is, except the young messenger, Ollie, and the man who was issuing the orders.

His sword still drawn, Damin turned to the older man. He was dark-haired and swarthy, and much younger than Damin was expecting, perhaps only in his mid-thirties. "Lord Axelle Regis, I presume?"

The Fardohnyan glanced around the pavilion at his captured men and then fixed his gaze on Damin. "Impressive. How did you . . . ah, the cliff. A clever ploy, sneaking up like that."

"I've been practising my sneaking manoeuvre on my stepsister," Damin informed him. "It worked a treat with her, too. Almodavar?"

"Yes, your highness?"

"Set a perimeter. I don't want any surprises until we're done here."

The old captain signalled four of the men to follow, leaving the rest to watch over the six Fardohnyans they'd already captured.

"Your *highness*?" Regis repeated with a raised brow.

"I'm sorry. Did I forget to introduce myself? How rude of me. I am Damin Wolfblade."

Regis looked him up and down, clearly sceptical. "*You're* the Wolfblade heir?"

"You seem unconvinced."

The Fardohnyan general shrugged. "The intelligence we received about Damin Wolfblade, sir, does not lend one to expect a man who would scale a cliff in the rain with a dozen men to capture an entire army."

"Well, that's what you get for listening to gossip. Your sword please?"

"You're assuming I'm going to surrender."

"If you want to die, I'd be happy to oblige, Lord Regis."

The Fardohnyan hesitated. "What are your terms?" he asked, although he made no move to give up either his weapon or his army.

"You sound the surrender and we'll stop butchering every man you have on the field at present."

Regis glanced around, perhaps debating his chances of calling for help. "If this was Fardohnya and our roles reversed, we wouldn't offer you mercy."

Damin raised his sword and pointed it at Axelle Regis's heart. "You mistake practicality for mercy, my lord. I have other plans for you and your men."

Regis thought on that, looked down at the sword against his breast and then glanced to the north, where the hidden cavalry lay in wait. "I have a cavalry reserve plenty big enough to turn the tide of the battle, your highness."

"Which you've left it too late to deploy," Damin reminded him. "But you don't need me to tell you that. You worked that out about an hour ago, didn't you? The only thing keeping you here now is that you didn't want to be seen abandoning your army."

"Unlike your High Prince who turned tail and ran the moment things started looking a little shaky."

Damin smiled. "Hotly pursued by your infantry, who fell straight into our trap, remember? Do you really have time for this, Lord Regis?"

The Fardohnyan hesitated and then slowly unsheathed his sword. He studied it for a moment, then offered it to Damin, hilt first.

Damin lowered his blade and took the sword from him, bowing in acknowledgment of the general's gesture. "Your surrender is accepted, Lord Regis. Issue the command to your troops."

"I'll need some of these men you've taken prisoner to relay the orders."

Damin allowed Regis to select two officers to carry news of the surrender, both to the cavalry and to the men on the main battlefield, the sound of which could be heard faintly in the distance.

"You'll be held hostage, of course," Damin told Lord Regis, once the men were dispatched. "Pending negotiations for your ransom, your release and your return to Fardohnya."

"I have no care about what happens to me." Regis shrugged. "My life was done for the moment Her Serene Highness set eyes on me. What will happen to my men?"

"They'll be moved back to Winternest," Damin informed him. "We have a mountain pass to clear. A few thousand prisoners of war should do the trick in no time, given it's their only way home. Who is Her Serene Highness?"

"Her Serene Highness, Princess Adrina of Fardohnya," Regis explained. "Hablet's eldest daughter. A demon disguised as a goddess."

Damin looked at him oddly, wondering if the humiliation of defeat hadn't sent the Fardohnyan general just a little bit crazy. "I see . . ."

Regis smiled thinly. "No, your highness, I doubt you do. But it's thanks to her I'm here and thanks to her there's not likely to be an offer of ransom made on my behalf."

"Does she have something against you?"

"She showed an interest in me, your highness. Only a
fleeting one, mind you. I'm sure she did nothing more than
flirt with me to relieve the tedium of the Winter Palace. But
in the eyes of Hablet of Fardohnya, looking at one of his
daughters uninvited means you've probably got your eye on
his throne and that's akin to treason. He doesn't trust his
daughter and the moment she looked at me, he started to
doubt me, too. Hence we find ourselves in this place, you
with a victory and I faced with death no matter which way I
turn."

Damin shook his head, thinking Hablet's court made the
troubles in Hythrun politics seem quite dull. "Is there no
chance you're mistaken?"

"I'm not even sure it wasn't Hablet who blocked the pass,
with the deliberate intention of stranding me here in
Hythria." He turned to the young messenger he'd been talking to when Damin and his men burst in. "Tell them, Ollie.
Tell them the message you brought me from our king."

The young messenger glanced at the Hythrun invaders
nervously. "He said . . . um . . . he said to tell Lord Regis
that his daughter, Her Serene Highness, the Princess Adrina
of Fardohnya, doesn't think he's worth saving. He told me to
tell Lord Regis that at her suggestion, King Hablet was going to abandon the general and his men to their fates."

"Tell him, at my daughter's behest," Regis quoted bitterly,
"we are leaving him to do what he can against the Hythrun
for the greater glory of his king and his family name, but
there will be no further support from Fardohnya."

"And all this because she *flirted* with you?" Damin asked,
shaking his head, partly in sympathy, partly in disbelief.
"What a nasty bitch. I'm sorry."

"You don't need to apologise. The fault is not yours."

A moment later the sound of trumpets echoed across the
foothills—Fardohnyan horns, sounding the surrender. The
noise was followed, a few moments later, by the distant call
of Hythrun horns, declaring victory.

Regis listened to the echoing trumpets with a morose expression and then turned to Damin. "It seems the day is yours, Prince Damin. Congratulations."

Damin glanced down at the curved Fardohnyan sword he was holding. It was heavy and unfamiliar and it represented more than even this Fardohnyan could know.

"Will you ride with me, Lord Regis? To meet the High Prince?"

"Will I be as surprised by him as I have been by you?"

Damin smiled. "Actually, the gossip probably doesn't do him justice. You'll find him to be everything you've heard and then some."

"And yet you follow him loyally?" Regis asked curiously. "Even knowing what he is?"

"I notice knowing what Hablet and his daughter are didn't stop you coming through the Widowmaker," Damin pointed out. "At least Lernen Wolfblade is family."

Regis shrugged. "We men do foolish things for pride and glory."

"Is that why you invaded Hythria? For pride and glory?"

"And to kill you, your uncle and your half-brother," Regis added. "I had quite specific instructions about that."

"Why does Hablet want me dead?" Damin asked. "I've never even met the man."

"He wants all the Wolfblades dead, your highness. I thought you knew that?"

Damin sighed, wondering if there was actually a single soul outside of his immediate family and close allies who didn't want him dead. "Well, he lucked out this time. Shall we go?"

Axelle Regis picked up his oiled cape, swinging it over his shoulders against the rain as he walked away from his command post and into his new role as a prisoner of war, the bitter miasma of defeat hanging over him as if he wore a second cloak woven from despair.

chapter 69

K alan Hawksword led the delegation to visit Princess Marla and inform her of the unfortunate events that had recently taken place at the Sorcerers' Collective. Accompanying her was the acting High Arrion of the Sorcerers' Collective, Bruno Sanval, the assassin, Galon Miar, and the head of the Krakandar Thieves' Guild, Wrayan Lightfinger.

Marla welcomed them into the High Prince's audience chamber, standing just below the podium where her brother normally sat on those rare occasions he was required to actually perform his duties as High Prince.

Bruno greeted Marla with a surprisingly courtly bow when they stopped before her. "Your highness. Thank you for agreeing to see us on such short notice."

Marla smiled warmly at the old man. "How could I refuse such an . . . *eclectic* assembly, my lord?" she replied, casting her gaze over the odd allies. "A sorcerer, an assassin, a thief . . . and my daughter. The reason for your visit intrigues me, Lord Sanval, almost as much as the company you keep."

"You know Master Lightfinger and Master Miar?"

"I'm acquainted with both of them," she agreed. "Although I admit I never expected to see either man in the company of the Lower Arrion of the Sorcerers' Collective. What can I do for you?"

The old man cleared his throat uncomfortably. "There has been an accident, your highness. At the Sorcerers' Collective. Involving the High Arrion."

"Alija?" Marla asked, feigning surprise. "I hope nothing ill has befallen my dearest cousin. Greenharbour just wouldn't be the same without her."

"It's more the ill that has befallen the Sorcerers' Collective," Kalan informed her mother, neither of them betraying the fact that this meeting was not only expected, but almost rehearsed. "Illness that was delivered by the hand of the former High Arrion."

Marla raised a brow and looked at Bruno. "The *former* High Arrion?"

"Lady Eaglespike is dead, your highness," Bruno told her.

"*Dead?*" Marla was genuinely shocked to hear it. Kalan knew her mother had been expecting news of her arrest, not her demise. "How can she be dead?"

"She attempted to draw on the magic of the Harshini directly, your highness. We all witnessed it happen. It was a tragic thing to behold."

Marla's gaze landed on Wrayan. He shrugged. "She's done it before," he explained, "only the last time she tried it, she was using a Harshini spell to protect herself from the danger of too much exposure. This time she didn't. Perhaps she was overconfident. Or she forgot the spell."

Bruno nodded sadly in agreement, which Kalan thought was a bit optimistic. Bruno Sanval had no more magical ability than she did, so for all he knew, Wrayan had killed Alija himself. In fact, Kalan wasn't entirely certain that wasn't exactly what had happened. She didn't intend to challenge him on it, though. The outcome of their meeting with Alija was everything Kalan could have hoped for and more. She wasn't about to start questioning their good fortune now.

"I have assumed her duties temporarily," Bruno informed the princess, "until we can arrange a new High Arrion."

Marla looked stunned. "But what would make the High Arrion attempt anything so foolish?"

"She was attempting to evade justice," Bruno replied gravely.

"Lord Sanval, I trust you have proof of this allegation," the princess warned sternly. "To accuse a High Arrion of any crime is a most serious affair. What was she accused of?"

"Murder," Bruno informed her heavily.

"Dear gods!" Marla exclaimed. "Who did she kill?" Kalan was quite impressed by her mother's performance.

She'd never realised what a good actress Marla was until now.

"It's more a case of how *many* did she kill, actually," Wrayan corrected.

"Talk about a gifted amateur," Galon added. "There's retired old assassins out there responsible for fewer deaths than Alija Eaglespike."

"And you have proof of these murders?"

"She confessed, Mother," Kalan said, her eyes meeting Marla's so only her mother could read the triumph in them. "She killed Ronan Dell and all his household; Kagan Palenovar; she tried to kill Master Lightfinger back when he was an apprentice; and then, to top it all off, she tried to commission Master Miar to kill him again today, in front of both the Lower Arrion and the Chief Librarian, Dikorian Frye."

"She confessed to *all* of this?" Marla asked, her shock quite genuine.

Kalan shared her surprise.

They were hoping to expose Alija's previous attack on Wrayan. They'd considered it an outside chance she would demand Galon kill Wrayan as soon as she recognised him, and with luck condemn herself a second time in front of two impeccable witnesses. But nobody had expected her to incriminate herself with the revelation she had ordered the attack on Ronan Dell.

They hadn't even suspected she'd had a hand in Kagan Palenovar's death.

"Regrettably, your highness, she did confess," Bruno replied.

"But how?" Marla demanded. "Did you just walk up to the High Arrion and enquire if she'd killed anybody recently?"

Bruno fidgeted uncomfortably with the cord around the waist of his formal black robes. "My first hint anything was amiss was when Kalan . . . Lady Hawksword . . . brought to my attention the fact Wrayan Lightfinger was visiting Greenharbour. When she told me he'd been living in Krakandar all these years . . . that he'd sworn an oath to the God of Thieves . . . well, I was quite beside myself, particularly when I learned he'd visited Sanctuary in his travels. We'd all assumed him dead, you see. Lady Kalan arranged a meeting and during our discussion he told me of the circumstances of his departure from the Sorcerers' Collective and his arrival among the Harshini . . ." The old man shook his head sorrowfully. "After that, things just began to snowball. Wrayan mentioned that Master Miar may have reason also to suspect Lady Alija of criminal activities, and that he had been courting her favour with the hope of proving her culpability. With Master Miar's help, we were able to secure the testimony of a slave trader who knew of the Ronan Dell massacre. Your own *court'esa* was apparently a victim of her machinations too, I regret to inform you. I admit though, until she confessed, I had hoped there was some plausible explanation for the evidence that was building against her."

"I share your shock and disappointment, Lord Sanval. It must be a bitter brew indeed you find yourself having to swallow. Is there anything I can do?"

"We are here as a courtesy, your highness," Bruno explained. "With the number of provinces under the governance of the Sorcerers' Collective, I thought it prudent the High Prince be advised of this situation, as soon as possible."

Marla nodded sympathetically. "Of course, my lord, I will send a dispatch to my brother at once, apprising him of the news. Do you have any recommendations about what I should advise him to do with the troops?"

"I'm not sure I follow your meaning, your highness. Surely that is a military decision?"

"Please, forgive me if I am presuming to quote Collective law to someone as eminent as yourself, Lord Sanval, but it was my understanding that if a Higher or Lower Arrion was removed for a criminal act, all decisions and rulings issued by that person following the act of committing that crime become void until they can be reviewed and judged on their merits." Marla shrugged, letting that sink in. "I realise I'm just a woman with no real comprehension of your laws, but the way I understand it, if Alija's first crime was the murder of Ronan Dell, doesn't that pre-date her appointment as

High Arrion? I could be oversimplifying the matter, but I believe that makes every ruling, every decision and every appointment she's made since she was appointed null and void."

Kalan stared at her mother, open-mouthed. Even she hadn't known about that law. How did Marla know these things, she marvelled. It was humbling to think that no matter how clever Kalan thought she was, her mother always seemed to be one step ahead of everybody else.

"Dear gods!" Bruno breathed in horror. "Your highness, I fear you may be correct. I hadn't thought about it." He was having great difficulty grasping the scope of the problem. "This is a calamity! A disaster!"

Galon looked at the others in bewilderment. "You mean everything Alija's done since she's been High Arrion is now invalid?"

"It may well be," Wrayan agreed. "The law was put in place by the Harshini when the Sorcerers' Collective was first created. It was meant to stop anybody profiting from a criminal act. You know, killing someone and then appointing your nephew to the post—that sort of thing. I remember Kagan telling me about it once. Or making me go look it up."

Wrayan's explanation solved the mystery of how Marla knew about the law, which relieved Kalan a great deal. It was hard enough being surrounded by real sorcerers. Having a mother with almost mystical powers would have been a little too much to bear.

"What does it mean in reality, though?" Kalan asked. "Are we going to have to go back and undo every decision she's made in the past twenty-odd years?"

"The decisions don't need to be unmade," Wrayan explained. "Just reviewed. But they can't be considered valid until they've been independently assessed as not benefiting anyone as the result of her crimes."

"That could take months. Even years."

"And we're at war, gentlemen," Marla reminded them grimly, "with no time for such a drawn-out process. May I make a suggestion, Lord Sanval?"

"Please, your highness, if you can see some way out of this dilemma, I would be most grateful for your wisdom."

"I'm not sure if I have the solution to your entire problem, my lord, but in the short term we do have a more immediate issue with the chain of command on the war front. Alija appointed her own son as commander of all the armies belonging to the provinces under the Sorcerers' Collective guardianship. In light of recent events, perhaps that command should be temporarily transferred to the High Prince? At least until the Fardohnyans have been dealt with."

"That would be a solution, your highness, but is the High Prince really up to . . . you know . . ." The old man's words trailed off uncomfortably.

"I believe the High Prince is surrounded by enough sensible men that such a transfer of command would not unduly burden him, my lord," she assured him.

"Then I shall draft the orders immediately, my lady, if you would be so kind as to arrange a messenger to carry them to the front."

"They'll be in Sunrise Province in a matter of days," Marla promised. "My second suggestion is that you form some sort of board of inquiry, not so much to question the High Arrion's decisions but to decide if, indeed, she was guilty of anything at all. If Alija died before she was formally charged with a crime, perhaps there might be a way to avoid the unpleasantness that comes with impeachment?"

"That is a wise suggestion, your highness. I thank you for your understanding. It grieves me deeply to assume the rank of High Arrion under such circumstances."

"I trust you and Lord Dikorian will handle the problem with wisdom and dignity," Marla replied.

"Dikorian?"

"He's now the Acting Lower Arrion, isn't he?" Marla enquired.

"Ah, well . . . no, your highness, he's not."

"Then who are you thinking of appointing, my lord?"

"Um . . . your daughter," the old man told her. "Lady Kalan Hawksword."

Marla's gaze fixed on Kalan. It was impossible to tell what she was thinking. "*You're* the new Lower Arrion of the Sorcerers' Collective?"

"Yes, Mother."

"This is . . . unexpected."

Kalan was delighted to think she'd done something that had taken Marla so completely by surprise.

"I am my mother's daughter," she said.

chapter 70

Tejay Lionsclaw spent a good two days pacing her tent, listening to the rain beating an incessant tattoo on her roof with no idea what was going on in the war camp, no idea what was in store for her, or even if they'd won the battle. She had only Kendra Warhaft for company and the young woman was kept as isolated as Tejay and had no more notion of what was happening outside the walls of their tent than she did. The slaves who tended them were not her own and the guards on her quarters were Dregian Raiders who didn't respond even when she asked them direct questions.

She was effectively alone in the world, cut off from everyone she trusted or thought she could rely on and starting to wonder if her misguided heroics were going to cost her much more than she'd bargained for.

It was all Lernen Wolfblade's fault, Tejay reasoned, as she paced the small empty space in the living quarters of the divided tent. If the High Prince had even an ounce of backbone, she might have got away with posing as a Warlord. He may have even thanked her for it. She was the one who'd sat in front of those damned soldiers, after all, facing the entire oncoming Fardohnyan army, just to make certain the archers got their arrows away at the right time. Had she received any thanks for her courage? Not a jot. Instead, they confined her and cut her off and were probably plotting to take her province and her children from her in her absence.

It was Damin's fault, too, she fumed. If that damned irresponsible boy had been where he was supposed to be when she and Lernen arrived at the command post at Lasting Drift, she might have had someone on her side. Instead, all they found was Cyrus Eaglespike, shocked to the very core of his being to realise the occupant of Terin Lionsclaw's armour was, in fact, not the Warlord but the Warlord's wife.

Damin, it turned out, had abandoned the field for some harebrained scheme he hadn't bothered to share with anyone, leaving Tejay to face the wrath and shock of Hythria's Warlords on her own. Her protestations that she'd simply taken the field at the last minute because Terin was unwell held up for as long as it took Cyrus to send somebody back to the camp to check on the missing Warlord.

Once it was clear her husband wasn't even in the camp, the whole damned thing began to unravel. Cyrus had had her arrested and bundled away before she could explain anything. Although he protested loudly on her behalf, Rorin could do nothing, because faced with Cyrus's fury the only man present in a position to overrule the Warlord of Dregian—the High Prince—turned into a quivering mass of blubber at the first hint of a raised voice and nodded his terrified agreement to every order Cyrus shouted after that.

"My lady!"

Tejay halted her pacing at Kendra's exclamation and turned to find Damin Wolfblade ducking through the tent flap. He was unshaved, muddy and looked as if he hadn't changed his clothes since the major engagement began two days ago.

"Where the hell have you been?" she demanded with her hands on her hips as she faced him.

"Winning the war for you," he replied, straightening up as the flap dropped closed behind him.

Tejay wasn't amused. "So nothing the rest of us did matters, I suppose?"

"Oh . . . I don't know about that. I hear there's a particularly grateful young Raider currently recovering in the physicians' tent, thanks to your heroic efforts. And that you faced down Hablet's entire army on your own. I heard you were wounded, too. Are you all right?"

"Don't I look all right?"

Damin eyed her up and down curiously. "You look fine, although after what you did in the command tent, my lady . . ."

"I wouldn't have *had* to do anything," she snapped, "if you'd been there to help me like you were supposed to. Or if that spineless uncle of yours had uttered a single word in my defence."

"Maybe you shouldn't have threatened to put him across your knee and paddle his bare arse in full view of the Fardohnyan army, then," he suggested.

"Who told you about that?"

"I've spoken to Rorin and Kraig already. Good morning, Lady Kendra. I hope this awkwardness hasn't been too hard on you?"

"Why are you being so nice to her?" Tejay demanded. "I'm the one that arrogant, woman-hating brute Cyrus Eaglespike berated in public like an errant child! Do you know he actually called me a whore?"

"Ah! That would explain his black eye, then."

"He deserved it."

"It's also the reason he had you arrested, Tejay."

"Well, now you're back, you can have him un-arrest me. Where were you, by the way? The last I heard, Cyrus was accusing you of fleeing the battle before it even started."

"I took Almodavar and twelve men and captured five thousand Fardohnyan cavalry with them," he told her, not completely able to disguise his smug expression. "Cyrus is having second thoughts about calling me a coward."

"Did you really capture five thousand men with only a

dozen Raiders, your highness?" Kendra gasped, thoroughly impressed. "How did you manage such a feat?"

"Cut off the head of a snake, my lady, and it doesn't take the rest of the body long to realise it's done for," he told her. When she responded with nothing more than a blank look, Damin added, "We sneaked up on their command post, captured their general and convinced him to surrender. The Fardohnyans are disciplined soldiers. They follow orders, even when their orders are to lay down their arms."

"And your brother, your highness? Lord Hawksword?" she ventured cautiously. "Is he . . . unharmed?"

"Alive and well, my lady, but you're going to have to take my word for that at present. I've got enough trouble convincing everyone Lady Lionsclaw shouldn't be executed. I'd really rather you didn't add fuel to the fire by consorting with Narvell."

"I understand, your highness," she said, with a graceful (if somewhat resigned) curtsey.

"Well, I don't!" Tejay exclaimed. "What in the name of all the Primal Gods do they think they can execute me for?"

"Fortunately for you, my lady, that's the problem. You broke tradition, rather than the law, I think. Cyrus is having a bit of a job thinking up a charge. But he's a resourceful fellow. I'm sure, given enough time, he'll think of something."

Tejay glared at him. "You think this is funny, don't you?"

Damin didn't bother to hide his amusement. "I wish I'd been there when you blacked his eye."

"If you'd been there, Damin Wolfblade, I wouldn't have had to. Did you really convince Axelle Regis to surrender?"

"I'm not sure how much of the credit I deserve. He'd already been cut adrift by Hablet, even before we drew him into the ambush. I think that's why he held back his cavalry. He figured enough blood had been shed by then. We just arrived in time to give him the option to back down gracefully."

Tejay looked sceptical. "He was probably more concerned about his horses than the men he might lose. Have you ever noticed that, Kendra? Men will kill without mercy and then get all misty-eyed if their horse falls over."

The young woman smiled. "I have noticed it, my lady. A most interesting phenomenon, I always thought."

"There!" Tejay declared, turning back to Damin. "You can stop thinking you're so damned clever now. Even Kendra agrees. It's all about the horses."

Damin at least had the decency to look sympathetic. "I will try to sort this out, Tejay, I promise."

"Don't let them take my province from me, Damin."

"I may not be able to stop them."

"You *have* to stop them."

"Isn't there someone you can marry, my lady?" Kendra asked.

"There you go!" Damin agreed. "Find yourself another husband. In fact, you should talk to Kendra about it. She's got one she doesn't want."

"Which reminds me, your highness," the young woman said to Damin with a tinge of guilt in her voice. "Is my husband well?"

"I heard he was wounded, my lady, but not fatally. I'm sorry."

She looked quite downcast at the news. "The High Prince informs me there will be no divorce if my husband lives."

"Then pray to Cheltaran his wounds turn septic," Tejay suggested heartlessly, before turning her attention back to Damin. "I won't marry again, Damin."

"Tejay . . ."

"Find a way to fix this," she ordered. "And don't treat me like a tradeable commodity. I stood there and faced down an army for you, Damin Wolfblade. I expect you to reward me the way you would any *man* who'd done the same for you."

"I'll do my best, Tejay. But I can't make you a Warlord, you know."

"Why not?" Kendra asked curiously.

"Well . . . because I can't," Damin replied.

"But you just said Lady Lionsclaw broke tradition rather

than the law by being on the battlefield. Doesn't that mean there's no law stopping her becoming Warlord?"

"A Warlord is more than a figurehead, my lady," the young prince tried to explain. "A Warlord is expected to lead . . . ."

"His men to war," Tejay finished for him. "I've already proved I can do that. What other qualifications does a Warlord need? Must I prove an able administrator? I believe I've been proving that for years. Must I have the right education? Speak to my brother. You know, Rogan? The one they're promoting to Warlord of Izcomdar because he's a *man*? He's sufficiently well educated for the position it seems and as we had the same education, that shouldn't prove a problem, either. Or is it the correct pedigree, perhaps, that makes one Warlord material? Well, what do you know? I'm a Warlord's daughter . . ." She glared at the young prince. "Feel free to stop me when I come to the essential qualities I seem to be lacking, your highness."

Damin opened his mouth to defend his position and then closed it again, no doubt because it occurred to him this was an argument he couldn't possibly win.

"It's not as easy as you make it sound, Tejay," he said with an uncomfortable shrug. "You know that."

"*Make* it easy, Damin," she ordered. "You claim you want to do the right thing by Hythria, so do it. *It's too hard* doesn't really wash with me as an excuse."

"I didn't mean that . . ." He sighed. "It's just . . . well, there are laws, Tejay. There might not be one specifically forbidding a woman from becoming a Warlord, but just the laws regarding inheritance would make it untenable."

"Then change the damn laws, Damin. As I've remarked before, you seem quick enough to suggest your uncle change the law when it suits your own agenda."

Before Damin could respond to that charge, one of the Dregian guards poked his head through the tent flap. "Your highness?"

"*What?*"

"Lord Hawksword wishes to advise a messenger has just

arrived from Greenharbour. He said to tell you the news is urgent."

Damin sighed impatiently. "Tell him I'll be right there." He turned back to Tejay. "I'll do what I can, Tejay," he promised. "But I can't guarantee anything."

He meant it. She could see that. But it didn't do much to ease her fears. "Don't let them take my province from me, Damin. Or my sons."

The prince hesitated, perhaps debating the value of any further empty platitudes, and then, without another word, he bowed politely to the two women and ducked out of the tent, leaving Tejay and Kendra alone with nothing but their uncertain futures ahead of them.

chapter 71

When he got back to his tent, dogged by the persistent rain that hadn't let up since the day of the battle, Damin was stunned to discover the messenger from Greenharbour was Wrayan Lightfinger. Narvell was with him and the two of them were standing either side of the brazier, talking in low voices while they dried their damp clothes. They looked up when he entered, Wrayan smiling wearily when he saw Damin.

"You look like I feel," the thief remarked, taking in Damin's less-than-pristine attire, as the young prince shed his dripping cloak.

"*Wrayan*? What are you doing here?"

"I've been seconded from the Thieves' Guild by your mother to act as a royal courier."

"Why you?"

The thief shrugged. "I'd like to say it was because she trusted me, but I suspect it had more to do with the fact the

High Prince has several sorcerer-bred horses in his stables
and I'm the only one she knows who can use such an animal
in the manner they were bred for."

"He got here from Greenharbour in two days," Narvell
added, obviously a little shocked at the notion himself.

"How is that possible?"

"Sorcerer-bred horses," Wrayan repeated. "You were fostered at Izcomdar, Damin. Surely I don't have to explain it to
you?"

Damin nodded in understanding. "According to old Rogan Bearbow, they were bred by the Harshini because of
their ability to link magically with their riders. He claimed a
sorcerer-bred mount will go for days without foundering if
he has access to the source of the Harshini power through his
rider. I thought he was joking."

"Well, now you know," Wrayan said, reaching into his
jacket for a small packet of letters which he handed to
Damin. "And I come bearing gifts."

"What's this?" Damin asked, after tossing the string aside
and breaking the seal on the first letter.

"Ah, now that one would be the decree from the new
High Arrion, Bruno Sanval, advising that all appointments
made by the former High Arrion, Lady Alija Eaglespike,
are null and void, pending a review of every decision she
made while in office. I believe it also temporarily transfers
to the High Prince control of the armies of Greenharbour,
Izcomdar—and probably Sunrise as well, if what Narvell
tells me about Terin Lionsclaw's fate is true—until the war
is concluded and the matter of heirs can be appropriately
dealt with."

Damin read through the first letter in stunned disbelief. He
was almost afraid to open the second document. "What's the
other one?"

"I believe it's a decree your mother drafted at your request
some time ago, formally lowering the age of majority to
twenty-five. Given the contents of Bruno's letter, and the
fact the heirs to Greenharbour and Izcomdar are currently in
the war camp, she thought it might come in handy."

"But Lernen refused to sign it," Narvell pointed out. "It's no good without his signature and his seal."

"The seal I can help you with," Wrayan announced, producing another small packet from the pocket of his vest and handing it to Damin. "The signature you'll have to arrange yourself."

Damin accepted the High Prince's seal from the thief and shook his head in wonder. "How . . . what happened?"

"Long story." Wrayan shrugged. "No doubt you'll get the full version from Kalan or your mother when you get back to Greenharbour. The short version goes something like this: Alija tricked Elezaar into thinking his brother was still alive and to save him from being tortured he told her everything he knew, right down to the colour of your mother's undergarments, then he confessed his crime to Marla just before he killed himself out of guilt, leaving your mother with no choice but to do something about Alija. So she hired an assassin to kill Tarkyn Lye in retaliation. Then Kalan got involved—she's a very scary young woman, your sister, by the way. Don't ever get on her bad side. Anyway, she, and your mother, and this assassin, Galon Miar—another long story I don't intend to get into right now—managed to manipulate Alija into confessing to thirty or forty-odd murders she's been responsible for over the years in the presence of the Lower Arrion and the Chief Librarian of the Sorcerers' Collective."

Damin stared at him. "You're joking, aren't you?"

"You had to be there, Damin," Wrayan told him.

"Where is Alija now?"

"She's dead. She drew too much power to herself and it killed her. You'd have to be a sorcerer to fully understand what happened."

"So what's happening in the Sorcerers' Collective?" Damin asked, stunned by the news.

"Poor old Bruno Sanval is losing his hair trying to figure out how he's supposed to deal with all this. I'm sure Kalan will have a few ideas for him. She managed to manipulate him into appointing her Lower Arrion, while she was at it. Did I mention that? I can't imagine what Rorin's reaction is going to be when he finds out."

Narvell smiled at the news of his twin. "She has been threatening she'd be High Arrion since she was ten years old. Lower Arrion by the time she's twenty-three augurs well for her ambition."

Wrayan looked at Narvell askance. "Trust you to think that."

Damin smiled too. Like Narvell, he admired his sister more than he worried about her. "I'm guessing Cyrus doesn't know anything about this, yet?"

"I've spoken to nobody other than you and Narvell since I got here, and given my journey was magically assisted, I doubt the news has beaten me here by traditional means. Unless someone sent a message by bird from Greenharbour, then he's probably none the wiser."

Damin looked at his brother. "Can you get Rogan Bearbow and Conin Falconlance in here? Quietly?"

"I suppose," Narvell replied. "Why?"

"I want to speak to them after I've spoken to Lernen. I shouldn't have any trouble getting Lernen to sign the decree—he promised me as much the morning of the battle. But I want to make damned certain that when we announce the new order of things, they're ready for it."

"Shouldn't you warn the Warlord of Pentamor?" Wrayan asked.

Damin shook his head. "Wherever Cyrus is, I can guarantee Toren Foxtalon will be one step behind him. We'll break the news to him at the same time we inform Cyrus his mother is dead."

Narvell picked up his cloak. "I'll go find the others then."

Damin nodded. "We'll meet back here in an hour."

Once Narvell had left, Damin turned to Wrayan. "I still have one problem neither your welcome news, nor these decrees, does anything to solve."

"Are you talking about Mahkas?"

Damin smiled ruefully. "All right, I have *two* problems neither your welcome news, nor these decrees, does anything to solve."

"What's the other one?" Wrayan asked, lowering himself wearily down onto the cushions surrounding the brazier.

"Sunrise Province. Tejay just suggested I have Lernen appoint *her* the new Warlord."

Wrayan held out his hands toward the coals to warm them. "Well, under the circumstances, you can't hand the province over to the Sorcerers' Collective, even if they were in a position to accept the guardianship. Appointing Valorian's mother as Warlord *would* preserve the inheritance for her son. And she'd certainly do a better job than the previous incumbent, from what I hear."

"But she's a woman!"

Wrayan frowned. "Don't ever say that in front of your mother, lad."

"I'm not saying that's the reason she can't do the job," Damin argued, exasperated that everybody assumed that about him. "I'm saying that's the reason nobody will accept her."

"Are you certain of that?"

"Well . . ." Damin hesitated as he realised he was relying entirely on his own reading of the situation. He hadn't even put the notion to anybody else to gauge their opinion. "Actually, I don't know for sure, but . . ."

"Let me ask you this, then. Do you think Tejay Lionsclaw is capable of doing the job?"

"Of course."

"And will it secure your throne in the future to have Sunrise Province as an unswerving ally?"

"You know it would."

"Then you have your answer, your highness."

Damin sighed. "I love Tejay like a sister. You know that. So does she. And I think she's a better man than half the Warlords in Hythria. But how do I get anybody to accept her, Wrayan? How would I get the Convocation to appoint her?"

"The High Prince has the discretion to appoint Warlords

as he sees fit, Damin. He did it when he appointed Terin's father, Chaine Lionsclaw, as Warlord of Sunrise Province. So you don't need the Convocation. All you really need to do is convince Lernen to make the ruling, which shouldn't be too hard given he's basking in the glow of your victory at the moment. As for the other Warlords, one of them is her own brother and you're about to hand two formerly underage heirs their inheritance years ahead of when they were expecting it. Don't you think—at least until the shine wears off your handsome gift—you'll get a bit of cooperation out of them?"

Still doubtful, Damin shook his head. "Cyrus Eaglespike would never allow it. And Foxtalon will support him, just on principle."

"Cyrus Eaglespike is going to be too busy for the foreseeable future distancing himself from his mother's crimes. He hasn't got the time to worry about who's appointed Warlord of Sunrise, Damin. If anything, the next few days are going to be his most vulnerable time. If you want to do this, you'd better do it now, when—for a few days at least—all the players are aligned in your favour. There'll never be another opportunity like this."

"What do you think my mother would say about it?"

Wrayan smiled. "I think she'd be delighted."

Damin frowned, still not convinced. "And what about afterwards? When things go back to normal and all the *players*, as you call them, aren't aligned in my favour any longer? What happens to Tejay then?"

"If you have any doubt about her ability to handle the aftermath, Damin, then you shouldn't even consider appointing her Warlord in the first place."

Damin smiled suddenly. "You know she gave Cyrus a black eye for calling her a whore?"

Wrayan laughed. "And you worry about whether or not she can handle the other Warlords?"

Damin picked up his damp cloak, and glanced down at the letters Wrayan had brought him. There was something else he wanted to talk to Wrayan about, but he'd kept his own counsel on the matter for so long now, it was surprising how hard it was to talk about it.

"Damin?" Wrayan asked curiously, sensing something was amiss.

He took a deep breath and faced the sorcerer. "If I told you I'd spoken to the God of War, would you think I'm crazy?"

"People pray to their gods all the time, Damin."

"I wasn't praying, Wrayan. He appeared to me."

To Damin's intense relief, the thief didn't seem to doubt his word. "When was this?"

"A couple of months ago. Just after I left Krakandar."

"What did he say to you?" Wrayan asked curiously.

"Not a great deal, in hindsight. Just a whole lot of stuff about honouring him. And that I was favoured by him."

Wrayan studied him thoughtfully. "Then you are honoured, Damin. Zegarnald chooses his favourites carefully."

"Do you think that's why we won so easily?"

Wrayan shook his head. "If Zegarnald had his way, you'd be fighting for months yet. The victory is yours, Damin. Don't belittle your achievement by thinking the gods intervened."

That idea cheered Damin considerably. "Have you ever met him?"

The thief nodded. "A few times. When I was in Sanctuary. I'm sworn to Dacendaran, though, so he didn't take much notice of me. Have you told anybody else about this?"

"Not a soul," Damin assured him. "I've got enough problems now without everyone thinking I'm a lunatic. Or worse, that I really have been singled out by the gods. That would be enough to make enemies out of some of my best friends, I fear."

"You're right about that, I suspect," Wrayan agreed. "And wise to keep your own counsel." He reached out and gripped Damin's shoulder reassuringly. "There'll come a time when it doesn't matter if people believe you've inherited the divine right to rule, Damin. But it isn't now."

"Then I'd better go talk to Lernen, I suppose. Help yourself to the wine and have someone bring you something to eat while you're waiting. You look exhausted."

"I will. And don't look so worried. You'll make the right decision, Damin. About all of this."

He shrugged. "Well, even if I'm wrong, it'll be a classic application of Elezaar's Eleventh Rule."

"Which one is that?"

"Do the unexpected," he replied, and then he refolded the letters from Greenharbour and tucked them in his belt to protect them from the rain.

With Wrayan settled in beside the brazier, Damin ducked back under the tent flap and headed across the muddy camp to visit the High Prince thinking—divinely sanctioned or not—if he succeeded in his quest, in the next few hours the whole make-up of Hythrun society was going to be turned on its ear.

chapter 72

The more Wrayan Lightfinger saw of Damin Wolfblade, the less he worried about the future of Hythria. Against the most astounding odds, Marla had raised an intelligent, capable and charismatic young man who would rule with fairness and common sense; a man who could be both ruthless and compassionate—the latter *not* a trait he inherited from his mother, Wrayan decided wryly. The prince old Kagan Palenovar, Laran Krakenshield and Glenadal Ravenspear had schemed and plotted and prayed they would produce was finally come of age. Their gamble appeared to have paid off, although how much of it was his upbringing, and how much simply his nature, Wrayan couldn't really say.

To learn even Zegarnald had smiled on this scion of Hythria didn't surprise Wrayan in the slightest.

Wrayan considered him carefully, several hours later, as he watched Damin Wolfblade break the news to Rogan Bearbow and Conin Falconlance that he had persuaded the High Prince to lower the age of majority to twenty-five, which meant they were now both officially the Warlords of their provinces.

It hadn't been an easy task, by all accounts. Lernen was feeling particularly peevish today and initially reneged on his earlier promise to sign the decree. Wrayan wasn't sure what Damin had done to get Lernen to put his signature and seal on the document eventually, but he did it somehow. Along with tactics and politics, Marla had obviously taught her son how to manage the High Prince when he was in one of his moods.

The two young men were quite stunned by the news, Rogan recovering more quickly than his younger companion. Conin Falconlance was a distant cousin still coming to grips with the notion he was even the heir of Greenharbour Province. Rogan, on the other hand, had been raised from birth to assume the role of Warlord of Izcomdar and had effectively been doing so since his father died in the plague, even though he'd been breaking the law to do it.

"And this law your uncle has signed, lowering the age of majority, cannot be revoked by the Convocation of Warlords?" Rogan asked, when Damin had finished explaining their unexpected change in circumstances to them.

"The next High Prince could revoke it, I suppose," Damin informed him. "But as that's me, and I turn twenty-five myself very shortly—the day after which I intend to ride back to Krakandar and take it from my uncle—I can't see myself doing that any time soon, can you?"

"It's a pity you can't lower the age to five," Conin joked. "That would take care of Sunrise, too, and then every province would have a Warlord again."

"Which brings us to the problem of what to do about Sunrise," Damin said.

"Have you found someone for my sister to marry?" Rogan asked.

"She doesn't want to marry again."

"But after what you've told us about the strife in the Sorcerers' Collective, you surely don't mean to hand the province back into their control, do you?"

"Certainly not."

"You have a regent in mind, then?" Conin asked.

"Not exactly."

Rogan glared at him. "Is this supposed to be a guessing game, Damin?"

"No. I just haven't really worked out how I'm going to break it to you, that's all."

"Perhaps you should just show them, your highness," Wrayan suggested.

Damin had introduced him as a royal courier and one of his mother's advisors. He'd omitted, wisely perhaps, the bit about Wrayan also being a thief.

"Maybe that would be better," Damin agreed. He crossed the tent to the beautifully woven hanging dividing the living area from the sleeping quarters and pulled it aside. Standing behind it, waiting for her cue, was Tejay Lionsclaw.

"*This* is your new Warlord?" Narvell gasped.

Rogan looked at his sister with a frown. "You can't be serious."

"Why can't he be serious, Rogan?" Tejay asked her younger brother, stepping into the main part of the tent.

Conin Falconlance stared at them in disbelief. "I'm sorry, Damin, but I fear Rogan is correct. The High Prince will never agree to a woman being appointed Warlord."

"The High Prince has already agreed to it," Damin told them. "It's a done deal, my lords. Say hello to the new Warlord of Sunrise."

"Damin . . ." Rogan began carefully, aware, perhaps, his sister probably wasn't joking when she threatened him. "I appreciate what you're trying to do here, but . . . this can't work. Surely you can see that. Even if the High Prince thinks it's a grand idea, the people will not accept a female Warlord."

"I think you underestimate the people of Sunrise Province," Tejay suggested.

Rogan turned to Damin, shaking his head. "Sunrise Province is too strategically important to be used as a testing ground for your socially enlightened agenda, Damin."

"I don't have an agenda," Damin replied. "What I have is a problem, which is that Sunrise doesn't have a Warlord. What I also have is a perfectly viable solution. Are you objecting because you think your sister can't do the job?"

"Of course not."

"Will it ease your mind if I tell you there is no Harshini law that prevents her appointment? They've never judged anybody on their sex. And the God of War certainly doesn't discriminate. Provided you worship him, shed blood for him, he doesn't care what gender you are."

"But what of the common people, sir?" Conin asked. "I fear Rogan speaks the truth. They will never accept a female Warlord."

"Do you know that for a fact?" Tejay asked.

"Well . . . I haven't asked them about it personally," he admitted, "but I can't imagine the peasants liking the idea . . ." His voice trailed off as he realised how indefensible his position sounded.

"I think you credit yourself with an understanding of the *peasants* that you don't really own, my lord," Wrayan suggested. "When was the last time you actually spoke to one? Not a slave or a servant in your employ, but one you might meet in the street?"

"Well, naturally, I don't speak to them myself . . ."

"Why *naturally*?" Narvell asked, glancing at his brother with a puzzled shake of his head, before fixing his gaze on the young Warlord. "Do you think it's unnatural to speak to someone not of your class?"

Conin looked quite offended by the question. "Does Charel Hawksword allow *you* to consort with the peasants?"

"Actually, he encourages it," Narvell replied, taking a step forward to confront Falconlance. "He says it stops the high-born from turning into pompous, self-important—"

"Enough!" Tejay snapped, glaring at the two young men. She turned to her brother, shaking her head. "If you want a reason why we need female Warlords, Rogan, take a look at these two as a shining example. Five minutes we've been discussing this and they're already having an argument about something that's got nothing to do with the discussion at hand."

Wrayan glanced across at Damin, who'd had the sense to step back and let Tejay convince the others herself. The prince was smiling faintly as he watched her, but made no move to interfere.

"That doesn't alter the fundamental problem with your appointment, Tejay," Rogan replied, obviously not unsympathetic to his sister's plight. "Even if I agreed with you ruling Sunrise, I just don't know how you're going to be able to hold on to it."

"The same way you'll hold on to Izcomdar, Rogan. By being good at what I do." She turned and looked at the others. "Besides, isn't holding on to the province *my* problem? If I take Sunrise and lose it a week, a month, even a year from now, you can all pat yourselves on the back about how right you were. In the meantime, I at least deserve the chance to prove I can do this, don't I?"

Rogan considered his sister for a moment and then nodded. "You're right, Tejay. If you can hold Sunrise, you deserve to keep it."

"You're *supporting* this?" Conin asked in surprise.

The new Warlord of Izcomdar put his hands on his hips. "I do. And so do you, young Falconlance."

"Why?" Conin asked. To Wrayan, he seemed more than a little taken aback by Rogan's threatening stance.

"Because the new Warlord of Sunrise Province is my sister and I'll kill any man who tries to interfere. If the people of Sunrise want to rise up and overthrow her because she's a despot, or a tyrant, or just a hopeless incompetent, that's one thing. But there won't be any outside interference, Conin. Not from Izcomdar. And certainly not from Greenharbour."

"Nor Elasapine," Narvell promised on behalf of his grandfather.

"Nor Krakandar," Damin also assured them.

They all fixed their gaze on the young Warlord from Greenharbour, who nodded reluctantly.

"There will be no interference from me," he agreed. "But I'd like to know how you're going to get Eaglespike and Foxtalon to agree to this."

"They don't have to agree," Damin said. "The High Prince has decreed this and the Convocation can't overrule him. But even if we needed the Convocation, five of the seven provinces are represented in this tent. We'd have the majority."

"I think I'd like to be there when you tell Cyrus," Rogan said. "Just to see his reaction."

"His reaction to the news his mother is dead is what I'm looking forward to," Narvell announced cheerfully. "Can we do it soon? And can I watch?"

"Grow up, Narvell," Tejay scolded.

"Sorry, my lady."

"Narvell does have a point, though, Tejay," Damin said. "We need to talk to Cyrus and Toren as soon as possible."

"No time like the present," Rogan suggested.

"I agree," Damin said, turning toward the entrance. "Almodavar!"

The old captain had been waiting just outside. The tent flap opened as he ducked inside. "Your highness?"

"Fetch the Warlords of Dregian and Pentamor here, would you, Captain? Use force if you have to."

Almodavar cracked a rare smile. "With pleasure, your highness."

The captain ducked back through the entrance and Damin turned to his companions. "This is going to be interesting."

Rogan shrugged. "I'm just looking forward to issuing orders to my own people that don't have to be approved by some foreign Warlord first . . ."

Wrayan didn't hear much more of the discussion. As Rogan was speaking another Raider slipped into the tent and approached the thief with a folded note. He opened it curiously and when he saw who it was from, he folded it again and followed the Raider outside.

"Brose Rollin!" Wrayan exclaimed, recognising one of his own men from the Krakandar Thieves' Guild. He was standing just outside the tent with Rorin Mariner. The man was splattered with mud and looked exhausted.

"Didn't expect to find you in the war camp, Wrayan."

"Didn't expect to find myself in a war camp, either. But I know how I finished up here. What's your excuse?" He glanced at Rorin. Wrayan had only been in camp a couple of hours himself. He didn't think anybody knew he was here. "And how did *you* know where to find me?"

"Damin told me you'd arrived when he came to see Lernen. I've been in the High Prince's pavilion for the last couple of days, helping out. And your man here is carrying a message for Damin, actually, not you. From Starros. When Master Rollin showed up just now, I thought you might want to speak to him first."

Wrayan studied the thief. He was a burglar; a good one, too. And always reliable. "Is something wrong in Krakandar?"

The man nodded wearily. "*Everything* is wrong in Krakandar, Wrayan. You can't imagine what it's been like since you left. The city is still sealed. People are starving. Everyone is terrified . . . I guess it's why we decided to do something about it."

"This sounds ominous," Wrayan said. "Who is *we* exactly?"

"The Thieves' Guild. And some of the other guilds. Well, all of the other guilds, actually. Once word got around about what we were planning, every man and his dog seemed to want to help. And that includes some fairly high-placed people at the palace, too."

Rorin looked at the young visitor in alarm. "What the hell are you planning, exactly?"

Brose seemed reluctant to confide in them. "Starros said I was to speak only to Prince Damin."

"You work for me, Brose Rollin, not for Starros," Wrayan reminded the burglar. "Answer Rorin's question. What are they planning to do?"

The thief hesitated. Behind them, a very unhappy-looking Cyrus Eaglespike and an equally peeved Toren Foxtalon approached the tent in the company of Geri Almodavar and a dozen or more Krakandar Raiders as an escort.

Brose waited until the two Warlords had entered the tent before continuing.

"We're going to steal the population of Krakandar."

"*What*?" Rorin asked.

"We're going to evacuate the city in secret. A week from next Restday."

Wrayan looked at Rorin. "Damin's going to love this."

"Can I speak to him?" Brose asked.

"He's got other problems at the moment. Your news is going to have to wait a little while, I fear."

No sooner had Wrayan spoken than an outraged bellow exploded from inside Damin's tent. Rorin and Brose both looked at the tent in concern and then turned to Wrayan for an explanation.

"Ah . . . now *that* would be the problem I spoke of."

"Has something happened?" Rorin asked.

"Nothing *you* don't already know about, Rorin," Wrayan told him. "I suspect that cry, however, was either the Warlord of Dregian Province learning his mother is dead, or Toren Foxtalon of Pentamor learning the new Warlord of Sunrise Province is a woman."

chapter 73

Luciena gave little further thought to Emilie and her morbid souvenir from Mahkas Damaran's infected arm. They were getting very close to the day the evacuation was scheduled to begin and she had a great deal more on her mind than what Emilie was up to. With Mahkas temporarily bedridden, she was much less concerned than she had been about her daughter in any case, although Luciena doubted they had more than a few days before Mahkas was up and about again, wreaking havoc and terror with equal abandon.

Mahkas's wound had been infected, not gangrenous, and once cleaned of the contamination, with the maggots eating the diseased flesh, he was already much improved. His temperature was almost back to normal and Darian Coe was talking about Mahkas being well enough to leave his bed in a matter of days.

It would have been so much easier for everyone if they could have kept him sedated until the evacuation was over, but Xanda wasn't willing to push their luck. Mahkas's temporary incapacity had been a gift from the gods, allowing much of the final preparation to take place. They were less than two days away from escaping this place and desperate to give the impression that nothing out of the ordinary was going on.

Something out of the ordinary was going on, however. Not sure what had woken her, Luciena guessed it was past midnight. She turned over restlessly, opened her eyes briefly and discovered Emilie standing beside the bed in her nightdress, holding a single candle, her face streaked with tears.

"Emilie?" she whispered, careful not to wake Xanda. "What's the matter, darling? What are you doing here? Did you have a nightmare?"

Emilie shook her head as she sniffed away her tears. "You have to come with me, Mama. I have to show you something."

"It's the middle of the night, darling."

"You *have* to come, Mama. It's important."

The child was obviously distraught about something. Luciena threw the covers back and sat up, rubbing her eyes. The movement disturbed Xanda. He reached across to her, his eyes opening when he found only emptiness where a moment ago there had been the warmth of another body.

"Luci?"

"Emilie's here," she told him softly. "I think she's had a nightmare."

Xanda opened his eyes wider and peered at them in the flickering gloom of the single candle. "Em? What's the matter, sweetheart?"

"You have to come with me," she insisted. "Both of you. I have to show you something."

There was a quiver in her voice that begged to be taken seriously. Without another word, Xanda climbed out of bed and walked around the big four-poster to his daughter. "Then show us, Emilie," he said, offering her his hand.

Emilie accepted her father's hand and with Luciena on her other side, she raised the candle to light their way and the three of them made their way out of the bedroom, into the darkened halls of Krakandar Palace.

Emilie led them to the day nursery on the ground floor. They encountered nobody on their strange walk, padding barefoot along the cold granite floors of the palace, their way lit by a single candle, the chill eased only by the occasional rug. She opened the door when they arrived and led her parents inside.

"What is it you want to show us, darling?" Luciena asked. She looked around the nursery, but on casual inspection nothing seemed to be amiss.

Emilie left her parents by the door and walked to the fireplace. The banked fire glowed red in the darkness. She reached up to the mantel and lifted down one of the ornaments, and then brought it back to the table where she placed it beside the candlestick.

"Do you remember this, Papa?"

Xanda nodded as he and Luciena approached the table. "Of course I do. It was a present to me from your great-grandmother, Jeryma, when I was six years old. Your Uncle Travin used to have one just like it."

"It got broken, didn't it?" she asked. "When your mama killed herself at Winternest?"

Xanda nodded again, unsurprised by the question. Years ago, Emilie had asked why she didn't have any grandparents and with surprisingly little fuss, Xanda had told her the reason. He hadn't told her much, but what he'd told her was the unvarnished truth. As for how Mahkas had retrieved the shattered pieces of Xanda's little horse and knight and rebuilt it for his distraught nephew—that story was a legend in this family.

"And then Uncle Rorin sealed the breaks again much later, didn't he?" Emilie asked, as if confirming in her own mind that she had the story straight. "When he first came to Krakandar?"

"I believe he was showing off his magical talent to Uncle Damin and the others," Luciena told her with a faint smile. "Is this what you wanted to show us, Em?"

The little girl shook her head and held out her hand. In her palm was the tiny blue thorn Darian Coe had extracted from Mahkas Damaran's arm.

"I wanted to show you this," she said, picking up the little horse and knight. Carefully, she took the thorn and placed it against the broken tip of the knight's lance.

"By the gods . . ." Xanda breathed in astonishment.

Luciena shared her husband's shock, wondering if she was imagining things. Perhaps she was still asleep upstairs and this was just her own nightmare, vivid and sharp, but a nightmare, nonetheless.

But it wasn't a dream, Luciena knew. And it wasn't a blue thorn they'd dug out of Mahkas Damaran's arm.

It was the missing tip of the lance belonging to Xanda's little blue porcelain horse and knight.

"Darian Coe said it had been deep in his arm for years," Luciena told her husband a little while later as he examined the horse and the broken tip, still too stunned to take in what it might imply.

Xanda put the horse down and looked at Luciena, his expression bleak. "Which means it's been there since the night my mother died."

"So it would seem." Luciena turned to her daughter. "Emilie, what made you think there was a connection between your father's old toy horse and the piece we removed from Mahkas's arm?"

"It was the colour, Mama. Walsark Blue. Uncle Travin told me once that Walsark is the only place in the whole world where they could make a glaze that colour." The child shrugged. "I didn't really understand what he was telling me. I just thought it was strange that the thing in Uncle Mahkas's arm was the same colour as Papa's little horse so I brought it down here to see if it was the same."

"But why tell us now? In the middle of the night? Couldn't this have waited until morning?"

Tears welled up in her eyes. "It was really bothering me once I started to think about it . . . about how they were exactly the same colour . . . so I snuck down here and put them together and that's when I discovered the little thing from Uncle Mahkas's arm really *was* the tip of the lance from Papa's little knight . . . and then I remembered what Darian Coe said about how long it had been in his arm . . . and I tried to figure out how it could have got there . . . so I went and saw Aunt Bylinda, but she didn't know . . ."

"You woke Bylinda?" Luciena asked in concern. "That wasn't very considerate of you, darling. She's not well."

"I know. I'm sorry. It didn't help much anyway, because

she didn't even seem to know what I was talking about. But it kept bothering me, Mama. I couldn't sleep . . . not until I worked it out . . . and then I realised the only way the tip could have broken off so deep in Uncle Mahkas's arm was if he'd been stabbed with it . . . and that made me think about your poor mother, Papa, and how she must have been arguing with Uncle Mahkas, maybe, before she killed herself and maybe that's why she did it . . . and then thinking about her fighting with someone so hard she'd want to die afterwards made me cry . . . and then I came up to your room because I thought you might know why . . ." She sniffled and Luciena gathered her into her arms to comfort her.

"Come now, darling," she whispered soothingly. "It all happened a long, long time ago. There's no need to be so upset about it now."

"Your mother's right, Em. Why don't you go back to bed? I'm sure there's a perfectly reasonable explanation for all this."

"Do you think so, Papa?"

He smiled. "I'm sure of it."

Rather than raise the household, Luciena took Emilie back to bed herself, and stayed with her until she'd drifted off to sleep. It was nearly an hour later that she returned to her room only to find Xanda hadn't come back to bed.

Curiously, she made her way back to the day nursery where she found her husband sitting at the table where she'd left him, turning the little horse over and over in his hands, staring into the darkness. The candle had burned down to a mere stub, but Xanda didn't seem to notice.

"I'd thought you'd be in bed by now."

"I won't sleep any more this night."

Luciena took the seat beside him and placed her hand over his. "It's like you told Emilie, Xanda. There's probably a perfectly reasonable explanation for all this."

"I know what the explanation is, Luci. He killed her."

"Mahkas?"

"That night is burned in my memory like it happened yesterday. My mother wasn't suicidal. She wasn't even particularly unhappy. I remember a letter had arrived. A Raider brought it to my mother. It was Raek Harlen, I think. After she got the letter she went as still as a rock. She didn't open it. Didn't read it . . . she just sat there with the letter in her lap, full of . . . I don't know how to describe it really. I used to think it was fear, but now I'm older and I look back on it, I don't think it was fear. It was anticipation."

"Do you know what was in the letter?"

Xanda shook his head. "I just remember a little while later Mahkas coming in to speak to her. He told us to go find Veruca, that we could have a treat, although I don't remember doing anything to deserve it. And then later—I don't know how long it was—Mahkas came out and told Veruca that our mother wanted dinner in her rooms and that he'd take Travin and me in to say goodnight to her."

Luciena frowned. "He took you to see her? Xanda, do you realise what you are saying? That he hanged your mother with a harp string and then took her sons back to discover her corpse?"

"Sounds like the Mahkas we all know, doesn't it?" Xanda suggested bitterly.

Luciena put her head in her hands, having trouble thinking even Mahkas could do anything so cruel. "But . . . it's almost inconceivable . . . he raised you. How could he kill your mother and then treat you and Travin like his own sons?"

"Look what he did to Leila and how he behaves around Emilie," Xanda pointed out. "It's not out of character for him."

She was having trouble digesting this. "It's not that I don't believe you, Xanda. I just don't understand why. What could possibly have been in that letter that would provoke him to kill your mother?"

"I'm not sure we'll ever know." Xanda shrugged. "Raek Harlen might have known what the letter contained, but he's dead now. The letter came from Laran Krakenshield, I believe, and he's been dead since Damin was a baby. He died on a border raid with Mahkas . . ." His voice trailed off. "All the witnesses are dead. All killed by Mahkas."

"Even Laran Krakenshield?" she said, wondering if Xanda's grief was getting the better of him. This was tipping over into the realms of the surreal. "Is that what you're thinking?"

"Ask any man who was on that raid, Luci, and they'll all tell you the same thing. The gods know I've heard the story often enough. Laran was unhorsed and wounded, but on his feet and fighting with Mahkas on his way to help, the last anyone saw of him. The next thing they knew, Laran was dead and Mahkas was apologising for not being quick enough."

"That doesn't mean he killed his own brother, Xanda."

"In a fight, one can kill just as effectively by deliberate *inaction* as they can by deliberate action, you know."

Luciena was getting a headache from trying to unravel Xanda's train of thought. "So, you're saying your mother got a letter from Laran Krakenshield and something in that letter drove Mahkas to kill her. At the very least, it made your mother angry enough to stab him with the nearest thing at hand, which turned out to be your little horse and knight. So he kills her, or at least she's now upset enough to kill herself . . ."

"Luciena, just consider how upset you'd have to be to kill yourself," he said. "And how long it'd take you to come to a decision like that. Suicides are not happy people, Luci. An hour before she died, my mother was restringing her harp. You're not going to take on a job like that if you're not planning to be around to play it."

"So whatever was in that letter, Mahkas was willing to kill for it," she concluded. "How do you know it came from Laran Krakenshield?"

He shrugged. "I think Veruca told me later . . . much later, actually. We were living in Krakandar by then. All I really know, other than who sent the letter, was that it happened around the same time as the Fardohnyans killed Riika Ravenspear."

"Who was Riika Ravenspear?"

"My mother's half-sister."

She smiled at him. "You people really do get around, don't you?"

"I know. It gets complicated. Anyway, she was kidnapped out of Winternest by the Fardohnyans in the mistaken belief that she was Marla. When they realised they had the wrong girl, they killed her."

"Perhaps the letter had something to do with Riika's death?"

Xanda threw his hands up. "What difference does it make now, Luci? It's all just idle speculation, really."

"What about the spear tip?"

"That just proves he was in the room with my mother, but we knew that. At best it proves she may have been angry enough to stab him with it, but it's not *proof* he actually killed her."

"How can I help, Xanda?" she asked, hoping she could do something to ease the pain in his eyes.

"Kill Mahkas."

"*Other* than that."

"Get yourself and the children out of here."

"It's only a couple of days away now."

"Less than that," he told her, glancing out the window. The sky was already noticeably lighter than it had been. "It's almost dawn."

"Another day closer to honouring Dacendaran with the entire population of Krakandar," Luciena agreed. "I hope the God of Thieves appreciates what Starros is doing for him. Although I worry we'll all be counted as his disciples after this for aiding the Thieves' Guild. What do you think?"

"I suppose," Xanda replied, but she could tell her poor attempt to change the subject was having little or no impact.

She took his hands in hers and smiled encouragingly. "Xanda, don't dwell on what this means. As you said, there's no real proof and nothing can be done at the moment. Besides, I suspect once Damin gets back, your thirst for vengeance will find plenty of blood to sate it."

"Do you really think Damin will kill Mahkas when he comes home?"

"You saw him the day Leila died, Xanda. You tell me."

Her husband didn't seem convinced. "He'll have cooled off by now. War may even have taught him a little common sense."

"Now, now . . . let's not go looking for miracles, my love."

Xanda frowned. "He's not that bad, Luci."

"I know. I'm only teasing."

"What do you think Travin will do when I tell him?"

"I don't know."

"Do you think Bylinda knows?"

Luciena shrugged. "She's been married to Mahkas a long time. Maybe she does. Maybe she turns a blind eye to that part of him. If you discount his tendency to murder members of his own family at the drop of a hat, or his unfortunate habit of beating people half to death when he's feeling a little peeved, I suppose he's not such a *bad* person."

Xanda smiled. "I know what you're up to. You're trying to cheer me up, aren't you?"

"Is it working?"

"Not really. I do appreciate the effort though." He leaned forward and kissed her cheek. "But for future reference, Luci my love, when you're trying to cheer someone up, fewer reminders of murder and mayhem would probably be a very good start."

Luciena leaned forward and kissed her husband's forehead, wishing again there was something she could do to ease the pain in his eyes.

And some way of speeding up time so that she could get her children out from under the roof of a madman.

chapter 74

It was an odd band who set out from Lasting Drift to return to Krakandar. Besides Damin, there was Wrayan Lightfinger, Prince Lunar Shadow Kraig of the House of the Rising Moon, his two bodyguards, Lyrian and Barlaina, and the messenger from the Thieves' Guild, Brose Rollin.

Damin had left Almodavar in charge of the Krakandar troops. He was, in fact, far better qualified for the position than Damin, and would supervise their post-battle duties and their eventual withdrawal from the battlefield more competently than any other man alive. Because of his age and reputation, even the younger Warlords deferred to his wisdom on occasion, so Damin anticipated few problems getting his men home once the aftermath of the battle of Lasting Drift was dealt with.

It was no easy task, cleaning up after a battle. There were thousands of dead to be buried, even more prisoners to cater for. They had to be counted and identified, not to mention housed and fed, until arrangements could be made to get them home. With the Widowmaker blocked, unless they were willing to march them, en masse, across Sunrise Province down to Highcastle on the coast (something Tejay was vehemently opposed to because of the manpower and cost of such an expedition), their only other option was to use the Fardohnyan prisoners to reopen the pass. The proposal even had the support of Axelle Regis, who—for the sake of convenience—had retained command of his army, albeit under the close supervision of Tejay Lionsclaw.

Her first task as Warlord would be to get the Widowmaker open again. If she could manage that without further bloodshed, if the trade routes could be re-established in a reasonable time, and the Fardohnyans returned home for a suitable ransom that compensated the Hythrun Warlords for the inconvenience of having to go to war, Damin was fairly certain she'd have no trouble holding on to her province.

As for Axelle Regis, his fate remained an open question. Traditionally, the generals of opposing armies were ransomed back to their sovereign, or given the option of falling on their sword, either of which seemed patently inappropriate in this case. Axelle could have won this war if Hablet had supported him—or if his daughter, Her Serene Bloody Highness, the Princess Adrina, hadn't decided to cut Axelle adrift once her interest in him waned. Damin silently thanked all the gods he could name that the succession in Fardohnya was through the male line and he'd never have to deal with the prospect of a Queen Adrina on the throne of Fardohnya when he someday became High Prince of Hythria. Hablet was bad enough. By the sound of it, his eldest daughter was infinitely worse.

The closure of the Widowmaker still bothered Damin more than he wanted to admit. Rorin insisted the pass had been closed by magic, which had given Damin more than one sleepless night since the surrender, wondering if the avalanche had been merely a lucky coincidence for Her Serene Highness when she decided she was done with Lord Regis, or if she'd somehow found a way to arrange for the Widowmaker to be magically destroyed.

The latter was almost too frightening to contemplate. There was a certain level of responsibility that came with being a prince and having access to sorcerers willing to do your bidding. Damin was fortunate, he knew. Because of their contact with the Harshini, neither Wrayan nor Rorin would ever do anything they considered immoral. Adrina of Fardohnya didn't appear to be nearly so restrained and if she'd found a sorcerer to do her bidding, the future was very bleak indeed.

They still had no idea who had been responsible for the damage—other than Rorin's suspicion the Halfbreed was involved because Elarnymire had appeared to warn him of the danger. Wrayan had done nothing to reassure Damin, either, when Rorin was telling them about his little adventure in the

Widowmaker, commenting that if the princess in question was beautiful then it certainly wasn't out of the realm of possibility that Brak might aid her if, in fact, the two had crossed paths.

But on hearing the full story, Wrayan had cautioned them not to read more into the situation than actually existed. In his experience, he assured them, Brakandaran steered clear of the halls of power and was more likely to be amusing himself with a whore than a princess. That left Damin right back where he started, wondering if the avalanche had been a lucky coincidence, or if Hablet's daughter had somehow found a way to arrange for the Widowmaker to be destroyed by a sorcerer.

Some of his other problems were easier to resolve. He made certain Narvell would keep an eye on the High Prince and not let him do anything too outrageous. Like all Marla's children, Narvell enjoyed the trust of the High Prince—when he was in the mood to trust anyone, at least. Although he wasn't quite as adept as his older brother at getting what he wanted out of Lernen, Narvell was certainly capable of arranging to get him back to Greenharbour in one piece, and with the war all but done for now, that was the best place for him.

On hearing the news of his mother's death, Cyrus had done exactly what Damin was doing, heading home immediately to deal with more pressing problems. Unlike Damin, however, he hadn't left his troops behind to help in the aftermath, but had withdrawn every Dregian Raider from the field.

He'd have taken Greenharbour's and Pentamor's troops with him as well, if he could, but, as Wrayan had predicted, Conin Falconlance was still grateful enough for his sudden elevation to Warlord to feel he owed Damin something, so he decided to stay and do the right thing by his new allies. Toren Foxtalon of Pentamor stayed for entirely different reasons. He'd allied himself with Cyrus because until the battle at Lasting Drift, Eaglespike had always appeared the strongest Warlord. Since the battle, however, since there

were suddenly three more Warlords whom he'd foolishly
never bothered with, he found himself quite lonely with only
Cyrus for support. With his only ally's mother being blamed
for countless crimes against Hythria he had a sudden attack
of Royalist sentiment and decided he should remain where
his help was needed most.

The Warlord of Pentamor's decision to stay eased the
last of Damin's fears about what might happen if he didn't
get back to the capital immediately. No Warlord was per-
mitted to enter the city with more than three hundred
troops, and his fear had been that if Conin Falconlance
and Toren Foxtalon left with Cyrus Eaglespike, the
Dregian Warlord would have had almost a thousand men
with which to attempt to avenge his mother. That wasn't
going to happen now. Not even Cyrus was going to attack
the Sorcerers' Collective with only three hundred men at
his back. He would have to fight to clear his mother's
name the hard way—through the law.

That had left Damin free to act on the disturbing news
Brose Rollin brought from Krakandar. He'd invited Kraig
along for the ride because he'd promised to see him safely
back to Greenharbour. Once this was done, once Mahkas
was dealt with, that was where Damin was headed. If the
worst happened, and he didn't survive the coming confrontation, Wrayan had promised to see the prince and his
bodyguards over the border into Medalon. They could find a
ship in Bordertown to take them south to a Fardohnyan port
where they had a much better chance of finding a ship heading to Denika.

It was the best he could do under the circumstances. Although he was more than a little grateful for the Denikan's
assistance during the battle, Kraig was a long way down
Damin's list of priorities at the moment.

What he *had* done, however, was remove their slave collars as soon as they were clear of the war camp. Nobody in
Damin's province seriously thought the Denikans had
brought the plague to Hythria, so there was no need to disguise them for their own protection here. Kraig had earned

the right to be treated according to his rank. Damin was determined to ensure that the Crown Prince of Denika returned home with a good impression of at least some small part of Hythria, even if it was only the small part of it that Damin was personally able to influence.

There was another reason for the small size of their party. They were all riding sorcerer-bred horses, having commandeered almost every mount in the war camp that had enough of the fabled bloodline in them to make them susceptible to magical manipulation. With Wrayan linked magically to the horses, they'd covered the first two hundred and fifty miles back to Krakandar in less than two days.

He made a silent promise to himself as they rode that he would find a way to equip every Raider in Krakandar with a sorcerer-bred mount if he could manage it. The ability to move at incomprehensible speed would give him a tactical advantage over his enemies that he'd be a fool to ignore. Of course, he'd need a sorcerer to make such a miracle a reality, but Wrayan lived in Krakandar and could probably be prevailed upon to aid his prince when the occasion called for it. Or he could bring Rorin to Krakandar. Provided Kalan would allow it.

Damin had cause to re-think his clever idea by the time they reached the Walsark Crossroads. Wrayan's ability was taxed to the limit controlling six horses. Each time he linked with the horses, Damin could see the toll it took on him. He trembled constantly, and when his eyes weren't burning like black coals from the power he was channelling, they were red-rimmed and watery.

When he looked at the thief as the crossroads appeared on the horizon just on dusk of the fifth day of their frenzied journey north, Damin realised that for the first time he could remember, Wrayan had visibly aged.

There was a delegation waiting for them on the edge of the sprawling refugee camp headed by Damin's cousin, Travin

Taranger. Xanda's older brother greeted Damin with relief and brought him up to date on the evacuation over a small camp fire just out of sight of the main camp.

The evacuation had begun three nights before Damin arrived, his cousin informed him, and Travin's best guess was that almost thirteen thousand people had already fled the city. Many of the refugees had made their way to Walsark, but many more had gotten as far as the crossroads and simply sat down to wait it out. Something had to happen; even the most ignorant beggar knew Krakandar was too strategically important to simply abandon it to a madman. Their prince would come to save them, they reasoned, or eventually the High Prince would send an army to secure Hythria's northern border. One way or another, something would have to give and the refugees had apparently decided the Walsark Crossroads was as good a place as any to wait for it to happen.

Travin Taranger was now left with the monumental and unenviable task of catering for the refugees and making certain they didn't starve to death, or worse, bring on another wave of the plague or some other devastating disease, by being crammed too close together in a disorganised and unhygienic refugee camp that sprawled as far as the eye could see in every direction around the crossroads.

"Do you have news of Xanda and Luciena?" Damin asked, when Travin finished his report.

"The children are safe in Walsark," Travin assured him. "My niece and nephews were among the first to leave the city, along with another four small boys who I believe belong to Tejay Lionsclaw."

"She'll be relieved to hear they're safe," Damin said. "In fact, you could probably make arrangements to send them straight back to Cabradell. I know their mother misses them."

"If only all our refugees were so easily taken care of."

"What about Xanda and Luciena? Didn't they come out with the children?"

Travin shrugged. "Xanda always intended to stay and

help. Luciena was meant to come out with the children, but according to her slave, Aleesha, the moment they stepped through the last tunnel, she gave her orders to bring the children to me, and then vanished back the way she'd come."

"So they're both still in the city. What about Bylinda?"

"No sign of her, I'm afraid. I'm not even sure she was privy to the plan."

"That's an understandable precaution. Can we get into the city the same way the people have been coming out?"

Travin shrugged. "Probably. They're still trying to get the stragglers out, but those who are left now are either the diehards or the lunatics. You know, the little old ladies refusing to leave their homes for fear they'll lose them. And the opportunists who think Mahkas may yet prevail."

Damin looked up at the sky. It had grown dark while they talked, but that wasn't necessarily a bad thing. It would be midnight before they reached the city even on fresh horses. Given Wrayan's exhaustion, Damin had no intention of asking the thief to get them to Krakandar any faster. He'd well and truly done enough.

He did want him with them when they entered the city, however. This mammoth effort was being coordinated by the Thieves' Guild. Damin wanted their leader with him when it came time to assert his own authority over the city again. If the guild started entertaining ambitions above and beyond honouring their god, Damin wanted Wrayan there to nip it in the bud.

He didn't really think Starros was going to be a problem, certain by now his best friend would have forgiven him for selling his soul to the God of Thieves. It just never hurt to take precautions.

"Do you have any news of Mahkas?" Damin asked finally, wondering what his reaction to this blatant challenge to his authority might be.

Travin shook his head. "He's been very ill, I know that much. I'm fairly certain the bulk of the population got away before he realised what was happening. And we've got over two thousand Raiders in the camp by now. But I've no news on what his reaction has been. Certainly no word about reprisals, which is something to be thankful for."

Damin frowned. "That means there are still another couple of thousand Raiders in the city. Who's in command of the men out here?"

"I don't know that anybody is. Most of the officers are still in the city."

"Then I'm putting you in command, Travin. Do you think you could have my Raiders outside the city walls by tomorrow morning?"

"*Your* Raiders?" Travin asked with a raised brow. "Last I heard, Mahkas was Regent of Krakandar, cousin, and you're just the heir-in-waiting with another six years of twiddling your thumbs ahead of you before you can claim anything."

Damin smiled. "Haven't you heard? The High Prince has lowered the age of majority to twenty-five."

"When did that happen?"

"About a week ago."

"How convenient for you, Damin."

"I thought so."

"And when exactly do you turn twenty-five?"

"I'm glad you asked that, Travin, because it just so happens that tomorrow is my birthday."

Travin looked impressed. "How convenient for you, Damin."

Damin didn't rise to the bait. "Can you do it, Trav? Get them organised and have them there by the morning?"

His cousin nodded. "I'll have them there. Will you have the gates open by then?"

Damin grinned at him. "It won't be much of a birthday party if the guests can't get in, now will it?"

Travin sighed at Damin's flippant reply. "In that case, my lord, we'll see you in Krakandar."

Damin looked at him oddly. Nobody ever called him that. "My *lord*?"

"Get used to it, cousin. It's the correct way to address a Warlord."

"I never really thought about it."

"Then your opponent has one up on you, Damin, because I suspect a day hasn't gone by in the past twenty-three years that Mahkas hasn't dreamed of what it means to be Warlord of Krakandar, and the winner of any prize is usually the one who wants it most."

CHAPTER 75

Empty of its population, the city of Krakandar was eerily quiet as Starros hurried through the darkened streets of the Beggars' Quarter in response to the summons he'd just received, demanding his presence at the entrance to the route leading through the sewers and out under the walls of the city. It was past midnight and he was exhausted. He hadn't stopped in three days. He'd been running back and forth like a madman, coordinating the various teams charged with getting everybody out of the city as quietly and efficiently as possible.

It was almost done now, however. The only people left in Krakandar didn't want to leave, and there was little Starros, the Thieves' Guild, or any other guild could do to convince them otherwise.

He wasn't sure what the problem at the tunnels was, and was hoping it was only a minor disaster awaiting him. He suspected it wasn't. Luc wouldn't have sent for him if it was something minor. He would have dealt with it himself.

When Starros arrived, he found a number of his men, who should have been stationed as lookouts, gathered around the tunnel entrance, which was housed in a warehouse near the outer wall of the Beggars' Quarter, normally used as a base by the slaves responsible for keeping the sewers free of debris. They'd commandeered the barn-sized building a few nights before the evacuation began, ensuring the cooperation of the slaves in question by promising the men their freedom once the job was done.

"Are we not worried about keeping a lookout any longer?" he enquired loudly, slamming the warehouse door behind him to get the men's attention. They were gathered in a tight, excited circle near the tunnel opening in the floor and if he hadn't known better, he would have sworn they were gambling.

The sound of the door slamming had the desired effect, however, and the men broke apart guiltily as he approached. He opened his mouth to demand an explanation and then realised he didn't need one. As the men fell back to allow him through, he discovered what was causing all the fuss.

"Damin Bloody Wolfblade."

The young prince turned to greet him. "Still using my name as a curse, I see."

Damin offered Starros his hand, but he didn't accept it, eyeing him up and down. The prince looked travel-stained and a little tired, but if battle had wrought any other changes on Damin Wolfblade, he could see no sign of them. "What are you doing here?"

Damin withdrew his hand with a puzzled look. "I got your message. Thought you could use some help."

"Aren't you supposed to be in Sunrise Province saving us from an evil swarm of Fardohnyans or something?"

He grinned. "Done that already."

"That didn't take long."

"The gods were on our side," he replied. "You're looking well."

"Yes," Starros agreed, unconsciously flexing his fingers as he neared the prince. "I am, aren't I? We need to have a little chat about that at some point."

"We *do*?"

Without warning, almost without thinking, Starros hit him. He'd been too well indoctrinated on fighting techniques as a lad by Almodavar to try punching Damin in the jaw, so he aimed for his nose. It was just a single punch, short, sharp and eminently satisfying. Damin staggered backwards, crying out in both pain and shock at the unexpectedness of the attack, but he didn't try to retaliate. Interestingly, none of the gathered thieves watching these two old friends settle their differences made any attempt to intervene, either.

"You sold my soul to the God of Thieves without asking, Damin."

The prince looked quite wounded by Starros's lack of appreciation, probing his bloody nose gingerly. "I thought you'd be grateful."

"He *is* grateful," Wrayan Lightfinger announced, stepping between them, perhaps thinking this wasn't really the time or place to settle this. Or maybe Wrayan recognised something in Starros's tone that didn't augur well for their friendship. Starros had been so surprised to find Damin returned, he hadn't even noticed Wrayan. The thief looked even more tired than Damin. In fact, he looked as if he'd aged ten years. That was remarkable in itself. Wrayan was part Harshini. He simply didn't get tired. And he hadn't aged in all the time Starros had known him.

"Wrayan! I thought you were still in Greenharbour."

"I heard what you were doing to my city," the thief said with a disarming smile. "Thought I'd better come back and see if I still had a job."

"Excuse me," Damin interjected nasally, his head tilted backwards as he pinched his nose with his left hand to halt the blood flow. "But it's actually *my* city, if you don't mind."

"Not yet it isn't," Starros warned.

"Only until I get to the palace," Damin assured him.

Starros studied him warily. He must have hit Damin in just the right spot. His nose was gushing blood as if he'd opened a vein. "Are you all right?"

Damin glared at him and then suddenly smiled. As peace gestures went, it wasn't much, but Starros knew Damin well enough to know it was probably all the apology he was ever likely to get. "I'll live."

Someone handed the prince a length of rag and he held it against his face to stanch the blood. Damin would go to his grave, Starros realised, thinking he'd done him a favour by selling his soul to the God of Thieves.

"It won't be easy, Damin. We've gotten the people out and as many Raiders as we dared, but Mahkas is still firmly in control of what's left and any troops still in the city are loyal to him. The only thing that's kept us safe so far is that he's been too sick to notice what's been going on. But Xanda tells me he was planning to be up and about this morning, so I don't imagine we have long before he realises what's happened."

"Where is Xanda, by the way?"

"He went back to the palace to find Luciena."

"Travin mentioned something about that. Why didn't she leave when she had the chance?"

"Xanda thinks she went back for Bylinda."

Damin thought for a moment before he spoke again. "If the real danger to Krakandar is Mahkas calling out the remaining Raiders when he realises there are no people left in the city, then we need to get to him before he does it."

"Now you're back, your highness, it shouldn't take much to get the remaining Raiders to lay down their arms," Luc North suggested, looking around at the circle of thieves, many of whom nodded in agreement.

"It'll be even easier if we can arrange for them not to pick them up in the first place," Damin pointed out. "But to do that, we need to remove Mahkas."

"Exactly what do you mean by *remove*?" one of the other thieves asked a little warily. Starros understood his concern. Even in support of the rightful heir, killing a Warlord was not something one undertook lightly.

"The High Prince has formally lowered the age of majority to twenty-five," Damin informed them. He took the rag away and gently probed his nose again. The bleeding seemed to have finally stopped. "I'm going to advise my uncle of this and ask him to stand aside and allow me to take up my birthright."

"And when he refuses?" Starros asked.

"Then as the legitimate Warlord of Krakandar, I'm well

within my rights to kill him." Damin glanced around the circle
of thieves as he tossed the bloody rag away. "Mahkas is my
problem, gentlemen. I won't ask any other man to deal with
it for me."

"Well, if you're looking for volunteers, my lord, there're
plenty of thieves left in the city who'd cheerfully kill
Mahkas Damaran for you. If you need the help, that is."

"Thank you," Damin replied. "I'll keep that in mind. In
the meantime, can we get to the palace without going
through the main gate? Through the sewers, perhaps?"

Starros changed his mind as he watched Damin. He'd
thought nothing had changed about his old friend, but he was
mistaken. There was an indefinable air of command about
him now. When he'd first come home to Krakandar, the
young prince acted as if he expected nobody to take him seriously. Now it was as if he knew he would be listened to, as
if he expected to be followed. It was a subtle difference, but
it was unmistakable and it sat so easily on the young man's
shoulders that Starros suspected it took Damin far less effort
to maintain this side of his personality than the frivolous and
flippant façade he'd maintained prior to Leila's death.

"We can go through the fens," Starros told him. "And
from there through the back gate and into the slaveways via
the palace storerooms behind the kitchens. I even have the
master key."

Damin eyed him curiously. "Taking your new career a little
seriously, aren't you?"

"And whose fault is it that I *have* a new career, Damin?"

"What about afterwards?" Luc asked, before Damin could
respond to the accusation.

"Afterwards?" the prince asked, the question catching
him off guard. He was still staring at Starros, obviously hurt
his friend wasn't more grateful for the way he'd saved him
from certain death.

"He means after you take back the city," Starros explained. "The Thieves' Guild has been instrumental in handing your city back to you, Damin. Instead of a sealed city
with four or five thousand Raiders that you'd have to lay

siege to for months, you've got a clear run to the palace, the prospect of few, if any, civilian casualties, and an opportunity to take the whole damned province without shedding more than a few drops of Mahkas Damaran's blood. That's got to be worth something."

Clearly unhappy about it, Damin hesitated before he answered. "We'll talk about it once the city is mine." He glanced around the circle of faces, expecting agreement, and then began heading toward the warehouse doors.

"If you want the help of the Thieves' Guild, we'll talk about it now, your highness," Starros informed him.

Damin stopped and turned to look at him, before he turned to Wrayan, who—significantly—hadn't followed the prince either. "You need to have a little chat with your newest recruit, Wrayan. The Thieves' Guild doesn't rule Krakandar."

"They do tonight," Wrayan replied, stepping up to stand with Starros. "And I'm afraid I have to agree with my newest recruit. How exactly *are* you planning to reward the Thieves' Guild for delivering your city to you, my lord?"

Damin was clearly shocked to find himself confronted with such a question. Years of friendship had lulled him into forgetting Wrayan ruled the dark underbelly of Krakandar City. That Damin had accepted the aid of the Thieves' Guild as his due didn't surprise Starros. Wrayan backing him against Damin without hesitation did, however.

Damin studied the two thieves in disbelief. "Are you serious?"

"Nobody's laughing."

"What do you want?"

"What are you offering?"

Damin glared at Starros, and took a threatening step closer. "How about I offer not to leave any marks?"

Starros didn't flinch. "You'll have to do better than that, Damin. We've risked everything for you."

"Horseshit!" Damin exclaimed. "According to Travin, you organised this evacuation as some sort of glorious prank to honour your god. There's more than a few refugees out there who think you did it just so you could sack the city in peace. You didn't even know if I'd get your message, let alone be here tonight. Don't try to make your little escapade appear noble, Starros, just because I happened to turn up at a convenient time for you to claim the glory."

Starros shrugged. "I'm a thief now, Damin. Thanks to you. I'm compelled to steal anything I can. Even glory when the chance arises."

Damin turned his impatient gaze on Wrayan. "We don't have time for this, Wrayan."

The sorcerer smiled, apparently amused by this power struggle going on between the two old friends. "Then I suggest you give him what he wants so we can get on with the real reason we're here."

Exasperated, Damin threw up his hands. "What do you want?"

"A general amnesty," Starros informed him. "No thief is to be held accountable for anything that goes missing until your rule of the city is established."

"So you *are* planning to sack the city?"

"Only a little bit of it." He shrugged. "And only from the people who can afford it."

Damin glared at him. "Let me get this straight. In return for the help of the Thieves' Guild, you want me to turn a blind eye to you and your little friends looting the rich houses of the city, until I can wrest control of it from Mahkas?"

"That pretty much covers it."

The prince thought about it and then, with a great deal of reluctance, he conceded defeat. "Very well. Until I open the gates of the city and let my army back in, you have a free hand."

Starros smiled. "See, that wasn't so difficult, was it?"

"That gives you about three hours, Starros. Make the most of them."

"You think you can remove Mahkas and regain control in three hours?"

"I think I can take care of Mahkas a lot sooner than that.

As for the rest of the city, the army is already on their way. Travin promises me they'll be here by daybreak."

Starros was impressed. He didn't think Damin would think to do that. *Mind you,* he reminded himself, *I didn't think he'd agree to the looting, either.*

Damin didn't seem amused Starros had forced such a concession from him. "You need to watch your back, Wrayan," the prince warned. "I'm not the only one with a realm in danger of being taken away from him by a madman."

Wrayan glanced at Starros and smiled. "I don't think I have too much to worry about. Besides, I'm not quite as attached to my kingdom as you are to yours. If I lose it to someone younger and smarter, I can always find another."

The comment surprised Starros a little, but before he could puzzle out what Wrayan meant, another group of thieves emerged from the tunnels, leading two Denikan women wearing unfamiliar leather clothing and a rather alarming array of weapons and following them, the largest man Starros had ever seen. The thieves automatically fell back as the big Denikan and his companions stepped out of the tunnel and into the circle of torches.

"So this is your city, Damin Wolfblade," the Denikan remarked, looking around the warehouse and its motley occupants with open curiosity. "Not exactly the reception I was expecting."

"Nor I," Damin agreed, looking pointedly at Starros. "What are you doing here, Kraig? I thought I asked you to stay with Travin until I'd secured the city?"

"Your cousin has far too much to do to be hindered entertaining foreign dignitaries, your highness. We thought we would be more help here."

"You and two girls are going to help us take a whole city?" a sceptical voice asked from behind Starros.

Damin glanced around at the thieves, who were all staring suspiciously at the newcomers. "This is Prince Lunar Shadow Kraig of the House of the Rising Moon, the ruling house of Denika," he announced, "and his bodyguards Lady Lyrian and Lady Barlaina. Prince Kraig has already aided us a great deal in devising a strategy to defeat the Fardohnyans when we were outnumbered two to one."

Starros studied the strangers curiously, wondering how Damin had come by such odd companions. "Well, if they've already helped you defeat thousands of marauding Fardohnyans, the few stragglers left in Krakandar shouldn't even raise a sweat. Are you sure you and your new best friends here even *need* the help of the Thieves' Guild?"

Damin stared at him and then inexplicably, he smiled. "I know what's going on here. And you haven't beaten me tonight, Starros. I'm letting you win because it suits me."

The prince might have acquired an air of command, but some things never changed. He still couldn't bear to lose. Not even on some vague point of honour. Starros shrugged, knowing his indifference to his friend's score keeping would drive Damin crazy. "Whatever."

"And if it takes me ten years," Damin added, "I'll find a way to get even with you for putting me in this position."

Hearing Damin admit that was really all Starros wanted. He hadn't got one up on Damin Wolfblade since that day twelve years ago, when they'd fought in the fens over Leila—the day Princess Marla had come home and found them fighting. It wasn't exactly recompense for having his soul sold to a god without his permission, but it was something. He was content he'd proved his point.

"Are we going to take this city or stand around here talking about it all night?"

Damin hesitated, obviously debating whether or not to push the issue, and then seemed to thrust the problem aside as he nodded in agreement.

"You're right, old friend," he said. "Let's go take my city back."

chapter 76

Mahkas Damaran had realised there was something seriously amiss when he couldn't find Emilie after dinner. His great-niece had been a godsend these past few weeks, helping ease the pain of Leila's dreadful death, even helping him forget The Bastard Fosterling for a time, the man responsible for her suicide.

At least, he consoled himself, *The Bastard Fosterling is dead.*

Xanda had assured him of it; so had every other man and woman in the palace that he'd questioned. They all agreed Starros was dead. And they all swore they had no idea where he was buried.

Not knowing the location of his body ate at Mahkas. He wanted to see The Bastard Fosterling's rotting corpse for himself. He wanted to be sure the filthy pig was dead. He needed to see an unmoving chest, feel the lack of breath, assure himself there was no pulse. If The Bastard Fosterling was dead, Mahkas wanted to be absolutely certain of it.

And just as nobody could tell him where Starros was buried, so nobody seemed to be able to tell him where Emilie was this evening, either.

He'd promised to take her riding again, as soon as he was better. His arm still ached abominably, but the pain and high fever of the infection was a rapidly fading memory. He still remembered Emilie sitting on the bed, holding his hand to comfort him, while Darian Coe sliced into his infected flesh. She was a good girl, Emilie Taranger. So innocent. So full of hope. So full of promise.

So much like Leila when she was a child.

And that was going to be a problem, Mahkas feared.

Emilie's similarity to Leila was a tragedy waiting for a place to happen.

The weak and misguided ministrations of her foolish mother had allowed Leila to be seduced by The Bastard Fosterling. Mahkas had convinced himself of that. Now he intended to make certain the same didn't happen to his beloved niece, Emilie. And it would, he was convinced, if he didn't take precautions. Luciena Taranger wasn't a fit mother; a blind man could see that. She was common-born, for one, just like Bylinda. The daughter of a sailor and a whore. Not a fit mother for the great-niece of the Warlord of Krakandar.

Although his wife had come from the wealthy merchant class, Mahkas realised now that money didn't make up for breeding. You couldn't buy class, any more than you could buy respectability. These commoners just didn't understand what it meant to be highborn; they had no real grasp of the privilege or the duty that went with being one of the ruling elite.

He'd been planning to talk to Xanda about it for days now. Once he was well enough, Mahkas intended to take his nephew aside and point out to him how his daughter was being ruined by her mother. He intended to use his own tragedy with Leila as an example of the perils of ignoring the warning signs. Xanda would be grateful for his advice, naturally, and would—Mahkas was in no doubt—immediately take steps to remove Emilie from the dangerous influence of her mother.

Of course, none of his advice would be any use unless he found Emilie so he *could* save her, and despite sending for her at least three times this evening, there was still no sign of the child. Finally, he decided to look for her himself. If her mother suspected Mahkas was about to have her excluded from any further contact with her daughter, she might be trying to prevent it by hiding Emilie from him.

He couldn't allow that, he determined, as he hurried along

the broad hall to her room. Emilie was his niece, his own flesh and blood. Her mother had no right to her at all. Luciena was simply the common-born breeding cow Xanda had used to give his precious daughter life.

He reached Emilie's room, full of righteous indignation about the way Luciena was spoiling his niece, muttering about her low birth in his rasping, whispery voice, the voice so cruelly destroyed by that ungrateful whelp, Damin Wolfblade.

Once he started thinking about Damin, Mahkas became so wrapped up in his own anger he didn't notice there were no guards on Emilie's room. He threw back the door and stalked through the darkened outer room and into the bedroom, only to discover her bed was still made and obviously hadn't been slept in.

He stared at the empty bed, the unlit candles, puzzled by what they might mean, and then he hurried out into the hall and glanced up and down the corridor. There were no guards at all, he realised. Not on any of the bedrooms.

And it was quiet. Unnaturally quiet. There were no slaves going about their business. No Raiders standing guard over the sleeping members of their ruling family.

It was as if he was the only living soul still in the palace.

Mahkas grew increasingly concerned as he checked each of the bedrooms, only to find exactly what he'd found in Emilie's room. The beds were made, nobody had slept in them. Even the young Lionsclaw boys were missing. He tried to call out, tried to summon Orleon to demand an explanation, by his voice couldn't be heard ten feet away, let alone echo through the palace commanding attention.

Angrily, he kept searching the rooms until finally he had a stroke of luck. He found Luciena in Bylinda's rooms. She was in the outer room by the settee, on her knees in front of his wife, begging her to go somewhere. The moment he saw Luciena, he knew his suspicions about a conspiracy were well founded. Everything about her—her words, her tone of voice, her anxious demeanour—all reeked of treachery.

The women didn't notice him when he first opened the door so he stood there a moment, listening to all his fears solidify into hideous reality.

". . . you *must* come with me, Bylinda," Luciena was urging. "This might be your only chance to get away from here."

"I have to stay," his wife replied in that damn irritatingly vague tone she'd adopted since his daughter died. "I have to stay near Leila."

"But we're not going very far," Luciena promised, taking Bylinda's hands in hers and squeezing them reassuringly. "Just as far as the Walsark Crossroads. Travin will be there. And the children. Damin will be there soon, too, I'm certain of it, and . . . Lord Damaran!" She jumped to her feet looking as guilty as a Karien sinner. "How long have you been there?"

"Long enough," he said in his rasping whisper.

She looked at him questioningly. "*Sorry?*"

Mahkas snarled with frustration when he realised she couldn't hear what he was saying. He stepped into the room and repeated himself, but the effect was lost with the second telling.

"Oh! . . . Well . . . then you'll probably want to come along, too," Luciena suggested with forced cheerfulness. "I was just asking Aunt Bylinda if she wanted to go . . . on a picnic." Luciena cringed a little as she spoke, knowing how foolish such a suggestion was, given it was after midnight.

"Liar!" he accused, his throat aching from the effort as he stalked across the rug to confront her. "I knew it! You're in league with Damin Wolfblade!"

"Don't be silly!" she said. "He's not even here. He's in Cabradell fighting the Fardohnyans."

"You're plotting against me!" he charged. "You're trying to turn my wife against me!"

"I'm tying to burn your life against a *tree*?" Luciena repeated with a puzzled look.

Mahkas wanted to scream with frustration, certain she was deliberately misunderstanding him, but he had no more hope of doing that than he did of making himself clearly understood. "Don't play games with me, woman!"

"Mahkas, I'm *trying* to understand you," she assured him soothingly, "if you could just speak a little more . . . loudly . . ."

"You heard what I said!" he declared, his shredded voice making him sound ridiculous. "And I heard what *you* said! You want to take Bylinda to meet Damin. Is that where everyone else has gone? To join my enemies? I knew it! I knew all along this ruse about a war with Fardohnya was just an elaborate lie! That ungrateful whelp! Leila would never have killed herself if he'd had even a modicum of compassion. It wasn't her fault! The Bastard Fosterling raped her."

Luciena took a step back from him as he ranted. That made him feel better. It was good when people feared him.

"Mahkas, are you sure you should be out of bed, yet? You've been very ill . . ."

"I'm well enough to see what's going on here!" he snarled, every harshly whispered word scouring his ravaged throat. "You're both as bad as each other! Common-born whores, the both of you, out to ruin our daughters."

"*Daughters*?" Luciena asked, a little confused. "You had one daughter, Mahkas. Remember? The one you whipped like a dog and then drove to suicide?"

Mahkas's right arm was still in a sling, but there was nothing wrong with his left arm. With all the strength he could muster, he backhanded Luciena without warning, throwing her back against the fireplace. Her head cracked against the polished granite with a sickening thud. She collapsed against it like a rag doll and lay there, unmoving.

Good, Mahkas thought with satisfaction. *That takes care of that problem.*

Then he glanced at his wife. She had risen to her feet and was staring at him with an odd expression.

"Why are you looking at me like that? You're the traitor here!"

"You didn't keep your oath."

"What oath?"

"You promised to protect us."

"*Us*? Who is *us*?"

"Leila and me."

"*Protect* you? I *killed* to protect you!" he croaked painfully. "I killed to protect Leila! You have no idea of the things I've done to make this world a place fit for my daughter! Don't you dare tell me I didn't keep my oath!"

"But you failed, Mahkas. Leila is dead."

"That's Damin's fault! Not mine."

She smiled distantly. "A month ago it was Starros's fault. Whose fault will it be next month? Mine?"

He stared at her, suddenly confronted with a stranger. "What are you babbling about?"

"You didn't keep your oath."

"For pity's sake, woman," he snapped, turning his back on her. "Shut up about that!" His throat was on fire. He needed to take something to ease it. Some honey, perhaps, in warm milk. That usually helped when he overdid things . . .

And he needed to raise his army. If he was under attack he intended to face it head on. *So Damin is at the Walsark Crossroads, is he? Well, we'll see how that murderous little ingrate reacts when I launch a surprise attack on . . .*

Mahkas cried out and fell to his knees as a sharp pain shot through his lower back. He grabbed at the site of the pain and discovered his hand sticky with blood when it came away. He barely had time to register that remarkable fact when the sharp sting struck again, a little higher, and he realised he was being stabbed a second time.

He turned to fight off his attacker, thinking, *This is what I get for not checking that Luciena was actually dead.*

But when he turned he discovered Luciena still lay unmoving by the hearth.

"*Bylinda?*"

As pale as a wraith, she was standing behind him, dressed in her mourning white, a small and bloody table knife held before her. If he hadn't seen the blood on her hands, he'd never have believed the blade dangerous enough to do any damage. Or that Bylinda would try to harm him.

His wife stared at him with eyes that seemed to be looking somewhere far away. "You didn't keep your oath," she said. Her voice was toneless, flat. Devoid of all emotion.

"For the gods' sake, woman!" he gasped. "Put that blade down before you hurt someone!" The pain in his back where she'd stabbed him was intense, but given what he'd suffered lately, not enough to incapacitate him. He held out his left hand, expecting her to hand over the weapon. "Give it to me."

"You didn't keep your oath," she repeated.

"I'll give you an oath now, you stupid bitch," he threatened hoarsely. "Give me that knife this minute or you'll rue the day you ever met me!"

"I'm long past that day, Mahkas." She glanced down at the blade, staring at it as if it was something she'd never seen before, as if the blood on it was some novel substance needing close investigation.

Wincing with the pain, Mahkas stepped closer, expecting to snatch the blade from her grasp. Instead, quick as a snake, she slashed the knife across his hand. He stared at the blood welling on his palm in shock, before fixing his furious gaze on his wife.

"Give it to me!"

"You didn't keep your oath."

"Stop saying that!"

"You didn't keep your oath."

"I swear by every god I can name, Bylinda, if you don't shut your fool mouth and give me that blade this instant . . ."

"Take it, then," she dared, thrusting it forward sharply.

He wasn't quick enough to get out of its way. The blade sliced into his right shoulder, sending a jarring bolt of pain along his infected arm. With the pain came the first metallic taste of fear as it occurred to Mahkas that not only could

Bylinda do him serious harm with that ridiculous little table knife, she intended to.

"Guards!" he bellowed as loud as he could manage. The cry came out in a strangled whisper. It was a wasted effort. Bylinda could barely make out his words; even if they'd been there, a guard in the hall would have no idea his master was calling him, let alone realise he was in imminent danger. The only other person in the room, the only one who might have been able to talk some sense into his wife, lay unmoving by the fireplace, blood seeping from her cracked skull.

Bylinda smiled humourlessly when she realised he was helpless. "Nobody can hear you."

Mahkas glanced over his shoulder at the door, wondering if he could make it out of the room before his wife caught him. He was in pain and bleeding from several small wounds, his arm was pounding and his throat felt as if it had been sanded with a rasp. Warily, he turned his attention back to Bylinda, thinking he might still be able to talk his way out of this. Bylinda didn't usually defy him. This was Luciena's fault. She'd poisoned his wife against him.

Changing his tack, Mahkas smiled at her. "If you give me the knife now, I won't punish you too harshly," he promised, reaching out to her again.

She shook her head. "You punish everyone harshly, Mahkas. Even your own daughter."

"Leila had to be taught a lesson, Bylinda."

"What about Darilyn?"

He hesitated, wondering what his long-dead sister had to do with this. "She's been dead for twenty-five years."

"You killed her, too, didn't you?" Bylinda accused. "In fact, I'm not sure which is worse—that you strangled your own sister with a harp wire or that you took those poor little innocent boys in to find her body and let them grow up thinking their mother had killed herself in disgrace."

Mahkas stared at her in horror. *How could she know that?*

"Luciena didn't know why you killed Darilyn," Bylinda

continued, "but I can guess the reason. It was something to do with Riika, wasn't it? Were you involved with her kidnapping, Mahkas? I remember Laran and you talking about it. I remember watching you, thinking how terrible it must have been for you to lose both your sisters like that. You sat there with a perfectly straight face and swore to your brother it was Darilyn who'd betrayed Riika, when all the time it was you, wasn't it?" She didn't raise her voice. She didn't even seem angry. If anything, she seemed contemptuous of him. "Did you kill poor Laran, too, or was it just a little bit of serendipity that he got himself killed before he discovered the truth?"

"You have no idea what you're talking about, woman."

"How could you even look at those poor children after you murdered their mother, let alone bring them into our home and expect me to raise them?"

Mahkas was rapidly losing patience with this. "Give me that damned knife, woman, before I—"

"Before you *what*, husband? Beat me? I don't care. You've taken the only thing I loved from me. There's no greater pain I fear now. And you know the worst of it? You've made me guilty by association. Your crimes are my crimes, Mahkas, because I never tried to stop you."

Threatening her wasn't working, so he tried changing his approach again.

"I'm sorry, my love," he crooned softly, moving a little closer. She had that faraway look in her eye again. He edged his way forward, thinking he could snatch the knife from her before she could attack him again. Once she was disarmed, he intended to beat her to within an inch of her life for this treachery. "Bylinda . . . darling . . ."

She stabbed him in the forearm this time, the knife in and out almost before he had time to register the pain. He cried out—a hoarse, useless, whispered cry nobody but Bylinda could hear.

"It hurts, doesn't it?" she said. "Being killed, a little bit at a time."

"I swear, Bylinda," he threatened, advancing on her angrily. "If you don't stop this nonsense . . ."

The knife took him in the shoulder this time. Before he could stop her, she changed her grip on the knife and plunged it downward past his collarbone and into the jugular. Blood spurting over them both, Mahkas collapsed to his knees with the shock and stared up at her, truly afraid of her now.

"*Bylinda . . .*"

"You didn't keep your oath," she said, looking down at him unsympathetically as she pulled the knife out and almost casually changed the bloody knife to her other hand and plunged it into his right shoulder.

"You lied to Laran." *Stab.*

"You lied to Travin and Xanda." She stabbed him again. "You lied to Marla."

And again she struck him, punctuating each accusation with her blade.

"You lied to me."

Again the blade sliced into him, the pain searing through his body as she attacked his wounded arm.

"And you lied to Leila when you didn't keep your oath."

"Stop it!" he rasped, not sure if it was the stings of her little blade, the loss of blood, or the torment of her accusations that was driving him mad.

"You didn't keep your oath."

She struck him again and he collapsed even further, on his hands and knees now, his back exposed to her. He felt the blade bite yet again, this time close to his spine. He could taste salty blood in his mouth and fear on his breath.

"Why . . . why are you doing this?" he cried, still not able to fully comprehend her cold, unrelenting rage.

"For Leila," Bylinda told him calmly, raising her arm to strike again. "I'm doing this for Leila."

chapter 77

The palace was asleep when Damin and his small band of invaders entered the reception room through the slaveways. Damin chose the upstairs exit from the slaveways because at this hour of the night, it was certain to be empty. The last thing they needed was to stumble over a squad of early rising slaves taking care of the ashes in the hearth of one of the more commonly used rooms downstairs.

They stepped into the cavernous hall, hurrying across the polished parquet floor with footsteps that sounded far too loud for comfort. When they reached the entrance, Damin halted everyone with a hand signal, and then he turned to face them.

"I'm guessing Mahkas will be in his bed at this hour," Damin told them softly. "So that's where I'm headed. Wrayan, I need you to find Xanda and Luciena. Starros and Kraig, ladies, you're with me. Luc, you and your people are with Wrayan."

The thief nodded. "What do we do if we encounter any resistance?"

"We won't," Wrayan assured him, but he was looking at Damin when he answered. Damin understood immediately. Between his magical powers and his status in the Thieves' Guild, Wrayan feared very few men. Besides, once they found Xanda, his cousin would be able to order any Raiders left in the palace to lay down their arms with a good expectation of being obeyed, even without Wrayan's magical assistance.

"And if we find Mahkas?" Wrayan asked.

"You come and get me. I'll deal with him."

The thief looked relieved that he and his men weren't going to be held accountable for the death of Krakandar's regent, regardless of how much everyone thought he deserved it.   .

Nothing more was said as the intruders left the empty room and turned in opposite directions down the corridor. Damin made no further attempt to conceal his presence. He strode through the darkened halls as if he owned the place. It was bad enough that he'd had to enter the palace by skulking through the slaveways. He didn't intend to skulk any more. Certainly not in his own home.

"Where do you want to look first?" Starros asked softly as he caught up with Damin's long-legged stride, looking around with concern. He would have been much more comfortable if they were skulking, Damin thought. Kraig, Barlaina and Lyrian, on the other hand were looking around with open curiosity as they followed him through the palace.

"We'll start with the bedrooms," he announced, making no attempt to lower his voice. "If what you're telling me about Mahkas being ill is correct, he may well be sound asleep in his bed."

Starros glanced at Damin sceptically. "Are we taking odds on that?"

They took the stairs to the next floor without encountering a single soul. Damin had wandered the halls of Krakandar Palace any number of times as a boy, but he had never before experienced such an eerie feeling of emptiness. It was as if the life had been sucked out of the building, leaving only an empty shell, haunted by painful memories.

The wing of the palace that housed the sleeping quarters was just as deserted as the rest of the building. Damin passed his own room, the one he'd shared with Starros as a child, Leila's room, the bedroom the twins had always called their own, the oddness of it all tugging on his memories of this place. He'd never seen this passage devoid of guards before. Never seen it plunged into darkness like this. Not a lamp was lit, not a single soul seemed to be in residence.

He hesitated when he reached Mahkas's room at the end of the hall.

"Is this where we will find your uncle?" Kraig asked.

Damin nodded. Immediately Lyrian and Barlaina began to reach for their weapons.

"He's a sick man and he's probably asleep," Damin informed them with a frown. "Let's not get too excited, ladies."

"You remain calm if you wish, your highness," Lyrian suggested tartly. "In my experience it's the *probablys* that usually require weapons. Besides, did we not come here to kill this man?"

This bloodthirsty need to inflict violence on someone—anyone—was an alarming tendency he'd noticed both women appeared to be suffering from, ever since he'd removed the slave collars and returned their own clothes and weapons after they'd left Lasting Drift. Everything was far too black and white in Lyrian's world, and he really didn't have the time to explain all the various shades of grey to her. Damin looked to Kraig for a bit of support, confident the prince would understand why he couldn't risk Lyrian and Barlaina bursting into Mahkas's room and slicing him into little pieces just for fun.

Kraig seemed to understand what Damin wanted of him. "You must not harm this man," he ordered his bodyguards. "It is Prince Damin's right alone to butcher this pretender."

He frowned, thinking the phrase *butcher this pretender* was a little extreme, but the prince's words seemed to have the desired effect. The women looked quite disappointed they were to be denied the opportunity to shed some blood and reluctantly returned their knives to the tooled leather sheaths they were wearing.

"Actually, why don't you two go with Starros and check the other bedrooms?" he suggested. That would keep them occupied and lessen the opportunity for butchering pretenders. "Just don't kill anyone without asking first."

Starros looked at the two women a little warily, and headed back down the hall with them, leaving Damin and Kraig standing outside Mahkas's door.

Damin hesitated, afraid of what he might find.

"You have come this far," Kraig said. "Don't falter on the brink of victory."

"Is it victory to kill a sick old man in cold blood?"

"Compassion is something one can only afford when one is through being ruthless, Damin."

The prince smiled faintly, not at the Denikan's words so much, as how similar he sounded to Elezaar. Physically, the handsome big Denikan and the deformed little dwarf had nothing in common, but in every other way they were soul mates.

"Then let's go butcher the pretender, shall we?"

But he got no further than putting his hand on the latch before Starros called out urgently from down the hall.

"*Damin*! In here!"

Abandoning Mahkas's room, Damin and Kraig turned and ran, following the young thief's cry into the next suite down the hall. Bylinda's room.

When they burst through the door, Damin discovered Lyrian lighting all the candles she could find in the room.

Mahkas Damaran—the man he'd come here to remove or kill—was lying on the floor near the settee.

At least, Damin assumed it was Mahkas. It was hard to tell with all the blood.

"It would appear someone has already butchered the pretender for you," Kraig remarked, staring down at the body.

Whoever had killed Mahkas Damaran had stabbed him over and over again until there was little left but a bloody carcass. He'd been stabbed so many times it was impossible to guess which of the hundreds of blows might have killed him. The rage, the pain behind such a vicious attack left Damin gasping.

"Luciena!"

Damin looked up and discovered Starros bending over his adopted sister's body, which lay lifeless and broken by the fireplace, the pool of blood under her head glistening in the candlelight.

"Dear gods! Is she . . ." he began, hurrying over to them, almost afraid to complete the question.

Starros shook his head. "She's alive. Help me."

Mahkas temporarily forgotten, Lyrian and Barlaina hurried to Starros's aid and together, the three of them lifted her gently onto the settee. Damin stared at her limp form, guilt warring with concern.

It was his fault Luciena had stayed in Krakandar with Xanda.

"Are you sure she's . . . there's an awful lot of blood."

"Head wounds always bleed profusely," Barlaina informed them, pushing Starros out of the way so she could tend to Luciena. "Bring me more light."

Lyrian hurried to comply and Starros stepped back as he found himself superfluous in the face of the Denikan woman's competence. Damin watched Barlaina working, wondering if it was Luciena who had murdered Mahkas so brutally.

And what might have driven her to it.

"Damin."

He glanced over at Kraig, wondering at his odd tone. The Denikan was standing by Mahkas's body, pointing to the floor.

With the additional light, a series of small, bloody footsteps were revealed, leading away from the corpse. Curiously, Damin picked up a candlestick and followed them. They led, not out into the hall, but into the bedroom.

Had Mahkas's murderer come and gone through the slaveways?

He opened the bedroom door and found it undisturbed. The bed was made, the entrance to the slaveways in the dressing room off to the left still firmly closed.

The footsteps led to the open window.

Was it an assassin, then, Damin wondered, *who finally ended Mahkas's life?*

The curtains billowed in a faint wisp of breeze and Damin caught sight of someone moving out on the roof. He put the candle down on the table by the door and walked over to the window, wondering if the assassin was still out there.

Were they so close on his heels they'd disturbed him in the act?

He pushed the curtain aside and froze when he realised

the figure standing on the edge of the sloped roof was Bylinda Damaran.

He turned to Kraig. "Find Wrayan," he ordered softly, thinking if he couldn't get his aunt back from the edge, then Wrayan might be able to force her back magically.

Kraig glanced out of the window, saw the figure perched on the edge of the roof and nodded. He was gone from the room by the time Damin climbed out of the window and began to make his way cautiously towards the edge of the roof, high above the paved courtyard of Krakandar Palace, where the blood-splattered figure of Bylinda Damaran stood, perched at the very edge of oblivion.

chapter 78

Bylinda looked up as Damin approached. Draped in her white mourning clothes and the blood of her dead husband, she'd been studying the drop to the pavement below as if debating something important within herself and Damin's arrival had distracted her.

She glanced over her shoulder at him and smiled distantly. "Hello, Damin."

"Aunt Bylinda."

"When did you get back? Luciena said you were waiting at the Walsark Crossroads." She spoke as if they were standing in the parlour, catching up after a long absence.

"I was going to . . . you *spoke* to Luciena?"

"Just before Mahkas killed her. She wanted me to leave the palace, to come visit you, but I explained I couldn't leave. I had to stay near Leila." His aunt sounded lucid, but her calm demeanour was at complete odds with a woman standing on the edge of a precipice.

Damin smiled at her reassuringly. Despite her rational tone, it was clear Bylinda had tipped over the edge of reason into insanity. "Luciena isn't dead, my lady. Just unconscious. She's going to be fine."

Bylinda nodded. "I'm glad to hear that. I've always liked Luciena. She's so . . . assured. Confident. I would have liked Leila to have grown up like that."

Damin inched his way forward as she was speaking, hoping to get close enough to pull his aunt back from the edge. The breeze was cool and, at this height, quite strong, and he was wearing riding boots, which (he discovered with alarm) gave him nothing like the sure-footed grip he remembered having as a child when he flitted across these roofs in bare feet.

"She'd like to see you, too, Aunt Bylinda. Why don't you come back inside so you can speak to her?"

Bylinda shook her head. "I don't think so, Damin."

"Bylinda . . ."

"Did you not see what I did?" she asked, turning to look down at the dizzying drop once more.

"Do you mean Mahkas?" he asked warily.

"I killed him."

Given the amount of blood she was wearing, and the footsteps he'd followed to find her, the news was no surprise to Damin. What did surprise him—and concern him greatly—was her calm, almost unnatural poise.

"Don't blame yourself, Aunt Bylinda. You merely got to him first. I came here to kill him, you know."

Bylinda glanced at him over her shoulder. "I realised that as soon as Luciena told me you were coming home. After what happened with Leila and Starros, there wasn't any other way this was going to be resolved."

"Bylinda, come inside," he urged, holding his hand out to her. "Nobody is going to hold you accountable for—"

"But I am accountable," she cut in, looking up at the starlit night. "Guilty by association. Mahkas's crimes are my crimes, Damin."

With that sort of reasoning, she was a mere step away from

walking off the edge of the roof. "Don't be silly. Nothing he did can be considered your fault."

"What if I knew?" she asked. "What if all this time I saw the signs and turned a blind eye to them because he was my husband and a wife must support her husband, even when she knows he's evil."

"I can't believe you did that."

"Then you are naïve, Damin. I knew Mahkas had something to do with Darilyn's death. And Riika's. I could tell by the way he was acting when he brought Travin and Xanda back to Krakandar after they buried his sisters. It wasn't his responsibility to raise those boys. It was your father's job. Laran Krakenshield was their guardian and he had a wife, so there wasn't anything stopping him taking on their care. Your mother should have raised your cousins, not me. But Mahkas insisted. He said he owed it to the boys. As if he was somehow obligated to them."

"Maybe he was just being generous . . ." Damin suggested, finding it a little bizarre to think he was standing here on the roof of Krakandar Palace trying to justify Mahkas's actions. He couldn't think of anything else to do. He had no idea what Bylinda was talking about. He knew who Darilyn and Riika were, of course. They were his father's sisters, both of whom died before he was born. But he'd never imagined Mahkas might have been involved in their deaths.

Bylinda fixed her gaze on Damin. "Don't confuse charity with self-interest, Damin. Mahkas was generous only when it suited him. Or when he thought it would make others think well of him. He did nothing that wasn't designed to further his own ambitions." She turned back to look out over the city. There were only sporadic pinpoints of light in the sea of darkness. Most of the city was deserted. "He married me because my family had money, you know," she told him, in a voice devoid of emotion. "It meant he wasn't reliant on Laran, you see. I knew that right from the start, but I didn't care because he was young and handsome and the Warlord of Krakandar's brother—who could have had any highborn woman he wanted—chose me, a simple merchant's daughter. You were born a prince, Damin. You have no concept of what that can mean to someone like me."

Damin had no idea how to answer that so he said nothing, letting her ramble on, wondering where the hell Kraig was with Wrayan.

"From the moment Leila drew her first breath he planned for you to marry her," Bylinda continued. "He tried so hard to make you love him because he needed your support and if you loved him like the father you never knew, then you'd give him what he wanted when you were old enough."

"It might have worked if he hadn't beaten Leila and Starros half to death," Damin agreed, hoping to keep her talking while he inched his way forward. While she was talking, she wasn't jumping.

Bylinda shook her head, seemingly unaware of the perilous drop before her, or the absurdity of having this conversation on the palace roof in the small hours of the morning with her husband lying dead by her hand in the room behind them.

"The irony," she sighed, "was he never understood you were far smarter than you let on. He thought you shared his delusions. He thought I shared them too, but that's my fault, because I let him think that."

"You can't know how things would have turned out if you'd acted differently, Aunt Bylinda."

"Do you think things would have worked out differently if I'd shared my fears with your father?" she sighed. "If I'd gone to Laran Krakenshield and told him my suspicions about Darilyn and Riika, when you were still a baby, Damin, he might be alive today, because forewarned, perhaps he wouldn't have been fool enough to trust his brother with anything, let alone watching his back in battle."

That accusation took Damin completely by surprise. "Are you saying Mahkas killed my father?"

Bylinda shrugged. "I don't know. But I am saying he

killed Darilyn, he undoubtedly had something to do with Riika dying, which is *why* he killed Darilyn, and even if he didn't kill Laran himself, he probably stood back and let the Medalonians kill your father for him."

Even knowing what he did about Mahkas, that seemed too much to comprehend. "I . . . I can't believe he'd do something like that . . ."

"Damin, you ripped his throat out for what he did to Starros and Leila. Why do you think he would balk at standing back to watch your father die if it suited his plans? It wasn't love that drove Mahkas. He didn't care that his daughter had been violated. He was distraught because he knew if you suspected—even for a moment—that Leila and Starros felt something for each other, you would have refused to consider marriage to his daughter."

"I didn't need to refuse it, Aunt Bylinda. It was never my decision. My mother would never have allowed Leila and me to marry."

"We all knew that, Damin," she agreed with ominous finality. "So did Mahkas. He just wouldn't admit it."

"Please, Aunt Bylinda . . . let's go inside . . ."

Bylinda didn't seem to hear him. Instead, she looked down. The faint sound of someone calling to her wafted up on the breeze. He didn't know who it was; some of the remaining Raiders, perhaps, or maybe some palace slaves had spotted the figure perched on the edge of the roof in the darkness. Then he heard a noise behind him and let out a sigh of relief as Wrayan climbed through the window.

The thief walked across the tiles with the assurance of one familiar with rooftops. He stopped beside Damin and studied Bylinda for a moment.

"Is she threatening to jump?" he asked softly.

"Not in so many words," Damin replied in a low voice.

"I saw what was left of your uncle. Did she . . . ?"

Damin nodded.

"And now she's riddled with grief and remorse and wants to kill herself, I suppose," Wrayan concluded. "What do you think I can do to stop her?"

"Get into her mind. Make her walk away from the edge."

"I can't."

Damin looked at him with concern. "What do you mean, you *can't*?"

"I can't coerce someone against their will. Even if I could unravel the shield on her mind quickly enough to get into her thoughts, if she really wants to jump I can't stop her, Damin."

Damin glared at him, but before he could answer, Bylinda turned to look at them, amused by their pitiful attempts to save her. "You can stop whispering about me, boys. I know what you're expecting him to do, Damin, but it won't work. I want this to be over and Wrayan can't make me do something I don't want, even with magic, can you, Wrayan?"

"No, my lady," the thief admitted. "I can't."

She looked back to the starlit sky, holding her arms wide. "I should have just jumped as soon as I got out here. I was meaning to. But it was such a lovely night and the wind was so cool . . . the skies so clear . . . the stars so bright. . . . It seemed a much nicer memory to take into the afterlife than the sight of Mahkas begging for his life." She suddenly smiled in fond remembrance. "No wonder you children used to sneak out here with a wineskin when you were younger."

"How did you know about that?" Damin asked, moving a little closer. Maybe, if he kept her attention on him, he reasoned, she'd not detect Wrayan closing in behind her. "We always thought our nightly trips out onto the palace roof were our best-kept secret."

"I *always* knew more than I let on, Damin," Bylinda said. "Don't you understand, yet? That was my greatest sin." She smiled at him warmly and held out her hand. Damin let out a sigh of relief as he reached out to take it and pull her to safety.

"Happy birthday, Damin."

She didn't jump so much as step off the roof. It happened so suddenly he had no time to react, no chance of preventing it. She made no sound as she fell, the only cry coming from someone in the courtyard, followed by a wet, thudding sound as she hit the unforgiving cobblestones below. Damin lunged for her as she went over the edge, but he wasn't nearly close enough yet to reach her in time. In his mad rush to save her, however, he overbalanced dangerously and suddenly found himself on his belly, slipping toward the edge, his smooth-soled riding boots offering no purchase on the tiles as he scrambled for a foothold.

Wrayan caught him by the arm just as his feet were going over the edge and with a super-human effort, pulled him upward until Damin was able to haul himself to safety. His heart racing, Damin flopped on his back on the tiles while he gathered his wits, the sound of his own racing blood the only thing he could hear, the image of Bylinda stepping calmly off the roof burned into his retinas, an after-image that refused to go away.

Breathing heavily from shock, grief and the nearness of his own brush with death, he blinked back the disturbing visions of Bylinda and glanced up at the thief standing over him. "Gods, Wrayan, I swear I tried . . ."

"I know you did, lad."

"I couldn't stop her . . ."

"Neither could I."

Damin pushed himself up onto his elbows. He could hear voices far below as the witnesses to Bylinda's fall hurried to her side in a futile effort to aid her. Then he glanced up at the sky and noticed the faintest hint of dawn edging over the distant horizon.

"It's nearly daybreak," he said after a time.

"Aye," Wrayan agreed. "It's been a very long night."

"Travin will be here soon. With the army. I guess we won't be needing them now."

Wrayan sat down beside him on the roof. "Be thankful, Damin. There are never any real winners in a civil war."

"Did you find Xanda?"

"He was down in the slaves' quarters with Orleon, gathering the last of the palace servants for the evacuation.

When I told him you were here, Starros went after them and called them back, so I suppose if you want breakfast, there'll still be somebody in the palace to wait on you, my lord."

Wrayan was taunting him, Damin knew that, but he was in no mood for it. "Is Xanda all right?"

"He's fine. He was worried he hadn't been able to find Luciena, though."

"She'll be fine. Mahkas only thought he killed her."

"There's something to be grateful for."

He slowly sat up, looking out over the darkened city, wishing he felt something other than powerless. If this was what it meant to win, for the first time in his life, Damin wondered if it was worth it.

He took a deep breath and climbed to his feet. He had too much to do, too much to mend, too much to arrange, to sit out here on the roof dwelling on his own grief. Mahkas was dead and Bylinda, for her own reasons—however alien to Damin— had delivered the justice she felt he so richly deserved.

Damin didn't grieve for Mahkas, but he did grieve for the heartbreak that had driven a gentle soul like Bylinda Damaran to commit a vicious murder. Of all the outcomes this night, the tragedy he hadn't seen coming was that one.

And now, thanks to Bylinda's sacrifice, he had what he came for.

I am Warlord of Krakandar now.

Damin stopped and looked down over the city. His city.

He'd almost forgotten, until Bylinda reminded him of it, that today was his twenty-fifth birthday. The responsibility for the lives of every man, woman and child in the province now sat squarely on his shoulders.

"Bylinda was right, you know."

"About what?" Wrayan asked, rising to his feet beside Damin to watch the sun creep over the horizon.

"It is a lovely night," he said, glancing up at the sky.

Wrayan glanced at him with concern. "Are you all right?"

He frowned. "If I say yes, does that make me a monster?"

The thief shook his head. "Don't agonise over it too much. Your mother deals with grief the same way. She's always at her most commanding when everyone around her is falling apart. At the very least, it makes you what they trained you to be, I suppose."

"What's that, Wrayan?" Damin asked sourly. "A heartless fiend?"

"No," Wrayan replied. "A Warlord."

Chapter 79

It was midwinter before the Convocation of Warlords could be held to confirm all the new appointments. By then the last remnants of the plague were gone from Greenharbour, Lasting Drift was just a place on a map once more, and in Sunrise Province, seven thousand or more Fardohnyan prisoners of war were camped around Winternest until the spring melt, when they could continue clearing the Widowmaker Pass.

Krakandar, Sunrise, Greenharbour and Izcomdar were all getting used to their new Warlords. It was the first time, Marla reflected as she nodded her approval of the buffet, that every province had a ruling lord at the same time in more than thirty years.

Rogan Bearbow's transition to power had gone smoothly in Izcomdar. He was the legitimate son of the former ruling lord and the population had never expected any other master. Greenharbour Province's transition had been similarly incident free. The Sorcerers' Collective had been grooming Conin Falconlance to rule for several years and his appointment was no surprise to anybody.

In Krakandar, Damin appeared to be enjoying a honeymoon period as the people got used to having their own

Warlord again. For the better part of the past fifty years (except for the brief two years Laran Krakenshield was Warlord) Krakandar had been ruled by administrators and regents. Finally, the people had a Warlord of their own, one they felt belonged to them. Damin had been busy consolidating his position these past few months and cleaning up after Mahkas.

It was a pity, really, that he had died under such tragic circumstances, Marla mused. For all his faults, Mahkas Damaran had kept Krakandar prosperous and safe, but his legacy would always be remembered as one of brutal tyranny. Mahkas would be remembered as the man who whipped his daughter into committing suicide. The man murdered by his own wife for his heinous betrayal. Nobody would remember it was Mahkas who constructed the third defensive ring around Krakandar City. His name would live on in infamy, any good he might have done buried and forgotten under the weight of his crimes.

Sunrise Province had been a little more problematic. Tejay Lionsclaw's appointment had almost caused a riot, but she was a capable young woman and had so far managed to keep the province from exploding into open rebellion. Marla was confident she would prevail and the fact the Convocation had confirmed her appointment today was another reason to be hopeful. Tejay was working frantically to clear the Widowmaker, fully aware that reestablishing the trade routes with Fardohnya was the quickest way to settle the population down. As Tejay had remarked a few days ago when she arrived in Greenharbour for the Convocation, happy, employed subjects with full bellies spent a lot less time plotting the downfall of their Warlord than hungry ones with too much time on their hands.

It wasn't an easy task ahead of her and of all the provinces, she had the most hurdles to overcome. Even with Axelle Regis's active cooperation in keeping them under control, the Fardohnyan prisoners of war were still a major problem. Just feeding them was putting a huge strain on a province that relied on trade through the damaged Widowmaker for its prosperity. Tejay had demanded the Convocation take some of the burden off Sunrise by contributing to the upkeep of the prisoners, a motion that Damin had supported and had bullied the others into agreeing to. It was a potential disaster avoided, Marla knew, but only the first of many. The trick would be identifying the next one and finding a way to head it off before it blew up in their faces.

Marla had arranged a reception following the Convocation to celebrate the confirmation of the new Warlords. It was the first time she'd had all her children under the same roof since the year she first took Luciena to Krakandar. It was a family gathering she organised, restricted to those she considered trustworthy allies.

Damin was over by the entrance, looking every inch the Warlord in his ceremonial armour, talking to his brother, Narvell, who looked so like his father it brought a lump to Marla's throat. He'd come to the Convocation as his grandfather's representative because Charel Hawksword was too sick to travel, which effectively meant anything Damin wanted at the Convocation—with Narvell's support and Charel's vote—Damin got. That included confirming Tejay Lionsclaw as the Warlord of Sunrise Province and the supply of foodstuffs to feed the prisoners of war until they could be repatriated back to Fardohnya.

With the support of Damin, Narvell, Conin Falconlance and her own brother, Rogan Bearbow, Tejay's appointment was a mere formality by the time the Convocation voted on it, and there was nothing Cyrus Eaglespike had been able to do to prevent it.

Next to Narvell was his twin sister, Kalan, dressed in her sorcerer's robes, proudly wearing the silver diamond-shaped pendant denoting her rank as Lower Arrion, chatting to Kendra Warhaft, whose smile was forced and artificial. Nobody had been able to change Lernen's mind about granting her a divorce. Damin had promised Narvell he would rule in her favour when he became High Prince, Marla knew, but that was probably years away and small consolation for either of the lovers.

In the meantime, Kendra was headed home tomorrow to return to her husband and her children. The only bright note in that sad arrangement was Stefan Warhaft's injury. He'd fallen from his horse during the battle and broken his back and was now paralysed from the waist down. Marla had heard a rumour that Rorin Mariner could have healed his fractured spine, but he'd found other places to be for days after the battle, until it was too late even for his magical skills to be of any use to the wounded baron. Marla chose not to investigate the report further. If the story was true, she didn't blame Rorin. If anything, she secretly admired the young sorcerer's sense of justice. Poor Kendra might have to stay married to Stefan Warhaft for the foreseeable future, but her husband would never be in a position to beat her again. The tables had been turned completely and he was now subject to his wife's whim.

Retribution, Marla reflected, had an interesting way of manifesting itself.

She watched Kalan chatting with her brothers and smiled. Marla realised her daughter had every intention of succeeding Bruno Sanval as High Arrion someday. She was quite certain her daughter would achieve her ambition, too. She was even prouder of Kalan's achievement than she was of anything her sons had done. They were born into their roles, trained from the very beginning to do them well and likely to win power simply by the accident of their birth. Kalan, on the other hand, had worked hard for what she'd gained. Any power she might wield some day as High Arrion would be hers alone and won by her own efforts. For a woman in Hythria, that was no mean feat.

Talking with Damin, Kalan, Kendra and Narvell were Xanda and Luciena. Her adopted daughter had recovered from her physical wounds inflicted by Mahkas Damaran, but Marla sensed a sadness in Luciena she suspected came from guilt over Bylinda's suicide. Marla intended to take her aside at some point and explain that it wasn't her fault. Luciena's involvement in that tragedy was none of her doing. She needed to stop blaming herself for it.

In another small group a little closer to the window, Rodja and Adham Tirstone were deep in discussion with Prince Lunar Shadow Kraig of the House of the Rising Moon and his two statuesque companions. Adham had recovered from his belly wound and was talking of returning to Denika with the prince, the trade possibilities between Denika and Hythria something both brothers were all but salivating over. Marla watched them talking, thinking Adham was salivating over more than the possibility of establishing a formal trading route to Denika. Adham had returned to Krakandar once he was well enough to travel. By all accounts, he and Lady Barlaina had struck up quite a friendship while he was recuperating, a suspicion Marla didn't doubt given the way Adham's eyes never left the young woman as she browsed the buffet.

Kraig and his friends were leaving tomorrow on one of Luciena's ships, his year-long adventure in Hythria thankfully at an end. It had proved a mixed blessing, this visit from a foreign dignitary. Although during the past few months in Krakandar he had been treated in the manner to which he was obviously accustomed, Kraig had seen the best and the worst of them and she did wonder what sort of impression Prince Lunar Shadow Kraig would take back to Denika with him. And how it would affect future relations with the southern continent. Damin and the Denikan heir seemed firm friends, however, any residual resentment about his treatment in the hands of his Hythrun hosts smoothed over by several months of Krakandar hospitality which had even included, so Marla had heard rumoured, a trip into Medalon to steal cattle. She had some concern over something called the seed game, too, and why Kraig seemed to think he had some sort of claim on their northern neighbour . . .

A gleeful squeal echoed through the hall as the Taranger boys chased their cousins through the party, ducking and weaving to avoid the adults. Ruxton's daughter, Rielle, and her husband Darvad had also come to Greenharbour with their family to see Rogan Bearbow confirmed as their War-lord and to see Ruxton laid to rest in a more permanent tomb. Their children had discovered kindred souls in Lu-ciena and Xanda's boisterous sons.

Out on the terrace there was another, much more intense friendship developing between Emilie Taranger and the two Miar girls, Karola and Mira. A year older and younger than Emilie, the three of them had been sitting cross-legged on the terrace for the better part of an hour, their heads close together as they traded secrets in the manner of prepubescent girls the world over.

Marla smiled, wondering how much trouble three girls aged nine, ten and eleven could get into, left to their own devices. Emilie hadn't been told the truth about Mahkas's death. Luciena and Xanda judged it unwise to disillusion the child about her beloved uncle and had blamed his infected wound for his untimely demise, and Bylinda's unbearable grief at his death so soon after Leila's for her suicide. Emilie seemed to accept the explanation and with the resilience common to most children, had almost put her stay in Krakandar completely behind her.

Then Marla spotted Galon Miar sitting near the window, as if he had one eye on his daughters and one eye on every-one else in the room.

She made her way towards him, smiling and nodding to her guests as she went. Galon rose to his feet as she approached and raised his glass to her. "Quite a party, your highness."

"I'm so glad you approve. I arrange all my entertaining to suit the Assassins' Guild."

"As you should," he agreed with a smile.

"What are you doing hiding over here, anyway?" she asked. "You're a guest, Galon. You even came through the front door, this time. Please, feel free to mingle."

"I was just looking over the family," he told her, refusing to rise to her taunt.

"For any particular reason, or do we highborn just fascinate you?"

"I was deciding which one of them I'm going to kill when you renege on your deal with us."

Unperturbed, Marla took a sip of her wine. "I've been thinking about that."

He grinned. "I'll just bet you have."

"Perhaps it won't be necessary for you to kill a member of my family, after all."

"You've decided to fulfil your agreement?"

She looked out over the room, deliberately avoiding his eye. "I've decided which of my children your guild can have as an apprentice."

"Is that right?"

"You can have my stepson, Kiam Miar."

"What a coincidence," he remarked. "I have a son named Kiam Miar."

"Fancy that."

He studied her curiously. "If we're talking about the same Kiam Miar, your highness, there is the minor detail of him not *actually* being your stepson. For that to be the case, you and I would have to get married."

"The things I do for Hythria," she sighed.

He studied her curiously. "Have you told anybody else about this?"

"Not yet."

"So I'm the first to know? I'm flattered."

Marla fixed her gaze on him, determined to set down the ground rules right from the outset. "You do understand this arrangement will be dissolved the moment you become the Raven, don't you? I'm doing this because the Assassins' Guild is leaving me little choice in the matter, not because I find you the least bit attractive."

"I understand."

"I mean it, Galon."

"If you insist," he replied with a knowing smile.

Marla frowned, wondering how she ever thought she could fool this man into thinking she was immune to him.

"Do you think your children will mind?" she asked, deciding on a safer topic.

"Kiam's already apprenticed to the guild, so I don't think he'll care one way or the other. But the girls will be thrilled. I couldn't shut them up when they learned you'd invited them to this party. Coming to live in a palace with a real princess should send them into raptures. Have you told *your* children yet?"

She shook her head. "I'm still trying to figure the best way to break the news to them that I'm planning to marry an assassin."

Galon looked at her oddly. "I'll be your fifth husband, Marla. I would have thought you'd have sitting the children down and telling them about their new step-papa down to a fine art by now."

Marla glanced across the room to where Damin, Kalan and Narvell were chatting with the others and frowned. "The last time I got married, Galon, my eldest child was only eight years old. He's just been confirmed as a Warlord in his own right. The situation is a little different."

Galon grinned. "Do you think he'll want to call me Pa?"

"He's more likely to call you out in a duel."

"You should be proud of him, you know."

She sipped her wine and glanced at her future husband. "I'll be sure to tell Damin you approve of him."

"I mean it, Marla. You've done a remarkable job raising your children."

"I've agreed to marry you, Galon. There's no need to keep flattering me."

"I'm not trying to flatter you. And I'm not just saying this because the young man in question is about to become my stepson, or because he's very large and fights like a lion and has the power to have me thrown into the lowest dungeon in Greenharbour until I rot if he decides he doesn't like me. Hythria has needed a strong High Prince for generations. We haven't had a half-decent one since the Harshini left. And somehow, in a court ruled by a depraved fool, you managed to raise a son strong and clever enough to become a Warlord in his own right. Rumour has it your other son is just as promising and I've had enough dealings with your charming daughter, Kalan, to know just how intimidating she can be. That's no mean feat, Marla. You shouldn't underestimate your achievement."

"My achievement?" she asked sceptically. "By all accounts I left my children to be raised by a homicidal maniac and the suicidal woman who eventually killed him. If there's any kudos to be awarded here, it should go to my children for turning out even remotely sane, given the circumstances."

"Don't beat yourself up over it," he advised. "Worse things have happened to a lot of people and they turned out all right in the end. Look at me."

Marla frowned. "Is that supposed to comfort me?"

Galon laughed softly. "I suppose not. But I did mean what I said. You should be proud. Although, Damin did make one mistake."

"What mistake?"

"Asking the High Prince to promote Tejay Lionsclaw to Warlord."

"Why was it a mistake? She'll probably prove the best Warlord Sunrise Province has had since Glenadal Ravenspear."

"But in supporting her, he let people know he's willing to go against tradition to get what he wants," Galon pointed out. "The whole of Hythria knows he's nothing like the current High Prince, now."

"I'm not sure Damin would see that as a bad thing."

"But it's not necessarily good for him, either. The Warlords like that Lernen doesn't try to rule them. You know that. Your son just proved he'll be a much different High Prince to your brother. He made enemies in this conflict. Enemies who may not have revealed themselves yet."

Marla shrugged philosophically. "Under the circumstances, I don't think he had much choice other than to do what he did. Besides, he's a Wolfblade, Galon. Being surrounded by enemies comes with the name."

The assassin smiled. "Well, look on the bright side. The truth hasn't made its way west of the Sunrise Mountains yet. The Fardohnyans still think he's just as bad as Lernen. All those tales of wild orgies, stealing other men's wives, *court'esa* of both sexes in the war camp with him . . ."

She looked at him curiously. "How is it you know so much about what the Fardohnyans are saying about us?"

"Thieves and assassins know no borders, remember?"

She studied him with some concern. "You seem to have excellent sources of intelligence, Galon."

"I doubt they're as good as yours," he remarked. "Between the intelligence network the Tirstone boys control and your contacts in the Thieves' Guild . . ."

"Do you mean Wrayan?"

"Interesting man, the Greatest Thief in all of Hythria."

"You've been talking to him?"

Galon nodded. "We're likely to be doing a lot of business in the future. It pays to get these things smoothed out early."

"Why would you have business with Wrayan?"

He raised a brow at her. "Haven't you heard? Maybe your sources aren't as good as I thought."

"Heard what?"

"Franz Gillam has offered Wrayan the Wraith—Greatest Thief in all of Hythria—the position of heir apparent to the Greenharbour Thieves' Guild."

"And he *accepted*?" she asked, stunned to think she knew nothing about this.

"Sure. Why wouldn't he?"

"He's head of the Krakandar Thieves' Guild for one."

"Well, depending on who you talk to, he's thinking of leaving because some young upstart in Krakandar turfed him out of a job, or he's leaving because he's discovered he's not aging the way he should and if he gets out of Krakandar now and comes back to Greenharbour, people may not notice."

Marla looked at the assassin curiously. Few people knew of Wrayan's Harshini heritage. That sort of observation could only have come from Wrayan himself. "You two really have become fast friends, haven't you?"

"We heir apparents have to stick together, you know."

She frowned and glanced around the room. "Speaking of Wrayan, have you seen him this afternoon? He was supposed to be here."

"He was out in the garden last I saw of him, but I'm not sure how long he was planning to stay. He said something about catching up with an old friend. Have you noticed Kalan was late, too?"

"No, I hadn't. But you obviously did."

"She scares me," he admitted with a grin. "I like to keep tabs on her when she's in the room."

Marla shook her head, wondering what she was getting herself into with this man. "I expect you to make an effort to get along with my family, Galon."

"And I expect you to make *your* children promise that if you become a widow again in the near future, it'll be because I died of *natural* causes."

Marla couldn't help herself. She laughed. "I wish you'd met Elezaar. He would have liked you, I think."

"Your *court'esa*? The one you say you killed?"

"He killed himself, actually. After Alija forced him into betraying me."

Marla tried not to dwell on Alija too much. Her downfall had opened a lot of old wounds. For Wrayan Lightfinger, it was a bittersweet victory. He hadn't known Alija was responsible for his former master's death. Although Kagan Palenovar had been gone for more than twenty years, Alija's surprise confession had staggered him. It had also driven home to Marla how ruthless Alija had been. How utterly without sentiment when it came to achieving her goals.

Ruthlessness wasn't a quality Marla was unfamiliar with. She often demonstrated the same single-minded, merciless determination when she had to. But Alija's crimes went beyond simple greed or power-grabbing. Marla knew why she did what she did. It was to protect her family, no other reason, and she didn't try to fool herself into believing her motives were any nobler than that. Alija, on the other hand, actually thought she was doing good. That's what had made her truly dangerous.

Still, things were finally reaching a point where she could relax. Damin was Warlord of Krakandar and, when the time came, would be a High Prince Hythria could be proud of. Narvell was doing well in Elasapine, the centre of Charel Hawksword's universe, vindicating the decision she made all those years ago, in this very room, when she decided the best thing for everyone would be for Nash to die in a tragic accident so nobody ever learned the truth about his treachery.

As for her only daughter, Kalan was Lower Arrion already and had proved perhaps the most astute and intelligent one of all.

Marla was just as pleased with her stepchildren. Luciena and Xanda seemed happily married and ran the vast Mariner shipping empire together as if the gods had granted them a licence to make money. Rielle and Darvad were obviously doing well in Dylan Pass. Rodja and Selena ruled the spice trade and now it looked as if they would be adding exotic Denikan imports to their empire. Adham still showed no inclination to settle down, but perhaps in Denika he would find what he was searching for.

That reminded Marla of something else. Now this awful business with Leila was behind them, she needed to start looking for a suitable wife for Damin. He was twenty-five and needed to think about producing an heir.

The Wolfblade line must go on, Marla was determined. She hadn't come this far to let it die out now.

"Your highness."

Marla turned to find Wrayan standing behind her. She smiled at him and took his hands in hers. "I was hoping to catch up with you. I've seen so little of you lately."

"Actually, I came to ask your forgiveness. I have to leave

early. There's somebody I have to meet and I couldn't arrange any other time."

"Some secret Thieves' Guild business I suppose?"

"Something like that."

"Did I ever thank you, Wrayan, for changing careers for me?"

He looked puzzled for a moment and then nodded. "Ah . . . you mean Alija?"

"You didn't have to kill her, you know. We had enough to hang her."

He looked at her curiously before glancing around to see who was near. "Do you think Alija was the first person I've killed?"

Marla looked at him curiously. She'd never really thought about it. "I don't know."

"Trust me, she's not. She won't be the last either, if I stay in Greenharbour."

Marla slipped her arm through his and walked with him toward the doors at the other end of the hall. "Galon told me about Franz Gillam's offer. I was a little offended to think you told him before you mentioned it to me."

"Galon's a professional colleague."

She looked up at him with a frown. "Is that what you're calling your relationship now?"

"*You* didn't tell me you were going to marry him," he accused. "So don't go on about *my* relationship with Galon Miar, when you're guilty of the same sin."

Marla sighed. "I haven't even told my children. Do you think I'm making a mistake?"

Wrayan shrugged. "He's a loyal Royalist, if that's what you're asking. And it does get you off the hook rather neatly with the Assassins' Guild."

They reached the doors and stepped through into the relative quiet of the corridor outside. Marla was still wracked with uncertainty. She stopped and made Wrayan turn to face her. "You've read his mind. Does he love me?"

The thief smiled. "Four husbands behind you and *now*

you start to wonder whether the man you're about to marry loves you or not?"

"I'm getting sentimental in my old age. Answer my question. Does he love me?"

"Do you have any reason to think he might?"

"That's not an answer, Wrayan."

"But it's all the answer I'm going to give you, your highness. I promised I wouldn't pry, remember."

"You promised you'd not betray any Assassins' Guild secrets you learned in his mind. You didn't promise anything about how he felt for me."

"But I have learned to know when to leave well enough alone," the thief replied. "I can tell you this much, though, if it will ease your mind. He has no agenda involving your children. Galon Miar knows what he wants and it isn't anything to do with Hythria's throne."

"What does he want?"

"You . . . among other things."

"Then he does love me?"

"I didn't say that."

Marla crossed her arms against a chill she feared came from her own guilty conscience. "You know, I used to be appalled by how ruthless Alija was. How utterly without sentiment she could be when it came to achieving her goals. But it's recently occurred to me that I'm no better than she is. I can be just as ruthless; I had to be, just to deal with her."

"Didn't Elezaar and his wretched Rules of Gaining and Wielding Power have something to say about that?"

She wished the dwarf was here now. "Rule Number One. Have a reason other than the love of power to reach for it."

"And do you?"

She thought about her answer carefully. "I only ever wanted to protect my children, Wrayan. Power for its own sake leaves me cold. I didn't do anything harsh, or ruthless, or even very profound, until I realised the only person in the world who could protect my children to my satisfaction was me."

"That's a noble goal common to mothers the world over, your highness," he assured her, "not a ruthless one."

She shook her head, unconvinced. "How many mothers the world over have killed to achieve it, though?"

"How many have had to?"

Marla smiled sadly. "Who'd have thought my two best and most trusted friends in the world would turn out to be a part-Harshini thief-turned-assassin and a dwarf slave? Or that my friendship would cost one of my friends his life and cause the other to commit murder."

"Elezaar would tell you that we'd done the right thing."

"He hated Alija. His opinion wouldn't have been objective."

"Well, you have your vengeance for him, your highness. I think he'd appreciate that."

"What were her final thoughts?"

"It's over and done with, your highness. Let her rest. She can't hurt you or your family now."

"Tell me. Please."

Wrayan looked at her oddly. "Did you *want* the gory details?"

"I don't need to be protected from them, Wrayan. What were her last thoughts?"

Wrayan hesitated before he answered her. "She was cursing me. And you."

"You're not just saying that to make me feel better, are you? I have broad shoulders, you know. I can bear the responsibility."

He rubbed his temples, as if easing a headache, and then looked at her. "The responsibility is mostly mine, your highness. I could have done something about Alija years ago. What's more, I should have. And it wasn't like I didn't have the opportunity. Gods! Even Brakandaran would have helped me if I'd asked him. Come to think of it, he even offered once."

"Why didn't you accept his offer?"

"Because I was doing exactly what you're doing now. Trying to convince myself I was better than that. That my motives were somehow nobler than Alija's. That I was the better person. But I wasn't. None of us are. We're all just human and we're flawed and we do what we have to, to keep the ones we love safe."

"Even if it means killing in cold blood?"

"Even that," Wrayan agreed.

Marla wasn't sure if she was comforted by Wrayan's words or disturbed by them. "Galon told me just now that I should be proud of my children, of the way they've turned out. Do you think they'd be proud of their mother if they knew even half the things I'd done?"

"Maybe," he said, "but if you want my advice . . . don't tell them."

"Because they'd despise me?"

"Because they might *not* despise you," he warned. "They might admire you, and then you'd really have a reason to lie awake at night worrying about the future." Wrayan let go of her hand and bowed politely. "I should go, your highness. The man I'm going to meet will wait on no one and I don't want to miss him."

"Go then. I'll see you later."

She watched him leave and then took a deep breath and headed back into the crowded hall. Looking around, Marla smiled. Here was everything she'd fought so hard to preserve, so hard to protect.

And she'd succeeded. Her family was safe. Fardohnya was defeated. The plague was done with. Hythria was secure. Alija was dead.

If only, she lamented silently, *Elezaar had been here to see it.*

Oddly, she was experiencing a few doubts but absolutely no remorse. She did have a vague sense of ineffable sadness, though, as she realised that an entire era had come to an end.

Revenge should feel better than this. More satisfying.

Victory, Marla decided, had a bitter aftertaste if you savoured it for too long.

But the threat of the Eaglespikes—and with them, the entire Patriot faction—was gone, now. For the first time in two decades, her first thought on waking wasn't wondering if

Alija Eaglespike was planning to destroy her family today. Marla smiled thinly, thinking it a sad comment on her life to discover the threat Alija represented might have been what drove her to greatness.

Elezaar would have been the first to point out *that* particular irony.

In a strange way Marla was free; in another way, bereft. Elezaar was avenged, her children were safe, her son was a Warlord, the Assassins' Guild was on her side and there was no Alija Eaglespike to rally the voices of discontent.

Elezaar had a rule for that, too. *Accept that which is unchangeable; change that which is unacceptable.*

Marla had lived by that rule all her life.

And tomorrow, she would wake in a world that she had finally made acceptable.

epilogue

The wharf district of Greenharbour City was massive. This was, arguably, the largest and busiest port in the world. It was loud and raw and a forest of masts stretched around the harbour. It stank like rancid fish, wet hemp, sweat and salt, yet it seemed to offer a safe port of call for every lost soul in the world.

It was not surprising, then, that this was where Wrayan had found Brakandaran the Halfbreed.

He hadn't been looking for Brak, just as he was quite certain Brak wasn't expecting to be found. Wrayan had come down to the wharves to check on the ship Luciena had arranged to transport Prince Lunar Shadow Kraig back to Denika. It wasn't one of her regular ships. Most of Luciena's fleet were coastal traders that rarely sailed out of sight of land, plying the trade routes between Hythria, Fardohnya and Karien. The voyage across the vast Dregian Ocean to Denika required a much larger vessel.

Luciena had contracted Captain Soothan to carry the prince home, but Marla was still concerned. She had invited Kraig here to discuss a treaty, been forced to protect him from raging mobs, quarantine him from the plague, hide him by having him pose as a sex slave, involve him in a war and then have him witness foul murder in Krakandar as the family settled its differences. Marla was convinced she had stretched the friendship with Denika to breaking point. She was justifiably nervous about sending their crown prince home, only to have the ship sink halfway to Denika because it was unseaworthy.

For no other reason than to ease the princess's mind, Wrayan had offered to check out the ship himself and make a few inquiries about Captain Soothan's credentials among his contacts in the Thieves' Guild.

The last thing he'd expected was to find Brak a member of Soothan's crew.

Once he'd found him, however, there was no chance he was going to let him get away without some sort of explanation. Wrayan had spent the last thirteen years fearing Brak was dead and he didn't intend to spend the next thirteen years wondering why he wasn't. Brak was reluctant to even acknowledge that he knew Wrayan, however, but had finally agreed to meet with him the following day in a tavern close to where the ship was anchored, if only he'd leave and stop making a fuss.

The time Brak wanted to meet was right in the middle of Princess Marla's reception, but it couldn't be helped. Even though he half expected him not to show up, Wrayan was waiting at the appointed time, figuring after all he had done for her, Marla would forgive his rudeness.

Somewhat to his surprise, the Halfbreed appeared a few moments after he said he'd be at the tavern, looking tanned and fit and every inch a born sailor.

"How did you find me?" Brak asked as he slid into the seat opposite Wrayan in a booth near the back of the tap-room.

"Hello, Brak, nice to see you too. I'm well, thanks, how are you?"

"I haven't got time for small talk, Wrayan, we sail on to-morrow's tide. How did you find me?"

He shrugged, disappointed Brak was feeling so unsociable. "Just lucky, I guess. I wasn't actually looking for you. Princess Marla asked me to check on an ocean-going vessel she hired to return someone to Denika, and there you were."

"I chose that ship *because* it was an ocean-going vessel on its way to Denika," Brak said, waving to the tavern wench to bring him ale. "She stays at sea for long periods of time. It keeps the gods away. They don't like to mess with Kaelarn."

Wrayan studied him curiously. "Are you dodging any god in particular?"

"Mostly Zegarnald and Dace, at the moment. They're both peeved at me for one reason or another."

"What did you do?"

"I quit my life of crime in the Sunrise Mountains, which didn't please the God of Thieves very much. And I meddled in Zegarnald's precious war, too. It came to a resounding halt a whole lot sooner than he was planning. He's pretty ticked off with me about that."

"How could you meddle in the war? You weren't anywhere near it, were you?"

"I was for a while. Zeggie had this great plan, you see, to flood Hythria with Fardohnyans and then put someone really smart in charge of the Hythrun defence so it would drag on for years. I took the liberty of changing the odds. Once the numbers evened up a bit, lo and behold, a victory! I didn't even really care which side won, just so long as somebody did. It's a popular misconception, you know, this notion that one should win a war to honour Zegarnald. He'd much prefer you keep on fighting."

Suddenly, a number of things began to make sense. "So it *was* you who blew up the Widowmaker."

Brak looked at him curiously. "How did you know about that?"

"Rory was there. He felt someone drawing on the source." Wrayan smiled and added, "He guessed it must have been you. But even if Rory feeling your magic wasn't enough to convince me you were involved somehow, Elarnymire popping up out of nowhere to tell him to run like hell probably would have given it away."

"Damn demons."

"Under the circumstances, I think Rory was grateful for the warning."

Brak's brows drew together curiously. "Rory? That lad we busted out of Westbrook? How's he doing?"

"Just fine," Wrayan assured him, determined not to let the Halfbreed change the subject just to avoid answering any awkward questions. "How are *you* doing?"

"Just fine."

"Shananara told me what happened with Lorandranek, Brak," he sympathised. "She said—"

"One more word," Brak cut in with a dangerous snarl, "and you will not see out the next minute, old friend."

Wrayan stared at him in alarm. Brak was deadly serious.

"I didn't mean . . ."

"I did."

"Then . . . let's find a safer topic. How long have you been a sailor?"

"This time?" Brak shrugged. "Not long. But I've been to sea before, you know. Several times. One tends to try any number of professions when one has several lifetimes in which to master them." He leaned back as the tavern wench placed his ale on the table. Brak winked at her before turning his attention back to Wrayan.

The thief sighed. Some things never changed.

"*What?*" Brak asked, with a wounded look.

"Nothing," Wrayan replied. He reached into his pocket and withdrew the chain he'd been keeping there. "I have something for you."

He placed the *couremor* on the table. The little crystal cube with its tiny dragon magically etched inside caught the sunlight coming in from the window and refracted the light in a spray of rainbow colours across the beer-stained table. Brak picked it up and looked at it with vague disinterest, before slipping it into his own pocket.

"Thanks."

"I used it to call Shananara."

"I gathered as much."

"She told me you weren't dead."

"Traitor."

Wrayan hesitated, wondering how far he could go before he pushed Brak too far, but he felt compelled to say something. And he had a selfish motive. If he could convince

Brak he should return to Sanctuary, even for a short time, there was the remote possibility he would allow Wrayan to accompany him and that would mean a chance to see Shananara one more time.

"They want you to go home, Brak. She said—"

"I don't have a home any longer," the Halfbreed insisted. He swallowed a good half of the tankard in one go and slammed it down on the table. "Are we done now? I have to get back to my ship."

Wrayan sighed again. It was worth a try. "Will I ever see you again?"

Brak shrugged. "Maybe. By the look of you, you're going to be around for a while yet. Provided you stay out of trouble."

"That's not likely."

"Well, take care of yourself," Brak instructed, rising to his feet. "Don't let Dace bully you."

Wrayan looked up at the Halfbreed. "I'll be all right. I'm the Greatest Thief in all of Hythria. When will you be back?"

"When they need me," he said, and then, before Wrayan could respond, he tossed a few rivets on the table for his ale, turned on his heel and walked away from the table without looking back.

The first novel in Jennifer Fallon's
brilliant new four-book epic

THE
IMMORTAL
PRINCE

THE TIDE LORDS BOOK ONE

A murderer somehow survives a routine hanging
and announces he is Cayal, the Immortal Prince—
a mythical figure in the legend of the ruthless and
immoral Tide Lords. Arkady Desean, an expert on these
stories, is sent to interrogate this would-be immortal and
prove he is a madman. But as Arkady begins to believe in
the Tide Lords, her own web of lies begins to unravel....

———— ❧ ————

"With her vivid style and snappy dialogue, Fallon embarks
on a rollercoaster ride of mortal and immortal machinations."
—*Nexus* on *The Immortal Prince*

"Well-crafted entertainment." —*Kirkus Reviews* on *Harshini*

 IN HARDCOVER MAY 2008

978-0-7653-1682-0 • 0-7653-1682-X • www.tor-forge.com

chapter 1

Hope seemed an odd emotion for a man about to be executed, but that was the only name Cayal could give the thrill welling up inside him as they led him up the steps of the platform.

Soon, one way or another, he told himself, *it will be over.*

He could see nothing with the black hood over his head, his other senses starved of input by the rough weave of his clothing. He gathered the mask was as much to spare the spectators as it was to offer a condemned man some semblance of privacy. It muffled sound, too, making the world outside seem remote, shrinking reality to only what he could hear and feel. The tall grim walls were gone, so were the overcast sky and the gloomy prison yard. He revelled in his sense of touch; relished the cold air on his bare chest and the musty canvas over his head that reeked faintly of other, successful deaths.

Cayal breathed in the aroma and hoped.

With luck, this might be the last thing he ever knew. Oblivion beckoned and Cayal was rushing to meet it with open arms.

"What the . . . ?" he exclaimed suddenly as a thick, heavy noose was tightened around his neck. He struggled against it, wondering what was happening. They should be ordering him to kneel, making him reach forward to the block.

He didn't want to hang. Hanging was useless. Futile. And likely to be very, very painful . . .

"No!" he cried in protest, but with his hands tied behind him, his struggles were in vain. He could feel the hangman checking to make certain the knot was secure and in the right place, just under his jaw below the left ear, the place guaranteed to snap a neck as quickly as possible.

"Any last words?"

The gruff voice sounded disinterested, the question one of form rather than genuine consideration for a dying man's wishes. For a moment, Cayal didn't even notice the hangman was addressing him. Then he realised this might be his last chance to object.

In a tone that was anything but repentant, he turned his head in the direction of the executioner's voice. "What's going on here? You're supposed to behead me."

"The executioner's on vacation," the disinterested voice informed him. "Read the charges."

The order was directed at someone else. A moment later, a shaky voice announced from somewhere on his left: "Kyle Lakesh, citizen of Caelum. You are charged with and have been found guilty of seven counts of heinous murder . . ."

As opposed to any other sort of murder, Cayal retorted silently, his anger welling up. *The headsman's on vacation? Are they kidding me?*

". . . For this crime, the Supreme Court of Lebec in the Sovereign State of Glaeba has sentenced you to death."

Cayal cursed behind the hood, certain nobody would see the irony. He'd killed seven men to get here. Seven worthless humans to get himself beheaded. *And the flanking headsman's on vacation!* Still, there was a funny side to this, he thought, wondering what the venerable members of the Supreme Court of the Sovereign State of Glaeba would do if they knew of the seven-odd million he'd killed before that.

"Is there any word from the Prefect regarding his grace's willingness to consider clemency?"

Another question of form, directed at the Warden. A last-minute reprieve could only come from the Duke of Lebec himself, an act that had only happened once in the past fifty years or so. Cayal knew that for a fact. He'd checked. When one was as determined to end their suffering as Cayal was, one did their homework.

Glaeban justice was harsh but surprisingly evenhanded, which suited him just fine. When you were deliberately setting out to be decapitated, there was no point in choosing a country known for its leniency toward killers.

The silence that followed the clerk's question put to rest any last-minute hopes Cayal had that they might not carry out his sentence. A moment later, he heard footsteps echoing hollowly on the wooden decking of the platform and felt a gloved hand settling on his bare shoulder.

"Ready?"

What if I say no? Cayal wondered. *What's he going to do? Wait until I'm in the mood?*

"I want to be decapitated," he complained, his voice muffled by the hood. "Hanging me is just wasting everybody's time."

"Do you forgive me?" the hangman asked in a barely audible voice. Cayal got the feeling that of all the questions the hangman asked of his victims, this was the only one to which he genuinely craved an affirmative answer.

"No point," Cayal assured him.

Blinded by the hood, he couldn't tell what the hangman's reaction was to his reply, and in truth, he didn't care. Cayal was beyond forgiveness. He was beyond despair. Just to be sure, he reached out mentally, wondering if there was any trace of magic left, but he could sense nothing, not even a faint residual hint of the Tide he once commanded. The magic couldn't save him from the pain he knew was coming . . .

Almost before he finished the thought, the platform dropped beneath him. He plummeted through the trapdoor without any further warning.

The rope tightened savagely, cutting off his breath. Cayal thrashed as the air was driven from his lungs, the knot under his left ear pushing his jaw out of alignment, snapping his neck with an audible crack.

Filled with frustration, Cayal jerked viciously on the end of the rope, choking, asphyxiating, hoping it meant he was dying. His eyes watered with the pain. His very soul cried out in anguish, begging for death to claim him. He thrashed about, wondering if the violent motion would complete the hangman's job. The agony was unbelievable. Beyond torture. White lights danced before his eyes, his heart was racing, lightning bolts of pain shot through his jaw and neck, he couldn't breathe . . .

Cayal cried out in a language nobody in Glaeba knew, pleading with the powers of darkness to take him . . . and then, with his last remaining breath, his cry turned to a wail of despair. He'd been thrashing at the end of the rope for far too long.

His cry had driven the remaining air from his lungs. His throat was crushed. His neck broken.

And still he lived.

They left him hanging there for a long, long time, waiting for him to die. It was the nervous clerk who finally ordered him cut down when it was clear he wasn't going to.

Cayal hit the unforgiving ground with a thud and lay there in the mud, dragging in painful breaths to replenish his oxygen-starved lungs as the noose eased, already feeling the pain of his dislocated jaw, broken larynx and neck beginning to heal of their own accord.

"Tides!" he heard the clerk exclaim as they jerked the hood from his head. "He's still alive."

The hangman was leaning over him too, his expression shocked. "How can it be?"

Cayal blinked in the harsh spring sunlight, glaring painfully up at the two men. Rough, unsympathetic faces filled his vision.

"I can't die," he rasped through his crushed larynx and twisted jaw, not realising that even had he been able to form the words properly, he still spoke in his native tongue; a language long gone from Amyrantha. Realising his error, he added in Glaeban, "I'm immortal."

"What did he say?" the clerk asked in confusion.

"Something about a portal?" the hangman ventured with a shrug.

Cayal took another deep breath, even more painful than the last, if that was possible, then lifted his head and banged his face into the ground, jarring his jawbone back into place.

"I'm immortal," he repeated in his own tongue. Nobody understood him. Even through the pain, with the failure of these fools to give him the release he craved, he found himself losing patience with them. "You can't . . . kill me. I'm a . . . Tide . . . Lord."

It wasn't until later—when the Warden came back down to see what was going on—that he'd recovered sufficiently to repeat his announcement in a language even these stupid Glaebans would understand.

"I'm . . . a Tide Lord," he'd announced, pushing aside the agony for a moment. He'd been expecting shock, perhaps a little awe at his news—after all, they'd just borne witness to his immortality—certainly not scepticism. "And as I've now proved . . . you can't hang me, I demand . . . to be decapitated!"

The Warden had been far from impressed. "A Tide Lord, eh?"

Ignoring the throbbing in his neck and jaw, trying to sound commanding, Cayal nodded. "You must . . . execute me again. Only this time, do it properly."

The man had squinted at Cayal lying on the ground at his feet in a foetal curl, smiling humourlessly. "I must do *nothing* on your command, my boy. I don't care who you think you are."

Cayal hadn't actually thought about what might happen if they didn't behead him. Not in practical terms, at any rate. He had wanted to end things so badly he hadn't allowed himself to consider the consequences, just in case it jinxed him somehow. Lukys would have called him a superstitious fool for thinking like that. But then, Lukys would have had quite a bit to say about this entire disastrous escapade if he'd known about it. Cayal wondered, for a moment, what had happened to him. It was a century or more since Cayal had seen any of his brethren. Perhaps, if he had, he might not have come to this, but finding the others was nigh impossible if they didn't want to be found. It was easy to get lost in a world of millions when there were only twenty-two of you.

So, alone and despairing, Cayal had waited until the lowest ebb of the Tide and then, quite deliberately and methodically, set out to put an end to his desolation.

And failed miserably; a problem he was only now—as he heard the Warden demanding to know what had gone wrong—beginning to fully appreciate.

"I am . . . Cayal, the Immortal . . . Prince," he gasped, between his whimpers of agony. The damage done by the noose and his anxious jerking about at the end of the rope was substantial. This wasn't going to heal in a few hours. Overnight, it might, but it was going to take time.

"You're a right pain in the backside, is what you are," the Warden muttered, turning to the guards who stood over Cayal, watching him writhe on the cold ground in agony as the healing progressed apace. "Take him to the Row while I decide what to do with him."

"Didn't you . . . hear me?" Cayal demanded as the Warden walked away, wondering if his inability to stand was somehow robbing his words of authority. The Warden seemed singularly unimpressed by the importance of his prisoner.

"I heard what you said, you murdering little bastard," the Warden assured him, glancing back over his shoulder at where Cayal lay. "And if you think acting crazy is going to save you from the noose, you can think again."

Crazy? Who's acting crazy?

"You don't know . . . who you're dealing with!" he tried to yell hoarsely at the Warden's back. The pain was unbelievable. Healing at an accelerated rate was a very nasty business.

"You've got a lot to learn about Glaeban justice yourself, old son," one of the guards informed him, hauling him to his feet. "Come on, your holiness. Your royal suite awaits you."

Cayal's legs hung uselessly beneath him, his shins banging against the stone steps as they dragged him up the narrow curving stairs to Recidivists' Row while they worked out what to do with the man who wouldn't die.

The man they refused to acknowledge as an immortal.

TOR

Award-winning authors
Compelling stories

Please join us at the website
below for more information
about this author and other great
Tor selections, and to sign up for
our monthly newsletter!

www.tor-forge.com